James Rice, Sir Walter Besant

With harp and crown

A novel

James Rice, Sir Walter Besant

With harp and crown
A novel

ISBN/EAN: 9783337046217

Printed in Europe, USA, Canada, Australia, Japan

Cover: Foto ©Andreas Hilbeck / pixelio.de

More available books at **www.hansebooks.com**

A NOVEL

BY

WALTER BESANT AND JAMES RICE

LIBRARY EDITION

London
CHATTO AND WINDUS, PICCADILLY
1887

PREFACE.

" WITH HARP AND CROWN " is a story of woman's fidelity, patience, and unmerited misfortune. Contrary to the usual practice in novels, and more in accordance with the experience of real life, Marion Revel's sufferings are rewarded —cynically, some critics, unthinking, said—by the withholding of life's supreme happiness. Who will deny that this is no strange and unknown fate? The years of self-denial, were women like Marion to look for the reward of selfish joy, would seem, in the end, a mockery and a waste. There are thousands such as she : their youth is spent in toil for others more helpless than themselves. They have no crown of husband and tender children. But in their calm and passionless faces, in the smile of content which reigns like the sun of heaven in their eyes, we know that they have their reward. Is there not in every family such a history, such a memory, such a woman? "Strength and honour are her clothing : she openeth her mouth with wisdom : in her tongue is the law of kindness : her own works praise her in the gates." It is nothing to her that the strong and the crafty, like Joe Chacomb, grow rich : that the helpless and the weak of will, like her brother Fred, live in idleness and eat the fruit of her hands. She is happy. For the sake of these good women, and for the real lesson of their lives, we have written this book.

W. B.

J. R.

WITH HARP AND CROWN.

WITH HARP AND CROWN.

CHAPTER I.

WHEN the Princess Belle-Belle in the story is ravished
from the castle, and carried off by the wicked sorcerers
and demons of the rabble rout, she meets her troubles resigned,
and leaves them unchanged. No anxieties of mind are able
to dim the lustrous splendour of her beauty, or to furrow that
fair cheek with the lines of trouble. She plunges into the
sea of sorrow with a sigh, but emerges with a smile. Prince
Florio is sure to be constant: her loveliness is not evanescent,
like that of ordinary damsels; she waits in patience, conscious
of the abiding disposition of her charms, and the fidelity of
her lover. Above all, she has no duties. Heroines are never
expected to do more than sit down. If the worst comes to
the worst, she has but to cry, in the attitude of a startled
fawn, "Unhand me, sir!" and straightway one at least of
her defenders rushes in, sword drawn, and frees her in a
twinkling from her oppressor. These dramatic rescues,
indeed, are nothing more than the Princess Belle-Belle expects. And when the last chapter arrives, after which comes
the real dulness of life, with tranquil wedded love and the
rearing up to virtue of Princess Belle-Belle the Second, she
steps to the throne on which, beneath the glare of the limelight, she poses a graceful farewell, ere she quits the agitated
waters of adventure for the secluded haven of safety. In the
after-years she will yawn, perhaps, over the peaceful present,
while she recalls the variety and the charm, the doubt and
the uncertainty, of the troubled past. It is a great thing

to be a heroine of romance; but then it is so different from being a heroine of reality.

For, to begin with, in real land, Princess Belle-Belle is not alone in her misfortunes. If she is torn from the delights of her childhood; if the fabric of fortune fall about her ears; if the grim order of destiny oblige her to pack up her traps, and be off and away from her earthly paradise—she does not go alone. The thunderbolts which strike one, strike many; the misfortunes which fall upon one, fall upon all her family; and the fair young princess, instead of bewailing her fate, must needs tuck up her sleeves, put on her oldest dress, and work with the rest and for the rest, oblivious, save when the respite of night brings time for thought, of all she has lost. Florio is gone. Ah! will he come back unchanged? The years are passing on; will they leave the cheek as fair, the eye as bright, the lips as ripe, the smile as ready, the dimples as deep? Poor Belle-Belle of reality! She forgets herself in her devotion to the rest; she lives out her life spending it for others. Hers is the self-denial which is the highest lot of poor humanity, and yet seems to us creatures of self the hardest and the saddest. When the winters have passed their appointed number; when her fair hair is touched with untimely grey; when the crows'-feet have fallen too early around her lustrous eyes; when her hands are rough with toil; when her face—her sweet, comely face—is lined with care; when her shapely figure is shrunken; when the thousand little graces and delights of her maidenly ways are forgotten and lost—Florio returns. He comes back to his Belle-Belle, but, alas, he loves her no more. Down falls the castle of cards; the chambers of imagery are despoiled of all their golden pictures. Were it not for the vision that greets her streaming eyes, and comforts her stricken heart, poor Belle-Belle would be sorrowful indeed. But she has gained the higher glory. To those who wait and work comes a reward not hoped for or expected. The peace which passeth all understanding is theirs at last. Theirs are the soft strains of rejoicing resignation; theirs is a crown, if they care to wear it, more glorious than any wreath of the Nemæan games;

theirs is the golden harp, with which to celebrate the mysterious victory over sorrow and disappointment—the solution
of the problem insoluble to the world, the final triumph of
Love over Pain.

We are on the highest slope of a breezy cliff, a foreland of
the glorious coast which makes North Devon the loveliest of
English counties. The path, mounting straight up from the
village below without any curve or winding, out of effeminate
regard for the steepness of the hill, has left the thick hedges,
which at its lower levels rise over it on each side, like an old
arch out of which the keystone has dropped, but which yet
preserves its stability. It has passed beyond the fringe of
flowers on either hand—the tall foxglove, yellow hawkweed,
pink herbrobert, and the white milfoil; it has emerged upon
the open down, where it runs along the edge of the precipice,
and looks out upon the tossing sea beneath and beyond. The
great waves of the channel show from this height no signs of
motion, save in the white lines of crested foam and wild sea-
horses' manes that lie flecked about the surface; the steamer
below, that is tossing and rolling as she plunges along, seems
to be moving on a sea of molten glass; the clouds that fly
across the sky cast their shadows before and behind them
upon the waters; and the face of ocean, as you gaze upon it
to its blue distances beyond, is as bright, as profound, and as
impenetrable as the face of the Sphinx rising out of the white
sands and warmed with the cloudless sunshine of the desert.
For that "multitudinous smile" which we quote so often is a
subjective thing. We see in the ocean, as in nature, what
we feel in ourselves: we are in a mood of laughter, and ocean
smiles; we are in a mood of sadness, and ocean is grave; we
are contemplative, and its face is like that of the owl-faced
Athênê for unutterable wisdom. On either side the hill descends rapidly; on either side the view is nearly the same.
To right and left is seen a circular cove, into which the waves
rush through the narrow mouth and sweep back, dragging
with them shingle, stones, drift-wood, seaweed—all the flot-
sam and jetsam of a wild coast. On either side are long

jagged teeth of rock, lying in slanting strata, stuck at the
entrance of the little bay like sharks' teeth, ready to grip and
destroy.   Behind the cove is the perpendicular face of the
rock, with ledges on which grow wild rose, honeysuckle,
blackberry, and bramble; and curving down to meet the
sands slide the long slopes of the hill, planted thickly by the
great gardener—Nature—with giant ferns, among which a
tall man would tramp, shoulder high, like some Titan among
the palms of a tropical island.   On the right hand is a narrow
ledge of sand, with rock that crops up in dentated edges, and
backed only by its bulwark of straight and steep precipice;
and on the left is a hamlet, consisting of half a dozen cottages,
and one pretty house standing by itself, apart from the rest.
You may distinguish it without the aid of any glass in this
bright and clear August sunlight.   It is little more than a
cottage, with its single storey rising above the verandah,
which seems to run all round it; it is covered to its highest
chimney pots with a flowing robe of clematis, fringed with
westeria and Virginia creeper.   It has a fair lawn in front,
stretching away from the sea; and if you were near enough,
you would see that its gardens are planted almost wholly
with roses—roses of every colour: roses white and red, of
York and of Lancaster; roses brighter than any that bloom
in the gardens of Gulistan; roses of Provence and of Auvergne;
roses of Gueldres, and roses of England.

Hard by the cottage is the church, never-failing adjunct of
the English hamlet—a grey old structure, too large for the
scanty congregation which on Sunday gathers within its
mouldering walls.   The pathway slopes down the hill to join
the cart-road—a Slough of Despond in the winter, and in the
summer a gridiron of Saint Laurence.   This winds in and
out among the houses; passes here by the mill-wheel, rolling
slowly round under the light pressure of the streamlet, that
drips rather than flows upon the broad feathers, and turns
round the creaking, strong machine; here by the gate of the
farmyard, where the pigs lie poking contented noses into the
reeking straw, content to believe that the days of transformation into bacon are yet far off, though the fiat has already

been issued, and the knife of fate been sharpened; here by an orchard, red and yellow with the apples that will soon be gathered and sent to the cider-press; here by the village school, where the voices of the children are rising in the afternoon hymn of dismissal; and lastly down to the shore, where the ruts are lost in sand and shingle. It is high tide, or else you might see the carts gathering the seaweed, which is drifted up in heaps; but now the waves are beating and lashing about the sides of the cove, and the one boat which belongs to Comb Leigh is tossing like a cork at anchor. If you look inland, you see a long valley stretching back far into the grey distance, where the mists of the summer afternoon lie over the hillsides, and wrap the trees that are nearer with the softness of a Claude landscape, and those that are farther with drapery of transparent muslin, through which, as through the Coan robe, you may see the leafy limbs all ranged in seemly order. The meadows lie between the trees—broad slopes, green with pasture land, or yellow with the ripened corn that waits to be cut. A fair English land-scape, meaning peace and prosperity and the blessing of heaven and earth.

And on the cliff, on the very highest part, between the path and the precipice, where a gentle slope affords ten feet or so of breadth on which to lie and rest and watch the sea, are two young people.

One of them—she—is sitting pulling a flower carelessly, and the other—he—is lying at her feet, looking now upon the sea beneath him, and now at the fair face above him.

It is a face a little irregular of feature, though oval of form; the forehead is too high, the chin a trifle too pronounced, the nose not quite straight; and the whole is crowned with brown hair, with just—as the sunlight falls slantingly upon it—the smallest tinge of gold to give it colour and warmth. It is a face where you might expect a pair of bright and restless, mutinous eyes; in their stead you find them clear and steadfast of expression—eyes whose depths a painter, could he study them, might take as models for the illustration of many virtues, but chiefly those of courage, truth, and love. If I were to classify women, as my own sex has been so often classified by philosophers, I should divide her, first of all, into two great sections by means of her eyes. For the eyes of some women mean love, and of some an incapacity for love. The former are the sisters, wives, mothers, and aunts to whom children of all ages passionately cling; the others are those whom we respect, or love perhaps, *as in duty bound*, because they happen to be near to us. Their hearts are cold; they love themselves more than their own; if they have children, they neglect them; if they have husbands, they slight them; if they have abilities or the faculty of imitation, they write movingly about domestic affections with that unreal twang that we know as well as the familiar gag of an actor. The girl sitting on the cliff had eyes that could love; they rested from time to time furtively upon the curly head by her knees, and on the comely limbs which lay stretched at full length upon the sward. Her head was bare, and in her lap lay the straw hat she had worn on her walk up the hill.

The young man broke the silence with a laugh.

"We have got metaphysical, Marion—another word for nonsensical. Have we nothing better to talk about after our long parting? And tell me, cannot you find some way of reconciling duty with pleasure?"

She turned her head a little to one side—girls in the country get these tricks and ways—while she thought a moment, before she answered—

"I do think that the way of duty is sometimes a very hard one. And when so many people are disappointed in the world, when we read of so many lives falling short of their ideal, oh, surely it is better to give up thinking of life as bringing pleasure, and only make up our minds to bear and do what is right!"

"You to give up the pleasures of life, Marion? You—why, Democritus in—in—a brown holland frock and a red ribbon!"

"The ribbon is not red, but magenta."

"Matter of detail; and—the prettiest little boots in the world."

She drew them back with a blush.

"Gerald, if life has pleasures and duties too, I think it has besides great nonsenses, which must not be allowed."

"Forgive me, Marion," he said, looking up with his frank smile. "Forgive me, and let me finish. Do you seriously propose to give up looking for happiness?"

"Ah, no," she replied, softening at once, and brightening like the face of a lake when the April cloud has passed. "No, it is not that, Gerald. I look forward to a great deal of happiness. I am happy now at home—I hope I shall be happy always, in some way or other; only I think it cannot be right to set your entire heart upon one way of happiness."

"I do so set mine," said the young man. "Marion, I think life is full of joys and glorious gleams of happiness. They call it stormy. Nonsense! it is a Pacific Ocean for calm and sunniness. See now, I am six-and-twenty, or very nearly; you, Marion, are already two-and-twenty. We have walked and talked together for at least twelve years—how many unhappy days have we known?"

"None, Gerald, thank God!"

"And how many shall we know? None, Marion, none!" He sprang to his feet, and looked out upon the sea, where the sun was hastening to his western bed. "It is an invention of old women and cowards that misfortune is always hanging over us. Why should we pitch our songs in a minor key because bad things happen? They will not happen to us; and if they do, our singing penitential psalms will not alter the course of events. 'If I ever wanted a thing,' Byron used to pule and cry, 'I never get it.' Then why the deuce—I beg your pardon, Marion—why could he not help himself to it? Did he expect it would drop into his mouth? I hate a man who sits and wishes, when he might be up and working. It is far better to have no wishes at all, to sit and wait like an Arab. I used to watch them, Marion, in the desert of Egypt, before I went to Brazil, under the blue sky of evening and night, in their attitude of dignity, while we smaller fry chattered. They are the only people who want nothing and hope for nothing; they accept and are contented. We who belong to a colder climate are for ever discontented with our lot; we grumble and struggle."

She laughed.

"No one, at least, will accuse you of being contented with things as they are. Are you as great a Radical as you used to be when you left us four years ago?"

"We are all Radicals at one-and-twenty, I suppose. But, Marion, I have found out now the truest happiness of life, and I mean to try for it."

"What is that, Gerald?"

"Marion, it is love."

She did not reply, but her cheek turned a deep red; and presently she became aware, without looking up, that his eyes were fixed on her. If you know people very well, and are thinking of them, you get to feel when they are looking at you, without turning your own eyes to ascertain the fact. Perhaps this is elective affinity, or perhaps it is biology, or perhaps we know all about a thing when we can give it a fine name. Scientific gentlemen, it is certain, when they have once called a millstone by a Greek name, are instantly enabled to see several inches deeper than other folk into it.

"Love, Marion," he went on, sinking again on the grass, and gazing into her face—"love requires two people. Let us two love one another."

"We always have, Gerald," the girl murmured.

"Always, Marion. How many times have we climbed this hill together, and sat here looking at the sea! We have been lovers always, from the days when I had to help you along if you got tired. Always we have loved each other, Marion. But I did not know how much, or with what kind of love, till I was coming back to England, and thought of you day and night. We used to be brother and sister, but we are that no more. The long separation has parted the old bond between us, but the new one has come in its place. I want you to be more to me than we have ever been before to each other. Marion, I want you to be my wife."

She was silent for a while.

"Tell me, dear, that you can love me with a warmer feeling than that of a sister for her brother."

She looked him straight and full in the face; there was no doubt, no hesitation there.

"I do love you, Gerald. I do not know how you want me to love you, but I am certain that no wife could ever love you more."

He took her hand and kissed it, softly at first, and then passionately.

"The thought has never been out of my mind, dear Marion, since I became a man. I have seen no other girl that I could love, and resolved to tell you my heart the first day we were alone together. Yesterday I was afraid to speak lest I might spoil all, lest I had made a mistake. Marion, we have made no mistake, have we? We love each other; we will give each other our lives. Speak to me, dearest!"

"If thy handmaid find favour in the eyes of my lord, and if—"

"No, Marion, you are not my servant; you are my princess and my queen."

And this time he did not kiss her hand, but drew her face down to his own, and pressed her lips to his. Marion's heart passed from her with the kiss, and she drew back blushing, confused, trembling.

Then Gerald began to tell her of the lives they would lead together, and the happiness before them; and as he talked, Marion grew cold, and her heart fell. She shivered.

"I feel," she said, "as if I had lost something."

"It is your hand that you have lost, my darling, for that is given to me."

"Not that, Gerald, not that," she replied. "Let us go home; I am cold."

The clouds had gathered up from the south, and were lowering black before them as they rose to go down the hill to Comb Leigh. Marion turned for another look at the sea the waves were black, and the grey face of ocean was troubled with the crows'-feet of innumerable cares. There was no sun-

B

light on the waters, and sea and cloud were blended together in the far horizon. Gerald passed his arm through hers, and ed her gently down the hill.

"Don't be saddened by a rain cloud, Marion dear," he whispered. "Life has got nothing to do with weather. Look at the lightning up the valley! One might as well hear evil in the growling of the distant thunder."

"It is not the cloud," Marion replied, bursting into tears, —"it is not the cloud, Gerald; but as you spoke to me, I knew that you loved me; I knew it was *coming*, and I felt so happy—oh, so happy!—all in a moment to know that you were really and truly my lover. I had not thought of it till the last few days, since you came home again, and we have been different to each other. And suddenly my happiness seemed to be dashed like a cup of water from my lips. What does it mean, Gerald? what does it mean?"

"It means that my Marion is the best and dearest of all the girls that ever lived, as well as the prettiest and sweetest. It means that she gave me her heart, and felt cold for a moment for want of it. And it means that my love is a little frightened to think what she has done, and all she has pledged herself to. See, dear, the clouds are rising again over the woods; there is the rift among them, and the bit of blue. Look at the glint of sunshine on the copper beech yonder. Everything is brighter for the rain, though it has been but a shower. See how the hills seem to start into light and colour again; that is a picture of our life, dear. Marion, Marion, stay here by the stile, and let me tell you again how I love you—so; let me press you in my arms. Dear, dear Marion, how I love you—how I love you!"

It was two hours later when they reached the bottom of the lane—Marion bright again, laughing at herself, and animated.

At the gate of the Rosery they stopped.

"I must go home," said Gerald. "Tell your father what you like, dearest."

"I cannot say anything even to Adie, Gerald. Come and tell papa to-night. Good-bye."

"Good-bye, sweetheart, good-bye."

He pressed her hands, and looked her full in the face with eyes of passionate longing—a look that Marion was to treasure up in her heart for ever. The first tender words and the first warm look of a lover are as sacred to a woman as the first little shoes of her eldest born. It seemed as if his eyes were on her and his hands in hers still when she recovered from the first tumult of her heart, and lifted her eyes to watch her lover, striding along the road that led up the valley to Chacomb Hall.

CHAPTER II.

CAPTAIN REVEL, on half-pay, of her Majesty's Navy— that service which we treat so badly and regard so proudly —was not in any respect like the mariner Ben Bowling, or Admiral Benbow, or Lieutenant Luff, the sailors with whom the literature of imagination has made the world familiar. He did not wear loose blue trousers and a pilot coat, nor did he hitch up his garments in moments of aroused virtue, nor did he drink rum, nor did he swear, unless under provocation, nor did he stand habitually with his legs apart, nor did he have a red nose. He was a sailor of quite the modern school, though now a man of between fifty and sixty years of age; being a rather quiet and precise man, with little of the self-assertion that usually comes from habits of command; modest of speech, and diffident in manner. He was pale, and had cheeks hollowed with study; short-sighted, and carried double glasses; and was absent, frequently wandering away from the topic, and having to be recalled by his daughter Marion. He was a student in literature and a dabbler in science, as great a gardener as Adam, and learned in flowers, especially roses, of which he had all the varieties that he could afford to buy. His face, with thin sharp features and delicately clear outlines, proclaimed his foreign extraction; for Captain Fabien de Lussac Revel was a Frenchman and the son of a Frenchman, although an English officer. Out of the great army of *émigrés* —who mostly, it must be confessed, left their country for their country's good—a few found commissions in the English navy, and fought as manfully against the France of the new *régime* as any Frenchman had ever fought under Jean Bart or Labourdonnaye. Among these was the Comte de Reville, who carried abnegation of his country so far as to Anglicise his name, and appeared on the Navy List as Lieutenant Revel. He never mounted any higher on the ladder of promotion, but he put his son into the service and brought him up as an Englishman. Captain Revel preserved the papers which proved his ancestry and his title, in case he should ever wish to resume it, and pleased himself with the comfortable reflection that his race was an ancient and honourable one, with a history as long as its pedigree.

He came to Comb Leigh when he retired from the navy, some sixteen years before our story opens, with three children, his half-pay, and a modest patrimony. He had married twice. By the first marriage he had one child, Marion, now aged twenty-two; by the second he had a son Fred, now nearly twenty, and a daughter, Adrienne, now sixteen.

Marion you have seen. Of two girls one is always the daughter of the house, the father's friend and confidante—the ruler, if there is no mother; the prime minister, if there is; and in any case the teacher and adviser. This was Marion. As for the son Fred, he was at Oxford, where it was felt certain that he would achieve great things. Adrienne, little Adie, was the plaything and darling, and, like all darlings, childish for her years, and exacting of much tenderness and sympathy.

It was a household full of tenderness. The captain was a soft-hearted man, fond of his children; the children, brought up in the seclusion of a happy valley into which the outer world penetrated rarely, believed that no one was so wise, so good, and so learned as their father. Those are the happiest families where all believe in each other, just as he is the happiest man who mostly believes in himself. The quality of self-conceit, if it is valuable for the individual, is priceless for the family. We all know those domestic circles, never tired of each other, in which Jack, otherwise a miracle of stupidity, is supposed to have the finest voice in the world; Tom, who got prizes at school, is the cleverest man in the world; Susan, the saucer-eyed, is the prettiest girl; and Jane, with a face like a frying-pan, the most remarkable. Marion Revel honestly believed that her brother Fred was far cleverer than his compeers, though he failed to get any prizes at all as a boy, and had not yet distinguished himself at college; while little Adie seemed to her the personification of brightness, affection, and beauty. To the outer world, Fred Revel was a good-natured, handsome young fellow, who took things as easily as if he had been born to ten thousand a year; to the unprejudiced observer, Adie was a girl with a face which a few years might render beautiful, and a figure which required the ripening of two or three summers before you could pronounce an opinion on it. And, up to the present, if the captain has had any anxiety about his son's future, it has not crossed his lips. In truth, he has had none. When Fred refused at thirteen to go into the navy, his father was grieved, but let the boy have his way. When he grew older and resolved upon going to the University, the captain, convinced that education was the finest thing in the world, devised with Marion schemes of pinching and economy, to get for the boy all the advantages of learning. He is at present making the most of those advantages. He attends the college lectures, at which undergraduates learn so much and are so thankful for; he has, through the thoughtful kindness of Oxford tradesmen, a fair mount occasionally, a tolerable glass of claret in his room, can give those little breakfasts by which the fatigues of study are dispelled, can decorate his apartment with costly engravings, and can partake in all the amusements of the place. Oxford and Cambridge are rich indeed in endowments, but they are richer in those fine philanthropists who force fine things upon inexperienced youth, and teach them lessons, never contemplated by the pious founders, in the luxury of that rich outer world to which few undergraduates will ever belong. Like so many of his kind, young Fred Revel, too, on his allowance of two hundred pounds a year, was living at the rate of a thousand in eight months, without as yet troubling himself as to what the end might be.

Ah, how pleasant it is, this paradise of the youthful fool, whose every banquet is a delight, and every noisy revelry a feast of reason! A dream from which the awaking may be bitter, but the recollection is sweet. We in England have much to be thankful for, and especially that we have two such places as Oxford and Cambridge, where for three years the poorest undergraduate may enjoy the privileges of unlimited tick, and feel all the reality of being rich. A great English University is like a dream of fairy-land; in it those who work and are good boys and are lucky get pocketsful of money for all the rest of their lives; those who lie idling in the sun or sit singing in the shade are patted on the head by their tutors, tempted to eat, drink, and be merry by the benefactors above named, and troubled by no difficulties or debts till the allotted time runs out. So the Sheikh of the Mountains took his young men into an Eden, where houris brought them iced sherbet and played with them upon beds of roses for three days and three nights; then they were taken out, and paid the penalty for the brief season of joy by a life of obedience and slavery. After all, they could remember.

The girls knew nothing of this pleasantness; girls are taught, very properly, to believe that young men are always engaged in intense study when they are not discussing points of philosophy. Marion and Adie thought that Fred was hard at work. When he came home, resplendent in the gorgeous costume proper to the High, he wanted a long holiday, and must put away his books. Moreover, he must tell them of the Oxford world. Fred was willing to listen to reason; during the vacations he was content to forego the improvement of his mind, and devoted himself, like the best of brothers, to boating, fishing, and his sisters.

This little Anglicised French family, living in the quietest place in all England, without any relations or connections in the country, where they had settled like Naomi in the tribe of Judah, had but one house where they could find intercourse with the outer world. It lay a mile and a half up the valley, and was called Chacomb Hall. There had been a hamlet of Chacomb and a race of Squire Chacombs from time immemorial. No Chacomb had ever distinguished himself; no event connected the place with the history of the country; the annals of the hamlet boasted no village Hampden, so that very likely there never was one there at all; and if there had been a Milton ever born among them, he was mute and inglorious, and so might just as well have been a Smith.

But for the Revels there was Gerald Chacomb. He was older than Marion by some four years, and had been her only friend and chief companion. The two, when Gerald was at home for his holidays, roamed about the hills together like Paul and Virginia, as loving and as thoughtful of each other, though of sterner stuff than that sentimental and unfortunate couple. They knew every bird in the woods by its call, every wild flower, and every tree; they were wise in the manners and customs of the smaller beasts of prey—weasels and polecats and martens, and their like—which lie hidden in the Devonshire woods; they learned together by long familiarity that neglected science of woodcraft which no books can teach; and when the boy, obeying the instincts of his nature, took to reading works of travel and natural history, it was to Marion that he read them, filling her soul as well as his own with images of the strange wild animals of those Southern lands, dim with the haze of perpetual heat, filled with the haunted silence of a tropical moon, and bright with the splendour of cobra, panther and jaguar. They sat side by side on the edge of the cliff, while Gerald read aloud of the mighty river, across whose broad bosom the green and gold serpents glide in the blaze of the sun; on whose shores lies the lazy alligator; and to whose waters come to lap, at morning and at eve, the chattering monkey, the sleek puma, and the giant python.

"It is over there, Marion." Gerald would point across the sea. "Only three weeks' voyage, and we could get there and see it for ourselves. When I am a man I will go."

When he was a man he did go. Nothing could stop him.

He left the University, and obtained a travelling fellowship, which, with the little fortune he had inherited from his mother, made him independent of his father's opposition.

Marion stayed at home, and tried to paint—it was her only accomplishment—the scenes which Gerald's letters described. She covered acres of paper with imaginary sketches, in which were reproduced his stories of the life he led upon the Amazons and Orinoco.

While he travelled, she, womanlike, looked on, watched, and waited, almost unconscious of the place he filled in her life.

Four years: it is a long time even in the life of a man whose years are like a piled-up sheaf, and whose days are hastening the swifter to their autumn, as the waters hurry the faster as they near the fall; but it is a great gap indeed in that period when a girl is becoming a woman. Marion was eighteen when Gerald Chacomb went away, full then of the trembling perplexities and twilight visions of the future which surround the way of a girl. She was twenty-two when he came back, a woman ripe for love; and Gerald Chacomb was doubly a man, because he was a lover.

CHAPTER III.

GERALD CHACOMB strode with swinging step along the road up the valley to Chacomb Hall, his heart aglow, his eyes aflame, his lips trembling with the recollection of the last two hours. Nor did he trouble himself to wonder how his father might take it. That consideration, indeed, one must own, was not one that often stood in the way of his resolutions. His plan was rather to treat the paternal permission as a kind of grace after meat; to act first and ask afterwards; to do, and then, with filial care that his father should have some part, to insure a kind of posthumous concurrence in the deed. And as he stepped along, his thoughts ran mainly on the life he would lead at Chacomb.

" The governor wants me to live at home and potter about among the Collection. Hang the Collection! Well, he will be happy. Marion will like to be near her own people, so she will be happy too. I should like to take her away with me somewhere, but I suppose that cannot be. My pretty Marion!"

About a mile from Comb Leigh he was awakened disagreeably from his meditations by the appearance of a man waiting for him by the roadside. He was a big, burly man, dressed in a fashion not often seen in the lanes of North Devon : a sober suit of black, with a tall hat ; his long-tailed frock coat swung back from his big, brawny shoulders ; and his waistcoat, as far removed from the M.B. type as is possible in a black waistcoat, showed an expanse of shirt front which might have been whiter ; his trousers were wide and bulged at the knees, as if he sat writing in them with his feet under the chair, after the manner of those to whom Nature has not been prodigal in the matter of legs—though his were long ; his hat was glossy, and yet not new ; and he wore no gloves. In his hand he carried a silk umbrella, which had seen slenderer days ; and about the whole appearance of the man there was manifest the desire to preserve somehow a respectable exterior. His features were coarse and common, but not more vulgar than may be seen in many a man who is bidden to sit up high at great festivals. When he laughed, which was often, he laughed with the mouth, and not the eyes ; when he smiled, the frequency of his smiles depending a good deal on the company he was in, he smiled with his lips, and showed his teeth. Strangers, who were apt to take a violent dislike to him at first sight, often found themselves before the evening was over talking confidentially to him, and next morning repented. His name was Joseph Chacomb, and he was Fellow of the Royal College of Physicians, and first cousin to Mr. Chauncey Chacomb, the squire of Chacomb Hall.

" You here?" said Gerald, holding out his hand with no very cordial show.

" I am, as you see, my boy," returned the other. " And

right glad to welcome the traveller home. Left the patients
with a brother poisoner. He is younger than I am, and his
conscience is clearer. Came down last night as far as
Exeter. You are looking in splendid condition. As for
your father, he is a different man already. You know, my
dear boy, his temper."

"Never mind my father's temper."

"I don't mind it. I am the only man who never did mind
it. In fact, I rather like it. If I was his son, I dare say I
should think a great deal of it. Being only Dr. Chacomb—
Joe Chacomb—with a practice like a joint-stock company
(Why? Because it's limited), I can afford to sit down and
laugh. However, he has made a splendid addition to the
Collection—an undoubted Dow, and he's now at home with
it on his knees. My cousin Chauncey ought to have been a
good father if he treated his baby—you, the only—as he
treats his Collection. But then your head was not by an Old
Master, eh?—after the manner of an Old Master."

Gerald was irritated, partly at a long-standing dislike of
the man, and partly owing to the interruption to his thoughts,
but he laughed.

"You are on your way home, I suppose. Captain Revel
is with your father. It wants two hours of dinner. This
Devonshire air, what an appetite it gives! If I lived here, I
would have two dinners a day and a supper. It must be
dreadful to be poor at Chacomb. Perhaps it is to escape their
country appetite that so many people come up to London—
that, and to get their medical attendance for nothing. Tell
me about your travels, Gerald. Your beard improves you,
and you've filled out about the shoulders. You are like your
grandfather: he was a fair Chacomb. Your father is a black
Chacomb. And I am a red Chacomb. We are nearly
prismatic. All the colours of the family represented in us
three. In the smoking-room to-night you shall tell me some
of your adventures, eh?"

He winked, and looked so knowing, that Gerald felt inclined to kick him.

"By Jove! I wish I had had your chances of seeing the

world.   But when I was one-and-twenty I was walking the hospital ; and ever since I've been making blue pills and brewing black draughts.   All the rest of the Pharmacopœia is humbug, Gerald.   With blue pills and black draughts I'd clear out half the sick wards of the hospital : beat doctors black and blue, eh ?   But never mind that.   Tell me where you went, and all about it.   The Squire is hazy in geography. I believe he thinks Brazil is in Africa."

Presently they reached Chacomb Hall.

The Hall was approached by an avenue of elms, under which the carriage drive ran, grandly arched over by branches so close together that the crowded leaves supported each other, and remained upon the trees till January.   The house stood on a slope : a great square modern house, with no pretensions to beauty save a western gable.   This portion was built of brick—a warm and soft brick, over which years had spread a mellow tinge ; two sides of it were clothed with ivy ; the third looked due west down the valley to the sea ; and in clear days—most days in North Devon are clear—you got a glimpse of Lundy in the far distance from the upper window. This bit, the last of the old Hall, had been mercifully preserved by that interposition of Providence which killed the former squire—a great builder—and gave the estate to his cousin, Gerald's father.

Between Chauncey Chacomb as a young man and the estate there had once been so many lives, that in accepting a clerkship in Somerset House at a hundred a year, he thought himself provided with all the goods the gods would send him. *Dis aliter visum.*   The owner of Chacomb had no children ; the two intervening lives fell in ; and Chauncey at thirty came into possession.

At thirty-five he took a wife.   Also, about this period he began to form those Collections of his which, he felt, could make him famous.   When he was thirty-seven his wife presented him with a son.   The same *annus mirabilis* was also remarkable for the acquisition of a rose noble ; an original Murillo, purchased through the agency and by the advice of Mr. Burls, the eminent picture dealer ; the picking up of an

ancient pike-head, which marvellously resembled the useful
end of a modern spud; and for the death of his wife, who
never recovered the effects of her confinement.

The Collection was the bugbear of Gerald Chacomb's boyish
existence. He knew every glass case and its contents. He
knew by heart the expository discourse with which his father
would explain his treasures while he exhibited them to the
unhappy wanderer whose steps brought him to the door. The
cases were placed in what Mr. Chacomb called his library,
though he never read, and his son had carried away the books
to his own side of the house, the old portion. The Collection
contained coins, flint implements, bronze ornaments, beads,
swords and daggers, and a multifarious collection over which
the rustic gaped and the antiquary yawned. For, in truth,
Mr. Chacomb's Collection was as valueless a set of trumpery
forgeries, worthless curios, modern antiques, and twopenny
bric-à-brac as might be picked up at Cairo, Rome, Naples,
Jerusalem, or any other place where the chief industry is
that of forging ancient relics. No bishop of the twelfth
century, travelling to Palestine for the good of his sinful
soul, was more eager after saints' bones than Mr. Chacomb
after any old fragment to which he could attach a history.
He had travelled, too, and brought home with him, after each
voyage, stones from the places he had visited. These got a
good deal mixed on the way; so that what had been a fragment from Luxor was exhibited as a specimen of the marble
of the Acropolis at Athens, and what had been knocked off
the long-suffering Sphinx was labelled as a stone from the
Colosseum of Rome. Young Mr. Chacomb, too, in his irre-
verence for the past, had still further jumbled and confused
things, by altering labels and changing stones—sins pardonable only on the score of youth and ignorance of archæology.

All his spare moments Mr. Chacomb devoted to writing
the catalogue of his Collection. It was a bulky manuscript,
which he constantly wrote, re-wrote, and corrected. Here
was recorded the history of each precious relic, told at length,
with all the circumstances connected with its find, and an
excursus on the probable connection of the treasure with the

political history of the period at which Mr. Chacomb's imagination chose to fix the date. The document was the repository of all that its author owned of fancy, history, or scholarship. His reading, such as it was, bore perpetually upon his catalogue. He bought journals of the archæological societies, and he hunted them for new hints with which to embellish his catalogue.

On the walls of the room in which the Chacomb Collection was placed hung a dozen masterpieces, to which the squire added as opportunity offered.

"I have," he was wont to say, "only a few pictures, but I am proud to say that they are originals."

In one sense they were originals, having been mostly painted for Mr. Burls, and at the request of that distinguished collector, by young men in his employ; their natural merits being improved by a resemblance, perhaps accidental, to one or other of the great masters. Any one can copy a picture in a gallery, but it requires a painter of genius to produce an original work in the style of a master. Latterly, however, Mr. Burls had few dealings with his former patron; for Dr. Joseph Chacomb suddenly developed a curious taste in oil paintings, and became the fortunate means of introducing to his cousin one or two *chefs-d'œuvre* of the very greatest value, which he obtained for him, on commission, at a comparatively small cost.

Gerald found his father, as usual, in the Collection. The glass cases were open; on the table stood his basin of water, his hydrochloric acid for treating the coins, his camel's-hair brush, and his labels. But instead of fussing, as usual, among them, the squire was sitting in an easy-chair by the window, nursing a blackened and smoke-dried picture in a tarnished gilt frame. And standing by him, eye-glasses in hand, was Captain Revel.

Mr. Chauncey Chacomb's appearance did not proclaim aloud his parentage of Gerald. For the son was fair and tall, square-shouldered and stalwart, while the father was short and dark. Gerald's face was round and comely, while his father's was sharp and hard. The squire, in fact, recalled

the old portraits of Richard the Third. He had the same
look of ability in the low, square forehead; the same cunning
which the limner always depicts in the expression of that
wicked Plantagenet: he was strong, like Richard; and, like
Richard, he was slightly deformed—though not in the same
way, for his right shoulder was higher than his left. This
gave his appearance an awkwardness to which no familiarity
ever quite accustomed his friends. His manner was always
cold, but with a studied civility. He smiled a good deal, but
not so often nor in the same way as his cousin, the doctor;
and he never deceived any living soul into the belief that
he was going to commit, for him or her, an unselfish act.
Chauncey Chacomb, as a clerk in the Admiralty, was unsocial
and unpopular. When the news came of his cousin's death,
there was an impious but intelligible expression of feeling
among his fellows that so great a piece of fortune might have
been bestowed more fitly upon one with more of the makings
of a good fellow. As a lady supplies with ceruse, rouge,
padding, and other artful agencies the deficiencies of Nature,
so Mr. Chacomb learned to wreathe his face in habitual smiles,
and assume a cordiality towards the world which he did not
feel. He was not cynical, but indifferent. He did not sneer
at people, nor was he envious of them, nor did he impute
unworthy motives, nor did he say bitter and carping things;
he was only cold and careless. To the aims and objects of
his kind, to the tendencies and movements of his kind, to the
sufferings and sorrows of men and women—to these hopes
and fears Chauncey Chacomb was dead. He loved but one
created thing—not himself, because he was too conscious of
his own defects to love Chauncey Chacomb, but his son; and
he had only one vulnerable point at which his hide of indiffer-
ence could be pierced by a simple pin's point—his invaluable
Collection.

When the rhinoceros, at whom you may discharge your
arrows and hurl your javelins till you are tired, actually feels
the prick of one which by accident finds out a thin place in
the hide carelessly flung across the creature's back, like a
railway rug over a lady's knees, he begins to rage and roar,

and makes things perilous for the black Nimrods in his neighbourhood. The rhinoceros, in fact, gets into a vulgar rage, and plays indiscriminate devilry. The elephant, on the other hand, if anybody hurts him, keeps his resentment to himself till the chance comes of paying off old scores. Then he puts his big foot on the offender, who is seldom strong enough to preserve much rotundity after the operation, and pretends, with an apologetic twirl of his trunk, that it was by accident.

Mr. Chauncey Chacomb, not elephantine in any other respect, had the nature of that glorious creature in this, that he nursed his wrath. When he was offended he smiled, and, taking the injury night after night to bed with him, tenderly looked after it, fostered and fed it, kept it always alive and flourishing, and looked on admiringly while the little ugly monster grew up into a great amorphous Frankenstein.

He brooded over a wrong. He pleased himself with inventing schemes of imaginary revenge, on which he would gloat, picturing the agonies of the victim and his own ungodly triumph. Twenty years before this story begins, he had received, as he thought, a great injury and a wanton insult from a man who unthinkingly scoffed at his ancient arrow-heads, and disputed the authenticity of his beloved rose noble. The man who did it had long ago forgotten the whole thing, but in Chauncey Chacomb's mind it was flourishing like an evergreen bay tree, growing ever taller and spreading wider, like a Norfolk Island pine. For twenty years he had been in almost daily intercourse with this man, dining at his table, walking and talking with him, asking and giving advice, receiving his confidences, and appearing, to all the rustic world of Comb Leigh, his dearest and most intimate friend.

And he hated him all the time. Day after day, and night after night, Chauncey Chacomb pursued the shadow of an imaginary revenge for an imagined injury. It was a sort of habit. Perhaps he would have done his enemy no harm had he found the opportunity. But the hatred, unforgivingness, and malice lay in his heart, like those little devils whom the magician puts into bottles—so lively and so harmless, *so long as the bottle is corked.*

This enemy who believed himself, who was believed by everybody to be Chauncey Chacomb's greatest friend, was the man who stood by him, looking at the newly bought picture, when Gerald and the doctor came into the room.

CHAPTER IV.

"I THINK I should have it cleaned, Chacomb," the captain said, looking at the picture with puzzled eyes. "See what you make of it, Gerald."

At first sight nothing was to be made out of it at all, except a perfectly black surface, covered with a dull and much cracked varnish, set in a dingy frame. Mr. Chacomb placed it on a chair before the window, and began to move slowly before it in a semicircle, so as to catch the light from every possible point of view, holding his hands, after the manner of art critics, slightly curved over his eyes. His attitude was one of speechless admiration. The doctor, with a gleam on his face which might mean amusement, and might mean incredulity, or, indeed, almost anything, took his place beside his cousin, and began a similar pantomime of observation with a grave countenance.

There was one thing especially noticeable about Dr. Chacomb, that the spirit of mimicry was so strong in him as sometimes to make him overact his part, and even to lead, by too zealous an impersonation, to the loss of many little *coups* carefully prepared beforehand. On the present occasion, with an involuntary glance at the other two, to see if they realised the humour of the situation, he crept with the squire slowly from left to right and from right to left, swaying his big shoulders and rolling his head, in grave imitation of his cousin, occasionally throwing in a gesture, a gasp, or an indication of rapture, as some hitherto unobserved beauty rewarded his inspection.

"What delicacy!" murmured Chauncey Chacomb.

"What fidelity!" echoed the doctor in a whisper.

"Splendid breadth of outline!" exclaimed the squire, bringing his forefinger round in a comprehensive circle, which finished by pointing to the fine proportions of the doctor.

"Majesty and height!" replied the doctor, with an upward sweep.

"You see it, Joseph?" said the squire.

"I do, Chauncey. Now that you point it out, I do."

"Then hang me," said the captain, who had no perception of the ridiculous—"hang me if I can see anything at all!"

Chauncey Chacomb answered not a word, but pointed to the centre of the panel.

Revel shook his head. The doctor sighed with pity, and nodded approbation.

"I suppose," said Gerald, "that we have not been able to catch the right light. I can see nothing at all; but I dare say I shall make it out presently. Perhaps there are duskier pictures even than this in galleries, and people admire them. Tell me what it is, father."

"I am studying it," replied Mr. Chacomb, solemnly. "There is a trunk, and—and—yes—it is a leg—an arm and hand, and what appears to be a head, but I am not quite sure. More delicate flesh tints I think I never saw. Revel, it would be a sin to have this masterpiece touched. Look at that curve — see — Hogarth's line of beauty anticipated."

"I see," said the perverse captain, "a daub of drab-colour paint, that looks as if it had been laid on by the brush of a house painter. All the rest is black panel, varnished by an apprentice. Come, Chacomb, you do not surely mean us to admire this?"

"Not unless you like, Revel. Eh, Joseph? not unless he likes," said the squire, chuckling.

"Certainly, Captain Revel, no one can force you to admire anything," said the courtier. "Still, if delicacy and breadth of outline fail to please you, what will?"

C

"Tut, tut," said the captain; "I may be a fool, but I cannot see anything."

"Gerald," said his father, "look at it carefully. Come where I am standing; here, my boy. You *must* see that leg," he added, almost piteously.

"There is certainly something, but I cannot — my eye wants your training, father—I cannot make out what it is."

The captain whistled softly.

"Mr. Burls said it was a Dow, did he? Well, it may be a Do; but I don't think it is a Dow."

At this simple joke they all laughed, except the squire, who had not learned how any one could dare to laugh at a picture of the Collection.

"What do you propose to call it?" asked the captain.

"Burls believed it to be the village Porkshop," the doctor said, modestly. "He promised to bring up all the details by a new process if—"

"I won't have it cleaned," the squire interposed, putting his hands in his pockets, and falling back in admiration.

"Nothing should induce me to have his confounded process applied to this beautiful thing. What are you doing, Revel?"

The captain, turning it round, was tapping the back with his knuckles.

"It is odd," he said. "The panel seems double. Lend me a knife, Gerald."

He cut the paper, and loosened the nails which held the board to the frame. Then behold a great marvel. For it was a false back, and behind it, on the reverse of the panel, lay the true picture, the back of which they had been admiring. A young girl's face, fresh as Etty, creamy as Greuze, bright as Titian, with the pearly tints of health and innocence — a beautiful painting, whose pigments were as unfaded as if they had been laid on the day before. It had been turned round for some purpose of preservation, and so had been left, forgotten and secure

—guarded only by some tradition that it was a picture— and probably lying among a lot of lumber waiting for a purchaser.

" Why, in the name of all that's— " the captain turned it round and round— "here's the picture itself; and, by gad, Chacomb, we've been looking at the back ! "

" Then it is a Dow, after all," cried the doctor with much presence of mind. " Dow, you see, Gerald; *dos* in French— back—eh? Ho! ho! Chauncey, my boy, we've been sold ! That rascal Burls ! Wait till I get back to town and have it out with him."

" It is the most extraordinary thing I ever knew," said the captain. " And a sweet little painting, after all. Chacomb, you are in luck. This damsel's face strikes me as a good deal better than the delicate—ha! ha!—the delicate flesh tints and the fidelity of touch. I don't think— "

Here he caught a glimpse of the discomfited squire, and, though little prone to extravagant mirth, sat down and fairly bubbled over with laughter.

" The back of the picture, after all. Only the back ! How about the flesh tints, eh? And the leg, and the line of beauty ! The delicacy and the fidelity ! Chacomb, we shall never forget it, never ! "

When Don Quixote, the Knight of the Rueful Countenance, experienced that adventure of the fulling-mills, which is known to all who are acquainted with his biography, he showed no more melancholy spectacle of discomfiture than Chauncey Chacomb at this sudden collapse of his newly acquired masterpiece. His frame shrank; his hands hung down; his face was pale, save where the cheeks were flushed with an angry red. The doctor had retired. One glance at his cousin had been too much for him; and stealing quietly through the window, he retired to a convenient spot out of sight, where he might sit down and laugh at his ease.

The captain turned the picture round, and set it in its proper place.

" This is almost worth sending to the papers," he said

"The prettiest little picture, too, Chacomb. Come, man,
you can afford to laugh, because you have won. Why, this
fresh, bright girl's face is worth all the sham Gerard Dows
you could buy in a lump of Burls and all his people."

But Chauncey Chacomb was too disturbed to answer.

"Come, Chacomb, you are not angry, are you? Even the
best judges get deceived sometimes. Though, of all the
wonderful things—how Marion will laugh when I tell her!
Now who could have suspected—who the deuce could tell
that the thing was hindside before? I've seen a sailor get
on horseback with his nose to the crupper; but hang me if
I ever saw a picture stern on before!"

"Angry?" echoed the squire. "Angry? No, why should
I be? As you say, we all make mistakes. My cousin there,
for instance—"

"Oh, I," said the doctor cheerily, who had returned refreshed—"I was the first to make the mistake. It was I
who put you all out. Laugh at me as much as ever you like,
if you must laugh. Ho! ho!"

He laughed as if he was laughing at somebody else.

"Yes," said Chauncey, with woebegone face. "Ha!
ha!"

It was an interjection with so little of the emotional and
spontaneous character about it that the doctor laughed the
louder.

"When I think of myself," he said, "in Burls's shop—I
went there, you know, with this thing under my arm—I will
never forgive Burls—never. 'What is it worth, Burls?' I
asked him. 'It's worth—' Well, never mind the price Burls
put upon it, because it would astonish you. 'It is a genuine
Gerard Dow'—Burls's own words, not mine. 'A Gerard Dow;
and I shouldn't wonder if it does not turn out to be the long-
lost Village Porkshop.' The long-lost Village Porkshop—
think of that, Chauncey."

"I never heard of that picture," said the captain.

"Perhaps not," the doctor went on. "Very few people
have."

This struck him as being a remark so true, and so apposite

to the fable he was inventing, that he broke into a new laugh.

"Excuse me, Chauncey; you ought to laugh, not I. But I can't help it, for the life of me. What I thought were flesh tints, he said was dead pig. Never trust Burls again, Chauncey."

The squire's face relaxed.

"Of course I was deceived," he said, rather hoarsely. "And as for the picture, Joseph, you may take it back, and—"

"No, don't do that," said the captain. "The picture is really a good one. Look at it again, Chacomb. Do keep it if you can."

The squire shook his head gloomily.

"No; I shall send it back."

But he kept it all the same, and the picture still hangs in Chacomb Hall, where those who now own the place tell its strange story.

Then the captain looked at his watch, and went away, Gerald with him. Chauncey Chacomb listened to their voices outside the house. When their steps had died away, he turned to his cousin, who was expecting one of the sharp speeches which the head of the Chacomb house was accustomed to use in moments of displeasure to such of his relations as owed him money. It was annoying to the doctor, because he wanted to borrow more, and was most sincerely anxious that his cousin should be kept in good temper. But the squire was not thinking of him.

"It is envy, Joseph," he whispered, with a kind of groan —"it is malignant envy. I am richer than he is, and he envies me and sneers at me. You saw it, Joseph—you saw how his lips turned pale with envy when he found the picture hidden behind the frame. He envies me my money, he envies me my Collection, and he even envies me my son— my Gerald."

The doctor was entirely confused with this sudden and unexpected turn; he began, indeed, to murmur that it was highly creditable to the captain, but left off in time.

"If I were like other collectors," the squire went on, "I should be annoyed at such an incident. It might be a blot on my reputation; but I can afford to disregard that. It is not even that he should be able to make up a story out of it, and laugh at me. It is the man's real nature that I see through and despise. That is the contemptible thing."

"It is," sighed the doctor, getting interested. "That really is the saddest part of the whole affair."

"I am glad you noticed it as well as myself. Joseph, let us two have one more look at this picture—what he calls the back of it—eh? Put it in the light again—so. What do you think? Tell me candidly, Joe."

The doctor's eyes glistened as he caught the cue.

"Think? What I thought all along, Chauncey; though Revel put me out a little at first with his confounded discovery. The real picture is here, after all; just where we were looking at it."

He glanced doubtfully at his cousin. The assertion seemed too daring. But it was received with credulity.

"I *knew* it all along—I was certain of it. We can't deny the girl's head, Joe—any one can see that. A modern thing, put in by some copyist. Pretty enough, too. It wants eyes to see the other, though. Let us look at it again. Yes; Joe, you are quite sure—are you quite sure that you see the details?"

"As sure as I was at the very first."

This, at least, was true.

"Ah, now it is our turn to triumph! Joe, if he makes a story out of it—'good enough to send to the papers,' Revel said—if he does, we shall have the laugh over him, eh? After all, you can't take in the real connoisseur."

"Burls would hardly go so far as to see a picture when there was none. I rely more on Burls and yourself than on my own eyes. But, there it is—why, Lord bless me, how can Revel—"

"Spite and envy, Joe; it is what we must expect in the world. Ah, sometimes one would be a hermit."

" You feel things too much, Chauncey. It is the goodness, you see, of your heart that runs away with you."

" Perhaps, Joseph, perhaps."

He had spoken in a braggart, self-satisfied voice ; but in putting the picture down, he laid it with the face upwards.

" Now," said the doctor, when the squire left him to dress for dinner, " I wish for once that I knew a little of my own profession. Chauncey has got a twist somewhere to-day. I thought he would have had a fit when Revel went away. Perhaps it is his heart going wrong, if I only knew it. Too much goodness—ho ! ho ! Humbug won't teach me, however, what I should like to find out. It is a good thing enough for the workaday world. Humbug doctors sick people ; humbug makes them thankful when they get well again ; humbug even, sometimes, makes them happy to go off ; humbug fills my scanty coffers ; humbug makes my clients believe in a couple of capital letters and a red lamp ; but humbug breaks down when you want it to be uncommercially useful. It pays all my bills, but it won't help me to read the problem of Chauncey Chacomb. Is he cracked ? Has my cousin dropped a tile ? None of the family ever showed any inclination to mania. But it looks queer. He rounds on his dearest friend, and slangs him. He gets as mad as a badger in a cask, without even being baited with the rubbish and the general foolishness of the Collection. As for this picture, which I bought without looking at it—who the devil would have thought that a picture could be hindside before ? However, Joe, my boy, you have not done so badly. You have sold it for ten times what you gave. You have had a holiday from the infernal shop ; you have got your travelling expenses paid, with a trifle over ; you are in hopes of borrowing the hundred pounds your creditors want so badly ; and you have got a whole bottle of port before you. I don't think, on the whole, that the original Joseph, in his palmiest and artfulest days, could have done much better for himself with Pharaoh than I have done with Chauncey. And then," he added, with some confusion as to scriptural sequence, " there is

certainly no Potiphar's wife in North Devon. Potiphar lives
in London."

Chauncey Chacomb locked the door with extreme care in
his own room, and then abandoned himself, with all the
pleasure of a secret voluptuary, to the rapture of unbridled
rage. He strode backwards and forwards, swinging his arms,
cracking his fingers, dancing, gesticulating, with fiercely
glaring eyes, as he gave full play to a revenge worthy of the
Furies, devising schemes of retaliation in which he had his
enemy at his feet and crouching before him. I believe, and
am firmly convinced, that if one half of the world were judges,
the other half would be condemned to undying torment; else
why the frequent "damn?" But then, the usurpers of the
throne of Minos, lacking that functionary's judicial coldness,
would presently repent and be sorry. To be sure, their repentance would not make the fatigues of Sisyphus, toiling
after his aggravating stone, a whit more endurable; but, to
the philosopher, the picture of judges and prisoners, both
justly unhappy together, might not be without its useful
lesson. At this moment Chauncey Chacomb believed that, if
an opportunity should occur, there would be nothing in the
way of revenge too dreadful to resolve upon. The laugh of
the captain had fallen upon his nerves like the lecturer's
oxygen upon the wire in the glass—that instructive experiment which we used to see at lectures before chemistry was
taught in schools—rousing and stimulating the dull spark to
a flame.

It is one of the advantages of a small place, where society
is limited necessarily to a circle of two or three, that the soil
adapts itself especially to the growth of the passion flowers
of envy and suspicion. In great cities they are reared with
extreme difficulty, and kept alive only with watchfulness and
attention. But in the country they grow like the giant lianes
in the tropics, twisting and twirling, strengthening and increasing, till they squeeze the spiritual life out of the tree
which has been their host.

In London we hate each other honestly, particularly we
who have reviewed each other's books, and been reviewed: it

is a keen emotion, but seldom roused. Nobbs hates Dobbs; when Nobbs meets Dobbs his liver is stirred to the extent of wishing he could knock him down, were he strong enough and were no one looking. If Dobbs is spoken of, Nobbs coarsely swears if he is of the old school, or calmly smiles—the smile of superior venom—if he belongs to the party of sweetness and light. For the rest, neither Nobbs nor Dobbs wastes time in thinking of each other. But in the solitudes of the country, hatred may become a cherished and a beautiful possession, the priceless pearl of imagination, the salt and spice of life, the chief thing which confers superiority, dignity, and the sense of power.

"I could kill him now where I stand," said the wry-necked little squire, who, like the majority of mankind, felt most largely the gifts of bull-dog tenacity and reckless daring when there was nothing present on which to exercise them. "I could kill him now, with his cold laugh and his sneer. He thinks I am his friend; how can I undeceive him? He thinks he can do what he likes with me; how can I show him the truth? He thinks he can direct and order me; how can I let him know—Gar! If I could crush him to powder beneath my feet; if I could sell him up, and send him and his beggars upon the streets; if I could ruin his name; if I could blight his hopes—I would do it. If, unknown to all the world, I could compass his end—I would—yes, yes, yes, I would do that too!"

And the squire burst into a short laugh, not the laugh of irony, or that of conscious power—these being impossible, except in works of fiction—but a laugh of pretended amusement combined with spite: it is a laugh that may be heard any day among men discussing those of their friends who are in the same trade with themselves. Its invention is said to be due to Sir Fretful Plagiary; but my own belief is that the distinguished dramatist appropriated that, as well as other beauties, from older men. Lucian, to my certain knowledge, laughs in much the same way, and perhaps earlier authors handed down the method to him. Chauncey Chacomb laughed, hitching up his uneven shoulder with an action

which seemed like imparting a confidence to his right ear.
Then he opened a secret drawer in an escritoire by touching
a spring. In it, among a lot of old jewellery and trifles, lay
the most commonplace of all worldly possessions—a simple
box, labelled "Cockle's Antibilious Pills." This he took out
and opened, gazing at the contents with a look which
amounted almost to rapture. To the superficial observer
the box contained only those blue-black globules and the
nasty white magnesia, put in by the philanthropic manufacturer to deter us from taking too many. To Chauncey
Chacomb the box spoke a whole volume, in folio, of evil
imagination and back-handed revenge.

"I wonder which of them it is," he said, sitting down and
shaking up the pills. "Who would think that it lies among
the rest, so like them all that the Devil himself could not tell
which it was. There were a lot of pale yellow crystals—
poisonous little deadly crystals—in a drawer in the laboratory
which Joseph showed me. When nobody was looking I took
a pinch. And in the night I made up a pill, rolling up the
crystals in the middle of coloured bread so that it looked like
a Cockle. He who takes that pill will have pains and con-
vulsions all over; and then he will bend back, like a bow
turned the wrong way, with his heels touching the back
of his head; and then he will go off altogether. Ha!
Revel would look well with his heels kicking the back of his
head. And dignified. Just as he was having his final curl,
I could whisper softly in his ear that I had done it, and
that it was a lesson to teach him for the future not to sneer
and flout at better men—yes, better men than himself.

"It would be dangerous, because some one else might take
the pill, and I bear no malice to any one else. Revel is my
only enemy. Perhaps the girls don't take Cockle's. But
then Fred might. If I could make sure that only the captain
would use the box, I could leave it on his dressing-table.
And I should watch and wait. A week, a month, a year
would pass, and the captain would be strong and well. Then
would come a day when he would feel a little queer. And
then—then—then—ah-h!"

He gave a sigh of infinite satisfaction, and closed the box, gazing at it with loving eyes, such as a mediæval bravo might have turned, after purging his soul by confession, upon his sharp and trusty stiletto. Then he replaced it in the escritoire, and locked up all safe. And then he rubbed his hands softly, dressed for dinner, and went downstairs just as the gong sounded.

For the moment, his ill-temper and malice had vanished. They came from time to time, like those familiars, formerly the plague of foolish old women, who, to be fed, sold their ridiculous souls to the Devil. Chauncey Chacomb allayed their voracity with dreams and schemes of revenge. Perhaps, had he been induced to carry his visions into reality, there would have been nothing left to dream about, and so the world would have become a thirsty Sahara of actual fact. The Tempter insinuates his abominable counsels into some of us with fancied evil. We dream of crime and wild revenge, wearying, not satiating, the worst passions of the soul; and to some the vision is dearer than one of luxury, pride, glory, honour, or even fair women.

The squire, then, having indulged his genius, fed his familiar, smoothed his mind, and crushed his imaginary enemy, came down to dinner in better temper. The doctor was cheerful, as he always was at dinner-time. Gerald was happy, if a little silent, and the talk went round as if no one of all three had a single thought in the background. This, you see, is the grandest achievement which our modern civilisation has wrought for us. It has enabled us to use speech so as to forget care, as well, according to the cynic, as to conceal thought. The squire put his secret hatred behind him; the doctor forgot his anxieties about money; and Gerald, as hungry as a man of five-and-twenty ought to be, forgot Marion.

As soon as dinner was over, the younger man left the other two with the wine, and went out. Presently they heard him crunching the gravel-walk beneath the elms. The squire's eyes contracted with an impatient expression.

"Not back three days," he said, "and off again to the

cottage. You see, Joseph—you see! He cannot be allowed
to spend a single evening with his father. Revel entices him
away."

"There are other attractions at the cottage besides Revel;
there are two young ladies."

"Cousin Joseph," said the squire, "do you forget that you
are speaking to a Chacomb, that you yourself are a Chacomb,
and that Captain Revel is a mere half-pay officer?"

"Cousin Chauncey," returned the doctor, unabashed, "I
remember that the Chacombs have been owners of this
pleasant and secluded little hamlet for a large number of
generations. During that time they have done nothing to
distinguish themselves, except to show that they can hold on
to what they have got. Do you forget that Captain Revel is
the last representative of an ancient and honourable French
house?"

"Bah!—a beggarly French title!"

"Whose ancestors were fighting men with the king, while
ours were ploughing Devonshire clays. So far as family goes,
my cousin, we must give in. To be sure, we—that is, you—
have got money."

"I would rather give it all to—to—to you, Joseph," said
Chauncey, flushing, "than that Gerald should have a penny
if he marries one of those Revel girls."

"Ay, ay?" the doctor replied, thoughtfully. Then he
looked up and laughed.

"To be sure, Chauncey, if you were going off before me,
which isn't likely, comparing your constitution and mine"—
he was as strong as one of the New Forest oaks to look at—
"I should say, leave me your money, by all means. Still, if
you do not want mischief to be done, you might perhaps keep
Gerald out of the way of it. You know that the best method
of handling the patent safety matches is not to let them get
near the outside of the box, eh?"

Here the squire banged the table, and used a strong expression—what some writers used to call a Saxon expression,
until we were taught that there never were any Saxons at all,
and reflected besides that the word is really of Latin origin.

" Everybody would think," the doctor went on, with a half-glance at his cousin's face, "that you wanted it. You and the captain are bosom friends; you go there, he comes here; the girls come here when they like; you— No, Chauncey, you really should not bang the table when all the glasses are on it. You have spilt some of my port on the cloth—a sinful waste of excellent wine. Before you bang again, allow me to take another sip."

" Finish the bottle," said Chauncey, rising abruptly; " I shall go into the garden."

He left his guest, and, passing through the open window, stepped out upon the lawn.

The doctor looked after him with a smile, and gave up his whole mind to quiet enjoyment of the port. When there was no longer any in the decanter, he rose thoughtfully, and followed his host.

Chauncey Chacomb was marching backwards and forwards, gesticulating. The devils, which had slept for a while, were awake again, and rending him to pieces. It was singular that the secret he had kept for so many years should be irresistibly torn from him by so foolish an accident as that of the picture. But it was so. He could no longer contain himself or his passion. Every feeling which overmasters a man must, soon or late, find expression, and take unto itself a confidant.

" Come, Chauncey," said the doctor, taking him by the arm. " I am a medical man, you know, and cannot have you exciting yourself. Relieve your mind, and have done with it. 'Give sorrow words,' as Shakspeare says; and if you don't tell me, tell somebody else. What a man like you, in good health, with a fine income and no debts, can have to trouble him, I don't know. But you have something. Repressed care, my friend, is like suppressed gout—it plays the devil with the constitution. That's why they say that care killed a cat, I suppose. I had a case last week of a man, about your age, but of slighter build, who choked, Chauncey, literally choked, not to use the technical term, with the effort of keeping something on his mind. As he was dying, he tried

to communicate it to me; but too late, poor fellow, too late!
—and he is gone. I believe if he had lived I should have
come in for something handsome in his will. There is another
man I attend every day, who is paralysed in the lower limbs
through getting into a righteous rage with his son, and trying
to keep it under. Give Nature way, Chauncey. You are
annoyed, and very naturally, because Revel found out what
had escaped you and me—eh? Bah! Sit down and swear
for five minutes and then forget it."

"Oh, if I could trust you!" groaned the squire.

"That seems an odd thing to say, after all these years.
Not trust me? Why, who the deuce have you ever trusted
except me? Who helped you to get the Collection together? Who watched and lay in wait for bargains for
you? Who stood between you and my lady when you
had the kick-up? Who has always been your best friend?
In the words of the poet,

> 'Who bailed him when they ran him in?
> Who backed the bill and nailed the tin?
> Who never flinched through thick and thin?
> 　　　　　　　His cousin.'

Not that you were ever run in, Chauncey—on the contrary, I
believe it was I who once—but never mind. The meaning is
clear. Come, old fellow, out with it. Make a clean breast,
or you'll be having—you'll be having—" he paused to think
what he could best frighten his cousin with—"you will be
having *angina pectoris*. That's a thing that comes of sudden
excitement. It catches you in the heart like the five claws
of a wild beast; grips there, and never lets go till it has torn
it all to pieces; and you die after five and twenty minutes of
agony. Give me your wrist. So. Good Heaven! a hundred
and twenty to the minute. And now put out your tongue.
My poor Chauncey, you must take care, you must indeed.
I think I ought to bleed you."

Chauncey sat down and gasped.

"I hate him, Joe," he said. "I hate him worse than I
hate mortal sin. Don't tell any one, but I hate him."

" Who? Gerald?"

" No—Revel, Revel! I've hated him for fifteen years."

The doctor looked at him with a puzzled expression. He saw for the moment no possible way to make anything for himself out of this revelation.

" He tramples on me; he insults me before my own son; he sneers at me; he gives himself airs of superiority. I hate him!"

The doctor remained thoughtful for a little while. Then he spoke professionally.

"Come up to town; go and travel; see other scenes and other people. If you hate Revel when you return, come to me again. No"—for the squire was going to speak again—" no, you have told me quite enough. I thought there might have been some reason; I mean—yes—tell me of something else."

The squire shrank back into himself again.

" Promise me, Joseph," he said, catching him helplessly by the hand, "that you will keep my secret. I can't help it," he added, piteously—"I can't indeed. The sight of him makes me mad. I want to kill him; I want to do him mischief. I lie awake and think about it at night. Tell me, Joe—you know I have always told you everything—we have no secrets from each other, have we? We never had."

" None, Chauncey, none," replied the mendacious physician, whose pocket-book was bulging with secrets unsuspected by his cousin. " I am thankful to say that I have always been as open with you as you with me—as open with you as you with me," he repeated, pleased with the roundness of the phrase.

"Then, Joe, tell me if you meant what you said—if you think there is any chance—any danger of Gerald falling in love with that Marion girl. If there were, I would—"

" What would you do, Chauncey?"

" I would cut him off with a shilling, Joe. I would leave all my money to you, I would, by gad—Chacomb Hall, and the Collection, and everything."

The doctor looked round him. They were in the centre of
the lawn: behind him stood the Hall; before him stood the
great trees of the avenue; on either hand stretched long
green glades up the hillside; a sweet breath of summer was
in the air; the sun was long gone down, and only the light
sapphire hues of evening left in the west; but the moon was
up—the full August moon, the harvest moon—pouring floods
of silver light on wood and copse, softening the straight lines
of the modern part of the hall, and bringing out into relief
every buttress and projection of the old western gable as
lovingly as if they had belonged to Melrose Abbey. There
was a deep stillness in the woods. To the doctor's heart,
weary with struggle, trouble, and the endless fight that
belongs to a man who is ever sinning and ever trying to
escape the consequences of his sin, the squire's words brought
a sudden hope like a ray of sunshine.

"Answer me, Joseph. Have you reason?"

"Perhaps, Chauncey, perhaps," said the doctor. "So you
would cut off your own flesh and blood for a marriage against
your permission?"

"I would. Mind you, Joe, Chacomb belongs to the
Chacombs. If Gerald does not get it, it goes to you."

"Lord, Lord!" said the doctor, "we talk nonsense. You
are only sixteen years older than I—and will outlive me.
Put such things out of your mind. As for Gerald, of course
he will marry to please you—sons always do," he added, in
a sort of undertone. "Come in, Chauncey. Let us have
some brandy and water after this cold talk. I must doctor
you. And don't trouble yourself about Revel for a while.
Control yourself, my cousin. We Chacombs should be strong
to act, but slow to speak. Your secrets are safe with me."

Gerald came home at twelve, and found the doctor smoking
a cigar outside the house.

They walked up and down together in the calm night.

"If I were you, Gerald, my boy," said the doctor, "I should
marry. It has always been my greatest regret that I did not
marry. Get yourself a wife, and soon"

"I mean to," said Gerald.

"Very proper. And I hope you will have the good sense to choose the right girl."

"I have chosen, if I may say so, the best and sweetest girl in all the world. I've known her nearly all her life, and there can be no mistake about her being the right girl."

"I am *very* glad to hear it, Gerald, very glad; and I am sure your father will be greatly pleased—greatly pleased. Good night, my dear boy, good night."

CHAPTER V.

IF there were rage and fury at the Hall, at the Rosery it was all love and calm.

Gerald and Marion were together on the sands, which the receding tide had left dry: without, the wavelets followed each other, caressing the beach and lapping gently against the edges of the great sharp rocks; the softest of moons was over their heads, the softest of breezes playing in their faces. Together they strolled hand in hand, with the soft warm pressure of early love. A woman unthinkingly lends her hand to be caressed, and, lo! her fond heart straightway glows with thoughts of unutterable happiness, and her charmed thoughts hover about the image of her lover, like the silly pigeon round the enchantress serpent. They were silent, because there was nothing to say. The immoral grammarians of every tongue have with one consent placed the verb *to love* first of all the conjugations, so that those who read may learn more things than grammar—*Io t' amo, je t' aime*, and all the rest. That said, little is left but to say it again, or to be silent while the pulses vibrate from one to the other, singing speechlessly, like the trembling strings of Anacreon's lyre, nothing but love, love, love, which swears to be unchanging and eternal.

From the cottage came the sound of a piano. Adie was playing, while her father was reading. Presently the

D

music ceased, and everything was still save the ripple of the waves.

"I suppose we ought to go in, Marion," said Gerald. "Reflect, dear, before we tell the world. There is yet time to reflect; no one has heard your promise but me. Think it all over again, and tell me, dearest, once more if you can love me."

There are many thousand stories yet to be written about human life, although so many thousand exist already. Fate shakes up the great kaleidoscope, and produces combinations without number; but there is one which never tires. On such a night a youth told a maiden that he loved her; on such a night she threw her white arms round his neck, and with self-abandonment most maidenly and pure, laid her face against his face, as he stooped his head to meet it, and whispered words, while her heart beat with the tumult of strange and new feelings, which were never to be forgotten or recalled.

"Gerald, you know that I love you, and—oh, gently, gently, Gerald dear."

He led her, trembling and glowing, back to her father's house, daughter still, but yet not quite the same. For maid Marion was pledged, and the golden cestus was ready to be loosed.

They found Adie standing on the steps of the verandah. She is a girl of sixteen—the age when childhood and maidenhood meet, and make each other ashamed, as the old thoughts of the one are beaten back by the new-born thoughts of the other; a tall and lithe damsel, with thin long limbs which want filling out. She is unlike her sister at every point. Her features are straighter and clearer; her blue eyes are bright, but they want the depth of Marion's; her fair hair hangs, as a young maiden's should, loose about her shoulders; she carries her head with a certain defiant haughtiness, unlike her sister's modest pose; and while Marion's lips are closed with the earnestness of duty and resolve, Adrienne's are lightly parted, as if catching at some unknown pleasure.

"You *are* come back, then!" she cried petulantly. "Gerald, it is too bad. Only home three days, and you monopolise Marion, the whole afternoon and evening. No, sir, I am too big to be kissed now; and I don't want my hair pulled, thank you. And, Marion, something has happened. Fred has written to papa, and there is a big bundle of letters come from Oxford, and papa is put out."

Marion's heart fell. Her brother Fred was one of that too numerous class of correspondents who write only when, as Adrienne said, "something has happened." That, in our euphemistic manner of speech, means something bad.

"What is it, Adie?"

"I do not know. The letter was brought this afternoon, but stupid Susan forgot to give it to papa till this evening. He turned quite pale when he read it, and of course won't tell me anything. Go in, Marion, and say what you can for poor Fred. I suppose he is in another scrape. Fred never writes unless he is in a scrape, Gerald. And ever since I have been old enough to be told things, the dear boy always has been in a scrape."

Marion, troubled, went into the drawing-room, where her father was sitting at his own table with a pile of papers before him. It was the family room. It was long, low, and narrow: it had a piano, a bookcase, and a table—the captain's—covered with books. It was Marion's studio, Adie's practising-room, and their father's library, all in one. When Fred was at home it was his lounging-room as well. Captain Revel's face, as he sat before the lamp and read his letters, was pale, and his hand trembled.

"Come in, my dear. Is that Gerald outside?"

"What is it, papa?"

"Call Gerald, Marion. We want his advice. Gerald, help me if you can. We are simple people here," he said, bitterly, "and do not understand the ways of the learned world. Read my son's letter, and advise me what I am to do. Listen, Marion, my child. It is your brother's latest freak."

Gerald read—

"MY DEAR FATHER,—I am sorry to have to tell you that I got into a mess at Oxford last June. I did not like to let you know the truth at the beginning of the Long, and I hoped the tutor would manage to get me out of it. But I find that he cannot. Perhaps he has himself written to you by this time. The fact is, I was rusticated for a year for a little escapade, in which I foolishly joined. Lord Rodney Benbow was the other man. We laid a train of powder round the court for a firework, which no one would have cared very much about, only Rodney would finish it up with a cracker or two at the Dean's door. The porter saw us, and gave information. So the Dons had us up, and made unpleasant remarks; and we were rusticated. I hope you will not be greatly annoyed. It will delay my degree for a twelvemonth, but that is all. You will be glad to learn that I have enjoyed the reading party greatly. We had good fishing, and very good fun all round. Lord Rodney wants me to join him in a journey up the Nile, and to the East, to last till the expiration of our sentence. He very kindly offers to bear most of the expenses. But of course I cannot accept his invitation till I hear from you, as I cannot ask him to pay the travelling fares. Rustication is not so very awful a thing, after all; and I daresay we shall get over it. Tell me if you would like me to run down to the Comb before we start for Egypt. Love to Marion and my little Adie.—Your affectionate son,
                                    "FREDERICK REVEL."

"Oxford is a place where young men are sent to receive the highest education the world can give," said Captain Revel, "and at twenty years of age they behave like naval cadets. He calls a public disgrace nothing. He talks of losing a year as if it was nothing. And he offers to go out to Egypt as if it was a part of the course. Gerald, you know all our family secrets—if we have any secrets. Advise me what to do."

Gerald hesitated.

"After all, it is hardly a disgrace, sir," he began.

"Not a disgrace? Not a disgrace for a man of twenty to

be firing crackers at his superior officer's door like a boy of twelve? Why at twenty I was cutting out slavers on the West Coast. It may be no disgrace at Oxford, but it is a sore disgrace at Comb Leigh."

"I mean," said Gerald, "that the offence is foolish enough, but not—not—in fact, it might have been worse."

"The boy is light-headed," groaned the captain. "A feather turns him; he has no more will than the shuttle-cock; he— "

"Papa," said Marion, "don't be too hard on poor Fred."

"It was for Oxford," the captain went on, pacing up and down the room, "that we saved and scraped, Marion and I—"

"Oh, never mind that, papa!"

"It was to give him the best start in life that a lad can have, and the best education, that I denied my girl here the training that she deserved. We pinched in her dress and in our living, Gerald; we made Marion governess to Adie when she ought to have been herself at school; we have lived cooped up in this little village when I might have taken her to see something of the world—in order that Fred might have the means of going to a public school and the University. And this is the end of it. He was to have brought credit on the old name—a name older and more honourable on the other side of the water than yours, Gerald, my boy—he was to be the pride of all of us; and see what it has all come to. Look at it, Marion—think of it."

"Nay, sir," said Gerald, "all is not lost because Fred has been unluckily foolish."

"All is not lost? No. All would not be lost if the boy would work, but he will not. This is the last blow. Fred has spent all our savings, Marion, my dear. There is nothing left. You did not read his postscript, Gerald. He tells me the tutor has sent on his bills. And here they are. He adds a remark that they may wait."

"O Gerald!" murmured Marion, "say something to help."

"May I look at the bills, sir?"

"Look at them all. It is a pretty collection for one year of Oxford life. Champagne, claret, water-colours, engravings,

boats, horses, for the son of a half-pay officer! You have
been at Oxford, Gerald. Tell me, if you can, that all young
men are so."

Gerald was silent for a while.

"Fred has been extravagant," he said. "Let us own that
he has been as foolish as a man well can be. Still, he is but
twenty."

"But twenty? Yes, with a long life before him, and,
like a ship with no ballast to keep her steady, without
principle."

"O papa!"

"Marion, shuffling words do not alter facts. Fred's life is
before him, and what will he do with it? 'Unstable as
water, he shall not excel.'"

"Let the debts wait," said Gerald. "As he has contracted
them, let him do what many a man has to do—pay them
afterwards. They will be a log about his neck for years,
but he will have to pay them in the long run."

"No, Gerald," said the captain, "we will not do that; will
we, Marion? We will not let a pack of cheating horse-
dealers and rascals make jokes on the name of Revel. We
will pay them every farthing, if we starve for it ourselves.
But he must never set foot again in Oxford."

"Perhaps," said Gerald, hesitatingly—"perhaps, captain—
if—if—if you would let me make terms with these fellows—"

"Thank you, Gerald; but I will not borrow of you. If I
want a loan, I will ask your father, my old friend. He will
do it for me. Fred's debts shall be paid. But the debts are
nothing, nothing—we can scrape for a few years more, and
settle them. As for the boy, all the world knows already,
I suppose, that he is rusticated—all the world except ourselves. He came home, sir, with the shame of the thing still
upon him, to play and sing and laugh with the girls whose
money he had wasted; and not a word to me, though he
knew I must learn it, sooner or later. Marion, say, if you can,
something in excuse for your brother. I can find nothing."

Marion's tears came into her eyes, but she could not say a
word. It was all too cruel.

"And he wants to travel—as a reward, I suppose, for his folly," said the captain bitterly. "I know what I will do; I will see your father, Gerald, and borrow the money from him to pay off all in full. I will go up to town myself, take the boy down to Oxford, and settle up every liability. Then he shall apologise to the college authorities, and take his name off the boards. I sent him there to work; and since he will only play, he may come to Comb Leigh and lay trains of gunpowder round the cove, if he likes. They cost less here."

Marion looked at Gerald.

"Perhaps, sir," he said, "I may be able to arrange for you. Let me go to town and see him. Let me bring Fred home to you. And—and—Captain Revel—perhaps a word or two of kindness may affect him more deeply than anger. You were good enough to take me into your confidence, you know."

"Ay, Gerald, ay; you can say what you like in this house."

"May I, sir? Then let me say another thing, though it is not a favourable moment. Captain Revel, accept me as another son."

He took Marion's hand.

"I asked this dear girl to-day," he went on, "to be my wife. Will you consent if she will—since she does?"

"Marion, Gerald, I did not look for this!"

The captain was silent for a while. The two stood before him like a pair of prisoners waiting their sentence. When he spoke, it was with the voice and look of one whose thoughts are far off.

"When Marion was born, I was angry and disappointed that the child was not a boy. When Fred was born, I rejoiced, because the old line might still be carried on. Fred's mother—well, never mind. Marion and I brought up the two babies. When Marion was only six years old, I repented of my disappointment, and thanked God solemnly for my girl, Gerald."

He stopped, and taking her head upon his breast, patted her face, while he went on—

"I have thanked God daily ever since for her. Not a

morning, not an evening, that I have not thanked Him for
His great gift of this my daughter. What Marion has been
to me and my house, who knows but myself? How can I
tell, even to you, who have known her so long, how Marion
has been the stay and comfort of my life? Marion, you have
wasted the spring of your time on your father and your
sister—"

"No, father, not wasted."

"Not wasted, dear," he repeated. "The life of love is
never wasted: it is like the rain which fertilises, and the
sun which brings forth; we see the fruits, and we forget the
way they grew. Not wasted, Marion; only spent and given
for us. You want to take her away from me, Gerald. It is
a great thing you ask, but it shall be as my child wishes."

"Gerald knows what I wish," said Marion simply. "But
not to leave you, father—not to leave you."

"Chacomb is not *very* far off," Gerald said.

"It will be as good as a hundred miles away when I have
to come to breakfast in the morning and find no Marion.
My dear, your father is selfish—he thinks of nothing but his
own comfort—forgive him, and go with your lover. I have
nothing to give with her, Gerald; but she brings you a heart
full of love—ah, Marion, my daughter!—full of love. That
is her only heritage, for her brother has wasted all the rest."

"Never mind her brother, sir," said Gerald. "You have
given me something of a right to interfere, and I will go to
town and bring him back to you to-morrow, if you let me."

"Ay, bring him back, Gerald. Tell him that he must
come home, and spend no more money, while we consider
his future. My heart is too full to-night to have any anger
in it. By Jove, I wish you could tie him up and give him
three dozen, and so wipe out all the score. Now leave me,
both of you, to go through these bills, and find out what I
shall have to borrow."

Not a thought crossed the simple sailor's mind that his old
friend—his companion of near a score of years—could possibly object to lending him any sum he might ask. Not an
idea that a Chacomb could object to an alliance with a Revel.

CHAPTER VI.

GERALD looked back at the captain as he drew Marion silently from the room. The papers lay spread beneath his hands, but he was not looking at them. His thoughts had flown back a long way beyond Fred and his debts; they were in the old time before Marion was born. His eyes were full, and his lips were moving. People who, in these superior times, believe in such things, might have thought him praying.

Outside in the garden, swinging her hat by the strings, and singing as she went, was Adie—untroubled, though she knew there was trouble. Hers was the light nature, which she shared with her brother Fred, of being able to disbelieve in trouble. She was impatient with people who took things seriously; she wanted everybody not to mind; she could not bear to see Marion and her father vexing themselves because Fred could not keep in the straight and narrow way; it was incomprehensible to her why anything should give trouble except sickness and suffering.

"I am glad you have come," she said, "because now, I suppose, it is all made right again. I heard you all talking, and poor Fred's name used a good deal, so I thought I ought not to listen, and went right away down to the cove. See what it is, Gerald, to be in a small house when you are not considered grown up, and must keep out of the way. Well, Marion, you have smoothed things, I hope, for the poor boy. Marion is the greatest peacemaker in all the world, Gerald."

"I am sure she is," said her lover.

"See, dear," said Marion. "It is past eleven, and you will catch cold. Let us go in."

Adie pouted, but obeyed.

"Good night, Gerald. You may kiss me if you like; it's very nice, but I don't think you ought to, you know; you don't kiss Marion. It *is* pleasant to have you back again, though I suppose I am too big now for the old games we used to have. But there's the swing still, and we can go fishing;

and I can play to you now, instead of Marion; and we can sing trios. Don't go off to any horrid places. Marion used to read your letters a dozen times, and got creeps and shivers over the snakes and alligators. Marion, I keep fancying I hear footsteps in the shrubbery. I was getting quite nervous when you came in. Good night, Gerald."

"Come, Marion," said her lover, when her sister ran in, "come to the gate, at least, with me. See, what a lovely night! Everybody is asleep; walk two steps up the lane with me. It has not been a pleasant ending to the first day of our engagement, dear Marion; but you will be happy in spite of Fred's weakness, will you not? After all, he is only a schoolboy, as you said."

"No, Gerald; but a man ought to be strong; it is his duty."

"I will go to town to-morrow, and see what I can do with him. We shall be back the day after, and—enough of Fred, dear Marion. Now, when no one is looking but the moon, which has seen so many kisses, put your arms round my neck, and promise me all over again. My love, it is too great happiness. This is what I dreamed of when I was abroad; it was for this that I came home. My dear love, my Marion, could there ever come a time when I should cease to love you?"

Ten minutes later Marion turned to go into the house. Gerald was walking home. Comb Leigh was all asleep. And then she heard, as Adie had heard, steps in the shrubbery.

She stopped and listened.

"Marion!"

It was a voice that she knew, calling her in low tones. She turned sick with dread.

"Marion, come here into the shrubbery."

She hesitated a moment, and obeyed.

"O Fred, Fred, Fred!" she whispered, kissing him, "how could you be so wicked and so foolish?"

It is Fred, hiding behind the shrubs for a chance to speak to Marion. His handsome face is clouded with a little care, but not very much. His blue eyes and fair hair are like

Adrienne's, as is the lofty carriage of his head. His chin is narrow and retreating, and the corners of his mouth are weak. But for beauty of form he is a very Apollo, and his voice is as sweet as a flute.

"I don't know," he replied. "I was wicked because I was so foolish; I was foolish because I was so wicked; and of course I have been a great ass. Don't reproach me, Marion; I came here for a little comfort, and you must not turn upon me."

"How can I help turning upon you? You are breaking my father's heart."

"Nonsense, Marion!—nonsense, sweet maid Marion!" he laughed flippantly. "People don't break their hearts for a trifle of money to be paid for their sons' debts. They get very angry, pay up, and then forgive them."

"Come in, and see him. Don't hide behind the bushes in your father's own garden, Fred. Be brave. Come in, and beg his pardon."

"I don't know about being brave," he replied. "If I hadn't gone such an awful cropper, I shouldn't mind so much; but addition is a beast of a rule in arithmetic when you come to bring it home to yourself; and I find that the people have all sent in their bills, and there will be the devil and all, and—"

"And, oh, Fred, why did you not tell us in June?"

"Well, you see, my sister, the fact is, I thought there would be a tremendous row, and—and—when I came down the tutor's letter arrived with me; so I took it from the postman, and thought it would be just as well that the governor should not have it."

"Do you mean to tell me, Fred, that you actually stopped a letter intended for your father?"

"That, Marion, is just exactly what I did do. No one knows it except yourself, and no one ever will. Now, Marion, don't go on and be silly. There's no great harm done, after all."

"O Fred, Fred!" she cried; "and you that we hoped so much of! It isn't only the debt and the folly and the disgrace; but oh, my brother, it is the terrible disappointment."

He shook off her hand from his shoulder.

"That's the way with the women. They cry and lament about nothing. There, Marion, don't make mountains out of molehills. A little debt and a stupid rustication. Now kiss me, and say you forgive."

"As if I should not forgive. But it is not my forgiveness that will do any good. Only come in and see him."

"No, Marion, I will not. I came down this evening—travelled with the mail that brought my letter—and hung about here while you were talking with Gerald Chacomb. Adie wrote to me that he was back again; but I could not see him through the trees. I knew his voice, though. If you were a different sort of girl, I should have thought you were spooning. Well, I want you to be my friend. Smooth him over. Tell him he need not worry about the debts. Oxford tradesmen always give long credit, and we will pay them somehow. And I want to go to Egypt with Lord Rodney. He's quite the best fellow in the world."

"And where is the money to come from?"

"It won't cost much. Rodney will pay for all but the travelling expenses. Don't you see the importance of keeping a friend like that?"

"Have you forgotten, Fred, that you have no money, that you have spent all that your father set aside for you, and that you will have to work your own way in the world?"

"Don't put things in such a bald, coarse manner, Marion. It's bad enough to be poor, without being reminded of it."

"What are we to do, Fred? Oh, what *are* we to do about you?"

"Just nothing, Marion. Let things go on by themselves. It is always the wisest thing not to fidget and fuss. My dear child, you are making a great deal of worry."

"Fred, you do not understand—you *will* not understand! There is no more money left, none at all; but that is nothing. It is you that we are anxious about—your future, your own conduct. Once more, will you come in and see your father?"

"No, I will not," he returned, doggedly. "I shall go back as I came. You had better go and tell him that I have been here."

"It would break his heart to learn that his son came home and waited outside like a—like a—"

"Like a burglar, I suppose."

"Afraid to go into the house and seek his forgiveness."

"Yes, I am afraid. It is all very well for you, Marion. You are his favourite. You have been his companion always. It is with me that he has always been stern and unforgiving. Poor little Adie and I are the children of his second wife. It is not our fault, I suppose."

"Fred, you are unjust."

"Very likely. I do everything that is wrong. I go to Oxford, and I live among gentlemen, and not among cads, as a gentleman. It costs my father a little more than he expected. I am unlucky enough not to get the scholarships and prizes you thought I should get. If you only knew the kind of men who do get these things, you would not think so badly of me."

"Gerald Chacomb got a scholarship, and was a fellow."

"Gerald Chacomb is a prig. Well, it is no use talking, Marion; go and fetch my little Adie out to give me a kiss. *She* won't reproach her brother when he is down on his luck. If she cannot help me as you can, she can tell me I have done nothing disgraceful or dishonourable."

"No, I will not bring Adie to you. She is in bed, poor child. Tell me what I can do for you, Fred—don't be cruel. You know there's nothing in the world I would not do for you. But, oh, if you would only come in with me!"

"Then I tell you what you shall do for me. To-morrow you will get my father to write me a letter sanctioning the Egypt journey; and—and, Marion, have you got any money?"

"I have ten pounds left from my own money."

"Then lend me that, my dear girl. I will give it you back as soon as ever I have any more. I must get back to London. Run and bring it at once, because I must be off."

Marion said nothing, but went away for her purse. It was

all she had, and with it vanished her last hope of any new dresses. But she gave it with a cheerful countenance, such as the Lord loveth.

"And now, Fred, what are you going to do?"

"I shall walk on to Barnstaple, and go up to town by the night train. Write to me at the Tavistock, where Rodney and I are staying."

"Fred, do not—do not spend more money."

"The Tavistock is the cheapest place in all London," he replied airily. "You could not spend money there if you wanted ever so much. Good night, Marion dear. You are the best of all girls, only a little inclined to sermonise. You will never get a husband if you are so solemn and serious. Come, give me a kiss. There—you are a dear girl—and now one for Adie. And now I will be off. Mind, I depend upon your good offices. You will—"

"I will do what I can for you—when have I not? And, oh, Fred—" remembering suddenly that Gerald was going to town on purpose to see him.

But Fred kissed her lightly on the cheek, and was gone.

Marion sighed, and returned to her father.

"You will be happy, child," said the captain, patting her cheek, "as you deserve to be, my dear—as you deserve to be. I am sorry that this other thing has fallen upon us on such a day; we ought to have been all gladness and joy for my girl's engagement."

"Do not think of it, papa, more than you can help. Gerald will go to town and see Fred; and we must hope for the best. Let us always remember our bright-faced boy, with his winning ways, and how we loved him."

She spoke as if her half-brother were about ten years younger than herself.

"Remember what you have always said about his weakness of will, and how he would fall into temptation—it was the fault of his nature: we must make allowances for all. Do not let him go to that wicked place any more; we will keep him here for a little, and try to make him steady. And then, papa, he is only a schoolboy—is he not?"

"I will endeavour, dear, to remember, and to make allowances. But the disappointment is grievous, Marion. After all, money spent is gone, and we are foolish to regret it. Only I can make no more now; and when I die, dear Marion, what is to become of those two helpless children? Who will provide for them? Thank God, dear, that your future is at least placed above starvation point."

"We are in better hands than our own, father. Now, go to bed, dear. Let me put up all your papers. See, here is a letter unopened among them."

"Another bill, Marion—another bill. I will look at it to-morrow."

He put it into his pocket, and shut up the packet of Fred's bills in his desk.

"My daughter"—he took her face in his hands, and held it up to his—two faces as honest, brave, and true as this world has ever seen, and both strangely alike—"my daughter, I am going to lose you. I, that have had the first place, shall have to be content with the second. It is the way of the world, and I do not repine, dear. Remember always, my child, that no husband can love you better than your father."

"I know it, father!" whispered Marion.

"I did not think I should be so moved, my dear, by anything. It seems as if I had so much to say, and no time to say it in. I feel as if opportunities for talking to my daughter would come no more, and yet so much is untold. It seems as if I were going—not my Marion."

"You are nervous, papa, dear. You will be better to-morrow."

"Good night, dear. God bless my darling! God preserve her from harm, and surround her with happiness and love."

The captain's voice broke down, and his eyes melted into tears.

So the girl's day, that should have been the happiest in her life, was spoiled by her brother's fault; and the night that should have been as a bridal night was mingled with a sense of bitterness that jarred upon her joy. Through her soul flowed the harmonies of love, but now and then the thought of her brother struck discordant notes, and marred the music. Somehow, in the education of our boys, we have dropped out one or two of the elements of morality. They do not learn in our great schools and universities the grand duty of looking things in the face. If they are taught the lesson of working first and enjoying afterwards, it does not seem to stick; and the simple principles of common sense, which should assign to every boy his own way of beginning the battle of life, are left to be taught by experience. Now, as Herodotus says, "Our lessons are mainly taught by our sufferings." Poor Fred wanted to enjoy. And, that he might enjoy, he had brought upon his father's house the common tragedy of a ruined home. Meantime, with his sister's last ten pounds in his pocket, he was marching gaily across the country, to catch the mail train from Barnstaple.

CHAPTER VII.

EARLY in the morning Marion was roused from sleep by a familiar signal. Not a lover's serenade, for Gerald was in his bed at Chacomb; nor by the voice of the lark leaving his watery nest; nor by the early crow of chanticleer; but by the rattling of gravel thrown up at her window. She knew it for the *réveille* of her father, and, throwing open the casemate, looked out—her face making a pretty picture, with the long hair loose, *crinibus solutis*, floating round and over it; her cheeks as dainty as a peach, and her dimpled mouth. Paint me such a picture, cunning limner. Put in a hand holding a white garment to the throat, lest the sun, who wants to see so much, should catch a glimpse of her marble bosom. Let her eyes be bright, but full and deep withal; give her oval face the curves that belong to the artistic mind, the mind that feels what others only see; give her eyebrows the slightest possible curve at the corners, to show a latent possibility of will; her forehead must be narrow rather than broad, but a little higher than sculptors have granted to Venus; over her face throw, if you can, some of the expression

of the great Love goddess; let there be a newly awakened
look of Venus. She is looking out of a square casement with
diamond panes; above and on each side is the thick thatch,
with green and grey for colouring, edged with deep shade;
swallows are flying in and out of the nests, regardless of her
presence; creepers are climbing up from below, and twisting
lithe tendrils round every little projection, and tossing un-
occupied arms about the open window as the wind blows
them to and fro. In the garden is her father. On his face
no signs of last night's trouble, for the morn is bright. He
has slept, and the good has driven off the evil.

"Dress quickly, Marion, and come down," he whispered,
loud enough for her to hear. "Do not wake Adie."

Adie was in her own room, next to Marion's, sleeping
soundly. The two servants, who completed the household,
were asleep too; for it was only five, and nothing astir yet
but the captain. Nothing? Everything. The birds were
busy with the early worm—the early worm was busy about
affairs connected with his own digestive organs. The swallow
hunted the fly, the fly looked about for the midge; and
nature wore that busy and cheerful aspect—we associate it
with universal joy and hymns of praise—when everything is
hunting and being hunted. There were sounds from the
village, whose life was already awake and hard at work: a
pump-handle was working noisily; a ploughboy was whistling;
cocks were clearing their throats; somebody was sharpening
a tool upon the grindstone; pigs were grunting; an ass—
probably a descendant of Lucius, the Golden Ass of Apuleius
—full of emotion at the brightness of the dawn, was greeting
Aurora with melodious bray; a child was crying—Nature in
her loveliest moods seems somehow dissatisfied unless she
can throw in a squalling child; a woman was scolding—if
all were harmony the sweetest morning would pall upon the
senses—but at such a distance as only to touch the soul with
a little jar, a saddened sense of dissonance; and the freshest
of breezes was lifting the leaves upon their stalks and waving
the branches.

Happiness wakes first; hope, next; trouble, last. The

E

unfortunate young gentleman in the picture, who is just going
to be awakened to fight the tiger for the gratification of Nero
and the delight of the Roman ladies, is very truthfully represented in that stage of dreaminess which precedes the happy
waking.   In another moment he will open eyes full of hope;
in the next he will turn to the roaring and hungry creature
who now pokes eager claws through the bars at him, eager to
slay and devour, and the trouble of horrid anticipation will
begin. Marion woke to happiness and hope. The only trouble
in her heart was the thought of her brother, and this, for the
nonce, she put aside.   It was one that could wait.

"It is *such* a morning, Marion darling," said the captain.
"Dress and come down, and we will go for a sail."

It was indeed a morning of the very finest—such a morning as makes those who have been pulled out of bed at six to
glow with conscious virtue, because it seems like the reward
of a good action.   Happy those who have only got up early
on fine mornings.   There are men—living men—who have
risen at six on rainy mornings, and so learned to probe some
of the deeper depths of remorse.

Then began a day which was destined afterwards to live in
her memory—so short, and yet so long—all her life. Not
one single detail was ever to be lost.   She remembered how
she knelt for a moment while her father called to her; how
she prayed quickly for him, for Gerald, and for Fred; how
she caught her straw hat—the dainty little straw, brown with
sunshine and sea breezes, that sat on her head like a crown
—and ran lightly downstairs into the garden and her father's
arms.

He took her face in his hands, kissing her on the cheeks
and on the lips and on the forehead in a comprehensive way
unusual with him.   Then he held her for a moment without
saying anything; and then he passed his hand through her
hair, which hung loose in pretty morning fashion.

"My daughter," he whispered, "and so I am going to lose
you."

"Not yet, papa; and not altogether, you know."

He shook his head, and let her go.

" Let us make the best of the bright morning, my dearest. I lay awake half the night thinking of you and Gerald and poor Fred, until it occurred to me that thinking would be of no possible use; so I gave it up and went to sleep. Never mind, dear. I will make it up to-night. Tell your father all about it, Marion."

" There is nothing to tell," she replied, reddening a little. " It was only yesterday afternoon that Gerald—"

" Well, dear, I am not going to ask you what Gerald said. You know that lovers' words are sacred."

" Gerald told me he loved me, that is all. He said he loved me even before he went away; and I knew nothing of it."

" But you were always fond of Gerald."

" Oh yes, papa—always fond of him; but not in that way. And it all seems so different now. I cannot tell you how different. The world is changed with me since yesterday."

" Yes, life is so. A woman leaves her father and her mother, and cleaveth to her husband. It is the rule of Nature."

" But I do not want to leave you, my dear father."

" No, dear. You do not want to, but you will have to leave me. Thank God, you can go happily with the man you love."

" I do love Gerald," she murmured.

" And so yesterday was the very first time that young man spoke to you on this important subject ? "

" Yes, the first time; unless, perhaps, it was the day before he left us to go to America, when we had our last walk together. I remember it so well. We were walking home through Chacomb Wood, listening to the birds. I was saying how stupid and lonely it would be without him, and he —but perhaps he did not mean anything."

" What did he say, Marion ? That is, if I may ask."

" He said that he hoped I should always find it lonely and stupid without him."

" Some prayers are granted," said her father. " One of the old philosophers—I suppose it must have been Socrates, because nobody else ever seems to have said anything at all

—used to say that men ought to be very careful what they prayed for. The gods, he remarked, sometimes give us what we ask for, and pretty fools we look then. However, Gerald's prayer seems to have been a reasonable one, considering everything."

"You are not jealous, are you, dear? You know I love you better than anybody in this world; better even—yes, perhaps better than my Gerald. But I love him too."

"No, dear, I am not jealous," said the captain, stoutly.

"Tell me you are glad, papa."

"Half-truths, my dear, as your poet Tennyson would tell you, are a very dangerous kind of falsehood. I am not glad on my own account. I am saddened, and a little confused to know what I shall do without you. But I am more glad than I can tell you for your sake, dear. You are going to marry the best young fellow in all the world. I do believe, the most honest, the truest, the most loyal, and the most generous."

Marion's eyes filled with tears.

"You are the best and kindest of dear fathers. Gerald is all that you have said, I am sure, and a thousand things more."

"You will have to find out how to manage your husband, you know, Marion. The old rule used to be, never to let him know how much you love him. That is nonsense. I will give you a better. Make him proud of his work, whatever it is. Keep up the flame in his heart; learn to follow him in his career; cultivate his ambition; never suffer him to think meanly of himself. Remember, my dear, that your husband's career is a more important thing than his love: keep him steadfast to the one, and you will have the other. The true *ars amoris* is the use of intelligent sympathy. You drive your husband with a light rein when you drive him to success."

"But I do not want to drive Gerald, papa."

"Do you not, dear? Chaucer's ladies confessed that what they liked best of all earthly things was power. But perhaps the women of the nineteenth century are wiser."

" I shall always be proud of Gerald."

" Yes, my dear; there are ladies who value their lords according to the market value of their abilities and attainments. Well, be happy, dearest, let who will be wise. You will go and put yourself under the heel of that young man; he will be your tyrant; he will order you and direct you—"

" Papa, papa, papa—*will* you be quiet? So long as he loves me, what matter what he does or says? People who love each other cannot help being kind and thoughtful."

" Come down to the cove, my dear, and let us get the boat ready."

The boat was tossing in the middle of the tiny harbour, fretting at the rope which held her, while the blue waves came rolling in over the bar of sand, and tearing themselves to pieces against the ragged rock on either hand. She was a strong and serviceable little craft, not afraid of a North Devon sea or a stiff breeze—one of poor Kingsley's keen north-easters—and as safe in a squall as a Portsmouth wherry.

The captain hauled in the rope, and Marion shipped the rudder while he went to the boat-house for mast and sails. If Marion had few accomplishments, she possessed one in perfection—the art of sailing. It was a kind of instinct with her. Had she been so fortunate as to live in the days when there were no boats, she would have been the first to arm her heart with triple brass, and invent a raft of some kind for herself. Fallen on days when there is little in this way left to invent, except torpedoes, she made herself as handy as any boy on the whole coast, from Burnham to Clovelly; good at the rudder, good at lowering the sail, good at keeping the boat's head before the wind, good at tacking, good at running, with gunwale touching the water, before the steady Channel breeze.

" The breeze is fresh, Marion." He took the oars, and rowed out of the cove into the sea beyond. " Now, then, up with the canvas; keep her steady; so! Now she feels it. Dip your nose in it; jump and dance, my pretty; show them a clean pair of heels." He was addressing the boat. "Isn't this better than lying in bed? And now, Marion, we are quite alone, and there is nobody but ourselves to hear—let us talk about your marriage."

"But I am only just engaged, papa."

"Gerald is six-and-twenty, dear—an age when a young man does not look on waiting with any rapture. This morning I will walk over and talk to Chacomb about it. I expect him to be as pleased as I am myself."

"Papa, I am afraid of Mr. Chacomb."

"Nonsense, Marion."

"It is not nonsense. Sometimes he looks so odd. I have seen him looking sideways at you, papa, when he thought no one saw him; and it was as if he wanted to strangle you. And we have known him all these years, and I never draw any closer to him."

"Chacomb has his reserved side, Marion, but he is a good fellow at heart; and he is very fond of Gerald."

"Ah, yes," said the girl, softening, "he is fond of Gerald. His voice drops when he speaks to him; his eyes follow him about; he forgets to hitch up his shoulder when Gerald is with him; and—and, oh, papa, he is jealous of you."

"Marion, you suspicious child, you are 'making up,'" said her father.

"No, I am not. It is all true. And suppose he were to become jealous of me after I am married?"

"Then he will be a great donkey, dear. Put these fancies out of your head. Chauncey Chacomb is as fond of you as I am almost, though he does not show it. As for me, I believe there is nothing that he would not do for me. For nearly twenty years we have been companions and friends. No, dear, we are happy in having such a neighbour as Chacomb, without thinking of his son at all. You will own it when I bring *him* back with me to-night to wish you joy. Look at the colours on that rock, dear; grey, purple, green, and black —a bluish black it looks from here. There are the cormorants flying about the point. We will come out some very still day, and try to sketch the light of these early mornings. But I shall have to come out alone soon, shall I not? Marion, when you are married you will take poor little Adie with you to see something of the world, will you not?"

They lapsed into silence for a while, wrapped in their thoughts, and watching the water as the boat flew before the breeze. The captain's face was composed and grave, but his expression was that of one who looks forward.

So they glided swiftly past the long shore of headland after headland; passing the peaceful villages lying in long streets behind the coves; catching glimpses of homesteads dotted here and there, and hearing the tinkle of the sheep bells from the high downs. Presently the captain shook himself together.

"I am dull for you, Marion; but I was thinking. Let us 'bout ship, and tack for Comb Leigh again. I was thinking about the old days—the days before you were born, my dear. Strange that the time should come back to me to-day so vividly that I thought put away and buried long ago. I never told you, Marion, about your mother's marriage; somehow we have not talked together a great deal about her, even when we have been alone.

"She was very beautiful, Marion—more beautiful than you, my dear. She was the most beautiful woman I have ever seen, and the best and kindest. You are like her so far. She was the daughter of a man in the position of Chauncey Chacomb—a country squire of Dorsetshire. Until I knew her father, I did not understand what was meant by county families and county pride. My dear, your grandfather was as proud as Lucifer. He had nothing whatever, so far as I could ever learn, no single point of distinction, to be proud of. He and his grandfathers had held their estates for a great many generations. During all these centuries, always opulent, always well educated, always with every chance of success, not one single man had ever distinguished himself. Most of the great Englishmen, somehow, do seem to come from the landed people; but your mother's family had not yet produced even a third-rate great man. However, the fact

remained that he was proud. I was only a lieutenant, with
very little except my pay. Mary loved me. I spoke to her
father, and was received with rather more contumely, I
thought, than he would have bestowed upon one of his own
footmen coming with the same request. I was a Frenchman; that was his first objection. 'No Frenchman,' he said,
'could possibly be of good family.' Thereupon I produced the
dear old genealogy—you know it, dear—with Charlemagne,
Godfrey of Bouillon, and the rest of them. He laughed at
the pedigree, which he politely insinuated was a forged one.
'If I had a pedigree,' he said, 'where were the estates?'
You see, he could not possibly understand descent without
estates. Of course, it was hopeless to explain to him what
the Revolution had done for us. Also it was hopeless to tell
him that, with his great fortune, it ought to matter simply
nothing—and would have mattered nothing in old France—
whether I had money or not. So, dear, as it was of no use
to expect anything from him, and time was valuable, we
took the law into our own hands, Mary and I, and ran away
together. We were married the same day at Southampton.
When your grandfather received the fatal news, he sent a
letter cutting his daughter off with the little portion he
could not touch. It is what you have now, dear Marion—
your fifty pounds a year. Then he struck her name out of
the big Bible, forbade her ever to be mentioned again, and
sat down with the consciousness of having behaved in a
manner becoming his dignity."

"Poor mamma!"

"She cried a little at first, but we made ourselves happy.
I had a little money to spend, and we went to visit the old
place in France, which I had never seen at all. Then we
agreed to live at Portsmouth until I could get a ship, for
which I had to wait about a year. Marion, it was a very
happy year, the happiest year I ever had. Only a year, and
then you came, my dear; and—and I lost your mother. So
I went to sea again; and—well, until you grew up, my love,
and could talk to me, I had very little happiness."

Of his second wife the captain never spoke to any one.

Fred and Adie had learned by some instinct to ask no questions about their mother. Nor had Marion ever ventured to lift the curtain which her father kept closed.

"And now, Marion, that you are going to marry into one of the oldest county families in Devonshire—as old as the Carews, or the Mays, or the Poles—we might, perhaps, think about a reconciliation. I have lived out of the world with you too long. You will be able, when you are married, to go into society; and I should like you to go with such family credentials as we can boast."

"But, papa, have we no relations in France?"

"Cousins in plenty, dear; and some day I will hunt them out, and we will go over and call upon them; and I will take my own name and title again for the occasion."

"I am glad," said Marion, "that in all the great family of humanity we have some one to call of our kin."

"To-morrow, dear, I will give you all your mother's letters. You shall read her love letters to me. I think I could not have shown them to you before your heart had learned what love means, and what those letters had been to me—how sacred and how precious. I want your mother to teach you, from her grave, something of what a woman can be to her lover and her husband. I should not like you to be married without learning for yourself all that these letters can teach. Enough talking, dearest. Here is Comb Leigh. Have you enjoyed your sail?"

"Yes, papa; but the talk more."

"Now, then. Hold her up, Marion—so—cleverly steered. There is Adie coming down to meet us. Breakfast—breakfast, both my daughters."

He kissed Adie on the forehead; but as they walked up to the house together, his arm was on the neck of his elder girl.

CHAPTER VIII.

PERHAPS if one were asked to name a time when his courage would be highest and his spirits most buoyant he would fix by choice upon a holiday morning in August, when the sun was shining. All the better, then, if he might be on the North Devon coast, watching the course of the south-west wind sweeping up the broad stretches of the Bristol Channel, and crisping the waves into foaming curls. Great, above all, is the power of the sun. When Aurora and old Tithonus, like a buxom young Cambridge bedmaker and an elderly gyp, have put out the stars and swept up the untidy clouds, the sun goeth forth to work marvels. We know very well how he brings with his breath the golden clusters to the laburnum, and the blushes with his staring to the young grape's cheek. What we do not sufficiently take note of is his power on the heart of man, bringing to it flowers and fruit as to a tree, and making tender sprays of imagination shoot up even in the most unlikely breasts. I believe that if you nail a scholar to a south wall, he will become a ripe scholar; and I am sure that a young prig, caught early, and trained like a pear tree, may be made to produce in time big word-criticisms in the ——. People who live habitually in the sun never nurse evil dispositions, or brood over fancied wrongs, or spend valuable time in anticipating evil. It is best, therefore, to be born in August, so that the first things your eyes rest upon in this world may be flowers, the clear sky, the sun, and faces which, like Ruth among the stooks, "praise the Lord with sweetest looks." I can hardly think it lucky to be born in March or April, when east winds blow. Children of those months are apt to grow up perverse, ill-conditioned, and of uncertain temper; and it is of course ridiculous for any one to be born between December and February. The folk of sunny lands, prone, it may be, to sudden storms—even to sticking wrathful knives in neighbourly ribs—are a gay and light-hearted people, dwelling together in amity, careless of the future.

The sunshine entered into Captain Revel's heart. He had no misgivings this morning—no doubt about the future. What had been dark was now bright. The sky was clear above him. He left the cottage to call upon the squire, Marion watching him as he slowly started on his journey. First he loitered for a few minutes among his roses; then he stepped into the road briskly, but stopped to hold a short conversation with a neighbour's dog, one of his oldest and most trusted friends. Then, apparently at the dog's invitation, he looked into the farmyard and inspected the pigs.

"O papa!" said Marion to herself, "do go on."

Then he stood for five minutes in the road, studying thoughtfully the mechanism of the water-wheel. Being quite satisfied at length with its working, he proceeded a few steps higher up. Here there was a smithy with the smith hard at work, the fire blazing and roaring, the anvil ringing, and the sparks flying.

"Now he will go in and talk to the smith," thought Marion.

The captain did not go in, but he stood at the doorway talking to the man. The sparks of the hammer ceased, the roaring of the bellows dropped to an occasional groan; and in the quiet of the noonday Marion heard the voices. Then the captain took out his pocket-book, and made a little sketch. Marion knew what he was drawing. Back at the end of the low, dark smithy, part of the roof had fallen in, and the sunlight streaming through the opening made shifting lights and shades among the blackened beams and the iron tools hanging upon the nails.

"I wish I was with him," said Marion.

The sketch finished, the captain nodded a friendly farewell to the smith, and proceeded a few yards farther. Presently there crossed his path a file of geese, following each other with heads down, outstretched necks, flapping wings, and as much importance in their manner as if they were a band of strong-minded women with a particular engagement.

now due, to go and sit upon a platform and demand that
everything should be all argued out again from the beginning, with a special proviso that no more knowledge should
be imparted into the controversy than each woman could
herself boast.

"Cackle, cackle, cackle!" cried the geese. "Leave us to
reconstruct the world: we know everything. Cackle, cackle
—we will teach the world everything; we will upset everything. Let the ganders lay the eggs. Cackle, cackle! Sage
and onions shall be cultivated no more. We will argue only
with those who agree with us. Cackle, cackle! We are the
wise and learned sex. Who is this two-legged creature in
the path? Let him go and lay eggs."

"Pardon, mesdames," said the captain, taking off his hat
and making a very fine bow, quite a reverence of the *ancien
régime*, to the little procession.

They crossed the road and plunged into the next field,
when they began to fall out with each other.

Then the captain went on.

Presently he came to where the road to Chacomb was met
by the path which ran down from the cliffs, the same lane
which Marion and Gerald had climbed the day before. Here
he stopped, and hesitating for a moment, took the turn to the
left, and began to walk up the lane.

"I thought," said Marion, with a little disappointment,
"that he was going to Chacomb Hall."

The fact was that the captain, wrapped in his thoughts,
quite forgot the purpose with which he started, and was now
taking his customary walk up the hill.

When he was out of sight, Marion went into the house for
something to read. New and recent literature rarely found
its way to Comb Leigh, and the most attractive volume she
could find was one of Pope's poems. She chose this, and
retreated to the shadiest place in the garden, where she could
escape the rattle of her younger sister's talk, and sat down
with the volume open before her. But her thoughts very
soon wandered far away from the poet. Ah, philosophers
and verse-makers, how many a time your books are opened,

and the characters, which never reach the brain, read by the
eye alone! The ghost of the little Twickenham poet was
looking down upon her from the spirit world. "She is
reading ME," he observed, with pardonable pride, to his friend
Bolingbroke. "She is reading MY poems. Observe, my St.
John, she leaves all meaner things to vain ambition and the
pride of kings. She could do nothing better. Prudent
nymph! Happy bard!"

First her thoughts wandered away to Gerald, and to the
sweet confidences of yesterday. There was the *novitas rei*,
the newness of the thing, which yet seemed, under all the
circumstances, as if nothing else could ever have been
expected. It was not strange at all. She belonged to
Gerald, she said to herself; but then, somehow, she always
had belonged to Gerald, and so that was nothing new. And
then she fell to wondering what Gerald's father would say,
and her thoughts yielding to the soft influence of the summer
season, she began, in dreamy fashion, with lids dropped, to
listen to the sounds in the air around her. The geese after
disputing with each other as to which knew most, through
personal wrongs in particular, about the rights of geese in
general, fell to pecking and snapping, quite like platform
ladies, and with such a cackle as may be heard on a Saturday
evening in Ratcliff-highway, what time the *placens uxor*
expects her husband to return with wavering step and
multiplying eye, bringing home the scanty residue of the
weekly wage. After this battle, the geese, arriving at the
conclusion that there was nothing to be got by arguing with
nasty, obstinate things who would not listen, retired to
separate corners and sulked, making savage dabs at tasteless
tufts of grass, and pitching, with more than usual vehemence,
into the unwary worm. All this time the blacksmith's
hammer was ringing on the anvil, the bellows was wheezing,
the flames were roaring. Presently the old village carpenter,
who was also a boatman, came along the road, swearing
softly and melodiously, because there was nobody to talk
to, at things in general, and bearing with him something
hot and smoking, which he began to daub over the bottom

of his boat. The smoke curled up, black and sooty grey,
darkening, where it spread, the clear blue of the sky. Then
the carpenter, too, taking his hammer, chimed in with the
blacksmith, the geese, the anvil, and the fire, with a steady
tap-tap, as he tinkered and cobbled the bottom of his old
craft. Every sound was separate and well-defined, but yet
seemed to blend together and make music. Marion's thoughts
passed away wholly from herself, and became a part of what
she heard; so that in the future, where this morning was to
live for ever, it seemed as if no precious moment had been
lost, nor one single thing dropped from her memory of what
made it sweet and beautiful. Besides the blacksmith, and
the boatman, and the geese, she became aware of the great
water-wheel going round with a steady burr-r-r in deep
undertone, like the pedal notes of an organ; there was a
grasshopper at the foot of an apple tree, pretending to be an
Italian and a *cigale;* there were those big, foolish fellows,
the credulous humble-bees, going about with their trumpets,
firmly convinced, and trying to convince other people, that
the devil was dead, and that "warm days should never
cease;" there were the pigs, fond and faithful lovers of the
present, grunting violoncello notes of satisfaction and content;
there was the turkey, whom the poetical Scott calls the
bubbly-jock, gobbling in the distance, with a melodious
gurgle as of an oboe played softly; with him were the ducks,
a material-minded race, whose hearts are too much set upon
things of this world—they quacked like the gentle flageolet
in its lower notes; there was a peacock who screamed, and
it was as if cymbals clashed; everything chimed in, as if
there was no shirking possible on such a day, but all must
help to swell the great concerted piece. The waves lapped
gently upon the shore, the leaves rustled in the light breeze,
and from the orchard came the twittering of the birds.
Marion knew how to distinguish them every one; that
was the cooing of the wood-pigeon; that the shrill pipe of
the wren.

"August is late for him," said Marion.

The chaffinch, somewhere invisible, added his monotonous

song; the little bluetit flew from branch to branch with a short, quick note, in impatience at the concert; the blackcap sang as if he was uncertain whether to imitate the nightingale or the blackbird; on the top of a rugged and twisted old apple tree sat the chiff-chaff, calling his own name as loudly as if he were playing a part in a burlesque; the yellowhammer, who also had words as well as tune, sang his refrain of "a little bit of bread and no cheese," with a tremendous emphasis on the *no;* and the great-tit added its two notes, like a saw grinding not out of harmony with the rest.

"There are more," said Marion to herself; "but I cannot make them all out."

As she listened, peace flowed in upon her soul with a rush like the bore of a tidal river; the music set itself to words; and voices sang round her—

"Gerald—Gerald—Gerald—my lover Gerald!"

Presently her head leant backwards, her eyes closed, and the volume dropped from her hands upon the grass.

"Observe, my St. John," said the rejoicing *umbra* of Pope. "she is closing her eyes to reflect upon the words of wisdom she has read in ME."

Nobody now took any more notice of the magnificent village orchestra; but all the instruments, including the birds, the geese, the pigs, and the waves, went on, which is an unfeeling way with Nature, just the same. The face of the listener lay turned a little to the left; the lips were parted with a smile; the wind lifted and dropped the brown hair upon the forehead; in the dimples, at the corners of her mouth, lurked a thousand little sleeping loves; the eyes, Marion's sweet and steadfast eyes, were closed. The girl is happy. Let her rest.

CHAPTER IX.

THE lane up which the captain was walking was a lane of set and serious purpose. It ran straight up the hill, bending neither to the right nor to the left, perhaps in imitation of bigger roads built by the Romans. It was paved with loose flat stones, like stepping-stones or stairs, and now and then made you desire, when they slipped from your foot and brought you down, to pile them in a heap, and use them to raise your Bethel instead of your woes, as recommended by the hymn. Nevertheless a pretty lane, set on either side with a hedge whereon climbed and clung the wild rose, its blossoms gone for the summer, but bright with hips; the honeysuckle, which is mercifully ordered to bloom from June till October; and the sweet wild convolvulus, which flowers whenever it gets any encouragement in the way of sunshine. Half-way up the lane there was a pound, erected once by a defunct churchwarden of Puritanical views as regards straying animals. As he was alone in his opinions, and died without disciples, no living thing had ever been impounded in it. Sitting on the topmost bar of the pound, his feet on the second rail, among the long grass and weeds which grew up in the interior of this sunlit dungeon, and poked spikey heads through the rails, was the very man whom Captain Revel wished to see—Chauncey Chacomb. The squire was, unfortunately, more moody, more savage this morning than the previous night. He was especially angry with himself, because he had let his great secret, the secret of his overpowering jealousy and hatred, pass from himself to the doctor. So felt Samson when he awoke in the morning, and remembered what he had told to Dalilah. He had noticed his cousin's strange and searching glance. He knew what it meant. It wanted no words for him to understand that Joe Chacomb thought him—Chauncey—to be going mad; and he knew, besides, that it was true. He had pressed upon his cousin that morning a cheque for double the sum he had asked for the day before, and both felt that it was to pay for silence. They had walked together gloomily after breakfast up the lane, and Joseph, tired of his moody companion, went on and left him on the rail, alone with his reflections. He did not look well. His face was pallid; his eyes were bloodshot, for he had been awake all night; his lips were twitching; there was a long, straight crease across his forehead; his right shoulder—the uneven one—was hitched up to his ear; his fingers were beating a tattoo upon the rail. What cruel fate was this that brought the two men together in such a place, and at such a time?

It is in the seventeenth century style—quite *rococo* now, and antiquated—to attribute disastrous events to the agency of the Devil in person. The more modern, perhaps the better plan is to avoid going quite to the bottom of things, and say that accident, circumstance, or chance led to such and such a conjunction of events. What are we to say? Is it design, or is it chance? One is taken, and the other left. One catches the train which is going to be smashed, but goes off jeering at the other who is too late, and is left behind upon the platform. One starts for Australia by the steamer which founders in the Bay of Biscay, while the other waits for that which is going to resist the storm. One gets a bullet in the head, while the other comes out of the battle with only his coat sleeve riddled. On this August morning, a man took a turn to the left instead of keeping straight on, as he had intended. Safety was in the one path, and in the other —death.

The rugged upland path led the captain's straying feet slowly up the flat stones which formed the rough steps of the lane. Before him, leading him insensibly, in fact, by the hand, stalked the fine actor who plays the principal part in the *Danse Macabre*. It is a defect in that otherwise admirable series of drawings, that every single sketch is a group of two, wherein the intention of the leading figure, despite his politeness—you will observe the gallant bearing of the Chevalier La Mort towards the ladies—is but too

F

apparent. A later artist would have represented the Disguise of Mors. He would have shown him as lurking beneath a stone in the shape of a viper, or flying through the air as an eagle, or crouching in shrubs like a panther, or even sitting on an old village pound by the side of mad Chauncey Chacomb, whispering devilry. But, in any case, the patient —or beneficiary—Dominus Moribundus, would have advanced to his fate with a step as cheery, a smile as jocund, a bearing as gallant, a countenance as unsuspicious, a heart as light, as Captain Revel.

He greeted Chacomb with a laugh, which reminded him of yesterday's humiliation—a laugh which set every nerve of the jealous and suspicious man tingling; a laugh utterly regardless of those morbid feelings which natures such as Chauncey Chacomb's generally mistake for evidences of superior delicacy and refinement.

"You, Chacomb?" he cried; "and up here? The very man I wanted to see. Come off your perch, man, and walk up to the top with me. Where's the doctor? Did Gerald go off this morning? How is the picture looking to-day? Ha! ha! We shall find it a breather for the next five minutes. Not so young as we were, we old fellows. How are the flesh tints, and the delicate outlines of the panel, eh? Ho! ho!"

Chauncey Chacomb screwed his mouth into what he meant for a smile, and slowly descended from his rail. If he was getting older—granted that he was sixty-one—so much the more reason for hiding the fact away. If he had made a mistake about the picture—and he was not so certain of that —it was an additional proof of bad taste in the captain to harp upon it.

"Not so young as we were, Revel!" he repeated. "None of us are, I suppose."

"I like the niggers for one thing," said Revel, leading the way; "they never know their own age within forty or fifty years. I once knew an old fellow on the West Coast who died at a hundred and twenty, as near as could be guessed, and refused to be comforted when he was being snuffed out, because he was cut off in his youth."

"I am not a hundred and twenty," returned the other gloomily.

Revel did not notice his bad temper. He was one of those men whose own tempers are so equable, that they are slow to suspect ill-temper in others. Nothing short of the wildest outbreak on the part of Chauncey Chacomb would have made the captain realise that his old friend could be actuated by any but the most kindly and cheerful sentiments.

"Look round, Chacomb, at the view up the valley. I do not know which is the best time in the day to mount this hill. I think such a morning as this, when there is no mist to hide the glorious breadth of colour. There was a light sea fog at six, but it has gone. There is a picture for you. It ought to be all the more enjoyable for being your own, eh? A more valuable picture than any in the Collection. Possession adds an additional charm of its own, I should think. I remember going to France about three and twenty years ago. I took my first wife there, in fact, for our honeymoon, poor thing, to show her the old place that was ours for a thousand years, until the Revolution swept us all away. It was on a summer morning like this. The ruins of the château are on the left bank of the Loire as you go down— the *digue*, you know, is on the other side. There is a town on the right bank, just a scrap of a town; a bridge over the river, which runs like a brook over its shallow and pebbly bed; and on the other side there is a little hill where they built the castle—one tower at each end, halls and chapels and dungeons between—almost a royal castle for the memory of abominable things; for my people were great sticklers for seigneurial rights. Very odd, Chacomb, that a man's heart glows with pride to remember that his ancestors were great rogues. The place is all in ruins now, but I went over it and spent the pleasantest day in all my life, pointing out to my wife the place where the thumbscrewing went on, where the rack stood, where the peasants were shut up on bread and water, and all the rest of it. It was just such a day as this, and we stood on the top of the tower, and looked over miles of as fertile country as there is in France. All ours once. I understood the pride of ownership for the first time, though I had no part or share in a single rood of land. I envy you, Chacomb."

The squire's head relented a little. It is undoubtedly a pleasant thing to be envied. The desire of exciting envy is, perhaps, next to the spur of necessity, one of the principal motives to work and stimulants to success. Those who deprecate the love of envy are themselves most liable to the passion—the poor and disappointed folk, not the rich and envied. I have known ladies who, I am quite certain, enjoyed their own fine things in proportion to the green and bilious feelings of envy they saw aroused in their friends and guests. If you want to see the highest enjoyment, chiefly caused by the awakening of profound envy in others, give a small schoolboy a watch and chain; a youthful schoolgirl a seal-skin jacket; or a charity child a fourpenny-piece.

"Yes, Chacomb," the captain went on, "I envy you. I wish I had broad acres and forest land of my own, as my grandfather had. It would help me now, at all events."

The squire, who was panting behind him, instinctively took his hands out of his pockets and buttoned up his coat. At all events, he would lend no money.

"Why now?" he asked.

"First, because I should have less anxiety about that boy of mine; and secondly, because I should not have to let my Marion go to your Gerald empty-handed."

The squire lifted his head, wagged it, nodded it, and grinned silently. Then he accelerated his pace, and lessened the distance between the captain and himself.

"Say that again, Revel. I did not quite catch."

"I say, Chacomb, that I am sorry to let Marion go almost empty-handed to her husband."

"Ah!" said the squire.

"When did Gerald tell you?"

"He did not tell me."

The captain went on, still striding in advance. It was

like one of those processions that may be seen in a mediæval manuscript. First marches the knight, chivalrous and frank; behind him goes the villein, with the thoughts of a villein stamped upon his face; with the latter, arm in arm, no less a personage than the Devil. The first walked with a light and springy step, the sunshine pouring over the hedge upon his face; he walked as one whose heart is full of hope; the second, crouching and bent, seemed to pull his feet painfully, step by step, up the ascent. He was in shadow, too, being much shorter than the other, save when a gap in the bushes allowed the sunshine to throw a gleam of light upon his face, which brought out the more forcibly the seaminess with which his passions were furrowing it. As for the third Person, he was invisible. Had it been otherwise, I would joyfully have described him to you in this place, and then my history would have been indeed original, unique, and priceless.

"Gerald did not tell you! Ah, he went off too early this morning. But you suspected, old friend, eh? You thought, perhaps, what might happen when the boy came home again?"

"I suspected? Yes, I did suspect," said the squire.

"I did not, Chacomb. You knew your boy better than I did. But it seems natural now: a thing so right and fitting for both that, though it was only arranged last night, it has settled down in my thoughts as completely as if it had been arranged from the beginning. To be sure, the pair have been always together, except when Gerald was away. You know the long letters he used to send her. There was not a word of love in a deskful of them; but it would be easy to read them now by the light of what we know, and find out proofs —eh?—of something deeper than friendship. I wish you joy, Chacomb, of your new daughter. Marion will make a fair châtelaine of Chacomb Hall."

The squire answered nothing, but twitched up his right shoulder with a half-glance sideways, as if to make sure that it was there. That portion of his frame might have been the chosen seat of an evil genius, from the attention he bestowed upon it in disturbed and anxious moments. A look of doubt, as if his way was not quite clear before him, crossed his face. Then he lifted his head and listened again, for the captain's heart was full, and he must needs go on.

"Gerald and Marion—Marion and Gerald—they have been in my thoughts together so long that it will be no effort to keep them together always. Gerald and Marion. It is a great happiness to me — a greater happiness, Chacomb, than I could have hoped or expected. Gerald has been to me always as dear as my own son. There is no boy to whom I would more gladly entrust my girl's happiness."

His son's praises only made the self-tormentor more angry. But he chafed in silence.

"I do think, Chacomb," the captain went on, "that Heaven is kinder to us than we can even ask. When things look darkest, comes a touch of fortune that lights up the whole atmosphere again. They looked very dull last night when I heard how Fred had disgraced himself. Did Gerald tell you that?"

"No—no! Disgraced himself? Tell me about that," answered the squire, quickly.

"He has been rusticated for a year."

"Ah!" The squire smacked his lips, and drew a long breath, perhaps of fatigue. "Was it—was it for anything more than usually shameful and dishonourable?"

"As you please to look at it. Gerald tries to make light of it. It was only a schoolboy freak."

"A schoolboy freak, you call it. Fred is only twenty, is he?"

"Very nearly. He is three years younger than Marion. The news came last night. I was gloomily looking over the letters and bills—"

"Fred has got into debt, then? Ah!"

"When the two came in, and told me all about it. Well, have had a long spell of fair weather: I must expect an occasional squall. But I have thought it all out, Chacomb.

I will tell you what I propose. I take it for granted, my dear old friend, that you are as pleased at the match as I am. Gerald will stay at home with you; he will be your right-hand man. Marion will show you what it means to have a daughter. You shall lend me money to pay off the prodigal's debts. We will have the wedding in September; and then I shall take the boy to London, put him to some work, and take care of him myself. Poor Fred is only a boy, after all."

As the captain enumerated each clause of his proposed plan of perfect happiness, the squire's right ear and shoulder came together with little jerks, each of great meaning.

"Oh, Fred is only a boy. And the marriage will take place in September. And you will go to London to take care of him. I see. Very good."

"That is what I think of doing. It runs in the blood, you see. My father, who was forty-five when he married, began with what you may call a good solid foundation of debt. The hereditary tendency passed over me, and has attacked poor Fred. Unfortunate that I did not foresee the danger. Then I should not have had to borrow off you."

"Quite so," said the squire, with a grin. "That's very unfortunate; extremely unfortunate—that is."

"Fred's debts come to about a thousand pounds, all told. Not so bad for the son of a half-pay officer, is it? But what should we have said if he had emulated the example of his great-great-uncle, the chevalier, who distinguished himself, a century and a half ago, by a career rather shorter and a great deal merrier? It only lasted six months. He was a private friend of the Regent, and a very particular friend of the Countess de Parabère. Some other young fellow ran him through the body, after one poor little summer 'on the chuck,' as we used to say in the navy, and they found his debts were half a million of francs. No one paid them, poor fellow; and history, while it drops a tear over the chevalier, has none for his creditors. There must have been something winning about the young fellow to make all the world trust him. Perhaps Fred is like him. At all events, Chacomb, this is the position of affairs. There is a balance of four hundred or so in the bank, all that is left of the money saved for the boy's education. Marion and I put it by, you know. There will be six hundred to pay. Now, I intend to ask you for that sum, Chacomb."

"Ah!" said the squire, who was growing purple in the face, perhaps with the exertion of going uphill.

"Yes, you shall lend me that sum, and I shall be able to pay you back when Fred gets an income."

"When Fred gets—ah!—gets an income," gasped the squire.

"It will be a few years—two or three years—first, I am afraid. But I shall devote myself to the boy. Never fear for Fred, Chacomb. Perhaps I have been too fond of my Marion, and neglected the boy. That shall be seen to—and at once."

The squire, answering nothing, began to swing his arms backwards and forwards. Over his face came the same expression which had alarmed the doctor the previous night, a look of uncontrollable passion, which surged up into his cheeks in bursts of crimson, and receded, leaving them pallid; which made his lips full and his mouth tremble; which gave unwonted fire to his eyes. But now the doctor was not present, and Chauncey Chacomb, with that invisible companion we have spoken of, had it all his own way.

As the captain spoke the last words, the lane came to an end at a field gate which led to the open down. The level of the summit was reached.

"Ah," cried Revel, "here we are at last."

Without looking round he vaulted the gate, and turned off upon the level, springy turf towards the edge of the cliff, followed by the other two, a little distance behind him— Chauncey Chacomb and the Devil.

"The grass is pleasant after the stony path," said the captain. "This is the place that my girl is so fond of. I believe she used to sit up here by herself, and watch the ships coming up the Channel—'silver sails all out of the west'—thinking that one of them might bring Gerald. I

will take you where she used to come: the very best place
for a good sea view, especially when it is fine enough to
see Lundy, between this and Clovelly. You may watch the
sea, if you like, while I read you my young scrapegrace's
letter."

Captain Revel was like the unfortunate draper in "Pierre
Pathelin," divided between his wool and his sheep, inasmuch
as his thoughts went from one thing to the other. They
were divided between Marion and Fred.

"And when we have read the letter, we will talk over
Gerald and Marion's affairs."

There was near them a fourth person lying on the grass,
whom Chauncey Chacomb had forgotten, his cousin Joseph.
He was reclining supine in considerable comfort; his head
was propped on a pillow made up of a little mound of tufted
grass, surrounded by one of the squire's soft felt hats—a new
and a very good hat—which he had crumpled up; he had
put on a new Tweed coat belonging also to the head of the
Chacomb clan—it mattered very little about the sleeves being
too short; he was smoking one of half a dozen cigars he had
thoughtfully taken from Gerald's own box, brought by him
from Havana; he occasionally tapped with thankfulness that
portion of his chest on which lay the pocket-book with
Chauncey Chacomb's cheque for £200; his legs were crossed
and his arms thrown out upon the grass, so that the warm
sun and the cool breeze could work unchecked all their beneficent will upon him.

His eyes were half-closed as he watched the blue wreaths
from his cigar rise daintily into the air, and the wind blow
them away, streaming like a girl's tresses by the sea-shore.
Near him sat a fat and motherly-looking ewe, pretending to
be pleased rather than frightened at the proximity of the
stranger. Every now and then he made faces at her, blew
the smoke in her direction, and even shook a menacing boot
at her. In vain: the experienced matron smiled like a
Celestial, but moved not. Ugly faces do not hurt, they
amuse; boots may shake, but do not fly off like flints and
pebbles; tobacco smoke is even pleasant in the open air.

To be sure, all sheep naturally have an aversion to the smell
within closed doors, because butchers' assistants have a habit
of smoking common tobacco in certain places, never named
among the race, where the associations are unpleasant. So
the sheep sat and looked on; while the doctor, in murmuring
tones, like one who eats the lotos in a land where it is
always afternoon, addressed her with honeyed words and
dulcet tones.

"Mother of mutton," he said, with a smack of his lips,
"fear not the stranger who comes with neither club nor
dog. Your children, madam, have gone, perhaps, to the
bourne which makes that stranger the man he is. The
lambs whom you imagine to be in exile in foreign lands
have worked up into these arms and legs, and this scientific
brain. 'Alas, unmindful of mint sauce, among the mint
they played.' There is thus, madam, if one may say so, a
kind of relationship between us. We may even one day
knit closer the tie that binds us. The grass which you are
champing—it is succulent, and eats short, I am sure, from
the expression of your open countenance—may perhaps, in
other forms, become part of the frame of the humble philosopher who addresses you. This, madam, is a law of the
universe: life preys on life, the strong devour the weak;
and though I sincerely hope that I shall not eat your ladyship and that your sphere of maternal usefulness may be
protracted for many a happy summer, you will acknowledge
that I must devour somebody, and may have to devour you.
Animals with brains are more dangerous to lambs than
animals with muscles. Your respected husband, madam,
Sir Timothy Ram—I believe it is a good old county name—
is a strong creature, but a mighty fool; the fox is a crafty
animal, and though he lacks strength, has hitherto managed
to preserve his independence. I, La Mère, if you will allow
me the expression, am both strong and crafty; therefore I
am to be feared by lambs. I will give you a wrinkle,
madam: never you work for yourself, if you can get any
one to work for you. Joseph Chacomb, O sheep of solemn
vacancy, is forty-five years of age; he has hitherto made

other people work for him; he proposes to continue that line of action; and he hopes devoutly never to do any more work at all. For his cousin Chauncey has blossomed into an Ass so enormous, that it would be an unspeakably sinful thing to let another have the squeezing and the plucking of him. Families should keep their hawks as well as their pigeons among themselves; and it is only Christian to do unto your cousin that which other men would do unto him if they could. Gerald, madam, is an ass of another kind. My own sincere prayer is that Gerald may marry Marion, and—"

Here his soliloquy was cut short by the sound of voices, or of one voice, and raising his head a little he saw Revel, with the squire following at his heels, walking as I have described across the down in the direction of the cliff. Naturally he did not see the third person, who was invisible.

"What the devil is the matter with Chauncey?" murmured the doctor. "He looks exactly as he did last night."

Just then the squire raised his face, so that the sunlight fell full upon it.

"By gad," said the doctor, rousing himself, "I believe there will be a row. Look at the captain pointing placidly with his stick to the sea, while Chauncey mops and mows behind him, like an ape who would like to swear horribly, but forgets the words. This grows interesting."

Chauncey Chacomb followed mechanically, his body bent and half crouching, though the ground was level; but his hands were spread out half-way between the hips and the shoulders, with quick restless movements; his eyes watched Revel's back with a strange intensity of gaze, which was like a wild beast's glare; his lips worked uneasily; his cheek twitched.

"I wonder if he *is* mad?" said the doctor, watching. "I've a good mind to go and spoil the row. I believe he must be mad."

He sat up to see better. The ewe, thinking the time for dissimulation was past, started to her feet and scuttled off in undisguised terror. But Dr. Chacomb was not thinking of her.

"I am sure," he said to himself, "that if Chauncey had a dagger he would stick it into Revel's back. He looks more dangerous than he did last night. There *must* be a row. Why does not Revel turn round? It would be fun to see him, just now, catch that charming expression on my cousin's face, when it looks most devilish. If they come to a fight I shall have to intervene, like the Queen's Proctor, or a policeman at a pantomime."

He had not long to wait.

The two moved on across the ground, which rose a little until it reached a sort of saddle-back, from which the turf sloped rapidly for eight feet or so, until it came to the edge of the cliff, which here descended almost perpendicularly to the sea. The figures stood out for a moment to the doctor's eye like two black silhouettes before the bright and sunny sky: the one erect and tall, the other crouched and misshapen.

Then the captain stopped.

"Here we are, Chacomb. The best place in all Devonshire on a fine summer's day; a place for lovers to sit and dream. I believe it was here that Gerald and Marion yesterday came to an understanding, as the country folk say. Ha! ha! Now we will sit down and talk it over." He turned round slowly, as a man does who is looking for a soft place to sit down upon. "Good God, Chacomb, what is the matter?"

The man's face was wild with boiling rage: his cheek was white; his eyes were red; his hands were raised to the level of his face, and held palms outward; his teeth chattered, but he could find no words. Chauncey Chacomb was mad, much more mad than when, the night before, he had poured out the secret of his foolish soul.

"Chacomb!" repeated the captain.

"I—I—I hate you!" stammered the other, feeling about

the air with his hands, as if searching for words. "I hate you! I would kill you if I could!"

He moved forward with a threatening gesture. Captain Revel, bewildered, stepped back. And then—then, all in a moment, the bloodshot eyes of the madman looked into space, for Captain Revel had disappeared. His foot slipped upon the smooth grass as he recoiled before the threatening gestures of his companion; he reeled and staggered; he fell head foremost on the slope; he caught with both hands at the short turf, but the roots came away from the rocky soil in his grasp; and, without a cry or a sound, he rolled over the edge of the cliff, and was gone.

When the fit left Chauncey Chacomb, he remembered, as in a dream, the captain's last look of horror, and it remained with him an accusing spirit till the day of his death.

It took him a few moments to realise what had happened. When he did, his madness being still strong upon him, he threw himself forward on the slope, at imminent risk of falling over, and lay on hands and knees, with his head projected over the edge. The cliff was about a hundred feet high, not quite perpendicular. Just above the water was a narrow ledge. On this ledge lay a helpless mass of clothes and broken bones, which had a minute before been Captain Revel. It still moved, so that he was not dead.

The wretched man cried and shouted, exulting like an Israelite over the fall of his enemy.

"Revel!"—the rocks rang out the name, and the echoes took it up, and repeated it along the black line of curved and indented cliff—"Revel—Revel—Revel—listen before you die. Gerald shall never marry Marion—do you hear? I will lend no money to your spendthrift son—do you hear? Fred and the girls shall starve—do you hear? I lend them money! I will see them begging their bread in the streets first. Do you hear? do you hear? do you hear? There you are, and there you will die. Ho! ho! ho! There you will die!"

Did the broken and shattered form of the man below catch the mockings of his enemy, as they rolled from point

to point round the coves and bays of the vexed shore? But
the harsh tones did not break upon the sleep of the innocent
girl by Comb Leigh Cove, to mar the beauty of her love
dream.

The squire felt with thankfulness that he had recovered
his powers of speech, and was going on with greatly in-
creased freedom and liberty of utterance, but found he could
not, being suddenly and violently pulled backwards by the
heels. It was his cousin dragging him up, at the risk of
his own life and limbs—a more perilous feat than the rescue
of a drowning man; for Chauncey Chacomb kicked and
writhed, shouting curses and imprecations on Revel, on his
cousin, and on Marion. Doctor Joseph, however, went
about his work with great coolness, and, after five minutes'
struggle, had his cousin safely on the level sward, with one
hand firmly in his collar, coat and shirt and all.

"Let me go!" cried the maniac; "let me go! Let me
see him die! Joseph, it isn't half enough to kill him. I
want to taunt him. Let me go! Suppose he were to die
before I have told him all. Oh, what a chance to miss!"

"Be quiet, madman, or I will squeeze the breath out of
your miserable little body. Be quiet, I say."

The doctor shook him backwards and forwards till his
struggles ceased, and then turned him round, and looked
straight into his eyes.

"Let me go, Joe," he whimpered; "let me go—please
let me go; and I will give you five hundred pounds. I
want just to have one more look—one more look. Ah, one
more!"

Here his voice died away in broken murmurs; and he fell
to shaking like one who has an ague. For he could not choose
but look back into the doctor's eyes, which seemed searching
into his very soul. He struggled to speak, but his tongue
refused to move; he tried to turn away his gaze, but he
could not: the mesmeric influence of the stronger will was
upon the weaker. His mania passed away from him, his
arms dropped, his lips closed. The doctor, still holding
him by one hand, made a pass or two with the other, and

then laid him gently on the inner slope of the sward, his face turned inland.

"So," he said; "here is a devil of a business! What is to be done next?"

What, indeed! He left his patient safe for a while in his mesmeric sleep, and crept warily down the slope. Where it shelved most steeply, close to the edge, he laid himself along the ground, and digging knees, toes, and elbows in the turf, he looked over. It was a fearful place; the cliff was inclined at a slight angle to the vertical, was stuck with small ledges and projections, on which the man had broken his fall, and so prolonged his pains. He lay on the lowest ledge, but now seemed motionless and dead. The doctor noticed that the projection ran along the base of the cliff, and apparently round the corner, and into a cleft in the wall, where Nature seemed to have designed a cove, but changed her mind owing to the difficulties of the undertaking.

"I might get down there," said the doctor; "at any rate, I can try."

He scrambled back, and looked again at his cousin.

"Sleep on, you miserable little madman," he said. "A pretty morning's work you've done. Sleep, you—you—you microcephalous imbecile, till I come back and kick you up."

Chauncey Chacomb made no answer. His eyes were closed, and he was sleeping.

"Had I known anything of the medical profession," the doctor murmured, "I should have locked you up last night. A strait-waistcoat and a little gruel, and myself for your private physician and adviser. What a chance—what a chance to miss! Everything," he added with a sigh, and hurrying along the cliff to the gap—"everything is in the hands of the man who has taught himself his profession. Joseph Chacomb, you were a fool, a very great fool, not to read in the days of your youth. I wonder if I can get down there?"

It was his only chance, for all along the road beyond the waves washed the bare faces of the vertical cliff. But here, where the ledge seemed to be carried round the curve of the rock, there was a deep indentation, as if a large knife had begun to cut a triangular stile, but failing partly in the task, had left a ragged mass at the bottom piled up by broken rocks and overgrown with brambles.

It was possible to get down as far as this by an active man; but beyond? Beyond it the waters ran into the gap, and at its mouth the cliffs stood face to face to make a gate. But the doctor thought it looked just possible to get round by the boulders and rocks that lay about the entrance.

"I don't like it," he said; "but I will try. I think Chauncey will do for half an hour."

He talked to himself, as was his wont, in cheerful tones; but his face was pale and his hand shook as he thought of the murdered man.

"Murdered," he said, half aloud; "murdered, if ever man was murdered!"

There was a kind of landslip at the end of the gap, down which he lowered himself step by step, holding by bramble and briar, clinging to projecting rocks, which gave way beneath his weight, creeping warily along the edge of precipices—not Alpine, certainly, but high enough to kill him if he fell—and dropping down smooth faces from ledge to ledge. But at last he stood above the water, where a single stone gave him a slippery foothold. He looked round him, and groaned.

"Chauncey, if I get safe out of this, I will make you pay for it."

It was a black and savage-looking place, in which the waves, though it was a comparatively smooth day outside, flung up jets and fountains of spray and foam, with loud whistlings and roarings, which sometimes frightened belated market women coming along the down after dark, when the weather was stormy and the wind high.

He looked round him, and saw at the back the cave, dark and yawning. He shuddered.

"I suppose the king of the octopods holds his throne

there. I hope his majesty is asleep. It would be a sweet thing to see his long claws coming out of the cave, and feel them catching me round the neck, and I without so much as a penknife—even a toothpick might be useful."

He clambered, clung, and crept along the black and sloping sides of the infernal hole, towards the opening. There he found his further progress stopped by a rough, serrated rock, standing like a sentinel to bar his way. He whistled in despair. The big, dark rock barred his progress, and he felt as if he could neither get forward nor back. Then he sat down, his feet dangling over the water, and began to reflect, looking at the boulder.

"I can't get over you," he murmured, "you big, black devil; but I might get round you. Suppose I was to fall in and be drowned, like a rat in a trap, as I believe I shall! It would serve me right, for getting down here at all. I should be found in a few years, perhaps, all that would be left of me—a button or two, a purse with some money, a silver watch: that would be the final edition of the works of this Josephus. Suppose, which is equally probable, that I have to wait here and starve slowly till the octopus in the cave thinks he is strong enough to throw off the mask and attack me. Chauncey, if ever I do get back, it shall be bad for you. No!" as he made another effort to get over the rock which barred him from further advance. He looked down into the dark depths beneath him. "That won't do. Pah! The crabs are mustering in all their force, and sending invitations to their relations. I can see them at the bottom, I believe. The lobsters will hear of it, and come without being invited. There are yellow starfish lying on the stones across the water—they have eyes, and are longing to be at me. There must be whelks, too, at the bottom. When they have eaten me, they will be caught and eaten themselves, from a stall, with pepper and vinegar, in Whitechapel. If I fall in, they will say that I went a-shrimping. Come, Joseph Chacomb, pull yourself together—pluck up."

He laid himself flat upon the rough and sloping surface, holding on by one foot and both hands, while he threw his

G

leg round till he met with a projection. Bit by bit he struggled on, panting and wheezing, for the doctor was not so young as he had been, till he found himself round the point, and with both feet on the narrow and broken ledge on which the captain lay. He made his way cautiously along, and in five minutes was kneeling beside the form which lay apparently inanimate upon the rock.

"Poor beggar! poor beggar!" murmured the doctor; "and to think that he might have been alive and well still if Chauncey had not been an Ass!"

He felt the pulse—the left arm was crushed and broken, lying under the body, but the right appeared to be comparatively uninjured. There was a faint motion—it takes a good deal to beat the life out of a man. The doctor dipped his hat in the sea, and, raising the head, poured the water over it. The captain's face was pale and white; from his mouth oozed the blood drop by drop.

"Revel," whispered the doctor, "Revel, can you speak?"

There was no answer; nothing to show that he heard, or comprehended, or lived—only the dull, slow beating of the pulse at the doctor's finger.

"Oh, that I were on the cliff now!" said Joseph. "What would I give for a boat? And how the deuce am I to get him, or myself either, out of this?"

He resolved to try the next point; and stepping lightly over the prostrate form, to which he could do nothing, he crept along the ledge in the same direction, and disappeared behind the next point.

It was half an hour later when he returned in Revel's own boat, rowed by a couple of farm boys. In the boat sat Marion. As the doctor—rough, coarse in grain, selfish, and cynical—looked at the face of the girl, so suddenly stricken that there was no time for weeping, no room for despair, the unaccustomed tears rolled down his cheeks.

They brought It, the poor crushed form, covered with a sheet, home to Comb Leigh in the boat. As they lifted the body, the doctor saw Chauncey Chacomb standing near. By his trembling limbs, by the wan light in his eyes, by his moaning and crying, he saw that the madman only partly understood what had happened, and how. As they bore the captain to the cottage, Chauncey followed with staggering step. His confused brain knew, in a bewildered sort of way, that he had somehow caused the thing to happen. He could not remember yet; but he was filled with a dreadful terror. He dimly perceived that there would be no rest or happiness for him any more: the seal of Cain, the murderer, was on his brow. But his victim's pulse yet beat, though feebly. For three long hours they waited round the bedside. Marion at his head, dry-eyed; Adie, weeping and sobbing at the foot of the bed; Chauncey standing helpless and silent, turning his bewildered eyes from one to the other. The sun shone in at the window, where the captain's roses climbed about, throwing their branches across the light, and making fantastic patterns in the shifting shadows of the floor.

Suddenly the watchers saw a change. There was a slight quivering of the limbs, and the captain opened his eyes for a moment.

" He is coming to his senses," the doctor whispered. " He hears, my girl; be brave."

" Father," she whispered, " do you know me?"

As she touched his poor pale lips with hers, he opened his eyes again, and looked at her in a strange, wondering way, with a tender pity in them. His thoughts were all with her— Marion saw it with a wild tumult of misery and happiness— all with her.

Then his lips parted, and she went closer.

" Marion," he whispered, " my poor, poor Marion!—I see it all! It was not my fault. Endure to the end, my darling—and always trust in God. My dear!—my dear!— my dear!"

His eyes both dropped as in very weariness; and presently the doctor, laying his hand upon the captain's heart, found that he had fallen into the sleep from which there is no earthly waking.

CHAPTER X.

A WEEK has passed; the coroner has come to Comb Leigh upon his errand, and by the help of a dozen farmers the inquest has been held. The conduct and appearance of Mr. Chauncey Chacomb, the principal witness, were remarkable: the reporter said that his overmastering grief did equal credit to his heart and to his head. In incoherent accents, and with hesitating tongue, he set forth what was well known to everybody present—how the deceased gentleman and himself had been almost daily companions for many years; and how, while they were talking together on the cliff, the captain's foot slipped, and he fell. Being asked by an intelligent juryman if he knew of any cause—orange peel now, a thing he had heard was fatal to many a man—why the captain should have slipped, he stated, after the coroner had called attention to the fact that orange peel would be a comparatively rare thing to find in August at the top of the cliff, that he knew of no cause or reason whatever. Being asked by another intelligent juryman if the captain was possibly unwell that morning—bile now, a thing often felt by himself, the questioner, after a market dinner—Mr. Chacomb said that Captain Revel had made no complaint as to biliousness. Being asked if the spot was considered dangerous, Mr. Chacomb said that, on the contrary, he had understood it to be a favourite spot for lovers to sit and watch the view, and that he had never heard of any one under those circumstances falling over. Another juryman interposed with the remark that it was very true, and he had sat there himself in younger days; whereat everybody laughed. From time to time Chauncey Chacomb, while giving his evidence, looked nervously at his cousin, who sat with his head down, but made no sign. The doctor's testimony was given with greater vigour, and bore internal evidence of careful preparation. It made, as he intended, a profound impression. He had heard, he explained, his cousin Mr. Chauncey Chacomb's cry for help, and on hastening to the place, and looking over the edge of the cliff, saw the deceased gentleman lying on the rocks below. He had then made his way to the spot by a breakneck path, which he described at length with pardonable aggravation of the difficulties, and had finally succeeded in getting round the point and hailing the boat. The jury were unanimous in expressing their highest admiration of Dr. Chacomb's heroism in attempting a rescue. They were also unanimous in concurring that Parliament should be petitioned to put handrails round all cliffs, and provide rope ladders in case of any one falling over. And then they brought in their verdict of "Accidental death." What other verdict was possible? Evil looks do not murder; and who was there except the doctor to say that the man slipped and fell, overcome with confusion at the threatening looks and gestures of his companion?

As for Fred, for whom Gerald had gone in search, he came home in time to attend the funeral. Not waiting for the paternal permission to go to Egypt, he had started at once, on getting the ten pounds from Marion, with a sanguine confidence that more would follow, and yet with some forebodings how his father might take it. At Paris he saw the news in *Galignani*, and hastened back. He bore himself steadily at the funeral, and the village folk congratulated each other that the captain's boy was so brave and fine a young fellow, and so admirably qualified to help his sisters.

Marion called upon him, indeed, at once for help, endeavouring to face the realities of the future. But in vain. Her brother would not look at the facts as they were. He put it off; he fenced with the necessity; he refused to read through the papers; he declined to let her know his liabilities. And yet he looked forward with a confident cheerfulness to a wonderful future; for with men of Fred's character it is the leading trait that they never can face anything real.

"You see, dear Fred, we *must* consider things; we have very little money—only the insurance; and we *must* consider what is to be done."

"I think, Marion"—with a yawn—"that it shows singu-larly little regard for my poor father's memory to begin this kind of talk the very first day after he is buried. And as for the future, I see no cause for any anxiety at all. I have already told you that Lord Rodney—"

"The firework man. O Fred!"

"Has promised to get me something good. What will it matter, then, that my father has left us no money? I hope, Marion, you will remember that, as the head of the family, I shall always feel it my duty to provide for you and Adie."

Marion repressed her rising irritation.

"Yes, Fred, it is very good of you to say so, and to think so; but Lord Rodney is in Egypt; we do not know when he will come back; and it will not do to trust to vague hopes. We have to pay off your debts first; and what are we to do till your friend finds something that will suit you?"

"Confound it, Marion, do not worry a man! If things look bad, staring at them won't make them look any better. Let us sit down and wait till they come round again. At all events, there is the insurance; and something will turn up."

Always a belief that things, if left alone, would right themselves; always that blind confidence which borders dangerously near the Paradise of fools. It is with certain natures infectious. Adie caught it of her brother. She, too, protested against the folly of anxiety about the future; she, too, found it a flying in the face of Providence to add up bills and think of ways and means; and, with Fred, would leave Marion alone with her papers, to wander along the leafy lanes, and to talk together of the merry days in store for them, and the pleasant paths of careless folly. It might seem safe to prophesy of Fred that there will be few more pleasant lingerings in the sunshine for him; but prophecy—since the school of the Prophets finally broke up and dissolved when Malachi left it—has been an eminently unsafe thing. Some things we know, of course, from long experience. The clever boy of the school becomes a pauper, after a thousand

failures; the good boy gets hanged, after a long course of
hypocrisy. Any one can prophesy so far; but what shall we
say about the bad and lazy boy? Observers have remarked
that though in after-life he continues to wallow in his laziness
and badness, like a pig of the flock of Epicurus, he too
often gets a good income, a pleasant life, and easy times.
"Women," Dr. Chacomb once said to me, "can always, unless they belong to the passive or stupid class, foretell the
future. Unfortunately their power is limited, and they are
all like Cassandra, inasmuch as they only see the bad things
that are coming." Still, that is better than nothing, especially
when you get predictions about your enemies' coming misfortunes. Why is it that one-half—the greater half—of mankind have been excluded from the Jewish Prophets? Had
it been otherwise, what a screaming sisterhood should we
have had! Fancy a dozen Deborahs pouring out the heart's
fulness of invective, exultation, and denunciation! Fancy
the lost splendours, the tragic predictions, of a wronged and
angry Hebrew woman!

Marion, left alone, went carefully through her father's
papers. The letters she put aside to be burned; the accounts,
and all that seemed to refer to money, she kept. And so one
morning, a few days after the funeral, she came across a
secret that sent the blood from her cheek.

A dreadful secret; a shameful secret; a secret that
touched the happiness and the self-respect of those dearest
to her; a secret that told her why, in the prime of early
manhood, her father, an ambitious and active man, could
resign his hopes for the future, and take refuge in a country
village, where he was unknown, and the thing could not
follow him.

"My poor dear father!" she murmured. "He suffered
this through all these years, and made no sign. What shall
I do, what shall I do to keep it secret? I may at least tell
Gerald."

But where was Gerald? He had disappeared. No letter
came from him, and he made no sign. It was strange. At
Chacomb Hall the two men thought nothing of it; Gerald

was not in either's thoughts.   At the Rosery there was one
at least who looked and waited all the day, who watched and
waited all the night.   But no news could come; for Gerald,
fresh from Brazilian lowlands, was working off a fever—
one of half a dozen left in his system as a parting gift
of the Oroonoko swamps—in a hotel at Boulogne, unable
to write, and fretting over the delay that kept him from
Marion.

It was at this juncture that Joseph Chacomb, quite unexpectedly and to his own astonishment, developed an entirely
new side of character.   He appeared as the man of sympathy.   During the bad days before the funeral he would
walk over every morning, and do what work there was
to do.   When that business was finished, he still came in
readiness to work at Marion's request.   She ended by liking
him and looking for him.   He was rough, and he took
dreadful views of human nature.   Still he was kind.   He
went through the papers with her—Fred's papers of debts—
noting things that might be reduced; while the culprit
himself was lying on the grass in the shade, or singing duets
with Adie.

"Well, there are all the bills before us.   Of course," he
said, "we are not going to pay half of them."

"But we must; Fred owes them."

"I know.   We need not pay one single farthing, I
believe.   They are debts contracted in his minority.   Fred
is not yet twenty-one.   Besides, they are all extravagant
debts.   You cannot make a minor pay for things manifestly
unnecessary.   Look here; an Oxford hack, no doubt a
broken-winded, spavined, knock-kneed roarer, at two pounds
a day; the tennis court at three and sixpence an hour, with
a few pounds added in for beer.   Where is their licence,
Miss Revel? answer me that—where is their licence?   And
what is this?   Rabbit coursing in a dog-fancier's back yard.
Could any British jury pass that account—even a jury of
small tradesmen?   Why, the thing is illegal.   Come, Miss
Marion, if you pay this bill, I will borrow a guinea of you.
give it to the Society for the Suppression of Cruelty to

Animals, and make them prosecute the rascal, with your brother for principal witness. As for these bills—champagne at a hundred and twenty shillings, claret at ninety, port at eighty-five—you will just leave me to do what I can for you."

"It is very kind," said Marion; "that is, if it is just."

"Of course it is just. There is one thing I should like to understand: why the young fellows at Oxford, who belong to exactly the same class as the young fellows at the hospitals, are so much better off in the way of tick. Show me, if you please, the London wine merchant who will trust a medical student with champagne, or even with the homely Bass. Lord, what a delicious time I should have had, with an undergraduate's credit at my back! Look here, again: a bill for badger baiting. Now, you know, that is too barefaced. Fancy having your badger baited on credit! Scoring up chalks for worrying a varmint in a tub! He's a glutton for enjoyment, Fred is."

He bundled all the bills into his pocket.

"Leave it all to me. I will do just the reverse of the unjust steward. I will sit down quickly and write off half: the champagne shall stand at fifty, and that will leave a handsome profit; the port at forty-eight, and that will be dear at the price; and as for the badger baiter, he shall not be paid at all. Miss Revel, the dishonesty of people is to the Christian mind appalling; to the unchristian mind—that is, to me—it shows how very, very few Christian minds there are."

"If they do not accept your offer?" said Marion.

"Then I button up my pockets. Then I say to them, 'Men and brethren, naked came ye into the world; naked, so far as I am concerned, shall ye continue to go through the world.' I beg your pardon, Miss Revel; I mean that they may then proceed to whistle for their money."

"But I could not bear to have Fred laden with debts, perhaps worried and persecuted by lawyers' letters."

"Could you not?" he replied, with a twinkle in his

eyes. "Fred would bear it with very great resignation, I am sure."

"Ah, yes, Fred has the sweetest of tempers," said Marion tenderly.

"Hum! I like tempers a little more snappish. Well, never mind your brother for the present. What can I do for you personally, Miss Revel? Do you propose to remain in this cottage?"

"We are your cousin's tenants—Mr. Chacomb's tenants. Did he ask you to put that question?"

"No, he did not. The fact is, Chauncey is knocked silly, quite literally. I never knew a man such mournful company as he is. Not that he was ever festive; but of late days—"

"You forget, Dr. Chacomb, that the last few days have not been festive days to any of us."

"Pardon me—I do not forget it. Well, Chauncey has made no allusion whatever to the subject. The question was dictated by my own curiosity—my impertinence, if you will."

"No, no; but I have hardly yet considered it at all. It is so strange to me, looking forward to the future; and yet we must. And Fred is no help to me as yet."

"Then let me be a help."

"You are very kind, Dr. Chacomb. I cannot tell you how grateful I am to you. Please give me your advice about this letter. My father had insured his life for two thousand pounds. I noticed, the day before his death, that very letter lying on his table, and gave it to him. He put it in his pocket, and it was found there afterwards. Will you read it?"

It was an official letter on blue paper, reminding Captain Revel that the days of grace for the payment of the premium would expire on the 13th of August, when the policy, unless the sum was paid, would become null and void.

"He died on the 12th," said Marion.

"Yes." The doctor looked grave. "I suppose we cannot put off the delay on the postman or anybody, can we? He got it on the 11th, or perhaps a week before, and forgot to open it. It looks bad, but it might perhaps be fought."

"What do you mean, Dr. Chacomb."

"I mean, Miss Revel, that your father's insurance policy is probably a piece of waste paper. You may light candles with it."

"But, Dr. Chacomb, it cannot be. My father has been insured for five and twenty years."

"It can be, because the company have made an iniquitous rule, and because his premium was not paid at a certain date. There is one chance, and only one. Considering the circumstances of the case, your father's long-standing policy, and the rest, the directors may concede the point."

"But, Dr. Chacomb, they *must* concede it. I suppose the directors are gentlemen."

"We are all gentlemen in this world. It is a *façon de parler*. The mistake is, to suppose that the fact of our being gentlemen prevents us from doing dishonourable things, especially when we are on Boards. There is the custom of the trade, which enables a man to break the eighth commandment without a pang. There is the necessity of making money, which really does blacken the moral eye; and when one is on a committee, you see, the moral responsibility is divided. Dirty things are done by directors, which not one of them would do by himself. The railway directors overwork their servants, and overrun their trains. The insurance directors pass an unjust law about the premiums, and rob the children of their inheritance."

"I wish I understood," said Marion.

"It is an easy thing," the doctor went on; "only the actuaries are afraid to let people know how easy it is. Life insurance is an admirable plan of making the long-lived people pay for those who die first. Of course no one minds living a little longer than his neighbours. So many people are born, so many die, every year. It is all, or ought to be, carefully calculated and made out; so that, you see, anybody knows at any time what is his expectation of life. Very well; when your father insured, five and twenty years ago,

he agreed to pay so much a year, so that if he lived long
enough he would pay for those who died young; and if not,
that he would be paid for by those who lived longer. He
was to go on paying all his life, and at a certain day; that
was in the bargain."

"Then all my father's money is lost?" said Marion.

"But there is something else. It happens that at any
time a policy has a surrender value, which is the greater the
longer it has run on. In other words, the insurance company
will always pay you a certain sum—which ought not to be
an arbitrary sum at all, but a properly advertised one—for
giving up the policy. Understand me: your father's policy
a month ago, after twenty-five years' premium, was worth a
large sum—nothing like his insurance, but still a large sum.
Now listen: the insurance companies have robbed us for
generations, and are robbing us still. As I have no shares
in any of them, I have no interest in hiding the fact. They
rob us in the surrender value, which they understate; and
they rob us far more when, as in your own case, a premium
is not paid, and they put into their pockets the whole of its
surrender value."

"Is there no help?" asked Marion.

"Perhaps; we will try."

He wrote the next day, explaining the circumstance.
He first asked for the insurance in full. The secretary
reminded him that the policy had lapsed. Then the doctor
referred the case to the board, which confirmed the secretary.
Then the doctor wrote a long and careful letter, setting
forth his revolutionary views as to surrender value. The
answer to this was referred to the actuary, who, not
having time to write an essay on the subject of life assurance, referred the doctor to the two great standard works
on insurance, and begged him to correct his views. The
doctor, who enjoyed the correspondence amazingly, thereupon prepared the Prospectus of a Company which pro-
pounded an entirely new system of insurance. No one took
any notice of his pamphlet, which fell flat upon the market;
and Dr. Chacomb, having some other work to do, allowed

the matter to drop. The following is an extract from the prospectus.

"Every man shall insure for himself, and not for his neighbour, and he shall insure for the expectation of his own life.

"If a man pay one pound at the age of thirty, his expectation of life being then about thirty-three years, he shall receive a policy, not to be forfeited, for the sum of one pound at compound interest for thirty-three years. In other words, he can leave his heirs the sum of nearly three pounds.

"The new insurance company is thus a savings bank, in which nothing but deposit accounts are kept, and from which no money can be taken.

"A man can use his own discretion, by insuring when he pleases, and for what he pleases.

"If a man, for instance, marries at twenty-four, he will be able to insure for a thousand pounds by paying a sum down of not much more than a quarter.

"It is a system which will require very little expense of management.

"The new company will take ten per cent. out of profits, but not more, and will be paid off; after which the rate of interest on insurance will be lowered.

"The new company will engage the services of Joseph Chacomb, Esq., M.D., as secretary and manager, at a salary of one thousand pounds per annum, guaranteed for five years, in consideration of the idea. Dr. Chacomb will also be the consulting physician."

It was a beautiful prospectus, and I have always thought it contained the germs of a just and prudent idea. But then I am not an actuary. As regards the letters, they gradually ceased, and the usual result happened—that the company won. But let us return to the present.

Marion laid before her only adviser a paper on which she had put down the family resources as clearly as she had calculated them. The list began with the insurance, through which the doctor ran his pen.

"We will talk about that afterwards. Now let us see. Deducting the arrangement I shall make with your brother's creditors, there will remain in the bank a hundred and fifty pounds; your own little fortune, settled on yourself, of fifty pounds a year; and the furniture of the cottage. Is this absolutely all?"

"I am afraid it is all we have. O Dr. Chacomb! do not say that they will take away all our insurance money!"

"I can say nothing till I have heard from the office; but let us talk as if they were going to be rogues—most men in committee are, you know. And so, my dear young lady, on that supposition, what do you propose to do with those two children playing on the lawn?"

They were literally playing on the lawn, and, with the carelessness that belonged to their character, laughing and singing while they played. Marion looked, and sighed.

"I have hardly begun to think about it. What can I do? What are we all to do? And oh, Dr. Chacomb, where is Gerald? Why does he not come to us?"

"We do not know. Surely, Miss Revel, if any one knew, you would."

It was an arrow shot at a venture.

"Yes; but I have not heard from him since he went to London. Where can he be? I am not able to think about anything else till I have a letter from him."

"She *is* engaged to him, then," thought the doctor, with great satisfaction.

"Have you spoken to Mr. Chacomb yet?" he asked, aloud.

"Not yet. Gerald was to have spoken. It was only the day before . . . . and when my poor father left the house for the last time it was on his way to Chacomb Hall, to tell his old friend—his old friend," she repeated, thoughtfully. "Mr. Chacomb does not like me. He never did. What will he say when he hears of our engagement?"

"What can he say, Miss Revel, except to welcome the daughter of his friend?"

"I do not know. I have sometimes watched him when

he thought no one was looking, and was perhaps off his guard. I think Gerald's father is somehow an unhappy man. He has feelings that he hides; secret thoughts that he does not like to show to the world. I have seen him look at my father—his daily companion—with an expression that seemed full of suspicion, hatred, and revenge. Then he would turn to me, and it was with eyes of dislike. I used to laugh, thinking of it afterwards. But I do not laugh now; for what may it mean to me?"

"It means that the squire will be proud of his new daughter, when Gerald takes you home."

"Ah, when Gerald takes me home! When will that be? Where is he now?"

"At all events, Miss Revel, Gerald is not a man to trouble himself much about what his father thinks. At least, I should not if I were Gerald."

This was a speech to which there could be no reply.

Dr. Chacomb arranged with her about his visit to Oxford, gave her the name of a solicitor under whose care she was to place the slender family fortunes, and left her for the time. On the lawn Fred and Adie were lightening the load of anxiety with an extemporised Badminton, though that pastime was not yet known to the world.

"Battledore and shuttlecock is a very healthy exercise, Fred Revel," said the adviser — "capital for children, I believe. Can you walk a little way with me?"

"With pleasure."

The young man's face did not manifest any lively emotion of joy, but he desisted from his game, tossed the toys to Adie, and lounged into the road after the doctor, yawning heavily.

"You find Comb Leigh dull after Oxford?"

"Dull!" said Fred. "It's dead and buried, put away and forgotten. However, under the sad circumstances, I must stay here to advise the girls, and arrange the future for them, dull though it is."

"Of course," said the doctor, with a smile of cynical delight, "they naturally look to you, as the head of the

family, for support and guidance. What would Marion do
with the accounts without you?"

Fred reddened a little.

"I wish I could support them," he said honestly. "I
sincerely wish I saw my way. Can you give me any advice,
Dr. Chacomb?"

"Let us sit down," said the doctor. "The road is dusty
at this season, and steep at all seasons. As the poet
says—

> 'These confounded long hills and rough, uneven ways,
> Draw out our miles and make them wearisome.'

I will light a cigar, if you do not object."

He lit one—it was one of Gerald's, the doctor having been
so fortunate as to secure the whole box in the absence of its
owner—but neglected to offer one to Fred.

"I like being in the country," he said, stretching his legs
in the shade of the hazel shrubs, and sitting on the grass by
the roadside, "if it is only for the comfort of a cigar in the
open. Comb Leigh is a delicious spot for a meditative
weed. Now, my young friend, you want my advice. Good;
I am forty-five and you are twenty. I have the advantage
over you of a quarter of a century. I wish it was the other
way about, because I would a great deal rather be twenty
than forty-five. But, as Horace says—

> 'The fleeting years go by, my friends,
> Time borrows what he never lends;
> Youth does not save, but always spends,
> Drinks all the wine that Heaven sends,
> And burns his candles at both ends.'

And so on. You are fresher from college than myself, and
may go on with the quotation."

"Tell me what you would advise me to take up as a profession?"

"That is the most difficult thing of all to do. Let us see.
Can you keep accounts?"

"No; I never could add up, except the points at whist."

"Do you write a good hand?"

" Am I a clerk ? "

" You would not be likely to pass any competitive examination, I suppose ? "

"Oh, no! That is why I am afraid—only I don't like to tell Marion so—that Lord Rodney's influence will not be of much use to me."

" Ah, some young fellows, without any turn for books, pick up a pretty fair living as parsons. Just now it pays better than it used to. Would you—? No? Very well, then. I put the law out of the question, because, without reading something, it is, I am sorry to say, impossible to get anything in the legal profession. Some men—myself included—do pretty well at the medical line, without injuring the delicate structure of the cerebellum over the preliminary studies."

" Nothing could make me read anatomy."

" Then we must leave the beaten paths, and try the unrecognised professions. My artless young friend, there are many pleasures in belonging to an unrecognised profession. You hold an uncertain social status, which has its charms ; you are a kind of Bohemian, which relieves you of many moral duties; you are not expected to exhibit any more virtues than you like ; you find the way open for association, particularly of a convivial nature, with crowds of good fellows, impecunious like yourself ; you are always devising new combinations for making money, which sharpens your wits till they grow as keen as a razor; and the profits, my young friend, the profits, if you do make a *coup*, are sometimes very handsome."

The doctor spoke with the enthusiasm of experience.

" But what are these professions ? "

" Their name is legion. I call myself a doctor; but I belong in reality, for my practice is but small, to the tribe of adventurers. Doing things on commission is the first method that occurs to me. You may sell anything on commission, but some things are not pleasant. I knew a man once, formerly in the Carabineers, who took to selling antibilious pills ; they gave him a very handsome per centage

indeed, but twelve months of the work aged him more than
five and twenty previous years of hard drinking. Some men
recommend shops to their friends, and get a commission
from the shopkeeper—members of club committees do it, I
believe, and it seems an easy way of making money; but
it does not last. You can't be always recommending people
to go to different places to buy things; and then the shop
people cheat you shamefully in your commissions. They
have no sense of honour, that class. A friend of mine in
this walk of life was once very cruelly treated by a cigar
dealer, after introducing a young millionaire who actually
smoked himself to death off his shilling Havanas. Coals
are not bad, though they have a bad name. But then, you
see, so many people go into coals. You want nothing but
an office, and you are not obliged to buy a single ton. You
get up the patter, and then you are a dummy, and all your
orders go to the real people, who pay you ten per cent.
Agencies are good, provided you can hit on one not yet
driven to death; but, Lord, the rapacity of people is dreadful
to think of! A gentleman adventurer in these days has to
fight very hard, whatever line he takes up. Literature, I
suppose, you would have no taste for, though some literary
friends of mine have managed to get along without reading
anything except old magazines and the *Annual Register*.
How should you like to be an advertising agent? It is a
business which depends entirely upon personal appearance
and manners. You would have a very good chance—a very
good chance indeed."

"I don't like any of your professions," said Fred. "It
does not seem to me that a gentleman would take up a single
one of those lines."

"A gentleman!" said the doctor, impatiently. "I should
like to write an essay, if I were an author—they are a scaly
lot, and thank Heaven I am not one—on the word. Formerly it meant everybody who wore the king's uniform;
now it means everybody who does not. Young man, put
your gentility in your pocket till you can afford to take it
out again. A gentleman out at elbows, and pretending to

be a gentleman still, is a sorry spectacle. Let us see if we can find anything else for you. Remember, however, that we cannot escape certain laws. If we have no money, we must work or starve. Obviously, the thing is to get the lightest work possible. You have been trained to nothing; you have to find some work that you can do; you have, in short, to prove yourself capable of inventing your own path in the world."

"It would not be quite the thing, would it, for the representative of a great French name to be selling coals on commission?" Fred asked, with his sweetest smile, and as if the question was a clincher.

"Representative — nonsense! Will your countship fill your pockets? Will it keep you and your sisters? Will it give you decent clothes? If not, forget it as fast as you can. I've known a good many loose fish in the world; the worst I ever knew was an Honourable without a farthing, who found it impossible to forget his birth. Look you, Mr. Frederick Revel, I like to call things by their right names. You have already wasted and squandered the whole of the little patrimony saved for yourself and your sisters by your father; and you have got nothing to show for it. You have been sent to expensive schools, and only learned the art of getting tick. You are twenty years of age, and you have your living to get. What will you do?"

"I do not know your right—"

"Very likely not. You may make up your mind to work, or you may make up your mind to parade your gentility. Gentleman, indeed! When shall we hear the last of the old, worn-out rubbish?"

Fred was silent.

"You must, if you work at all, begin with the humblest kind of work—farm work even—or you must take up with some such line as I have shown you. Of course you may, if you please, live upon the very small fortune and the exertions of your sister."

"You presume, sir," said Fred, "on the trifling services you have rendered us. Your advice is insulting and ungentlemanly. I shall not live upon my sister's exertions, nor shall I become a tout and a cad. You will please to give me no more advice."

He turned on his heel, and left the doctor.

"I know the breed," said Joseph, watching the young man as he hurried down the lane with impatient gestures—"I know the breed well. They kick and fume when they hear the truth. They are full of noble sentiments; they are your lip gentlemen. I know the receding chin, the shifty lips which curve into what novelists call a sweet smile; and I know the bright eye, with what the same gentry call a hundred laughs lying in it, which looks as if there was nothing but sincerity and unselfishness behind. I suppose the lad got it from his mother. Wonder who his mother was? 'The dancing eye,' as they call it, means a callous heart. I never knew a fellow with it yet who would budge a step to oblige anybody. That is an aphorism presented by Joseph Chacomb, Esq., M.D., to literature generally. The dancing eye means the callous heart. It's very neat. Give me the quiet eyes of Marion. Happy beggar, Gerald!—unless he's got into trouble. Wonder where he is? Maybe gone dead, like the captain; in which case—" he was growing calmly meditative in the bright sunshine, and lay back making his gentle reflections, and yawning—"in which case, ah-h! it wouldn't be bad for me. I should begin by locking up Chauncey.

"Wonder if I was like that boy when I was twenty-one. Think not. I knew more of the world. There were the makings of a very fine man about Joe Chacomb, only he had not the fair start. Might have been different—Joe might —if he had had the Chacomb rents instead of the little Ass up yonder. Forty-five last month, and nothing done yet—no money in the Funds, nothing to chuck away in foreign mines, and nothing in the Bank. As for his moral character, Joe's best friends—that is, the men who know him best—don't believe he has got any morals at all. Once Joe was a mealy-faced boy, with a rosy cheek. Joe was one of the little cherubim; sang anthems, Joe did, in a church

choir, with a white nightgown on, like a blessed angel.
Life is rum—very rum. Joe would be uncomfortable now
among the blessed angels.   He wouldn't know how to
handle his harp; he's forgotten the treble of all the anthems,
and can't sing bass. Joe makes schemes of plunder; Joe
borrows without intending to pay back; Joe wants to see
Gerald marry the Revel girl, and get cut off by his idiotic
father. Joe is no longer a cherub at all—unless he is one
of those unlucky cherubs who've tumbled down.   After
all"—he sat up and stretched himself, with a yawn—" we
are as things have made us. Joe isn't any worse than his
neighbours. It is beautiful weather, and this is a lovely
cigar."

CHAPTER XI.

DURING these days Chauncey Chacomb kept entirely at
home, and refused to go outside the gates of the lodge.
His cousin, who watched him with an interest growing
daily, observed that a curious change was creeping over the
squire's expression.   His very features seemed changed.
There had been formerly a look of cunning and suspicion
latent in the man's face, which always made themselves felt
in the sharp, quick upward glances of his small keen eyes.
That was gone. His occasional wild glances, apparently
uncontrollable, which first roused the doctor's suspicions,
disappeared as well.   There were no more bursts of a jealous
rage, perhaps because the object of the rage was dead; but
in place of all these there was left a settled gloom, a sadness
which never varied. The spare form was shrunken. Chauncey
Chacomb had become smaller; his head was lower between
his shoulders; he stooped as he walked; he noticed nothing.
If his cousin plied him with wine at dinner, he drank it,
and remained as dismal as if it had been cold tea. He made
no reference to the absence of his son, paid no attention to
external matters, and made no sign of interest in anything,
except that he heard the name of Revel with a visible shrink-
ing and horror. The worst sign was that he neglected

the Collection; he forgot to correct the Catalogue; he locked up his drawers, and left the keys on his dressing-table; and he spent the day in wandering aimlessly about from room to room.

"Go," said Joseph Chacomb one morning, pushing him into the Collection room—"go and potter about as you used to; that will do you good."

Chauncey made no resistance; but when, an hour later, the doctor opened the door, he found him sitting in a straightbacked chair, in the middle of the room, his thoughts far away from any of his curiosities.

Then he watched his cousin more closely. He observed that every day after breakfast Chauncey manifested a keen desire to be left alone. One morning he pretended to go out, but returned after the space of five minutes. He found that Chauncey had crept away to Gerald's rooms, which were, as has been stated, in the western gable, the old part of the house. Hither, when Chauncey began to make his Collection, had been transported gradually the old shelves of books which once formed the library. They were ranged in rows in Gerald's study, Gerald's bed-room, and the room which Gerald used for his workshop: an old and curious library, consisting almost entirely of French eighteenth century books, those works of learning in which the French of that time excelled. People got together materials in the sixteenth century; they learned in the seventeenth; they boiled down, digested, annotated, and correlated in the eighteenth. Every kind of subject was treated of in this cyclopædic collection, which was especially rich in books on medicine. The doctor, stepping silently over the carpets in the direction pointed out by the footman, passed through the open doors, and found Chauncey in Gerald's bed-room. He was not sighing over the vacant place of his son; he was not shedding a tear over the portrait of his son's mother, which hung upon the wall; he was not thinking of son or mother either, because he was thinking of himself. He was standing at the shelves, with a book in his hands, swiftly devouring the contents. Dr. Chacomb marked the eager and concentrated gaze of his eyes, as he read page after page, turning over swiftly, as if he sought for something that concerned himself. Presently he put back the book with a heavy sigh, and sat down. The doctor marked the volume—it was an old calf-bound octavo, whose gilt lettering was faded so that he could not read the name, but he saw its place among the rest. Then, having made his observation, he slipped away, and presently his cousin came out, with a dejected air, and crept like some scared and sick animal into the shade of the trees of his park. Then the doctor sought the place, and took down the volume. It was a French treatise on hallucinations and diseases of the brain.

"I thought so," said the doctor. "The poor little beggar has quite gone out of his wits. We may as well see what he has been reading, anyhow."

He carried the book away with him, and read in it that night before going to bed. There was a strange and dreadful fascination about the pages. They fixed the eyes on the letters, while the vivid images of haunting heads seemed to crowd round the reader, to float around his brain, and to whisper in his ears. The doctor threw it away at last, with a shudder. Before getting into bed he opened the window and looked out. On the lawn, a silver sheet lit by the splendid harvest moon, was walking backwards and forwards his cousin Chauncey, swinging his arms, tossing them over his head, rolling about as if he were drunk. He looked at his watch. It was two o'clock.

"I wonder if he has been carrying on this game every night," he murmured. "Upon my word, I don't like it. Why, hang it, he might come in and murder a man while he was asleep."

He hastened to lock and bolt the door, and then, feeling a little safer, he went to bed and to sleep.

Next day he tried to rouse his cousin. He made him go with him for a walk, almost dragging him by the arm.

"Chauncey," he said, "you are getting worse company than ever. I wish I could only hear you swear a little.

Try, my dear fellow, just one small damn, to break the ice."

Chauncey shook his head mournfully.

"I fear I shall never swear again, Joe," he murmured. "Never again."

"Don't say that, Chauncey," returned his cousin, really affected at this dreary prospect; "you are young yet, and while there's life there's hope. Pull yourself together."

But he would not be coaxed into cheerfulness.

Then the doctor tried bullying. It was after dinner. Now, Joseph Chacomb, who was not at all times—owing to pecuniary conditions—accustomed to what the Americans call a square meal, was making the most of his stay at Chacomb. The dinner, when he was at the Hall, was like Mr. Cook's tours—personally conducted. He ordered it and looked after it himself, down to the potatoes, which he liked served as a separate dish, to remind him of the merry days when he was a student in the Quartier Latin; and to the beer, which he drank from a tankard, to remind him of hospital days in London—for the doctor liked to be sentimental over his dinner. In the same spirit of poetical reminiscence, he chose every day a bottle of Chauncey's best and oldest port, of which he drank every drop, to remind him of the aspirations which had once filled his brain. Naturally, after the port he wanted conversation, and then found himself with a man who neither spoke nor moved.

"I would rather sit with the Aldgate pump, Chauncey. Hang me if the pump would not be a more lively companion. At least it could wag a handle. What are you staring at? Do shut your eyes, man; and if you must stare, look at me."

His cousin was sitting with his short legs tucked under his chair; his uneven shoulder was level with his right ear, and his head bent down to meet it. The room was dark, save for a pair of wax candles on the table; the windows were open, for it was a sultry night, and thunder was in the air. Chauncey Chacomb was staring straight before him, into the darkest part of the room, with a steadfast gaze.

"Don't glare in that way, Chauncey. It's simply disgusting to a man who wants to be cheerful. Tell me, my dear fellow," he continued, quite softly—"tell me, if you can, what you see every night. Tell me why you go out into the park when you ought to be asleep."

"Always the same thing, Joseph—always the same thing. I see Revel's eyes. There—there—there!" he shrieked, as a gleam of summer lightning lit up the room for a moment. "He is here himself. I saw his face as well as his eyes. And yet he is dead. Joseph, help me! Oh, cousin Joseph, help me! It is dreadful to see a dead man's face."

His voice dropped to a low wail. He sank his head into his hands, and bowed himself upon the table, covering his eyes and moaning.

The doctor shivered, and looked round him uneasily. The dining-room was dark with crimson paper and heavy hangings.

"I hate a place where there is no gas," he murmured. "And I hate a room like this, which nothing will light up. Here, Chauncey, old man, wake up! We will go into the drawing-room, and light all the lamps and candles. Come, I will play you backgammon for sixpence a game, if you like."

This was genuine self-denial on the part of Joseph, because he hated backgammon; and, like a great many poor men with grand ideas of money, he despised sixpences. Chauncey got up, and followed his cousin in silence. Presently, he recovered so far as to take an interest in the game. He won three in succession, and putting up the sixpences in his pocket, went so far as to chuckle. But then he relapsed suddenly into his former moody state, and sat intently watching nothing.

When the doctor had put him to bed, with a little dose of morphia, he proceeded to consider the position.

"Which," he said, "I cannot say I like. It is not interesting, and it does not promise to be profitable. I am wasting my time here—time is valuable at five-and-forty—when I ought to be back in town. Things will go wrong if I stay idling here, and I do not understand what I shall gain by waiting on. I believe Chauncey has gone mad; but I don't see just yet how that will do any good to me. That Revel girl runs in my head. I believe I shall end by seeing her eyes just as Chauncey sees the captain's. Perhaps something has happened to Gerald; but it is no use expecting that. Let us see. Gerald comes back; Gerald marries the girl— as if that ought not to be enough for any young fellow. His father cuts him off—but his father is mad. Then who is to prove it? Suppose I say he is sane. The worst of making calculations about what is going to happen is, that what you expect never does happen. The best scheme is disconcerted by the one thing that is least likely. After all, the cleverest man is the man who knows how to use things as they turn up, and at once. It is no use making a book on the events. I shall wait and see what turns up."

The time wore on, with no news from Gerald.

"Let us wait still," said the doctor.

But it was weary waiting for Marion. The past was gone, and with it all the promise of golden fruit. The future was dark, the present was a blank.

One day—a fortnight after the death of her father— Marion could bear the suspense no longer. At least she could see Mr. Chacomb, and tell him all.

It was in the morning—such a morning as that when she sat in the garden and fell asleep, to be awakened by the tramp of feet that brought back her dying father. The house was quiet and lonely, for the other two had gone out together. The sight of the flowers, the wind in the trees, the songs of the birds, all fell upon her nerves like blows upon some heavy instrument. She left the cottage, and turned into the lane that led to Chacomb Hall.

She met no one on the road. Had she been in a mood to mark them, the flowers of early autumn were springing in the hedges at her feet, and she would have rejoiced in the sounds and sights of Nature which called to her unheard as with a voice of sympathy. But Marion had no eyes or ears.

She was listening to the voices of her thoughts, which were sad and heavy. In a fitful way, as people do when they are disturbed by some great sorrow, she noticed little things which passed across her brain, assuming great importance for the moment, and then vanishing. Behind those evanescent images lay the shadow of her sorrow, and with it the heavy prescience of more trouble. She recalled the words of her father, the last time they were together; the last talk with her lover—and where was Gerald? Dark and boding were the spectres of her brain, like those of Sisera's mother when her son lay murdered by the woman whom Deborah blessed above all women. "Why is his chariot long in coming?" But she could not return answer to herself even in words, "Has he not sped?" She came to the stone pillars and the iron gates of Chacomb Hall, and looked up the long avenue of elms, cool and shady, which led to the house. Then, after a moment's hesitation, she left the road, and walked quickly up the drive. On either hand lay Chacomb Park, with its broad stretches of grass and clumps of trees. At the end of the avenue she could see the western gable, with its warm red brick, its pointed roof, and its latticed windows. These were Gerald's rooms. Her pulse quickened when she saw them. Perhaps—perhaps there might be news of Gerald. Presently, in the shadiest and darkest part of the avenue, where there lay on either side thick plantations, there came across her path and stood in front of her—as Apollyon met Christian—the man she partly hoped but greatly feared to meet: Gerald's father. When he saw the girl coming, he threw up both his arms, and cried aloud—

"Why do you come here? What have I to do with you? Why do you come to me in your black dress? Do you accuse me? Do you dare to say I did it?"

"Accuse you, Mr. Chacomb?" she stammered.

"Then why are you here?"

"I came to ask if you know—if you have heard anything about Gerald."

"Gerald—Gerald?" he replied, impatiently. "What is

all this about Gerald? He is away—he has been away for
four years. Stay; my memory is confused. Gerald came
back again. He was at home for four days, and now
he has gone. I forget things very strangely. Where has
he gone to?"

"You are not well, Mr. Chacomb?"

"I am quite well. That is, Marion, I am not well, and
the doctor watches me about. I have dreadful dreams.
Sometimes I think I did it."

"Did what?"

He looked cunningly out of his small eyes.

"No—no; I am not going to tell you that. Let us talk
of something else."

As he spoke a change came over him, and he seemed to
become quite suddenly quiet, self-contained, and impenetrable.

"You came to ask after Gerald, Marion?" he said.
"Pardon my brusqueness this morning. I was thinking of
other things, and am not quite well. Yes; it is a great
anxiety to me that I do not know anything about my son.
He is, however, sure to return soon. The sad news, when it
reaches him, will bring him home. He was always fond of
your poor father."

"I hope he will come back soon," said Marion, sadly.
"Do you know that we are going away, Mr. Chacomb?"

"No. Are you going away? Actually going to leave
the cottage? Where shall I find another tenant? Going
to—where are you going to?"

He spoke as if he was uncertain whether to be pleased or
sorry.

"We are going to London. We have no money at all
now. The wicked insurance people refuse to pay my poor
father's policy. We are going to sell all that we can, and
move to where we can get employment of some kind—whatever kind may suit us."

"Ay—ay," he replied. "Well, Miss Revel, you have
my good wishes, my very good wishes. I should think that
your brother's talents would be quite certain, directly they

find a proper scope, a fitting channel, to put your sister and yourself in affluence."

"Poor Fred! I fear we cannot depend entirely upon him. I shall try to get some work for myself."

"Quite right; quite right. Many ladies get work for themselves nowadays, I hear, and do not mind it very much."

"It is not a question of whether we mind it or not," said Marion; "we have to do it."

"Dear me, dear me!—that is very sad."

"I want to talk to you about Gerald, Mr. Chacomb," said Marion, blushing.

"My son Gerald. Yes, yes—oh, certainly," said the squire blandly.

"Tell me, Mr. Chacomb, did Gerald say anything to you ever about me?"

Mr. Chacomb shook his head, and looked surprised.

"Did he tell you that—that we were engaged?"

"He did not," said Mr. Chacomb, with decision.

"I suppose he had no time. We were engaged, with my father's consent—"

"Oh, with your father's consent! Your father agreed to it, did he?"

"The day before—before the dreadful day my father went out to talk it over with you. He met you on the hill; did he say nothing—nothing at all to you?"

"How could he find time to say anything, Miss Revel?"

"Then I must tell you, for it is right that you should know," said the girl. "Gerald told me in the afternoon—we were sitting on the very place where my father fell—that he—he loved me; and I accepted him. In the evening we told my father."

"Gerald had a father too," said the squire.

"He promised to tell you about it. Why did he not?"

"Young lady," said Mr. Chacomb, with dignity, and slowly, "you had better take the very first train to London, you and your brother and sister. It may save future unpleasantness. As the engagement has only been entered upon for one day, to speak correctly, I think we may consider at once that it has never been made. You think me unkind. Perhaps; but I wish you to know the truth. Understand, if you please, once for all, and clearly, that under no circumstances should I have consented to your marriage with my son—under no circumstances—none. And certainly not now—certainly not now."

She looked at him with much the same eyes as he remembered in her father. He was staggered for a moment, but presently went on again, with dignity—

" It would be best for all of you to go away at once, before Gerald returns. I can explain to him my reasons, if I choose to do so, for refusing my consent. It never could have been given, remember. Gerald Chacomb is heir to the Chacomb estate; he must marry position and wealth. Besides—but my reasons have nothing to do with you."

" Nothing," said Marion, proudly. " At least, I have told you I am engaged to Gerald. What your reasons may effect with him I do not know, and cannot tell. But I am engaged to Gerald until he releases me. Now I understand—now I understand."

" What do you understand ? What do you mean ? "

She looked at him steadily, trying to put a sudden gleam of conviction into her words.

" Now I understand the expression that I used to catch sometimes in your eyes, when you looked at my poor father. Mr. Chacomb, you hated him. I know it now. And you rejoice at our misfortunes. You were with him at his death. You have not told us yet why, when you two were together on the cliff, my father, who had walked there a thousand times, fell over, and only one was left. Why did my father fall ? "

The words were spoken at random, but the man turned pale and trembled. He answered nothing, but his lips moved.

" Why did my father stop and fall ? " repeated the girl.

" I do not know," he stammered—" I do not know. How can I tell? He slipped, he fell. You heard my evidence at the inquest. Go and ask everybody if it is not true. How dare you say such things? How dare you ask such questions?"

"Why did you hate him, Mr. Chacomb?" she went on, quickly. "Was it because he was kind, and you are cruel; because he was unselfish, and you are selfish; because he was loved by everybody, and you—are not; because he was frank and sweet-tempered, and you are jealous and suspicious? Were these your reasons, Mr. Chacomb, for hating a good man?"

She stopped for a moment, and continued, with a softer voice—

"You are Gerald's father—that is why we tried to like you. I see now that it was labour lost. When Gerald and I marry, it will not be to come here. Your permission will not be asked. I shall never pretend to love you, any more than you can love me. For I know too much—I understand too much. But I am engaged to Gerald still, and shall remain pledged to him until he releases me himself."

The blood ran hotly to his cheeks, and he moved his hands uneasily.

"You shall never marry him—do you hear? You shall never marry him. I would rather that Gerald was lying dead before me in the path. I would rather—rather—"

She interrupted him fiercely—

"Rather say I fell from the cliff, Mr. Chacomb."

The words fell from her lips before she understood their full meaning. They produced a strange effect upon him. He shifted his feet, and turned his head about as a man troubled with a sudden sharp spasm of pain. But he mastered this, and drew himself upright, reaching to the shoulder of the tall girl before him.

"Then," he said, calmly, "if you will have the truth, hear it. Marry my son if you like—marry Gerald if you can. But if you do, you will marry the son of your father's murderer. Yes," he continued, as she recoiled with a cry —"his Murderer. I did it. I pushed him over the edge.

I always hated him, and I never, somehow, got a good, safe opportunity till then of doing him a mischief. He drove me mad, too, all the way up the hill, talking of you and Gerald, and what fine things he was going to do when you were married, with my money — my money. I had no knife, or pistol, or anything to kill him with, or I should have done it when I was walking behind him in the lane. He laughed at me the day before about my pictures, too. It was not likely I was going to forget that. So, when we came to the edge, I pushed him over. He fell very quick, Marion, so that I had only a short opportunity of seeing him roll over and over; but I lay down when he was gone, and mocked him from the edge. I think he heard what I said—at least, I hope so. If I had you in the same place, Marion Revel, I would push you over too. It is a nice wild spot for lovers to sit and talk, is it not? and a nice wild spot for people to wreak their revenge on their enemies. I cannot harm you here, because I should be found out; and my constant principle is never to be found out. For instance, I had thought of poisoning him with a pill, but I kept putting it off because I was afraid. I am glad now that I did not. That damned cousin of mine finds out most things, and he is always watching and following me about. He would have found out, very likely, if I had used the pill. Well," he went on, with great steadiness, "you know the truth now. I do not suppose for a moment that you will want to marry Gerald after what I have told you. Take my advice, and go to London at once, to avoid any more trouble. I am a dangerous man, and if you don't accede to my wishes, I shall very likely do a mischief to your brother Fred, or perhaps to your sister. Go at once, I say, and before a worse thing happens."

The girl, stunned by the cruelty and horror of the thing, could make no answer. Mr. Chacomb's voice rose to a shriek as he began his last sentence, but sank into a sort of moan as he finished it; for he saw before him the doctor, walking up the avenue.

He came straight to the squire, and took him by the arm.

"Better go in, Chauncey—go in, and wait for me. Go, I say!"

Then Mr. Chacomb turned quietly, and walked away.

"Has he been talking wildly, Miss Revel? I am sorry you met him. Chauncey is a little—no, if you please, not a little, but a good deal upset just at present. The suddenness of the calamity of last week affected his nerves, and he does not know what he says. You see, he is quite amenable with me: he knows his excitable nature, and obeys orders at least."

"Is it excitement? Is it madness?"

"Who can say what is madness and what is not?"

"I know he hated my father," said Marion. "That must have been madness. But now, I know more. Poor Gerald!" she added, softly, "it is very hard on him; and now it must all be over."

"Why must it be all over?"

"I cannot tell you. It is another secret that I must bear in silence. Dr. Chacomb, help me, in the name of Heaven, to get away from this horrible place. The air stifles me. I am always finding something new and dreadful. There is murder in it, and madness, and horror. Oh, what shall I do —what shall I do?"

"Tell me what Chauncey has been saying. Has he been talking wildly?"

"No; he has been talking sense. Ah, me! he has been talking sense."

"Then it is the first time for a week and more. Miss Marion, if you will tell me nothing, I can only obey your orders. You shall go to-morrow, if you will. I will send after you the furniture that you will want in London. Perhaps it will be best to get out of his way, and to go at once. Now let me know how I may help you with Gerald."

She clasped her hands tightly, to keep down the tears that rose to her eyes and the sobs to her throat.

"It is too much to bear," she moaned—"it is too much. What have I done, what has my poor father done, that he should be punished like this? It is but a week ago—no,

I

a week ago we were in wretchedness—only a fortnight ago
the world was bright and happy. I had his love, my dear
father's love, and Gerald's too. But that was only for one
day. I had one day of the most perfect happiness that a
girl can have in this world. I had Gerald's hand in mine;
his lips touched mine; I saw his eyes soften as they met
mine—oh, what happiness, what happiness! It all vanished
in a moment. And now his own father, my Gerald's father,
sets between us a barrier that can never be passed. I must
give him up."

"Let nothing that Chauncey Chacomb has said make you
give up Gerald," said the doctor. "He is mad; how mad I
cannot say, but mad enough to make his words wild. Forget
what he has said."

"I cannot forget what he has done. Oh, cruel, cruel!"

She sat upon a fallen trunk and sobbed. Joseph Chacomb
watched her with a pity which penetrated even the triple
folds of selfishness which wrapped his heart.

"I will go," she said. "Thank you for all your kindness
to me. I cannot tell you how I thank you. We will go to
London to-morrow. Anything, anything to get away from
this dreadful place. I will write a letter to Gerald, and send
it to you for him. When he comes back you will give it
him. Promise me that, without my permission, you will not
tell him where we are."

"It is odd," thought the doctor, "that now, at this most
important juncture, when I ought to want her to marry
Gerald above all things, my own interests seem nowhere.
Can I be growing sympathetic—I, who have always been
preaching self-interest? It is only a troubled girl, only a
woman breaking her heart, and I must needs help her because
she bids me."

"I promise," he said. "You shall do with me as you
please. I will keep your address a secret till you bid me
speak. But think again. Do not set the words of a miserable creature like Chauncey Chacomb against the happiness
of your life. Do not turn Gerald away because his father has
said harsh things. If Gerald were here himself to plead—"

" Ah !" she caught at the words with a gasp. " If Gerald were here himself it would be harder to say, but sweeter to remember. We should part in love, and I should have his farewell. Now, oh, now what will he think of me—what will he think of me ? for I can tell him nothing."

" In God's name," cried Joseph, moved out of himself, " what has Chauncey said ? What mischief has he brewed in your mind ?"

She shook her head, and gave him her hand.

" Good-bye. I will write you a letter for Gerald to-night —if I can, if I can."

She left him, and sped swiftly down the avenue, with bowed head.

Joseph Chacomb looked after her with something like moisture in his eye. Then he blew his nose.

" I have not felt so," he said, " since I went to the Adelphi for the first time, and saw Celeste play Janet Pride. I thought I had mastered the weakness. What the deuce ! It was not I who made this girl's trouble ; it was not my fault, I suppose, that Chauncey broke out in a new place ; it was not through me. I believe that Chauncey—and what can he have told her, I wonder ? Things in this world never go straight. It is just as I said last night : make every allowance and the most careful calculation, have your combinations arranged like a professional bookmaker, down comes an accident that no one foresees, and smashes it all up. Only a week ago—to be sure, I did think Chauncey cracked, even before this last business—I saw the most beautiful, the most fortunate chance. Gerald, who is as headstrong as a mule, was going to marry the girl, in spite of his father ; there was going to be a grand family kick-up ; the crooked little animal, with a brain as unsettled as his body, was going to leave everything to me. I know his life is a bad one, and this place, with its lovely income, was going to be mine. It is too bad, upon my word ! No will would stand a contest with Chauncey as mad as a hatter. The servants will talk, if no one else does. It is a splendid stake missed. And now we must confine ourselves to smaller operations. At all events, let us borrow all we can. The wise man, like Joseph Chacomb, gathers his roses while he may. Poor Marion! the girl's eyes are enough to melt the heart of St. Anthony."

Six days afterwards—the Revels gone—Gerald appeared, worn and weak from his fever, and ignorant of what had happened. Joseph Chacomb told him in a few words.

"Gone? Marion gone? And without waiting to see me?"

"She is gone. All the village children are crying after her still; but she has left a letter for you."

Gerald tore it open.

"What is this?" he cried fiercely. "Do you know the contents of this letter?"

"I know," said the doctor, "that she asked me to give you a letter containing her farewell to you, and that she made me promise not to give you her address without her permission."

"It is your doing! I believe this is your doing!" the young man burst out.

"It is not," returned the doctor. "I am innocent of any knowledge even of Miss Revel's reason. She refused to tell me. You may believe me, Gerald, when I assure you that I wanted above all things to see you married, and to her."

"Then who—do you know—for God's sake tell me something!—do you know anything, the smallest thing, that could make her write this letter? Read it, read it slowly, and try to account for it."

The doctor read as follows:—

"DEAR GERALD,—A thing has happened which will prevent our ever being to each other what we hoped to be. Think kindly of me—indeed, it is not my fault! I pray you earnestly not to try to see me. Forget me, and forget the words we spoke to each other. That can never be thought of now which you hoped for then, and I too—God knows. You may believe that it is no light matter which forces me to write this letter.   MARION."

" What does it mean? I cannot understand it. I was seized at Boulogne with a touch of my old marsh fever, and have had a baddish fortnight. The moment I could travel I returned, to find this letter, and the place deserted."

" Yes, and the captain in the churchyard."

" Have you no clue? Man, you were here the whole time; you must know something."

" Gerald, if you want to know why Marion wrote the letter, you must ask your father. I do not know what he said to her, nor why she wrote the letter."

The conversation took place on the way from the Barnstaple railway station, whither the doctor drove to meet Gerald. Nothing more was said till they reached the Hall.

" Where is my father?" the young man asked.

" With his Collection, I believe. Gerald, be patient with him; he is excited and worn by the captain's sudden death."

Gerald pushed the doctor roughly back, and ran up the steps. Joseph Chacomb heard him open and shut the door of the museum, and groaned.

" Now all the fat is in the fire. Anyhow, it is only hastening the inevitable row. We shall have to lock up Chauncey to-night with a strait-waistcoat, I suppose. Dear, dear, what a pity for me, and for Marion too, poor girl, that things could not run smoothly!"

He never knew what passed between the father and the son. He heard loud voices, which died away; he heard the shrill notes of Chauncey Chacomb; he heard his cries and entreaties. In ten minutes Gerald came out, white and trembling.

" Go to my father, cousin," he said. " Do what you can for him. Hide him—for God's sake hide him from people, lest he should talk. Treat him kindly so long as he lives, for I shall never see him again."

" What have you said, Gerald?"

" Do not ask me. If he tells you, you will keep it secret, for the credit of the name. Joseph "—he gasped for breath, being perhaps still weak from his recent illness—" I am going away, away from England. I cannot bear to stay here. I leave my father to you, mind. He is to be your charge if I never return. Tell Marion, when you see her, that I accept the inevitable, but I love her still."

"I will take care of your father, but why—?"

"Again, do not ask me. Has that fellow taken out my luggage? Very good; then it may remain in the dogcart. I shall drive back to the station. Perhaps I will write to you from London."

He seized the reins, and drove away, leaving the doctor speechless.

Then he went to see his cousin. Chauncey was sitting, calm and composed, at the window. He raised his eyes heavily when he saw the doctor, but did not speak.

He maintained a perfect silence for four days. The doctor began seriously to think of a private asylum. Then came a letter from Gerald, telling in the fewest words possible that he was starting immediately for Southern Africa, and would be gone when the letter arrived.

"I ask," he said, "for no news, because there can be none but bad news. I leave no address, and shall not go to the post-office at the Cape or Natal for letters. Perhaps I shall come back again in a few years. Perhaps not at all."

Joseph Chacomb read the letter to Chauncey in the evening.

"I had absolutely made up my mind, Joe, that Gerald should not marry that Revel girl. I hate her as much as I hated her father. Did you hear how she turned upon me, and forced me to tell the whole truth—the whole truth, by Jove? Well, I told Gerald just what I told Marion."

"What did you tell them, Chauncey?"

"Marion found it out herself, and taxed me with it. As no one was looking, not even you, I confessed it all at once, and laughed at her. She did not look so scared as you might have expected; only her eyes were something like the captain's when he fell; but not so wild—no, not so wild: there never were eyes so wild as those. But they reminded me, you know. And when Gerald came in just now—Gerald is a handsome boy when he is in a rage—I told him too. He looked like his mother, very much. It is odd how little that boy resembles me."

" What, in Heaven's name, did you tell them ? "

" Why, Joe, where is the use of pretending between ourselves? You know as well as I. You saw me do it. You saw me with your own eyes push him over the cliff. That was why the only evidence you gave at the inquest was how you tried to rescue him. *I* understood—yes, I understood perfectly well. You cannot deceive a man of my penetration."

" Let me look at you, Chauncey."

" Look at me as long as you like. You thought I was mad. I thought so myself for a little while. But I am not. I was never cooler in my life. It is true that I lost my composure a little when Gerald swore he would never return home again. That was natural with such a fine boy as Gerald—a boy to be proud of—only I am quite sure he did not mean it. He can never, you see, marry the daughter of the man I murdered. No, Joseph, you are a clever fellow, but you will not make me out to be mad. That is past even your medical skill."

" Chauncey, pull yourself together, man. Think, think what you are saying. I saw it all, from the beginning."

" I know you did, Joe—I know you did. And very good it was of you to hold your tongue. Very good and thoughtful indeed. To be sure, you were always a kind-hearted fellow."

" I saw it, I say. Chauncey, you did not touch the man : he slipped and fell. Your hands were six feet from him, and more."

" Kind of you, Joe—cousinly. Let us keep up the family honour, *outside*, and say so everywhere. You and I know better."

" What am I to say to this man ? " cried the helpless physician. " How am I to persuade him? Good heavens,

Chauncey, I tell you that you did *not* push Captain Revel over the cliff."

" Quite right, when you speak so loud."

" Who the devil is to speak soft in such a matter ? Chauncey," he said, in a stage whisper, " you did not—you did not—you did not do it. It is a delusion which you will shake off when you recover."

" I am recovered," said the squire. " I know well now. I see the whole scene before me. But let us talk no more about it. The inquest was ' Accidental death.' So that I am quite safe. Only it will be well to keep things quiet to ourselves, will it not ? "

" Quite off his head," murmured the medical man—" quite ! Come, Chauncey, come, my poor cousin," Joseph pleaded, " put this awful hallucination out of your mind."

"Do not be a hypocrite, Joseph Chauncey. I hate hypocrisy where it is unnecessary. So would you, if you had had, like me, all your life, somehow or other, to pretend. I pretended to be in love with Gerald's mother. I pretended to be fond of your society—"

"Gad!" cried the doctor, "this is like a horrid nightmare."

" I pretended to be the special friend of Revel ; I pretended to like his girl ; and I pretended to be sorry for what has happened. But I was glad, Joe—I was glad—only for one thing."

" What is that, Chauncey ? " asked the doctor, catching at a possible means of restoring him.

" It is, Joe, that I understand now what the Lord did when he put a seal on Cain's forehead. He has put one on mine, and I feel it hot and heavy. It grows hotter and heavier every day. I expect it will be like red-hot steel before I am dead. But I must bear it, and everything else. You will not hear me complain, Joe, whatever I suffer. It is upon me day and night—day and night. It would have been better that I had never been born, for I have lived to be a murderer."

Then the doctor, by a stroke of inspiration, bethought him all at once of his own utterances on the cleverness which is able to make capital out of things as they happen, rather than to speculate on things that might happen.

He rose solemnly, and standing before his cousin, a great burly person, over a misshapen, withered little man, like a big schoolmaster over a small boy, shook his forefinger—a very large, fat, and red forefinger, terrible in its shaking as Jupiter's nod—at his face.

"Cousin Chauncey, when people are mad, they are sent to asylums. If they make a noise, they are put into strait-waistcoats. If they fling themselves about, they are put into padded rooms. If they do not obey the keepers, the fellows kneel on them and break their ribs, and then say that the foolish madman did it himself. They tickle the soles of their feet with feathers; they put them on bread and water; they never let them go out in the open air; they laugh at them, and mock them; they give them no books to read; they shut them up with gibbering idiots, who dangle their hands—so—and drive them really mad with their dreadful grinning; or else with raving maniacs, who glare and roar, and tear with their claws. Cousin Chauncey, you, I am sorry indeed to perceive, are gone mad. But at present I am the only man who knows it. I shall be good to you, and hide it—so long as you help me—from the world. But I must treat you, for the future, as you behave to me. I shall manage your affairs for you; put a proper person into the house to have charge of you when I am in London; receive and lay out your money for you; take care of your estates for you; and, so far as I can, prevent your making a fool of yourself. In return, you shall have your liberty, and shall do whatever you please within bounds; only you will hold your tongue. Try to get rid of me, and I shut you up; try to shake me off, and I lock you up in an asylum. Gerald is gone, and I think he will come back no more to England. I am the heir. Make a will, and I will prove that you were mad. Rebel if you dare; try to get away from my protection if you can: you are in my power, cousin Chauncey, and very thankful —very thankful indeed—you ought to be that you have got a physician in the family to take care of you, hide your little failings, and—and spend your money for you, by gad!"

CHAPTER XII.

EAST and west of Tottenham Court Road—a thoroughfare whose great shops have not been able to redeem it from a vulgarity which enters into the soul of those who journey upon its flags—there run lines of parallel streets, this part of London being as regular as the city of Philadelphia, U.S.A. When they were originally built, a hundred and forty years ago, they displayed in their fronts a good deal of aristocratic hauteur and coldness, befitting an expensive and fashionable part of town. Their coldness remains, but their haughtiness has vanished. The streets are not vulgar, but vulgarised. Queer trades are carried on in the houses; brass plates, shutters, and window blinds bear announcements of callings alien to the general experience. A modeller of human limbs, a stippler of photographs, a wax flower maker, a valentine and lace-paper manufacturer, a maker of playing cards, a painter of fans, a Parisian artist engaged upon the petty trifles on which we waste our money at Christmas and Easter: these are some of the professionals who live side by side in Lowland Street, Tottenham Court Road, in such amity as is consistent with trades which are not in rivalry. The majority of the ground floors belong to the offices and workshops; the first and higher floors are let out either on a system of flats, or in separate rooms to ladies and gentlemen who are, as a rule, occupied elsewhere during the day. It is to apartments in Lowland Street that the gallant young draper's assistant of Oxford Street brings home his lovely bride. It is here that the tutor (London B.A.), who gives lessons at a shilling an hour in all the sciences and most languages, finds a lodging adapted to his modest wants. It is to this retreat that the translator and the literary compiler, whose days are spent in the British Museum, return when midnight closes the public-house. Here are third-rate actresses and actors; here are betting men, whose sphere of action is limited to the suburban fixtures; here are City clerks, who, by chumming together, are able to afford one festive evening in the week at the Oxford; here are the young and hopeful who look for better days; here are the old and battered, praying that the worse days may not become the worst; here are those who pretend to have fallen from affluence, and pride themselves, like Lucifer, upon the depth of their fall; here are those, once gentlefolk indeed, who would, if they could, fain forget the past and be contented with the present. The romance, the contrast, the poetry of London are not always where we have agreed to place them. Where life is assured and easy, the romance is of the drawing-room school, which ripples rather than disturbs the surface. Among the reeking and foul purlieus of the courts, about which not even a penny paper, trying to work up to the highest sensational level, dares to tell the whole, horrible truth, the romance, if there is anything that is not real, is brutally and repulsively tragic. Perhaps it is among these strugglers in byeways for life, these hangers-on to the ornamental robes of civilisation, these people who profit by the foibles and vanities, rather than the necessities of their fellows, that a deeper romance may be found, in which life is really earnest, and the situations are really melodramatic.

No. 15 Lowland Street, stands at the corner which marks the confluence of that thoroughfare with Euphrates Row, a place of less pronounced respectability. It is on the south side of the street; its door bears two plates, one of brass: on this the name of Ruddiman represents as was supposed a generation or two back, a landlord long deceased. The plate has remained, a monument of his worth, destined to last as long as the brass, and entirely unexpected in life. Immortality sometimes takes a shape not looked for. The other plate, a brighter and a newer one, is above it. It is in zinc, and proclaims the fact that here is Mr. Rhyl Owen's Academy.

The door itself is decorated and furnished with a row of half a dozen bell handles, each of which is attached to its own room. In the window of the ground floor is a card, setting forth that lessons may be procured from Mr. Rhyl Owen on moderate terms, in book-keeping, French correspondence, Latin, arithmetic, and penmanship in all its branches. At the back of the house, where once stood the garden, in the old times before Euphrates Row was a modern encroachment on the privacy of Lowland Street, they have built the school-room—a long and low apartment, whence may be heard, at morn and afternoon, the buzz of many lessons, the voice of the admonisher, and the wail of the admonished. That is the select academy of Mr. Rhyl Owen. In the evening it is let out as a genteel dancing school, to a professor with a respectable connection, whose daughters assist in imparting a knowledge of the art, and in maintaining the lofty tone of the establishment. Ladies of the ballet are not admitted to these lessons. Once a year—I am sorry the anniversary will not fall within the limits of this book—a ball is given: tickets of admission for lady and gentleman, half a crown each; refreshments, provided by the eminent host of the Grapes, of course are extra. The staircase of the house is dingy, and one which is sometimes swept, but rarely cleaned. The wainscoted walls are blackened at about the height of four feet six, where people's shoulders have rubbed against them for five generations; but it is a broad and handsome staircase—not so stately as one of those in the decayed houses of Soho, but a staircase which shows conscientious work and no contract. The house, as compared with most in the street, is thinly populated. On the third floor front dwells a lady who may have heard of seventy springs, but as all her life has been passed in London, she has never actually seen one. She lives on her means, and is reported by the outside world to be possessed of a comfortable income. It may be so, and it is perhaps nothing but a miserly disposition which makes her lie in bed rather than light a fire, dine habitually off bread and butter, and find a banquet in a plate of cold beef bought at a cookshop in Euphrates Row.

Perhaps, however, it is her ostentatious cleanliness which
favours the idea.   One of the bedrooms at the back of the
same floor is occupied by a young gentleman of four or five
and twenty, who lives with his sister downstairs, and is
supposed to be engaged "in the City."   On the second floor
there lives a hermit.   This class of thinker is not so numerous
as in the old days when—as in the sixth century, before the
Caliph Omar came to change things—the whole of Palestine
resounded perpetually, day and night, and from end to end,
with the litanies of those who fasted and sang, and the howls
of those who flogged their own sinful backs.   I have, myself,
only known one or two cases of the modern hermit.   One
was a man who got into the habit of living quite alone, never
going out of his chambers except to dinner, and then always
to a restaurant close at hand, where he sat daily on the same
bench and had the same food.   He is still living, though
prematurely grey.   The other was the case of Mr. Lilliecrip,
the hermit of Lowland Street.   He was not a religious
hermit, so far as the public knew, nor did he sing litanies
like a Benedictine, nor did he flagellate himself with a cat-
o'-nine-tails like a repentant garotter, nor did he fast and
macerate himself like a Ritualist in Lent.   But he had earned
and maintained the character of a hermit by simply never
going outside his own door.   He had the two rooms, back
and front, and the voice of rumour was busy with him.   He
was reputed rich; he was said to be a nobleman in disguise;
he was as great a mystery as the Man with the Iron Mask;
he was a great criminal, he was a murderer hiding from
the law; he was a forger, afraid to go into the streets; he
was a political spy, obliged to keep himself dark; but, above
all, he was fabulously, enormously, tremendously rich, and
could buy up the whole of Lowland Street and never feel it.
On the ground floor, as has been stated, is Mr. Rhyl Owen;
with him his daughter Winifred, of Her Majesty's Telegraph
Department.   And the first floor, together with the bed-
room of the third floor back above mentioned, is let at twelve
shillings a week, taken by the quarter and money paid in
advance, to a family consisting of two young ladies and their

brother. The elder of the two paints all day at her easel
when she is not copying at the National Gallery; the younger
sits at home and watches her sister, or goes out with her
brother to walk along the streets and look at the shops.
For it is four years since the captain died. Comb Leigh has
long since passed away into the dim twilight of the happy
past. The Revels—Marion, Fred, and Adie—have descended
together to the level of Lowland Street, and to the life that
is called "from hand to mouth."

It is an evening in April, when the advent of spring
makes itself felt in the heart of London by longer daylight
and colder winds, rather than by any of the gracious phenomena familiar to lovers of nature in the country. All the
children are in the street, playing noisily; the nearest clock
has struck six; a German band blows at the corner with an
energy which shows temper as well as tune; and the cold
wind which, outside London, has stripped the apple tree of
its blossoms, turned the lilac flowers brown, curled up the
young leaves of the roses, and killed every little peachlet
which was beginning to swell out on its tiny stalk, is
sweeping through the streets and round the corners, driving
the shavings and bits of paper round and round in the areas,
rasping the housemaid's elbows, and painting the children's
legs a lively red. Where does it come from, this bitter
wind of the east? Does it always blow across the flats
which stretch from Ostend to the Ural Mountains? And
what manner of people are those who dwell beneath its bane-
ful influence?

On the ground floor of No. 15, Mr. Rhyl Owen is engaged
in putting away his tea-things, having prepared and eaten
that meal by himself, according to his usual wont, after the
dismissal of the boys. The room is at once his dining,
sitting, and sleeping apartment. A turn-up bedstead of the
old-fashioned kind, constructed to look as much like a wardrobe as possible, stands in one corner; a wooden arm-chair
is in the window; a cupboard by the fireplace holds the
crockery of the *ménage;* two or three hanging shelves

contain Mr. Owen's library, which consists principally of
translations—not used as cribs, but forming, when he is not
engaged upon Plutarch or the Book of Proverbs, his favourite
reading; for Mr. Owen is as fond of Homer, Virgil, and Ovid
as any other schoolmaster, though his mastery of their
original tongues is defective. The table is equally divided
between a pile of exercise books and a girl's workbox;
an easy-chair stands by the fireplace, and one or two
other chairs complete the furniture. The tenant of the
room is small in stature, like Zaccheus, Tydeus, Julius
Cæsar, Napoleon, and most of the other men known in
history. His face is seamed, crow's-footed, crossed and
furrowed by a thousand lines, every one of which represents a vexation or a disappointment. His short and curly
hair is an iron grey, and stands up all over his head, giving
him a look of perpetual surprise. He wears neither beard
nor whiskers. His eyebrows are thick and black, as if he
was of a fierce and determined nature, which he is not.
On his large and bony hands the knuckles stand out like
cairns upon a hill-side. His lips are large and mobile;
his eyes are as bright as a ferret's. He is dressed in a
long black frock, once a coat belonging to a taller member
of society; its extreme rustiness proclaims its durability,
and furnishes a proof that English honesty is not yet
become a byeword and a proverb among the nations, in
spite of the sizing of cotton and the manufacture of shoddy.
Round his neck is a voluminous black tie. His linen, for
it is Friday evening, might be cleaner with advantage.
His legs are encased in trousers of a dark grey. How
much his garments bulge at the elbows and the knees,
how their folds and sinuosities betray the habitual disposition of their master's legs beneath the chair, it would
be long to tell. On his head he wears a black skullcap.

Mr. Rhyl Owen placed the tea-things in the cupboard,
reduced the fire to a minimum, and taking his pipe from
the mantelshelf— a long clay—loaded and lit it. Then he
looked all round the room, like a dog who searches about for
the most comfortable place, took a book from the shelf, sat

down in the wooden chair, with his back to the light, and
heaved a mighty sigh.

Just at the moment when he took the first whiff a knock
came to the door, accompanied by the rustle of feminine
garments. He listened for a moment, and an expression,
half of fear, half of annoyance, crossed his face.

"If that's Mrs. Candy," he called out, as the door
partly opened, "you needn't say, ma'am, what you came
to say. I caned your second to-day, and I caned your
eldest yesterday, and I shall do my duty upon both boys'
trousers to-morrow if they deserve it. So you may take
your boys away or not, as you like, Mrs. Candy. There's
the national schools," he went on, in a lower voice, as if he
was working off an angry mood; "there's the young cox-
comb of a certificated master; he knows everything. He
ought to be caned for conceit, and I should like to have the
job. 'Wisdom is too high for a fool.' You had better send
them there. And there's the Roman Catholic schools, where
the priest ought to be caned, and I should like to have that
job too."

"It isn't Mrs. Candy, Mr. Owen," said a voice from
outside.

"If it's the milk, you must come again, then; I've got
no money."

There was a little laugh.

"It isn't the milk."

Mr. Owen walked to the door with the solemnity that a
schoolmaster of many years' standing naturally acquires, and
opened it himself.

"Oh, it's you, Miss Adie, is it?" he cried, with a changed
voice.

"May I come in, Mr. Owen?"

"Surely, surely; come in."

She came in—the Adie Revel we left four years ago, a
young girl of sixteen. She is twenty now, and a woman;
her figure is tall and shapely; her face, with features perfectly and absolutely regular, is set in a framework of light
and waving hair; her eyes are of that limpid blue which

seems as full of expression as the eyes of Sappho or Heloise; her lips are parted in a smile, which seems one of perpetual content—it is the smile of a nature which looks for little more than to get the greatest enjoyment possible out of life; and the expression of her eyes, which seems so deep, is as yet but the light of youth and health. Love, quickener of the real nature, has not yet come to transform the maiden. The sorrows of her life have passed over her as the breath of evening over a sea of molten glass, and left no trace behind. Her dress is of a cheap and common stuff, but it is made, by herself, in that perfect taste which almost deceives even feminine appraisers of the marketable value of other women's costume. It falls about her in folds as graceful as if it had been of silk, and fits her slender figure as if it had been made in Regent Street. Round her neck she wears a blue ribbon tied in a simple knot—her only ornament. But she is so beautiful that she wants none, it is pleasure enough to look upon her; and if you listen while she speaks, you hear a voice as clear and musical as any bell, if somewhat thin— a voice which seems to be the fitting organ for a soul of infinite depths.

"Come in, my pretty," said the schoolmaster, the lines in his face softening all over, just as the lines in an old building soften when the sunshine suddenly falls upon them. "Come in and sit down, and talk to me. I've had my tea, and I have lighted my pipe, but I am grumpy."

"Poor old man!" said Adie, touching his cheek with the tips of her fingers. "Why is he grumpy?"

"Miserrimus," said Mr. Owen, bringing his chair from the window to the fireside, and putting back the coals he had taken off—"Miserrimus (nominative case, masculine gender, superlative degree, from *miser*, wretched) is the adjective that describes a schoolmaster. It is told that Dionysius the Younger sank to the lowest depths of misery, and became a schoolmaster—the lowest depths, you see: that is how men gird at the profession. Shakspeare puts a Welsh schoolmaster like me upon the stage to be laughed

K

at. No one ever forgot that Louis Philippe had been a schoolmaster. Johnson was called a pedagogue all his life. Not a cheating, yard-of-tape measuring counter-jumper among them all but thinks the schoolmaster an inferior animal—not one so poor to do him reverence. Lord! Lord! what does it matter, Miss Adie? We get our holidays, and then we can go fishing, and forget our troubles. And, after all, there's the blessed pipe. And Solomon says a word or two for us—'Receive knowledge rather than choice gold.' What made you come down and see me, young lady? Not but what I am proud to have you here."

The girl turned red for a moment.

"I came down because I was all alone upstairs, with nothing to do, and—and—oh, Mr. Owen, give me some tea. We have got no money, and I am so hungry."

"Tea? To be sure, to be sure." He got up, and began to bustle about, laying another stick on the fire. "Why, what in the name of——. Surely Miss Revel hasn't had any misfortunes. Wait a minute, my dear, wait one moment. The kettle is on the sing. Hungry! I have been hungry myself, and it's a dreadful thing, Miss Adie—a dreadful thing."

She laughed.

"Oh, not so very dreadful. Marion went out yesterday to sell some pictures, but could not get her money, so we had no dinner. This morning we finished all the bread for breakfast, and Marion went out again directly afterwards, and has not come home since. I worked till I was tired, and then I went to sleep. But sleeping won't make up for no dinner."

"Where is your brother?" asked Mr. Owen shortly.

"He's gone into the City. But Fred will look after himself—he always does."

"No dinner to-day, and none yesterday. Both days I had a beautiful dinner, and just now I was grumbling!"

He shook his head as if he was sick of the selfishness of human nature, dived into the cupboard and produced a piece of bacon, from which he cut two or three slices. The girl looked on with ill-disguised eagerness while the bacon was cooking in the little Dutch oven. When it was ready, she devoured it with the natural eagerness of an appetite sharpened by the absence of dinner for two days.

CHAPTER XIII.

MR. RHYL OWEN sat opposite, watching his guest with loving eyes. He was a soft-hearted creature, though he was the master of a Commercial Academy; and it went to his heart to think that this fair young creature should actually want the commonest necessaries of life. He cut the bread and poured out the tea with zealous solicitude.

"Is it good? is it refreshing?" asked he. "Now, do have another slice—some more bread: eat plenty of bread with it; and now the tea—we must do without the milk, because I've drunk it all up myself—a greedy beast! Some people like a bloater with a meat tea. I say bacon's more wholesome. As for sprats, now, I suppose a young lady like you wouldn't look at them."

"I would have looked at anything five minutes ago. O Mr. Owen! I am so much obliged. It is so horrid to be hungry."

She finished her tea, and then looked up, with her familiar laugh.

"That's right," he nodded, and smiled back. "Already you look filled out in the cheeks, in a manner of speaking; though you're not, no more than your sister, like my Winifred for plumpness. Tell me, Miss Adie, you are not often so bad as this upstairs, eh?"

"I don't think we have ever been quite so bad before, even before Marion was able to sell her sketches. But then we have been thrown back. It was necessary for Fred, who must have a good appearance when he goes into the City to look for a secretaryship, to have a new suit of clothes, with a great-coat, this weather. That took all our spare money, as you may guess. Then we have had to pawn things—

my father's watch and chain, and even his sword. You may think how Marion liked that."

"My dear, you had better not tell me more than you think right," said Mr. Owen, with some delicacy about hearing further particulars.

"Why not? It is no use pretending to be proud—we have nothing to conceal; we have been ladies and gentlemen —now we are not, I suppose. What else is there to say? There is no shame in being poor."

She laughed, but she spoke a little bitterly.

"Poor Miss Marion!"

"Yes, it's hardest on Marion, isn't it? because she does all the work for us. Besides, she was the eldest, and had been most with poor papa. I hope she will bring some money home with her."

"Perhaps your brother—"

"Oh," she laughed again, "Fred never brings any money home; he takes all the money out. But that will do about myself. How have the boys been to-day—good?"

"Boys never are good. They are born bad—original sin, you know—and it is our duty to thrash them till they grow good. Listen, there's some one at the door again. If it is Mrs. Candy, she is coming to have a row. Perhaps it's— Why"—his face lit up all over with pleasure—"it's actually Winifred, home two hours before I expected her."

It was Winifred. She came running into the room, threw her arms about her father, and gave him two great smacks, one on each cheek; then caught Adie by the chin, held her face up to the light critically and kissed that too.

"You are the prettiest girl in all London," she whispered.

Then she took the lid off the tea pot and examined its contents, put in some water, and got another cup and saucer. Then she threw off her hat and jacket; and then everything ready, she sat down and prepared to enjoy herself in a businesslike manner.

"It is perfectly delicious," she said. "Tea made, Adie to tea with us, and a fire. Father, this is worth living for, isn't it?"

He sucked his pipe and nodded.

"Bread and butter, Adie, dear. How sorry I am I wasn't home to have tea with you! No, I won't have any bacon, thank you. There are times, father, when you feel yourself a man to be envied, eh? Your daughter in the Civil Service, like a proud young competitive clerk; a young lady to tea with you; and your work for the day done. Good work, too. Adie, I am always proud of my father's work."

She read her father's moods by his face, and spoke accordingly.

"I tell him," Winifred continued, looking sideways at the little cloud which still hung upon her father's brow— "I tell him it is noble work which he is doing, the best work a man can do, to raise these poor boys out of ignorance, to bear with their ways, and try to make them like himself."

Mr. Owen shook his head with mild deprecation, but he enjoyed it.

"Nonsense, father! Every teacher wants to make his disciples like himself, else what would be the good of teaching? A schoolmaster ought to be learned; you are learned, father."

"Pretty well, my dear, pretty well. Cæsar at my fingers' ends, as you may say; and as far as Compound Interest, perhaps, you might find it hard to meet my match."

"He must be sober. Why, father, who could be soberer than you?"

"Yes, my dear; I am too poor to drink if I wanted to."

"He must be just."

Mr. Owen nodded, as much as to say that Lowland Street Academy contained the justest of men.

"Merciful, too, with his justice."

He nodded again, with emphasis.

"By the way, father, who was that I heard crying yesterday?"

"Candy Secundus," said her father shortly.

"Poor Candy Secundus! Poor little Sugar Candy! Do
you know little Sugar Candy, Adie? The dearest little
fellow, with blue eyes and curly hair, and always getting
into scrapes. His mother keeps the baker's shop over
the way. What did poor Sugar Candy do, father?"

"Justice comes before mercy," said Rhyl Owen. "'Chas-
tise thy son while there is hope, and let not thy soul spare
for his crying.' Candy Secundus brought a piece of chalk
in his trousers pocket, and chalked upon my desk—my desk
—these lines:—

> 'Taffy is a Welshman;
> Taffy keeps a cane;
> When I get a big man
> He shall have it back again.'

Candy Secundus will remember his verses for some time
when he comes to sit down. I expect Candy's mother will
come to-night to give notice."

Winifred looked graver. The withdrawal of one boy from
the little school meant the loss of a pound a quarter, a
sensible item in the modest household.

"I will go round and see her presently," she said. "Perhaps she will be reasonable."

As the light fell upon her, the low fire on the left and
the gas just turned on overhead made pretty effects of
colour in the twilight. You may see that she is not a
beautiful girl—not beautiful in the sense that Adie with
her regular features and calm eyes in a perpetual repose,
is beautiful. Look again: you see a face full of mirth
and animation; a nose rather short and perhaps a little
too broad; lips half open, showing the whitest teeth behind;
and more still, cheeks as soft as peaches and set with
a pair of dimples—*petites fossettes d'amour.* Her chin is
strongly accentuated and rather pointed, for Winifred has
a will of her own; the tiniest and daintiest little pink
ears nestle beneath a cloud of rebellious locks of light
brown, which escape from their assigned places, and float at
their own, own sweet will; a face full of affection, enjoyment,
and possible passion; and, to crown all, a pair of grey

eyes which have caught the sunshine of June, and give
it back through all the year—eyes always ready to laugh;
eyes fearless and trusting; eyes that enjoy the world, and
are aglow with the fire of her youthful blood, in which the
lover—when the lover comes—will see "a fountain of
gardens, a well of living waters, and streams from Lebanon."
Her fingers, long and delicate, quiver when she speaks,
as if she was working the telegraph still. As she sits, as
she moves, as she speaks, you feel that you are with a girl
whose nervous system is strung by nature to concert pitch,
so that one note out of tune would set the whole ajar.
The other girl, Adie Revel, beside her, is at present calmly
and dispassionately happy. She has had enough to eat
—that is sufficient for the time. Like the owner of the
Splendid Shilling, she can say, "Fate cannot harm me;
I have dined to-day." She has no more care for the
next day than when we left her last, playing Badminton
with her brother. Like the soft-eyed deer, she lies in the
sun and warmth, enjoys what the present has to give, and
is a philosopher in this—that she leaves the gods the rest.
"Heaven," we know, "which sees the future, keeps the
issues in the darkness of the night; nor does it forgive the
man who trembles before what is coming, more than is due
to human uncertainty." Adie had never read Horace;
but she agreed with so much of his philosophy as not to
tremble at thinking of the future. Now Winifred thought
perpetually of things that might be coming: she thought
of Marion, who worked for the three; of Adie who could
not work, but sat at home and hoped for better things;
and she thought—she thought too much—of Fred: Fred
the handsome, Fred the indolent, Fred whose very faults
made him interesting, because they were not the faults of
the class among whom she had been brought up. A young
man of Lowland Street or Euphrates Row, if he departed
from the paths of rectitude, which was not uncommon, was
to be seen smoking pipes at public-house doors, reeling
home at night, or even in extreme cases of moral obliquity,
marching handcuffed between two men in blue, or escorted

from the doors of Bow Street Police-office to the door of
her Majesty's omnibus. The Lowland Street youth did not,
like Mr. Frederick Revel, wear trousers and coat closely
resembling those of Bond Street; they did not spend the
day in the fashionable end of the town; they did not
frequent West-end billiard rooms; nor did they despise
the companionship of other young gentlemen in the street.
Perhaps it was the contrast of Fred Revel with this
other young man which made Winifred think so much
about him.

The old schoolmaster, retreating from the table to his
place in the window and his book, left the two girls to
their talk.

"Poor dear!" said Winifred. "To think of your going
without your dinner for two days! Why did you not
tell us?"

Adie laughed.

"That is nothing, providing we don't have to go without
our dinner to-morrow and the next day. But I dare say
Marion will get some money; she always does find money
somehow."

"Perhaps your brother will get a proper place soon."

"Poor Fred! He says, Winifred, that some people are
born to work and some to spend, and he certainly was not
born to work. Sometimes I think that Fred will never get
any more work to do at all. You know, he does try; he
goes into the City, I believe, at least once a week—and
everybody knows it is in the City that you pick up rich
posts. Once he was made secretary to a company. His
friend, Lord Rodney Benbow, got him the post. To be
sure, the company broke up in a month; but then, as Fred
says, it gave him the business experience that he wanted.
Winifred, don't let Marion know that I told you about our
distress; she is proud, and would not like it. As if it
matters now," she said, with a bitter laugh—"as if it
matters for all the world to know how poor we are! Let
them know. We have not a single friend to care whether
we starve or not."

"O Adie! you have me."

"It is a horrid thing to be poor," she went on, passionately. "It is a cruel thing, a wrong thing, a wretched thing to be poor. Marion seems to think it enough if we get our miserable meals day by day."

"Give us this day our daily bread, Adie," said Winifred.

"I know. But my bread ought to be more than breakfast and dinner and tea. I want things, Winifred, that other girls have. What is the good of life where there is no pleasure—nothing but working day after day to get enough to eat?"

"But we cannot have all we want to have," said the telegraph girl, letting her thoughts loose vaguely in the field of boundless impossibilities.

"Why can't we? Once I had all that I wanted; it was not much, to be sure, for I was only sixteen, and satisfied with little. Now I am twenty, I want to live."

"Adie, do you think it is right to talk so?"

"Right or not, I do so because I think so. Yesterday I went out with Fred for a walk. He will not take me to Regent Street or the Park, for fear of meeting his old college friends. You see, Winifred, this is the only dress I have got. I can trim it up after the fashion, but I can't turn it into a new dress. Fred keeps up appearances better—I do not know how. Well, he is ashamed to be seen with his sisters in the street. We walked part of the way down Oxford Street, turned to the right up Berners Street, and then, after seven o'clock, when all the gentlemen were having dinner, and Fred was not afraid of meeting any one he knew, we went down Bond Street and Piccadilly. As we came home through the squares, the people were driving off to dinner; in one or two houses we could see them sitting down, ladies and gentlemen—ah, happy people!—dining properly, and with servants to wait. Some other people, not so happy, but better off than ourselves, were going to the theatres. We came home. Neither Fred nor I had a single sixpence between us. When we got home, we found Marion sitting with a single light, trying to draw an outline. She had no

money either. Fred smoked, nobody spoke, because we
were all three too miserable; and about ten we went to bed.
We had had neither tea nor supper, and Marion sat all the
evening with her head on her hand. Poor Marion! Poor
Fred! Poor me! You don't mean, Winifred, that I should
like this life?"

A grunt escaped the lips of the schoolmaster, but he said
nothing. Adie looked up for a moment, and went on, in a
lower voice—

"Fred keeps up his spirits and mine too, as well as he can,
the dear fellow. He is always cheerful; he says that something will happen to make us all comfortable again. But
it is worse for Marion, because she has all the work to do,
poor thing! She is different from both of us, I think; and
takes things more seriously. To be sure, where should we
be without her?"

"When Fred—I mean your brother," said Winifred—
"gets the place he wants, it will be better, will it not?
He will do something for you. It would be dreadful for
him to go on for ever allowing Marion to work for both of
you."

"That is what he says and thinks. Fred has, only you
would not think it unless you knew him as well as I do, the
noblest of hearts. He says that this living on the proceeds
of Marion's work is killing him, and I am sure that he is
getting thinner. He declares that he is ready to take any
kind of work that offers. Of course, you know, Winifred, it
must be such work as a gentleman can do. Now and then
Dr. Chacomb suggests something; but Fred has got an
aversion to the doctor, and his way of looking at things.
Above all, as Fred says, he is a gentleman, and, if he pleased,
a nobleman."

"Yes, dear, I know."

There was another grunt from the schoolmaster.

"I read once," he said, without looking round, "of a
nobleman in France who fell into poverty. He resolved on
giving up his title and forgetting his rank. He handed
his sword to the Mayor of Bordeaux, and went away.

When he came home after twenty years, enriched by trade, he demanded back, and received again, the sword of his ancestors."

Adie listened politely.

"You had better tell Fred that story, Mr. Owen," she said, with a laugh. "I should like to see Fred depositing my father's sword with the Lord Mayor of London while he went about, on Dr. Chacomb's suggestion, as an advertising tout. That was the last advice, I believe."

"There are good families in Wales," said Rhyl Owen, "as well as in France. My father, Ap Rhyl, whose father was Ap Owen, used to boast of our descent from Llewellyn, who was a king. Yet my brothers and I had to work for our living, and never grumbled at it."

"Never mind, father," said Winifred. "You do not quite understand."

"But Adie, disinclined to discuss the question, had risen.

"I shall go upstairs now," she said. "Good night, Mr. Owen." She went to the chair, and held out her hands. "I am very, very much obliged to you."

"Child," said the schoolmaster, looking up at her, "stoop down, and let me whisper. If you have got no money tomorrow, you and your sister come down here at one o'clock —we will go shares. And, Miss Adie, make your brother do some work, and try to get some for yourself. Don't leave everything to Miss Marion."

Adie nodded her head, laughed, kissed him on the forehead, and left him. It was two years since they came to the house. Rhyl Owen and his daughter were not, as she and Fred confessed to each other, strictly of the upper classes, but they were kind. Adie loved little attentions, and craved for the outside signs of affection. Winifred was her only companion, and, when Fred was not at home, she allowed herself a greater approach to familiarity with Winifred's father than her aristocratic brother would have approved of. At all events, she felt that he would have shuddered if he had seen her actually kiss the forehead of the little Welsh schoolmaster.

"Not even a University man!" he would have said.

"Winifred," said her father, abruptly, "he's a worthless chap."

Winifred changed colour. But she knew whom he meant.

"He's a worthless chap, Winifred, my girl," he went on. "He hangs about billiard tables, and borrows money of gentlemen. Sam Beagle, who is head waiter at the Guards' Club, told me he heard Lord Rodney talking about him, saying that Fred Revel cost him a sovereign every time he met him, and he'd be dashed if he'd stand it any longer."

Winifred was silent still.

"As for the girls—the young ladies, I mean—it's a good thing for you and me that they came here. It isn't often that we get the chance of knowing a real lady. As for Miss Marion—Lord! when I think of that girl, Winifred, and how she toils and slaves, my blood boils—it boils, I say. There, I've broken my pipe! Give me the other one, my dear. As for Miss Marion, I say, she's a good woman. Who can say more?"

He got up, and stood before the spark that lingered in the fireplace.

"What does Solomon say about a good woman?" He took a Bible, and opened it at the Book of Proverbs, and read—"'She riseth while it is yet night, and giveth meat to the household. . . Strength and honour are her clothing; and she shall rejoice in time to come. . . . In her tongue is the law of kindness. . . . Many daughters have done virtuously, but she excels them all. . . Let her own works praise her in the gates.' That is Marion Revel. I have watched her for two years. She is the good woman of Solomon, and she is more—she is the true Christian, Winifred, because she thinks and works for others, and not for herself."

"And so do you, father, dear."

He stroked his chin.

"In a measure, my child. Yes. It is the task of the teacher, I read in a book the other day, to lose his own

interests in those of his pupil.   The anxieties of one become
the sufferings of the other ; he feels with his scholar—"

"Poor little Sugar Candy," said Winifred, thoughtfully,
with a gleam in her eye.

Her father caught it, and laughed.   He was a silent man
out of school, because he talked so much in school hours that
quiet was needful.   He was a grave man, because he could
not indulge in the natural mirth of his nature before the boys ;
but the old Adam broke out sometimes, as it did now.

"Ho! ho!" he laughed.   "Candy Secundus will become
a great poet:

> 'Taffy was a Welshman ;
>   Taffy had a big cane ;
> When I get a big man
>   He shall have it back again.'

Ho! ho! ho!   If little Candy does not turn out a great
man, my dear, they will tell of this day, and how his brutal
schoolmaster flogged him.   Dear me!   Schoolmasters are
a misrepresented race!   I dare say Orbilius in Francis's
'Horace'—there is the book on the top shelf—was a merry,
soft-hearted, and gentle creature, only Horace never understood the right side of his nature.   Perhaps Busby used to
cry at night when he thought of all the boys wriggling on
their seats."

"Winifred," he went on again, after a few meditative
puffs of his pipe, "think over what I said, my dear.   He is
a worthless chap.   You went for a talk with him on Sunday
afternoon."

"Yes, father, but Adie was with us.   Oh, you don't
know!"   She took his face in her hands, and squeezed
the wrinkled and crow's-footed eyes and nose together.
"You don't know anything about it, father.   Why, the
Revels are quite above us.   Fred is a gentleman, an Oxford
man, a scholar, and a Count—think of that—only he is too
proud to take the title.   And what am I?   Only a telegraph
girl, father."

She laughed as she spoke, but the tears came into her
eyes.   She brushed them away quickly.

"And now, father, I shall go round to Mrs. Candy's, and find out if she is angry with you. I shall pretend to ask for a loaf, you know. We can't have the school dropping to pieces just yet, can we? Dear old father, you have yet to work a year or two longer, until your daughter can make money enough to keep you."

Left alone, the schoolmaster sat down and pondered. The house was quiet and lonely. He thought of his bright and pretty girl; he thought of the idler whose fancy she had caught; he wondered what was best to be done. Outside the house, in the street, the children shouted and played; within there was the silence of the grave. And he thought of the two friendless girls above him, and one of them so helpless.

"Between most of us and starvation," he said, "there's only the mercy of the Lord. Thank Him, it's a thickish plank."

Presently he heard a heavy foot mount the stairs, and stop at the Revels' door.

CHAPTER XIV.

THE visitor knocked at Miss Revel's door. Getting no reply, he gently turned the handle and looked in. Its only occupant, Adie, was sitting in the dusk at one of the windows, pressing her cheek against the glass, and gazing, with her thoughts far away, at the passers below. The gas from the street and the shop over the way lit up the room. In the softened twilight and the dim illumination you could perceive that the room was comfortably furnished with easy chairs, a sofa, a piano, and a few water-colour paintings. The light was not strong enough to show that the covering of chairs and sofa was worn in holes and faded, that the carpet was ragged, that the piano bore marks of age and use. An easel stood at one window, and by it a small stand with paints and canvas. In the centre was a table covered with work, over which Adie's fingers had been busy during the day. She was not idle, for she kept the wardrobe of her sister and herself, and maintained, in spite of all difficulties, the neatness of her brother's linen. The new-comer, who was indeed no other than Dr. Chacomb, stepped across with the noiseless tread affected by some heavy men, and laid his hand gently on Adie's.

"You?" she started. "I did not hear any one open the door. I thought you had deserted us, Dr. Chacomb. It is nearly six months since you came to see us last."

"I got very little encouragement in my last visit," he said. "I am not quite certain that I ought to come here again at all."

"Did Fred say anything to annoy you? You remember that you annoyed *him* very much."

"So that he had the right to annoy me in return, you mean. No, it was not your brother's little outbreak of temper. I hardly know what that young man could do which would annoy me. He might surprise me, certainly. If he were to get his living in any honest way, it would surprise me. But he would never annoy me."

"Do not say unkind things about Fred," said Adie. "For my own part, I should be extremely sorry to have him making his living as an advertising tout; and that, you know, was what you advised him to become."

"That is about the only thing he is fit for," said the doctor.

"Well, if it was not Fred, who was it—Marion or myself."

"As it was not you, it was of course your sister."

"I declare," said Adie, pettishly, "It is too provoking. What did Marion say or do, I should like to know? You are absolutely the only decent creature left in the world— not to speak of dear little Winifred Owen—that comes to see us, and you take offence at some nonsensical fancy of your own. Oh, why are men so stupid?"

"Hardly a nonsensical fancy," said the doctor. "It was real hard fact. Where is Marion?"

"I do not know. She went to Burls's shop. Perhaps

she stayed there to finish off something; perhaps she had to go over Waterloo Bridge to Hermann's. She may be in any moment. Sit down and be comfortable, and tell me all about it."

"Tell me first how you have been getting on since last I saw you."

"We have been getting on worse and worse. I think we did have some money, a little, left when you came last. That is all gone now. And Marion has not been doing very well for the last three months. At present we have nothing."

"Nothing?"

"Nothing at all. Not a sixpence in the world. We paid our rent for the quarter out of Marion's dividends. Then we had a little money left to live upon; we have got nothing now, and out of that we have to save up for next quarter's rent, and live besides. It's like what papa used to call a midshipman's half-pay."

The doctor was silent.

"Yesterday we had no dinner. To-day we have had no dinner. I do not know what poor Marion has done; but I went downstairs, when I was so hungry that I could not bear myself any longer, and asked Mr. Owen to give me something to eat. I've had bacon, and bread and butter and tea."

"And Fred?"

"Fred is like the sparrows: he picks up his dinner in the street," said Adie. "I wish I could."

"No money, no dinner. Why did you not send to me, child?"

"Why did you not come to us?"

"Did not Marion tell you anything?"

"No. Marion tells me nothing about herself. Tell me what was the matter, Dr. Chacomb. Perhaps I can help to put things right. Heaven knows we can't afford to give up our only friend."

"It is a very simple matter," he replied. "I asked Marion to marry me, and she refused."

" Oh ! "

Adie found nothing else to say before a statement the whole bearing of which she could not immediately realise.

" You, too, I suppose, think it absurd," said Dr. Chacomb.

" I have never thought anything about it at all," she replied ; " because this is the only time I have heard about it. But it does seem at first as if it was too bad that you can't know us without wanting to marry one of us. Why isn't all the stupid love taken out of the novels ? No one would think of it at all unless for them—I am sure Marion and I don't—and then we could live together and be happy."

" Childish talk," said the doctor. " You don't understand. Now listen, Adie, and see if you can understand this. When you knew me four years ago, I had no money, and was in debt. I used to run down to Chacomb to borrow, when I was hard up, of poor Chauncey. I had a mouldy little surgery—I blush to think of it—at Islington, with half a dozen patients, and what is called a general practice. I was lazy, because I had nothing to do. I was forty-five years of age, and a failure. You remember me then. Try to compare me now with what I was. Tell me what you thought of me."

Adie laughed, and shut her eyes. It was great fun to tell Dr. Chacomb the exact truth, and not to offend him.

" I shall not be complimentary," she said. " You were a red-faced man—such a red face !—and Fred used to say you drank too much."

" Fred was always as fond of me as I am of him," said the doctor, smiling. " But Fred was right."

" You wore black trousers that bulged dreadfully at the knees, and a coat that never—whether you walked or stood or sat—hung anyhow but in bumps and folds. Your boots were worn down at the heel, and you had a horrid black waistcoat which was frayed at the pockets."

" Very likely," said Dr. Chacomb. " The pockets were worn by searching for the coins which were not there. Those devils of pockets ! I remember them, too. They

L

were my purse, and the reverse of the purse that Peter Schlemyl got—"

"Who was Peter Schlemyl?"

"I forget now, except that he sold his shadow, and that he got instead of it a purse, out of which you could take as much money as you pleased, without putting any in. Now, you could put as much as you liked into my pockets, and there never was anything there. The gold changed into silver, the silver into copper, and the copper into nothing at all. But pray go on with your description. It grows interesting."

"I think I have finished. Stay—you had immense red hands. I used to wonder how it would feel to have hands of such an enormous size. Your hair was thick and matted; your lips were very large, I remember, and very red, you had great black eyebrows, and your eyes were fierce and strong—they seemed to take in everything, and to want to order everybody about. Altogether, you were not quite nice, somehow. Comb Leigh did not suit you."

"Good," said the doctor. "On the whole, it is a clever portrait. But that was four years ago. Light the candles, look at me again, and tell me if the portrait will do now."

"There is only an inch or two of candle left, and what are we to do for more when these are gone?" said Adie. "Never mind, we can go to bed in the dark. There, Dr. Chacomb."

"What do you see now?" asked the doctor.

"No," said Adie, "I will not describe you any more."

The portrait, indeed, no longer represented Dr. Joseph Chacomb. His face, lit by the candles, had lost its old red hue, and was now pale, but not pallid; his large eyes—formerly, to the young girl's fancy, so fierce—were softened and grave; above them lay eyelids heavy, as if with thought. His eyebrows were no thicker than is befitting to a man of great mental and physical strength. His lips were large, especially the lower lip; but you may remark the same prominence in that feature in the photograph of nearly every great statesman, lawyer, or preacher. His hair, grown thin at the temples, was strong, closely knitted, and not yet touched with grey—a sturdy crop of brown curls. His large hands, from which he had removed the gloves, were now white and shapely. He was dressed by Poole, in such garments as belong especially to the prosperous physician—a black buttoned frock, and grey trousers in which no trace of Adie's ancient "bulge" was visible. A pair of double eye-glasses in gold hung from his neck.

"Of course I knew," said the girl, "without the candles, that you were greatly changed. I was only talking of what you used to be. You are not offended, are you?"

"Not at all; but I want you to understand all about me, and that very clearly. Look at me again. Am I younger or older than I used to be?"

"Younger, to look at."

"If a man is younger to look at, he is younger in reality. There is no wearing of wigs about me; it's all Nature's handiwork. I am exactly what you see me, and I was exactly four years ago what you knew me then. I ought, by all the rules of life, to be four years worse—fiercer in the face, redder in the eyes, clumsier in the paws; but I am not, you see. I am ten years younger; I am not red-faced at all. You have never asked me what has effected this transformation."

She shook her head.

"I will tell you."

"If it is a story, let me put out the candles. You can talk by the gas-light just as well."

"Rubbish! Let them burn out; I will give you plenty more. Listen to me, child. When the unsuccessful man putteth off his unsuccess, he lays aside his bad habits. Of bad habits come red faces and fierce eyes; of unsuccess come old coats, down-at-heel boots, and bulgy bags. Failure in a man is like a fallow soil to the fields, because it causes all manner of ill weeds to grow. When you knew me first, I was a failure; now I am a success."

"I am glad to hear it," said Adie. "I wish you would teach Fred the way to become a success."

"Fred! As if any teaching would do him any good! But have you no curiosity? Do you not care to ask what I have done?"

"No," said the girl. "Men are always doing something to make money. It seems to me to matter very little what they actually do, so long as they get it, and give it to their daughters."

"There is no critical faculty at all," said the doctor, "in the feminine mind. If Eve had only been told not to inquire how Adam made his money, we should all have been gardening in Paradise this day. I never did like gardening, for my part, so I am mightily obliged to Eve. Then, Adie, since you do not ask me, I must tell you. You have never heard, I suppose, of the Royal Hospital for Gout, supported by voluntary contributions?"

Adie shook her head.

"You see," she said, "I never had gout. It comes of eating and drinking too much, I believe. We are not at all likely—Marion and I—to get gout. Perhaps Fred may get it some day."

"I am its Founder," he said with pride. "Of all my projects, it is the only one which I have pulled off. The rest, poor innocents, perished unborn. But one is enough. I founded it. Alone I did it. I hired the building, got my secretary, and organised my management. It is now a flourishing institution. I am the chief consulting physician. We appeal especially—it is a stroke of real genius this, if you could only understand it—to those who have never had the disease. The funds come in, and my fortune is made."

"Do you mean that you take all the money that people send?" asked Adie in her innocence.

"No, my dear young lady. That would be an elementary proceeding unworthy of my genius, and leading to unpleasant interviews with the magistrates. My fortune is built upon my reputation, and that is based upon my hospital. I am now the leading specialist on gout. Dr. Porteous, of Savile Row, pretends to be my superior; but you will not believe that."

"Very well," said Adie innocently : "I will not."

"My income is over four thousand a year, and it goes on increasing like a snowball. You understand so far?"

"Yes. You have got more money than you know what to do with."

"Not quite. However, this is what I am coming to. I want to marry Marion. If she will have me, I will take you away to a pleasant house at the other end of town. You shall have a carriage to ride in. Do you hear?"

"Ah!" cried the girl, her colour flushing.

"You shall leave this place, and go into the country, to the seaside—wherever you please. You shall have money to spend, and as much as you want. You shall associate with ladies and gentlemen again. You shall dress as a young lady of your beauty—you know what a pretty girl you are, Adie—ought to dress. You shall have lessons in all young ladies' accomplishments. You shall pick up the threads of your life where you dropped them four years ago, only they shall lead to a life broader and more famous, and fuller in enjoyment. You shall belong to the world that you envy. Only you must help me."

"How can I help you?" she asked, with lips apart and brightened eyes.

"Will you if you can?"

"Will I not? Would I not do anything, anything to get out of this dreadful place, and feel once more that to-morrow's food at least is ready and certain? You know that Marion is reserved. I cannot go to her and say, ' Marion, you are a great goose to refuse the good luck that offers for both of us.' If I were even to hint at it, things would be worse than ever. There must be no appearance of my helping, even if I see a way."

The doctor considered.

"'Time is precious to a man when he is on the verge of fifty. There are only ten years more of enjoyment before him. I want to marry at once, Adie, and waste none of those valuable years. First of all, however, I must help you. Don't be proud, child. You have no money?"

"Not one penny. I told you so."

"Then you must not refuse to take some. I suppose you keep house while Marion paints?"

"Yes."

"I think you had better not let her know, if you can help it, that I have given you anything. Only take care that you always have plenty to eat. See, here are five pounds for you and Marion, for your housekeeping. I put the money into your hands on the condition that you do not give it to your brother to waste. Spend it on yourselves. Let Marion, if you like, believe that it is careful housekeeping. And as to helping me, you can only do it by letting Marion feel, day by day, the misery of poverty."

Adie considered.

"That may seem cruel, but it is really kind. As soon as Marion begins to realise that her compliance means your restoration to the world of respectability, she will comply."

"But about Fred. You will help the poor boy too, won't you?"

"I am not at all obliged to provide for Fred," said the doctor; "but I will do what I can for him. Fred shall not be forgotten; that is all I can promise on his account. It is you that I should like to see happy and well provided for, my dear child. I want to have you with us for a year or two before you marry and leave us; to see you enjoy yourself at balls and operas and theatres; to bring a little more plumpness to those fair cheeks of yours."

The doctor had got her hand in his, was bending his face to hers, and you might almost have thought by the look of his eyes that he was making love to her. But he was not: it was only a way that he had, and the natural pleasure which every well-regulated male mind feels at having a girl's soft hand in his own.

"I should like, my girl, to make you happy, as well as Marion. Are you afraid of me?"

"But Marion must be made happy first," said Adie. "How do I know that you will be kind to her, as well as to me? Marion is not so easy to get on with as I am; she takes everything so seriously, you know. And, besides, it is not me you want to marry, but Marion."

"If you are not afraid of me, why should Marion be? If you would not laugh at me, I would tell you that I love her. I do indeed. I have always loved her."

"Have you? It seems very funny that you should love Marion. You are such very different people. Perhaps, though, that is the reason why you love her. But I do not want to laugh."

"What would you say if I told you I loved *you*, Adie?"

"I cannot imagine such a thing to happen at all," she replied. "It is no use speculating. One thing you may be quite certain of: if you were Blue Beard himself, and I were only going to be the last wife but one, I would marry you if you asked me, to get out of this doleful life. Yes, I would. And if I were Marion, I would marry any one who would give us enough to eat. If I were Beauty herself I would marry the Beast with pleasure, if he would give me proper dresses and the things that make life comfortable as well. I would do anything for more money, Dr. Chacomb—anything, I declare."

"Have patience a little, Adie," said the doctor, smoothing her hair with his palm. "Wait till I bring home Marion for my bride, and you shall have all you want. I am not quite Blue Beard, nor yet quite the Beast; but tell me," he added, sentimentally, "would you mind having me for your brother-in-law?"

"Not a bit," said Adie, truthfully. "I should rather like it, I think. You are the only gentleman we know, and I am sick of starving. Fred never does anything for us; I can do nothing for myself. What are we to look forward to? You are quite sure you will not do anything horrid after you are married? Because, you know, I should feel miserable all my life if poor Marion were made unhappy through me."

"Trust me, Adie," said Dr. Chacomb; "and help me if you can. See, you have forgotten the money."

Adie took up the five glittering sovereigns, and held them in her hands, holding them to the light with an admiration

that had a sort of tremor in it. She had never before had
so much money given her all at once, and the gold represented a boundless vista of rich and luxurious probability.

"It seems wrong, somehow," she said, "to take your
money. Suppose nothing comes of it, after all. Suppose
Marion will not be persuaded to marry you. Suppose you
reproach me for doing nothing. Mind, I cannot promise
much. I will do what I can, because I think it is the best
thing for us all, not because I want it by itself, and very
much, to happen. And you will perhaps turn round then,
and say I took the money from you."

"Joseph Chacomb, Adrienne Revel"—in less prosperous
days he would have said "Joe Chacomb"—"Joseph Chacomb
has faults. He is sometimes called overbearing, chiefly by
his enemies; but do not forget that he comes, like yourself,
of gentle blood. We are the Chacombs of Chacomb. My
cousin Chauncey, poor fellow, and I are now alone to represent the family, unless Gerald turns up again. You may at
least trust Joseph Chacomb to be a gentleman."

"Good night, then, Dr. Chacomb, and thank you."

"Hush! I hear Marion's step."

The pair separated guiltily, Adie slipping the money into
her pocket. The man's ear was quicker than the girl's, for
immediately afterwards the door opened, and Marion Revel
came in.

Four years of hard and careworn struggles have placed
their mark upon her. She was little more than a girl when
we saw her last, with the buoyancy of girlhood still on her;
she appears a woman of thirty now, by her wasted cheeks
and her faded look. She is dressed, like Adie, in a cheap
stuff, cut and trimmed by her sister in the fashion, so that
she might not look dowdy. Her gloves are worn and mended.
She has something of the air, without the meekness induced
by incessant obedience, of a nun or a Sister of Mercy. Under
her arm she carries a parcel, which Adie recognises, with a
heart-sinking, as the packet of drawings she took away with
her in the morning.

"You, Dr. Chacomb?"

She put down her drawings, and held out her hand, with a smile which suddenly brought back all her youth. She was only twenty-seven, after all—that halting-place in the growth of womanhood where youth and beauty meet, the time when a girl may be at her sweetest and freshest, or may be *blasée* and worn out. Marion should have been at her sweetest and freshest, but for the sad reasons of hard work, anxiety, and insufficient food. The Princess of Fairy-land can live on nothing; her tears nourish her, as they did the Psalmist: her hopes sustain her; her faith cheers her. In Real-land the Princess grows pale and weak when she has not a good dinner every day. In her distress she lives chiefly on tea and bread. After a while her spirits fail, her faith declines—all for the want of proper food. Rabelais makes great Gaster the first Master of Arts, the first great inventor, the deviser of every art; he should have gone farther still, and made him the nourisher, the support, stay, prop, and comfort of love.

"You, Dr. Chacomb! It is a long time since you came to see us last."

"It is not my fault if I do not come oftener," said the doctor. "You have only to say that you like to see me."

"Of course we like to see you. You are our last link with the past. If it were not for you to remind us that things were really what we remember, Adie and I should get to believe that we had been all our lives in Lowland Street."

"Yes," said Adie; "sometimes I believe we were. Comb Leigh seems a dream."

She took her sister's packet of drawings, and looked inquiringly. Marion shook her head.

"I have had a weary day, dear, and very little luck. Mr. Burls swore, in his pretty fashion, over the forest birds, and would not look at the wild flowers. But he has promised to get me some work, doing curtains and backgrounds for a portrait painter, if he can. Then I walked over Waterloo Bridge, and saw Mr. Hermann. I think I dislike him worse than Mr. Burls. He was not in his office, and so I came home. Oh, I forgot to say that I waited for five hours at

Mr. Burls's, and began to copy a head for him. So I have
not wasted the day. And Adie—?" She looked wistfully
at her sister.

"I have been alone all day. At six o'clock I left off work,
and went down stairs to have tea with Mr. Owen. Winifred
came home early. Then Dr. Chacomb came in, and we have
been talking. Let me take the poor pictures, dear. I wish
Mr. Burls had his head between them, so that I could squeeze
it—like this—to a jelly, the horrid man, for swearing. I have
promised to see Winifred again this evening," she added,
mendaciously. "I will leave you with Dr. Chacomb. Good
night, doctor."

"Why do you reproach me with not coming, Miss Revel?"
he began. "You know the reason."

"There is no reason," she returned, with a little bitterness.
"That is no reason at all. You asked what you knew you
never could have; you were foolish—or were you kind?
Perhaps you only thought of my happiness, to ask. But you
might have known—surely, no one could have known better
than yourself—how utterly impossible it was. You promised
never to allude to it again."

Dr. Chacomb waved his hand. Nothing more strongly
marked the difference between the man now and the man of
four years ago than the attitude in which he stood, the air
with which he listened, the gesture with which he received
the young lady's appeal. Everything betrayed the man of
self-possession, of experience, of reserve—the man accustomed
to converse on equal terms with those whom a former generation called persons of quality. Now, anybody can be a
gentleman of Bloomsbury, of Camberwell, or even of Islington,
but it requires some adaptability to put on the air of the
middle-aged gentleman of Belgravia. As for the young gentleman of that district, he is born, not made, like the poet,
and cannot be imitated. Those who attempt to copy him
are like Icarus, who flew too high; and, like him, they fall
and perish miserably.

Four years ago, Dr. Chacomb would have been nervous,
shy, and ill at ease with ladies; four years ago, with Marion

herself he found himself expressing sentiments that smacked of Bohemia in the language of Bohemia; four years ago, the gifts and graces of life were like the latter letters of the alphabet to the algebra lecturer, his unknown quantities. He is polished now : the same man still, but with the outward veneer of self-control. What *does* it matter, perhaps, how selfish, how cruel, how licentious your disposition may be, provided the veneer is thick enough to prevent anybody finding it out ? And if even your wife never discovers the faults that lie seething beneath, if her only complaint of you is that you show—being at heart a Blue Beard for philandering, a Nero for cruelty, and a Louis Quatorze for selfishness—a certain lack of sympathy, a strange reserve as to things holy and good, why, civilisation has done something. Success had civilised the doctor.

He waved his hand with a gentle sweep of deprecation.

"Nay," he said, "I hardly promised never to open the subject again. On the contrary, I came to open it to-night."

"You have news ? "

"None from Gerald. No line has come from him since he left England. I have told already what we know. We traced him to the Cape; from Cape Town to the Trans Vaal Territory; then we lost sight of him. I have no news to give you of Gerald. Believe me, Miss Revel, in spite of my own hopes, I am sorry to have nothing to tell you—of him."

"I believe you, Dr. Chacomb. You are a true friend."

"I would have shown that a long time ago, had either you or Gerald told me at the time of my cousin's strange hallucination, and what he said. He has it still, Miss Revel. I heard to-day from the person who has charge of him. The belief is on him stronger than ever. In other respects he is calm, rational, and consistent; in this alone he is mad, hopelessly mad. He believes that he murdered your father."

"At least he hated him," said Merion. "There is no delusion there."

"Yes, he hated him; he hates his memory still. But that

is nothing; it is all part of his madness. Forget Chauncey
Chacomb, Miss Revel! The poor lunatic never did your
father any harm, save in thought. He is quite innocuous;
and if you were to go and see him, he would probably sit
down and cry."

"I could not bear to see him."

"But never mind Chauncey Chacomb; I came here to-
night on a different errand. I came to ask you, Miss Revel,
once more how long you are going to mourn over a lost
love."

"Always, Dr. Chacomb."

"It is not as if you had been married. Even then a
widowhood of four years in one so young would have been a
great deal to give."

There was an innate coarseness of feeling in the man
that success and veneer could not wholly hide, and which
made itself felt in such speeches as these. You know how
vases of a debased period still proclaim the vulgarity of
their form, however they are painted or gilded. Dr. Joseph
Chacomb considered Marion's obstinacy as something con-
ventional and affected, like the prolongation of her mourning
by a widow who ought rather to rejoice over her emancipa-
tion. What was the good of it? Fish swim in the sea as
good as those which lie in the fishmonger's window. If
Gerald was gone, there were other lovers to be had, notably
himself. It irritated him, this constancy. And yet had
he been asked to give up Marion, had he been told that
there were plenty of girls as good as Marion in the world,
he would have laughed at the impossibility of finding one
that could be to him what Marion might be. He really
loved her. Perhaps, too, there was a little pity in his
feeling towards Marion. She had been so happy, and was
now so poor. Quite selfish men very often nurse the luxury
of pity with great enjoyment, and even endeavour, when
possible, to combine relief to the unfortunate with more
enjoyment for themselves. If, for instance, Dr. Chacomb
had come across Jephthah's daughter lamenting among the
mountains, he would have been moved to the deepest pity

by her beauty and her distress combined; while ugly virgins in basketfuls might have wept without attracting his sympathy. Most likely, after a little consideration, he would have proposed to remove the cause of her tears by an immediate elopement and secret marriage at the nearest sacred grove or high-place of Baal.

"A very great deal to give," he went on. "You are young, but you will not always be young. You have given already to the memory of that poor boy the best years of your life. Be reasonable, Marion."

"I try to be reasonable; but it must be in my own way."

"I came to see you to-night," he went on, "in order to make one more appeal to your common sense. See, now," he said with a little dropping in his voice—it was remarkable that he did not take her hand as he had taken Adie's—"see, Marion, you do not absolutely hate me."

"Indeed, I do not hate you in the least. Quite the contrary. I am always very glad to see you."

"There it is, then. Half the battle is won if you have overcome your dislike to me. I know that when you first made my acquaintance, appearances were against me. I was horribly poor: I was desperately in debt; and I had fallen into coarse habits. All that is altered now. There is nothing to prevent any lady from marrying me."

She shook her head and answered nothing. It was the second time and she knew what would follow.

"Then it is surely something that I am getting rich more rapidly than I could ever have hoped or expected. There is no profession in which money accumulates faster than mine, once you make a start. I've made a splendid start."

"I'm very glad indeed—for your sake."

"Be glad for your own, Marion. I wish I was a younger and a more eloquent man, to persuade you the better. Be glad for your own; I want you for my wife. In all the world I don't think I have a single friend—not a man, woman, or child to whom I can tell whatever I have on my mind. When you are struggling, it doesn't matter; but when you are rich and comfortable, you want a companion. It is not good—Scripture warrant—for a man to be alone. When I sit at home, after a dinner that a duchess—yes, a duchess—would enjoy, I cannot drink a bottle of port as I used to four years ago, because I must consider my nerves for the next day's work. I hardly can smoke now. I don't care to read. And thus it is that I want a wife to talk to me. Be my wife, Marion."

She shook her head again silently.

"I will be kind to you; I will indeed. You shall never hear a harsh word from me. I will consider your wishes in everything; you shall have the direction and ordering of the whole house. I shall be contented to make money for you to spend, provided I can only see you my wife."

He began to tick off on his fingers the special advantages she might derive from a union with himself.

"Look at yourself, now—toiling and moiling for a miserable pittance, and putting money into other people's hands. What have you had to eat to-day? Next to nothing. Adie told me. You have actually suffered privation—you. What will your work lead to? More misery, more starvation, more wretchedness for you and your sister. I offer to take you—and her—out of it all."

He ticked this off as a telling point, and went on again after a moment's consideration. The man was tremendously in earnest; but each sentence jarred upon the girl's nature, and made compliance with his wish the more impossible.

"Adie, now. Do you think it right and proper that she should be living in this style, brought up as she was? She is twenty years of age, as beautiful as Helen of Troy, and full of longings for the good things of the world. Remember that it will be your own fault if she continues to go on like this. Why, I've known girls, out of desperation "—he stopped for a moment—"do all sorts of things. Marion, think of Adie before you give me up."

Tick the second. Then he played what he thought a stronger card.

"There is your brother Fred. He has been loafing about town for four years, living on your exertions. Now I tell you candidly and honestly that he will never do any work at all. He does not want any. I know the London loafer. Every day makes him fonder of the billiard tables, and less inclined to work. Fred *couldn't* do any work if he had any to do; it is impossible for him now, even if it was possible for him four years ago. You will have to go on working for him as well as for your sister. You will see him descend lower and lower. He is already at a tolerably low level. You will watch the last pretence of trying for work disappear, and the last scruple at depending upon your exertions; you will see the very last flickering spark of his honour die."

"Dr. Chacomb!"

It was a good blow, and he repeated it, thinking he would drive the nail home.

"You will see the last flickerings of his honour die out bit by bit. He will lose all that you have admired in him. Well if he does not bring disgrace upon your name. I offer you relief from this infliction. I will myself provide for your brother."

The girl made him no reply, but her head sank lower.

"Gerald is dead," he went on—"of that be very certain. Gerald is either dead or he has forgotten you, and his father, and the past, all of us together. Do you think that he would not have written had he been alive? Do you still believe that on the word of a madman, accepting a wild statement which he never even tried to question or to prove, he would have stayed away for four years, and made no sign? Why, anything might happen. His father's life—Chauncey has got heart disease—hangs upon a thread; the estates might come to me. You might have married some one else. Nonsense! Gerald is dead, or Gerald has ceased to think about you."

"If he has ceased to think about me, that is no reason

why I should cease to think about him," said Marion. "If he is dead, let me mourn for him still."

"No, Marion." He lowered his voice, and his eyes, under the rolls of fat eyelids, assumed a softer light. "No, Marion, mourn no more. You have had enough of misery and sorrow; let the dead bury the dead. The memory of your father's death must not cloud the whole of your life. There has been too much mourning. Come back to the world, and take your place among the ladies of the world, the sweetest and best of them all. I swear there is no one like you, Marion—no one among the countesses and people —wherever I go. Come out of this dreary and starving den, where you lie hidden and forgotten. Good God! to think that you should dream of going on here, and like this, for ever!"

"Not for ever," said Marion—"not for ever. There *is* an end appointed."

"Yes, and it is appointed by *me*," said the doctor, with an earnestness which perhaps redeemed the audacity of the statement. "Be my wife, Marion, and all shall be well with you. I am hungering and thirsting for you. Come to me, and I will make you happy. Come to me, and your sister shall be happy. Come to me, and I will rid you of that idle, good-for-nothing rascal, your brother."

As he spoke, the door opened, and the idle rascal himself appeared. He had a cigar in his mouth, and stood for a moment looking at the doctor, as if uncertain what to say. He lifted his hat, took the cigar from his lips, and stepped in with an air of easy dignity, such as might belong to Alcibiades in his early days of success, wealth, and an easy conscience. The doctor saw with admiration how handsome the young man was, with what a fearless confidence he held his head, how clear and honest was the look in his eyes, how frank and gallant was the pose of his figure. He was well dressed, too, and wore a hat of the newest and glossiest. It was not till after he got home that Dr. Chacomb was able to put it to himself with indignation how, while his sisters were starving, their brother was so fat and well-looking;

how he could afford cigars whose perfume spoke of nothing less than sixpence a-piece; and how an idler and a loafer had the impudence to look so independent.

"You will rid my sister of the idle rascal, her brother," said Mr. Frederick Revel, quietly. "It is not the first time, sir, that you have volunteered your advice; but I hope—I believe, it is the first time that you have openly insulted my sister by abusing her brother. Leave the room, sir!"

It is one of the easiest things in the world to say; but unless the words take effect instantly, the order has to be repeated.

Dr. Chacomb looked at the young man as if he had not spoken; or, rather, he looked through him, fixing his eyes thoughtfully on a sketch upon the wall behind him.

"Leave the room, Dr. Chacomb, unless you wish to go through the window."

"Fred!" cried Marion. "Dr. Chacomb—for Heaven's sake!"

"Miss Revel," said the latter, "I will call and see you again, when we shall not be interrupted. There will be no going through the window, so far as I am concerned."

"Understand, sir," cried Fred, fiercely—no one, not even the laziest of *lazzaroni*, likes to be called an idle rascal—"that I object to your coming to this house at all."

"I thought," said the doctor, with a smile, "that the lodgings were taken, and—and, in fact, paid for by the exertions of your sister. Perhaps I was wrong."

"I object to your presence here; I will not have it. My sisters are under my care and protection."

He looked for the moment as if it really was by the labour of his hands that they were housed and maintained.

"Your care and protection?" Dr. Chacomb shook his head slowly "They have done great things for the young ladies. They provide your sisters with good lodgings, companionship of their own class, plentiful food, and abundance of pocket money—"

M

The young man interrupted him with an impatient gesture.

"Your sisters ought to be, and are, no doubt, infinitely obliged to you. Mr. Frederick Revel, do not talk nonsense. You must try bounce with other people. Remember, sir, the time will come when even the self-sacrifice of a sister will fail you, when the devotion that has kept you in idleness so long will be tired out, and when your own petty tricks to keep up the appearance of a gentleman will break down. Miss Revel, you will not forget what I said. You have but to order me, and I will free you of the burden "— he spoke very slowly, shaking his finger at Fred—"of this idle, good-for-nothing, spendthrift brother of yours."

Marion held out her hand. Frederick threw himself into a chair, with a futile effort to preserve his dignity.

"Do not," Marion murmured—"do not be hard on poor Fred. We are as we are—what God made us, I suppose. And—and—Dr. Chacomb, do not desert us. Try to be kind *to them*, and forget me."

CHAPTER XV.

THE starving poet whom Pope in England, Boileau, Saint Amant, and Regnier in France, have held up to the derision of posterity, lived in a garret, sometimes sharing his pallet (whatever a pallet may be) with a fellow in starving aspiration. Many an unfortunate young gentleman, with a turn for imitative scribbling and a capacity for idleness, has imagined that to be uncomfortably poor and to live in a garret are necessary conditions of the poetic life in its embryo. This belief sweetens the water of affliction, and spreads the crust of poverty with Sicilian honey. It is, therefore, useful. Chatterton, Savage, Béranger, Mürger— the name is legion of those who have lived at the top of the house in their youth, though not all have survived that period and come down. But there comes a time when the imagination takes sober tints, and expectation of success changes into certainty of defeat. Then the poet curses his garret, with all that thereto appertains—the narrow limits of its four walls, the stairs which lead to it, the wind which blows down the chimney, the wretched furniture which helps to make it unlovely, the prospect from the chimney tops, his own bad luck in being born a bard.

Mr. Richard Carew—whose character might be gathered from the simple fact that his friends always called him Dicky and nothing else, so that had there been a thousand Richards in the field, or rather at the public-house bar, there would have been but one Dicky—was arrived at the time in the life of a genius when the early hopes have been blighted, and disappointment has been accepted. He is thirty years of age, and is certainly as poor as when he began, perhaps poorer, because his wardrobe is more scanty. He has been in the profession for ten years, during which time the heartless world has allowed him to remain in the garret where first he slung his hammock. He has now— the bitterest blow of all—come to disbelieve in his own genius. *He has left off trying.* That is fatal. So long as you continue to write there is hope—*qui scribit laborat;* glimpses of true art are caught by him who is always copying or endeavouring to draw, however thin be the vein and Minerva unwilling; felicities of expression come of their own accord to him who continuously writes, like a happy combination of colours to him who shakes up the kaleidoscope long enough. Dicky, however, has for the last three or four years forgotten the ambition which led him to abandon the usher's desk at a Devonshire provincial academy, and change it for the garret of a genius. He has sold the little library of great authors whom once he studied. He reads no more except to copy; he writes no more, except to perform, with as little trouble as may be, the daily task.

The place is in Lowland Street, two doors from No. 15. The garret already alluded to is not the apartment one would choose for luxury. It is long and narrow, with a sloping roof. It is furnished with a contempt of luxury worthy of Diogenes. Although the residence of a literary man, there are no books in it; and although the home of a genius, there are no sheets of writing-paper on the one table. Perhaps, however, he works with his brain. The place is low and close, in spite of the chimney, which acts as a ventilator. It contains a chair or two, a chest of drawers, a table, and an iron bedstead, whose sheets and pillows are crying aloud for a bath. It is eleven in the morning, and the tenant of the room is lying on his back in the bed, with his hands joined under his head, and his eyes wide open.

"I suppose," he growls, "that the longer I stay in bed, the hungrier I shall get. Why can't a man sleep it off?"

He got out of bed with an air of disgust, and began to dress. Dicky Carew boasted a shock crop of red hair, a face which would have been a figure-head of health but for the redness of his nose, and a profusion of whiskers which stood out on either cheek, imparting to what Nature intended for the emblem of meekness the look of extreme ferocity.

If it were fair, which it certainly is not, to reveal the secrets of a gentleman's toilet, one might illustrate the simple severity of Mr. Carew's manner by one or two striking particulars. Some children of the present luxurious generation, for instance, would be too proud to wash their only pocket handkerchief with their own hands. Dicky was not. He whistled, indeed, over his task, with the ease and freedom which a happy conscience imparts to an habitual duty. It might even have been objected that he spent more time in washing the linen than in washing himself.

"The consumption of soap is awful," he murmured, looking at the wasted cake. "I must really get to the Museum early to-morrow"—a *non sequitur* at first sight as profound as the celebrated typical case of Stoney Stratford, except to the initiated few.

A daily inspection of his wardrobe was necessitated by reason of its extreme scantiness; for Dicky, like Diogenes,

St. Francis, or St. Anthony, scorned to spend money on raiment and fine linen. Still, it is known to all that seams will separate in which we have too long placed our trust; buttons will fail on which, forgetful of the mortality of perishable things, we have relied too confidently; edges in conspicuous places will fray and fringe.

He looked first at the heels of his boots, and groaned aloud; they were worn to their junction with the upper leathers. The thought forced itself upon his mind that in a day or two it would be absolutely necessary to have them heeled, or even to reject them altogether.

"I've read of a Frenchman," he said, "who discovered that his boots wore out on the pavements of Paris as fast under a republic as an Empire. I believe the free institutions of England are more fatal than either to the heels of boots. Where can I get the money for new heels? I wish there was another Revolution."

He observed that his trousers showed signs of unforeseen decay about the knees, and his heart sank.

"Show me," he said, almost fiercely, "the capitalist who can afford two new pairs of second-hand machine-made reach-me-downs in a single winter. Where is he, I say? Produce him."

His coat, which was originally a black walking coat of fashionable cut, had been for some months slowly turning green. Dicky laid it over a chair where it could catch the full effect of the sunshine, and retired a few steps to watch the effect.

"It's beautiful," he said, "regarded as an effort of Nature in her most sympathetic mood, and as something to talk about for people who've got what art critics call the 'vivid passion of sight.' The coat is better altogether than Joseph's. No such depth of light and shadow could be got out of a coat of many colours. You want a single shade, such as green, growing out of an originally black ground, but in different gradations; a touch of green on a foundation of black, in places where the nap gets rubbed off between the shoulders — those Museum chairs do wear the shoulders shamefully; where it buttons across the chest, a pale green with a lustrous shimmer; where it's simply shiny, the right cuff for example, it's like a piece of imitation Bohemian glass; the deeper artistic feeling comes out in the folds of the tail as it hangs gracefully from the figure. If all the world were artists; if everybody had the æsthetic eye of a—a—Nicolas Poussin, one would wear that coat with pleasure and pride. As it is, I should like to have a new one, and I can't get it."

He investigated his pockets one after the other. There was a penny in one, some loose tobacco in another, a pipe in a third, a pencil with some paper for notes in a fourth.

"I have heard—or did I read it once when I used to read books?—of a man who found a half-sovereign in his waist-coat pocket. Perhaps—no, there's no half-sovereign there. As for breakfast, I must go without. I shall be able to raise a couple of shillings from old Lilliecrip, I dare say. That will carry me through the day. Eleven o'clock, Lilliecrip at twelve, writing till three—nothing to eat till half-past, even if I do get the two shillings.

"Now if I had only not gone to the Harmonic last night—only not gone—my head would have been clearer this morning, and there would have been five shillings in my pocket instead of a penny. What's the good of a penny?"

He took it out and held it up disconsolately.

"A bronze penny. In the good old days, a penny had its value; it was a good lump of copper; you could buy things with it. England has never been merry England since copper pennies went out."

The clock chimed the half-hour. He took his hat.

"I may as well go," he said. "There is not much to make one linger in this retreat."

He twirled his hat thoughtfully.

"What a hat for a gentleman and a genius! It was a Lincoln and Bennett once, and figured on the stage. I believe Toole played in it. Ah, it looked very different in its youth, I dare say. It was glossy and black, for certain; now it's shiny and brown. It used to be brushed regularly, no doubt; now it's a very dangerous thing to brush it. I am sure it must have had a stiff brim both before and behind; now it's so limp that it can't be taken off except from the top, like a priest's biretta. It was once of fashionable build—Lord! Lord! who would think so now? I should date that hat, I think, at 1860, or thereabouts."

He put it on his head, a little to one side—which gives, as every one knows, from the commander-in-chief to yesterday's recruit, a smart and even a rakish air; put up his note-book, felt for his pencil and keys, took from the corner a coloured cane—quite a gentlemanly cane, which was the pride of his heart, and which he handled as delicately as a Life Guardsman on a Sunday afternoon—and went downstairs.

On the second floor he stopped, looked doubtful, shook his head, and tapped at the door. A voice replied, and he entered.

"You needn't trouble to ask me this morning, Mr. Carew," said a querulous voice; "I've got no money to lend, or to give, or to throw away."

The voice came from an easy-chair by the fireside, where a very old woman sat propped up with pillows.

"My dear madam," said Dicky, with the sweetest manner in the world, "I am sure I never thought of borrowing even a sixpence of you; I am only anxious to repay you the small sums which—let me see"—he produced his note-book—"it was—how much was it?"

"Three pound four and tenpence."

"Let us say, between friends, and to make it round money, three pounds five," said Dicky, making a careful note of it. "My aunt from Westmoreland is coming to town, I expect, in a day or two. She will—"

"I don't believe you've got an aunt in Westmoreland at all," returned the lady in the chair. "Whenever you owe me money it's your aunt in Westmoreland."

"My *dear* madam," Dick replied, with unction, "is it

possible you mistrust *me*, your old friend, Richard Carew?
You must be unwell; you suffer this morning, poor dear.
Let me shake up the pillows." He crossed the room delicately, and adjusted the cushions of the great chair in which
the old woman sat propped. "Poor dear soul! And yet
there's the look of youth in her eyes still."

"Go away, do," said the old woman. "My granddaughter
told me when she went to rehearsal this morning not to
lend you another sixpence if you was to beg for it on your
bended knees."

"I did not come to borrow," said Mr. Carew. "Can we
not be disinterested for a moment in this world? You will
not deny—come, now, deny it if you can—that your eyes
once played the very devil with the fellows."

"Perhaps they did, Mr. Carew, perhaps they did," she
replied, twinkling and mollified. "But long ago. Lord
bless me, I played with the infant Roscius at Drury Lane:
I was the Player Queen to his Hamlet. Eyes? Ay, to be
sure. Why not? Fellows were fellows, then, too."

"They were," said Dicky; "I've read of them. Gad,
ma'am, I was born too late. Those hands, too. What delicacy in the shaping of the taper fingers! Blood shown in
the almond nails—"

"Very likely," said the old lady, looking complacently at
her withered old fingers. "My mother was on the stage
before me."

"Ah! Possibly — who knows? — Royal blood; pearly
nails; pink and rosy palm. Don't think I only come to
borrow money, ma'am. When hollow hearts—you remember
Byron?"

"I used to know him."

"Happy man! 'When hollow hearts shall wear a mask,
will break your own to see, Then, Dudu, let me only ask if
that resembles me.'"

He grasped her by the hand, cast one eye on the mantelshelf in hopes that a casual shilling might, as had happened
once or twice already, be lying ready for the borrower's
hand, and left her, creeping out with sympathetic tread.

Outside the door he winked and smiled, and shook his head a great many ways.

"Breaking up at last, poor old girl! Many's the pound I've had out of her. Memory seems going at last. On Sunday it was four pounds eight and sixpence. She's forgotten one pound three, as near as I calculate it. Now, that's all clear gain."

On the ground floor he tapped again. There was no answer, so he opened the door uninvited, and looked in. A comely woman of forty-five was busily ironing, crooning a tune all to herself the while. She looked up in his face with a pleasure which was quite unaffected and real.

"Why, Mr. Carew," she said, "I thought you were out and about hours ago. I haven't seen you, not these three days."

"I have been composing, Mrs. Medlar," he replied, "since daybreak."

He pressed his hand upon his forehead and sighed heavily.

"Lor! and poetry too, I dare say."

"Poetry it was," said the mendacious one.

"Do you"—Mrs. Medlar sat down before the fire with the hot iron in her hand, occasionally tapping it with the point of her finger, lest it should take advantage of the position to get cold—"do you feel that it exhausts you very much, Mr. Carew? I have heard now, from a gentleman that used to deal at my husband's shop—poet for a tooth-powder and perfumery in quite a large way of business, he was— that what with the rhymes, and the names, and the ideas, it was sometimes enough to make him feel as if he must take a little something, or drop."

Mr. Carew staggered, but caught the back of a chair for support.

"Those were the lower flights," he said, in a sinking voice. "Efforts like mine, Mrs. Medlar, are attended with more trying consequences. At this moment, I feel, I really do feel, as if I had not even breakfasted. Now you'll laugh at that, I suppose."

This statement, at least, was true.

"Poetry seems like ironing, almost," said the lady. "You work on and on, never thinking, and all of a sudden down you drop. I was just feeling a little faintish myself when you knocked."

Dicky groaned.

"Those who lead public opinion must suffer," he said. "There are martyrs to literature of whom the world knows nothing."

"Poor dear!" said Mrs. Medlar. "I know what it is to work, and get the reputation, and that, and all the while no one thinking of your poor insides. I've seen my own brother come home from leading a West-end funeral as limp as that thread paper, and as green as a cucumber. He was one of them as wants constant support, little and good. The honour and glory of the funerals was not enough, he used to say, to make up for the fatigues and the long waiting. Some of them took biscuits in their pockets, but he'd never give in to it—he had that feeling for the look of things. The sinkin', he used to say, gave him the real mournful look."

Dicky looked round the room. It was a comfortable room, combining the requisites of kitchen, dining-room and *salon;* for Mrs. Medlar was a widow with a property of her own, and of an orderly and saving disposition. But it was not the furniture—for with this Mr. Carew was already tolerably familiar—which attracted his attention so much as the shelves above the sideboard. On the lowest of these was a plate, half covered with a basin; and on this his eyes were riveted.

"Excuse me for interrupting you, Mrs. Medlar," he said, with a winning smile of perfectly disinterested curiosity; "but *is* there—do I see in that plate—sausages? Really, now, they *are* sausages. Do you know, my dear soul, that I feel as if a fried sausage, well browned and crisp, was the one thing that I want at this moment to pull myself together."

"Then," said Mrs. Medlar, rising with alacrity, "why didn't you say so at once? A sausage you shall have, and two if you like."

"Generous heart!" muttered Dicky, taking a seat, and stroking his chin while he gently wagged his head. "O woman, at the hour of tea, a ministering angel she. My own lines, Mrs. Medlar. I will finish the whole poem when I have time, and dedicate it to you."

"If it was only the hour of tea, Mr. Carew."

By this time the sausages were in the frying-pan. "Only the hour of tea." Evidently her words had a meaning not on the surface.

"Ministering angel! If you were Mrs. Carew, it should never be anything but the hour of tea all day long."

She turned the sausages and looked round at him with a smile. Mrs. Medlar's face was a compound of good-nature and shrewdness. She knew pretty well what her literary friend wanted, and she was resolved to keep a tight hold of it for herself—namely, her little income. She knew, too, that Mr. Carew was at best but a humble member of the profession ; she could not but compare his worn and seedy raiment with the gorgeous apparel in which her late husband rejoiced ; she saw very well that Dicky was often partially, and even sometimes wholly, intoxicated ; she had, on one lamentable occasion, helped him to bed with her own hands. Now the defunct had never returned the worse for liquor, except on proper and expected occasions, such as an Odd Fellows' feast. It was quite certain, again, that Dicky had no money in the bank. All her notions of things right, things respectable, things becoming, were upset by the behaviour of this Bohemian. And yet she liked him. He came at irregular intervals and made love to her, borrowing half-crowns which he never repaid ; he made the most solemn protestations of affection when he was in distress, and in moments—literally moments—of affluence he forgot to tap at her door at dewy morn or balmy eve, and left her as neglected as Horace's Lydia. And yet she liked him : it did her good to have the vagabond with her and to scold him ; it soothed her to hear his tale of love, the only thing in which she believed him. He came generally in the evening when he had no money, and therefore nowhere else to go, and sat drinking whatever she gave him—contentedly, it must be owned; for Dicky's tastes were catholic, and so long as the liquid had any, even the least, intoxicating qualities, he was happy in consuming it. They tell a story of a Lincolnshire farmer who was accustomed to get drunk every night off brandy and water, and who paid a visit to a Somersetshire cousin. To his astonishment, the cider offered for the evening refreshment produced no effect; and after the twentieth tumbler he was heard to moan, "This is weary, weary work." Dicky Carew would never have found any weariness, provided the right conclusion—the state of drunkenness, in fact—might be seen in the dim future. But yet the widow liked him.

"Tea!" she repeated, dishing up. "If I were to offer you either tea or mild ale at this moment, which would you take?"

"Generally, I should say tea," said the poet; "but after my labours of this morning, which have made me nervous, it would be better for me to take mild ale."

She gave him a shilling, and pointed to a jug. He disappeared, and presently returned with a comfortable head of foam upon the vessel. She noticed, with a quiet smile, that he neglected to give her back the change. It was a forgetful way he had.

He sat down to the sausages while his hostess cut his bread. A pound of sausages, as every man knows who has lived in chambers and had dealings with Mr. Tucker or Mr. Prosser, consists of six. Mrs. Medlar had fried four. These rapidly disappeared; but instead of grace after meat, Dicky's eyes wandered from the empty dish to the two remaining sausages, looking as innocent as babies and as attractive as infant pig in their clean white skins. It was a mute appeal, but it was unsuccessful; for Mrs. Medlar, to place herself beyond temptation, put them away on the top shelf.

"Now, Mr. Carew, take your beer. Leave me just one glass for my own dinner, and then you may go away."

He took the jug with both hands, and slowly tilted it upwards. When it finally left his lips—it was always a subject of regret with Dicky that he was obliged to take breath twice in a quart—it was empty. He anticipated any reproaches that might fall from the widow's lips by seizing his hat with one hand, and her own fingers with the other.

"Affectionate and self-denying nature," he murmured, " when we are married—"

"Married, indeed!" said Mrs. Medlar, trying to snatch her hand away, and wounded in her tenderest feelings at the absorption of all the beer. "Married, indeed! When will that be?"

"The days," he continued, "shall be one everlasting round of sausages, beer, frying-pans, and ironing. You resemble Diana when you fry, and recall the statues of Juno when you iron. And when you drink beer, I am reminded of Venus, who was born of the foam."

What he meant was not clearly comprehended by Mrs. Medlar; but it was intended, and therefore was taken, for a compliment.

"If you meant it," she said; "but there, you don't. You tell the same tale to a dozen women. As for flattery, I believe you could flatter a donkey's hind leg off. I like a man to be real, I do."

"Flattery! O Mrs. Medlar—may I say, Almina?"—this was her baptismal name. "Almina! 'When hollow hearts shall wear a mask, will break your own to see; Then dearest, pray, your conscience ask, if that takes after me.' I wrote the lines this morning, thinking of you; and yet you talk of flattery. But farewell; when a few more moons have worked their baleful will upon this fragile form and laid it in the dust, you, as well as the nation, my Almina, will know what you have lost. For the sausages," he added, in a tragic voice, pulling his hat as hard over his eyes as the limpness of the brim would allow—"for the sausages and the beer, madam, I thank thee."

"Ah," she said to herself when he was gone, "it's all very well, Mr. Carew; but you don't get over me this way. Before we go to the altar, if ever we do go, I shall make the lawyer tie me up fast and make no mistake. Let me keep my own

to myself, and then we'll see about marrying. I believe he's
artful enough to make love to one of the young ladies at
No. 15, where he goes every day. He'd better not; if he
does, I'll County Court him. He's good company, too. Pity
he drinks. But, Lord, after all, it would be a poor tale to
drag round with a feller that can't keep out of the public,
and only because he's good company."

The object of her thoughts, refreshed and strengthened,
was on his way to No. 15.

"It was providential," he said, "quite providential, that I
did not get up when I woke up first. At the very best it
would have been tea and bread-and-butter with Mrs. Medlar,
and now it's been sausages and beer."

Arriving immediately at No. 15, he assumed a business-
like air, straightening his back and throwing his head well
up. He proceeded slowly up the stairs to the second floor,
at which he knocked, and entered with quite a new manner.
Dicky had several at command. With Mrs. Medlar he was
the hard-worked, sentimental, struggling man of genius;
with the employer to whom he gave a part of every day, he
was the careful and mechanical amanuensis; with Marion
Revel, whom he adored at a distance, he was the melancholy
and disappointed student; with Adie and Winifred, he was
the dashing and high-spirited young bachelor; with Fred
he put on the semblance of a Lothario and man of fashion in
disguise—his seediness was temporary, his pecuniary em-
barrassments were the result of reckless expenditure, the
humility of his position was merely parenthetical; with his
companions of the British Museum and the evening harmonic
meeting he was a jovial, daredevil fellow, whose spirits were
always at fever-heat, likely to stick at nothing, who considered himself the greatest of living writers, though as yet
he had failed to convince the world of the fact, and who
looked forward to a proud and glorious future. In none of
these disguises could he succeed in deceiving a single person
except himself, on account of his unfortunate habit of getting
drunk whenever he possessed or could borrow the necessary
money. And when, after the usual amount of gin-and-

water, Dicky's brain grew clear, but his power over it weak, so that fiction gave way to reality, he appeared in a uniform, simple, and consistent character: its fidelity of colouring in the less attractive details grew sometimes monotonous and an excess of repetition was even irksome to his audience: for he then showed himself what he actually was, a good-for-nothing scamp who had once dreamed great things, and failed to accomplish even small things. He had grievances in the shape of *coups manqués*—splendid dreams which had come to nothing. He lamented the past, wept over the present, and groaned at the prospect of the future. Dicky's friends began by laughing at him; they ended by finding him a bore. He had, it is true, one or two redeeming points: he was generous, provided his generosity was not exercised so far as to cause him to give up present enjoyment; he was kind-hearted, inasmuch as, if he were to marry Mrs. Medlar, he would spend her money but not ill-treat her; and he had a touch of humour of a pleasant if a common type.

His income, an extremely precarious one, was derived from two or three sources. He contributed paragraphs, literally at a penny a line, to the *Weekly Intelligence*, a paper with an immense circulation, whose proprietor had narrow views as to the marketable value of literary merit. This paper was remarkable for the bold and startling views it advocated on the subject of religious reform, as well as for a rooted antipathy to the monarchical and aristocratic institutions of the country. He was also connected with a small weekly sheet called the *Christian Clerk*, which was at once Anglican, Evangelical, and Conservative. For this paper he wrote short articles of an improving and constitutional tendency. These he got from the works of a few forgotten divines of the last century preserved in the British Museum. And from the two sources together, taking one week with another, he probably contrived to make as much as seventeen shillings a week. As his lodging only cost him four shillings and sixpence, that left him twelve and sixpence for living, luxuries, and the com-

forts of life.   But he had another resource.   I do not
mean Mrs. Medlar, who might be counted as a third.   On
the second floor of No. 15 lived, as has been stated, a certain
Mr. Lilliecrip, of eccentric manners and retiring customs.
Dicky Carew went daily, excepting Saturdays, to Mr. Lilliecrip's lodgings, and there, closeted with the tenant from
twelve to half-past two or three, wrote at his dictation.
What he wrote, or what he did there, he was bound, under
the most tremendous oaths, and penalties almost Masonic,
never to reveal.   For the services thus rendered he received
the honorarium of fifteen shillings weekly,   This, therefore,
brought his weekly income available for *la nourriture* to
twenty-seven shillings and sixpence.   He never bought any
clothes unless he was absolutely obliged ; and as a gentleman
can always get enough to eat, counting breakfast, dinner
and supper, for eighteenpence a day as a maximum, it
follows that Dicky had exactly seventeen shillings a week
to spend in drink.   And he nobly spent it all.   He drank
in the morning, at noon, and at night.   He drank whenever
he could.   He had been three years with Mr. Lilliecrip, and
during the whole of that time that gentleman had never
once offered him, Dicky used to reflect with indignation,
even so much as a glass of pale ale.

   "You are late," said Mr. Lilliecrip, looking at his watch ;
"a quarter of an hour late, sir, and time presses.   Let us
begin at once."

CHAPTER XVI.

"YOU are late, Mr. Carew," said Mr. Lilliecrip, severely ;
       "a whole quarter of an hour late."
   Dicky's employer was sitting at a table, a pile of manu-
scripts before him, which he was annotating and correcting.
He lifted his head, showing a face perfectly pale and colourless.   It was a long face, and there was plenty of it, because
the cheeks and chin were hairless, while on the lip was

a heavy white moustache. His hair was long and silvery white; his features were of a kind you do not easily forget, being straight and regular; his forehead was high, but narrow; the upper part of his nose had that very delicate carving which goes with persons of strong artistic tendencies, but little sympathy; his eyes were clear and bright, but rather shifty. It was a face still extremely handsome, though its owner was well on the shady side of sixty, and might in youth, when the expression would be a little different, have been of wonderful beauty. But it was a face of which Dicky, at least, was heartily weary. Its changeless set regularity, in which not a wrinkle or a crow's-foot but seemed in its appointed place, was a kind of nightmare to him. He hated this man, who was his chief support; he loathed this daily task of sitting at the table and writing, without being allowed to say a word himself, or to ask a question, at his master's dictation; he kicked against the decrees of Fate which bound him to Mr. Lilliecrip's rooms; he envied those happier brethren who were able to lounge all day in the reading-room of the Museum. But though he dared not rebel openly, in secret he nursed daring plans of revenge, and would imagine, while he was writing, little dramas, in which Mr. Lilliecrip and himself were the only figures. The former was at his mercy, he should implore for pardon—Dicky never clearly made out in his own mind how the situation was to be worked up to—and should be spurned with contumely. He should pray for a day's grace, and should be reminded bitterly, but with overwhelming dignity, of his bond:—"The bond and no more—give me the bond." He should be dismissed into misery with the mocking laugh of revenge. There was a story which Dicky had once read, of a man who, for some unexplained reason of his own, hounded down and persecuted another, following him from one scene of distress to another, and thence to a worse, with an insatiable thirst of revenge. This story Dicky appropriated to himself, and used to rehearse it mentally while he wrote. His imagination was as active as his brain was lazy; and while his fingers moved mechani-

N

cally, whole dramas were working themselves out in his mind, consisting entirely of separate *tableaux* without any connecting plot.

"Come," said Mr. Lilliecrip, "let us go on."

Dicky took up his pen, adjusted the blotting pad, and waited.

Mr. Lilliecrip slowly rose, and began to walk up and down the room with hands behind his back. Dicky recommenced the melodrama of revenge where he had left it off the day before; but his eye, as mild as that of a milch cow, only showed habitual attention to the words for which he waited, while his fingers expressed by their attitude an eagerness to begin, almost bordering on enthusiasm.

The Hermit was dressed in a long, grey, cashmere dressing-gown, which reached to his heels, and was tied round the waist by means of a bright crimson silk scarf. Falling open, it disclosed a shirt front of irreproachable fit and brilliant whiteness, set with small diamond studs; his neck was adorned with a collar, in which was a tiny black ribbon in the neatest of bows; his hands were small and white—the hands of a gentleman. As he passed at each turn before the looking-glass on the mantelshelf, he stopped and looked at himself with the complacency of self-satisfaction. His figure was tall, thin, and stooping; his expression was cold, self-contained, and repellent of familiarity; his step was firm and elastic.

"Where did I leave off yesterday?" he said. "Let me consider."

"We were with William the Fourth, sir," said his secretary.

"With William the Fourth. I was engaged on that part of my personal recollections which are concerned with William the Fourth. Yes, yes."

He looked in the glass, and carefully brushed off a tiny speck of dust which had settled on his nose. Then he resumed his walk, thinking. Dicky sat motionless, pen in hand. Once, two years before, he had ventured to blow his nose during a period of silence, but had been so pointedly invited to disturb Mr. Lilliecrip outside, and on his way up rather than in the room, that he dared no longer so much as to cough.

For fourteen long years this man had never left the two rooms in which he lived; for fourteen years he had lived a perfectly lonely and solitary life. There was but one man, besides his secretary, with whom he sometimes exchanged a word—Mr. Rhyl Owen—who went for him, under promises of strictest secrecy, to a certain lawyer at monthly periods for money. He spent every evening of his self-tormenting life, and almost the whole day, absolutely alone; and he chose for his retreat a shabby genteel second floor in the heart of London. Why?

And yet he was not unhappy. The sturdy health he enjoyed, the clearness of his eye, the steadiness of his nerves, the coldness of his manner, showed that he was happy in his own way. Why had he left the world? He was no self-starving ascetic; that was clear from the appearance of a kitchener complete in all its parts, with a bright array of stewpans, pots, and culinary apparatus for which his servant, a woman, brought him every morning, before he was up, and set out in readiness for him, a basket with the day's provisions. In the evening she came again, and put his dishes in the cupboard out of his sight for him. His bookshelves contained half a dozen works on cookery; the rest were all French novels, chiefly new ones; and with these and the periodicals, the Hermit found enough to read. His day was uniform, and perhaps monotonous: he took breakfast at ten; at twelve his secretary worked with him till half-past two or three; till six or so he was busy preparing his own dinner, to which he devoted his whole mind. After eating it and taking a glass or two of claret, his evening was free for reading. He was, it will be seen, a recluse of quite a different stamp from those of history. Nor was he without other amusements. A chess table stood in the window, on which he would work out problems and send them to papers. He had a piano, on which he discoursed with sufficient skill, but without pretensions to artistic

cultivation, and he amused himself sometimes with making
water-colour sketches.   The subjects of these—as Dicky
knew, having often seen them on the table—were all varia-
tions of a single theme.   They represented military life in
various phases.   There were the awkward squad, the church
parade, the regimental steeplechase, the garrison ball, the
mess-room, the billiard-table; and there was besides a
picture which Mr. Lilliecrip painted again and again.   The
treatment varied and the figures, but the background was
always the same—cold, snow, and ice; a handful of men,
sometimes one man alone, wrapped in great coats and armed,
creeping warily to trench work; among them always one
tall and handsome young man, in whom Dicky recognised
his employer, the mysterious Hermit of Lowland Street.

A battle-piece hung upon the wall; over the mantelshelf
was a sword; these were further proofs that the solitary had
been in the army.   Why, then, had he taken a hatred to the
world and left it?

Perhaps he did not hate it: the papers and periodicals
proved that he took an interest in what went on.   The latest
Army List on the table showed that he followed the promotion of his old officers; and what was the meaning of those
piles of manuscript which he was perpetually reading,
dictating, and correcting?   And yet he hid himself, so
jealously hid himself that high and close wire blinds were
adjusted to the windows to prevent his face being visible to
the street or the opposite houses.   He appeared to deny
himself in nothing.   A box of cigars, of a choice brand, stood
on his sideboard; a row of pipes were in the rack; with
them a jar, the end of whose being—the holding of tobacco
—was accomplished, and the room had a fine and constant
perfume of smoking.   There was a spirit case; and once, the
door of the sideboard having been left open, Dicky caught
sight of a pile of bottles, some of them with silver tops.

"Champagne!" he murmured, with bated breath.   It was
a drink which he often dreamed of, but had never tasted,
even in its humbler forms.   And if the man was so rich as
to afford all these luxuries, why did he live in Lowland

Street?   Why did he live alone?   And why, Dicky thought
with indignation and sorrow, why did he give a paltry fifteen
shillings a week to his secretary?

"I was at William the Fourth—yes—ascended the throne
1830, and died 1837.   Of course.   Are you ready?"

"Quite ready, sir."

"The first time I saw the Duke of Clarence was in the
year 1818, when I was myself a child of eight.   I was in the
Park with my mother, an old friend and sincere well-wisher
of the royal and gallant sailor.   He took me in his arms on
being told who I was; pressing me to his breast, his royal
highness, who was remarkably fond of children, said: A
damned fine child—a monstrous great boy—a chip of the old
block.   I congratulate you, Lady ——, on your son.'   As he
put me down I felt a tear fall upon my cheek—one of the few
that William the Fourth was ever known to shed.   I did not
know then that my father and he had been fellow-midshipmen
many years before.   The Duke of Clarence never forgot an
old comrade."

Dicky wrote down this interesting and illustrative anecdote
with a sense of greatness being thrust upon him.   He was
in the presence of a man who had been in the arms of royalty.
He instinctively gathered up his feet under the chair, so as
to hide the state of his heels, which were really not fit for
the companion of kings to see, and listened for more.

"The next time was in the year '36.   His Majesty was
pleased to send for me, being informed that I was in the
neighbourhood of Windsor.   I found him on the slopes, and
he conversed with me for half an hour, chiefly on questions
connected with the state of the army, a subject in which he
was supposed to take little interest.   Opposed as I was to
his Majesty's rigid conservatism, I felt myself obliged to ask
permission to state my views at length.   This he granted,
and dismissed me, after hearing them, with every mark of
gracious condescension.   I feel bound to say that on this, as
on every other occasion, I found William the Fourth most
affable, clear-headed, and intelligent; and I bear witness the
more readily to this effect, because detractors have sneered

at his Majesty's abilities: these were, in reality, of no common order. I had at one time the idea of writing a political history of the reign of William the Fourth, but was deterred by the private nature of much of the information which I should have used.

"History is based upon lies, and it is impossible to get at the truth. That is only known to the diplomatist, who never talks: it dies with him. When I was in Vienna, Metternich confessed to me the whole secret history of the campaign of 1815, which I shall write as soon as I find time. Who would have guessed that Waterloo was a put-up thing?

"Wellington I knew well. He was very fond of entertaining me, during long evening talks, with stories about Napoleon's generals. His opinion of them greatly varied. Marmont, he said, was a devil of a fellow. Massena kept him awake at night. Soult never made him forget to say his prayers for a week. 'Gad!' he used to say, 'even you would have had your work cut out with Soult.' He thought a great deal more perhaps than I really deserved of my personal courage and military genius. It was generous of him.

"Talleyrand was excessively fond of boiled pork, broad beans, and pease pudding. He told me once, dining at the Austrian Embassy, that he could have wished to be an Englishman, in order to enjoy the oftener what he considered our national food. It is not generally known that he ordered it to be served every day when beans were in season.

"Sir Robert Peel, Lord George Bentinck, Bulwer Lytton, Lord Melbourne, and I, were once taking supper after a late debate. After midnight, we set ourselves to foretelling the future, a thing which the military diplomatist alone can do with certainty. It is now thirty years ago, and I remember, though I do not boast of it, that I foretold exactly the war between Germany and France, being only out a trifle in the year: I placed that too soon. Bentinck, who was really a man of the highest genius, prophesied that very same evening the escape of the prisoner of Ham and the beginning of the end for Louis Philippe. Could Ezekiel himself have done more?

"When these men died, England had no great men left. The legislators and diplomatists of the present day are pigmies in comparison with the school to which they belonged. The great art of the diplomatist, according to their traditions, was to know the exact moment to *invent*—to invent with freedom and facility, and to invent with a truthful face. I have often heard poor Lord George declare that an evening with Austrian and French diplomatists was like a short campaign; everything depended upon the accurate gauge of your adversary's truth. Have you taken that down correctly, Mr. Carew?"

"All down, sir—'gauge of truth.'"

"Good—another sheet. 'Recollections of Lord Melbourne.'"

Dicky obeyed, and—his thoughts wandering—proceeded to write without catching the meaning of the words. The drama in his mind meanwhile was going on. "Spare me, Carew—spare me! You have the secret of my life; you have in your power the honour of a house; you can blight a noble name. Be merciful as you are strong."

This was the masterpiece of Dick's imagination, and a part of the duologue with which he amused his weary occupation. He was writing something quite different, but no doubt it was almost as great nonsense.

"There was a time, old man, when you spurned the humble amanuensis. He came up thirsty; you had champagne in the cupboard, and there was a refreshing tap at the nearest corner, but you offered him neither ale nor wine. His boots were down at heel, and you had not the humane generosity to present him with a new pair; he was hard up, and you knew it, and never raised his pay. Old man, I'll have my bond!"

"—A cry was heard, which reached from St. James's Palace to the lonely smoking-room of the club where the disappointed peer sat brooding: 'Long live our youthful Queen!' He sprang to his feet and uttered a cry of grati-

tude.—Is that down? Take care; these are among the
most precious of my recollections."

He spoke in a slow and deliberate manner throughout, so
that his secretary might easily follow.

"I was reading over what you wrote yesterday, and I find
that your inadvertence allowed me to make a statement
which is ridiculous. You actually permitted me—you, my
private secretary—to state that Beau Brummell, Count
d'Orsay, and Prince Albert were my guests on the same day
at the Star and Garter."

"You said so, sir."

"Nonsense. How could I say so? If it was not true,
how could I say so? Take care, Mr. Carew, take care.
I am afraid you do not pay proper attention to accuracy.
Had I not detected that mistake my enemies would have
certainly accused me of inaccuracy, and perhaps the very
authenticity of my recollections would have been impugned.
I looked for better things, Mr. Carew."

Dicky saw his anticipations of a rise in salary vanish and
become the shadow of a hope. It was hard on him, because
he was afraid of interrupting Mr. Lilliecrip in the full flow
of reminiscence, and he certainly had described a banquet
in which, he being the host, the late Prince Consort, Beau
Brummell, Count d'Orsay, and other distinguished personages
had figured as his guests.

"Would you like me, sir, to take the memoirs away with
me, and revise them by the help of the *Annual Register*?"

"Certainly not, sir. You will understand that you have
no right to breathe a word as to these memoirs. Should
you do so, remember *that I shall hear of it*. You will then
lose, not only your present employment, but any future
honorarium which I may think of bestowing upon you."

This Hermit, it will have been perceived, was engaged in
the preparation of Personal Reminiscences. In order to
avoid the raising of expectations doomed to be disappointed,
it may be mentioned at once that his personal reminiscences
were a series—an immense long series—of personal lies,
figments, and imaginations, of which the world had never

seen the like.   He had not been in contact with any of the great men whose names he used so freely; he had never spoken to one of them ; but he wanted to do something that would live after him, and he was gratifying the vanity of a morbid mind by compiling a gigantic work of pretended memoirs.   He proposed to bequeath these to the British Museum, with an injunction that the packet was not to be opened for seventy-five years.   The man was preparing a lie, which with its dulness, heaviness, and stupidity was likely to weigh heavily on posterity, unless these very qualities caused the imposture to be detected.

Mr. Lilliecrip sat down again, and passed his white hand across his forehead.

"I am fatigued to-day, I think.   My memory is sluggish. Tell me, Mr. Carew, without mentioning names—the world is nothing more to me, and I care not to hear its names— what people think of me, or what that small part of London in which you move thinks.   What is said about me ? "

Here was an astonishing thing for the Hermit to ask. For more than three years Dicky had worked with him, and had never exchanged a word save on necessary subjects.

"What do they say ?   Do they talk about me ? "

Dicky remembered that the conversation, only the night before, had turned exclusively upon the Hermit : had he been of an entirely truthful nature, which unhappily was not the case, he would have repeated for Mr. Lilliecrip's information the speech he made on the occasion.   It was as follows : he delivered it with much freedom of utterance, being then in the first stage only of intoxication, standing before the fire, and waving a pipe in his right hand :—

"Gentlemen, with regard to my esteemed friend, whom you call the Hermit of Lowland Street, I am not, as many of you are aware, allowed to reveal the important secrets which my mysterious employer has been good enough to intrust to my care.   He is, however, as you may imagine, no mystery to me.   Is he rich? is he nobly born? is he generous? is he princely in his disposition?   I say nothing. I answer neither Yes nor No.   What is the reason for his strange retirement? Gentlemen, I must not tell you. It was only this morning, in the splendidly furnished suite of chambers, externally humble, where we transact our business—chambers in which everything is as magnificently appointed as in Windsor Castle, or in my noble friend's ancestral halls—"

"He is a swell, then," said a listener. "By Jove, he must have done something *very* bad."

"It was only this morning he said to me, 'Carew, if there were any other man in the world to whom I could confide my history, I would not give you this trouble. I feel that you are my only true friend, and I fear I inflict too much upon you.' He had the goodness to say that—"

"Wouldn't it be better, Dicky, if he were to ask you for the measure of your feet, and buy you a new pair of boots?"

Dicky took no notice of this personal allusion to his poverty.

"He went on to say that what he offered me now was nothing, simply nothing, compared with what he was going to give when— But I am speaking too freely. As for the ridiculous honorarium which—pah! gentlemen, I blow it away like this cloud."

Later on in the evening, Dicky, growing truthful under the influence of gin-and-water, wept as he confessed, amid the smiles of his friends, the mean and curmudgeon-like spirit of the Hermit, and the degrading task of writing from dictation which was his daily lot. It was curious that at no stage of intoxication would he confess the nature of his employer's papers.

However Dicky did not, in answer to the question of his master, think fit to communicate the substance of his speech.

"They *do* talk, I suppose," said Mr. Lilliecrip. "It is not a usual thing for a man to immure himself in four dingy walls, and deny himself society, is it?"

"They talk, sir: they will talk, you know—even quite common people."

Dicky was a little embarrassed.

" What do they say then ? "

" Well really, sir, wild talk mostly. It would offend you, perhaps."

" Offend me ?   Do you really suppose—   Come, Mr. Carew, what do people say of me ? "

" They don't know what to say about you.   Some think you are the rightful Sir Roger Tichborne in hiding for something done in the Bush."

" Good.   Go on."

" Some say you are the real heir to a crown, and paid to keep yourself out of the way."

" That is better."

" Most believe that you are a murderer in hiding, and there's more than one has given information of you to the police, in hope of getting a reward.   I have heard of people consulting old newspapers of fourteen years ago to find out who was watched by the police then, and they have stood me drinks, sir—dozens of drinks—in order to find out any little hint that may help them."

" This is interesting," said the Hermit.   " A cheap way of getting popularity and notoriety, too."

" They call you the Hermit of Lowland Street, and there's a man connected with the *Daily Firework* wants to make an article out of you."

" Tell him he'd better not," said the Recluse.   " Tell him, if he does, I'll find out all about him—his debts and his sins, his weak places and his discreditable doings—and I'll ruin him.   Tell him that."

He actually impressed Dicky with so deep a sense of power in reserve, that he accepted this threat as quite within his reach, and went on—

" Some think you must have forged a will, and are living on the proceeds ; or else that you are a—"

" Bah ! " said the Solitary.   " It is stupid.   What does it matter what they say ?   About yourself now, Mr. Carew ? "

Dicky's heart beat.   Here then, was the long-looked-for opportunity.   Now for the increase of salary.

" I was about to venture, sir, to speak of myself. Three years is a good spell at fifteen shillings a week—"

" You were about to say that you were sorry the work was not worth more than half; and you would have been right, Mr. Carew, quite right."

This was a damper.

" What *I* was about to say was, that your appearance is discreditable, and that I shall advance you the money to purchase a new suit, to be stopped out of your pay at the rate of five shillings a week. That is all, Mr. Carew."

He placed a packet with money in his hands, and nodded dismissal.

" Stay—stay; there was another thing. I hear now and then a pleasing voice singing in the room below me to the piano. I am absolutely careless about the world, but you may tell me anything you know about the voice. No, sir— no gush; no names. I want nothing about the history of these people—quite commonplace and vulgar people, in a commonplace and vulgar street. Answer me without un-necessary words. Rich or poor? "

" Poor. Were rich."

" Is the owner of the voice young and pretty, or old and—"

" Young and pretty. Twenty."

" How many in family? "

" Two sisters. Ladies. Unmarried. One is an artist."

" That will do, Mr. Carew—that will do. To-morrow, if you please, be more punctual. Remember what I say, that if in your drinking bouts—I know your habits, sir—you let out what you do here, you will repent it in such sober earnest as you little dream of."

Dicky retired humbly. With regard to the money, his first thought was naturally to spend it in a wild and rollicking carouse; but better thoughts prevailed. How if Mr. Lilliecrip found him out? How if, in the blindness of his wrath, he should carry into execution his threats, and make *him* repent?

" To be sure," Dicky reflected, taking comfort, " I am a soft-hearted man, and I repent very easily."

"Strange," said the Hermit, "how that voice haunts me. For the first time these fourteen years I want to see another face. What is coming over me?"

As he spoke, the voice began again to a simple accompaniment of the piano, singing a simple ballad to an ancient tune. It was Adie, taking one of the few pleasures left to her, to sing and play while Marion painted.

He stood still and listened. Presently it ceased, and he caught the low ripple of girlish laughter, and the voices of girls talking. His heart beat and his knees trembled.

"I am a fool," he said. "I am fooled by that idiot, Carew. He takes some vulgar little milliner animal for a lady, and a rosy cheek for beauty."

He spent the rest of the day over his dinner.

In the evening his man of business, Mr. Owen, knocked at his door. Mr. Lilliecrip was sitting by the fire in the soft light of a moderator lamp. He was in evening dress: this Hermit, had he donned the friar's serge and lived in those miserable quarters on the river Coquet whereof the ballad sings, would have made it a rule to change the simple gown and the rope for black coat and white tie in the evening. He was playing with a cup of coffee, and lazily thinking of taking a pipe over the latest novel. On the entrance of the schoolmaster he finished the coffee.

"Pray excuse me a moment, Mr. Owen," he said, with great politeness, "and take a chair."

Mr. Owen placed a chair in the middle of the room, and sat himself down, with his feet under it, in such a position that he could not be accused of curiously prying into anything while the owner was not in the room. Mr. Lilliecrip, however, returned immediately, wearing a velvet jacket and a smoking cap.

"Always change your evening coat, Mr. Owen, before smoking; the tobacco *will* linger about the cloth."

Mr. Owen grunted. The advice is superfluous to a man who has but one coat.

"I have been for the money as usual," he said. "Here it is—thirty-three, five, seven. Count it."

The Solitary counted it, and dropped it in his pocket.

"Messrs. Crackett and Charges want to see you. They say there is an opportunity for advancing your interests."

"I told them to send no messages, and to write me no letters. I will not be worried with investments."

"That's all, then," said Mr. Owen, rising abruptly.

"One moment, Owen—your advice, if you please. There's a girl downstairs."

"Two," said the schoolmaster—"three, in fact, counting my Winifred, and I don't see why she shouldn't be counted."

"Nor I, I am sure. Count her, by all means. One of the three is pretty, I am told—not that I care, of course; not that it matters to me."

"They are all three pretty, and as good as gold."

"There is one that sings."

"They all three sing. What is that to you?"

Mr. Rhyl Owen was gruff of speech with Mr. Lilliecrip, the result of fourteen years' occasional communication with that gentleman.

"If he's not polite with you, he'll bully you," said Mr. Owen, thinking about him. "He is a cur that licks your hand one minute and bites it the next."

"What are the girls to you, Mr. Lilliecrip?"

"I am sometimes a little lonely. Do you think that one of them—they are all, I suppose, poor—would like to come up here, and sit with me, read with me, talk to me in the evening?"

"No, she would not. None of them would," the schoolmaster replied, with great decision.

"I would pay her, you know."

"Mr. Lilliecrip, two of them are ladies, and the other earns her bread in a better way than talking to old fools."

"You are rude to-night. Am I not fit company for them, do you mean?"

Mr. Owen was silent.

"Come, sir, tell me what you do mean."

"I mean, Mr. Lilliecrip, that neither of the young ladies shall come up here if I can prevent it. They are real ladies, born and bred. As for that, my Winifred should not come here either."

"Well, well, Owen, I cannot afford to quarrel with you, or else I should have to find some one else to go out for me. Perhaps you are right, people might talk if a young lady came to my rooms alone, though I am surely grey enough and old enough."

"Old enough, certainly," said Mr. Owen, drily. "The young lady's brother lives in the house, too. You had better speak to him about it."

"Ah!" Mr. Lilliecrip changed colour, but very slightly; "is he—is he a gentleman, too? Lowland Street seems to be suffering from an invasion of ladies and gentlemen."

"Oh, yes—he's a gentleman, and a fire-eater too. Lord, Mr. Lilliecrip, put it out of your thoughts. Why, he'd murder you, that young gentleman would, so fierce as he is, if he'd even the thought of his sister visiting you in this room. We must first know who and what you are, Mr. Lilliecrip, and why you have shut yourself up."

"And a pretty girl?"

"They are both beautiful girls; and one is a lovely creature. God bless her!" said Mr. Owen, getting up to go.

When Mr. Lilliecrip was left alone, he began to ponder over his cigar. After fourteen years of solitude, the thought of a beautiful girl being in the same house, the possibility that she might enliven his room by her presence, agitated him. How should he get to know this beautiful girl?

"It is strange," he said; "I cannot understand. Fourteen years of peace and content, and to-night—all from a voice and a few words; one would think I was only beginning the prison. Could it be possible for me to leave the place and go out again?" He rose, and walked up and down the room, his face working with the emotion of some disturbing memory. "No, never!" he cried; "never! I will stay here till I die!"

CHAPTER XVII.

THE April mornings are sunlit at six, even in the heart of
London, and there is a fine painting light for those
who are able to get up for it. The early morning was
Marion's time of peace and quiet labour; she would be
alone. How great a blessing it is to be alone for an hour
or two in the day can only, I suppose, be appreciated by
women who live together. It is one of the many evils of
poverty that the poor have no solitude possible. As the
social ladder descends, the necessity of a life in common
becomes more marked. The suburban villa has its three
sitting-rooms for a family of half a dozen; but the ladies of
the "lower middle class" have to sleep, eat, read, work, and
play in the same room.

In the early morning, when the air is clear and bright,
Marion took fresh courage, and clothed herself with new
faith and hope. Above all, she worked: that soul is never
quite unhappy which can take a healthy pleasure in work
for its own sake. Marion was, for the first time, after four
years of copying, engaged upon an original picture. She
was ambitious, as most young painters are. She did not yet
fully understand that a work of art must be a copy of Nature
itself, and not a reminiscence or a reflection; and her picture
had the fault of being drawn from the inspiration of other
masters. There are plenty of such pictures in every Royal
Academy—you find a familiar touch here, and another
there; you are reminded of one master here, and another
there. Nature is at second hand—the light hardly fits the
season; the flowers do not fit with each other; the primrose
and the nightshade are painted blossoming side by side; and
yet, for some subtle grace and secret charm of their own,
the pictures are bought and loved. It was so with Marion.
She had chosen an Italian subject, who had never been in
Italy; she had put in Italian flowers, who knew not an
Italian summer; country figures, who had never seen a

contadina; an Italian sky, who had never been out of England; a dress which was never worn under the canopy of heaven; a light which never shone on earth or ocean; and yet, for one redeeming touch it had, the picture was warm with life and feeling. She had taken a scene from Browning's "Pippa passes," a poem which—if its author had only for once been able to wed melodious verse to the sweetest poetical thought; if he had only tried, just for once, to write lines which should not make the cheeks of those that read them to ache, the front teeth of those who declaim them to splinter and fly, the ears of those that hear them to crack—would have been a thing to rest himself upon for ever, and receive the applause of the world. To the gods it seemed otherwise. Browning, who might have led us like Hamelin the piper, has chosen the worse part. He will be so deeply wise that he cannot express his thought; he will be so full of profundities that he requires a million of lines to express them in; he will leave music and melody to Swinburne; he will leave grace and sweetness to Tennyson; and in fifty years' time, who will read Browning? Let us return to our sheep.

Marion had chosen the place where Pippa passes singing :—

> " The year's at the spring,
> The day's at the morn,
> Morning's at seven,
>   The hill-side's dew pearled ;
> The lark's on the wing,
> The snail's on the thorn,
> God's in His Heaven,
>   All's right with the world."

Oh, strong poet of the densest tympanum, to write those third and fourth lines—

> " The hill-side's dew pearled ! "

Was there ever such a stuttering collocation of syllables to confound the reader and utterly destroy a sweet little lyric?

Pippa was Adrienne, Marion's model. She was passing in the bright early morning, singing as she went, unconscious

of her words, and dangling her grapes before her; a figure
full of health, youth, and beauty; Adrienne with the least
possible darkening of the eyebrows and the hair; not an
Italian face at all; sweet-lipped Adie, tall, delicate, graceful
—not a silk-weaver, not Pippa, not a workwoman, not the
heroine of Browning's noble dream; an English girl, in a
bright clear sunshine, with strong shadows, which lay black
under the vine-leaves and behind the stones, and set off her
sweetness as a crystal mounted in an ebony setting; and
behind the unconscious girl a face and the back of a head—
the face of a man who catches the words.   They strike his
ear with a force the girl knows nothing of; the glamour of a
devilish passion falls from him, and he sees the awful thing
—too late—in its true light.   In the head of the woman that
looks to him you may, if you can, imagine the wonder that
is in her unseen face, and the horror of the awaking.   Pippa
sings her song and passes—

> " God's in His Heaven,
>   All's right with the world."

The picture was nearly finished; the principal figure—a
half figure—was completed; the heads were worked up; only
the flowers and accessories were as yet to be filled in.

Marion worked contentedly from half-past five to eight at
her canvas.   She was not unhappy, provided there was money
to give her two children enough to eat: it was all she worked
for now.   If she dreamed of anything better, it seemed a long
way off.   She was their natural protector: to her they were
the two children always, helpless, not quite to be trusted; a
little perverse—at least, one of them—but always lovable,
always to be treated with a fond consideration.   At eight
Adie appeared, and began to make the breakfast.   This was
the happiest time that the girls had.   In the evening there
was always the drop of bitterness in the cup, the discontent
of comparison, the absence of their brother.   In the morning
they were alone, for Fred seldom rose till nine or ten, and
they could talk.   Presently Marion, keeping silence on the
doctor's proposals, began to talk, as usual, of money matters.

"Five shillings, Adie, dear," she said, giving her that amount. "It is not a great deal for a long day's work copying, is it? But it is as much as Mr. Burls would give me. After all, I dare say it is more than one deserves. Why do they always pay women so much worse than men?"

"Because they are not strong enough to knock the cheats down and beat them, as men would do," said Adie vindictively.

She took the money, and dropped it into her purse, where Dr. Chacomb's five pounds were lying: the accusing jingle of the coins reminded her unpleasantly of her promise, and struck her soul with a note of remorse. It was as if she had sold herself to deceive her sister.

"It is enough, at any rate," she said, "for to-day. You shall have some dinner when you come home, dear. Not a dinner-tea; you shall have some steak, and I will get you a pint of claret, if—if—oh, if Fred does not want it all. You want a little wine so badly, dear."

"Let Fred have two shillings, Adie, and I will do without the claret. Besides, it is ridiculous for us to talk about wine, with our fortunes at this low ebb."

"Marion, you are looking pale. Do not work so hard; things will get right somehow—I am sure they will. Fred says he has always felt certain they will."

Marion shook her head. She was not hopeful this morning; perhaps because the sky had clouded over since she left off work for breakfast.

"Fred will get a situation," Adie went on, trying to talk cheerfully, and working the talk round, somehow, to a point. "That is, if he gets friends to back him up. The poor boy wants friends badly, if only to keep him out of the billiard-rooms. Perhaps I shall be able to get something to do; but it seems as if I can do nothing at all. I might teach French, it is true, if anybody would believe that I knew it. Marion, let us talk it together every day, for fear of my forgetting my only accomplishment. I cannot play well enough to teach music, and I know nothing else—nothing. My dear, I am horribly helpless and selfish. I let you work day after day for us, and never seem to do anything."

"Adie," Marion patted her cheek, "I do not want you to do anything."

Adie sighed.

"Marion," she whispered, laying her arm on her sister's neck, "Marion, tell me, if you saw a way—if any one told you of a way, would you not like to escape out of all this dreadful misery and poverty? Think of yesterday and our starving. Think of my having to go and beg Mr. Owen to give me something to eat. And Fred coming home at night smoking an expensive cigar, with no money left of all he took from you the day before. Oh, the shame of it!"

There were times when Adie's view of Fred's conduct was harsher than Marion's.

"Let us face the present," said Marion, conscious of what her sister meant. "See, dear, I shall take the pictures to Mr. Hermann. He always buys what I bring him, though he does not give much. Mr. Burls said that if he had any money he would have given four guineas a head. Mr. Hermann ought at least to give me a guinea each—that makes five guineas, and then we will have a little claret to do us both good."

It seemed a very small matter to Adie—this chance of five guineas—in the face of all the possibilities opened up by the doctor.

"But, Marion, suppose a way were to lie open unto us? Suppose—O Marion, you who work so hard for us all, what if we could get back to something like the old life again, and be at rest?"

Marion looked at her inquiringly. She knew, by a sudden intuition, and by the flushed cheeks and drooping eyelashes, that her sister had been talking to the doctor, and about herself.

"If the way were not impossible, Adie."

"Oh, what could be impossible? Marion, dear, you know what I am thinking of. It seems such a simple thing. And think what it means for you and me and Fred. Only try to think. Servants to wait upon us again; ladies and gentlemen to talk to; dress—proper dress—to wear; money to spend. O Marion! how can you say it is impossible? It would not be to me."

Marion heard her sister with a heavy heart.

"What did Dr. Chacomb say to you?"

"He told me he loved you; and he asked me to speak to you myself. I promised I would, Marion; was I wrong?" Marion caressed the fair cheek that looked up to her.

"Don't talk to him again about it, my dear. Try to realise only that it is impossible, and that we must face the present. Have patience and a little hope."

"Sometimes I have hope. Sometimes I think Fred is right, and we shall all three go back to take our proper place like disinherited princes and princesses; and sometimes, Marion—it is too selfish, when you do everything for us—sometimes I think you might do more. Don't say it is impossible, dear. I have been lying awake half the night thinking it all over."

"My poor child," said Marion, taking Adie's face in her hands, "my poor child! it is so hard that you should be unhappy."

"And you, dear; is it not hard for you too? Is it quite impossible, Marion? See, dear"—she spoke hurriedly, as if the subject was too much for her—"see, dear, here we starve and are miserable; with *him* we should at least be warm and comfortable, and have no anxiety — think of that. Think of waking up every morning without feeling that there will be no dinner the next day unless we work for it; think of not having to find money for Fred's extravagances; think of being able to wear decent things; think of the change we should have in our lives. He is kind, Marion; I am sure he is kind. To be sure, he is not very young; but what of that? He does not want your love, he says; he only wants you to marry him, and then he will try to get your love afterwards."

"My dear, could I marry any one unless I loved him first?"

"Why not? I would. If Dr. Chacomb had come to me instead of to you, and asked me to marry him, I should have jumped for joy. Love! What is all the nonsense people talk about love? I cannot understand it. I want to be well dressed and rich—that is the real happiness."

"You will know better later, Adie. Do not let us talk about it any more. Dr. Chacomb knows that it can never be. I told him so last night. I think he is kind, too; but it is impossible, Adie. Do not say anything more about it. Put it quite out of your thoughts, and let us try to make the best of the little we have."

"But we have nothing," said Adie, with her musical laugh, "nothing at all. Marion, I have often read about the duty of being contented with little; but not even the books which are the hardest about duty, and make it the most difficult to get to Heaven, ever say anything about the duty of being contented with nothing. Be reasonable, dear Marion, and discontented."

It was after breakfast that this conversation took place. The girls always took their breakfast first, the head of the family appearing later.

As Adie finished her philosophical remarks, Fred appeared, fully equipped for his journey "into the City." His way there might have seemed, to any who saw him start, a circuitous route, for on reaching Oxford Street he invariably turned west. It does not do, however, to be always guided by appearances. He may have "fetched a compass," like St. Paul, and worked round by way of Battersea. His equanimity, disturbed by the doctor the evening before, was completely restored. After all, he was—and he knew it well enough—an idle rascal. He never had done anything, and he hoped to pass wholly through life without doing anything. Besides, Fred's anger was like a fire of chips—it exhausted itself, and was quickly spent. Storms in shallow lakes quickly subside. This morning he was fresh, and even radiant.

Marion's artistic instincts furnished, perhaps, one of the reasons why she never grew tired of this idle and good-for-nothing brother. She loved him for his beauty and his grace. It was always a pleasure for her eyes to rest upon the lines of his form. His face, which to a man seemed wanting in depth, was to her as full of depth and possible emotion as the illimitable sea. She made perpetual excuse for him; she cheerfully gave him all she could; she made him her type of that divine beauty which, man or woman, the best of us dream of and long after. Her face lit up when he entered the room and kissed her in his lordly, off-hand way.

"A lovely morning, Marion. Are you going far? Adie, sew a button on my glove for me, please. Will you come for a walk this afternoon? I can be back at two o'clock for you."

He went to the window, and looked out. A cloud crossed his face.

"Marion, I think that, considering the state of our finances and how unlucky we have been of late, it is hardly a time for charity."

"What do you mean, Fred?"

Marion was getting together her portfolio.

"I mean that the woman I have seen you talking to once or twice is hanging about in the street, intending no doubt to waylay you directly you leave the place. Now, Marion, please remember charity begins at home. We cannot well afford out-door relief just now. No doubt it is extremely creditable and respectable to have a pensioner—even such a disreputable pensioner as that."

Marion's hands shook a little; but she steadied herself.

"I dare say she will not want any money, Fred. Now I am ready. Give me good luck, Adie, dear."

Fred watched her from the window.

"There are the usual children hanging about her skirts," he said, impatiently. "Really, I think Marion considers herself a mother in Israel. If there is a child in trouble, or a woman in distress, Marion must be consulted. Why cannot we live unknown, and not talked about? I fully expect Marion will be reported in a daily paper for a philan-thropist."

Presently he saw the woman he had noticed cross the street.

"I thought so," he said, impatiently. "Upon my word, you know, Adie, it's too ridiculous. Here we are, almost starving, and Marion throwing the money away upon street beggars! She has crossed over—I knew she would—and is begging of Marion. Now they are talking at the corner. Now they have gone off together. Who *is* the woman, Adie?"

"I don't know. I asked once, but was told not to ask any more—some poor woman who knows Marion."

"I shall make it my business," said Fred, pompously, "to inquire. I am the head of the family, and I will not have secrets kept from me."

"Don't be a goose, Fred. You are no more the head of the family than I am. As if anything you could say, or I either, would turn Marion an inch from her own path. Poor Marion!"

"I wish I could see the way to persuade her to make money," said her brother. "Look at this canvas—she spends half her time over a thing like that!" It was her unfinished painting. "What will she do with it? Who will buy it? And when I proposed to her to make a steady income by giving lessons, she refused. Just the same the other day, when I saw an advertisement that would have suited me admirably: 'A gentleman by birth and education wanted to advance about twelve hundred pounds in a sleeping partnership'—sleeping, Adie—'from which he will draw at least a hundred per cent. by way of profits.' Think of it, you know—nothing to do but to draw twelve hundred a year or so! I showed it to Marion, and asked her to sell out her little fortune and lend it to me. She refused. She said nothing would induce her to part with the money, not even to make my fortune with it."

"Yes, Marion told me about it. You see, Fred, if you had lost the money — which you most likely would have done — where should we be? Now, if everything else fails, we always have the fifty pounds a year to fall back upon."

"Just like women," Fred growled; "they never understand the simplest rules of investment. I could make that miserable fifty into five thousand if I had it!"

"O Fred! you will never make your own fortune or ours either, poor boy! sit down and have your tea."

He complied with the invitation. Adie sat opposite, and talked.

"Such a chance, Fred, too, as Marion has missed. Oh, such a chance! We shall never have another like it—never!"

"What chance, Adie?"

His face flushed, as hers had done, at the mere thought of being rich.

"Fred," she put on her most solemn tones, "a rich man wants to marry Marion!"

"A rich man?"

"And to provide for you, and to take care of me. But she has refused him—twice."

"Who is it?"

"It is Dr. Chacomb."

"I would rather she married the Devil!" he said, hotly.

"Don't swear, Fred."

"I would. Do you know that he has insulted me—that he insulted me last night even? He called me— well, never mind! Marion shall never have my permission to marry Dr. Chacomb."

"You *are* a goose, Fred; you really are. You cannot really think that either of us is going to ask your permission to do anything we want to do. Be sensible, if you can. Play at being the head of the family, as you call it, outside, where perhaps they don't know that Marion works for all and provides for all—poor Marion!"

"Are you too going to turn against me, Adie?" he asked.

"No, Fred. I shall never turn against you. You are like me. We are both of us the same; and you are my very own brother. You *can't* help yourself, my poor boy, any more than I can. And if anything happened to Marion— Well, let me tell you about it, without any more heroics! Dr. Chacomb is a very kind-hearted man. I should live with him and Marion. We should have a carriage, and a box at the Opera, and—"

"Dreams, Adie! The man has no money. He lives on what he can borrow from his cousin!"

"But he *has* money, I tell you. He is rich. He is a successful physician, and the founder of the Royal Hospital for Gout. Why, he makes five thousand pounds a year, he tells me. O Fred! what a brother-in-law, if Marion would only see it!"

Fred became thoughtful.

"Does he do all that? I know how to find out. There's a chemist fellow comes to our billiard-rooms—not a gentleman, you know—who knows all about doctors and that class of people"—Fred always spoke of persons who earned their livelihood as "that class of people." "Now I think of it, Chacomb did have a respectable appearance last night when he came here. I don't like him, Adie. Hang it! you can't like a man who calls you an idle—Well, but if he *has* this large income, and if he will take care of you and look after me, I shall not let any prejudice of mine stand in the way. I withdraw my opposition, Adie."

"That's very good of you, Fred," Adie laughed.

"I do not forget," the young man went on, "the house to which I belong, whose head I am. It has always been usual for the representative of the name to have a voice in the alliances contracted by the members of the family."

"That's very grand, my dear brother; and it is a great blessing to feel that we have a head with a proper sense of dignity. If you had arms as well— No, Fred, I won't tease. But Marion won't have him."

"Adie, suppose—I only say suppose—the doctor were to shift his proposal to the younger sister. What would you say?"

The girl reddened.

"I told Marion that I should jump for joy. But I don't think I should. I like Dr. Chacomb very much—I do, indeed; but I don't think I could marry him when it came actually to the point. However, that is not to the point.

I am quite sure that he will not ask me, and I am also quite sure that he is as rich as he says he is. Besides, Fred, if poor Gerald never comes home again, he is the heir to Chacomb."

Fred whistled.

" So he is, so he is. Adie, we must try and bring it off if we can. My dear child, fancy going back to Comb Leigh, the masters of Chacomb!"

"Oh, the delight! Fred, fancy sitting by the dear old beach and hearing the waves beat against the rocks again! Oh, think of the cliff, and the garden, and the flowers. You and I would live in the Rosery: we would walk about as we used to do, and lie on the grass and eat strawberries, and have piles—piles of roses in the drawing-room every day, and all the new music. I should wear white all the summer."

" And in the season we would come to town," said her brother, flushing with enthusiasm.

" Yes; and you would give me a pony carriage, wouldn't you?" Then she burst into a laugh that ended in a sob. " But it's no good. We are here—*nous voici plantés*—in Lowland Street. Marion will not have him, and we grow poorer every day."

Their faces dropped, and the sunlight of imagination disappeared behind a cloud.

Quoth Fred, after a little pause—

" Have you got any money, Adie?"

" Marion gave me five shillings, and—and—Fred, don't be angry, but Dr. Chacomb offered me five pounds when he heard that we had no money—all in gold—and I took them. Here they are."

She spread out the sovereigns, with Marion's poor five shillings, on the table, and looked up at her brother in a little doubt.

He knitted his brows with the gravity of Epictetus the moralist.

" That was wrong, child. That was very wrong. Women never seem to have the same sense of honour as men.

You ought not to have taken the money. Remember that men never take money of each other, unless they win it at billiards, cards, or betting. Then of course, it is a different thing. I could not myself, for instance, poor as we are, accept money of any one—even offered me by my best friend."

This was very noble, and Adie felt proud of a brother distinguished by sentiments so honourable.

Then his eyes fell again on the money. It lay glittering on the table, representing a really large area of enjoyment.

"Five pounds," he said. "I wonder how long it is since I had five pounds? Not since I was at Oxford, I believe. Look here, Adie, what are you going to do with it all?"

"It is for housekeeping."

"Yes, you must take care not to have any more money from Dr. Chacomb. I will make a note of the amount."

He took out his pocket-book, and entered it, date and all, with solicitude.

Adie looked guiltily on.

"Oh, I wish I hadn't taken it! I will tell Marion when she comes home, and we will send it back. Fred, it was very wrong of me."

"N-no," said her brother, "I don't think that is necessary. Adie, it just occurs to me that I owe a little bill at the Sheaf for billiards and things; and there is my account at the tobacconist's; and I want a new pair of gloves, and my boots are giving out. There is a sovereign, too—a debt of honour—which I ought to pay; and I should like to buy something for you—it is a long time since I gave you anything, my dear sister; and—and I think it would be best to pay off all these things at once."

He laid his hands upon the whole heap of money, and kept them there.

"O Fred! not *all!*"

The girl's look, and the tone of entreaty, spoke a whole volume of woman's endurance and man's selfishness.

"Four pounds will do, Adie. That leaves you, you see, one pound five shillings, counting what Marion gave you—

more than a whole week's housekeeping in advance. Better say nothing to Marion about the money; and tell Dr. Chacomb, with my compliments, that I am going to repay his small temporary loan with interest—when I get a post."

He dropped the sovereigns in his waistcoat pocket and went away, leaving Adie rather sick at heart, and perhaps a little confused between the delicate distinctions of the code of honour which permitted her brother to borrow without repaying, but forbade his taking what was offered.

The woman waiting for Marion crossed the street when she left the house, and stood before her. She was a woman who might be of any age from five and thirty to fifty, with a face which was pretty once, and eyes which formerly might have been bright. She was thin, careworn, and poorly dressed. As she stood waiting her lips moved—she was talking to herself. As Fred had remarked, her appearance, whether regarded as a pensioner or not, was disreputable.

Marion turned pale when the creature confronted her.

"You promised me you would not molest me. You promised I should never see you at all," she cried. "Why can you not write, as you engaged to do, to the post-office? How dare you come to my very door?"

"I saw him," she replied, "at the window. What a handsome boy it is! Ah me, where did he get his curls from? Where did he get his dimpled chin and his bright eyes? Tell me that, Marion Revel."

"Remember, if you break your contract—if you venture to speak to either of them, if you let them suspect who and what you are—I will help you no more, and you may do your very worst."

"Tell me how *she* is," asked the woman. "I did not see her."

"Adrienne is well and happy—at least, as happy as our poverty will allow."

"I have not caught a glimpse of her for three months. I hoped that to-day she would put her pretty face at the window just for me to see it again. Oh me, oh me! Last

Christmas Day it was I saw her coming home from church
with a girl—quite a girl of the lower classes. Such a difference as there was between Adrienne, as tall and straight as a
poplar, with a face like a countess—where did she get her
face and figure from? tell me that—and the little chit with
her, all dimples and curls and chubby cheeks! Such a contrast; a beautiful contrast for me to look at! Marion Revel,
you never could have had such a figure, not when you were
at your very best, four years ago; and now you've gone off
sadly, poor thing! All your good looks gone, like me. It's
dreadful to think how care and trouble spoil a woman's figure.
That's where men have the great advantage over us women.
Why, if it had not been for all my troubles, I should have
been a lovely woman still."

"Our sins make our troubles," said Marion.

"Do they? Then, Marion Revel, you must have been a
greater sinner than anybody would think."

"Come," said Marion, "I cannot waste my time. What
do you want with me?"

"Money, of course. What else can I want?"

"I have no money. I sent you ten shillings last week. I
cannot afford to give you more than five shillings a week. If
I give you more it is robbing *them*."

"And if it is robbing them, it is all in the family, Marion."
Marion shuddered.

"There are others besides them to consider. Look at that
finger." She held out her left-hand ring. "What does that
mean? Turn over in your mind what that means, and let me
know what you are going to do."

"Where is the money gone that I gave you last week?
Tell me the truth."

"Yes, there is no reason why I should tell you any lies
about it. It is all spent except twopence. And the rent to
pay. How is it spent? It is spent on myself. What did I
buy with it? I bought bloaters and bread for the boy to
eat, and gin for myself to drink. What do I want more for?
To buy more bloaters and bread to eat, and more gin to drink.
I've had a misfortune, too. Rickety Jem was knocked down

by a cab as he was selling papers in Fleet Street, and he's so bruised that he can't walk. Poor little Jem! It's a creditable thing for me, isn't it, to have a son selling *Echoes* for a halfpenny? Give me some money and let me go, Marion Revel."

"I have only sixpence."

"Then give me that, and send me some more."

Marion took out her purse.

"The purse would pawn for eightpence," said the woman. "Give me that too."

"No, I shall not. Here is the sixpence."

"And you talk about being poor! Why, the things you've got on you could put in for at least thirty shillings. There's the malachite cross, that's good for three-and-six. There's the jacket; why, any one would lend you ten shillings on the jacket. There's your gloves—real kid; well, they is patched a bit, and wouldn't fetch much. And your gown! Marion Revel, it's disgraceful if you don't give me more than sixpence, with a whole fortune on your back. I thought your father's daughter was not so selfish."

"How dare you name my father?" cried Marion, roused to frenzy by the dreadful importunity of the woman. "How dare you let the name of Captain Revel pass your lips? Now do your worst, if you dare. Go up and tell that innocent girl who and what you are. Make her more unhappy than she is —it is the utmost that you can do. Do this if you please; but if you do I will give you nothing—nothing. Now let me go."

The beggar began to whimper and cry, using the corner of her shawl in lieu of a pocket handkerchief to mop up imaginary tears.

"You're the only friend I've got in the world," she moaned, "and you throw me over because you are afraid I shall tell. Is it likely I should tell? Do you think I am going to give up five shillings a week? Marion Revel, is it likely, I ask you? And the boy ill at home, and crying for food, and I've got no money. Oh! oh! oh!"

"What shall I do? What am I to do with you?" cried

the poor girl, in despair. "Is there no work for women in the world?"

"It depends," the other replied. "For such as you there is work and pay; for such as me there is only work and starvation. I can make cardboard boxes, and get two and twopence, bar stoppages, for twelve hours' work. That is all I can do. Just now there are too many of us wanting to make cardboard boxes, and I can't even get that; so I must come to you and beg. Get me some more money, Marion Revel!"

"If I do, you will only ask for more again when that is gone."

"Yes, I shall. I shall go on begging till I die. I wish I was dead. I wish I was laid in my workhouse grave and all my troubles over. But what would become of the boy?"

Marion sighed heavily.

"I will try and get you some money. If I can, I will bring it myself this afternoon. If I fail, you must try something else."

"I might go on the parish—that would be a fitting end to it all. Sometimes I think I will go and steal something. Marion Revel, I can hurt you in more ways than you think of if I like. I can do worse than tell *them* the truth. I can go before a magistrate for petty larceny, and give my real name and history. Mind you, I never lost my real name; I can bear it still if I like. So can the boy—little Rickety Jem. How would you like that?"

The woman passed from whining to threatening, and back again. She was uncertain in her behaviour. She alternated between the burden of her misery, which made her whine, and the feeling of the hold she possessed over the girl, which made her threaten. Either weapon was equally efficacious; for the blow which she could inflict was not upon Marion, but upon the other two.

"I can do no more," Marion said. "Go away and leave me. You have made me unhappy enough. I have told you what I will try to do, and what I shall do if you dare to injure those who are dear to me. Now go."

The woman pulled her shawl closer round her and flitted away. When she got round the nearest corner, she looked about her. There was, of course, a public-house in the street. There are always in London two things in full view—a public-house and a church. The population may be broadly divided into two great classes—of those who worship at the former and at the latter place. The woman belonged to those who worshipped at the bar. She made sure that Marion was not looking after her, and crept into the place that is open all day long, a pit for those who like to tumble in. A moment afterwards she came out, wiping her mouth; but she bore herself more upright, and faced the world with a brighter air.

This was Marion's secret—the secret she had discovered on going through her father's papers, the thing she had to keep away from her brother and sister, and to hide from all the world. The knowledge of it made her ashamed; the thought of it weighed her down; the burden of it kept her in the poverty of misery, when she might have been in the poverty of simple comfort.

The woman was, as Fred idly put it, her pensioner—not by choice, but by a dreadful necessity. She had to be kept from starvation for the sake of the dead man lying in Comb Leigh churchyard, and for the sake of the two "children," who knew nothing of it. We have to bear our troubles as we can; but Marion's burden was all the harder because it was so much heavier than her brother or sister were able to suspect.

CHAPTER XVIII.

HAVING no more money, Marion had to walk, carrying her parcel of paintings. From the Tottenham Court Road to Waterloo Bridge is a long step; of that, however, she thought little, provided only she could sell her pictures. The man she was going to had already bought one or two sketches, small things, and at a moderately low price. He

lived in Stamford Street, and called himself, on a brass plate,
picture dealer and restorer.   He was a German by birth, but
had been long enough in England to speak English fluently,
with only the sweet German accent, so as to interchange a
few of the consonants, such as the labials and dentals, in
that remarkable and pleasing manner peculiar to his country-
men.   His name was Gottfried Hermann, and he was said to
be descended from the children of Israel, which is by itself
a passport to everybody's favour.   As for his religious principles, they were no doubt deep and genuine, the result of
profound investigation and anxious thought; but as his
daily practices were beyond everything scoundrelly, and his
walk, or rather his creeping, in life was mean, tortuous,
and shady, it would be perhaps superfluous to inquire into
his creed.   The Americans—a much more practical people
than ourselves—make it a rule never to ask after the religion
of a stranger.   They like, on the other hand, first to make
sure of his honesty.   Perhaps we shall some time or other
adopt this, among a few other laudable Transatlantic
customs.

In every profession there must be perforce some whose
natural place is about the lowest steps.   We have not all of
us learned to climb.   To some of us climbing is not agreeable, to others it does not seem profitable.   Mr. Gottfried
Hermann was one of those who stand about the lowest steps
of picture dealing.   He was also one to whom that position
was the most pleasant.   On the higher levels he would have
found the air too bracing, the wind too keen, the light too
brilliant, the situation too exposed, the sensation to a retiring
and sensitive man suggestive of standing in a pillory.   For
his own part, he preferred to work in the dark, or rather in a
sort of twilight of his own creating.

He was a fat, round-faced man of fifty, with a certain
stamp upon his expression which, rightly or wrongly, we are
accustomed to regard as indicative of habitual self-indulgence.
He smoked a great-bowled German pipe, which might hold
half an ounce or so, all day long; and he sat at the front
window of his house in Stamford Street contemplating the

passers-by when he was not studying a picture. There grew up from the area a thin and skeleton-like vine, which threw its slender arms across his window, and gave an air of verdure and Eden-like innocence to his features, as they beamed behind the sickly leaves in summer. In winter the tree suggested the similitude of the spider in his web.

This morning, the leaves being not yet out, and only a green budding visible along the branches, he had the spidery look as his flabby face shone through the panes. He was not alone. A man in the last depths of shabbiness was with him, standing hat in hand, a suppliant.

"Give me work, Mr. Hermann. I can do it well and quickly."

"Tell me about New York first, what you was doing there."

"I was copying there."

"Aha! he was gopying. Zo, what was he gopying?"

This impudent rascal habitually adopted the use of the third person in talking to those who asked for work, with the deliberate intention of insulting his visitors, and an inward chuckle at the thought that most of them did not know they were being treated as servants, and were too miserable to resent it if they did.

"I was with Messrs. Fourbe, Gredin, and Fripon, the largest picture dealers in America."

"I know them, I know them. Let him sit down and tell me all he can about their business."

"There is not much to tell. They had good copies of pictures made in Rome, Dresden, and Florence, and their chief business was to have more copies made from them."

"And they sold them as originals. Most unbrinzibled."

"No, they were sold as genuine copies by good living artists, made on the spot. It is a safer business. They used to have a canvas stretched on the wall, and I and two or three others copied all day, as quickly as we could. As fast as the pictures were finished, they were cut out and framed. Mostly they were sold by auction. I've got a very rapid hand, sir."

"Goarse," Mr. Hermann replied. "Ferry goarse, that kind of work."

"You see, sir, copying does not require the fine painting, Mr. Gredin used to say, that is expected in an original."

Mr. Hermann shook his head.

"Go away. I give you ten days. Make me a—a—a—let me see— a Greuze; you can do all styles, ja wohl. Yes, a Greuze, and—and I shall see. What is this?"

He took a picture that was standing with its face to the wall, and laid it on the table.

"That is a Linnell."

"Is it a gopy or is it an original?"

"If it was anywhere but here, I should say it was an original," replied the man. "I know enough of the trade to be quite sure that it is not an original, or else it would not be here."

"Ha! ha! He is right this fellow. He is right. Let him go away now, and come back in ten days with the Greuze."

The man left him, and Mr. Hermann watched him down the steps.

"Ah, he is poor. He has done someding. I will find out what. Himmel, here is the pewtiful young lady, Miss Reffel. I am glad she did not meet that other poor teffel."

He saw Marion coming up to his door, and went to open it himself.

"Gott pless me!" he cried; "it's Miss Reffel. Come, my tear young lady, come in. What a bleasure to see you, and what a plessing to know that you are well! Come in, and show me what you have prought me. It will be coot; oh, it will be coot. I know that it will be coot. There—sit down. You may look at the bictures while we talk. There's a pewtiful thing, now. Give me the liddle barcel—zo—yes—zo. What do you think of that for a real and genuine Linnell—a rare and pewtiful Linnell?"

It was a delicious, soft, warm, sunlit scene—a field of standing corn, with a tree at the right hand, and a wood behind. Creeping up in the background, a thunder-cloud.

"It is a very nice picture," said Marion; "but it looks to me like a copy."

He laid down Marion's parcel unopened, and held the picture to the light.

"A gopy!" he jerked out, angrily. "A gopy! Why does she think it is a gopy?"

"Perhaps I am wrong," Marion replied; "but I should have said, on looking at it, that there could be no doubt about its being a copy. However, if you are sure—"

"If I am sure!" he echoed. "Why, if I am not sure, who the teffel can be sure? I beg your bardon, young lady, but if ever there was a genuine Linnell—why, there—never mind; let us look at the things in the liddle barcel."

He opened it, and began to turn over the pictures one by one, talking all the time as he held them to the light.

"I don't want to buy any more bictures. I think I shall never buy any more so long as I live. There's more bictures bainted than beoble to buy them. Times are ferry hard, Miss Reffel."

"Indeed they are, Mr. Hermann, else I should not be here; but you must buy mine, if you please, because I want some money."

"Flowers and fruit. Yes, ferry bretty—ferry bretty inteet. But no one looks at flowers and fruit now. It is a real bity to see a young lady of your talent waste her brecious time over flowers and fruit. You might as well go to the Zoological Cardens and baint the monguies. It would be pedder to baint the monguies. Beoble like monguies, and they don't like flowers and fruit. One, two, three—three bictures of beaches and crapes. What shall we say for this boor lot altogether?"

"I was thinking of a guinea a-piece," said Marion humbly.

Mr. Hermann held up his hands in a kind of horror.

"A kuinea?—twenty-one shillings a-piece for liddle things like those? My tear young lady—oh, tear! oh tear! It's ferry difficult to refuse a sweet young bainter like you. Why am I not a rich man? What shall I say to this young lady? Miss Reffel, if I was to give you a whole kuinea a-piece for these liddle pictures, I should be a ruined man. I should have to go back to my liddle vive and my liddle children in Jairmany mit nozing. Gottfried Hermann would be pangrupt."

He emphasised his assertion with many and weighty gestures of his fat white hands, and much nodding of his very large head.

"Then what could you give me?" asked Marion. "Please remember, Mr. Hermann, that I am very poor, and that you are—"

"Ferry poor too—oh yes!—ferry, ferry poor, I am. Come, let us regon up together. I shall keep these liddle bictures in my place for two years; then they will go to America; they will be framed; there will be the gommission. It's the gommission zuks away the brovit. Ah, if only we could do without the gommission—those wicked sgoundrels! Now, let us see. I keep the bictures two years, say fife shillings interest—that is nozing; dey go to America with lots of others, say fife shillings more; framing, fife shillings more; gommission, ten shillings; there is twenty-fife shillings: profit to myself—I am ferry poor, Miss Reffel—five shillings, that's all. What is a poor liddle five shillings? But it is all to oblige you, my tear girl. Ah, I would lose eferything to oblige a young lady, and a sweet bainter like you. That's thirty shillings. Suppose they give in New York—bicture dealers are an unbrinzibled lot—most unbrinzibled" (he shook his head, as though he and his English brethren were models of virtue and honesty)—"suppose they give us forty shillings; that's the outside figure. I will risk that, Miss Reffel, to oblige you; and it makes—ja, zo—yoost ten shillings a-piece."

He took out his purse and counted out three half-sovereigns, which he pushed over to Marion.

"It seems very little," she said. "Could you not—"

"My tear young lady, you have seen the figures—be reasonable."

The sight of the money was a temptation not to be resisted. She took up the three little gold pieces, and put them in her purse.

The honest Mr. Hermann went on with his examination of the other pictures.

"Scene by the seaside—zo; light a little too strong—yes. A head—zo." It was the head of Adrienne. "Where did you get this face? Did you draw it from vancy, or did you gopy it? Is it a bortrait?"

"It is my sister."

"Himmel!" he replied, with a glittering eye. "Her sister—it is her sister! What a face! what a pewtiful face! Young lady, I will give you a whole kuinea for this bicture. I will give you a kuinea for every one that you baint like it. Ah, what a face! It is a Fenus—mein Gott, a new Fenus. Make me more of her, make me lots of her, and you shall make a liddle vortune out of your zister. Bring her here to me to talk mit me; I should like to see this lovely Fenus, this young Miss Reffel. Is she a bainter too? Bring her to me."

Marion hesitated for a moment, but she took the guinea. After all, it was money, and she wanted it.

"Zo"—he pushed aside the water-colours.

"You have forgotten the seaside piece," said Marion.

It was so—the forgetful Mr. Hermann had pushed this with the rest into his portfolio.

"Ah, yes—zo; I had forgotten. Let me have this liddle bicture with the rest, Miss Reffel, because I am so ferry poor."

"No," said Marion, strictly; "give me a guinea for that picture, or I will take it away. Why, there are four days' work in that picture."

"Four days only! and she asks a kuinea—nearly two kuineas a week! What a grand thing to be a water-golour bainter! Two kuineas a week! I will gif vifteen shillings for it."

"No,"

"Then seventeen. Come, Miss Reffel, come. We are old friends."

"No; let me have it back; and let me go."

He took it out, and held it up. It was a pretty little thing —a reminiscence of Comb Leigh, with the water dancing in the little cove, the brambles climbing over the rocks, and on the left the old carpenter cobbling the bottom of the boat, while his tar-pot sent up its straight, thin column of smoke, marring where it ascended the clear blue of the sky. It was more than pretty, as the dealer saw; it had feeling and truth in it as well as beauty; it was a picture which if it had a good name at the back of it, would be worth thirty or forty pounds at least.

Mr. Hermann placed it back in his portfolio.

"I suppose I must," he said; "a young lady always does what she likes with me. Here is a kuinea, and I shall have to save and scrabe to make it up. Baint me more heads, Miss Reffel, of your sister. Baint her in gostume. She would do for Haidée; she would do for Marcuerite; she would do for—mein Gott! how she *would* do for Codifa. Baint her in dress and out of dress, and I will gif you a kuinea for efery one, efery one—a whole kuinea. I will."

"My sister is not a model, Mr. Hermann."

"Then make her a mottel. Why is she not a mottel?" he replied, angrily. "If she is ferry poor, and you are ferry poor, why is she not a mottel? You may as well be a mottel as starve, I suppose."

As Mr. Hermann in his younger days had sat in the Life School himself, he thought strongly on the subject of models. Moreover, as his wife, his mother, his sisters, and in fact his whole family, had been in the profession, it was not likely that he would hear the calling spoken of slightingly.

"I hope we shall not starve," said Marion. "Thank you, Mr. Hermann. May I bring you any other pictures, even if I do not paint my sister's face again?"

"I could put you in the way," said Mr. Hermann, looking musingly at the girl—"I could put you in the way of making a large sum of money; oh, a ferry large sum of money."

"How could I do that—by painting?"

"Yes, by bainting; only it must be by bainting things for me. When pictures are ordered, I must have them bainted, and I think you could baint them well. That Linnell was bainted for me by a young man I know; and yet, you see, you found it out at once."

"I thought you said it was genuine?"

"So I did, so I did; but that was only to try you. Now, young lady, I will tell you some of the real secrets of the bicture trade, and then you can make money for yourself. I am always generous with the young ladies. I would do anything for the young ladies—anything in the wide, wide world; and I am going to put a fortune in your hands—a fortune—if you can work it properly."

"I am sure I am very grateful."

"Now, listen; don't inderrupt. That Linnell—how was it done? My young man goes to an exhibition, and then to a private gallery, and then to Ghristie's, and so on—wherever they have got any Linnells. He is not allowed to sit down and make a gopy, so he takes the gadalok, and, when nopody is looging, he draws a tree from this picture, and a field from that, and a bit of field flower from another, and then, my tear, he goes home, my young man does, and he makes a Linnell by himself, all gomplede—a new Linnell, that Mr. Linnell himself would not know from one of his own, made up of liddle bits taken from half a dozen bictures he bainted himself; and then he brings it to me, this gleffer young man, and if the bicture is well done, and deceives a stranger, I gif him—I gif him fife pounds for that bicture—fife pounds, young lady."

"And what do you do with it?"

"What do I do with it? I sell it, my tear, I sell it to the bicture tealers, who sell it to other bicture tealers, and it goes round the trade, and then about the world. Mein Gott! if all the calleries in Manchester and America were emptied, there would be more Linnells and Codmans than fifty men

could baint in fifty years. And such a lot done by my young
men—oh, such a lot! I've got the glefferest young men you
effer saw. Not this one," he pointed to the 'Linnell' which
lay on the table. "He shall go—he shall go to the teffel;
he used to baint well, but he has done bad lately. I am
afraid he is a young man of bad morals. I think he trinks."

"What you want me to do," said Marion, who had grown
very pale, "is, as I understand, to go round the exhibitions
and sale-rooms, take a bit from one picture, and a bit from
another, patch up the whole in a single painting, and call it
after a modern artist."

"That is it, my tear young lady; that is yoost what I
want."

"Then, Mr. Hermann," she said, "you are a villain."

"Eh? mein Gott! Miss Reffel!"

He laid down his pipe, and looked at the girl with feigned
surprise.

"I say you are a dishonest, wicked man, Mr. Hermann. I
will have no dealings with you. Give me back my pictures,
and take your money, and let me go. Give me back my
pictures."

She laid her hand on the portfolio.

"Not so fast, Miss Reffel—not so fast. The bictures are
mine; I have bought them. I shall not give them back."

"Then, Mr. Hermann, I will tell everybody who you are.
I will warn the world against you."

"Who will you tell?" he asked, a shade of anxiety crossing
his face. "Who will you tell, Miss Reffel?"

"I will tell Mr. Burls, the picture dealer."

He burst into loud laughter.

"She will tell Purls! Ho! ho! ho! She is going to tell
Purls! Eh, my tear, how Purls will be astonished! I
suppose never was a man so astonished as Purls will be
astonished. Purls the honest, Purls the truthful! Eh,
mein Gott! what a plow it will be to Purls! Go and tell
Purls, my tear; go and tell Purls immediately."

He laughed again. The idea of Mr. Burls being told was
too much for him

"Go and tell all the tealers, Miss Reffel. Ah, they will be almost as much astonished as Mr. Purls—good Mr. Purls! Ho! ho! ho!"

Marion had no reply to make.

"Gome, my pretty young lady—gome, Miss Reffel, do not be angry about nozings. Sit down again. Most of my young men go off the same way when they first hear my plan. Then they get poorer and poorer, and then they gome to me to get rich. Sit down and listen; only one moment. See, the Manchester men want bictures; the stockbrokers and the goddon-brokers want bictures; the New York merchants want bictures. They can't all have bictures; they won't have gopies; but they don't know bictures. Then they go to the tealers, and the tealers go to each other, and one after the other they come to Gottfried Hermann. They come to me. I am the benefactor of the world. Wherefer the English language is spoken—wherefer there are rich beoble who want bictures, there you will find the works of my young men. Without me bictures by modern masters would be so tear, that they would haf to puy bictures from the liddle sgrubs. Think of that. By my help the goddon-brokers look at their walls and say, 'That is a Linnell;' ho! ho! 'That is an Eddy;' ha! ha! 'Here is a Leighdon, and there is a Roberts.' Won't you sit down, Miss Reffel, and listen quietly? You are such a ferry nice girl, that I should not like to see you go off in a rage.

"The best of it is," he went on, "that they puy the bictures because they think it is a goot infestment of their money. Ho! ho! They leafe them in their last wills and destamens to their heirs as ferry precious broberty. Ha! ha! But when they are sent up to Christie's, they are sometimes found out, and the heirs are sold. Ho! ho! ho! what an infestment of money—eh? It serves them right, because if they would puy the bictures of young artists like yourself, Miss Reffel, they would get the falue of their money. They would—mein Gott, they would. Sit down, young lady, and listen to me. Don't go away in a rage."

"I will hear no more," said Marion. "Find some one else to work your cheats for you."

"You will come back, young lady—you will come back. You will get no one to give you such a goot price for your bictures as Gottfried Hermann; you will come then, and work with my young men, and make pewtiful Eddys and Leighdons and Linnells. Oh, yes; you will come back in a liddle time; you will come back to your friend, and I bear you no malice, my tear young lady—no malice at all. I like you for it; I do indeed. Good-bye, Miss Reffel. Oh," he cried, as she left the room, "do baint your sister for me in oils; baint her as Cotifa, and I will gif you ten pounds. I will indeed—ten pounds, mein Gott—ten pounds! How pewtiful she would look as Cotifa!"

CHAPTER XIX.

MARION was more than outraged by the proposals of this unholy alien, this German producer of new and original pictures—she was humiliated. If you want to humiliate your enemy beyond endurance, ask him to do something which shows the very small respect in which you hold him. To the frailer vessels of humanity, indeed—those of ornamented porcelain and coloured glass—it is worse to be asked to do things dishonourable than it is actually to do them. Men who negotiate foreign loans, men who bull and bear the stock market, men who promote bubble companies, "salt" mines, draw up prospectuses, advertise sherry, send ships to sea that are bound to sink, direct bankrupt life insurance associations, "adapt" plays, and abuse their rivals in anonymous criticism, —all these can bear their heads proudly, and believe themselves honourable and upright men. Ask them confidentially to join in cracking a crib, fencing a wipe, or any of the humbler and less remunerative forms of treachery, and lo! their self-respect collapses like a pricked balloon. For a discreditable proposal implies discredit. Marion had borne a great deal without repining. She worked all day for a miserable pittance, she saw others reap the fruits of her labours: this was all part of the condition of poverty; it did not make her seriously unhappy. Never before this had she been asked to join in fraud; never before this had the sweet waters of Hope in her heart been troubled by such a prophecy as Mr. Hermann's, that she would come back soon, poorer than ever, and be glad to take his offer.

Should she ever go back so ruined and lost as to accept the foul proposal? Were there, then, such depths of misery as would drive the unfortunate to give up even the semblance of honour? Was it hopeless to struggle with the world? And were all the avenues barred by the middle-man, to rob and plunder those who must sell or starve?

Alas, how many have given an answer! Ask of the middle-man, if he will tell you. Look behind the curtain, the kindly veil which hides the dreadful features of truth. See at their toil the slaves of those who take the work and sell it, and grow fat upon the proceeds. There are such fat and noisome grubs in literature, but it is in art that they chiefly flourish. They starve the struggling artist into submission; they cheat and plunder him; they lie to him, and steal from him; and when his last spark of ambition is extinct, they make him the instrument of their forgeries. It is no fiction, but a miserable truth, that Gottfried Hermann exists and drives a roaring trade, keeping in his pay the men who have been starved and cheated by Burls. The middle-man bars all the avenues.

For the moment, Marion felt as if she was in the bonds of a stern necessity which was dragging her downwards, and there seemed no escape. It was in vain that she fought against the feeling. It seemed that the man spoke truly of coming events. She would have to go back and humbly ask for work—work of any kind, in order that she and hers might eat a morsel of bread. And there came upon her brain, for a while, the black pall of despair, when the mind is shrouded with darkness that can be felt; when the distinction between good and evil, for which Adam gave up Paradise, is lost again, and the earth seems to be hell; when there is no more hope, and the voice of God is silent.

She would have to go back. She shuddered at thinking of his soft and flabby face, his fat white hands, his oily voice. It came upon her quite suddenly what he meant by asking her to paint her sister for him—girls do not understand these things at first. The thought was like a shower bath. She shook herself together, and dared once more to resolve. Never, come what might—poverty, disappointment, distress —never would she go back to that man again.

She had wandered, wrapped in her gloomy thoughts, as far as the Horse Guards, when this sudden rage seized her. She crossed the road, and went into St. James's Park. The sun was shining—it had been shining in the streets, indeed, but poor Marion did not notice it there. Here it fell among the young leaves of April, and flashed a twinkling, fitful light, unlike the steady glow upon the foliage of summer, on the bushes and shrubs putting on their brand-new spring apparel. Here, too, the wild ducks, who habitually take up their winter residence, because it is a safe and secluded spot, in St. James's Park, were reminding each other of important appointments at the back of the north wind, made eight months before in those iceless seas where the secret of the Pole is hidden; the swans were beginning the soft nothings which precede their brief-lived marriage ties; and the sparrows, who are a practical folk, as a rule, and always intent on business, were feeling the soft influence of the season, as well as Marion and the nursemaids, who had the park to themselves. She turned to the left, and walked along the banks of the lake, while calmer and more hopeful thoughts gradually came back to her. Her hands, which had been tightly locked, unclasped, and she looked around her. After all, whatever happened, they were not utterly destitute. She had her fifty pounds a year, enough to give her some little standpoint from which to resist the enemy. They were cast down, but not utterly forsaken; by some means or other she would contrive, and perhaps— But she checked the rising hope that perhaps something would turn up. That is only the hope of a helpless person. However, perhaps her own picture—the thing into which she had thrown all her soul and all her powers—might somehow advance her. Of course, she never entertained the least trust in the promises and expectations of her brother. She was the family bread-winner ; he was the family spendthrift. It was all part of the great Providential design : some families have an invalid ; some have one of weak intellect ; hers had one who could not work. In fact, it had two ; but poor Adie, who could not make money, had her functions, and kept house for them all. I feel almost ashamed to add what is so apparent to all, that Fred's helplessness in no way diminished Marion's affection for him. It had even ceased to irritate her. She made a never-ending series of excuses for him ; he was her charge ; it was her duty to work for him.

Perhaps it was the soft spring air that brought Marion's thoughts back to a peaceful channel ; perhaps, too, it was the sunshine and the warmth that made her think of Gerald, long lost, and that short love chapter in her life. Some people like a novel that is all love ; I am sure a life ought to be all love, and especially that love which cannot be written in a book, the best love of all, which follows the short-lived fever of passion. The memory of Marion's brief romance left its enduring mark upon her mind, making her softer, more womanly, more open to sympathy, more ready to pity and forgive. That is love's special function. Those who can-not love are cruel, selfish, and unfeeling, like Narses. Those who can, very likely have every kind of vice, but they have the possibilities of affection, which means self-denial. "Joys," said Blake, painter and poet, "impregnate." The fruits of even short-lived happiness are tenderness, thought for others, and the gracious sacrifice of labour. Among women, those are best who have been loved and have loved ; among men, those are best who have staked their happiness upon the faith and truth of a woman. You stake your love, perhaps, and lose, but oftener you win ; and always you are a gainer for having dared to stake.

Marion paced the gravel backwards and forwards, thinking of these things. Presently she became aware of a heavy step behind her. The step seemed familiar; it drew up to her, and she saw that it belonged to Dr. Chacomb.

"I saw you," he said, "as I was on my way to the hospital. May we have a little talk?"

"If you will only talk about—if you will only not talk—" said Marion, thinking of the last night's conversation.

The doctor bowed gravely.

"You have only to express a wish, Miss Revel," he said; "besides," he added, airily, "the time has not come round yet."

"The time?"

"Yes. I began to think it possible six months ago. I asked you then. You said, No. I asked you again last night. You said, No. I shall ask you again in a little while—"

"And I must say No then. O Dr. Chacomb! do not ask me again."

"I must, Miss Revel. If you say No, I shall ask again, and again after that. I do not despair. You have owned that you do not dislike me. I trust to time, though a man can ill afford time at nine and forty. Meanwhile, I am consoling myself with hard work."

"I am glad that you are succeeding."

"Thank you. Trust me, dear Miss Revel, that I shall not obtrude my suit upon you more than I can help."

If the man would only not make such speeches! Who could help being irritated with him?

Marion turned the conversation.

"Tell me about your hospital."

"Would you be interested to hear about it? Let us sit down. There is a seat, and I really do think the east winds have gone at last. Now, what shall I tell you? I had an inspiration, as the French say—they are very profane, the French. I saw there was no hospital for gout. I saw that the best way for a physician to get himself a practice was to start an hospital. I borrowed money of Chauncey Chacomb, my cousin, and I started mine."

This statement was not strictly accurate. He should have said that he had taken money from Chauncey Chacomb, inasmuch as he was receiver of the rents, and accounted to nobody. A dishonest receiver might have pocketed the whole. Dr. Chacomb, wiser than the Unjust Steward of the parable, frankly confessed that he borrowed the money. The fact of the lender not being consulted was, of course, of no consequence.

"I borrowed money from poor Chauncey," he said, "and I started this hospital. It is now in full swing. Out-patients in the morning, seen by my assistants; in-patients visited every day by myself, physician-in-chief; and private patients received at the institution itself, as well as in Adelaide Street, Carnarvon Square. The hospital is supported by voluntary contributions. Some day I will show you the prospectus, drawn up by the secretary—a clever fellow: I picked him up cheap—who might have done great things in literature but for his unfortunate crook of the elbow. As he only crooks it at night, it does not matter to the hospital; and I take care to keep him poor."

"And you are now a great physician?"

"Hum! I should say Yes to anybody but yourself. But you, Miss Revel, are a sort of touchstone. I like to tell you the exact truth. I am not a great physician—there are no great physicians; but I have learned things of late, and I am as good as any of my brethren—a good deal better than Dr. Porteous, of Savile Row, who pretends—the pompous old donkey!—to be the leader in gout. Wait a year or two, till I have snuffed him out."

He snorted, and looked as angry as a writer whose pet field has been invaded.

"I am sure you are a good physician."

"I use new medicines, and they say I am a quack. Quack! quack! quack! Any man can say that. I do not follow the English Pharmacopœia, and I am not too proud to learn from other people. I chalk out my own line. Medicine in this country, my dear young lady, is dead; the doctors are smitten with the disease of stupidity. They neither inquire, nor invent, nor experiment. They do not dare try a fresh drug."

"Perhaps it is as well not to try things that have no properties."

"Nonsense! Everything has properties, if you can find them out. The dandelion and the nettle, the buttercup and daisy, have properties, if you analyse them. But the doctors cannot analyse. Every weed in the hedge has properties, but we are afraid to move a step to find them out. Do you think Nature makes things just to look pretty? If you want to know what herbs are worth, you must go, not to the botanists, who are only able to give you the Latin names; nor to the doctors, because they will say that the plant is not in the Pharmacopœia; but to the old women of the villages, and gather their knowledge. We are getting so civilised that we must be cured as we are taught, by books. The old women are fallen into disrepute; they die and their knowledge dies with them—more's the pity! But they *know*."

"And you have consulted them?"

"I have gone about picking up hints," he replied, "and I have learned things. I have found old women who can do with foxglove, henbane, hawksweed, and nightshade what we doctors cannot do with all the nastiness compounded at the wholesale chemists', and sold at a profit of a thousand per cent. My old women learned the art from their mothers, who learned it from theirs, and so on, till we get to the Witch of Endor. As for her, I have myself sat at the feet of the Witch of Endor, only my old woman never heard of Samuel, and therefore could not call him up. I would have asked her to, by gad! like a bird, if I thought Samuel knew anything about drugs for gout."

"Then you ought to cure everybody," said Marion.

"No. There is a time for every man when, by the rules of his constitution, he is bound to die. No doctor can stave off that day; all he can do is to prolong life till the day comes. My patients want to be told their time. I pretend to know it, and I refuse to tell them. I am, of course, a great humbug. Men ought to live their appointed time, and then die of old age. Medicine is not of much use—it can only help you on to your limit; but if you catch one of the big diseases, like cholera, or typhus, or scarlet fever, or diphtheria, off you go, and no doctor in the world can help you.

"Stay," he said; "you said something yesterday about my cousin Chauncey and Gerald. I have got a letter to-day from his housekeeper, a very worthy person, whom I sent down there to look after him. Would you like me to read it to you?"

"Is there anything about Gerald in it?"

"Now, my dear Miss Revel, how can there be? Is it likely? Pray believe me when I assure you that if I heard anything about Gerald, even though it were to destroy my own hopes, I would tell you immediately. But I shall not. Poor Gerald!"

He shook his head solemnly, and opened the letter.

"Chauncey is quite sane, except upon one or two points. He is fully persuaded that he murdered your father, and he has little hallucinations on minor subjects, which are of no importance."

They were certainly of no importance to Marion, but they were of considerable importance to Chauncey, inasmuch as they led him to believe that he had no control over his own affairs; that the doctor spent his money for him, ordered his household for him, gave him a housekeeper and a guardian, and administered everything for his own behoof and special advantage.

"You see," he added, "I go down as often as I can—about once a fortnight—to see that the place is kept up."

"Dear Comb Leigh!" murmured Marion—"when shall I see it again?"

"Whenever you like—whenever you like! Nothing in the world could give me greater pleasure than to take you to Chacomb."

"And Mr. Chauncey Chacomb?"

"As if it matters what he thinks about it!"

"Thank you," said Marion. "I do not think I can ever go to Chacomb Hall, after what has happened."

He was a coarse-grained man, this doctor, she thought.

"Well, when you like to come. By the way, do you remember the picture with the back turned outwards? It was the thing that drove Chauncey so wild at the last. He made me say that I agreed with him, and thus your father laughed at him. He has got that picture hanging in his own bedroom now, and he looks at it every day—the back of it, I mean—with the hope of bringing out the details. Poor Chauncey! He never was a good fellow; and I think I like him as well now that he is known to be cracked as when he was only foolish, but considered to be of sound mind."

"But people—his tenants—consider him of sound mind still, do they not?"

"No; they only pretend to. They know well enough that he is off his head. We have had to observe a few precautions—nothing very serious, but still a few—and they have been noticed. The housekeeper—a most worthy, estimable woman—writes to me to-day, and I will read the letter. I have not had time to look at it yet."

"My dearest Joe"—("I beg your pardon," he stopped and choked)—"My dear Dr. Chacomb—It is a fortnight since you were down here, and I hoped to see you last Saturday"—("I could not go," he explained, "on account of dear Lady Strongwater's gout, which threatened to fly to the stomach; I was up with her all night")—"I hoped to see you last Saturday. Your patient has been going on pretty well, though full of tantrums, as usual. He has been very fractious for the last week, but he does not want to see you. In fact, I think, in his present mood, you had better not come. Last week nothing would suit him but going to the cliff where the accident took place. I believe he wanted to roll over himself. I refused to let him go; so he said he should wait till midnight, get out of window, and go and throw himself down where Captain Revel fell. Then I gave in—had a little party made up of Jem "—(" You remember Bos'n Jem, Miss Revel ")—"Charles, the stable-boy and myself. We all set off to walk to the cliff together. Directly we got outside the gates, he said it was ridiculous, and marched straight back again. Then he went to the Collection and cried; said nobody cared for him."—(" It is one of the features of hallucination, Miss Revel, that the patient cries if he is put out.")—" I prescribed port with his dinner, and we got him comfortably to bed."—(" Very good, very good. A bottle of port is a fine thing for hallucinations. If you feel low, wind yourself up. Sound medical maxim.")

" Poor Mr. Chacomb!"

The doctor seemed to forget that he was reading this interesting epistle aloud, and went on with it.

" In the morning he was quiet, and we had a talk."

Here there was a gap, because the writer had taken another sheet. The doctor looked at this, changed colour violently, and crumpled the letter in his hand.

" Well," he said, with an effort, " there's nothing more— nothing of importance. My poor cousin is hopelessly gone. I shall not lock him up, because he can do no harm where he is, and the treatment I prescribe for him will be best in the long-run. As it is, as it is—" He shrugged his shoulders.

" Yes," said Marion; " when Gerald comes home again he will thank you."

" You think—" he began.

" I am sure. Whenever I think of it, I feel the same assurance. Gerald is coming home. It is impossible that he should be dead, and that I should not know it."

" That is superstition."

" I cannot help it. We feel the presence of the living with us; why should we not feel the fact that they are alive? Gerald is alive at this moment; and I think, because I feel it so much more strongly now than I did a year ago, that he is coming home."

" Good-bye, Miss Revel," said the doctor, abruptly. " Put poor Gerald out of your thoughts, and—if you can—put me, my poor unworthy self, in his place."

He walked down the gravel path with his heavy tread, which was so silent on a carpet, and disappeared.

"What a fool I am! Why should I want to read Julia's letters to Marion without reading them myself first?"

He took the letter out of the envelope again, and read it.

"MY DEAR JOE"—("Hang her!")—"It is a fortnight"—("I read all that to Marion")—"And now I have got something important to tell you. I knew that you would never marry me, in spite of all your promises; and for the last three months Chauncey has been urging me to marry him on the sly. So yesterday we went quietly to the registrar's office, where I had had the notices put up"—("The deceitful little devil!")—"and now, if you please, I am Mrs. Chacomb, of Chacomb Hall, Chacomb."—("The deuce you are!")

"Chauncey is very good to me. It is all nonsense to say he is mad; he is no more mad than you, and he declares he will prove it."—("The devil he will!")—"He is a little flighty at night, and sees faces in the dark—so would any one in this lonely house. He hears voices, which everybody might hear in such a quiet place. Dear Joe, you know that I never could and never did love anybody but you; but when this poor little man kept begging and praying—and you away in London—and offering to make me a lady, a real lady, I thought I could do nothing better than take his offer."—("Nothing better, ma'am, nothing better; and I'm deuced glad of it;" but he spoke with a little bitterness.)—"I do not expect the county ladies"—("Eh? Ho! ho! the county ladies!")—"will call upon me just yet; but I'm going to send a notice of the marriage to the papers, and I can wait. Remember, my dear Joe, for the memory of old times, my husband and I will always be happy to see you whenever your professional duties will allow you to come.—Always your affectionate cousin,   JULIA CHACOMB."

"The cheek of it!" said the doctor. "The confounded impudence and cheek! I send her down to obey my orders and, by gad, she marries him! And now she thinks to be

the mistress of Chacomb, does she? We will see, we will
see. Julia, my girl, I've known you in the ballet, and I've
known you in the burlesque; I've known you on the quiet,
and I've known you on the rampage; but I never knew you
to try such a big game as this before. Never mind, Mrs.
Chauncey Chacomb the second, you haven't got over Joseph
yet. I shall go down next Saturday and bring this young
couple—ho! ho! he's fifty-eight and she's forty, if she's a
day—to reason. I shall let them know who is the master of
Chacomb. I shall put my foot down. Very well, Julia—
very well."

CHAPTER XX.

SATURDAY morning was an off-day with Dicky, so far as
Mr. Lilliecrip was concerned. He was wont to spend it
at the British Museum, in preparation of the articles, paragraphs, and letters which formed his tale of labour for the
Weekly Intelligence and the *Christian Clerk*. He was awakened by the street cries, which in London do duty for the
dogs of rural solitudes and the lark of the poets. He rose
hastily, for a thought flashed across him in his dreams,
piercing the innermost marrow of his soul.

"Good heavens!" he gasped, rushing his toilet, so to
speak—"eight o'clock already; and to-morrow is Sunday.
Never mind, I may be in time yet."

He did not, as when we saw him last, waste time in
lamenting or apostrophising the deficiencies of his wardrobe.
On the contrary, he huddled everything on as fast as possible,
reduced his curly and abundant locks to something like
smoothness, and hastened downstairs.

At the door of the ancient dame of whom mention has
already been made, he met her granddaughter, Miss Ethelreda Vyvyan, commonly known as "Ready Vyvyan" by
those who knew her best, and familiar to public eyes and
ears in connection with the Royal Hemisphere Theatre,
where she took second parts in burlesques: an accomplished
young lady; one who had a strong, if not a melodious voice,

and who could be trusted to get through a song without
absolutely losing sight of time and tune; who could dance
passably; who looked charming in "page" costume—she
preferred it "full page," she said; and who was pretty
enough for the simple costume of the theatrical village
maiden with short skirts, silk stockings, and a coquettish
hat.   But she was happiest in a costume *à la Henri Quatre*,
which displayed more of the figure than womankind in
western Europe have thought necessary since their conver-
sion to Christianity. "Popsy," her grandmother called her;
and what her surname really was, or her Christian name
either, I am sorry to say, I do not know. She was carrying
the breakfast milk upstairs, and looked as fresh and bloom-
ing as if she had not come home after a late supper at two
o'clock in the morning. Seeing the poet, she set down her
milk, and laughed and clapped her hands.

"How are you, Dicky?" she asked, with a familiarity that
spoke of old and confirmed friendship. "How are you this
morning, old boy? None the worse for last night? Let me
look at you: eyelids rather red, cheeks a little twitchy,
tongue a little dry—got a fur upon it, I should think.
You've been going it, Dicky Carew. Coming in to pay poor
old granny her money? Not you."

"The fact is," said Dicky, "that I am going into the City
to draw my dividends."

"Walker!" was the vulgar rejoinder of this young lady.
She accompanied it with a gesture which we may briefly
indicate by saying that it betrayed a complete mastery over
her limbs, and an early training for the ballet. "Walker!
How much do you owe the old lady? Never mind; you'll
pay me some day, whenever I'm hard up, and it will wait.
I've got lots of money now. I say, Dicky, come and see me
to-night. Better! I'll give you a pit ticket. New piece.
Heroine jumps from the flies into a cascade of real water.
'Heaven help me, I am lost! Death before dishonour!'
So—" She took an imaginary header over the banister, and
posed. "Not one of them, not even Dardie Duncan, had
the pluck to take it, except me; and, bless you, if you've got

good eyes, it's as easy as—as saying you are off to draw your
dividends; only it wouldn't do to miss your tip. Better
come, Dicky."

"I can't," said Dicky. "I am going to dine this evening
with the Countess of Grasmere, else I should be quite at your
service."

"Lord! Now I am going to have supper with Prince
Bithisnozoff, the Russian swell, and a few of his very particular friends, at the Prætorium, after the curtain drops.
Bet you my supper, Dicky, will be a good deal jollier than
your dinner. I suppose you'll get new heels to your boots
first, and take the swallow-tail out of pawn, for her ladyship's
dinner? Good-bye, Dicky."

She disappeared singing the last burlesque melody. A
moment afterwards she reappeared.

"Dicky, old boy," she cried after his retreating figure,
"I heard you go upstairs last night at half-past one. You
only tumbled down—altogether, that is—once and a half,
and carried your boots and hat quite safely all the way up.
I felt for you, poor fellow! What a dreadful thing to
go to bed sober! Haven't you got a bad headache this
morning?"

Dicky made no reply, but ran down the stairs.

"She's a remarkable girl, Popsy," he said, outside the
house—"a very talented and agreeable girl. I never quite
know whether she is chaffing, or whether she wants me to
marry her. Poor thing! I suppose it's the latter—all girls
do, somehow. Poor Popsy! More broken hearts."

Perhaps it is as well that we do not know always in what
estimation we are held by our friends. Certainly, nothing
was farther from Miss Popsy's thoughts than to marry Dicky
Carew. I heard, indeed, last month that she had gone to
church with a highly respectable young walking gentleman
from the provincial stage, and that they were both going
out to California on a professional engagement. Marry
Dicky Carew, indeed! Popsy knew a great deal better than
that.

At the bottom of the stairs, on the ground floor, he passed

the hospitable door of Mrs. Medlar; but he crept softly by on tiptoe.

"It is the shrine of material comfort," he murmured. "She is fat, she is fair, she is comfortable; she has still many summers of buxomness before her; she has at least a hundred and fifty pounds a year. When I sow my wild oats, I will marry Mrs. Medlar, and let the others pine away in cold neglect."

It was half-past eight, and he had a clear half-hour before him. He spent it, and fourpence, in a coffee-shop, where a cup of fragrant mixture, whose component parts contained no beans from sunny Mocha, with a slice of bread and butter, formed his breakfast. He had but little appetite for a breakfast, and sighed not for luxuries. Contentment, after all, is a continual feast. At five minutes to nine he arrived at the gates of the British Museum. As the clock struck nine, he passed through them.

Nothing but the strongest sense of duty could induce me to reveal what followed in the next few minutes. This, however, is too imperative.

It may be known to some of my readers that there exists in the British Museum, for the use of readers only, a lavatory furnished with the customary jack towels, and supplied with soap. Mr. Carew sought this retreat with a calm, deliberate, and thoughtful air, as if he were about to remove the dust of a long walk, prior to study. Arrived there—he was happy in finding himself the first—he proceeded—oh, Dicky! Dicky! —to pick out and appropriate to himself the largest and best tablet of soap. The careful way in which he did this, the critical inspection of the soap, the honourable sense which led him to take but one, and leave the rest for his friends, all pointed to habit. This was too true. Among a certain body of advanced thinkers, moral philosophers whose code was based upon a broader view of right than most can boast, there had grown up, little by little, a custom of avoiding the small and annoying expense of buying soap by taking what was put out in the lavatory. They annexed for themselves what was meant for mankind. They substituted the particular for the general. By long habit they had grown inured to the custom, so that it had now none of the stings of conscious sin; and though they never spoke of it among themselves, they had come to regard the soap as a grateful but silent testimonial of regard from England to her men of genius. They may have been, and doubtless were, men of the keenest and most delicate sense of honour in other things; but there are, as everybody knows, secrets in every profession. Go to! We waste our breath in proclaiming the sins of other trades, but carry on our own. Let the publican put quassia in the beer, cocculus Indicus in the stout, fusel-oil and potato spirit in the sherry; let the grocer sand the sugar; let the parson play at being a priest; let Mr. Burls and his crew go on selling copies for originals; and let the obscure literary hack appropriate the soap in the lavatory, as he appropriates his "copy" in the reading-room. It is humble work that he does, and poorly paid. Grub Street has been, it is true, long since abolished, but its former tenants have only migrated. When an Improvement Society destroys a rookery, the rooks only go somewhere else. Pope's poets and pamphleteers are dispersed at night; but in the day you may find them all in that vast circular apartment, where light, pens, ink, blotting-paper, and warmth—everything but air—are given, with the noblest library in the world, without money and without price, to those who like to use them. Far be it from me to defend Dicky's custom. I only record it. The librarians lament the loss of engravings from the books, which are cut out and sold by the more needy among the readers for one penny apiece. But the daily loss of the soap has never yet, to my knowledge, formed the subject of a paragraph in the annual report, a complaint posted up in the room, or a parliamentary commission.

Mr. Carew wrapped his soap in paper, and deposited it in his coat pocket. Then he repaired to the reading-room and began his work.

His labours—for he had postponed everything to the last day—were of a divided nature. The mission of the *Weekly Intelligence* was to show up the aristocracy in their true colours, to paint the bloatedness of our prelates, and to represent faithfully the down-troddenness of the British workman. It was also devoted to the purpose of hiding from the workman who bought the paper the fact that he is in these latter days falling into such a condition of mind and body as no class of artizans have ever before experienced, inasmuch as he is incapable of combining except for the purpose of getting higher wages and lower hours, that he has ceased to take an intelligent interest in his work, that he lives for himself alone, and that he drinks away all that he can spare from a half-starved household. To conceal these home-truths, and to reveal the other falsehoods, was the *raison d'être* of the *Weekly Intelligence*. Dicky, who was on the staff, was entrusted with the easy work of showing up the vices of the great.

On the other hand, the *Christian Clerk* was a paper of an altogether different tendency. Its object was to circulate among the Church congregations. It aimed at being the friend of churchwardens, and the companion of all Anglican vestrymen. It had no theological bias, but prostrated itself before everything that wore a white tie, and could use the letters M.A. For licentiate persons it had small respect. Dicky was an old and valued servant on the staff of this organ. He was regarded by the editor as an unfortunate and misunderstood man of genius. There was scholarship in his papers, lucidity and strength in his arguments, and a certain solid style, he would say, which one might look for in vain among other ecclesiastical papers.

Dicky began vigorously to look for material for the *Weekly Intelligence*. He took down half a dozen old volumes of the *Gentleman's Magazine*, all thumbed and worn by the exploring fingers of countless predecessors.

He had his paper ready at his right hand, and pen in hand to note anything that occurred. For some time the search was fruitless. His rapid eye ran up and down the columns without finding anything.

"I seem to know them all by heart," he groaned. "It's disgusting to see how men find them out."

Then he took down another half-dozen, and began a new search. After a little he found something that seemed to suit his purpose, and began to write.

"In the yellow and faded pages of an old magazine"— Dicky always began his little anecdote paragraph this way— "we discover the following curious and interesting pieces of information."

And so on. By dint of going through a dozen volumes of Sylvanus Urban. he managed to pick out what amounted to nearly a column and a half of small type. There was a riddle, the wording of which he altered a little; there was a short account of a gentleman's seat, showing that it was one of the oldest mansions in England, to which Dicky added that its owners were the most profligate; there was a notice on the York Assizes, where no fewer than five and twenty were left for execution, two being respited—the indignant writer called attention to the fact that the judges were gentlemen; there was a report of an action in the West Indies, in which Dicky remarked that the common sailors, who did the fighting, got no mention. And so on, all being flat, stale, and unprofitable; for Dicky was long past the time when he used to try to put things pleasantly, and his *réchauffés* were served up week by week, without the slightest disguise.

The *Weekly Intelligence* finished, Mr. Carew turned his attention to the *Christian Clerk*.

This was a more important business. He was engaged upon a series of brief papers on the ecclesiastical questions of the day, and it behoved him to exercise considerable care to steer clear of theological difficulties. As Dicky's only principle in literature was to steal everything he wrote, and never to read without an eye to plagiarism, it was first of all necessary to discover safe ecclesiastical material. He found this among the pamphlets of the last century, a *corpus* of good work too often neglected by the starveling small fry of literature. If by any remarks of mine I can turn the petty plagiarist into a new, fruitful, and wholesome preserve, I shall be glad to indicate to him the road by which Dicky

Carew might—alas, that I must write the word *might!*—
have risen to literary distinction. Dicky was the original
discoverer—he kept the discovery to himself—of the pamphlet. He loved it of all ages, but he loved it most for
practical purposes a hundred years old; for then it was sure
to possess some of the graces of modern writing. He would
transfer anything he pleased simply by copying it out.
Now, in earlier work there was often a passage, a turn of
thought, or a phrase, too majestic in its roundness, or too
involved, for the modern scribe. In such cases, Dicky had
all the trouble of taking the idea and writing it over again
himself. But the pamphlet kept for fifty or a hundred years
in the wood, so to speak acquired a fulness, a mellowness,
and a delicacy of flavour quite unknown in the ephemeral
productions of the day. He felt safe even with pamphlets
thirty years old. They were quite sure to have been written
by a man whose age would be somewhere about forty, so
that the probability was very much in favour of his having
gone to a world where plagiarisms are not sharply looked
after—where, indeed, such things are impossible. Armed
with one of these, Dicky boldly dipped his pen in the ink,
and copied whole paragraphs, regardless of possible consequences.

On this day he wrote a careful and elaborate argument,
from the Anglican point of view—*i.e.*, from a modern pamphlet dated about the year 1843—in favour of Church
Establishments. The writer of the pamphlet from which
he cribbed, one of the Oxford movement of that date, had
not yet become convinced of the desirability of Church
freedom with a view to reducing the laity to Church discip-
line, and therefore advocated Church and State. His suc-
cessors have learned better. Nor had he yet, as those of
the following generation have done, taught himself that
overweening respect for authority which enables the Ritualist
to see a friend and certain protector in Rome. Therefore
he talked about the " errors " of the Roman Catholic Church.
Dicky modernised his work to suit what he understood to be
the latest phase of thought. At the close of his argument

he allowed himself a few phrases of a really eloquent piety, with texts which he found at the end of the pamphlet. They were of the kind he liked—sonorous, well rounded, eminently Christian, and dogmatic.   When Dicky folded up his papers in two parcels that evening, addressing one to the printer of the *Weekly Intelligence* and the other to the printer of the *Christian Clerk*, he felt that he had done a good day's work, and earned the humble stipend which he was receiving for labours of such great importance.   The one envelope was full of blasphemy against all authority, divine or worldly; the other was, as hotel advertisers say, " replete " with the sweetest, the most sentimental, the most pious adhesion to all constituted authority, and especially to the Anglican bishops.

It was then five o'clock, and it must not be supposed that the day's work had been conducted entirely without refreshment.   Not so.   A select circle, comprising half a dozen of the choicer spirits, were wont to meet at one, and after the simple dinner of a chop or a sausage, with half a pint of stout, discuss the more abstruse literary topics over pipes and gin-and-water.   Those who were in funds sometimes carried on these Tusculan disputations with such ardour, and so long, as to be too late to return to the Museum, in which case they would find their MSS. and the books from which they had last been stealing kept for them the next morning by their friends the attendants.

They were a seedy and generally a morose crew.   Dicky alone among them preserved a cheerfulness which was mostly due to his splendid constitution.   They were engaged in copying for scholars, in compiling for third-rate publishers, in inventing blood and thunder stories for the lowest periodicals, or like Dicky himself, in writing for the papers which appeal to the class just removed from pauperdom.   How they drifted into the calling of "Letters" it is hard to say. Perhaps one or two of them had been gentlemen, and had been scholars.   Possibly most of them had deserted the lower ranks of clerks, or begun, like Dicky, as ushers in commercial academies. Not one of them deserved better pay or higher consideration than he got; not one had a right to complain that he served a hard master, because all were such bad servants.

Among these friends Dicky drank a modest allowance—three glasses—and returned to his duties. It was the third which inspired him with the happy thought of adding the final clauses of pious ejaculation above referred to. Perhaps it was the same glass which confused the keenness of his vision to a certain extent, and made it possible for him to commit the most fatal mistake of his life; for when he addressed the manuscript, folded and neatly tied up, by an inadvertence that he was destined to regret all his life, he sent off the packet destined for the radical and even atheistic *Weekly Intelligence* to the mild and religious *Christian Clerk*, while that intended for the *Clerk* was addressed to the *Intelligence*.

He then made the best of his way to the offices of *Clerk* and *Intelligence*, which were in two neighbouring streets, left his copy, marked "immediate," for the printer, and then began to think what he could do with himself till seven, the earliest hour possible for the commencement of a "night." Dicky especially disliked walking, because it wore out the heels of his boots, and yet he generally found himself condemned to pace the stony-hearted streets alone with his thoughts for nearly two hours every day, the time between the closing of the Museum and the commencement of the symposium. To be alone with their thoughts is to some men a perennial source of happiness. To Dicky it was exactly the reverse. For solitude led him to look back at the past or forward to the future. Neither of these prospects afforded him the slightest pleasure.

CHAPTER XXI.

WHEN Dr. Chacomb left Marion, she remembered the promise made to her pensioner, and hurried away from the Park. If you have a constant drag and drain upon your resources, you come, after a time, to regard it as a necessary evil, like a humpback or a stiff leg, and cease to think of it in the light in which it first presented itself, of an intolerable nuisance. Provided Mrs. Spenser confined her applications for help to herself, Marion hardly minded. It was but so much a week added to the burden she had to bear. The chief thing she feared was that some time or other this excitable lady would break her promise, and invade their lodgings, where Adie might see her.

Mrs. Spenser, desperately poor, as has been shown, lived in about the most ignoble neighbourhood in all London, always excepting certain portions of Pentonville. It was in Sun Court, St. Giles's, a place where every room held a family, and many rooms held more than one family each. She lived there with her son, called, by reason of a St. Vitus's dance which possessed the boy, and impelled him to kick out at odd times, to the discomfiture and indignation of passers-by, Rickety Jem. She had one room for herself and her son, and they slept in opposite corners. Try, if you can, to realise the degradation of a woman who had indeed once been a lady, when she had one room for herself and her boy of fourteen. The infamies and miseries of poverty can all be summed up in this. Nothing—not even insufficiency of food, insufficiency of clothes, or abject dependence—is so great an evil as the enforced huddling together in one room of a whole family. It is too horrible to tell of, too horrible to think of.

Yet the people in Sun Court were not exceptionally vicious or wicked. There are courts—one I know of, only a few yards north of Mecklenburgh Square—where a decently

R

dressed man who ventured to pass through in the daytime would be infallibly set upon and robbed, and where if a policeman dares to show his burly form he is saluted with flower-pots rained upon him from the windows, with other casual manifestations of an unpopularity that belongs to a class rather than to an individual. In Sun Court anybody might pass through at any hour with impunity. The policeman was looked on as not a friend exactly, but as a necessary evil. The inhabitants were harmless, except in one particular, that they were poor. When people are poor, however, they are dangerous. It is a fact well known to modern legislators, just as it was known to Julius Cæsar, that a well-fed man is contented with the order of things. That is why, if a member of Parliament shows signs of making himself disagreeable, he is presented with something good in the shape of a commissionership.

Mrs. Spenser lived partly on what she could extract from Marion, and partly on what she earned as a maker of cardboard boxes. Her son contributed his share by selling the *Echo*, cigar-lights, and such penny papers as he could beg from gentlemen at the Metropolitan railway stations. It was a miserable and precarious livelihood. She was a miserable and a discontented woman. She held herself aloof from her neighbours, on the plea that she was a lady. She tried, but ineffectually, to keep the boy separated from the other boys in the street, on the ground that his father was a gentleman. The people in the court called her Lady Spenser—a title which she accepted with a kind of gratitude.

How long does it take to reduce a lady to the lowest dregs? how long a gentleman to the level of the habitual criminal? It is a question one hardly dares to ask. We may pass from one stratum of life to another with greater ease than we like to think of. The descent of Avernus is steeper than we imagine. The difference between those who wear respectable clothes and those who do not is less than we are pleased to think. Thousands have found it easy to step across the gulf, and once across, all must perforce stay there. For the heaven of respectability is like Abraham's bosom, as described by Josephus—inasmuch as, if you once get out of it, you can never get back again.

It was not Marion's first visit to this dreadful den. She had been there once, a year before this. Then it was a bitter frost, and the depth of winter. She went to the place, resolved to tell the woman that she could do no more for her: it was when her resources had dwindled down to her fifty pounds a year. She thought it would be an injury to her own two helpless ones to do anything further for this wretched creature, who repaid her kindness with ingratitude, and threatened as often as she begged. But when she saw the miserable tenant of the room wrapped in a single blanket, without a fire, without a penny, trying to forget hunger in sleep, while her boy ran about the iron-bound streets crying his *Echoes* and his cigar-lights, her heart melted, and she refrained from saying what she meant to say. Since then, through fair weather or foul, whether she earned much money or little, the woman had her share of it. She was alternately defiant and humble. She threatened still, and begged. She was intemperate. She had not improved at all, and she was always a bitter grief and burden to Marion; but she could not be cast off.

It was a greater moral shock than the poor girl had ever known, to see this woman when they came to London—to know what she had been, and to see what she was. But the first visit to her lodging formed an epoch in her mind, because it revealed to her some of the dreadful things which lie unheeded at one's feet. For the first time in her life she found herself face to face with a hopeless misery which she could do next to nothing to alleviate, and that little at the expense of those who were also dependent upon her. And yet the woman had a claim too.

A lady—was it possible that she could ever have been a lady? What remains of ladyhood, what traces of the delicate blossoms which are nurtured by gentle breeding, could be discerned in this poor fallen creature? Surely none, save in her speech, which was soft and clear, and not yet disfigured by the toads, snakes, efts, and other dreadful things which fell from the mouths of her neighbours. That was all. The current of her thoughts—like a river whose mouth gets silted up, and so forms broad and malarious lagoons—had lost all settled purpose, if it ever had any, and was now dispersed in the marshy flats of food-providing. If this was certain, she began to think of the day's luxuries—now the maximum of gin obtainable. She looked for nothing more; she hoped for nothing more. When she looked back, which was seldom, she was tormented with Dante's worst sorrow, the remembrance of former happiness. She had no hope for the future, because she never looked forward. As for the present, she knew now of only three evils in the world—cold, hunger, and pain: she acknowledged two delights—warmth, and the imaginary paradise of intoxication. She was a ruined and hopeless woman. But such as she was—a miserable outcast, a creature lost to virtue, an unrepentant Magdalene—she had a claim upon Marion.

Marion found her working at her cardboxes. There was no carpet, no blind or curtain, and no furniture except a table and a chair. Mrs. Spenser had the table covered with the materials, which she was cutting and shaping with wonderful dexterity. Her features in repose were haggard, but regular. She had once, assuredly, been beautiful. A mattress lay in the corner, the sunlight upon it streaming through the dirty panes of glass, and falling full on the face of a boy who lay there upon his back. He was a sharp-faced, bright-eyed boy, nearly fourteen years of age; but he looked very much younger, because he was so small and thin. He was dressed in the merest rags. By his side lay a blanket. He was barefooted, his cheeks were hollow and wasted, his skin had the flush and brightness which belong to consumption, and he had a hacking cough.

"Is this your—your son?" said Marion, with some hesitation.

"That is my son," Mrs. Spenser answered. "Don't interrupt me; I've got some work come in, and I am in an industrious mood. I've promised Jem some tea by and by. You can't sit down, Marion Revel, because I've only got one chair, which I want. Tell me what you think of my boy. Tell me who he is like. Is he like me, do you think? Look up, Jem, and show the lady your face."

Jem turned his face obediently. Marion stooped, with a shudder, and patted his cheek. The boy was exactly like her sister Adie.

"Have you brought me some money, Marion Revel? If you have, put it on the table. You are a wonderful girl to come here at all. I wish I could get on without your help. I'm in a better temper than I was this morning. Don't be angry with me, will you? And don't think about what I say when I lose my head. I could not hurt *her*, you know."

She was changed since the morning, and spoke with a certain softness pleasant to hear.

"I can spare you ten shillings. Will that do?"

"It isn't much, but it must do."

"There's the rent, mother," said Jem, with a sharpness beyond his years. "Don't you forget the rent."

As he spoke, a St. Vitus's trembling of the limbs seized him, which explained at once why everybody called him Rickety Jem.

He half rose from the mattress, in evident pain.

"It is the cab that ran over him yesterday," said his mother. "Lie down again, my boy."

"I was going to get you the gin, mother."

Mrs. Spenser did not blush for shame; but she laughed, which was her only equivalent.

"Presently, my son. He knows his mother's ways," she explained. "I told you all about them long ago, Marion Revel. You can't say I ever hide anything from you."

"Alas, no!"

"Nor much from the boy. You shall hear. Jem, my beauty, who was your mother?"

"A lady she was; and much good that is to us."

He seemed to separate the mother who was a lady from the mother who was not.

"Much good indeed. It does not prevent her from making cardboxes for a living. Who was your father, Jem?"

"A gentleman he was. And much good that is to us."

Marion started.

"Don't be afraid, Marion Revel; the boy has nothing to do with you or yours. What else was he, Jem?"

"A villain; and mother was a fool to run away with him."

"What will you do to him when you meet him?"

"Kill him if I can," said the boy, viciously. "Rip him up, and cut him down, cos he's done all the mischief."

"There," said his mother; "some day or other I shall meet the boy's father—no matter when, because I can wait. Then my boy Jem will be tall and strong. He will remember the little catechism I taught him. You'll remember it always, Jem, won't you?"

She went on working her deft fingers, manipulating the card, and cutting the bright-coloured paper with swift activity while she talked.

"You'll remember when you meet him—he is a tall and handsome man—very tall and very handsome, careful about his hands, dresses expensively. He has got a face something like yours, Jem, when your face isn't like mine. You will be sure to know him. Get him in a secret place, and murder him. Tell him what it was for. Ask him if he remembers Carry—ask him if he tried to find out what became of his Carry; and then murder him. Marion Revel, this is good training, isn't it? It is all I am able to give him. His name, Jem, is Lillingworth. He was a captain once, in the army. Now you know all about it."

"Oh, it is too dreadful!" said Marion. "Jem, you know your mother is not in earnest."

"She is, though," said Jem, nodding his head—"real good earnest. She makes me say that patter every day. Lord! I know all about Captain Lillingworth. He's my father, and I've got to kill him."

"No, no; it's only make-believe, Jem. Do you not know it is wicked to talk about killing any one?"

"Wicked!" said his mother—"as if he knows anything

about religion! Do you think *I* could teach him religion —I?"

"Have you never been to church, Jem?"

He shook his head.

"Not such a fool as that," he said; "one of the boys was nabbed last Sunday for just looking inside. Got locked up all night, he did, and never done nothink."

"Have you never been to school, Jem?"

He shook his head again.

"One of the boys says we shall all have to go soon, and get whacked."

"Can you read?"

"Yes, I can read some, but not much. I can read the bill for the *Echo*. See, I can write a little, too." He took a piece of chalk out of his pocket. "There"—he traced on the door the letters E C H O, only the C was turned backwards—"that spells 'Echo.' I've made it wrong somehow. Never mind, all the boys mostly can write 'cept me, and I'm learning myself."

"Does he know nothing at all, this poor boy?" asked Marion.

"Nothing," said his mother—"nothing. Best that he should know nothing. We have been thrown upon the streets together, he and I. Let him live in the streets all his life. We shall both die there."

"One of the boys knows a hymn," said Jem, after thinking the matter over. "He learned it to me. I can say it all a'most—

> 'Adama Neeve was made of clay,
> Such was his petty cree—'

I forget—yes, 'his petty cree.'" (Perhaps he meant pedigree.)

> 'And in the garden he could play
> If he'd obedient be.

> 'Adama Neeve he looked about;
> There were apples red and brown,
> And he got a stick, and they turned him out
> 'Cos he knocked the apples down.'

There's more, only I've forgotten it since the cab ran over me."

"Don't look at the boy that way, Marion Revel," cried his mother, stopping her work for a moment. "And what are you crying for? He's all right."

The boy proved upon the spot that he was all right by a violent fit of coughing, followed by a terrible shaking of his limbs, which seemed dislocated for the moment by the energy of St. Vitus.

"We've had a bad winter, and a long winter, too—that's given him a cough; and then came the cab. But we shall get on now, sha'n't we, Jem, my pretty?"

Jem nodded and winked, trying to look jolly; then he shivered, and pulled the blanket round his neck. From time to time the fit seized him, when his limbs tossed themselves about without his control, and his teeth chattered.

"It is too dreadful!" Marion murmured. "What can I do for you—what can I do?"

"It is not so dreadful as it looks. So long as the weather is warm, I don't mind so much; and Jem is a good boy, too —ain't you, Jem? When he's well he'll bring home sometimes a couple of shillings a day, won't you, Jem?"

"Once I brought home three shillin's."

"So you did, Jem; so you did."

"That was when I held the gentleman's horse, and he gave me half-a-crown and thought it was a penny."

"I spent it all," Mrs. Spenser explained, defiantly. "Jem had none of that windfall, poor lad."

"One of the boys—" Jem began again.

"You *must* do something for the boy," Marion said. "Perhaps I shall be able—"

"Marion Revel, you let my boy alone, and I will let your brother and sister alone—that is a bargain. If I choose that the boy shall grow up as he is growing up, that is my business; we shall be revenged so, somehow, on his father. I am a miserable woman, and he is a gutter boy. Some day we shall find him out."

"Do not think of revenge. What good will revenge do?"

"You are a fool, Marion Revel!" the woman replied, in her clear silvery tones and her quiet manner. "Revenge is what I dream of. Every day that I wake in this den, and feel myself lower than I was yesterday, I think more and more of revenge. I want to make *him* suffer as he has made me suffer. I want to curse him through his son. He'll feel that, if he can feel anything, when he sees him."

Then Jem had another attack of coughing.

"One of the boys—" he began again, but choked.

"Let the man come here," Mrs. Spenser said. "Let him come here and look at the boy. Let him see us both; let him think what I am, and what I used to be before he came, with his handsome face; and then let us two, Jem and me, haunt him and follow him about wherever he goes—won't we, Jem?"

"All right," said Jem, whose notions of a vendetta were as yet imperfectly developed. "All right, mother. Rip him up and cut him down."

"Now go, Marion Revel. No; if you give me any more money, I shall only spend it on myself. If you give me any furniture, I shall sell that for drink when the fit comes upon me. I have got enough money now, and Jem shall have some tea to-night."

"And shrimps, mother. Let's have shrimps."

"Yes, and shrimps and bread and butter. That's what Jem shall get. I shall have gin."

She had preserved throughout the same defiant air. When she saw the tears in Marion's eyes, she became more defiant still. When the girl patted her boy's cheek, she had a pang of jealousy; when she took her money, she laughed with a little triumph. She was never quite certain whether to regard Marion as an enemy or a friend, but leaned to the former.

"Let me come again to see Jem."

"You may see him any day you like; all you have to do is to go down Holborn, where he hawks the *Echo* and his cigar-lights. Ask any boy there for Rickety Jem."

"I'm Rickety Jem," said the lad, with pride.

"Don't you see he is ill? Don't you notice his cough and his bright eyes? And look how thin his cheek is," said Marion.

The mother tossed her work aside, and took the boy's head in her hands.

"Don't try to frighten me, Marion Revel. The boy's going to get strong and well. They are growing pains he has, and the winter's made him weak. Is not that so, Jem? Why, I feel him getting stronger every day."

"All right, mother," said Jem. "One of the boys said as another boy said as I wasn't going to be long for this world. Then we all laughed."

"Go away, Marion Revel. You will bring bad luck on my boy and me. You ought to, I'm sure. What can one of your name bring me, except misery?"

"Won't you let me come again to see the boy?"

"No—yes. Come if you like. What does it matter After all, you are a good woman, Marion Revel." Her voice sank a little, but she raised it again. "It's a pity you're fallen off in your looks, because you were once a very pretty girl—a very pretty girl indeed. And now your figure is quite gone, Marion." She had resumed her place at the table, and her fingers were nervously playing with her cardboard and scissors. "Sixteen years ago, now—you must have been eleven, and the others were seven and five. They were both like their mother, I remember, but you were like your father. A grave little girl you were, full of queer sayings. O Marion! do you remember the questions you used to ask—such questions, which not even your father could answer?"

The tears came into her eyes as she recalled the old days, and her voice became unsteady. She waited a moment, and then went on, in a clear and deliberate tone—

"I used to lie awake at night and think of the other two, Marion; but I don't dare think of them any more—it drives me mad only to see either of them at your window. Not to see them at all, and to think of them still, would have driven me mad then; but I had my boy here to nurse, and that kept me in my senses. God knows it would have been better for me to have lost them quite. Sometimes I used to wonder what I did it for. Now I have long left off wondering or thinking why I was so wicked and so foolish. But once I used to think a good deal about it. It was after he left me—left me like a flower he had put in his button-hole one day and thrown aside the next. He was a cruel and a selfish man; he made me repent the very day I did it. He never spared a woman in his passion; he used to boast that to my very face, when it was too late; he used to give me the shameful history of all the women he had led astray."

"Do not think of him," said Marion.

"Years ago, when Jem was a little baby, I used to think of him every day and every night. I used to curse him. One of my prayers was heard—just think of that—because I learned by accident that he disgraced himself, and was obliged to leave the army. That was something, but not enough. No, I want to see him lose all the money that gets him the things that he loves, and go down to the grave in miserable poverty like this. He likes luxury of any kind: let him make his dinner off a crust of bread, and his supper off a red herring on lucky days. Then I shall be satisfied. No," she added, "it is not true. I shall never be satisfied, because I never could forget what I lost. O Marion! Oh, the days gone by! Oh, the happy, peaceful days when I was loved and trusted, and my children put their arms round my neck and said their prayers."

"God will forgive," whispered Marion.

"But will *he* forgive? No: it is impossible. I haven't done any harm to God," she said, wildly. "I could face Him. It is the *other*. How could I ever bear to look at him again?"

"He has long since forgiven every sin against himself, because his own are forgiven. Oh, believe it, and let your poor heart be softened."

Marion bent her face and touched those guilty cheeks with her own pure lips. The woman shrank back with a little cry, and covered her face again with her hands. It is hard to follow the current of a mind like that of this poor creature. For the first time, Marion seemed to have roused in her some sense of human regret, if not repentance. She was not, then, utterly insensible. I believe that prison chaplains and matrons tell the same story. There is no man or woman so hardened but that there is some weak point. Marion had found the weak point. A little sympathy, a little patience, silence on certain points connected with the past—these things seemed to touch her.

But what hope, what future, was there possible, even if the better nature were thoroughly awakened?

She sat silent at the table, and then she began again with the pasteboard and the scissors; then she spoke in a whisper, like the far-off murmur of a shell—

" I don't think," she said, not looking up—" I don't think there is a single woman in all the world except you, Marion, who would do what you are doing. Oh, how hard they are, all of them, and unforgiving! Not but what it's right and what we ought to expect, Marion. You must not bring yourself to any harm through me. Would *they* like it if they were to find out? Do you think you ought to come here? Remember everything. Make your heart hard against me, my poor girl. I am only a drag upon you. I take away your money as fast as you get it; and you are afraid that I shall say or do something to frighten the other two. Do you think you *ought* to come here?"

The soft, dreamy voice ceased. Then there came a change in her face, swift and sudden; but Marion could not see it, any more than she could see the suspicions in her brain.

" Let me come again for the boy's sake. It is dreadful to see him so ill and so ignorant. Let me come and teach him something."

Mrs. Spenser dashed the hair from her face, and sprang to her feet, standing on the mattress where her boy lay—large-eyed, wondering, expectant from long experience of a row— like a tigress over her cub.

"No, no!" see cried. "Leave my boy alone. You ought
to hate him; you ought to wish him dead; you ought to
loathe his sight. Marion Revel, why do you come here at
all? What right have you in this house? Go away, and
wait till I ask you for more money. I shall work no longer.
Why should I work for twelve hours a day to earn two and
twopence? Go you and make money to keep me and the
boy, as well as those other two helpless creatures. Go away,
before I do you a mischief. Jem, you miserable son of a
miserable mother, take this shilling and crawl out and
get the gin. Now, Marion Revel, what do you say to
that?"

CHAPTER XXII.

THE sunny nature, as we call it, is one so greatly lauded
and envied that it goes to one's heart to criticise it.
Nevertheless, the truth is that "sunniness" very often comes
from sheer insensibility, and a dislike to disagreeable things.
I fear that the sweet good temper always shown by Fred
Revel, and his affectionate behaviour to his sisters, took
their origin in these natural causes. He had small capacity
for sympathy, a profound inability to calculate the chances
of the future, and was impressed to so high a degree with a
sense of the beauty of things beautiful, that it was, with
him, almost a disease. Naturally, therefore, it cost him no
effort to regard his sisters with affection, especially the
younger, whose beauty he could see was a thing quite rare
and unapproachable.

He thus made up in a measure for his laziness by his
affection. He repaid devotion by gentle words, and even
caresses. When he was at home—which was not often—he
was at the orders of his sisters. He had been known to
spare Marion a journey to Burls's shop; he would sometimes
lie on the sofa and read to them; on Sunday he had occasionally gone to church with them; and on Sunday evenings,
when Winifred Owen always came upstairs to have tea with
his sisters, he stayed with them, helped in the preparation

of the simple banquet, sang with Adie afterwards, and comported himself with all the steadiness of a Sunday-school teacher.

Unfortunately, these loving natures are like bindweed, convolvulus, or clematis, inasmuch as they are apt to spread the tendrils of affection in unexpected directions—other, in fact, than those of sisterly affection. It was not enough that the young man should be loved by his sisters—that is a kind of affection which does not satisfy; he craved for the deeper and fuller stream of passion. He found it with Winifred Owen; and at this period of the history their love passages had already gone a very great deal farther than even Mr. Owen, jealous for his daughter, suspected. It is not, therefore, surprising to hear that, when Winifred's work at the telegraph office was finished, it often happened to her to find Fred Revel waiting to take her home.

The same thing happened to many of the young ladies in the department, and was indeed so common an occurrence as to excite no other feeling with those who went home unaccompanied than that of envy. None of these telegraph clerks, however, were waited for by persons of their own sex. It was also remarked that the gentleman who came for Winifred Owen possessed personal attractions of a higher order than most of the cavaliers in waiting. The girls of her Majesty's telegraph department are not, it must be understood, given to the dangerous practice of casual and meaningless flirtation. You will not meet them at theatres with gentlemen who hail from the Temple, nor are they to be accosted in Westbourne Grove by invincible young City men. Not at all: their behaviour is as circumspect as their position is respectable. There is no line of work in which a girl's reputation is safer than in the telegraph offices. Add to this, if you please, that her Majesty's Government—which is piling up pyramids of material for repentance in making contracts for work, which ought to be done at first hand, with people who get their profit out of the underpaid women in their employ—has not yet, happily, applied the dire and dreadful rule of supply and demand to the telegraph service.

The girls are honestly paid and fairly worked, and they are not bullied like the poor girls in shops; so that they retain their self-respect.

Of course, it was the one piece of folly wanting to fill Fred's cup that he should fall in love. Perhaps, if he had done it a year or two before this, when his indolence was not as confirmed as a bodily blemish, it might have been good for him. In a healthy state of education we shall train up the boys to fall in love as a duty at two or three and twenty. As it is, those of our youth who permit themselves this natural emotion at so early an age are the uncalculating and the sanguine, like Fred Revel.

How handsome he was, as he waited for the girl clerks to come out, and watched for Winifred among them! As yet, their wooing had the subtle charm of secrecy; and Fred belonged to the girl, though she alone knew it, by ties that could not be broken.

Her pulse beat higher with pride as she took his arm, and walked with him down the unfashionable street of Newgate. She loved him. It is assuredly not the first time that a woman has given her heart to a man whom she knows to be —soften it—deficient in the more robust virtues. The worthless ne'er-do-well has for her some secret charm of manner which the world fails to detect. Was not Mrs. Medlar in love with Dicky Carew? Was not Bluebeard idolised by every one of his wives in turn? Did not Acte, the sweet and pure-minded Christian, love Nero, the Anti-Christ? As if we wanted examples! Winifred loved this handsome and indolent young Absalom, who, for his part, loved the bright-eyed little telegraph girl as much as it was in his nature to love anybody.

"We must be more careful, Winifred," said Fred, in his airy manner. "You know what they say—I mean in the lower classes, of course—about keeping company? What an expression! They will think in Lowland Street that we are keeping company, will they not?"

Winifred had heard the expression employed in her own department.

"They have not the chance," said Winifred, squeezing his arm; "we are too clever for them, because we always part at the corner of Tottenham Court Road."

"Not to-night, my love," he replied. "I have got some money; let us have a drive in a hansom through the parks."

"Fred, dear," she said, timidly, "I should like it so much —oh! so much! but would it be quite right? Do you think we ought? You know yesterday poor Adie had no dinner, because there was no money."

He was silent for a moment, and something like a blush crossed his face.

"I did not know," he said. "We will walk."

They walked, and he talked.

"I wish your father liked me, Winifred. It is a bore, considering everything. I met him on the stairs this morning, and he stopped to say, with a long face, 'Young man, the soul of the sluggard desireth, but hath nothing. Have you found any work yet?' Any work, you know; as if I was a common clerk or a railway porter."

"Well, but, Fred"—Winifred was jealous for her father— "what else should he say? You do want work, do you not?"

"Say? Anything. But then, Winifred, you do not understand—how should you?" He laid his hand upon hers. "What a pretty little hand it is! I think I shall never get tired of it—and mine, isn't it?"

"All yours, Fred, dear."

"Let me buy it a new pair of gloves."

To be sure, Winifred's gloves were a good deal worn, and showed signs of frequent repair. I do sincerely believe that her character will be greatly raised when I state that she had the courage to refuse a new pair, on the same ground as she had refused the drive—the plea of poverty.

"Then, Winifred, if I must not give you anything, let us go somewhere where we can have a quiet talk together."

It was, as has been stated a chapter or two back, in the sweet spring month of April, when the sign of the zodiac— whatever the zodiac may be—is Gemini, the twins, as we call them, but the older astronomers named the Maid and the Man—that is to say, it was the acknowledged season of love. Over in the west—for it was seven o'clock—the sun was going down behind a lurid mass of sapphire, smoke, and blood-red cloud. Fred hurried his companion away from the tumult of Holborn into the quiet retreat of Lincoln's Inn Fields. He opened the gate of the gardens with a key, to which he certainly had no right, and took Winifred into the quiet gardens, where the lilac was bursting into bloom, the trim lawns were fragrant from an afternoon shower, and the tulips were gorgeous in their short-lived splendour: a Cockney garden, if you please, but pleasant and sweet to the girl.

"Let us walk up and down here," said her companion. "It is always quiet and undisturbed, and we can talk."

The gardens were quite deserted—there was no one to listen to them, no one to see them, no one to disturb them. An ideal place for a London idyll. Winifred's lover walked beside her, as beautiful as Apollo; his head thrown back with a careless grace that you may see in the early portraits of Byron, his eyes flashing, his lips, like Adie's—half parted, the very type and ideal, to outward seeming, of early manhood, full of noble thoughts and lofty aims. He looked strong and resolute, because he was dreaming great things as he walked. He was on a Royal Road to greatness—such greatness as means wealth and comfort; and was marching along it in imaginary state and splendour, with Winifred beside him.

She did not share his dreams, this simple girl who was in love with him, but she looked up at him with eyes that drank in long draughts of admiration. Heavens! that such a hero—so brave, so handsome, *going to be so good*—should see anything in her, the telegraph girl, to love; and what—what must be the nobleness of the man who could so stoop beneath him as to marry her? Yes, to marry her. Winifred was married; Fred Revel was married; they were actually married to each other. They went to the parish church one Sunday morning—Mr. Owen never went to any church at

s

all, but stayed at home, to read either Plutarch or the Book of Proverbs—where the banns had been put up among half a hundred others, and were married; and no one, not a soul, knew anything about it. It was just before her father's warning, which, like many a prophetic announcement, came too late to be of any use; and the words never ceased to ring in her brain.

"He's a worthless chap, my girl."

"Winifred," Fred began, bending his gracious head with such a sweet condescension as the king who reigned in Shushan from India to Ethiopia might have observed to that fair Jewess Esther after her twelvemonth's washing in oil of myrrh and sweet perfumes, or as Solomon bestowed upon the nameless nymph whose lips were as a thread of scarlet— "Winifred, my darling, do you think, like all the rest, that because I have done nothing yet, I *can* do nothing?"

The girl shook her head at these assuring words. Of course she did not.

"And suppose—suppose, Winifred—that I were to come to you with such a position as would be worthy of you—"

"Fred, I am only a telegraph girl, but, oh, so proud of you!"

"The wife takes her husband's position," he replied, with the grandest air. Had he been the Earl of Burleigh, his condescension could not have been greater. As my wife you will be, not Mrs. Revel, but Madame la Comtesse. Would you like that? For I intend to resume the title which my father dropped as soon as we get back into our old position."

"But—but—oh, I am not fit to be a great lady."

"You will learn, Winifred—you will easily learn. Marion and Adie will teach you. You are quick and clever. I shall not be ashamed of my wife."

"To be your wife before all the world!" she gasped. "It takes away my breath."

"Sit down," he said, "and let us talk about it calmly."

He placed her on a garden seat, and sat by her, taking her hands in his. It was as yet all too much happiness for the girl, who with him could only breathe and feel.

"They call me idle, I know," he said, thinking over Dr.
Chacomb's accusing speech. "They think I am good for
nothing but loafing about and playing billiards. It is not
true, Winifred. Adie will tell you, if you ask her, that I am
always thinking about what I shall do. Why, I am ready
to do anything—anything that a gentleman may do, and
never afterwards be ashamed of. They shall see—they shall
see what I will do."

Winifred was wholly carried away by the infection of his
ideas.

"Adie is right," she cried. "She always says you have
the noblest of hearts."

"Adie is the best girl in all the world. Now, Winifred
dear, I am going to tell you a great secret."

"What is it, Fred?"

"Do not laugh, and do not tell any one. When I was in
France with Lord Rodney Benbow, I was told by a woman
from Algiers, an Arab woman, that there were to be great
troubles before me, but that after three or fours years all
would be smooth. Then my father died suddenly—killed by
a fall, and then all our troubles began. As for Adie and
myself, we have always felt that we should pull round
somehow."

"But do you believe what a fortune-teller says?"

Winifred had been brought up in a healthy contempt for
the petty supernatural.

"No—that is, I believe we shall get out of the hole we are
in somehow. Of course, I do not believe what a fortune-teller
says"—but he did—"and I have plenty of irons in the fire.
I will tell you: first, I have put down my name at the
Colonial Office; then I have applied for a nomination to the
Foreign Office. If these do not come to anything I have
promised a man I know—not a gentleman—a bonus of ten
per cent. on any good thing he gets me. Unfortunately, all
the secretaryships are given to men who can put capital in
the company. Besides this, Dicky Carew thinks he knows a
paper where they would like a man to send West End things
to them." Fred spoke as if he belonged without a doubt to

the highest stratum. " Out of all this something will come,
surely. What would you like best? They might make me
governor of some small West Indian Island to begin with.
Should you like that? 'His Excellency Sir Frederick Revel,
K.C.B., Governor of the Starboard Islands, accompanied by
Lady Revel, has returned to England on furlough, and
yesterday dined with the Queen at Osborne.' That would
read well, wouldn't it? Or they might make me secretary
of legation at Vienna. Society is not so good at Vienna as
it used to be, I fear, but we need not be too particular; and
it is a place where we could make ourselves comfortable. Or
perhaps you would prefer being attached to the embassy at
Paris? There may be a better chance for a diplomatist,
especially one of French descent, in Paris."

" O Fred!"—the prospect was altogether too dazzling, and
she gasped, " I can never become a great lady—never! I shall
only make people laugh at you, for marrying such a simple
girl. How will you like to have ladies laughing at my want
of manner?"

" I have thought of all that," he replied, as if the thing
were quite settled, and nothing left but to arrange the
details—" I have thought of all that. Before we leave town,
you shall live for a few weeks with a family who will form
you. Your taste in dress is already perfect—almost as
perfect as Adie's; and yours is a style of beauty which can
bear ornament, which hers can do without. I think you would
look very well with a diamond spray in your hair. I saw one
the other day in Bond Street which I thought would just do
for my pretty little girl. I mean some day to deck you up
in all the dainty things that money will buy. Then, if you
like, you shall learn some accomplishments—playing, singing, languages—all the little trifles that women pick up so
easily." He spoke as if they came by nature, or were to be
learned in a week or two. " The chief business is, of course,
the cultivation of manner and style. You must be, above all
things, *chic*. We should have to sink the school and the
connection with the—eh?—the Government department."

" Fred, I could never learn to be ashamed of my father."

"Ashamed? no, I suppose not. Only it will not do when we are in society to put the fact of the school in the foreground. A countess, you know, may be the daughter of anybody, but she does not generally tell all the world about it."

Winifred was silent. This kind of talk jarred upon her.

"And now that we are united, Winifred," the Prince went on, in a lordly way—"now that I have married you and made you happy, you will take pains to fit yourself for the position you will occupy, will you not?"

"Yes, Fred," she answered him, humbly. "I will try all I can; only you must tell me what to do. Perhaps Adie will help me."

"But remember, dear, it must be a profound secret. I do not want anybody, not even Adie, to know anything about it. I can meet you in the evening, when you leave the office, and we can walk home together and talk; but no one need know till we are able to tell them—till I am able to take you away altogether."

"Oh, let me tell my father, Fred—poor father! And he loves me so!"

"Certainly not—on no account. I would rather you told Adie even—Only wait a little while, dear child, and we will tell all the world. Wait just a little. They must give me something good, with all my interest." At the moment he pictured to himself the whole of the Upper House tumultuously pressing his claims on dispensers of official sinecures. "Why, a commissionership in the Poor Law is worth about a thousand a year, and nothing to do for it. I should not be at all surprised if Rodney got me that."

"Are you quite sure, Fred?" (Winifred remembered what her father had told her. She blushed to remember that it came through a waiter)—"Are you quite sure that Lord Rodney is your friend?"

"Sure, Winifred? Why, we were friends at Oxford, and we got rusticated for the same thing. Then we were to have gone to Egypt together, only I did not get so far. Friends! why, Rodney would do anything for me—anything in the world."

It was an *idée fixe* with the young man that his one acquaintance in the world who had position had also unbounded influence, and was exercising it for him day and night.

As a matter of fact, Mr. Owen's information was perfectly correct. Lord Rodney, who had as yet no influence whatever, was tired of constantly lending money to a man who seemed incapable of doing anything for himself. He resolved—and his resolution was arrived at, unluckily, just before this very evening—to give Fred Revel no more money.

"Come, Winifred," he said, "there is no one here; put your arms on my neck, so. Now kiss me, and say you love me."

She did as she was told.

"And I have made you happy?"

"Yes, very happy. O Fred, Fred!" she burst out crying —"you *will* leave off going to billiard-tables, and—and— work, and be good to your sisters, will you not?"

He was moved by her tears, but very angry at her words. Work! Leave off billiards! Trifles of this kind, when he was glowing with the prospect of future greatness!

"That shows the kind of thing people say of me," he replied. "Well, there is nothing to be done but to leave the beastly hole where we are now, and go somewhere else. I shall see Rodney to-morrow, and tell him that he must get to work in earnest for me."

"Forgive me, Fred."

"I forgive *you*, my dear," he said, magnanimously; "but I do not forgive people who try to set you against me. There, let us have no more tears. Come, my dear, you are married to me now, and you must believe in me, you know."

"Yes, Fred."

Winifred was very humble as they left the garden. She clung to her lover's arm, because her eyes were full of tears, and her brain was turning round and round. He was silent too, because, as will happen in every fool's paradise, a word of the girl had knocked over his palace walls about his ears. It was as if the sun was suddenly hidden behind the clouds.

Was Lord Rodney his friend?

If not, then he had nothing to hope from any one.

Would he give up billiards, and work and be good to his sisters?

Two of the four sovereigns he had taken from Adrienne were in his pocket still. Where were the other two? And what about the debt—the debt of which his sisters knew nothing?

They parted sadly at Tottenham Court Road, with a silent shake of the hand. The young man walked along Oxford Street, moody and miserable. Presently he came to a door at which his feet stopped of their own accord, and without any volition on his part. Then they turned to the right, went up certain steps, and entered a room where three or four men were playing billiards.

The marker nodded familiarly. As Fred took down his cue, he whispered to him—

"The bill falls due in a day or two."

"Renew it, then, as you did for me last time."

"Can't, Mr. Revel — can't. The other party wants his money."

Fred made no answer. He replaced the cue, and presently left the billiard-room, to wander backwards and forwards in the street.

Work? He *could* not work.

Winifred went home. Her father was out, and she sat down, trying to think over what had happened. She was as sad as her lover. Was this right? Was this the way in which young ladies should be wooed, won, and married? Why, he had made sure, to begin with, that she loved him. So she did; but it seemed strange that he should assume it from the very first. And he had ordered matters his own way, without a word of remonstrance from her. She had begun the wifely obedience while yet a maid.

"He is a worthless chap."

Her husband! Husband of a fortnight—married in St. Andrew's, Holborn.

Her father's words rang in her brain with a dreadful pertinacity. She knew that they were true. In her heart she knew that all these fine promises would end in nothing. She foresaw the unhappiness she might be bringing upon herself. And yet, like Marion, towards whom Fred might sin seventy times seven and still be forgiven, she loved him none the less. For it was the strange property in the boy's character that all women who knew him loved him, and all men who knew him liked him; and yet all, somehow, despised him.

She loved him; that was all. She went to her bed-room at the back, and prayed for him. She gave him what she had—her prayers and her love.

When her father came home at nine o'clock, he found Winifred bright and cheerful. The simple family supper was on the table, and the lamp was lit.

Winifred was rather silent.

At ten she put her work together. It was her wont to leave her father to smoke his pipe by himself.

"Father," she whispered, kissing the rugged and wrinkled face, which looked always so beautiful and kind to her— "father, if Fred Revel turns out different to what you thought, you will take back your words, won't you?"

"What words, my dear?"

"You said he was worthless. You meant that he could do no work, you know."

"Winifred!" he started up in his chair, took both her hands, and looked at her. She tried to lift her eyes, but could not.

"No, father, no," she sobbed; "ask me no questions."

He drew her to his knees, and held her as he had held her many thousands of times, when she was a little thing, and he was father and mother both to her. His left arm was round her waist, and her head was on his shoulder, and he was soothing and patting her cheek.

"My child, my daughter, my own Winifred!" he said,

"tell me what you like—what you like, my dear. Forget what I said. No doubt I am a fool, and he is full of good qualities—as good as he is handsome ; and nobody could be handsomer than he is. Only remember, my dear, what I have taught you. A virtuous woman—her price is above rubies. Be good, my child. Promise me—no, promise me nothing ; only be good, my child."

She left him presently, but the schoolmaster had no sleep that night. His passionate Welsh nature was on fire with indignation against the handsome boy who had stolen away his child's heart. He walked up and down the room ; he lay down, but could find no rest.

"If he does her any harm," he said ; "if he plays his game of gentleman with my girl—I—"

In the morning, he was quite grave and silent during breakfast, making no observations at all out of Solomon's Proverbs. Winifred gave him his tea, with downcast eyes. When she rose to go to her work, she said, hesitatingly—

"Father, you do not think the worse of any man because he is poor, do you ? "

He shook his head and brightened up, seeing his opportunity.

"A good name," he replied, "is rather to be chosen than great riches ; and loving favour rather than silver and gold. Winifred, find me, if you can, a single question that Solomon does not answer. Go to your office, my dear, and don't fret. 'A merry heart doeth good like a medicine.'" When she had gone, his face clouded again. "I wish," he said, "that the passages about fools and folly were not so fresh in my mind to-day. Solomon had a wonderful eye for a fool—'The father of a fool hath no joy.' To be sure, I shall only be his father-in-law."

Then the clock struck nine, and he went into the school and caned Candy Secundus. Invigorated by his anxiety, he inflicted upon that culprit a most astonishing punishment ; insomuch that when he went home, his mother drew the inference of greater criminality than was absolutely the case, and gave the unfortunate boy a second caning before he went

to bed, to enforce and underline the lesson. To Candy
Secundus, therefore—it is a remarkable instance how men
and women live unconsciously for each other—Fred's wedding
brought two chapters of Lamentations, forming both a morning and an evening lesson.

CHAPTER XXIII.

IT is not an easy thing for a physician to get away from
patients, even at the beginning of the London season.
But it was absolutely necessary for Dr. Chacomb to see his
unfortunate cousin after this new misfortune which had
befallen him. For his own part, he took the blow with the
serenity of one who had received many buffets from fortune.
If there should be a child, farewell to his heirship. If the
woman played her cards well, farewell to his rule at Chacomb.
In any case, it was a serious check on his projects; for he
meditated great improvements on the estate. Taking the
position of a country gentleman, just as the heir presumptive
to an earldom might almost consider himself a peer, he gave
his attention to questions affecting land, contracts with
tenants, drainage, high farming, and other things. He
talked over these subjects with authority, as one personally
interested, and, in fact, enjoyed the additional importance
accruing to him as the future possessor of a goodly
heritage.

No light owned by Dr. Joseph Chacomb was at this period
allowed to burn under a bushel, or, indeed, to burn at all
save at such times as might be beneficial to himself. He
owed, in fact, everything to the Chacomb estate. An adventurer, a shady general practitioner, a projector of companies
which, if they were floated, always came to wreck, a haunter
of tenth-rate clubs, where very questionable gentlemen associated to drink and tell stories, he found suddenly, ready to
his hand, the rents of his cousin's property. He borrowed—
who could resist the temptation of borrowing? He founded
with great pains his Royal Hospital for Gout, on which he

mounted the ladder of professional reputation. He left his old companions—the bond of friendship among the impecunious is like that among savages, uncertain and liable to sudden tempests of suspicion. He put off the habits and language of their class; changed his channel of thought; cultivated those manners which make the man; and became —a gentleman.

It required careful observation and long familiarity now to distinguish any trace of his twenty years' vagabondage in the polished doctor. He even became an author, and published that treatise of his "On Gout and its Cognate Diseases" which is still the standard work on the subject, although Dr. Porteous, of Savile Row, always declared that it was translated from the French—a language which Joseph Chacomb had learned in its purity in the Quartier Latin. He had a solid-looking house in Adelaide Street, Carnarvon Square; he had a professional carriage, with the Chacomb arms, and the soberest of liveries; he had a large medical and general library; he had a servant—the prince of servants —a man whose manners proclaimed him born to be a master of a college; he had a circle of acquaintance, creditable in themselves, and likely to advance his reputation; he gave dinner parties, at which he told admirable stories. All these things were done and established. Chauncey Chacomb might develop into a Brigham Young in the matter of wives without affecting the doctor's position, credit, and prosperity. All this was his by right—subject, of course, to the few thousands he had borrowed. He was unmistakably chief physician of the hospital, he had undoubtedly composed a great work, and his doors were besieged by clients.

If there was an air of mystery about the doctor's antecedents, that helped him. Joe Chacomb the adventurer was gone and forgotten. In the new doctor, who sprang suddenly into reputation, people saw a man who was reputed to belong to an excellent Devonshire family, to be the heir of a large property, and who had spent the greater part of his life abroad in the pursuit of science—one who had travelled much, and observed a great deal. Dr. Porteous went so far, indeed, as to hint that perhaps he had travelled in the Isle of Portland, but that did no harm.

His prospects and professional name could not be hurt by Chauncey's conduct. What the doctor felt was a mixture of chagrin that he had been outwitted, pity for his cousin, and anger with himself for not looking after things more closely.

Outwitted by his own creature—the woman he had sent down because he could trust her; a woman whom he had known for twenty years, and whom he had employed as the first matron of the new hospital until he thought she would be more useful as housekeeper to Chauncey!

"It will be worse for her in the end," he said. "I know her. She will find it grand at first to order the people about; then she will feel dull because no one will call upon her; then her temper will break out—Julia always had the devil's own temper; and then—poor Chauncey! It's a deuced annoying business."

Chauncey, too, whose muddled brain was growing every day feebler and less able to bear excitement; who followed him about like some tame pet when he went to Chacomb: who was only to be trusted because he was harmless—what would be the effect of a nagging and discontented woman upon him? His health was daily failing—he wanted the gentlest treatment; and here was a headstrong and self-willed wife, in whose clutches he would be as a little child.

Joseph Chacomb was a kind-hearted man, albeit there were certain specks and blemishes, already indicated, on his character. He felt that Chauncey, now that he was clearly cracked, and that Gerald was lying dead in some African swamp, was specially under his own care. Chauncey belonged to him, and he would not brook any interference in his conduct of this interesting case.

Who could help feeling pity for a man so shipwrecked and afflicted? particularly when his hallucinations were accompanied by a sincere trust and faith in himself, the doctor.

It was a disarrangement of his comfortable plans. Chauncey

would not last long. Far from him the desire to wish his end—that would be unworthy of a man in his position; but soberly, in the nature of things, he could not disguise from himself, he said, the fact that Chauncey could not last long.

And then?

Chacomb Hall, with Marion.

The doctor was lonely in his grandeur; his evenings were dull and stupid. Sometimes he even longed for the jolly old days when he would take his pipe to a club where certain jovial fellows might be found, and where present Insufficiency of means—an admitted fact not to be disguised—did not prevent the flow of cheerfulness. He was not a reading man, and he had gradually got into the habit of imagining Marion sitting opposite to him, playing to him, presiding over his house, acting hostess to his guests.

"She is a lady, by gad!" he would say. "Dress her up, put a little more fulness in her cheeks, give her eyes a look less anxious, take that droop out of her mouth, and she'd be a credit to an earl. She's worth fifty of her sister. With those two in this house, with Chacomb Hall to fall back upon, what society is there in London that would not be open to me? I should get known to—to Cabinet Ministers, perhaps. I would get a title—Sir Joseph Chacomb, Baronet, M.D., of Chacomb. It is quite time that a Chacomb should distinguish himself. Dr. Porteous would go into an apoplexy. Perhaps there would be a little—eh? a little Joseph, successor and heir. I should like to have a son; I should like to bring him up as I ought to have been brought up myself. What a splendid boy the son of Joseph Chacomb, properly brought up, would be!"

It will be seen that the doctor was human in having this weak side to his character. He could be sentimental; he liked to dream—being as a rule, the most practical of creatures— of a future consisting wholly of domestic bliss.

"The old lot would laugh," he said to himself, "if they heard me. What fools men are! When one fellow blusters

against religion, and society, sham morality, and the rest of
it, the other fellows imitate, if not believe him : they bolster
up their miserable make-believe of social revolt by the example of the man they think the strongest. Lord, Lord! Joe
Chacomb was the advanced thinker; he was the materialist;
he was the man who believed nothing and feared nothing.
Look at him now; and where are all the rest? Gone back
to the hearth—*Christiani ad focos*—sitting as meek as mice
with their wives and children; going to Church every
Sunday; churchwardens; attendants at lectures; moral and
religious parents, acquiescing in the order of things as they
are; forgetful of the old discussions. Do they really forget, though? Is Paris as if it never existed? They used
to admire Joe Chacomb, who was afraid of nothing. By
gad! they shall admire me more now, and with better
reason."

CHAPTER XXIV.

DR. CHACOMB went down to Devonshire, and arrived at
Chacomb in time for dinner. He did not think it
necessary to announce his intentions. The house looked
quiet and even deserted; the gravel walks were half grown
over with grass; the beds, which ought to have been gay
with spring flowers, were bare; there was no one about the
place; the front door, generally open, was shut. What could
it mean? He walked to the back of the house, and entered
by the stables.

In the hall there was no one; in the breakfast-room no
one; in the dining-room, drawing-room, and library no one.
He thought of the Collection-room. Chauncey Chacomb was
sitting there in a corner, his head half resting on the uneven
shoulder, his face the image of despondency. He started to
his feet, however, when he saw his cousin, and rushed to
meet him in a kind of rapture.

"Joe!" he cried—"cousin Joe! O Joe! why were you
not here a fortnight ago?"

"Why did you not write to me? Come, Chauncey, this

is not the way a bridegroom should look. Cheer up, man; pluck up spirit, and be happy."

He shook his head dolefully.

"Happy!" he groaned. "Happiness and I parted four years ago, when I did—you know what. If you'd come a fortnight ago, you might have prevented it."

"My dear Chauncey, you are not a child in leading-strings. Come, sit down, and tell me all about it. Where is she?"

"She's upstairs in her bed-room, with her maid. She's trying on all the dresses. There are hundreds of them lying in drawers, just as my lady left them. She's got them now, with the jewellery, and she spends all her time pulling the things on and off again. She has sent away every one of the servants except the two grooms, because they were not civil, she says. And so here we are in this big house, we three— she, I, and the little maid, the only one she kept out of the whole lot. And, Joe, I am afraid."

"Nonsense, Chauncey; what should you be afraid of?"

But the doctor did not like the look of things.

"I am afraid of being robbed. Look at my Collection, left by itself all night. Why, some one might break in and carry off the very gems of the whole. I want to leave it, too, to the National Museum just as I have put it together."

"Very good, Chauncey, so you shall. I will charge myself with that part of your intentions, at any rate. But no one will steal into your Collection, be sure; no one knows the value of these things."

"That is not all," he went on, whispering. "I am afraid of her, Joe—I am desperately afraid of her. When night comes, I go away and lock myself up in Gerald's room—you know: the west wing, where there's only one door of communication, and I barricade that for fear she should get in."

"By Jove!" said the doctor, "this is conjugal felicity. This is an encouragement for a young bachelor like me to get married, isn't it?"

"Once in, I feel safe. I've got my pistols loaded, and there's a chain on the door. They shall never take me alive, Joe—never!"

"Come, Chauncey, do not talk nonsense."

"You I can trust; you would never betray your cousin, if only for the sake of old kindness, to say nothing of the family name. I never regretted telling *you*, Joe. But oh! if I had only kept it back from *her!*"

"Really, Chauncey, I must say, considering what humbug the whole thing is, it was worse than folly to tell her."

"It was not my fault, Joe. Why did you send her to me? It was lonely in the evenings, and I got to sit with her to escape the—you know—the faces, because I was miserable and afraid of being left alone. Then we used to have brandy and water, and she would talk to me. She's a clever woman. O Joe! what a clever woman she is! And she hid nothing from me, you know; told me all her life—"

Joseph smiled.

"How she had been on the stage, and all. The evenings were pleasant after she came; and then I told her how lonely I was, and how miserable; and one night—O Joe!—one night I told her everything, everything from the beginning. She heard me right through, and the next day she said that to make it safe I was to marry her right off. Because, you see, I was in her power."

"In her power? Ugh!"

The doctor's disgust that any one besides himself should have this man in his power was too great for any words.

He grunted.

"Go on, Chauncey. A pretty mess you've made of it for yourself and me too. Go on."

"She gave me no rest after that. She was at me all day. She made me tell the story of—you know—till I used to go into the woods, and shout and scream—I could not help it, Joe, indeed I could not—in order to get the dreadful thing out of my head. Oh, miserable wretch that I am! Why did the Lord suffer this evil to fall upon me? Why did I hate the man who never did me any harm at all, but only good? Joe, Joe, she went further; she said that if by any one telling, or any subsequent inquiries being made, I should be taken to Exeter—Exeter!" he cried, with a pitiful sob in his voice, "where I've been a county magistrate myself—tried for murder, and "—he dropped his voice to a whisper—"hanged, Joe, you, she said, would only be transported for life, as an accessory and accomplice."

"Oh, I am to get transportation for life, am I? Good, Mrs. Chacomb; very good."

"Buy her off, Joe—buy her off. She is dangerous."

"Not she, Chauncey. Don't be afraid. What else did she say?"

"She said you sent her down here because you thought she was your tool, and would do what you told her to do."

"She's a devil!" growled the doctor, moved to pity and wrath by the sight of his cousin's misery. Most people would resent the ill-treatment of a servant, pet, or slave, always supposed to be their own peculiar property. Chauncey was Joseph's own property, and here he was actually being bullied and ill-treated by somebody else! "Chauncey," he explained, "I give you my word of honour that I sent you this woman because I thought she would be an intelligent and kind-hearted housekeeper for you, and because, my dear fellow, I was afraid to leave you by yourself."

"Yes; it was very kind of you, Joe. I have not been myself since that dreadful day. Then she made me marry her; told me that it was the only escape for me from you; that she knew how to manage me, and that— Hush, here she comes."

The door opened, and the second Mrs. Chacomb sailed into the room, gorgeously attired in silks, which would have looked more than splendid had they been in the fashion; as it was, they were twenty years behind it, and so presented a grotesque appearance.

"Joe!" she cried—"I beg your pardon, Dr. Chacomb. My husband always calls you Joe."

"Pray call me Joe, Mrs. Chacomb,' he said, politely. "We are cousins, you know, now. We are not what we were once."

Which was true.

"We shall have dinner as soon as you are ready, Joe,"

T

she replied, graciously, but with an obvious uneasiness.
"Why did you not say you were coming? I am afraid you
will fare badly."

As he left the room the doctor heard an angry whisper—

"What have you told him?"

"Nothing—nothing," replied her hapless lord and master,
relapsing into his usual melancholy taciturnity.

Joseph came down again quickly, and gave his arm to the
ex-housekeeper with much ceremony. He noticed with surprise that she squeezed it affectionately.

The dinner was wretched—a fowl badly cooked by the
little maid, and potatoes nearly hard. To make up, there
was a bottle of port, which appeared to be a standing part
of the evening meal, put out for the use of Mrs. Chacomb.
The doctor took his share, however.

The conversation languished, and Joseph found it insuffer-
ably dull. The woman at one end of the table, with her airs
and affectations, disgusted him; the man at the other moved
his innermost soul to pity and contempt; the little girl who
waited on them, the only other creature in the big house,
trembled at every movement of her mistress.

"Where are your servants, Mrs. Chacomb?" he asked,
when the girl had left them.

"Gone, Joe," she replied, with a greater confidence in
using the Christian name than she had shown before dinner.
"Gone, and a good riddance too."

"Get some more—get some more at once. Chacomb Hall
must not be left to the care of a child."

The woman resented his tone, but said nothing.

They did not adjourn, but sat round the fire after dinner,
in silence.

The clock struck nine; the squire rose solemnly, and
shook hands with his cousin.

"Joe, you are more than welcome here. I am *very* glad
you have come. Keep on coming. Come as often as you
can."

Then he took a candle and went away.

"My husband's habits are peculiar," said Mrs. Chacomb.

"At present he occupies the empty wing—Mr. Gerald's wing."

"I see."

Then the little girl brought brandy and cold water, and asked if there was anything else.

"You have looked to all the locks and bolts?"

"Yes, my lady."

Mrs. Chacomb had taught her to say "my lady," as a sort of reminder that she was no longer a housekeeper.

"Then you may go to bed."

"Do you mean to tell me that the poor child sleeps all alone in the empty servants' room?"

"No; she sleeps in the little room next to mine—the dressing-room."

And then the two were left alone in the great empty house, about which not a sound was heard save the cracking of the furniture and the wind in the trees outside.

"Lively, Joe, isn't it?" asked Mrs. Chacomb. "This is how I spend the evenings. I am not going to carry on like this always, though, and I let you know it."

"Julia," said the doctor, "what did you do it for? You have really made a great fool of yourself. I expected better things."

"Why does any woman marry a man who is a fool, and old to boot? Because he is rich."

"Of course, and because he is cracked, and you thought you could do what you liked with his money."

"Well, you've been doing what you like with it for four years."

"I was his cousin; you were, Julia, his housekeeper."

"Never mind what I was. I *am* his wife."

"So I suppose. And what if there was to be a row?"

"Ah, that would be bad, would it not?" she replied, with a cunning smile. "I should have to confess that my husband is a murderer, and his cousin an accomplice."

"Julia, don't be a fool. You don't mean to say you believe—"

' I do, though. I believe every word of it."

"Then leave off believing it, and try to be rational. The row I mean is quite a different thing. Suppose I was to say, 'This man has been forced into an unequal and unhappy marriage by a woman whom I sent down to take care of him —a woman who wormed herself into his confidence and traded on his fears; who found out the point in which his lunacy shows itself, and persuaded him that his hallucinations were a reality.' What should we see then?"

"I don't know, Joe. It would be an interesting thing to see."

"Do you imagine, Julia, that I cannot prove the death of Captain Revel to have been the purest accident?"

"What proof have you?"

"Read the account of the inquest, if you can get it. If not, wait till my proof is wanted again."

"I believe it would be awkward, in spite of what you say, if I were to declare that there is no hallucination at all."

"Melodramatic, Julia—not awkward at all. Effective, but useless. It reminds me of Sadler's Wells days, when you were an innocent and jolly young actress, not a scheming woman, compassing a selfish end by cruel means. Yes, cruel, Julia. It was a cruel thing to torture him as you did; and mark me, if you do it again, if you dare to allude to his miserable delusion, you leave Chacomb Hall at once. There, if you refuse, I take the thing into my own hands, and get a separation, exposing all the means—the unworthy means— used to force the poor man into a marriage with you. How would you like the servants one after the other giving their evidence?"

A random shot, but it told.

She was silent.

"One more thing, my friend Julia. Whatever power you had over Chauncey as his housekeeper you have lost by becoming his wife. You can't give testimony for or against your husband. It is a cruel and wicked law in most cases. In yours, my dear creature, it seems a most beneficent regulation. So, you see, you have been too clever for your own interests."

"At all events, I am his wife. And now, Joe, we will leave all stupid talk about delusions. Chauncey may be mad or not, just as you like. Meantime I am the mistress of Chacomb Hall. I mean to receive the rents, and to have things exactly as I please."

"I was coming to that point next," said the doctor. "The fact is, that the news of your marriage forced me to look into my own rights and powers. You know that I have managed the Chacomb property for four years. Pray understand at once that I intend to go on managing everything down here —and everybody. I am resolved that the Chacomb property shall be wisely administered, and the present owner shall be kindly treated. If you attempt to interfere, I will separate you from your husband on the ground of his lunacy. I nominated myself before as the trustee of the estates, and if I meet with opposition I will be nominated by the Court of Chancery. Be under no false impression of your own import-ance—you have none. You are of less account now than you were before your marriage, because then you were a trusted servant, and you are now—or you may be if you choose—a suspected enemy."

"Pray go on," she said. "I am to be nothing, I suppose."

"Nothing at all. You may keep up your own dignity as before. You will be under my orders, or you will leave Chacomb Hall."

"What are your orders?"

"Kindness and care for Chauncey; that the place is kept up properly; a quiet and decorous life for yourself."

"And if I refuse?"

"Separation, and as small an allowance as I can persuade the lawyers to make you."

"And Chauncey?"

"In that case I should get him a keeper of the other sex."

She poured out some brandy and water, and gave it him with a cheerful smile.

"Joe," she said, "you know I would not be such a bad lot as to round on your cousin, whatever he's done—though how in the world you can call it a delusion the Lord only knows. As for your orders, why, you dear old boy, when did I ever disobey you, except in marrying that poor little undersized Richard the Third sort of madman? Let us be friends."

"Only on condition of your carrying out faithfully all I want," said the doctor.

"Of course I will," she replied, with a wonderful clearing up of her face. Some women look so much better when they are humble and obedient. "Then let us have no more quarrelling. After all, I do like a masterful man. As for you, Joe, you always were masterful. I give in. I will do whatever you like. Shake hands, old fellow, and forget the row."

He shook her ringed and jewelled fingers with more ceremony than she cared for. A little of the old ease and familiarity would have been more agreeable to her.

"We will be friends," said the doctor, "so long as—"

"Yes, yes, I know. You shall be obeyed. Did I not always obey you when you hadn't a red cent in your pocket, and was only Joe Chacomb—rattling Joe—marching about behind the scenes as if the place belonged to you? Those were the real jolly times. Oysters and stout—"

"Oysters were sixpence a dozen then," said the doctor, with a sigh of sympathy. "The wind used indeed to be tempered to the shorn lamb. How the deuce do medical students manage now, I wonder?"

"You sang a good song then, Joe."

"I did," he said, shaking his head.

"Do you remember that night when we had supper after Boxing Night at the Wells? Lotty Vandeleur—Wicks her real name was—and I danced after supper, for you to decide which danced best. You gave me the prize, I remember. This was the step."

She sprang to her feet, gathered up her skirts, and began to dance after the old-fashioned Columbine manner, which had, perhaps, certain advantages over modern burlesque dancing. It was a curious sight, this stout and jolly-looking woman of forty gravely pirouetting, with her heavy silks gathered up under her arm. The doctor looked on and laughed.

"Let me smoke, Ju, and it will be almost like old times."

He lit a cigar, and they fell back on talk, and reminiscences of a *jeunesse orageuse*. At two o'clock in the morning he got up and shook himself together.

"By Jove!" he said, "we were almost forgetting that I am forty-nine and you are forty. Good-night, Ju."

"Good-night, Joe. *On revient toujours à ses premiers amours.* As if you are ever going to forget the jolly days when you were young. Lord! I saw Lotty Vandeleur the other day—she keeps a lodging-house in the Hampstead-Road—and we talked about you. Joe, you were a bad boy— oh, a shocking bad boy! You are only better now because you are richer."

"Good-night, Mrs. Chauncey Chacomb."

"Good-night again, Dr. Joseph Chacomb, Physician to the Royal Hospital for Gout. Butter would not melt in your mouth now, would it? You do not remember the taste of oysters and stout, do you? You never heard of a ballet, did you? You never sat up half the night, with a houp-houp-houp-la! tra-la-la-la! and a party of youth and beauty, did you? Gravesend on Sunday is a thing you never heard of, isn't it? O Joe, to think that we should ever get old and be hypocrites! To think that we can only last ten years or so, and then have to give up being jolly, and pretend we like being miserable! Isn't it too bad? And, Joe, Joe, did you ever think that I should be such a fool, such a great, big, silly fool, as to marry that—that—"

"My cousin Chauncey, Julia? I did not think it, nor did you. But you did it. To know ourselves, Mrs. Chauncey, is the end of all philosophy."

CHAPTER XXV.

MARION was at work before Adie was dressed or Fred had risen, when a letter was brought her, addressed Marion Revel, *tout court*—without, that is, the ordinary gracious prefix of Miss or Madam. The writing was slovenly and half educated, the spelling was loose; but the postmark was Comb Leigh, and Marion tore it open with a trembling hand. She read it with bewilderment.

" MARION REVEL " (it began)—" My husband has received the letter you caused to be sent to him. He wishes me to say that he will give you nothing. That is all. For my own part, I beg to assure you, with the most profound respect, that you can do no harm to him, and that you had better not try it on. I defy you.—Yours to command,

"JULIA CHACOMB.

" *P.S.*—I know all about it."

There was a second postscript, written in a shaky hand, outside the envelope—

" She won't let me send you any money. Ask Joseph.— C. C."

What did it mean? Marion read and re-read the letter. Presently Adie appeared .

" Read that extraordinary letter, Adie, dear. Tell me what it means, if you can."

" It is from the new Mrs. Chacomb. I met the doctor yesterday—"

" Adie, I hope you remembered your promise not to speak to him about—"

" We did not talk about you, dear. I told him about Fred and the five pounds; and he laughed, and offered to give me some more."

" You did not take it?"

" No, Marion, I did not. Then he told me about Chauncey

Chacomb. He has married his housekeeper. I suppose the name of the lady is Julia. Evidently it is from her. Poor Mr. Chacomb! He used to be kind to us in his way."

"But what does the letter mean?"

"It means, Marion, I suspect—it means that Fred has been writing for money."

"O Adie, he would not—he could not!"

"He could, because he has written at different times to everybody who would lend him any. My dear Marion, Fred is one of those lazy lilies who neither can nor will toil and spin. He only borrows."

"But from Chauncey Chacomb! Oh! it would be impossible for him to borrow of Chauncey Chacomb."

"He wrote once to the doctor, I know, because the doctor told me so; and he is always writing to Lord Rodney Benbow."

"O Fred, Fred, what will become of us?" sighed Marion.

She thought of what the doctor had prophesied—that all the nobleness left in her brother would drop out of him little by little, till there should be no spark left at all; and she felt that this was a beginning of the end. What was she to do?

"It is clear what will become of Fred," said her sister, who was in a harsh mood towards her brother, in consequence of the embargo laid upon the four sovereigns. "It is clear enough that Fred never means to do anything except live upon his friends. Marion, don't say anything. I am as fond of my brother as you can be, but I am not so blind to his faults. I told you about the money yesterday. In the evening there was nothing left; he had paid away the whole of it in a single day. He does not go into the City at all, as he pretends; he spends the whole day—think of it, Marion, the whole day long—in billiard-rooms, playing pool for sixpences. When he is lucky, he wins ten or fifteen shillings a day, and sometimes more; with this he goes to a restaurant, and dines well. When he is unlucky, he makes you give him money for dinner, and dines well too."

"Don't, Adie! You are unjust."

"No, I am true. Whatever we do, Marion—whatever *you* do, for I can do nothing—we shall be always burdened with the weight of our brother, who is more idle than the shifting shadows."

The door opened, and he came in, fresh from dressing, radiant, handsome, and graceful.

Marion gave him the letter to read.

"Who is Julia Chacomb?" he asked, with the least possible blush.

"Mr. Chacomb is married again—to his housekeeper."

"Oh, I wish I had known it," said Fred.

"Frederick, is it possible that you have written for money to Mr. Chauncey Chacomb?"

"Yes, Marion, I have." He tried to put on a defiant and even consciously innocent air, but it was a failure; his eyes dropped before her look. "Yes, Marion, I have."

"Do you often write to people for money?"

"Sometimes I do. I write to whomever I think will help me. I am the head of the house, and I act as I think best in the interests of us all."

The girls looked at each other—Marion in dismay.

"Fred, I am in earnest," she said, after a little. "You are not to write to any one again for money. It is dishonourable."

"I am the best judge of that," he said.

"Then judge so for yourself. Above everything, remember, once for all, that I will not have any letters written to Chauncey Chacomb. There are reasons—O Heaven! are there not reasons?—why we can never, never, not in the last extremities of poverty, apply to Chauncey Chacomb."

"You talk strangely, Marion," said her brother.

"You talk wisely, Marion," said her sister.

"You forget, perhaps," continued Frederick, "that I am the master of my own actions."

"No, I do not forget. You will do what you think best

without any interference from us. But one thing I can do—"

"Marion!" cried Adie, alarmed.

"Adie, let me say it for once, and have done with it. The time is come when we must understand each other. Our father was the most honourable man in all the world—thank God for it!—and we, Adie and I, try to follow in his steps. You may stay with us as long as you will do the same. We shall not grudge you all you want, if we can afford it. We will give you what we can, and we will spare and save for you. But I will not, I cannot, keep even my own brother in the same house with me if I cease to think him—a gentleman."

Fred was perfectly silent.

"Fred, dear," she continued, caressing his head as if he were a child, "will you promise me—promise me, my dear —to write no more such letters? If we cannot give you quite all the luxuries you would like, we will give you all we can. The other day Adie went without food all day in order that you might dine well. You took all the money that our only friend had given her. To-day you shall have what we have, only leave us enough to buy something—it matters little what—to eat. Do what you like, my brother, if you cannot work or find work to do, but spare us dishonour. Let us keep our name, at least, from the mouths of people. Surely this is but a little thing to ask you."

Fred rose with something like an oath upon his lips; but it was bravado, not rage. He was not so hardened as not to feel the justice of his sister's reproaches.

"Let me go, Marion. One would think I was a—a—devil —a fiend. Is it I who keep you starving? Is it I who keep you living in this miserable hole, when—"

"It is, Fred—you, and nobody else," said Adie. "Marion has made nearly three pounds a week for months. With that and her own income we could all three live in a cottage, where there was fresh air at least. Out of the three you have taken two. And what have you done with it?"

"Why should I not write to Chauncey Chacomb? He

was my father's best friend—his only friend. It is his duty to help us. Marion, you forget yourself strangely when you lecture me on points of honour. Remember, if you please, that I have all my life associated with gentlemen and men of honour. I have—"

"Once more, my brother, understand me clearly. So long as I can make the money for you I shall not complain, provided—I will not repeat it."

He left his breakfast untasted, seized his hat, and went out.

"I am glad you spoke, Marion dear," said Adie; "not that it will do much good, but it shows Fred what we think. My dear, I will try to get something for myself to do—I will indeed—so as to relieve you a little."

Marion shook her head, and laughed through her tears.

"Poor Adie! I do not think you will do much good, but you may try. Women's work is not for girls who have no training and no art. Go and consult my wrinkled little friend, the schoolmaster. You can get nothing but good advice from him."

"Why cannot I paint like you, Marion? It seems so easy."

Adie's notions of art were limited. She could understand colour, as was proved by her dress, but she had no more feeling for form than generally belongs to her sex. It is strange that the sense of beauty—the sixth sense—is so deficient in one-half of the human race. Men very early learned it: witness the names in that brief chronicle of antediluvian women. Eve's name means breath of life: she is simply the mother, because poor Adam, who had no means of comparison, probably failed to appreciate her beauty at its true worth. Presently we get other names, which show the birth and the progress of Art, which is the recognition of beauty. Adah, "the beautiful," and Zillah, "the shadow," are wives of the first antediluvians who had a discerning eye. After Zillah came her daughter Naamah, "the lovely," who marks the period when men first began to be carried out of themselves by the radiance of a woman's beauty. The way was thus prepared for Helen. Philandering is, indeed, of extreme

antiquity ; for Lamech, who " slew a young man to his hurt "
—probably out of jealousy—was its inventor. But neither
Naamah, nor Zillah, nor Adah understood, we may be sure,
her own beauty, or the reason of the power she possessed
over men.

Fred Revel went away in a sore and savage frame of mind.
Marion's plain speaking humiliated him—everything that
was true seemed to humiliate him. And, moreover, there
were anxieties and difficulties of which Marion knew nothing
—which, if he dared to tell her, might bring some excuse for
his letter to Chauncey Chacomb. He was in a sore scrape—
a far worse scrape than Marion suspected.

Life looked black indeed to the young man as he turned
into the street that bright spring morning. It was not only
that he had spent on himself money which might have given
comfort to his sisters' lives, nor was it that he had written
letters to every man who might help him with money. As
for the former, perhaps he did not know the sacrifices daily
made on his behalf, or if he knew, he set the knowledge aside
with the reflection that the condition of things was only temporary, and would be changed—as soon as he got his appointment ; and as for borrowing money, anybody might do that.
To be sure, in every man's case there is a limit to the borrowing power ; and Fred had arrived at his extreme tether, without being known, in any single case, to have repaid again.
He borrowed, like Dicky Carew, from everybody—even from
that worthy himself. Unlike Dicky, whose little earnings
were always encroached upon by his own habits of lending to
brethren in distress, Fred Revel never lent to any one. What
he got he spent in fostering the delusion that he belonged to
the wealthy—at least, to the easy class. It was not selfish
so much as foolish. He lived for ever in that fool's paradise
about which we have spoken before. He told himself a
thousand times a day that better days were coming, and he
looked for the better days to that most unsteady of supporters,
a patron. Some men are so weak that they *cannot* place the
real situation before themselves ; they live in an atmosphere
of self-deceit of their own making ; they veil their figures

in a cloud, which hides the contours and obscures the surroundings.

There was one great reason why Fred should not run in a groove with the rest of the world—he had no money, and he could not work. That was it: he could not work. He had never been able to study at school. It was a grand mistake to send him to Oxford. He cared nothing for reading. Unless he had work in the open air, he could live but one life—that of the *lazzaroni*, who bask in the sun, and let the days slip by. He ought to have been a sailor.

Modern society takes no account of these unfortunates; and yet it is this class which feels most deeply the consequence of man's first disobedience and his fall. They are the brethren most to be pitied, for, with them, the earning of bread by desk labour is torture, mental and physical. We do not pity them even—we only despise them. The average workman has no words to express his contempt for him who cannot work; the structure of society has no place for him. Perhaps, in a more advanced civilisation, the disease will be recognised as a somewhat uncommon but incurable phenomenon, and hospitals will be provided, with gardens, music, dancing, and art—everything but lovemaking, because the disease may be hereditary—for the lazy ones of the earth. Of course, the accidental possession of money will not be considered an excuse for keeping out of the hospital; that, on the other hand, will help to furnish the less fortunate with the graces of life.

There was, then, a more bitter sting than Marion knew of when she roused herself to say, for the first time in her life, words of bitterness to this shallow-hearted and feather-brained brother.

And then there was Winifred to think of.

He walked, with those uneven steps which mark a mind ill at ease, and with quick, impatient gestures, to his favourite haunt, the billiard-room. No one was there but the marker, practising with infinite patience a stroke with which to astonish the habitual players.

"I want to know," Fred began—"I want to know if you can do anything for me about that money I borrowed?"

"Nothing. I told you so at the beginning. That's the sixth time running I've made this stroke. If he won't renew, you must pay up."

"I can't pay up."

The marker whistled meaningly, and chalked his cue.

"I have tried, but I do not know what to do. It's thirty-seven pounds three and tenpence."

"Thirty-seven, three, ten. Ah! And, counting interest, say forty; there is always something or other which they put on. Saul is a devil of a fellow at totting up."

"You took me to him."

"I did—that's quite true. I told you he would let you have money, and he did. At good interest, and on security, Saul will let anybody have money. He would discount a bill for the devil himself, with pleasure, if there was a respectable name at the back. You signed a paper, and took what he gave you."

"Ten pounds and a box of cigars. That was all I got."

"It doesn't seem much; but there, you know, you would have it; and you were so certain that you would get your appointment before this, that you would have taken a thousand of he'd let you. Come, now, don't blame me."

"What can he do?" Fred asked, in an anxious tone.

"I don't know. If there is any way of getting his money back, he will try that way. If there isn't, he'll make it hot for you some other way. Lord bless you, I knew how it would happen. I've gone through it all myself, only it was a long time ago. You must pay up, or he'll put on the screw."

The speaker was a short, thickset man, whose beard was grey, and his hair touched with grey—a man well on the shady side of fifty.

"I saw it all coming from the very beginning, and here it is. You have got a nice, light touch with the cue, and you come here for the sixpenny lives. You bounce about your family; but you've got no money, and know no trade. There is only one trade open to you."

" What is that?" asked the young man, with a flush.

"Mine. I was a gentleman once. Not for very long; but a gentleman to begin with. My father served His Majesty King George III., and carried colours in the Peninsula. How did I come down to this? By the very same road that you are travelling, Mr. Revel; exactly—the very same road. Young gentlemen who dislike work, and can play billiards, take to playing for money. Those who play billiards for a living always end in marking at billiards for a living. Lord bless you, it's as plain as a pikestaff. Go the round of the rooms, ask them all to tell you what brought them to it, you will hear much about the same story. You wouldn't shake hands with me now, would you? I don't mind it, my boy—not a bit. My word, I was a much finer fellow than you at one time."

He sat down, and prepared to reveal his own story with considerable enjoyment.

"We wore whiskers then, and no beard—only Cavalry men wore a moustache. We had long hair brushed in waves. We had frock-coats tight at the waist; high shirt-collars and large neckties. I think I see myself now—going down Bond Street, with Captain Rook and Lord Deuceace, arm-in-arm, as if the pavement belonged to us. They both went to the dogs worse than me, poor beggars! There, you've read Thackeray's History of Deuceace, of course. I always wanted to sit to Thackeray myself, only I never got the chance. I would have put him up to a tip or two.

"As to being satisfied with my present aristocratic mode of life, I can't say I am. Would I change it? I certainly would if I could. But there's only one state of life for which I would change it, and that's a regular allowance—say three pounds a week, enough for my quiet brandy and water and my pipe. After all, it is not so very bad. None of the crew ever come here; and if they did, they would not know their old chum. As for the broken-down ones—that's most of the set—we never speak when we do meet. We pass on, and pretend not to know each other. Deuceace went to the bad altogether, as you know, perhaps. I think the turf *is* worse

than the billiard-table. Here, you see, you only ruin
yourself. Over the races you ruin the poor devils who *will*
bet as well. Cards are bad, because in the long run you take
to playing with marked packs. That's what Captain Rook
came to grief over. When I last heard of him it was from
Charley Fetherstone. He saw him at the Grand Prix in
Paris, with a *pari mutuel*, and in the evening came across
him in a two-franc hell. Now, at billiards you may play
dark, and that isn't a nice thing for a gentleman to come to;
but, damn it, that's the worst you can do. No one can say
a worse thing of me than that. After all, as you see, you
can always pick up an honest living when you've forgotten
that you are a gentleman."

Fred groaned. The marker warmed up in his recollections,
and went on :—

"Charley Fetherstone has not done so well, though. He
would combine the three: gambled, betted, *and* played
billiards. A very dashing and brilliant fellow he was; but
somehow it all came to nothing. He should have stuck to
one thing, you see, like me. What with being ducked
for a welsher at Hampton, expelled his club for turning up
the king at écarté, and getting known all over London for
dark play, he hadn't a chance in the end. I met him a few
months ago carrying a pair of advertising boards. Think of
that! And Charley once the dandiest young fellow in all
New Bond Street. I was coming along here, with my old
briar-root in my mouth, when I came alongside of him. I
saw his eyes flash, and then he dropped them, and plodded
on like most of the board-carrying lot, noticing nothing.
I couldn't help myself. I had five shillings in my pocket—
two half-crowns—and I slipped one into his hand. 'Take
that, mate,' I says—rough, you know. 'What's this for?'
said Charley, staring at me, with the best bit of acting you
ever saw in your life—'I never saw you before, mate.' 'No
more you did, old fellow,' I said; 'quite so—no more you
did. We never clapped eyes on each other till this blessed
minute, did we? That's why I gave you the half-crown.
Better luck to you, Charley Fetherstone!' He never

answered, but he dropped his head, and went on plodding in the mud.   Poor devil! poor devil!"

Fred listened with a swelling heart.   Was all the world, then, going to prophesy disaster?

"Well, young gentleman, that's all.   I've told you your lines as near as I can read them.   You can play billiards, and you *can't* work, and you don't want."

Perhaps he spoke out of pure kindliness, and from a desire to warn the young man; perhaps from the cynical depths of a dark experience.

"What security did you give Saul for the money?"

"A bill of sale on my furniture."

"Very well, then; let him have the furniture.   What does a young fellow like you want with furniture?   Your chambers are in the Temple, are they not?   Let them clear you out, and be hanged to them!   Go home and put everything valuable in your pocket.   I remember when Dick Latitat, the lawyer—he's a judge in India now—found out there was going to be an execution put into his chambers, he moved everything out at dead of night to a friend who lived opposite, and in the morning, when the Philistines came, the spoil was gone.   Not that I should advise you to do that, because a bill of sale is a serious thing.   Let them take the lot, and you'll be easier about it."

Fred sat down on one of the seats that ran round the room, and looked blankly before him.   A billiard-marker! Dr. Chacomb had advised him to become an advertising tout. Such was the opinion of the world about him.   He could not even reply to the marker's prophecy; for it seemed as if suddenly the very foundations of his life were giving way beneath him.   Where could he get this money?   And if he did not get it, how to break the blow to Marion?   For he knew well enough the immediate effect of his inability to pay.   He had given, in fact, a bill of sale on the furniture, nominally his own, in his capacity as "head of the house."

"Come, don't give way," said his friend.   "You owe me a matter of five shillings or so; we will chalk that off, if you're so hard up as all that. Try and borrow the money. See Saul, and ask him to make terms."

Fred went away and sought the money-lender. He was a middle-aged man, dressed in sporting guise. He sat in a little office, without any sign of office-work except a safe; there was a table, and there were chairs. The table was covered with sporting papers, and Mr. Saul was reading one of them. His manner was not calculated to prejudice a stranger in his favour: it was uneasy, while it affected ease; it was half familiar and half distant; the manner of one who is an Ishmaelite in the world—feared and distrusted by the very men whom he most obliges. It is the penalty of the profession. Money-lending, the mystery of the hangman, and the discharge of the duty of sheriff's officer may rank together as the three least desirable of callings.

"True to time, Mr. Revel," he said. "I expected you in a day or two. Sit down. Come to discharge your little account? It is not due yet, though—not for three days. Let me see." He consulted a note-book, and opened his safe. "Here is the account—thirty-nine nineteen and eleven."

"Why don't you say forty at once? And to think that it is only six months ago, and all I got was ten pounds!"

"I beg your pardon, Mr. Revel. You took ten pounds in gold and a box of most valuable cigars, which you might have sold for— Ah, well, we need not go into that. Shall I write you a receipt?"

"No; I have not got any money."

The man looked at him with a feigned surprise.

"No money? That is awkward, for the note will be due in three days."

"I can't help it. You must give me a little time. Come, Mr. Saul, you do not want the money to-day or to-morrow. Give me a month to look about me."

"That is not the way to conduct business, Mr. Revel. The little trifle—it is certainly a very small sum—is wanted by me imperatively, to make up a large sum due to a friend, a debt of honour. In fact, I must have it. You gave me a bill of sale, did you not? Yes. Really, it would be very disagreeable— Come, Mr. Revel, you will go away and borrow the money of some friend, I am sure. I would not press you if I were not obliged. I tell you what I will do. Find me a good name, and I will do another bill for you. I will give you three days yet." This was a gracious concession, because three days is the exact space allowed by the law. "You shall have three days, and then— But no doubt we shall have a better account in that time. Anything like good security, my dear sir, good security—reversion, mortgage, post-obits, the name of a good friend—I will oblige you in any way possible. You shall never call *me* a hard man."

There was one chance yet. He would go and see his old and long-suffering friend, Lord Rodney Benbow. Lord Rodney's wild oats had long since been sown. He was going in for political life; he was private secretary to the Earl of Cromarty; he was proposing to stand for a family borough in the Conservative interest at the next election; he was already a most respectable man; and it was not at all his intention to keep up an intimacy with a man like his former friend Revel, who was just hovering with uncertain wing on the outskirts of civilised society. He received him, however, with a show of the old cordiality, and shook hands with him.

"What is it, Revel? Are you in a mess again?"

"I am always in a mess."

"You certainly always are. How much is it this time?"

"Forty pounds. I borrowed it six months ago. Got ten pounds and a box of cigars of Saul the money-lender."

"I know the scoundrel well."

"I gave a bill of sale for it on the furniture."

"I was not aware that you had any furniture."

Fred coloured. He had not thought it necessary to inform his distinguished friend of the exact conditions of his life.

"And now you cannot meet it. Well, let the man clear off the sticks. I suppose the furniture of your chamber is not very precious to you." He, like the marker, thought Fred was living by himself. "He will probably lose by the bargain. Let him come and take it."

" I thought that perhaps you would—"

" Lend you the money ? My dear fellow, I haven't got it. Do you know that I have lent you more than fifty during the last two years ? I don't want to bother you about it, and I dare say you will be all right some day ; but a younger son has not too much to spare. Why don't you do something for yourself ? "

" Did you remember to speak about my application at the Colonial Office ? "

" I did. It's no good, my boy. They are pestered with applications. There are seven hundred names down at the Colonial Office already. They will not give you anything. You must abandon the notion of a Government appointment altogether."

" And at the Foreign Office ? I know French."

" Everybody knows French. Come, Revel, let me speak frankly. You are going downhill. It's a bad sign when a man borrows sovereigns. And now there's this business of the bill. Set to work on something—what the deuce does it matter what ? A man can do anything nowadays. Why, my younger brother is going into a merchant's office next week. Don't fly into a rage with an old friend. Give up running after shadows. You will get nothing from the Government, nothing at all ; there is no department of the Civil Service that you can get into by examination ; and as your father did not do the sensible thing with you, and give you a chance in the army, you must try something else. Be reasonable, old boy. You and I were too much together once. It did not hurt me much to get rusticated, but it played the deuce with you. Try and see things in their right light. Give up family tradition and Oxford prejudice, and take anything. No one whose opinion is worth anything to you will think twice about what you are. And now, Fred, my boy, good-bye. Let the furniture go to the money-lending fellow ; give up billiards and the West End, and go in for work, like me. If I can help you, I will. Only let the world see that you can help yourself."

Fred mechanically took his hand and left him. It was

dismissal. There was no hope from that quarter, nor from any other. In three days' time the money-lender would execute his threat and sell them up. Sharp lessons, but they came, like the admonition to the unfortunates in Tartarus, too late.

> " Discite justitiam moniti, et non temnere divos."

" Admirable advice ! " says Scarron the scoffer ; " but what is the good of it *down there ?* "

Quite so. Fred had learned from the doctor that he was a lazy *vaurien* ; from Marion that he had disgraced and dishonoured himself by writing begging letters ; from the billiard-marker that his ultimate profession was undoubtedly to mark at billiards ; and from Lord Rodney Benbow that he was certainly going downhill. It was quite true ; but he had got lower than anybody knew, and now he was going to be found out by Marion. All the humiliations he had experienced were nothing in comparison with this. Winifred would know it, too. Adrienne would know it. They would have bare walls for shelter, for everything would be seized. What could he do ? How fend off the blow ?

Winifred would cry, and believe him when he told her something in mitigation of the offence ; Adie would laugh bitterly, and smite him with winged words ; but this was nothing compared with the reproach he would read in the eyes of Marion.

CHAPTER XXVI.

" AND now, Adie," said Marion, " let us forget Fred's sins, poor fellow ! See, the picture is finished—actually finished. I can do no more to it."

" I am sure," said Adie, who was a critic after the fashion of those who, in trying to say smooth things, always contrive to wound the vanity of an artist—" I am sure I have seen many worse pictures in the Exhibition."

Poor Marion !

If she had shown her sister a poem, Adie would have

assured her, with a genial smile, that she had seen worse verses in print; if a tale, that inferior productions had appeared in the *Housemaid's Journal*. And then Adie would have thought that she was conveying a rare and merited compliment to her sister.

" I *do* like the face of the girl," she said—as if, bad as the thing was, there were some merits. " I suppose because it is painted after me. And it all seems so pretty, and you are very clever, Marion."

" Not that it is the slightest use," she went on, dolefully. " You will not be able to sell it, I suppose, unless Burls takes it of you for a tenth part of what it is worth. Marion, we are an unlucky family. Sometimes I think we shall never get out of our degradation."

" Not degradation, Adie."

" Yes," she said—" disgrace and degradation. You toiling day and night for nothing; I dependent on you. Fred playing billiards for sixpences. It *is* disgrace, Marion."

She had lost all faith in her sister's power of success. Two years of drudgery seemed to her conclusive that Marion would never be an artist.

" I will tell you a secret, Adie. Dr. Chacomb is going to try for the Royal Academy with it. He is coming here to-day."

" It is very good of Dr. Chacomb," replied her sister, who was in a despondent mood—" very good indeed. But it is no use. They won't take it; if they take it, they will hang it where no one can see it. It will not be sold, and then you will have it back again—poor dear Marion ! "

" Perhaps the bad luck will turn, Adie. At all events, it is always right to go on working. Don't be down-hearted, dear."

" I must be. I found out another thing yesterday. Promise me, Marion, if I tell it you, to keep it a secret."

" What is it, Adie ? "

" Winifred Owen is a very pretty girl, Marion."

" Well ? "

" And a ladylike girl."

"Yes."

"And—and—how should you like Winifred Owen to become Winifred Revel?"

Marion only opened her eyes.

"You may make up your mind to that event, my dear," Adie went on, with the calmness of despair. "It will be quite a marriage of romance. He has nothing; she has nothing. They will live upon love, without even a cottage. What do you think of it?"

"Poor Winifred!" said Marion. "I will speak to Fred at once."

"No, do not, Marion—let things go on. Now you know why I am so cross with him this morning. It does seem too bad. He ought to be content with dragging his sisters down, and spare poor little Winifred. It is too late, Marion. She loves him."

"How do you know, Adie?"

"Because I can see, my dear; because I have got eyes in my head; because when girls love people they look in one way, and only one way; because Winifred is carried away with his good looks and winning ways. Poor Fred would win the heart of an icicle if he set about it in earnest."

"It may stimulate him, to be engaged."

"No, Marion. Nothing will ever stimulate Fred to do any work. I know my dear Fred. He will just go on for ever as he is going on now; he will spoil her life as he has spoiled yours. Poor little Winifred! And how can they marry? Think of living on, year after year, in love with a man whom you cannot hope to marry. Marion, what is the matter? Are you ill?"

For her sister's cheek paled, and she sat down suddenly, as if Adie had struck her some sharp blow—which, indeed, was the case, though she did not know it.

"Poor Fred! He does not tell us any more, as he did at first, what he does and where he goes. That is the worst sign. I feel as if we were becoming outcasts. Why are we alone in the world in having no friends and relations? Where are your mother's people, Marion? Where are mine?

Where are all our French cousins? Surely the Revolution did not kill everybody. Did my father have no friends among his brother-officers who would help us if they were asked?"

"My dear, have patience."

"Patience! O Marion, I think we have had patience enough. I hate it—this cramped, miserable life. I have no more patience with it at all. Our hopes are bound by a fraction or so, more or less. We live from day to day; we tremble at shadows; and we are wretched because poor Fred spends a few shillings on himself."

Then the doctor came, and the topic was necessarily changed.

He planted himself in front of the picture, and began to criticise it.

"I am not really," he said, "a judge of pictures at all. I only pretend to be, like the rest of the world. This, however, seems to me a pretty painting. I never saw a dress like that; but then painters put any dress they like on their models. I never saw a sky like that—'light that never shone on earth or ocean'—but then I never saw lights like those in Turner's pictures. 'So much the worse for you,' Turner used to say when any one objected to his light that he didn't see the colour. The flowers look faithful, and the leaves seem as if they were shaking in the breeze. How do you make things look as if they were alive? Miss Revel, you are an artist. I am not a critic, and so I can tell the truth. There is genius in the picture. Now let us take it away. I have got the frame ready, and it must go in to-day or to-morrow. As for the face, it's yours, Miss Adie: that is another way of saying that it is so beautiful that no one ever will believe it can be true to life."

"That is right, Dr. Chacomb. Say something more to me, just to put me in a good humour. I want a little coaxing and petting this morning."

"It's a lovely face, Miss Adie," he went on. "Your sister has caught the laugh in it. That's the prettiest thing of all in your face, that it always seems to laugh. Perhaps it is your eyes that laugh. You ought to be the happiest girl in the world."

"Isn't he delightful, Marion? I know I ought to be, Dr. Chacomb. I've got the 'makings,' as Fred says, of any amount of happiness—tons of happiness; but who could be happy in such a frock as this? And, oh! if you could only see my boots. Now you have said something pleasant to me, go on with Marion's picture."

"Well, then, I have spoken about it to a patient and friend of mine, an R.A., and got you such little influence at work as may be useful when it comes to hanging. I did not say the picture was by a lady, because the R.A.s don't like ladies. Even Ruskin says that women cannot paint. Did you ever hear how a lady first became a student of the Academy? She sent a drawing in under an assumed name; no one knew anything about the artist; it was accepted, made some noise, and then they found out. But they could not turn it out again, of course. That was some years ago, in the year '60, and plenty of ladies have been admitted since then."

"And you think your friend's interest will help?"

"I hope so. You see, there are so many pictures by Academicians, and so many by well-known men. When these are all provided for, the new and unknown painters have got to take their chance. And for most of them it's a mere toss-up. Some must be taken. Yours is a good deal better than many that are taken; but, pardon me, there are many of the rejected which would show well even by the side of this picture. There, you see, interest comes in."

"And if it is taken?"

"Then it shall be sold; then you will have commissions in plenty; then you shall see your way to a comfortable—perhaps a large—income every year; then, my dear young ladies, you shall say farewell to Lowland Street, and rejoice the world to which you belong."

"Dr. Chacomb," exclaimed Adie, with enthusiasm, "I love you; upon my word, I adore you. You never come here without raising our spirits and giving us hope. You are not mocking us ? You really think that one may reasonably look forward to something this year—say a journey in a van to Epping Forest with the ladies and gentlemen of Elephant Row—they went all together last year, and came home at midnight. Or perhaps one may pray—it's no use praying for anything unless it is reasonably probable—for a new dress for both of us; or what do you say, Marion, to hoping —just tempting Providence by a prayer, you know—that we may see our way to take lodgings where we may behold a field and a tree ?"

" Really," said the doctor, " you may hope all these things. And if you will permit me—"

" I will permit you anything, doctor, if Marion's picture gets into the Academy."

" You hear ? " And the doctor called Marion to witness. " She permits me anything. That means a visit to the dress-maker's at least."

So he went away, carrying the picture with him.

" My dear," said Adie, " it is such a pity—oh! such a terrible pity ! "

" What is a terrible pity ? "

" That it cannot be, Marion. The doctor is the best friend we have ; and, Marion, he is a friend out of love to you. Do you think he looks for no reward at all ?"

They were interrupted again. This time their visitor was a tall, thin man, with stooping shoulders, very long white hair, and a curiously pale face. They had never seen him before, but from Dicky Carew's description they knew their visitor for the famous Hermit of Lowland Street.

They knew him by his tall and stately figure, by his hand-some face, by his cold air, and by the studied carelessness of his dress. It was noon, and he was attired in morning costume of the latest fashion. He wore gloves, and had a flower in his button-hole ; he carried a new hat, and but for his white, colourless cheek you would have taken him for the freshest importation possible from New Bond Street.

" Pardon me," he said. " I have to ask a thousand pardons for this intrusion. I live over your heads, and it is, perhaps you know, a great many years since I left my rooms. I see no one except my secretary. If I fail in the politeness due to two most interesting and charming young ladies, you will, I am sure, be good enough to excuse my *gaucherie* on the ground of my recluse habits."

Marion bowed. She took a dislike to the man at once. Adie would perhaps have laughed, but the solemnity of the address overawed her.

"I learned accidentally," he said, looking from one to the other, "that one of the young ladies is an artist."

"I am an artist," said Marion—"or, rather, I try to be an artist."

"Thank you," he said, looking at Adie. "One of the ladies —perhaps both—plays and sings very charmingly."

"My sister," said Marion, "plays and sings so as to charm me at least. I presume you have overheard her, upstairs. If you will let us know what time will least inconvenience you, we will observe that hour."

He bowed and smiled.

"It is not to speak of your music that I have broken my rule," he said. "I hoped, when I resolved to quit an un- worthy world, to make no more acquaintance—never to ask, never to know, if I could help it, any one's name with whom I might be obliged to converse. I hoped to pass the re- mainder of my existence in absolute silence and seclusion."

He waited, to let the preamble take effect.

"That must be very disagreeable," said Adie. "I don't wonder at your being tired of it. And all the time you have been locked up did you have no one to talk to but Mr. Carew?"

"My secretary?" he asked, with a studied elevation of his eyebrow, as if he had only heard his name once or so— everything about this man was false, affected, and *maniéré*. "In fact, I think I have heard that his name is Carew—an old Devonshire name, too; an instance of the many survivals, among the lower classes, of good names."

"Dear me!" said Adie, in her light frivolous way. She was quietly enjoying the spectacle of this visitor, who was as awkward as an owl in the sunshine. "I should not advise you to tell Mr. Carew that he belongs to the lower classes."

"Adie," said her sister, "we have not learned yet to what we owe this visit."

"Pardon me"—her visitor could not take his eyes off Adie. "A curious resemblance; the sound of your sister's voice—are you sisters?"

"Yes, we are sisters."

"Ah! it is not with you," he said to Marion. "I was struck at first, but that is nothing. I am forced out of my solitude by a pressing want, in which you may help me."

"Do you want to talk to somebody?" asked Adie. "Is it that the unworthy world is actually going to be forgiven?"

The young lady, whose face and voice reminded him of some old acquaintance, and who treated his solemn airs with no more respect than if he had been a quite common creature, disconcerted him hugely.

"Do not speak to me," he replied, "of the world; I hate it—I hate it."

"The world," Adie went on, "is a large ball or sphere, flattened at the poles, something in the shape of an orange. It rotates upon its axis once in every twenty-four hours, and revolves round the sun, which is the centre of the planetary system which we ignorantly call the universe."

"My dear Adie!" Marion cried.

"Geography, my dear Marion—it is so in all the books. The world is a very large thing, and it must be a very big heart to hate it."

"It is not the world I hate." The Hermit swayed himself backwards and forwards with a deprecating gesture. "I hate mankind. I have found men ever cruel, negligent, and unjust. I have met with nothing but selfishness in my communications with men. I have ceased to expect from men anything but slander, obloquy, and treachery."

"That seems very bad," said Adie. "How did men find you?"

He straightened himself, and assumed the most effective pose he knew, his right hand thrust in his waistcoat, like Canning.

"They found ME," he said, "the soul of honour, in things small as well as great; they found ME, a chivalrous gentleman of the old school, one who feared not the face of man, and bowed before the face of woman."

Marion felt inclined to yawn. It was a vulgar and commonplace inclination, but she felt it.

"Pray, sir," she asked, "what can we do for you? You do not know who we are. We have not the pleasure of your acquaintance. May I ask again why you have called upon us?"

"It is an affair of business," he said, descending to prose. "I want some drawings made from these rough sketches, and I thought that perhaps you might be able to do them for me."

"Let me see them," said Marion.

They were the subjects which Dicky had so often seen commenced and recommenced—drawings in water-colour, in sepia, and in pen-and-ink of garrison scenes, and drawings of camp life.

"You want them copied?" she asked. "But they are finished sketches already, and so much better than I can do myself."

"I want you to make an oil painting of one," he said. "Choose which you think best."

She laid one aside—a simple drawing of a single figure emerging from a tent, in ice and snow, looking with a wild expression of terror as he buckled on his sword.

"That is a curious subject; shall I take that?"

He snatched it from her.

"No. I did not know it was there. I will choose one for you."

He took a drawing full of life, energy, and verve, representing a garrison steeplechase.

"Yes, I can do this; but you have got the same face in the central figure."

She looked at the first, and then at her patron.

The face was the same ; but it was his face—his own face. She saw that in a minute, in spite of the change which twenty years had brought to a face once gallant and gay, and still handsome.

He passed over the remark in silence.

" If you will kindly," he said, with a resumption of his cold politeness—" if you will kindly attempt a reproduction, a *pasticcio*, of this little unpretending sketch, I shall be happy indeed. I am so selfish "—he turned to Adie—" that I shall try to make your charming sister the accomplice in these innocent pleasures of mine. If I could, by any persuasion, enlist you in the same cause—"

She shook her head.

" I assure you," she said, " I do not paint at all ; and none of my pleasures are innocent—not dove-like, that is, like your own."

" I mean," he replied, " that if you would sometimes condescend to visit the cell of a Solitary, you might cheer the hours of retirement with the sweetness of your voice. Saul, you know, had David."

" Yes," said Marion, " and threw his javelin at him. My sister, Mr. Lilliecrip—I think that is your name—cannot pay visits to your rooms, nor can I."

" Pardon me again." He smiled, so as to lay bare a whole row of white teeth. " I find that I am more spoiled for society than I had anticipated. I should have known that my invitation was contrary to the *convenances*. Pray forgive me. Only, perhaps, you will not allow my rudeness to interfere with your usual practice on the piano. Let me, at least, have the pleasure of hearing you play and sing, as you have been accustomed to do."

" If you want society," said Adie, in her *naïve* manner, " I don't see why you are a Hermit. If you remain a Hermit, that must be because you do not care for society. If you want cheering up, why not go back to the men you have found so very, very wicked ? "

" I hate society," said the Solitary.

"Adie, dear, we have no excuse for asking this gentleman anything about his private affairs. I will try to copy your picture for you, sir, and I hope you will be satisfied with the result; but I do not promise much."

"I will come down, if I may be allowed, from time to time, to advise in its progress," he replied. "Tell me if I may be permitted to intrude upon this sweet solitude, the abode of the twin muses, the sisters of singing and painting, Euterpe and Poly—Polyhymnia, I think, unless it was Proserpine; but my classical memory is weak."

Marion was annoyed at the man's florid language.

"You may come," she said, shortly. "Indeed, you have a right. Good-morning, sir."

"Marion," said Adie, when his step was well up the stairs, "this is a day out of an Arabian Night. Isn't he too funny?"

"Do not let him come here when I am out," said Marion. "Promise me not to go up to his rooms, or to talk to him. I don't like the man."

They heard, presently, his footsteps over their heads, walking backwards and forwards.

The Hermit was in a fever. He had actually seen and talked to two young ladies, after fourteen years of incarceration. He was worse than Simon Stylites, who could at least, if he wished, wink at his fair devotees; he had not even that consolation. He read perpetually his yellow French novels of intrigue, and he fed his mind upon the distorted unrealities of the Second Empire. But here was reality; and he trembled now that he met it.

"They are perfectly delicious," he said. "As for the younger, I seem to have met her before, somewhere—who is she like? But the elder girl, with her deep eyes— Ah! if I could win her, I would—yes, I would give up even my Hermitage, and go back to—to"—he shuddered—"to some part of the world where no one would know anything about me."

In his nervousness he had left all his sketches with Marion.

CHAPTER XXVII.

ADIE left Marion over the sketches, and sought the society of Mr. Owen. It was a half-holiday, and she knew that she should find the schoolmaster alone in the deserted school-room.

There, in fact, he was. The sun, shining through the open windows, made the empty desks and deserted benches look bright and pleasant. He was sitting at his desk, ensconced comfortably for the afternoon with Langhorne's " Plutarch," but he did not look sorry to be disturbed by the girl who so often came down to talk with him. Plutarch, no doubt an incomparable author, has no chance, even with an old school-master versed in the wisdom of the book of Proverbs, against the voice and eyes of a pretty girl. The life of Aristides, and the comparison between him and Cato, are most improving studies ; but even to an instructor of youth it is more cheerful to read a page of life.

Therefore Mr. Owen gave his visitor the one chair in the room, and sat himself down, with crossed legs, on a bench before her. With his matted hair, his seamy and wrinkled face, his spectacles, and the tips of his short fingers touching each other, he looked the very effigy of wisdom. The owl-faced goddess whom Dr. Schliemann found at Troy was not more sagacious of aspect.

"And so, Miss Adie, you want my advice about work, do you ? Sit down, and let me think."

"If I could find anything that I could do ; but, Mr. Owen, I am so lamentably ignorant. I know French, to be sure, and I can play and sing a little ; but that is all. As for history, I assure you I hardly know Alexander the Great from the Great Mogul."

"That's because you don't read Plutarch," said the schoolmaster.

"And my geography is worse. I really should not know

whether the map of America was upside down or not, it is so long since I looked at it."

"There is no upside or downside either to a map. I caned a boy to-day for not knowing the frontiers of China. To be sure, I did not know them myself."

"Then you ought to be ashamed of yourself for caning the poor boy, Mr. Owen," said Adie.

"It is the duty of the boy to know his lessons, and the duty of the master to awaken his instincts. It is for example, 'Smite the scorner, and the simple shall beware.' The only way to do that is by caning him. Draco, you will find, in Plutarch's Life of Solon, punished everything by death, 'because,' he said, 'the smallest offences deserve death, and there is no greater punishment for the most heinous.' As for the schoolmaster not knowing everything, it is, as everybody knows, a part of his professional baggage to pretend to know everything. My dear, if the boys, who are demoniac by nature, found out a weak point in my knowledge, I should lose my authority over them. Just look at the range of subjects: Latin and trigonometry; French and writing; book-keeping by double entry and geography; chemistry, so as to march with the age—bless you, a schoolmaster is nowhere who does not march with the age—Euclid, algebra, and history; the Bible! The wonder is, that the brain stands it all. But it isn't the amount of knowledge, my dear, that makes a good schoolmaster feel like going cracked, but the amount of pretension. Well, we are as honest as we can afford."

"I do not want to teach," said Adie—"I am far too stupid and too impatient. But there are other ways."

"There are," he said, "fifty other ways. Wait here, and look at Plutarch, while I go and get a little book of notes. I made it up two or three years ago, when Winifred was casting about for a profession. Sometimes I have thought about sending it to the papers. You shall hear."

"Now"—he returned with a penny note-book, filled with figures and references—"I am not going to read you all this, but only a part. Listen! Axiom First. I've ruled it all out, like Euclid, in axioms, definitions, and propositions. Axiom the First—you will have to grant this—'No woman wants to work.'"

"Granted," said Adie. "That's true, I suppose; nor any man either."

"No; that is the great difference between the sexes. Man does like work, and woman does not. She likes to sit in warm corners, and talk. Axiom One's allowed. Axiom Two: 'If a woman is obliged to work, she likes to work as little as possible.'"

"Of course."

"Axiom Three: 'She likes to get as much money as she can, and to be her own mistress!'"

"Yes, I suppose so."

"We are getting on capitally. Axiom Four: 'A woman ought to get the just price of her labour.'"

"Of course she ought."

"She grants everything, this young lady does," said the philosopher. "She's got a brain fit for Euclid himself. Axiom Five: 'There ought to be no difference, provided the work is the same, between the wages of women and those of men.' That granted too? Very well. We are getting on famously. These are the introductions to a great science; but as yet I've only had time to work out one or two propositions. What a discoverer I might have been, if I'd only had the time to work for myself! Fancy reducing all social distinctions to theorems, like Euclid, only more interesting. First Proposition—this is a startler: 'All employers of women ought immediately to be hanged by the neck.'"

"Oh, what a dreadful proposition!"

Adie took the word in its usual, not its Euclidean sense, and understood Mr. Owen to mean that he wished to introduce a Bill into the Legislature for the sole purpose of instantly destroying this large and influential class.

"Immediately," he repeated; "without trial, without jury, without counsel—all on one rope; and I would pull at the other end."

"Mr. Owen!"—for he looked quite flushed and excited, and began to stump up and down the school-room, jerking about his short legs in a really alarming manner.

"Second Proposition: 'No woman ought to be allowed to work for money.'"

"But if they must?"

"Let me say my say, and then you shall talk. There are three millions of women earning wages. Sixty thousand are milliners. Stay, let me read my list."

He found the place in his book, and read:

"'Milliners, 58,460; shirtmakers, 26,875; machinists, 10,724; bookbinders, 5272; florists, 4260.' But the list only accounts for 105,691; and I forget now whether it extends beyond London. Besides these, there are bead-makers, lace-makers, bonnet-makers, book-folders, boot-closers, factory girls, shop girls, bandbox-makers, match-makers, nurses, cigar-makers, and thousands of other trades. Now, how do they get paid? Don't answer me."

He stopped, and tapped his forehead, in reflection.

"'Third Proposition: 'It ought to be penal to make or take contracts.' Penal, Miss Adie—imprisonment for life, without hope of commutation.

"Now, for money. My Winifred is in a service—a Government service—where they pay the men better than the women for the same work. However, she is quick—bless her little fingers!—and gets a guinea a-week. But you would not like to be a telegraph girl?"

"I do not know what I should like, I am sure."

"Dressmaking. That is almost the worst line of any. If you live in the house you get two or three shillings a week, and your food; if you live out, you get fifteen shillings and no food. Fifteen shillings! Think of that, and in London, where even the worst room cannot be got under five shillings. Say two girls live in it together, for economy; there is half-a-crown for rent. Eating and drinking cannot be got under eighteenpence a day, because the poor creatures are unable to buy and cook their own food, but must give a profit to eating-houses; that leaves exactly two shillings a week—five pounds a year—for keeping up a respectable appearance, and dressing as the poor things must dress. Why, no servant in the country, no poor lodging-house maid of all-work, is paid so badly. My dear, try to think what the girls do. They work for twelve hours a day, and sometimes more. When the season is over they are turned off. Of course, they have no share in the profits, although the success of the firm depends on their needles. What right—what right, I say, have the masters to the great fortunes they make out of the girls? The fine ladies never think; and when the girls go wrong—but there, never mind.

"Day workers, again. They make eighteenpence a day—nine shillings in all. Worse off than the poor creatures in the shops.

"Shop attendants. Do you know that they make them wear black silks, and stop the money out of their pay?

"Florists. Do you know that they have to work from five in the morning till eight, nine, and ten at night?

"Barmaids. They are kept in the house on the condition that they attract gentlemen—paid for degradation.

"Cigar-makers. They make cigars faster and better than men. They are paid forty per cent. less than men.

"And listen to this. Woman's skilled labour is worth sixteen shillings a week at the outside; man's unskilled labour is worth eighteen shillings a week as a minimum. There is not a man in this country—not a single stupid, illiterate lout—who, at the ordinary rates of pay, cannot, by fetching and carrying, earn more than a woman skilled in a mechanical trade.

"There's a lower depth still, my dear—a lower depth, for which a judgment ought to fall upon this country, and it will. It's the Government contracts. They contract for what they ought to make themselves; they pay the middleman, to save themselves the trouble of preventing themselves from being cheated; they pay a price which they know to be inadequate, and they look on while the contractor grinds the face of the poor to fulfil his bond. Because, my dear, he will have his profit, that is quite certain; and unless he can cheat the Government, he will starve his labourer. There are thousands of women in this country doing Government work, for contractors to make their fortune; and no one to lift up a hand, and ask that labour for the nation shall be paid a fair and honest price. A woman working a machine for an army contract, for twelve hours a day—think of working a machine twelve hours!—can earn two shillings and twopence-halfpenny a day; and that less stoppages, if the foreman has a spite. Six times twelve are seventy-two — seventy-two hours a week for thirteen shillings and sixpence! Most of them widows, too, with families of children. There are nearly a million of widows in this country, and more than half are earning their own living.

"There's philanthropists, now—they talk of teaching women trades; but why, my dear, why? To get their labour cheaper, and make the middle-man richer. If philanthropists wanted to help, they would teach the women to form trades unions."

All this time, Mr. Owen was walking up and down the room, faster and faster, growing every moment the more energetic as he denounced the oppressors of womankind.

"They are all in league together, I tell you. Woman is to be the beast of burden because she is the weaker vessel. We are no better than Australian savages. We treat our women as they treat theirs—make them do the hardest work, and take the best pay and the best food for themselves. My dear Miss Adie, it's shameful, it's intolerable, it's horrible. If I could make them understand—I mean the fine ladies—the evils they cause by their apathy, not only to the poor women with whom they have no sympathy, but with the women of their own class, for whom they make the path of sin easy. But there, you don't understand. How should you?"

"I understand, at least, that women are very badly treated. But you have not told me of anything that could help me. What are girls like myself to do, Mr. Owen?"

"God knows!" he replied, shaking his head. "The Lord only knows what young ladies find to do who have been brought up to nothing. Some of them go out for governesses —keeping a governess is the modern way of pretending to educate the girls as well as the boys, for a tenth part of the cost; but the examinations all over the country are making it more and more difficult to find good places, except for girls who have taken degrees. Some of them try law-copying, another name for slow starvation; some of them make pretty, useless things, and send them to places where they pretend to sell ladies' work. Nobody ever buys anything there, and after a bit the things come back again spoiled by being knocked about a shop."

"The world seems a much more wicked place than I ever thought it," said Adie.

"It is, young lady—it is a great deal more wicked than any one ever thought it. It is so wicked, that the heart of man cannot conceive its wickedness. There is so much misery in it, that no one would dare to write it down; there is so much wrong wanting to be set right, that no one dares stir a finger for fear of disturbing everything. In this country we sit and wait, hoping that no one will trouble us; and one day we shall see some noisy demagogue go up and down the face of the country, raising such a storm as England has never seen, for his own selfish and miserable ends."

"Don't frighten me, Mr. Owen," said Adie, really frightened at the passion which the schoolmaster threw into his words. "Tell me, is there nothing at all for me to do?"

"Some young ladies take to art, like your dear sister, but they are few; some try writing, but not one in a thousand makes anything at that; some go on the stage, but there are not many young ladies on the stage—more's the pity for the theatre: one or two have taken to lecturing, and that's the worst line of anything else in the world. The history of woman's work, Miss Adie, is what I have told you in my axioms. Women don't want any work to do; they have not been trained to it; they are not accustomed to unite for purposes of self-protection; they are the victims of every dirty-souled draper and man-milliner who is content to get rich on the profits made by starving his work girls. Proposition One, first class, first boy—boy—I beg your pardon —Miss Adie Revel, what is Proposition One?"

"Every employer of women, including the Government, ought to be hanged immediately."

"Prove that proposition, first—young lady of the first class."

"Women are cheated out of their proper pay; skilled women do not receive wages at the same rate as skilled men, and they have to work too many hours. Men who oppress them ought to be punished. The best punishment is caning—"

"First boy, take care."

"I mean hanging. You wouldn't cane me, Mr. Owen, would you?"

"Finish the proposition first."

"Well, it is finished, isn't it. So that they all ought to be hanged."

"*Quod erat demonstrandum.*"

"Say that in English, Mr. Owen."

"*Quod*, which—the pronoun; *erat*, was—verb imperfect; *sum, fui, esse*—*demonstrandum*, gerund in *di-do-dum*, to be demonstrated. First boy, go up a place. Now the Second Preposition."

"'No woman ought to be allowed to work for money.' But I cannot prove that. It seems to me that women ought to be allowed to work for as much as they can get."

"I want to see women working at things which do not bring in money," he explained. "And why? Because there are plenty of men in the world to do the useful things. When these come to be too few, we shall invent more machines. If women were prohibited from getting their own living, the men would have to do all the nasty jobs that they have put on the women—boot-work and the like. Boys could do the things which require lightness of touch, and do them quite as well, too, as women."

"But you would not let the poor women starve, would you?"

"No; the State should keep them, and keep them in comfort. Ah, it's a *pons asinorum* in my new Euclid that women ought not to be allowed to work for money; but it's coming round to it by degrees. We don't like to see our women cultivating the fields, as I am told they do in France. Soon we shall come not to like to see them at hard work of any kind; and then the man who is found guilty of ill-treating his girls will have a bad time of it. Why, I heard the other day of a woman employed in a white-lead factory, who had to walk four miles to her work and four miles back, work ten hours, and earn nine shillings a-week. Her employer was a gentleman, of course—they all are. My reform will sweep all such gentlemen off the face of the earth. Now, first class, attention: Proposition Three."

"'It ought to be penal to make or take contracts.' Come, I know all the beginning, Mr. Owen."

"Prove it, first boy."

"I can't, please, my master."

"First boy, you will have to go to the bottom of the class. Listen. When a contract is made, the maker secures his own profit first; when he has to make a lower offer, he sticks to his own profit, and screws the loss out of his *employés* if he can. When coal went up fifty per cent. the miners would have got nothing; only they showed a bold front, so they got ten per cent. When coal went down, the men got locked out till they agreed to a reduction of fifteen per cent. Who wins by that? The masters, whichever way the wind blows. The women cannot unite, because no one has taught them how; and so they suffer by every contract that is made, and you can't prevent it."

"I don't quite understand, and I think I have had enough of trading for one day. But, Mr. Owen, you have not answered my question. Tell me what I can do to earn some money."

The old schoolmaster took the girl by both her hands, and looked in her face. It was a face so pretty, and yet, somehow, so helpless. In every feature it spoke of a want of support.

"My child, you have got, or your sister has got, a little money. She has her art, she has health and strength; pray God that you may have to do—nothing. And believe me, it is the happiest condition for all women on this earth to do nothing. Stay at home, my dear, and nourish high and noble thoughts; keep up your courage, and trust in God."

He led his pupil to the door with the gallantry of a Castilian, and dismissed her; but the talk had revived old thoughts in his brain, and ideas that he had long since abandoned as impracticable and useless. He sat down and tried to read Plutarch with his usual calm, but in vain. The beloved pages of Langhorne had no charm for him. He put the book down, and began to pace up and down the schoolroom, working out one more of those golden dreams of an impossible future which while they last, make a man divine.

"I see," he might have said, had his vision shaped itself into words, "I see a time when men shall acknowledge that the truest chance for the world is to cultivate and raise the women. They shall form associations which shall enable girls to work, if they must work, for their own profit. Rich people shall help the girls to found their own co-operative workshops. The minimum of pay for work done shall be regulated. They shall have the boy and girl put on an equal footing at school; the maid and the youth on an equal footing at starting in the world; and the only superiority shall belong to the married man who has his family to support. The family shall still be everything; but the woman's place in the social circle shall be sacred. Somehow or other, rich women will understand then that their own luxury, their vanities and indulgences, have done more than anything in the world to retard the progress of their sex; they will see that these are the chief means by which the lower class of women is kept down, and the sex is put to rebuke through the temptations of which the pure and virtuous are the principal cause.

"It is a curious world," he said, waking from this foolish dream—"it is a curious and a wicked world. When our

Lord said, 'Judge not, that ye be not judged,' and when He bade the guiltless one to throw the first stone, He meant more than the people understood. We can none of us separate ourselves from the sins of the world. We all help to cause them. The purest young lady helps when she goes to the shop of the man in Regent Street who starves his work-girls on fifteen shillings a week. We help by what we say and by what we do. We are all entangled in a mesh and network of wickedness. We are none of us better, one than the other. And last night I was hard in my thoughts about Fred Revel. Lord be merciful to me a sinner!

"Solomon says that the labour of the righteous tendeth to life. Did he ever know of shirtmakers and machinists getting three farthings a shirt, and having to find their own cotton? I doubt it's a more complicated world since his time—eh? We want a new King Solomon. There's comfort in Proverbs, and there's a verse for nearly everything; but sometimes it breaks down. To be sure, we are never told that Solomon was a prophet. He hadn't the gift of seeing the grinders of women's labour in the future. And after all" —his face brightened up—" there's something: 'He that by usury and unjust gain increaseth his substance, he shall gather it for him that will pity the poor.' Aha! Solomon is always there."

CHAPTER XXVIII.

MARION turned idly over the sketches her new patron had left with her. There were some fifty or more water-colours, executed with great power of drawing and considerable feeling for colour. But they were nearly all alike. They represented the Hermit in his youth—the likeness was quite unmistakable—in various scenes connected with the army. He was riding a race; he was presiding at a convivial gathering; he was acting on a stage; he was dancing; he was fighting; but none of the portraits seemed so exactly characteristic as the one which he had snatched

from her hand, showing himself—his own actual face—wild
with terror amid those dismal surroundings of cold, misery,
and death. Why should a man paint himself deliberately as
a coward?

Men, however, as Marion might have known, do reveal their
own natures who get to giving secrets to paper. There was
a murderer, some time ago, who came home after perpetrating
the deed, and wrote on a slip of paper, by way of rough
note for after-entry in a diary, a memorial of his own crime:
"Fine and hot, killed a little girl"—a circumstance which,
if I remember right, so far prejudiced the mob against him,
that they wished then and there to rend him into small
pieces. But Marion was no psychologist; she had never
learned to reason and to analyse, as lawyers say—which is,
being interpreted into English, to impute the worst motives,
and then to try and prove them. Therefore, she wondered.

Presently, turning over the drawings, she came to a head.
There was nothing very much, artistically speaking, to attract
her attention. The head was dressed in the fashion of hair
common twenty-five years ago—not a very pretty fashion.
It was not well painted—not nearly so well as the later
sketches. But Marion looked at it with an astonishment
which took away her breath.

For it was the head of her sister. The same graceful pose,
the same careless parting of the lips, the same contour, the
same eyes. Only the chin and the shape of the head were a
little different. How could the Hermit have got Adie's face
to draw?

And then she dropped the picture with a sinking heart.
It was not the portrait of Adie, but it *was* the portrait of—
Mrs. Spenser. Haggard, worn, and wasted as the woman
was now, she yet preserved a likeness to her youth; and here
it was. Marion tied it up in paper, for fear her sister might
find it, and began to think.

The man, whoever he was, must have known Mrs. Spenser.
But when? and under what circumstances?

"It cannot be," she said—"he must have seen Adie on the
stairs or somewhere, and drawn her."

And this, again, was impossible; because Adie's head was never dressed like the hair in this picture.

She took it out and looked at it again.

Then she put it back, with a prayer that, if the man had known Mrs. Spenser, he might never be moved to speak of her. And she resolved to have as few dealings with him as possible.

But the accident, which might mean nothing, made her as uneasy as Robinson Crusoe when he spied the single unaccompanied bare footprint on the sands—Surely the finest incident that ever occurred to any novelist.

She began her copying work, Adie being, as we have seen, in conversation with Mr. Owen.

Presently Dr. Chacomb came back to her, beaming.

"I have shown your picture to my patient," he said, "and I think I may congratulate you. He likes it. I will not tell you all the flattering things he said of you or of it; nor the faults he found in it. But you may be certain that it will be taken, and nearly certain that it will be sold. Are you satisfied?"

"More than satisfied," said Marion.

"I have bought you some flowers in Covent Garden on my way—quite the simplest wild flowers. Here is a rosebud. It must be a Devonshire nosegay. When shall we get back the roses to *your* cheek, Marion?"

Sometimes he called her by her Christian name, and there was a lowering in the man's voice, as if he was stepping down from some imaginary platform of pretension. To the world he was loud-voiced, self-reliant, and ready to advance to the front.

"The flowers are beautiful"—Marion evaded the question of her own cheeks—"and we are very much obliged to you, Dr. Chacomb, for that and everything else."

"May I sit down and talk for five minutes, before I visit my gouty patients? They are all swearing in chorus at every moment's delay."

"Then go at once, Dr. Chacomb, and relieve the poor people."

" In five minutes. Let me have a little five minutes. The atmosphere of this room is a rest to me. One is out of the world here, looking at you quietly painting."

Marion began to feel afraid, and looked it.

" I am not going to make love to you," said Joseph Chacomb. " I like to be with you. So long as you know that I love you, that is enough. Do you think a woman ever understands her own power over a man ? "

" I never thought about it."

" You make me young again. All the old feelings that I had forgotten come back to me. That is it, Marion. You freshen up my withered old heart as—what is it the Psalmist says ?—the shadow of a great rock in a thirsty wilderness. You are the shadow, and my life is the thirsty wilderness. But with you all the old thoughts come back, just as if I were a boy again, singing in the choir of the parish church, only with a little more vigour."

" But how can I do all that ? "

" I do not know. It is so. Those worst parts of life, which the moralist is always lamenting, one, after all, Marion, very easily forgets. I have been worse than most men, I suppose, because I kept it up till forty-five, and the average run of men knock off at thirty. I had a rackety time for five and twenty years. London, Paris, and Vienna taught me pretty well all there was to learn ; and I think I started in practice with as extended a knowledge of human nature as most young physicians."

" If you are sorry for what is past, is it not better to think no more of it ? "

" But I'm not sorry, you see. I enjoyed the whole run. Hang it, I enjoy everything ! I like my present life ; I like pocketing fees, and going about in a carriage to see rich patients. But I sometimes think I liked the old life better, when I made a precarious living, and chiefly by borrowing from Chauncey Chacomb. It's a very pleasant thing to sit among a lot of good fellows, and talk all night. There's an excitement about letting the morrow take care of itself. It is delightful to be out of society, and to please yourself what you do and how you live. There is a freedom, too, about the city of Prague which you cannot get anywhere else."

" What is the city of Prague?"

" It is the capital of Bohemia."

"Then you are not sorry, after all, for wasting so many years?"

" Yes, I am. I am confoundedly sorry. Only I liked the time. If it was not for that, I should not be afraid of meeting old friends, who might remind one of disagreeable things. And I dare say I might be able to repent now, which I cannot, just when I can afford it for the first time in my life."

It was not quite the repentance that Marion might have wished, but she let that pass.

" Then there is the third kind of life," he said, "and that is what I want to lead with you."

" The five minutes are exceeded, Dr. Chacomb," said Marion. " Goodbye."

" I had a letter from Mrs. Chauncey Chacomb the second to-day. She tells me your brother has written for money, and she has answered the letter. I hope it was not a rude and vulgar answer."

" Fred ought not to have written. There is the answer."

" I shall see her on Saturday. You shall never have such a letter as this again. Chauncey wants to do what he can for your brother, and smuggled a letter to me. What can he do?"

" Nothing," said Marion, shortly. " We want no help from your cousin."

She knew that Chauncey Chacomb was a prey to hallucination; but she could not bear that they should turn to him for help in any, even the direst, necessity. It was enough for her to know that Chauncey bore her father an insane and meaningless hatred.

The doctor had spoken of meeting old acquaintances. On the stairs he found himself face to face with a gentleman who had red hair, and plenty of it, a red face, and very seedy attire. Dr. Chacomb changed colour, and drew himself up to let the other pass.

"Hallo! Joe—Dr. Chacomb. Who the deuce would have thought of finding you here?"

"I beg your pardon, Mr.—Mr.—"

"As if you didn't know me—Dicky Carew. And what a swell you are, Joe! What are you up to now? Is it true that you've come out strong in the pill and powder line, and cut your old friends?"

"I have business of importance, Mr. Carew, and must wish you good morning. Have the goodness to address me in future by my surname."

"I will, Joe—I will. I always do, in fact, when an old pal has got up in the world. Not that you and I were ever exactly pals in the strict sense of the word. I don't think, for instance, that I owe you any money. But you *have* been seen at our nightly free and easy, Joe—I mean Dr. Chacomb —haven't you?"

The doctor tried to push past him, but his old friend stood on the stairs facing him, with one arm laid on the stair rail and the other propped against the wall, so that it was impossible to get by without using violence; and Dicky looked so genial, so glad to see him, that Joseph Chacomb became Joe again.

"Come, Dicky," he said, "I am not best pleased to meet you, because I am out of the old set now, and cannot be as I was before. You understand that, perfectly?"

"Lord bless you!—yes. I understood it in a minute. Can you, in those togs, be a pal of mine, while I am in these? Not to be thought of, Joe—I mean Dr. Chacomb. And so you've got on in the world—that's quite clear. Pride, nowadays, instead of going before a fall, comes after a rise. When I rise, Dr. Chacomb, we will be haughty together."

"I am doing very well. And you?"

"Life with me," said Dicky, "is stationary. The stream of Time flows on without stopping, but brings no change to me. Perhaps, some day, the world will be sorry to think—"

"What are you doing now? Are you on any good paper?"

"On two admirable papers, if they only paid better; and in a Hermit's good graces, if only he valued my services higher. Doing pretty well, Dr. Chacomb; rising steadily, I think."

"Let me look at you," said the doctor. "Ah, I see. The old story, Dicky. I see it in your eyes and in your cheeks; it's telling on your nerves. Knock it off. Good morning."

"Yes, Joe," said Dicky, trying to intercept him, "I will consider your advice, which I am sure is based upon the soundest"—

"Good morning, Mr. Carew," said the doctor, pushing past.

"One moment, Dr. Chacomb—one word only. At this juncture, owing to my aunt in Cumberland not having remitted me my rents, my editor being away on a holiday, and my publishers being, like myself, in temporary embarrassment, I should be very much obliged if you would lend me half a sovereign. The money shall be repaid on Saturday morning, at half-past ten punctually, and at any spot that shall be most convenient to you to meet me."

The doctor produced the coin, and handed it to Dicky, who, directly he touched it, sprang up the steps rapidly.

Seeing Miss Revel's door open, he looked in.

"Good morning, Miss Revel," he whispered, with a face like the morning sun for redness and for smiles.

"Is that you, Mr. Carew? Are you going upstairs?"

"Yes. Are you quite well, Miss Revel? Ah! And Miss Adie quite well, too? Ah!"

Then he went a few steps higher up.

He stopped, for a thought struck him.

He turned round, and began to slowly descend the stairs.

Then he sped swiftly, so as to give reflection no chance, for the nearest public-house.

"I know it is bad for me," he said, with the glass in his hand; "but it doesn't do to be always thinking of oneself—it isn't Christian."

CHAPTER XXIX.

FLUSHED mentally and facially with the effects of this self-denial extraordinary, Dicky Carew mounted the steps which led to his employer's rooms three at a time. He did not observe at first—being a little late, and perhaps on that account anxious to begin work without any preliminary remarks—a singular change in his patron's appearance. When, however, he was seated, and ventured to look up, he was astonished. The Hermit had exchanged his long Cashmere dressing-gown—which gave him, owing to his great height and thin figure, something the air of a jointed telegraph post—for a new and fashionably cut walking coat, designed for a man of five-and-twenty. He had reduced his white hair to a more practicable length, trimmed his white moustache after the fashion of the modern youth, wore a pair of pearl-grey trousers, and a flower in his button-hole. In fact, he had postponed the morning interview with the secretary in order to call upon his fellow-lodgers. Dicky, beside this elderly dandy, looked almost supernaturally shabby. The Recluse was standing before the glass, still adjusting and trimming, with the air of a *petit crévé*. Somehow, too—was it the effect of a little rouge?—his cheeks, contrary to their wont, seemed to have upon them a faint tinge of colour, a delicate bloom, very pretty to look at. By craft and mysterious art, known only to himself, this lonely dweller in a cave had made himself look some twenty years younger. He might now have passed for a man of thirty-five to forty, prematurely grey.

"I am here, sir," said Dicky, taking up his pen and adjusting his pad.

It was then that he looked up and observed the remarkable change in his employer's costume.

Mr. Lilliecrip grunted, and tied his neck ribbon again, catching the full effect of the light upon the downward stroke of the right hand end.

"Hold your tongue," he added, tearing off the tie in a rage, and taking another from a box. "You have interrupted me in an inspiration which may never come again. How dare you speak unless you are spoken to?"

The inspiration referred to his tie: his secretary understood him to allude to something about George the Fourth, the Prince Consort, Washington, or Tippoo Sahib—all of whom seemed somehow mixed up together in those extraordinary memoirs.

Dicky waited submissively, only letting his imagination loose on that little drama of revenge of which I have already spoken. This old buck—this elderly Hermit, dressing himself in the glass to gratify a perfectly meaningless vanity—how if he had him at his mercy!

"Had it been myself," thought the secretary, "dressing to partake of the buxom, the ripe, the juicy Medlar hospitality, or to escort Ready Vyvyan—I know she loves me, poor little Popsy—to the theatre; or going to meet Winifred Owen on her way from the telegraph like Fred Revel; or to take Miss Marion Revel—the angel—out for a walk, if she'd let me, which she never would, it would be a different thing. There might be some sense in *my* wearing pearl-grey trousers, a lemon-coloured waistcoat, diamond studs, and a flower in my button-hole. But for an elderly Hermit, for a miserable Solitary—pah! it's disgusting; it makes one sick. I should like to spoil his beauty for a week."

"Tell me, sir," said Mr. Lilliecrip, turning to him with an imperative air—"tell me if this necktie sits properly. What do you think of the angle? Does it not rather spoil the perfect regularity of outline of the features? Give me your opinion, if you are capable of having one on so important a matter as dress."

"I am not a valet," said Dicky, sulkily.

"I forgot—no. You are one of those failures of civilisation called a copying clerk. Not a valet—no. Beau Brummell once told me—"

"Were you his valet?" Dicky asked, with a fierceness which surprised Mr. Lilliecrip, who made no answer, but proceeded with his tie. At length it was finished.

"Now, sir," said Mr. Lilliecrip, in his coldest voice—
"now, sir, you are late again. I have warned you already,
mind."

The beer was up in Dicky's brain by this time, and he felt,
with a glow of self-respect, that Mr. Lilliecrip had really
better not go too far. When the humblest worm has had
two glasses of beer in the morning, over and above its usual
quantity, that worm will turn and present a warlike front.
Under ordinary circumstances, it is a mistake to suppose
that a perfectly sober worm will ever turn. In this case,
Dicky was emboldened by the success of his remark.

"I am ready," he repeated, doggedly. "Go on; go on,
Beau Brummell."

"Where did I leave off yesterday?"

"I forget," said the scribe, with a laugh. "I think you
were dining with William the Conqueror, after you van-
quished Henry the Eighth at Waterloo."

Mr. Lilliecrip looked daggers, but answered nothing.
Dicky noticed, however, that his hand trembled, and nerved
himself for war.

The Recluse took a paper, and read it over.

"You have spelt developed, Mr. Carew, with two *p's.*
That is the French way. I thought you were totally ignorant
of French. I see, by the way, that you are: Fouché appears
on the next page with the wrong accent. So that you
are unacquainted—I mean only partially acquainted—with
English. Of course, in a tenth-rate literary hack one does
not expect much; but surely, in the intervals of penny-a-
lining and drinking at public-house bars, some of the imperfections of an early education might be repaired by the help
of a little industry."

If he had accused him of shabbiness, of intemperate habits,
of extravagance, of unpunctuality, of any ordinary small sins,
he would have borne it patiently. But to be accused of an
illiterate education, it was too much. The lightning played
round Dicky's eyes, and for a moment he was like Achilles
resenting the insults of Agamemnon. Aided, perhaps, like
that illustrious hero, by the goddess, he repressed his wrath,

and answered with a mildness like the thyrsus of Bacchus, because it concealed a sharp point—

"In which paper did I spell the word wrongly? Was it the one where you described the only time you ever went to the theatre with Walter Tyrrell, the murderer of William Rufus; or the occasion on which you were invited by Richard the Second to meet Sir William Walworth at a State dinner in the Tower?"

Nothing could justify this speech, not even that second visit to the house of call. Still Dicky felt, though the glove was in a manner thrown down, that such an extemporaneous plunge into English history reflected the greatest credit upon him. He wagged his head as if more might come, and took up his pen again.

"I am ready, sir," he repeated, in his mildest manner. "Pray go on."

Uneducated! imperfections of an early education! He, who had been captain of Biddlecombe Grammar School, and afterwards assistant master at a commercial academy at Exeter, until an unpleasantness connected with the master's daughter, needless to relate, had driven him forth, and sent him to seek his fortune in London! Imperfections of an early education! Dicky's feelings were cruelly outraged; but he repressed himself, and repeated, calmly—

"I am ready, sir."

Mr. Lilliecrip, who had seated himself opposite his secretary, looked at him curiously and nervously. The offensive remarks addressed to him in reference to early kings of English history appeared, however, to produce no effect, after the first shock, upon his calm and cold air. On the contrary, they made him look colder of aspect. He waited a little, and then went on, as if nothing had happened—

"'At one of the Chiswick parties, it matters little in what year, I had the pleasure of meeting Talleyrand.' Have you taken that down, Mr. Carew? There are two *l*'s in Talleyrand."

"'I had the pleasure of meeting Cardinal Wolsey,'" said the secretary.

Really, some fate was possessing Richard. *Raro antece-dentem*—his sin was finding him out. It was all that fatal second glass of beer.

"Talleyrand," repeated Mr. Lilliecrip, mildly. "'The diplomatist, although then considerably advanced in years was in his best spirits, and said some of his happiest things. Among others that I remember—"

"Remember!" echoed Dicky. "Ho! ho! ho!"

Not a loud laugh, but an offensively quiet one, as if the producer was enjoying a joke all to himself.

Mr. Lilliecrip took no kind of notice.

"'Among other things that I remember was a reply he made to a young nobleman of ducal rank, who wished to silence the talk of certain lacqueys. 'Young man,' he said, 'let us listen to your betters.'"

"Capital," said Dicky. "Have you forgotten the rest of the story?"

"Sir?"

The voice was as cold as steel; but Dicky was protected with the armour which goes with Dutch courage, and felt it not.

"I always want to write down the end of your stories," he said. "Did the noble entertainer at Chiswick kick out Cardinal Wolsey—I mean Talleyrand? or did the noble scion of a ducal house kick him out? And what view did Henry the Eighth take of it? Were you beheaded on Tower-hill for laughing at the Cardinal's impudence?"

"When you have finished your morning's work, sir, we shall exchange a few words."

"I am ready, sir," said Dicky, again with the look of humility. Only he spoiled his submission by a chuckle, and a soft "Ho! ho! ho! Henry the Eighth!"

"'It is not generally known that the way to eat asparagus' —there is only one *r* and no *h* in that word, Mr. Carew— 'was for a long time the subject of much social discussion. I once dined with Queen Adelaide, after she became a widow, in private. There was no other guest, and she was good enough to give me her views on this important point. 'I tell you,' she said, ' because I am glad to interchange thoughts with a man like yourself, who has made all the minutiæ of social life the subject of his profound study.' "

" Did she say all that ? " asked Dicky. " Oh, oh ! "

Mr. Lilliecrip pursued his story.

" ' For my own part,' said the dowager queen, ' I always eat it with my fingers.' She did so in effect, and I imitated her example.' "

Dicky saw no opening for any caustic remark after this brilliant anecdote, and Mr. Lilliecrip dictated—still in his cold, impressive manner—two or three more anecdotes, which were also too vapid to present the slightest opening for any comment, involving nothing more than an innuendo against the virtue of a noble lady deceased, and another greatly dishonouring a celebrated statesman, also deceased. Then he took a bundle of papers, and tossed them across the table to Dicky, ordering him to read them aloud for his correction.

Dicky proceeded to obey mechanically. Presently he observed that his patron was staring straight before him, obviously not attending. His imagination was in that fine state of activity which is peculiar to a condition of chronic nightly intoxication, gently stimulated by a " hair of the dog that bit you " in the morning. And he gave it full play, reading in a sonorous and even melodious tone, while the unconscious Mr. Lilliecrip sat with his thoughts wandering.

I regret to say that he made nonsense of the invaluable Memoirs ; more than that, as he saw that he was not observed, he introduced irrelevant and even improbable matter, with anachronisms of the wildest kind, and anecdotes of his own invention. Never had Dicky been so carried away by the force of his own imagination. Like a pent-up stream, the waters of fancy gushed and bubbled out, and, like the winter torrents in a thirsty land, they brought ruin and destruction with them, instead of fertility and smiling vegetation. Impunity emboldened him. Now and then he looked up ; but seeing Mr. Lilliecrip motionless, he proceeded with his fatal comedy. After reading in this irreverent and burlesque manner for a quarter of an hour or so, he might, had he been looking off the paper at the moment, have remarked a sudden change in the Hermit's eyes—only for a moment. His lips twitched, his colour came and went, and then he sat as before —his cold, calm eyes still gazing into space, as if he was thinking of something far away.

" The first time I ever saw Peter the Hermit "—Dicky was reading with a full richness of tone which showed his own enjoyment of the situation—"the first time I ever saw Peter the Hermit was on the occasion when the then Dean of Westminster, against the opinion of the leading clergy, introduced him to the Abbey to preach a charity sermon for the Crusade. They collected eighteen marks and a groat, a large sum for those days. The whole was handed to Peter, who put it in his pocket with a genial wink. After the collection, we dined together—a quiet dinner at the Ship, for Peter was fond of whitebait. King Richard was there, Sir Robert Peel, Mr. Gladstone, Bismarck, Saladin, the Dean and Bolingbroke. Nobody else but myself. The conversation turned after dinner upon gallantry. I was astonished at the freedom with which the English statesmen expressed their opinions, especially Mr. Gladstone. Peter told some capital stories. I only remember one, and that, I am sorry to say, I am unable to repeat. The taste of the age, as is well known, was then different to our own. Peter was no exception, and Sir Robert enjoyed a free anecdote. As for Saladin he broke his chair with laughing. The secret history of the Crusades has yet to be written. If I have time I shall write it.

" It is not generally known that the ' Wandering Jew ' was staying in Lowland Street, Tottenham Court Road, about ten years ago. He had lodgings on the second floor, where he used to cook his own meals. His name was never uttered to anybody except myself, and I have promised not to reveal it unless he gives permission. He was a cheery bird, fond of singing the ' Steam Leg,' which was his only song ; but he was a grumbler, and often complained of fatigue. The knowledge of drinks which he had gathered during his long peregrinations was extraordinary, and many is the artful

compound he has brewed for me. I have the receipts, and
mean to write them out at the end of my Memoirs. He
always declared dry champagne to be the best and most
wholesome of liquors. After that he placed Allsopp—when
you have it genuine. He did not like quassia in his malt.
I never could get him to tell me whence he drew his supplies;
but he seemed to have letters of credit on all the banks in the
world. He was a man of innumerable *bonnes fortunes*. He
loved kidneys for breakfast. He once said to me, after a
night of it, 'Lord——, a man of your transcendent abilities
ought to do something for the world, if it is only to double
the salary of your secretary, and to offer him an occasional
glass of ale—'"

"Enough of this buffoonery, sir," said Mr. Lilliecrip,
rising, with great solemnity. "This is Monday. We will
consider our engagement at an end from this moment. I owe
you, I believe, at the rate of three shillings a visit, the sum of
six shillings. There is the amount. Leave the room!"

For the moment Dicky, who was still in the full flow of
recollections, hardly comprehended the blow. He dropped
the papers, and gazed stupidly in Mr. Lilliecrip's face.

"You hear me, sir. Leave the room! Not a word of explanation or apology. Go; and let me see your face no more."

Dicky made haste to seize the six shillings—that was, at
least, something tangible. Then he pulled himself together.
As it was quite clear that he was dismissed, and he saw very
plainly that he had done for himself entirely, he concluded
not to go without relieving his mind in some degree of his
real feelings.

"What, because I enlivened the monotony of your rubbish
by substituting some better stories of my own? Come forth,
Hermit of the Dale—don't be unreasonable!"

Mr. Lilliecrip turned paler, if that were possible.

"I have known," says Dicky, assuming an air of dignity
quite beyond his income, "for a long time that the pretended
Memoirs were nothing but falsehoods, which you intended to
palm off upon the world as real Memoirs and recollections.
Why, man, there is not a page in the whole collection but

will confute you as soon as it is printed, if it appears in the next ten years. And if it is kept dark for fifty, the dense stupidity of the thing will damn it infallibly. Besides which, my own self-respect was at stake in being a party to this impudent forgery."

"Give me back those papers, sir, and leave the room."

Mr. Lilliecrip trembled visibly as he spoke. Perhaps a hermitage of fourteen years' duration does not strengthen the nerves.

"No," said the rebellious secretary, folding them up—"I shall keep these; I mean to show them about. I shall tell the whole world what a humbug lives in Lowland Street. By Jove, there are the names of living statesmen among them. I will go to them, and let them know what is preparing. Your name and your pursuits shall be published, sir. You shall be made notorious. We shall find out who it is has been living here by himself for fourteen years. And you shall know what it is to call Richard Carew an illiterate copying clerk."

He paused, for Mr. Lilliecrip was of a ghastly pallor. Then Dicky hardened his heart, and went on—

"For three years I have endured you, and I am glad it is over. You Pagan pretender, you treated me like a dog. You unchristian monk, you gave me the wages of a dog. You had no more consideration for the man who worked for you than if he had been a machine. I always longed to tell you my mind, and now I have. Unholy Hermit, you are a humbug!"

He produced the papers, folded up in a roll, and flourished them in his enemy's face.

"Now I have you in my power," he said, melodramatically. "Now, impostor, hiding away because you are ashamed or afraid to face the world, I can do what I please with you. You shall be unmasked. You are in my power. Ha! ha!"

It was quite the realisation of his dream, and a thing altogether to be enjoyed.

"This is too much," cried the Recluse. "Give me back my papers, or I will force them from you."

" Will you fight me for them ? " asked Dicky, who was as plucky a man as ever drank Devonshire cider. " I wish you would. My wind is not so good as it was, but I could double you up like an empty thread-paper. Or will you ring the bell, and send for a policeman ? If you do, I will stay here till he comes, and make you go before the magistrates, and give your real name. All Lowland Street will come too. I shall tell the magistrate that I would no longer be a party to an abominable deception of posterity, and am before him in consequence."

He placed the roll in his pocket, put on his hat, and took up the clouded cane of which he was so fond.

" You will see me again, Simon Stylites," he observed, at the door. " I resign your employment. I shall look in upon you in a day or two and report progress. I am going to be your bugbear. For the present, good morning."

He left the room with a loftiness of bearing which pleased himself immensely. His soul was in a tumult of pleasure at the recollection of the many fine things he had said ; nor was it till some hours afterwards, when the flurry of his spirits had in a measure subsided, that he began to realise the importance of the salary he had lost.

It was to Mrs. Medlar that he communicated, first of all, the news of his revolt, and the eloquence with which he had conducted the business of the final scene.

" But you have lost your salary, and how will you live ? "

This was a new light, in which he had not thought of regarding the situation.

" Go back and make terms, Mr. Carew," she said—" go and offer him the papers back again for what he will give. Lord ! what's the use of being proud ? Why bite your nose off to spite your face ? Make it up again. You know his secrets."

" Viper ! "—he did not mean Mrs. Medlar—" Viper ! I do. I shall grind him to powder beneath this heel."

" Well," she replied, " there isn't much left to grind with ; and if you don't make it up with him there won't be any sole left either. However in the world could you go to be so foolish? The usual thing I suppose—a drop of something. Now, mind, Mr. Carew, you don't marry me unless you take the pledge."

She offered him no refreshment; she gave him no applause. It was as if Amadis de Gaul, after his proudest achievement, when he conquered the giants of Armenia and carried them away captive to the enchanted Princess of the Island of Morocco, had been received by the chosen of his heart with a scoff and a question instead of an accolade or a chaste salute.

Dicky felt the reception deeply.

"For thy sake," he might have said—"for thy sake, Lady Medlar, have I recovered the self-respect of an honest man. What if the spirit which prompted the deed was fortified and encouraged by a draught of Burton—old and mild?"

Alas! many a notable jest has been lost to the world through the want of appreciation of those who first hear it. And there are some women, love they never so madly, who cannot convert their husbands into heroes.

CHAPTER XXX.

IT must be owned that Dicky, face to face with the immediate loss to his income caused by his freedom of speech, felt next morning a little out of spirits. He did not follow Mrs. Medlar's advice, and humiliate himself before his enemy, having an instinctive assurance that it would serve no useful purpose. On the contrary, he carried his plunder, the roll of manuscript Memoirs, to the British Museum, to read them, with a view of doing what mischief he could to the man who had dared to call him illiterate.

Away from the personal influence of the Hermit, whose cold and measured manner never failed at the time to impress the amanuensis with a profound sense of truthfulness, Dicky found it horrible to realise the prodigiousness of the vast collection of lies. They were gross, palpable, and foolish lies. They were slanderous. They betrayed themselves. They

were full of anachronisms; dead and living men were mixed;
and they had not, as some of these anecdotes of social life
have, the spice of ill-nature and epigram wanted to make
them attractive. The Hermit was a poor storyteller. The
stories he told were like those of the very bad French
novelists who lived under the Consulate and First Empire—
their works are nearly all out of print, but you may get hold
of them now and then if you search—who have no other
recommendation than a gush of language without parallel in
literature, and comparable only to the mouth of a main
drain. The Hermit was not only a weak and foolish man—
weak on the side of personal vanity, foolish in shutting himself up because he had a spite against the world—but he
was a man full of morbid desires and tastes. He courted
notoriety. Men have been known, for the sake of notoriety,
to abandon wife and children, pass as martyrs, and take up
the most unhealthy forms of extreme opinions in a party cry.
No one, so far as I know—except Mr. Greville and my
Hermit— ever deliberately contemplated the purchase of
immortality by the production of clap-trap and sensation
memoirs.

Dicky read and made notes, thinking best how to turn his
plunder to his own gain and the discomfiture of his enemy.
Mr. Lilliecrip called him illiterate! Ah! And copying
clerk. Good. Pretended that he had no acquaintance with
French—did he? And but a partial acquaintance with
English. Very rich—very correct indeed. Dicky would be
revenged; but he did not yet quite see his way. Presently
the clock struck one, and he was reminded of the dinner
hour.

There are many shady retreats in the neighbourhood of
the British Museum where the weary student may find
refreshment—there used to be one, indeed, in the institution
itself; but the authorities, who in the cause of knowledge
are inexorable, discovered that the country people preferred Banbury cakes to Babylon bulls, veal and ham pies to
mummies and marbles, and so at length removed it.
Among the neighbouring hostelries, the one chosen by

Dicky and his immediate circle of friends owned a sanded floor, a large fireplace, and half a dozen wooden cribs, with settles, like those of the Cheshire Cheese and the Cock—a device by which the proprietors persuaded the unthinking that their steaks and chops had a hidden virtue unknown to places where the floor is carpeted and the seats are cushioned.

He was still suffering from the excitement natural after a battle in which barren honour was the only result on which he could pride himself. He dined alone, although there were friends in the other boxes. After his chop, he ordered a glass of the beverage which best he loved, whisky and water hot, and lighting a pipe—you may smoke in this establishment—began to think how to recover his losses. Fifteen shillings a week. It was a good deal to lose. It was half his income.

While he smoked, stirred his grog, and meditated, he was disturbed—agreeably at first—by the entrance of a man he knew.

He was a very big man, with whiskers which grew all round his face and stuck out under his chin, leaving that feature free and clean. This gave him a truculent expression. He looked all round the room, and spotting his man, who was no other than Dicky, strode noisily across the floor, and banging his fist on the table, uttered these remarkable words, in the deepest bass ever heard—

" You precious scoundrel ! "

The other gentlemen in Dicky's walk of life who were dining at the time naturally took a lively pleasure in the prospect of a row ; there was a general silence, and craning of heads round the divisions.

" You precious scoundrel ! " the stranger repeated. Then, observing the presence of others, he addressed the company generally.

" Gentlemen, I put it to you. You shall judge what a villain this fellow is. I have engaged him for the last two years on a paper—a property of my own, gentlemen. You, as literary men, will appreciate the care and trouble I have had to nurse this property. My own child, gentlemen. I invented the title; I found the capital to start it; I bore the loss for six months—though I could ill afford it. This double-dyed blackguard—"

"Draw it mild—I say," expostulated one of the hearers. "It isn't parliamentary."

"No, sir, I repeat, this double-dyed blackguard, to whom I have paid—ah! paid Enormous sums of money—"

"Well," said Dicky, driven to desperation—"it was seven and six a week. What is it I've done? Tell me quickly, can't you? Play up your pretty pipe, shepherd."

The big man gnashed his teeth at this allusion to his voice.

"This snake in the grass, gentlemen—but I must tell you that mine is a Christian paper, and a Church paper. It is no other than the *Christian Clerk and Vestrymen's Bosom Friend.*"

It is difficult to explain why the countenances of the assembly relaxed, and their faces broadened with smiles. But so it was.

"The *Christian Clerk*—my property, my title. You will hardly believe, gentlemen, that after being in my employ on that paper for two years—after receiving, as I said, Enormous sums of money—he sends me last week a collection of infamous paragraphs, bringing the clergy into ridicule, attacking the aristocracy, and breathing nothing short of open infidelity! Would you believe that, gentlemen? And I trusted him, gentlemen, and printed it all, without even reading his proofs."

There was a universal shout.

Dicky, in a cold perspiration, saw at once—with a fearful foreboding of what would happen next—what *had* happened. He said nothing, but looked mutely round the well-known faces for sympathy.

He received none. They were all laughing, except the unlucky proprietor of the paper, who raged in their midst.

There was one other exception. In the box next to Dicky's but nearer the door, there sat a bearded gentleman, perhaps

the greatest Bohemian of them all, who, instead of laughing
with the rest, fixed his eyes on the injured editor, and gravely
wagged his head, expressing by this movement his profound
sympathy with the *Christian Clerk*.

Then Dicky laughed himself, and the merriment was
general. But a worse thing happened. Another man, whose
face was only too well known to Mr. Carew, opened the door,
and looked up and down the room. Seeing the person he
was in search of, he darted with a tigerish bound and something like a yell towards Dicky's table.

"Now, sir," he cried, in a profound voice, and banging his
fist on the table with a crash that rattled the crockery all
over the room—"now, sir, what have you got to say to me?"

"Nothing," said Dicky—"only take care of the plates, and
don't destroy the property. They charge a great deal here
for a broken glass."

There was instantly a dead silence.

The man was a very little man indeed, with an immense
head and bearded face, a very ferocious type of man—one
who would have called himself Lucius Junius Brutus in the
first years of the Revolution, and paraded the streets bawling
"Death to Tyrants!"

Dicky knew him, too; but he was now reckless.

"Destroy the property?" echoed the new-comer. "De-
stroyer of property yourself. Tell me again, what have you
to say? I will expose you among your friends. Listen,
gentlemen. This man has been on my staff for two years. I
have learned to trust him. He has written for the *Weekly
Intelligence—my* property, gentlemen."

There was a grin of universal expectation on every face,
except that of the hairy gentleman above named, who caught
the little man's eye, and shook his head with a sympathising
gravity.

"The *Weekly Intelligence*. No doubt many of you here
are subscribers." There was another grin at this hypothesis,
which showed too amiable a confidence in the purchasing
and reading powers of his audience. "This man here wrote
for me."

"Are you," asked the proprietor of the *Christian Clerk*—
"are you the editor of that infamous journal? And do you,
sir"—he turned to Dicky—"do you dare to say you wrote
for the *Christian Clerk* at the same time that you wrote for
the *Weekly Intelligence?* Hypocrite!"

Dicky wagged his head, but answered not.

"Infamous journal, sir! What do you mean?" cried
the little man. "I'll make you know, sir; I'll teach you,
sir."

As he advanced, the big man retreated, being, indeed, an
egregious coward. But before he left the room he shook his
fist at Dicky.

"You are discharged, sir. You are discharged. Ask for
what I owe you, if you dare."

As he left the room, the sympathetic man of letters rose
and left too. In five minutes he returned, and turned his
grave and thoughtful face upon the other editor.

He was still haranguing the room. He told how he had
trusted in the Radical principles of the man before him; how
he believed him superior to the trammels of superstition;
how he denounced kings, priests, and nobles, with a cheerful
vigour which raised the circulation of the paper—

"Then you ought to have raised my pay," said Dicky.

—How his own confidence grew to such an extent that he
even allowed the proofs to pass unread; and how—gentlemen
—how on the last Sunday morning his attention had been
called by a friend to an article in which the bishops and
clergy of the Church of England were held up to general
admiration as possessing all the virtues.

There was no sympathy with this editor any more than
with the first. He looked upon the grinning faces around
with a disgust too great for words. The bearded and long-
haired man near the door preserved a calm and even sad
demeanour when the editor's glance fell upon him, only
raising his hands in deprecation of Dicky's iniquity.

"Now, Mr. Carew," he wound up, "you shall not say I
tried to cheat you; there's your money in full"—he threw
three half-crowns upon the table—"and take your discharge."

He put on his hat with tremendous vigour, and, hurling defiant glances right and left, walked swiftly out.

The man who had not laughed went out after him.

Dicky, in the midst of acclamations, rose solemnly.

"It's all true, gentlemen," he said. "I wrote for both those papers, and I must have mixed the articles. Anybody who knows of a vacancy may recommend me."

"If I hear of any, Dicky, that I can't fill myself, you shall have the office," said one of them.

The second clause of the proviso exactly suited the sentiments of the rest, who all repeated it, with slightly verbal alterations. Then the man with the long hair and the ragged beard came back, with transfigured and radiant countenance.

He had secured both jobs.

That man, the only one who saw the opportunity and seized it, is now in comparative affluence. He is the principal literary prop of the *Christian Clerk*—whose circulation has trebled during the late Christian revival—and he has led the *Weekly Intelligence* to dazzling heights of revolutionary audacity, in which even the editor himself sometimes feels dizzy. Of course his pay is trebled too.

The moral is obvious.

It was with a heavy heart that Dicky turned into the street when the afternoon *séance* finished. No occasion for him to go back to the Museum for the present. The pamphlets and the magazines might rest undisturbed. His occupation was gone, and with it his salary.

Presently he reflected on the cause of the sudden downfall of his worldly prospects; and he remembered that a third glass of gin and water was the cause of the fatal exchange of "copy" for the papers, while an unwonted early visit to the house of convivial hospitality caused the outbreak with the Hermit.

Then he met Miss Ethelreda Vyvyan in Holborn, on her way home from rehearsal. She skipped up, in her artless and cheerful manner, and slapped him on the shoulder.

"Dicky, my boy, the grandmother is ill—poor old girl!—and you must pay up."

" Pay up, Popsy ? "

" Don't call me Popsy, because it's cheek, and I won't allow it. I am Ethelreda Vyvyan, of the Royal Hemisphere Theatre, if you please. But you must pay up, old boy, whether you call me Popsy or Ready ; and it's close upon five pounds. I'll toss you whether we make it five-ten or a fiver clear—come."

" I'm going into the City instantly," said Mr. Carew, " to see my lawyer. He is engaged in selling out some stock for me."

" Ah ! and going down to Westmoreland afterwards to see your dear old aunt, who sends you such regular supplies, are you not ? Now, Dicky, pay up, and no more humbug between friends. I wouldn't bother, old man, if I didn't want the dibs—I wouldn't, really."

" I haven't got any money, Popsy. That's the real truth."

" Then give me what you have."

" I've got nothing, Popsy, except a pound ; and I must pay my rent, mustn't I ? Your Dicky would have to find a lodging in the ' cauld, cauld blast.' Oh ! shelter me."

" Dicky, it's pretty clear you've been going it a little too free. Now, take my advice, and stop it. You can pay grandmother at so much a week, if you like ; but no shirking. Come and see me to-morrow morning, and tell me what you are going to do."

Poor Dicky ! He was going to do nothing—there was nothing to do.

Then he began to curse his ill fortune.

Then he advanced a step, and cursed his fatal habit of drink.

Then he became suddenly and strongly repentant.

And then, giving the rein to these wholesome meditations, he wandered up and down the street, revolving wholesomely the evil effects of drink, till he came upon a place where a card was posted in the window inviting all to enter and take the pledge.

Dicky thought of Mrs. Medlar's advice, obeyed the invitation, and, without further consideration, put down the penny, and took the oath.

At half-past nine that evening there was a knock at Mrs. Medlar's door.

It was Dicky Carew. He was leaning for support against the doorpost. His hat was at the back of his head. He carried the clouded cane, but it was broken. His knees bent beneath him. He bore the external appearance of one who had been drinking, not wisely, but too well.

Mrs. Medlar looked at him with rising wrath.

"What have you got in your hand?" she asked.

"Itsh pledge," Dicky replied. "I've come—tell you—Mishush Med—Med—Medlar—followed advishe, ekshlent advishe—took pledge, thought you'd like—look at it. Besht of women. Thought I'd pleashe you!"

CHAPTER XXXI.

AS for the head of the Revel house—the unlucky Fred—he was spending his three days of grace in a condition of absolute terror and remorse. He saw the hour approaching —he counted the strokes—when the home, such as it was, of his sisters would be literally stripped; and he did not dare to tell the secret. He sat and listened, pretending to take an interest in their hopes and plans. He did not dare to tell his wife—the wife whom he did not dare to own. As always happens, he repented when it was too late. I do not know whether his repentance was quite of the kind advocated by the Christian preacher; but it was deep and real, because he was extremely sorry. He knew that there was going to be a *mauvais quart d'heure*, and he did not at all see his way clear to making things pleasant when the furniture was actually carried off. He foresaw the winged words of Adie, the tears of Marion; and he dreaded the explanation he should have to offer to his wife.

For ten pounds and a box of cigars he had bought this misery. It was the dearest purchase he had ever made.

Frederick Revel was not a young man who preferred evil to good; nor had he what is meant when we talk of the vices of a young man. He did not, for instance, like Mr. Richard Carew, fall about the stairs on his way to bed. But he loved the semblance of an easy life, and he desired above all to keep things smooth. Had he been a prophet in Israel in those days when the kings liked to have pleasant oracles, though Rabshakeh, with the Tartan of Esarbanipal, was already knocking at the gate Gennath, Fred Revel would have sat before the king with smiling face and brow of unclouded sweetness, prophesying the most delightful future. For the sake of keeping things pleasant for himself, he was content to take Marion's money day by day. In order to make life more pleasant, he fell in love with Winifred. And not to disturb the existing pleasantness, he had forborne to consult his sister when he borrowed the money for which they were all of them now going to pay.

A contemptible young man? Well, yes—if you please. The curious thing about life is the way in which these contemptible young men sometimes manage to get liked. Everybody liked Fred. The women liked him for his bonny face, and that sweet smile of his which came so easily, meant so little, and yet seemed to mean so much. Men liked him, too—that is, men of a sympathetic turn—why, it would be hard to say, but principally because he was always in a good temper. Fred spoke ill of no man, because he harboured no malice. He never clashed with any one, because he had no ambition. He never refused to listen, and never grumbled at his own lot. Think what it is to be a man who is nobody's rival, who envies no man, who is in no one's way, and who is always genial, friendly, and in a good humour. A most contemptible young man; but there are plenty of his kind, like those pretty, fair-weather craft lying at anchor up Haslar Creek. A young man whose ideas of pleasure would expand with his available powers of spending and borrowing, but who would never cease to desire enjoyment of some kind, were it only that of the Neapolitan beggar—to lie in the shade, and enjoy the softened reflection of the glaring sun from the opposite wall. A young man to whom work of any kind is so distasteful as to be impossible: a man without a backbone.

The day before the fatal morning, he made a little effort to communicate the trouble that was impending.

It was after breakfast. Marion was engaged upon her work. Adie was preparing to go marketing. Fred was walking up and down the room restlessly.

"Marion," he said, "I want forty pounds."

She remembered a former request that she should invest money in a sleeping partnership.

"What is it for, Fred?"

"Never mind what it is for. Will you let me have it?"

"How can I? I have not a quarter of the money."

"Pshaw! always the same story. Have you not fifteen hundred pounds in the Stocks? Can you not sell out a paltry hundred for me when I ask you?"

"My poor Fred," she replied, "how often am I to tell you that the income we get from that sum is our only stand-by, and that nothing—no necessity, however pressing—shall make me part with it?"

Even then—had he only told her! But he did not dare.

She put on her hat hastily, and went out of the room, on her constant and never-ending errand of work and money. He looked after her, and groaned. His last chance of raising the money was gone.

In the language of certain writers, Fred was not quite bad, because he was sorry to think of what was coming upon him. All the rogues who somehow miss general abhorrence may be defended by much the same plea. The French jury brought in extenuating circumstances for the man who had murdered his father and his mother, on the ground that he was an orphan. We are told that M. Kakistos is not wholly a villain, because he loves his mother, or because he sheds tears of repentance before his flogging, or because he has given a sovereign to convert the natives

of Fiji, or because he assures the chaplain that he is sorry
for having murdered his grandfather, tortured his grandmother, beaten his wife, and starved his children. Where
is the old-fashioned villain, all wickedness, and as hard as
nails? Nowhere. I declare that he is extinct—gone out
with cock-fighting, the P.R., the highway robber, and
Jonathan Wild. But plenty of things as bad as those he
used to do are perpetrated by smooth-handed young gentlemen like Fred Revel. What he had done was as bad. And
yet he was no vulgar rogue, and would have scorned any
action which might seem to him openly dishonest.

And what would Winifred say?

A man of so gelatinous a nature ought not to have fallen
in love at all. Of course, love is intended to imply intelligent
selection. It involves an average vigour of mind, a certain
amount of determination and pluck—none but the brave, we
know, deserve the fair. It means perseverance, because every
petit commis who marries on a hundred and twenty pounds
a-year is proud of having achieved, by industry and the display of extraordinary talents, a position which enables him
to bring his bride to her cottage home. It means self-
reliance; because no one would get engaged who was not
full of trust in his own abilities. It makes, in the popular
estimation, a great many lesser things—notably, a proof of
the unselfish nature of the young man, in giving up everything, club life, independence, liberty, and the rest, for the
sake of a woman.

Yes. But Fred, unfortunately, flew in the face of the moral
philosophy of love by slipping into it because it was pleasant,
and by marrying secretly because that was more pleasant.

What is to be done with a man whose only notion of life
is to have and to enjoy? It is fitting that sorrow and vexation should fall upon him. It is well to read him stern
lessons which he must learn, whether he likes it or not, and
may lay to heart if he chooses; but what about those on
whom his actions bring trouble? There are three women
now—at first there were but two—who will mourn and
lament if this young man come to harm.

He was a worthless chap, said schoolmaster Owen—who ought to know a worthless chap when he saw one, if experience is any use. It is not for me to defend him, or to ask for any sympathy. From his childhood upwards, he had grasped at pleasure as the only good. He was blinded by his own passionate desire for enjoyment. He could not see beyond the present, he could not suffer more than the present pain. Why people liked him it is impossible to say, except that it was because he was so sanguine and so light-hearted.

But here is a point of difficulty. He was, being a poor man, quite useless, and morally inferior. Suppose he had been rich, what a wealth of good qualities would have covered over and hidden, so that they could never have been suspected, these faults which bad fortune brought conspicuously to the front. He could not work, it is true, having no power of application; nor could he refrain from present enjoyment if it was in any way to be obtained; but these were defects quite unlikely to be noted in the daily life and conversation of a wealthy man. On the other hand, he was as handsome as Apollo; he was physically brave; he was truthful; he was honest and honourable in such general dealings as required no money; he had proclivities in the direction of art; he was of good taste, and as generous as Alcibiades. In fact, Fred often reminded me of that gallant who, in his turn, seems to have moulded his character on the well-known model of Absalom. Probably tradition brought the story of Absalom to Athens by way of Tyre and Cyprus.

Whence it follows that prosperity, and not adversity at all, has uses as sweet as the fire to a bottle of port on a frosty day. I believe I should myself—but of course we should all be better, once out of the mire of savagery and over-feeding, were we free to go our own way, cultivate our taste, and gratify our sympathies. Lord, make and keep us rich. Amen.

Fred appeared this morning in a state of agitation quite irregular and previously unknown. For the first time in his life he was ashamed of himself. He was in the position of a criminal about to be arrested, to whom escape was impossible.

He had trifled with his breakfast, and eaten nothing.

Marion, busy with her thoughts, took no notice, and presently went away on a commercial visit to Mr. Burls. Adie, who poured out his tea for him, saw there was something wrong, but forbore till Marion was gone.

"Now," she said, when the door was closed upon her sister, "what is it, Fred? Tell me."

"Nothing," he replied faintly.

"Don't talk nonsense. Tell me everything."

"Can you bear to hear everything?" he asked, in a hollow voice, not at all feigned.

"I must, I suppose, some time or other," said his sister. "Come, Fred, dear, don't be a baby. Take your finger out of your mouth, and let me have a clean breast at once."

"Well, hang it, Adie, you might be a little sympathetic. You know how unlucky I've been."

"I do know that, Fred." She patted his hand with her soft and slender fingers, and sank down at his feet in a pretty, unstudied attitude—all Adie's attitudes were unstudied. "I do know, Fred. You've been so unlucky as to be born with a great desire for good things and no money. So have I. I am exactly like you. Nobody could be more unlucky than you and I. Let us sympathise together. Poor Marion is not too lucky either, because she has to work for all three of us. Let us sympathise with her too."

"Three months ago, Adie, I was hard up," he began solemnly.

"Why, my dear boy, what were you yesterday, or four months ago, or any time since I first knew you? You were hard up when we were in the nursery together. For goodness sake do not look so solemn, Fred; you frighten me."

"Do let me go on, Adie; it is no laughing matter. I went to a man named Saul, a money-lender, and asked for an advance. He came here to see the security."

"What security?" asked Adie, with quickening apprehension.

"The—the furniture, you know."

"But that is not yours. It is Marion's."

"It is mine and yours, I suppose, as well as Marion's.

My father left no will. At all events, it is too late to ask whose it is, because he came here and took an inventory. Then he made me sign a bill of sale—"

" What is that ? "

" And gave me ten pounds and a box of cigars. The bill was dated at three months, and it was for thirty pounds. Now it has mounted to forty. And, Adie, the bill falls due to-day."

" But, Fred, you have no money. Tell me, can he take you—O Fred! can he take you to prison ? "

" No, but he can take the chairs and things. Hush! "—he turned very pale—" I hear steps on the stairs. They are coming up now."

Adie sprang to her feet, with a sudden horror upon her.

The door opened, and Mr. Saul appeared alone. But there were two men behind, and a van drew up to the door.

" Now, Mr. Revel," he said, taking off his hat with a bow to the young lady, " this is the day, you know, and I suppose you are ready to meet your liabilities."

" No, I am not."

" Hum! That's awkward. Then you have found a good name, perhaps ? "

" No, I have not."

" Well, you will give me fresh security ? "

" I have none."

" Not a single friend to help you ? Not any to help this young lady ? Not any other property ? "

" None—nothing. You must do what you please."

" Ah! Well, I am very sorry, but we must proceed to remove the furniture. Benjamin, you may come in."

Two men came in, and without further ceremony began to put chairs together and move things about.

" What are they going to do, Fred ? " cried Adie.

" They are going to take away all our furniture," her brother replied.

" I am very sorry, young lady—very sorry indeed, to place you to any inconvenience ; but the law, you know—the law."

" But it is not my brother's furniture. It is my sister's, all of it."

"That's awkward too, because he said it was his own."

The men went on in a swift business-like way. In three journeys up and down stairs they had nearly dismantled the room.

"Not my music too," Adie cried, as a profane hand was laid upon her music stool.

"Everything, Benjamin," said Mr. Saul.

"Everything?" she asked. "Are you going to take our wardrobes?"

"Everything, Benjamin," said Mr. Saul, addressing his assistant, and not looking at the girl.

"Oh, stop!" she cried, "stay till my sister comes home. I think she will be able to pay off the money, or some of it. Spare our room, at any rate."

Mr. Saul waved his hand with dignity in the direction of Fred, as much as to say, "You see the real culprit. I pity, but cannot help you."

In the presence of the men Adie said nothing to her brother, who walked backwards and forwards with flushed cheek and restless step.

"Can't you stop them at all, Fred?" she asked. "Must everything go? Oh, what will Marion say?"

He seized his hat and rushed from the room, leaving the girl alone with the men.

"Show me," she said, "your authority for taking these things."

Saul drew out of his pocket the bill of sale.

"There is my authority, young lady. I would advise you not to resist it."

"Resist it? I resist it? How can I? Will you let me take one or two of my own things? They are in the other room."

"Benjamin," he replied, "go with the young lady into her room, and bring me what she wants to take away."

"No, sir," she said proudly. "If I am to have the company of you and your assistants in my own room, I shall leave you to do your worst. The worst is to take away everything, is it not?"

"That is the worst," said Mr. Saul. "I assure you, if I had known that I was advancing money on the security of furniture used by a young lady, I would have refused the loan—I would, indeed."

"That is your worst. Then I will tell you that you are a cheat, and a thief, and a villain. You gave my brother ten pounds, and you exact forty. You are a Shylock."

Mr. Saul, who had not expected to meet any one in the place except Fred, looked a little disconcerted.

By this time the furniture was reduced to the carpet, which the men began to take up.

"How glad I am," said Adie, "that Marion's picture is gone !"

"Eh? What? Picture?" Mr. Saul was evidently alarmed. "Where is the inventory ? Why the devil, Benjamin, can't you tick off things? Where's the picture?"

"Pictures—there—here you are," said the assistant.

"Now, remember, young lady, if anything has been taken away, pledged, or lent, or sold, it is fraudulent, and will lead you and your brother into serious trouble. Benjamin, there's something about a picture that I don't understand. Go up to Mr. Revel's bedroom, three-pair back; look into the cupboard first, and then go out on the roof. Ah! I am a Shylock, am I? I've had to do with real ladies before now —not ladies in Lowland Street, with a brother who lives by billiards—real ladies, and I've always found something put out upon the roof. Go and look well on the roof, Benjamin. There you'll find the picture, no doubt. *My* picture."

"I wish my brother was here to thrash you," said Adie, with flashing eyes. "You cheat him because he is made to be the prey of such creatures as you; but you would not dare insult him before his face. When he is gone, you insult me. Of course, no one expects from a money-lender the smallest resemblance to a gentleman; but one might expect some trace of civilisation. Costermongers, even, are careful in their speech when they talk to ladies. Money-lenders, I suppose, rank below costermongers."

The words were brave enough, but the girl's heart was

swelling within her. Mr. Saul made no reply, but presently cursed Benjamin roundly because his visit to the roof produced nothing.

Then the carpet was taken up, and Adie remembered her friend the schoolmaster.

He was in school, presiding over his little band of twenty scholars, divided into two classes. They were the sons of the small shopkeepers in Lowland Street and its environs—people too proud to send them to the National Schools, where they would have learned quite enough for all their wants in life, and feeling a glow of pride at the reflection that Johnny and Harry were learning Latin. Rhyl Owen, meantime, taught the children what he could, in the old-fashioned method of instruction, accompanied by the quick, old-fashioned method of stimulant. He was perched on his chair, with his little legs tucked under it, his long coat sweeping to the floor like an academical robe, and his puckered face bent over a battered copy of Cæsar. He was finishing off the grammatical portion of his lecture, and with one eye on the clock, which pointed to a quarter before twelve, was beginning a short address on the character and exploits of his author.

"What is it, Miss Adie?"—becoming suddenly conscious that the young lady was standing in front of his desk. "Silence, every boy, or I will cane the whole school, from top to bottom. Fifty lines for Smith—half an hour for Bumpus —all the school an hour to stay in."

"Come out as soon as you can, Mr. Owen," she whispered, with a tremulous voice. "Come out and see me; we are in terrible trouble."

The schoolmaster looked again at the clock. It wanted eight minutes to twelve. Nothing the parents disliked more than the dismissal of their boys a moment before the time. It was so much defrauded of their rights. Fortunately, he heard a clock somewhere striking the hour.

"We are five minutes slow," he said. "Boys, you may go. Those I told to stay in just now shall be let off for once."

All took up their books and were off in a moment, except two.

"There's Candy Secundus and Holybone Primus—kept in as usual," he explained. "Stay, I'll cane them both instead, and let them go. I shan't be a minute working them off. Come here, you boys, and be caned. You deserve it richly, both of you. Candy Secundus first, because he's the worst."

He grasped his cane and descended to the field of action— the small space in front of his desk, which acted as a narrow arena, there being just room, and nothing to spare, for the caning of a boy. It was also the intellectual gymnasium, being used for the standing of a class, and such scholastic evolutions.

"No," said the girl. "Let them off this time. I am sure they have done nothing very bad. Go away, boys, as quick as you can; Mr. Owen is the kindest master in the world, and lets you off."

They needed no second invitation, but grinned and dispersed themselves. To be sure a caning more or less mattered little.

The schoolroom empty, Adie sat down, and gave way to the tears that her pride kept back before the men above.

Mr. Owen waited patiently, standing before her with the cane still in his hand, and as if she was a culprit, and he was about to administer punishment.

"When you are composed, my dear," he said at length, shaking the instrument as if he meant to begin as soon as she was ready.

"I must cry," she said—"I am in such a rage that I must cry. Oh, Mr. Owen, it is worse than when I asked you to give me something to eat, and that was bad enough. Fred has been borrowing money, and they are carrying away all our furniture."

"How much money?" Mr. Owen asked. "I've got— don't tell Winifred, because it was meant as a surprise for her—I've got twenty pounds in the Post Office bank. Will that be of any use? Come with me, my dear—no, you stay here, while I go and see what can be done."

He found Mr. Saul superintending the removal of the bedroom furniture.

" What is the amount of the debt ? " he asked.

" More than you can pay, old shaver," Mr. Saul replied, with a fine politeness. " Now, don't interrupt by asking conundrums, but just get out of the way."

" What the devil do you mean ? " the little Welshman cried, in a boiling rage. " I'm a friend of the family—"

" A pretty family—" the creditor began.

" Look here," said Mr. Owen, turning up the sleeves of his coat, which were much too long, in case matters should take an assault-and-battery turn, which he ardently desired. " Look here—I've asked you a civil question, and got an uncivil answer. I'll break every bone in your great fat body, you lumbering money grubber ! "

There was little doubt, from the fiery and Early Briton-like expression of his eyes, that he would have done it—Cadwallader and Caractacus must have been awful warriors to tackle : one wonders how the Romans worried through with the job. Mr. Saul collapsed. That is, he became civil.

" I'm sure I don't want to say anything against the family. The young man will make me lose a lot as it is, and that's enough, I take it. But perhaps you will pay the amount. It's a matter of above thirty-nine nineteen. Say forty."

That was too much. Mr. Owen groaned aloud.

" Can't you give us a day or two to look round ? "

" Why, you've already had three days. Be reasonable, now. Benjamin, wake up. Hang it, one would think you were working by the hour ! Now then, sir ; there's the case —cash advanced, bill of sale on the furniture ; no money forthcoming, furniture sold. Is that straight and fair, or isn't it ? If it isn't, pay the money on the nail to me, Mr. Saul, of Thavie's Inn, and the goods shall all be taken out of the cart again."

Mr. Owen retreated.

" My dear," he said, " is there no one else to ask ? "

" Of course there is. There is Dr. Chacomb. Oh, even Marion would not mind my asking his help in such a strait as this. He will be at the hospital now."

Mr Owen had a short interview with the great physician,

who was in the very rush and flow of business. But he came away with the schoolmaster instantly.

"I know Saul. I've had dealings with him. Here—hansom! Now then, Mr. Owen, jump in."

"Fred Revel is a more worthless rascal than ever I thought him," said the schoolmaster.

"You know him—yes, you know the family? I have heard of you, Mr. Owen, and your daughter."

"Yes, I know him," said the schoolmaster savagely. "Curse him!"

"Ah, you would like to punch his reckless young head. It's no good, my dear sir, not the least good in the world. He belongs to a tribe on whom kicking would be quite thrown away. I am sure you must have observed, in your professional experience, some boys who are none the better for all your benevolent caning, and would be none the better if Solomon was in your chair."

"I have," said Mr. Owen. "Candy Secundus is a case in point. And I've often thought that Alcibiades must have been another. He once boxed a schoolmaster's ears, and does not appear to have been caned for it, as he should have been if it had been me."

"No doubt. I am going to see Mr. Saul, and get the sticks back again. No experience will teach that boy anything."

Mr. Owen got down at the usurer's office, and hastened back to comfort Adie.

He found her in the dismantled and empty room. With her, Marion.

"I could sit down and cry, Marion," she was saying, "if there was anything to sit down upon. But one cannot cry standing, it's too ridiculous. It's like the nuns in the picture. And, besides, it won't bring back our things."

"Where is Fred?" Marion asked.

"I do not know. He ran away, and left me to face the enemy by myself. Marion, don't say anything to the poor boy."

Adie, as we have seen before, reserved to herself jealously

the right of reproaching her brother—a right which she executed in secret, and with discretion.

"What could I say, Adie? The thing is, what are we to do?"

"Come downstairs, Miss Marion," said the schoolmaster. "You shall have Winifred's room, and Winifred and Miss Adie shall have mine, and I will sleep up here on the floor till you get your things back."

"And Fred?" asked Marion.

"Fred may sleep on *his* floor," replied Adie. "As he has done all the mischief, let him have some of the suffering."

"Mr. Owen," Marion said, "how shall we thank you?"

She took his hand, and looked her thanks with swimming eyes.

"He wanted to lend us all the money he had in the world," Adie cried. "I thank him," throwing her arms round the little man's neck. "I thank him—so."

She kissed him a dozen times, till his cheeks burned with unwonted glow, and his eyes looked as fiery as Prince Llewellyn's, or those of the bard praying that ruin might seize the ruthless king. Then, because his heart was full, he pulled himself from the girl's embrace, and hurried downstairs.

"Adie—" Marion began.

"Marion," interrupted her sister, "please, don't look so solemn. Now listen, and reproach me afterwards. Things were too serious for thinking about what was proper, and so I just sent that dear little man to the Hospital for Gout, and told Dr. Chacomb."

Marion sighed.

"Yes, dear—that's just what I did. As Dr. Chacomb does not want to marry me, there is no pocketing of what they call maidenly reserve. Besides, I want my dresses back again. If they were to be sold, we should have—just think —not a single thing in the world except what we stand in. Not even a clean collar to put on."

But they had another and an unexpected friend, who now tapped at the door. It was Dicky Carew.

"Miss Marion," he began, in a breathless way, "am I too late?"

"What for, Mr. Carew? We have had our furniture seized, that is all."

"But it can't be sold at a moment's notice. They had no business to carry it off at all. I saw them removing the things in the van, and asked whose they were. Then I hurried round to my place to get some papers. Please wait a quarter of an hour if you can."

He left them again, and they heard him run upstairs and knock at the Hermit's door. He was in his dressing-gown, reading his valuable Memoirs.

"Mr. Lilliecrip—" Dicky began.

"You need not make any apologies, Mr. Carew—they are worthless. Nothing would induce me to employ you any more. You have brought me back my papers, I suppose?"

"Apologies be hanged!" he replied. "I've lost more than your appointment since I saw you last. That is not what I came for, Mr. Lilliecrip. And as for the papers of yours in my possession, what would you give to get them back?"

"Eh?"

"What would you give me, supposing I sold them to you back again? Mind, they are worth a great deal. They are worth all my revenge, because I intended showing them about. I was going to make you a general laughing-stock. I was going to take it out of you for my three years' servitude. Now I offer to sell them to you. What will you give?"

Mr. Lilliecrip gasped for breath.

"Come, now, my jovial Hermit"—Dicky, being quite recovered, was able to afford a little geniality. "Come, now, friar of the lonely dell, set the muscatel a-flowing. Ah, stay, gentle stranger." Dicky pointed to the cupboard. "There's no rest like the tap for the Pilgrim of Love."

"You would—ah!—you would like a glass of wine?"

"I would, strange as it may appear. Palmer with the sandal shoon and cockles in thy hair, I would for once taste of thy hospitality."

Mr. Lilliecrip opened the cupboard door. Dicky's wildest dreams were more than realised, for it was full of bottles with silver foil.

"Moselle or champagne, Mr. Carew? Or perhaps you would prefer sparkling Burgundy?"

"Sparkling Burgundy sounds rich," said Dicky; "but I should like a whole bottle of champagne just for once. Come, holy father, brother cellarer, brother cook, and brother treasurer to boot, let us have a bottle of the creamiest and the driest. I am like Byron, because I can't resist the offer of champagne. And I am not like Byron, because I was never offered any before. Corkscrew, aged Ascetic."

Dicky was master of the situation, and he felt it. Besides, a state of absolute destitution as regards income is not at first without a certain exhilaration, a gentle stimulus to the spirits.

He took a tumbler, poured out a glass, and drank it off, with a nod and a smack of the lips.

"'Gad!" he said. "Do you positively mean to tell me that you mortify the flesh day after day with this"—he poured out another, and drank it—"this nectar? 'The Pope he leads a happy life'"—another glass—"only three tumblers in a bottle? I should like another. But no."

He finished it, and sat on the table, dangling his legs, with a beaming countenance.

"Come, Solitary of Sahara, what will you give me for this precious manuscript? Here are your recollections of King Pharaoh, and how you dined with Rehoboam. Here is a bolster of about the liveliest lies ever put together. What shall we say for this lot? Refuse, and they go, with a history of the Hermit of Lowland Street, supposed by some to be the Wandering Jew, to the *Daily Firework*. I shall get the job. I shall write three columns in leaded type. Buzwing, who attends our evenings, will do the leader. You will be so shown up to derision, so illustrated and exemplified by every big name, from Gyges to Napoleon, that on the whole I think you will wish you had not quarrelled with your private secretary, and never gone into the hermiting line. Come, what shall we say?"

"You have me at a disadvantage," replied the Hermit, whose face, during Dicky's harangue, had expressed every shade of terror and dejection. "I wish to have the papers

back: that is quite true. Your presence is offensive, and I
wish to see you gone; and I wish also to buy your silence."

"Buy them all," said Dicky—"buy them all," rollicking
reveller and lonely tippler. I am in a hurry. Thirty pounds
will buy the lot."

Mr. Lilliecrip hesitated.

"Thirty pounds before I count three, or I go.   One.

"But I—"

"Two—Th—"

"I consent."

Five minutes afterwards, Dicky rushed down the stairs
again, holding in his hand six bank notes, white and crisp,
for five pounds each. Marion was alone in the empty room.
He lost all the bounce he had put on with his late employer
as he opened the door, and came in quite humbly.

"Miss Revel," he said, stammering, "I am very sorry.   I
know something about those money-lenders.   I—I—have got
a little money by me—put away in a stocking, you know.
I've brought it to you. Take it, please, and let me fetch all
the sticks back again. It's only thirty pounds."

"Oh! Mr. Carew.   But I cannot."

"You must, Miss Revel.   You will, I am sure, to oblige
me—no, not to oblige me; for the sake of your sister."

"But, Mr. Carew, why do you—"

"Because you—oh! it's for your own, Miss Marion.   No,
don't turn away.   I know well enough what a distance there
is between you and me.   Dicky Carew is not blind; he understands more than people think.   Suppose he has dared to love
and respect you for three years, he has known all the time it
was nothing but such love and respect as a servant may pay
his mistress.   God bless, you Miss Marion!"

"Mr. Carew, I cannot take your money.   I cannot, indeed."

At that moment the door opened, and Mr. Owen appeared
again.

"My dear young lady," he said, "I've got my money.
Mrs. Candy—she's a good soul, though a little short of
temper—advanced it out of the till on my Post Office bank-
book.   Here it is—twenty pounds.   We can buy back some

of the furniture, at any rate. They have only got the right to take what will pay for the bill."

Dicky Carew patted him on the back.

"Good man," he said—"you shall give the boys a half-holiday for this. Now, Miss Revel, you've got enough to defy the money-lender and all his malice. Let us go together, Mr. Owen, and pay off the sharks."

But there was yet another visitor—Dr. Chacomb.

He entered in his quiet and self-possessed manner, shook Marion's hand slightly, and nodded to Carew.

"You here, Carew? Miss Revel, I am happy to say that the little difficulties are removed. The man will send back your things at once; and you will have no further trouble about the matter."

"We are deeply grateful, Dr. Chacomb."

"Not at all. The rascal abated half his claim directly he saw that he had me to deal with. He will place his men at your disposal, and you will only have to see that everything is put back exactly as they took it away. Good morning, Miss Revel; I am going down to Chacomb to-morrow; but I hope to have the pleasure of seeing you next week."

"Now," said Dicky, with fallen face, when he was fairly gone, "I shan't have the pleasure of getting your things back for you. I've sold my revenge for nothing but a speech. What a pity! What a pity!"

"And now," said Mr. Owen, grumbling, "I shall have to take back this money to Mrs. Candy. Miss Marion, do keep it for me."

CHAPTER XXXII.

THIS was Marion's darkest hour. When the bill of sale was settled, and the furniture brought back again she had a letter brought by a ragged little girl from her disreputable pensioner, Mrs. Spenser. It was written in her usual strain—half of command, half of entreaty.

"Come to me at once, as soon as you can. The boy is very ill."

Marion obeyed the letter. This was a case in which not even the doctor, a kind of *deus ex machinâ*, could interfere in her behalf. The thing had to be faced by herself. It was her own secret.

The woman apparently had time, between the sending of the letter and Marion's arrival, to recover her spirits. She was sitting at her table as usual, at her work, singing to the boy, who lay on his mattress, propped up with pillows and a bundle of clothes. His childish face, with its bright, questioning eyes, looked profoundly pathetic to Marion : it seemed as if his intellect had been stopped at the age of six or thereabouts, when he might have been a child of great mental promise and vivid imagination.

He had grown thinner in the few days since Marion last saw him ; his cough was worse, and he sank back from time to time upon the pillows. The St. Vitus's dance was more frequent and more violent.

Marion came in unobserved. The boy's mother was singing an old nursery song with open doors while she worked. Rickety Jem nodded his head, drummed the floor with his stick, and tried to join in the chorus.

> " Soldier, soldier, will you marry me,
>   With your musket, fife, and drum ?
> Oh, no, pretty maid, I cannot marry thee,
>   'Cause I've got no coat to put on.
> So she went upstairs to her father's chest,
> And she brought him a coat of the very, very best,
>   And the soldier put it on.
>
> " Soldier, soldier, will you marry me,
>   With your musket, fife, and drum ?
> Oh, no, pretty maid, I cannot marry thee,
>   'Cause I've got no boots to put on."

The boy got up, and tried to brandish his crutch as he limped up and down in time to the tune. It was a very feeble effort, for the rickets seized his limbs, and he fell back again, with a cough that seemed to tear him to pieces, upon the bed.

Marion remembered the old song—but in a place how different !—and the singer too.

The boy, recovering from his attack, cried out for more, just like a child.

"'Soldier, soldier!' Go on, mother, finish the song."

> "She went upstairs to her father's chest,
>   And she brought him boots of the very, very best,
>   And the soldier put them on."

"Now the last!" cried the boy, impatient—"when she's given coat, and hat, and boots, and all."

> "Soldier, soldier, will you marry me,
>   With your musket, fife, and drum?
> No, pretty maid, I cannot marry thee,
>   'Cause I've got a wife at home."

The boy drummed on the floor and laughed at this simple ditty, singing it over and over again in his piping voice.

"You remember that song, Marion, of course," said the woman, half defiantly, as she looked round and saw her visitor.

"Yes," she said simply. "How is the boy?"

"Tell Marion Revel how you feel, Jem, my son."

"Better," said Jem—"ain't I, mother?"

"He was very restless last night. That was why I sent for you. I want him to have a doctor. This morning his cough is not so bad as it was. At least, I don't think so."

Rickety Jem looked up in Marion's face with his weird smile. The likeness to Adie struck her more, as the features grew thinner and the eyes brighter. She kissed him on the forehead, and the boy shrank back, half ashamed. Like an Australian savage, he hardly knew the nature of a kiss.

"He's so thin," said his mother. "What can I give him to get his strength up again? Show me your arm, my boy."

He drew up his sleeve, and showed an arm about the thickness of Marion's finger—a thin stalk of an arm, a mere transparent strip of fragile bone.

"Don't look at me like that, Marion Revel," said the woman. "He has had plenty to eat—it isn't that. I have not spent the money in drink. Nothing at all has come into the place except tea and milk. The boy has had

it all. It's more than a month since he went out of the
house, and was run over by the cab. He's never been the
same child since. But always the best of boys to his poor
mother, isn't he, Jem? Always the best and most affectionate boy in all the world."

Jem laughed.

"Some of the boys got no mother. Some of the boys got
mothers as beats them. Some of 'em are afraid to go home,
even in the winter. One boy ran away, and went to sea."

"His mind runs on his companions still," said Marion.

"They've been his friends since he could walk. He knows
nobody else. He has been to no other school."

Marion sighed.

"When I go out again," the lad went on, "the boys'll ask
me where I've been. I shall tell 'em I've been having milk
and eating oranges. Ah! when shall I go out again, mother?
I'm tired of coughing, and the pain in my back won't go."

"Soon, my boy, very soon now," returned his mother;
"when we have some warm weather—when the summer
comes again."

Marion's eyes filled with tears.

"Let me bring a doctor to see him."

She had written to Marion expressly to ask for a doctor.
Now she suddenly turned from her purpose.

"What good? I know, Marion Revel, what you think.
It is quite true, and it is coming. I have felt it coming for
four weeks. Lie down, Jem, dear, and have another orange.
If you lie down you will not feel the pain so much. There,
my child, now you will be comfortable. Go to sleep, my
boy—go to sleep, my darling."

The boy complied, and closed his eyes as if asleep.

"He lies like that, quiet and still," murmured his poor
mother, "for hours. It's to make me think he is getting
well. But he is not. Oh! he is not. I know it. And
what shall I do without him, Marion? What shall I do.
Hush!—speak low. It's the great mercy of God, after all,
that he should go—isn't it? I don't mean to me, because
there is no mercy left for me; but for him, for the boy. It's

better that the child of shame and guilt should die, and the sooner the better. What is before him if he lives?"

"And for yourself"—Marion took her thin hand in her own—"for yourself; can you bear to let the child go?"

"Bear!" she replied, with a great and sorrowful cry. "Ask me if I can bear this miserable life? What have I not borne for fourteen years? Do you think there is anything that such a woman as myself cannot bear? Oh! Marion Revel"—she burst into low and bitter weeping—"*he* ought to forgive me; he would forgive me if he knew what my sufferings have been. Not to take me back—never that; not to let me kiss my son and my daughter—his children and mine—never that; not to take his name again, no—not that; but only to be near him, and to feel that he has quite forgiven me. Your mother will be his wife, Marion, *there*. She was a good woman, like yourself. Some people are born good, and it is no merit of theirs; but if I could only be his servant!"

"My dear, believe that he has forgiven. Be quite sure of that; do not doubt. Ask God's forgiveness too."

"That's not what I think of," she said truthfully. "It is of *him* that I am always thinking."

"You must think that the boy will only go before."

"Where am I to go, mother?" cried the boy, who caught at the last words. "Not to the hospital. Don't send me to the hospital. There was one of the boys went there—him that used to turn Catherine wheels alongside of the 'buses—and they cut off his legs, and he never came out again. Died, he did. Then they cut him up to see what he was made of."

"No, not to the hospital," said Marion—"to a much better place; to a place where there is always happiness."

"And oranges?"

"Yes; finer fruit than you ever dreamed of, Jem."

"And lemonade, and milk?"

"Everything is there; and for anybody. There are fields and flowers."

"One of the boys came from the country, he did. He's always talking about fields and flowers."

"That is it, Jem. You will go to the country—a much better country than this."

"Mother, why are you crying? Shan't we go together?"

"Yes, boy—yes," she answered. "Where you go, I go. God shall not separate us, shall He? Marion," she added, after a pause, "you will forgive me, won't you? I have suffered so much that I am not always mistress of myself. I know how good you are. There is not one woman in ten thousand such as you, that would come to see a woman such as myself. Do not think me ungrateful. See, I try to keep myself from drink. I am always sober now."

"I do not think you ungrateful—only—only—do one thing that I ask you—teach this poor child a single prayer."

She drooped her head, and answered nothing. Only she did not refuse.

"Jem," said Marion, "you have a Friend whom you cannot see, but who sees you. Would you like to ask that Friend to help you? Listen, and say after me."

The boy listened, and learned.

"Now you know it—say it aloud. Never doubt that this great Friend hears. Do not be afraid to say it every morning, and every evening. When you are in pain, and when you are awake at night, say it for yourself, and for your mother, and for me."

The boy said his prayer. He understood little enough what Marion taught him as yet; but he obeyed, being a docile child, and unaccustomed to such gentle ways as Marion's.

While he prayed, his mother, her head bowed between her hands, crouched at the foot of the bed—like a slave, who longed, but feared, to meet her Lord.

CHAPTER XXXIII.

MR. OWEN spent the remainder of the day lying in wait to catch the author of the mischief, Mr. Frederick Revel, with whom he wished to exchange a few words.

He caught him in the evening, as the unhappy young man

was stealing back, expecting to find a "desolated hearth," with perhaps his sisters, and his poor little wife, sitting on the bare boards, weeping.

"Come with me, Mr. Revel," he said, leading the way to the empty schoolroom, where he took up the position of vantage, by sitting at his desk—Fred standing before him like one of his boys. The wrinkled face of the pedagogue was full of trouble; he stammered and hesitated.

"I've said nothing about it yet," he began, without explaining what *it* was. Fred knew what he meant. "Nothing about it. But I have seen what is going on. Now, sir, what have you got to say for yourself?"

Fred shook his head, implying that he had really very little to say.

"I told her at the beginning of it all that you were a worthless chap." He went on: "She said you were the soul of honour. I told her you were a lazy chap; she said you were longing to find work. I told her you were eating your head off; she said that you were pining away and getting thin with sorrow at finding nothing to do. That was a month ago and more. What have you found to do since?"

"I have been unlucky, Mr. Owen."

"No, sir!" taking up the cane, and bringing it down, *emphasis gratiâ*, on the desk, with a crash that made the young man jump in his shoes—"no, sir! you have not been unlucky, you have been idle. You have gone on eating your head off at your ease. You have not tried to find work. You despise a man who does honest work—you despise ME. Good Heavens! I daresay you despise your own sister. Solomon says, 'The sluggard is wiser in his own conceit than seven men that can render a reason.' *You*, to despise honest work! —you who have spent your days in a billiard-room! You have borrowed money till your old friends will lend you no more; you have never looked for work at all; and, to crown all, you have gone to a money-lender—a blackguard money-lender, who dared to insult me when I asked him a civil question—and got advances on your sister's furniture. When the scoundrel came with his bill of sale, and seized the sticks, where were you? Ran away—ran away! He robs his sisters, this man, and runs away; and then he dares to ask my girl, *my* Winifred, to marry him!"

The situation was such that the young man did not even dare to resent this plain speaking. It was true; and, moreover, the speaker was his own father-in-law.

"Was it your fault that the furniture was not sold at once? Has your sister Marion got to thank you that it is all brought back safe?"

"Brought back! How? By whom?"

"By Dr. Chacomb, if you must know," growled the schoolmaster. "Not but what there were others willing and anxious to help."

"I am glad," said the culprit humbly.

"You ought to be sorry. But what have glad and sorry got to do with the business at all? What are you going to do about my girl?"

It was a most unfavourable opening for announcing his marriage. It was as if an Eton scholar, just under the rod of Dr. Keate, was about to choose that moment for announcing his passion for the headmaster's daughter. The news must be postponed.

"It's all true," he replied—"quite true, and I am—but what does it matter, as you say, about glad or sorry? I mean to keep my promise to your daughter—to Winifred."

"Do you?" cried the peppery Welshman, in a tremendous rage. "Will you? Here is condescension! Here is an affable young fellow for you! He brings misery on his sisters; he keeps them poor; he refuses to work; and now he tells me that he is ready to keep his word with my daughter—the honest daughter of an honest man. Why, sir, if it depended on me, I would knock your head off your shoulders. I would refuse to let Winifred see you any more. I would turn you into the streets to starve. But it does not depend on me, unfortunately. There are your sisters to be considered, and my girl. The devil of it is, that Winifred loves you; and I can't get over that. Sooner than grieve my lamb, she should marry a murderer, if I thought the murderer would love her in return. But don't think it is an honour you are conferring on our family, Mr. Revel; because, I tell you plainly, I looked for better things for my daughter."

"I suppose," said Fred grandly, "that you wanted her to marry some miserable little counter-jumper."

"I did. I looked to see her marry an honest man—counter-jumper or not—who would make his living as God should order, try and do his duty, and not be ashamed of his handicraft. It's a poor sort of family pride that sets up one trade over another. And you—what trade have you got at all? What are your expectations, sir?"

"I have none," said Fred. "I hope, however—"

"You had better give up hoping. You have no expectations, no money, no friends, no trade, no skill, and you propose to marry my daughter! Truly, you are the most hopeless man in all this wide world. Remember that you will have to show you can keep her first."

"You do me wrong, Mr. Owen. I give you my word that I should not be ashamed of any trade. I would do anything, if only to show you and Marion that I am not so helpless as you think me. I only want an opportunity."

"In that case," said the schoolmaster, the boys meet here every morning at nine. You shall come here to-morrow, and work my classes for me. There's your chance."

Fred turned pale. It was, to be sure, a chance. But what an opportunity! Work, in his vague brain, meant, at the best, a gentlemanly lingering in an office for a few hours in the day; at the worst, writing at leisure, in an armchair, by a comfortable fire. But work of the kind proposed by Mr. Owen was too terrible. Assistant, usher, understrapper in a wretched London academy—teacher of small tradesmen's sons! Possibly, considering that Mr. Owen's cane was not wholly intended for ornament, he would be expected to take his part in its use.

"Well," said the schoolmaster, "what do you say? I give you an opportunity. You shall work here as my assistant for a month, without pay. Then I will try and get you

a place in a larger school, where they will give you—well, I
daresay you might get as much as thirty pounds a year to
begin with, board and lodgings for ten months in the year
thrown in. You'd be a made man then," he went on, with
a queer light in his eyes—"wouldn't you? Thirty pounds
a year, and all found. Walk out with the boys on half-
holidays; look after them in play-hours, and— Eh? why,
in a few years, you might be thinking of marrying my girl.
Come, Mr. Revel, it's the best chance I see for you. You
are an Oxford man, too—though you haven't taken any
degree—and that always counts for something. Do you
know Latin?"

"I—I—yes—of course I do."

"Then construe me this piece. Stay a moment. Where's
the translation?"

He opened a Horace, one of the books that stood for show
on his shelves, and finding a place at random, took down
Francis's translation to keep himself safe with. Out of
Cæsar, Mr. Owen's Latinity was shaky.

"Now then—

'Qui fit, Mæcenas . . . .'"

"I am rusty. I have forgotten my Latin and Greek."

"Well, there are other subjects—algebra—Euclid."

"I never learned mathematics at Oxford."

Fred spoke as if mathematical science belonged to a lower
stratum of society than his own.

"Then we come down to geography and history, arithmetic, English, writing."

"It's no use. I can't be a schoolmaster."

"Mr. Revel, if you want to marry my daughter, you've
got to work. Now go. Make something of yourself, or
give up my Winifred."

"What am I to do?" he asked, almost piteously.

"I will tell you." The schoolmaster bent his face down
within a couple of inches of Fred's, and said, in mysterious
tones, "Go abroad."

"Go abroad?"

"Ay, go abroad. The world is wide, and there are places where they want strong arms. Find them out. Go there, make your fortune, and then come back here for Winifred."

Fred made no reply, but left him.

The diplomatic schoolmaster nodded and winked when he was gone.

"That was a good stroke," he said. "Now we shall get rid of him."

Why should he not go abroad? Anywhere abroad. There was nothing for him to do in England. He was only a drag upon his sisters. He could not help his wife. Why not leave wife and sisters for awhile, and try his fortune somewhere?

And then his sanguine imagination began to picture an Arcadian scene of prosperity, plenty, and happiness.

He walked away to St. Martin's, to meet his young wife, gathering at every step fresh ardour of resolution.

"Winifred," he began eagerly, "I have something very serious to say to you. No, nothing wrong. There has been a row at Lowland Street; but it is all hushed up now, and smoothed over. A bill of sale—nothing you would understand—an old debt of mine. That is not it. I have seen your father."

"O Fred, did you tell him?"

"No. I was afraid to tell him after the shindy. He let me have it, on his own account, for idleness. I will spare you, my dear," he said, with commendable feeling, "the details of the interview. For your sake, I bore it all. And the end of it is—"

"What, my dearest? Oh, tell me—tell your wife."

"The end is, that I must go abroad."

"With me, Fred? Not, and leave me at home?"

"For a time, Winifred, I fear I must. See, dear, it will be better so. You do not know, my love"—he spoke naturally and simply—"the dangers I run in London. My dear, a man told me the other day that the only end for such a life as mine was to become a billiard-marker. Your father says I am ruining Marion. I see no prospect of getting even the smallest appointment. I have been running after shadows all this time. Now, be brave, my girl, and let me go."

Winifred tried to be brave, but could not.

"Abroad—across the ocean, somewhere—I shall find an opening. I have made it all out clearly, Winifred. I make a clearing in the forest, run up a log hut—only a shanty at first. I live in the woods, planting, sowing, weeding, and all the rest of it. I shoot the wild game for my dinner. And as soon as I have made a nest—in about a year or so—I shall write to you to come out too. Think of leaving this dingy London, and living in the most beautiful climate under the sun, with the most delicious fruits, no need of money, and no lack of good things. Above all, away from all this —bah!—this struggling mass of people, fighting and quarrelling for their ill-gotten gains."

He spoke enthusiastically, as if he had been all his life pining for a return to the Saturnian rule.

"But Fred—O Fred!—is it real? Will you be able to do this? Do you think you can really and truly work in a field like a labourer?"

"Out there there is no such thing as gentlemen"—Fred's notions of America, it will be seen, were confused—"a man may take off his coat and work without losing caste. Besides, it is the desk work that I hate; that is horrible and detestable. In the open air, in the sun, where there are no billiards, and where you want no money—there I could work. Yes, and you should never be ashamed of your husband."

"Fred! as if I could be ashamed!"

"You must let me go. I will be a burden on Marion no longer. Who knows what dreadful thing may happen next?" He was still thinking of the billiard-marker's prophecy. "My old life is finished, Winifred; let me begin a new."

This man a "worthless chap"? This man as idle as a gipsy? This man as prodigal as a Guardsman? Every pulse in Winifred's veins cried "No."

"We shall not be parted long, love," the young hero went on. "I will write by every mail. You will try to keep your heart up; you will not forget your husband—will you?"

They were at the door of the Lowland Street lodgings.

Fred was in earnest for once. He would be rid of the whole trouble, and try fresh fields. All weak natures, when anything goes wrong, want to go away, and begin life over again. Some years ago when there was a crash in the ice, and some half-dozen men were missing, it was found that a few—those who knew how to seize an opportunity—had taken advantage of the accident to disappear in the flesh, leaving debts, wife, children, and other impedimenta behind them. Fred proposed to do exactly the same thing, only he did not intend to desert his wife.

"I *must* go," he said—"I must go. I feel choked. It is as if I was being dragged down, and was dragging Marion and Adie, and you, my poor little girl, too. See, love—here I cannot shake off the feeling that I am a gentleman. I could not bear that one of the old Oxford set should see me at some miserable work. Out of England it will be different. Come, dear, take my watch and chain—the chain is sham, because I had to pawn the real one long ago; but the trinkets are gold, and so is the watch. It is all I have to give you. My dear—my dear—"

"You are not going now, Fred; not now—not to-night?"

He held her tight in his arms, kissed her twice, and was gone.

He walked straight to Dr. Chacomb, told him what he proposed to do, and asked for the loan of enough money to pay his passage to any port in the States by the first steamer.

"There is some stuff in the fellow, after all," said the doctor. "Of course there is. How could your sisters have a brother with no good at all about him?"

When Fred shook hands with the doctor half an hour later, his eyes were soft, and his voice a little husky—

"I will send the letter to-night," said the doctor. "And— and—Fred, if I have been a little rude sometimes—that's right; you forgive me. Write to me when you get out; and depend upon it that I will look after your wife. Sly dog, sly dog! You will come home a man. Good-bye, and *bon voyage*."

Fred's letter was to Marion. He told her what he had

done. He wrote with his heart full of sorrow, and made no protestations. When she had finished the letter, Marion came to a postscript which startled her more than all the rest.

"*P.S.*—Winifred is my wife. I married her two months ago, and against her will, poor thing! And I made her keep the secret. Be kind to her, as you have always been the kindest of sisters to me."

Marion gave the letter to Adie, and crept downstairs to Winifred's room, where the schoolmaster, listening disconsolately, heard the sounds of weeping and sobbing. He knew, somehow, that they were crying for Fred, and it made him angry.

Then Marion came and told him all the truth, and would hear of nothing but an immediate and general amnesty.

"And it is my bullying," said the schoolmaster, "that drove him away."

She left her new sister in her father's arms. Winifred told him all, talking and crying, till she fell asleep, and lay there, dreaming that she was with her husband, all the night. Every time she moved, and murmured "Fred," a pang of rage and jealousy went through Owen's heart; but he fought it down, and greeted his daughter, when she awoke, with a cheerful smile.

CHAPTER XXXIV.

"COME out, Chauncey, or I will do more mischief."

The voice was that of Mrs. Chauncey Chacomb. She was standing in the great hall of Chacomb, before the single door which led to the wing known as Gerald's rooms, with which this door was the only means of communication.

"Come out, Chauncey. It is six o'clock. Come out, and you shall have port with your dinner."

There was no reply.

"Chauncey," she went on, "I know you are listening on the other side. Open the door at once, or I will send Charles with a hammer to break it down."

"You can't—ho! ho!—you can't. The door opens your way, and I've barricaded it inside."

"Joe"—she turned to the doctor, who had arrived, and was surprised to find that his cousin had locked himself up for four and twenty hours, and still refused to come out—"Joe"—she was in tears—"it isn't my fault. I have done nothing to him. How can I help it if he turned rusty?"

"Cannot you get in at the window?"

"The ground floor windows are all secured with shutters, and he has got a pistol, loaded. He says if anybody puts a ladder to the first floor window, he will shoot him dead first and himself next. Joe, what a fool I was—oh! what a double fool—to marry this wretched little lunatic!"

"Try him again. Speak softly to him. If you do not succeed, I will try. Now, Julia, forget that you are his wife—make believe to be his housekeeper again."

She laughed.

"I wish I was. Chauncey—I mean Mr. Chacomb," she said, in her sweetest tones, "dinner will be served soon. Will you have it sent in to you, or will you take it with me?"

"Neither," he replied. "I shall stay here. I've got a box of sardines and a case of claret. I shall dine off them."

"This is dreadful," said the doctor. "Does he often go on like this?"

"No; but for the last week he has been very queer. I've got four men sleeping in the house, and I think he is frightened. He thinks they are watching him."

"Julia, I am disappointed in you. I thought you had more tact. Now, we *must* get him out."

"I can't. It's no use bullying me, Joe. If I had the patience of—of Moses and Aaron, I could not help flying out at him now and then. Is it my fault if he locks himself up? Can you say that I have ill-treated him? Have I beaten him? Have I starved him? Have I asked him for money?"

"No—no," said Joseph. "I hardly suppose you have. At least, not much. But there is such a thing as contrast. Now, the first Mrs. Chacomb, you know, was a lady—"

" And I am not. Well, never mind. If it was miserable here when I was housekeeper," she went on, "it is fifty times as miserable now I am the mistress. No one comes to see me. I go nowhere. I have no money; but that is your doing."

"It is, Julia," said the doctor, with a smile. "I like to manage the Chacomb revenues myself. I have brought you the weekly allowance. When you choose to put the household on a proper footing, you shall have an increase. That's enough for the present."

"I wonder if a lawyer could force you to give me more?" she said, looking discontentedly at the coin.

"You had better try. I still preserve a few letters of yours, Mrs. Chacomb. It will not be difficult to prove that you used your position here to gain an ascendency over the weak brain of a lunatic, and forced him to marry you on the vague threat of doing him a mischief. Where will you be then?"

"Don't be cross, Joe. It isn't like your old self. Lord! I wish the good old days could come back again. Do you remember me as Perdita the Perfidious, at the Wells? You were a good fellow then, Joe. You hadn't been spoiled by getting a fine practice, and going about to see countesses. You didn't sit down to a finicking pint of claret to your dinner. You drank all the stout and the port you could lay your hand to, in those days. You didn't snap up a pretty woman then for a word here and a word there. Ah! Joe, you were a very different man then."

"I was, and you were a very different woman then. Hang it, Julia, it's twenty years ago! You are Mrs. Chacomb, of Chacomb Hall, now—a very grand lady."

"Very grand indeed! Oh! if I had only known. What do you think my lord did the other day? Forbade my going out in the carriage—told the grooms not to take me out. When I ordered the carriage round, they laughed in my face. Do you call that being mistress of Chacomb Hall?"

"It was an extreme measure on the part of my cousin," said the doctor, twinkling. "I did not think he had so much pluck. Of course, you acquiesced meekly."

"No doubt," said Mrs. Chacomb. "Ju Cathnor always was a weak, easily-put-upon, worm-like thing in her younger days, wasn't she, Joe? Wasn't she?" She danced up to her old friend with an airy flourish of her hands—a reminiscence of bygone times. "It's likely she'd acquiesce. I will tell you what I did, Joe. First, I dressed myself properly. Then I made my little maid call the grooms to the kitchen, and give them beer. (Beer is the real magnet for the male feet. Champagne, as you know, draws the feminine tootsicums.) Then I stepped out, and got into the carriage, and waited. In a few minutes my gentlemen came out, and harnessed the horses for their daily drive—little thinking I was inside. When we had gone two or three miles, I ordered them to put down the head, and drive me a good round. You should have seen their faces. When we got home, I let them have it, both of them. They won't forget the rough side of my tongue for a bit. And after dinner I let Chauncey have it."

"Ah! I thought we should get to the bottom of the barricade some time or other."

"It is not the slightest use in the world," she pursued, "nagging Chauncey. You get no fun out of it, and no satisfaction. He only opens his eyes wide, and stares straight before him, as if he were looking at ghosts. And it isn't any good lifting your voice to him: he doesn't even listen. Always that far-off look."

"I'm glad you don't feel it necessary to lift your hand to him," said the doctor.

"I've done that, once or twice; but, Lord! it's boxing the ears of a man who takes no manner of notice. Many's the time I've boxed your ears, Joe—when you richly deserved it —till you've sworn again."

"Some people swear easily. It's a habit of which I have broken myself."

"Ah! the jolly old days, when we went to Richmond on Sundays, Joe—you, and I, and Jack ——. Well. So I determined to punish him. I got up and went straight to the Collection. I took half a dozen things called Roman lamps —you know the trumpery—and I brought them back with

me. 'Now, Chauncey,' I said, 'I'll teach you to insult your
wife.' Then I put them under my heel, and scrunched them
up, every one."

"And then?"

"Then Chauncey shrieked as if he'd been killed, and ran
away. It was last night. Since then he hasn't come out,
and I can't persuade him. You heard me try."

"We must persuade him. Go and fetch—stay."

He went away, and came back with an apostle spoon, a
rusty spur, and one or two fragments of pottery.

"Now, we will have a little drama. Threaten to break the
things to pieces."

She nodded. The time was half-past seven, and the evening had fallen. The great hall was empty and dark, save
for the two figures and a single candle on the table. It was
a long and lofty place, running the whole length of the house,
with windows at the end. Originally it had been designed
by the builder as a sort of state dining-room. Screens stood
here and there, and the hall did not communicate directly
with the outer door. But both the outer and the inner door
were open. The two figures moving in the big hall in the
twilight looked weird and spectral.

"Now, Julia."

"Chauncey, will you come to dinner?"

"No, I will not. Go away and leave me."

"Chauncey, will you come out, for the first time?"

No answer.

"Chauncey, will you come out, for the second time?
Chauncey, if I ask you for the third time, it will be the
worse for you. I have got in my hands a valuable silver
spoon, with a label on it—out of the Collection."

"My apostle spoon—my apostle spoon!" he moaned,
behind the door.

"That isn't all. I've got a rusty green old spur, which I
can bend with my fingers. Now, Chauncey, if you don't
come out at once, I will bend it and break it into little
pieces. It's only rubbish."

"The spur of King Canute!" groaned Chauncey.

"And break the apostle spoon into fifty fragments. O Joseph!"

For at this point of the drama the doctor seized her by the wrist, with a violence that was perhaps a little over-acting the part, and made her shriek quite naturally.

"Cousin Chauncey," he said, in his deepest tones, "what is this? Why do I find you locked up and barricaded in this way?"

Then arrived the very luckiest moment in all Joseph Chacomb's life.

For just then a strange face showed itself at the door of the hall, that inner door which led to the outer porch. A white face—a face bearded like a pard, full of expectancy and curiosity. Neither of the actors in the little drama saw it. Finding that he was unperceived, the owner of the face stole across the hall softly, and crept behind one of the screens. Then he listened.

"Is that you, Joe? Is that my cousin Joseph?"

The voice of Chauncey sounded hollow and faint.

"It is, Chauncey. Open the door, and come out."

"Send _her_ away first," he cried. "I only want to see you."

"Go to the dining-room, Julia," said the doctor. "Wait for us there. Order dinner. I will bring him out in five minutes."

She obeyed, and swept away, brushing the floor with her long silk train; and the doctor heard her ring the bell.

"At all events," he said to himself, "we shall have dinner. Now, Chauncey, make haste, and open the door. I shall be here till Monday morning, and you may trust yourself entirely with me, you know. Open the door, and tell me all about it."

There was a great drawing away of boxes, pieces of furniture, chairs, and other things, by means of which Chauncey Chacomb had effected his barricade. Presently, his steps were heard in the space which he had cleared, a chain was taken down with a clinking, locks and bolts were undone, and the squire of Chacomb appeared. Marriage had done very little good for him. When the Cambridge Don, who married late in life, was asked how he found the state of wedlock, he said that the breakfasts were better, but the dinners not so good. Chauncey Chacomb would have said, with truth, that everything was not so good. As a house-keeper, Mrs. Cathnor had been a pink and paragon. She kept the servants in order. She kept up the house. She regulated his expenditure. She looked after his comfort. She was submissive in appearance, and she ruled in reality. Now that he had married her, all was changed. She ruled, and professed to rule. She had dismissed all the old servants, and could not bring herself to engage a new set. She had no sense that an old country hall should be kept up with a certain amount of state. Above all, she had neither fear, respect, nor reverence for the master of the place; and she bullied him.

He was very miserable to look at. Thin in the face, stooping, his right shoulder a good deal more raised above the left than it had been four years ago; his eyes closer together —half shut—with a thousand crows'-feet and wrinkles round them; and a general look of suspicion on him, which only cleared away when he saw that his cousin was standing in the hall alone.

He ran to meet the doctor, with hands outstretched, and an eagerness that was affecting.

"Joe," he cried, with a sort of sob—"cousin Joe, the only friend I have in the world, since Gerald went away. How glad I am to see you! How glad I am you came to-night!"

"Tell me all about it, Chauncey."

The way in which the poor creature clung to him struck the doctor with pity and remorse. Of course, it is under-stood by this time that Joe Chacomb's better points were exactly such as to be brought out into full blossom and fructified, so to speak, by prosperity and the sense of power. Still, at no time had he been a stony-hearted man. Pity is an artistic emotion; it soothes the avenues to the brain and the more delicate sensations, just as soup prepares the way for dinner. Hence, so many marriages are founded on pity. Amadis the Invincible, Sir Bors the Lady-killer, are not bad fellows at bottom ; it goes to their heart to see fair Melusine grow thin and pale.

"Cousin Chauncey, cheer up," said the doctor. "Let us be jolly, man. You can't undo what you have done, but we may make the best of it. We will go back to the old times, and have a bottle of port for dinner, shall we ?"

Chauncey shook his head.

"I haven't enjoyed my glass of port," he said, "for four long years. I must not expect to enjoy it now. Joe, can't you persuade her to go away from me ?"

"I might," said Joe. "Gad ! I never thought of that. But I might. When would you like her to go, Chauncey ? I think she is best in London—everybody is best there. Of course, I should not let her call upon me, and should give orders not to admit her."

"Of course," said Chauncey. "So should I, if I could get rid of her."

"I will do what I can, Chauncey. Now, why did you barricade yourself ?"

"She talks, she scolds, she sings, she—she boxes my ears, Joe. And whether she talks, or sings, or scolds, it is all the same ; for her voice goes through me like a saw, and makes me see ten thousand devils. When I hear her at night, the room is peopled with faces—not all of them Revel's face, only a good many. Some have Marion's face ; so that I am sure she must be dead."

"She isn't dead. Nonsense, I saw her yesterday."

"Joe, how the devil could I see her face with the face of her father unless she was dead ? Now, answer me that."

"Upon my word, I can't answer you that. But Marion is alive, poor girl !"

"Her brother wrote to me last week for money. He said they were starving. But she wouldn't let me send any. Now I remember, Marion's name was mentioned. Then she must have died since then."

Evidently the poor man's hallucination was stronger than ever.

"Come to dinner, Chauncey," said Joe, with a shudder.

"Joe, you won't leave me, will you? Come and sleep in Gerald's room. I will have the little room. It will be very comfortable to wake up and hear you snoring. It is quiet,—so very quiet, when the faces begin their long procession. Promise me not to leave me. Oh, I am afraid of her. Yesterday she broke into the Collection, and broke my valuable Roman lamps. To-day, she was threatening to destroy King Canute's spur just as you arrived. She's a dreadful woman, Joe—oh, a dreadful woman! I never knew that such women could be found. I have read of them, but I thought they only lived in novels. Joe, take her up to London with you—take her right away from me. Let me get rid of her. O Joe! Joe!—what should I be without you?"

The listener, bending low behind the screen, heard and marked all this. As the two went arm in arm to the dining-room, he followed with noiseless step, listening still.

The dinner was as bad as when the doctor last visited Mr. Chacomb.

"Upon my word, Julia," he said, trying to get his knife through the joints of a large barn-door fowl—"upon my word, the state of your larder is too monotonous. We had tough fowl the last time I was here."

"We have tough fowl every day, I think," said Chauncey humbly.

The listener had followed to the door of the dining-room, which stood open. The room was lit by four candles only, which formed an island of light in the midst of a great darkness. So dark it seemed to him, that he was standing in the doorway looking at the party, without the fear of being observed. Facing him was Chauncey, who sat at the side. At one end was Mrs. Chacomb, at the other the doctor—the usual order of things being reversed.

"Joe, said Chauncey, quite quietly, laying down his knife and fork, " give me a glass of sherry, Joe—thank you. Yes, thank you, it is quite clear now. I told you that last night I had a great vision; quite a remarkable procession of faces passed my pillow."

" Ay, Chauncey, you did say something about it. You

are like the prophet Joel. Julia, this fowl is disgraceful. Well, cousin, and what about the vision? Tell me what it meant?"

"They came trooping past me in thousands: an endless file of human faces without bodies—thousands of them, Joe. Every minute there would be a Captain Revel among them; then a Marion Revel—all dead people, you know. One face I missed among them, and I thanked God, because I knew that he must be alive; it was the face of my son—my Gerald. But he is dead too—"

"Chauncey!" cried the doctor, "take another glass of sherry, and then go on with the wing of your fowl."

"Chauncey," said his wife, "if you talk like that at dinner, just when people are trying to be happy and enjoy themselves, after all the misery you've made me undergo on your account, I will come round and shake you. I declare I will."

"Manners, Mrs. Chacomb!" said the doctor. "Ladies in society do not shake their husbands. Nor do they threaten to do it."

She tossed her head, and poured out a glass of claret. There was no servant in the room, the little maid having retired to the kitchen, where the grooms were helping her to dish a very bad pudding.

"Now Gerald is dead, too," resumed the squire; "for I have just seen him."

"My poor cousin," said the doctor, "do be good enough not to talk in this creepy way. It's not pleasant at dinner. Take another glass of wine. Did you get the port, Julia?"

Chauncey, as usual with him, was staring straight before him; and, as usual, the others took no heed to the direction of his eyes. Then he set down the glass which he held in his hand, and half rose from his chair.

"Chauncey's worse to-night than I have ever seen him," the doctor murmured. "His wife has frightened him out of the few wits he had left."

"It's strange," the squire said. "The other faces passed away, but this one remains. Revel only turned his sad eyes upon me, and disappeared; so did Marion—her eyes are like her father's. Gerald remains. I see more than his face—I see his whole body in the twilight. He is pale. He has grown thin. His beard is long, and his eyes are sad. He moves. He comes this way. Gerald!—Gerald! My son!—my son! Speak to me."

He threw himself forward, with his arms extended, and fell, face downwards, upon the table, with a fearful cry.

It was echoed by his wife, who turned her head, and saw the form that her husband had seen—which he thought to be a spectre.

"Father," cried the stranger, "it is no vision. It is your son."

But his father moved not.

The doctor was the first of the three to recover. He seized a light, and threw it upon Gerald's face. Then he, too, turned very pale—so pale that his friends would not have known him. Then he put down the candle, and said, very softly, as if speaking to himself—

"Gerald come back!"

"It is Gerald," the stranger replied; "and more than thankful, my cousin, for the trust my father has in you."

"You know—what do you know?" asked the doctor.

"I was present just now in the hall. I listened—forgive me—I overheard all that my father said—"

"Wonder if he overheard all that Julia said?" thought Joseph.

"—and I thank you from my heart. You have earned my everlasting gratitude. Father, will you not shake hands with me?"

"Voices and faces—faces and voices," murmured the poor little squire, trying to look at things as they were. "I see them, and I hear them. Joe, tell me what is real."

"This is real, Chauncey. Your son is real. He who was dead liveth. I wonder if that's in the Bible," he murmured softly—"sounds like it. The prodigal—no, the wanderer has come home again. Let us kill fatted calves, and drink—drink old port—wine of Shechem. Sit down, Gerald. Have you had dinner?"

Dr. Chacomb was nervous, and talked a little at random.

"Here is a tough old hen." He pointed to Mrs. Chacomb in his agitation of spirit. "Here is your new stepmother." He pointed to the fowl in the dish. "Sit down, and make acquaintance, and eat and drink."

Gerald bowed coldly to Mrs. Chacomb, and sat down But he did not eat much, or drink either. The doctor ate and drank for everybody. The squire sat gazing steadfastly at his son.

"Gerald," he murmured from time to time, between his teeth.

Presently he got up suddenly.

"Joe," he said, "give me a sleeping draught. Make me sleep a long while. I haven't slept for a fortnight, and I don't know which are ghosts and which are realities. The room is full of ghosts now."

The doctor and Gerald took him to his own wing.

Mrs. Chacomb waited for them for two hours. Then she rose in a rage, and went to her own room.

Chauncey went to bed and to sleep. The other two sat up and talked. Gerald told of his travels—how he had been stricken down by fever in Central Africa, and had been tended by faithful negroes. The doctor told how he had started the Hospital for Gout, and was now a prosperous man.

"And my father, Joe?"

"Your father's hallucinations are stronger than ever. That woman I sent down here as housekeeper. She made him marry her."

"Was it—was it all hallucination?" asked Gerald.

"Every bit. I was there. The man fell off the cliff. I have told your father so a hundred times, but nothing moves him. Nothing ever will now."

Gerald sighed.

"I fear I was hasty in going away. However, I have formed the mode of my life. I am going back again as soon as I have shaken off a little of this jungle fever."

"Back again? With all this before you?"

"Yes, my cousin. It is my fate, I suppose. Every man must work out his fate, eh? You are not four years in Africa without believing in fate, let me tell you. Do you ever see the Revels now?" he asked—quite carelessly, Joseph noticed. "I must call upon them when I go up to town. That will be in a few days. You can give me their address, please."

He did not ask what they were doing, or anything about them, which was remarkable, the doctor thought.

Then he began to talk about his stepmother.

Next day, Mrs. Chacomb, with a great array of boxes, took the mid-day train to London. It is sufficient to say that she lives in considerable comfort and some splendour, but by herself, in a suburban villa at Dalston. Once a month or so, on a Sunday afternoon, Dr. Chacomb drives over to her. She is a widow now, and entertains her friends with long histories of the splendours of Chacomb Hall, and her own great doings with the other county ladies.

When Chauncey awoke it was high noon. He was lying in Gerald's bed, and by him sat his son, in the flesh—no ghost at all.

"Gerald"—his voice was hollow, and sounded far off—"I have had a miserable time since you went away. Now and then I know that I am suffering from hallucinations, but they come again. I know now that it is all a delusion. Think that it is so. O Gerald, do not believe your father a murderer, whatever he may think himself! Ask Joe."

"I do not, sir. Trust me, I do not."

"Joe will tell you, Gerald. Remember, Joe has saved my reason—what little reason I have—and my life, too. Always let Joe do what he likes in this house. Give him money if he wants any. Remember, Gerald, it was Joe who saved your father from the madhouse."

Then he thought he should like to get up and see the Collection. The doctor had pieced together the lamps with cement, and he saw no change. Nor did he ever, at that time or afterwards, make the slightest allusion to the second

Mrs. Chacomb: she passed out of his mind like one of his old dreams.

After a month or two he took to lying down, a habit which gained upon him. And now I do not think he will ever get up from his bed any more.

CHAPTER XXXV.

AFTER Marion undertook the Hermit's commission, he began to exercise his privilege of coming to see how the picture progressed every day, showing an almost feverish anxiety about it. Not that he cared about the copy, which was his crafty pretext, but the society of the young ladies filled him with a delight unspeakable, after his long imprisonment. It was, to some extent, a return to the world—a very limited and humble part of it. Mr. Lilliecrip was one of those men who, like La Fontaine and Oliver Goldsmith, expand and show their sunniest side in the presence of ladies. He resembled those poets in no other single quality, being, as has already appeared, as untruthful as a Syrian, as boastful as a Gascon, as selfish as a Fakir, and as cowardly as a Fantee. But the pleasure of seeing for half an hour a day these two girls, of talking to them, hearing the rustle of their dresses, watching the waves of their hair, breathing the same atmosphere with them, filled his life now with a delight quite new to it. He was attracted, too, by some strange resemblance in Adie's face, manner, and voice to one he had known many years before. Fancy an imprisonment —voluntary, but still an imprisonment—for fourteen long years, during which nothing beautiful in the shape of womanhood has been near the prisoner. Then imagine the opening of a door by which, while the captivity is maintained, its rigour is alleviated by the talk of young ladies. Then try to think with what a boyish joy, what beating of the heart, what pleasant excitation of the nerves, this Recluse would creep nervously down the stairs every morning, and knock at the door of the room which held those angels of a better world. He dressed with the greatest care. He manipulated his long white hair, letting it sweep back from his brow with the flow of an ancient Gallic warrior. He covered his long fingers with rings. He decorated himself with diamond studs. He made up compliments, writing them out before-hand, and studying how to bring up the conversation so as to drag them in. He acted over again in his imagination what he had said in the morning. He even, in his ardour, neglected his dinner, and made for two or three successive days a repast perfectly simple.

The change in his life coincided with the severance of his connection with Mr. Carew. The rude, low-bred, and pain-fully true words spoken by his secretary gave his nervous system a great shock. To be sure, Dicky, whose manner was truculent and even threatening, had abstained from personal violence, a thing to which Mr. Lilliecrip had an almost sacerdotal objection; but his criticism put him, for the time, out of conceit with the Memoirs.

Men's imaginations take hold of strange forecasts. Mr. Lilliecrip, obscure in life, pictured to himself a posthumous glory equal to that of Mr. Pepys, and second only to Saint Simon. He was, so far, like Chauncey Chacomb, who desired to be remembered after death as the collector of the Chacomb Museum. The doctor, on the other hand, was contented with the good opinion of his contemporaries. Their praise, he was wont to say, leads to pudding.

But what pleasure could a writer of Memoirs feel in work which even a common scribe and quill-driver like Dicky, his late secretary, declared was too stupid to be read, too clumsy not to be detected as an impudent forgery? Undoubtedly, too, it *was* a forgery; though, by the practice of long years, Mr. Lilliecrip had come to regard it as a genuine series of reminiscences. There are liars who have reached to such a point that they cannot speak the truth—imaginative liars; liars of principle, habit, method; liars who like to believe that they are telling the truth, who build a palace for their soul and live in it always, adding to it, decorating and im-proving it. Mr. Lilliecrip was one of these. Just now, after the rude assault of his secretary, the palace walls seemed too much knocked about for the place to be habitable, and he felt like one who has been turned out into the cold.

And so he basked in the sunshine of the first floor. He appeared every morning as radiant as Tithonus refreshed by kissing Aurora's rosy fingers. He brought compliments with him—good old-fashioned compliments with a fine crusted flavour—these the girls laughed at; flowers, which they liked, and early fruit—things which no one can ever refuse. And yet, as he felt with irritation, he made no headway in their good graces. The man, callous as regards others, was morbidly sensitive about himself. He felt what was thought of him; he almost knew what was said of him. If he had overheard Adie's opinion of him, he could not have been more certain what it was.

This it was.

"Marion," said the young observer, "I don't like him. He was a gentleman once, I suppose; but I don't like him. He is never real. His compliments are foolish, and his pretensions ridiculous. Considered as a Hermit, he is a disappointment. Hermits ought to have dirty faces and to wear serge gowns, with nothing between that and their tender skins, to punish them for being hermits—the nasty creatures! Mr. Lilliecrip is dressed like a young gentleman of Regent Street. Lilliecrip, too—what a name! My dear, he has done something."

He did not impress her at all. She only laughed at his magnificent talk, and almost openly mimicked him. He saw that she criticised him. As he spoke, moved, and dressed *pour l'effet*, it was natural that he should be on the watch perpetually to see what sort of effect was produced. He liked to walk up and down the room, a habit which his long years of solitude had given him, just as if he had been in the Zoological Gardens. At the table by the window Marion was at work with her water-colours; Adie in her chair, at work on some of her own devices. Between them he walked and talked, generally of himself; but always in a guarded manner, as if there was something to hide.

"My old friend, Lord Cardigan," he began once, naming an officer whose exploits the younger generation know only by hearsay—"my old friend, Lord Cardigan, once advised me seriously to cultivate Art as an occupation—of course, not as a profession."

"Dear me!" said Adie, in her flippant way. "That is a very interesting anecdote. Tell us another, Mr. Lilliecrip; and then I will try to remember how I once sewed a button on my cuff."

"Ah, yes—very good indeed, my dear young lady, very good. It reminds me of poor D'Orsay's best days."

"Mr. Lilliecrip, what do you go about under false pretences for?" asked Adie.

"My dear!" expostulated Marion.

"I mean, of course, why do you live in a wretched house like this, where the world never comes?"

"Because the world never comes here," said the Solitary, with a sigh.

"I am sure I wish it did," Adie went on. "But the world is a very pleasant world to those who have money. You have money, I suppose, Mr. Lilliecrip?"

"Money, yes, and—and—rank," he added, as if the word dropped out unawares.

"Really! are you Sir John Lilliecrip, Baronet, or General Sir Arthur Lilliecrip, K.C.B., or Baron Lilliecrip, or Earl Lilliecrip, or the Marquis of Lilliecrip, or His Grace the Duke of Lilliecrip? You can't be His Royal Highness Prince Lilliecrip—can you?"

Mr. Lilliecrip made no answer to this sally, which visibly disconcerted him.

"Adie, dear," murmured Marion.

But her sister went on.

"Tell me why you wear that ribbon in your button-hole, Mr. Lilliecrip?"

He had assumed a slender scarlet ribbon, like that worn by the Legion of Honour in France.

"It is nothing," he answered, pretending to hide it. "A small personal distinction, bestowed upon me in 1848 by the Emperor of Austria, on the field of battle."

"Dear me!" said Adie, who did not believe a word of it. "I like to hear about battles. Tell me the history. Did he make you kneel, and knight you on the spot?"

He gravely shook his head.

"Pardon me; it is an affair of history. I can hardly, even to gratify a lady's desire, tell the story without revealing— revealing what it is best to keep concealed.

"Can you not understand, young ladies," he went on—by this time he was standing in the window, where a reflection of the sunlight from an opposite window fell full upon his face and head, and lit him up with a kind of aureole—"can you not understand, without putting me to the pain of explaining, and thereby uncovering what it has been my fixed resolution to conceal, the sad history of a deceived and disappointed life? Suffice it that I found, at the age of forty— late, you may say—the world a mockery, its pleasures a vanity, the profession of friendship hollow, the vows of women false."

"I cannot understand that at all," said Adie; "that is, speaking for myself. I find the world's pleasures charming, and I believe women are always true. Marion, dear, can you understand that the pleasures of the world are vain? You see, Mr. Lilliecrip, we have known so few of them that it would not be fair to judge. When I have gone on a little way further, say half as far as you, I might possibly agree with you; but at present I can only say that I do not understand it at all. It seems to me stagey to talk in this way."

Mr. Lilliecrip was staggered. The girl's way of catching him up in an elaborated sentence put him out. He leaned against the window for a moment, and considered.

There was a woman in the street below, staring up at the window, with haggard look. A woman in rags—a disreputable woman. She came with hurried steps into the street; but when she arrived at the door of No. 15, she hesitated, stopped, and crossed over to the other side. Then she walked up and down, gazing with all her eyes at the windows of the first floor—those of Marion's lodgings.

It was a bright morning; the sunshine was reflected across the street upon one of Marion's windows. There, presently,

this unquiet watcher—for she walked up and down, talking
to herself, clenching her hand, and clutching her wretched
shawl round her wasted figure—saw a head appear, clad in
long, white hair, and standing out in the sunshine as if it
were a silver head set in ebony.

When she saw it, she started; then she looked again,
bending forward and straining her eyes, as one who wants to
catch at every vantage point of sight. The head turned a
little, and she saw the full face for a moment; the figure
straightened itself, and she saw the slope of the shoulders.

Then like a mad dog, she ran up and down the kerbstone
in misery, with eyes full of rage and terror.

And lastly, as if she had no more control of her limbs,
she shrieked aloud, and running across the street, dashed
open the door—which was, as usual, left ajar—and rushed
up the stairs to Marion's room.

"Let me try to make myself clearer," Mr. Lilliecrip was
going on, in those clear, calm tones which convinced Dicky
Carew against his better knowledge that the man was truthful.
"You are both far too young and inexperienced to feel the disappointments of a man who was for twenty years in search of
a career. Wealth and rank; family connections and—if I
may say so—hereditary intellect; accomplishments and—if
I may be allowed to speak of it—personal distinctions—the
Victoria Cross, the Iron Cross, the Eagle of Russia, the Cross
of Maria Theresa, are a few of my rewards. All these things,
dear to most people, to me were vain. What are they, indeed,
compared with a disappointed heart? In diplomacy, I looked
for truth and honour, and found falsehood and treachery; in
war, I looked for courage and found cowardice; in friendship,
I looked for devotion and found self-interest; in love, I looked
for fidelity and found betrayal. Everywhere self, everywhere
luxury, everywhere interest, everywhere falsehood. England,
my native England, where is the ancient virtue gone?"

"That sounds very pretty," said Adie. "But suppose you
had started like me, without expecting too much. As for
myself, I look for nice people, and I pray for money in order
to put myself in their way."

There was a step outside the door, which Marion heard, and, lifting her head, waited for a knock; but none came. Had no one spoken, they might have heard a loud quick breathing outside. But they could not guess the wild passion that held the woman there motionless till she could bear it down low enough to find her voice again.

"It was my leading principle through an active life," went on this pompous moralist, "to seek out Virtue. Rarely have I found it. At last, after repeated trials and disappointments, I resolved to quit the world for which I had toiled in vain, and endeavour to find in solitude such happiness as my meditations alone might give."

"Meditation and mutton cutlets," said Adie. "I have heard they go well with claret. It all sounds like a piece of an old novel."

"Young lady, forbear to scoff at a man who has seen Courts, who knows the roar of battle, who has lived in cities, and who, with all his experience, can proudly say with Bayard that he is a knight *sans peur et sans reproche.*"

He delivered himself in measured speech, raising his figure to the full height of six feet two as he spoke, and folding his arms with an attitude which spoke volumes. He swelled out, too, like the frog in the fable, and looked bigger.

Adie felt abashed at the rebuke and at the aspect of the godlike man. Still, in her frivolous way, she might have answered, had not the door been flung open. There stood the woman—the same whom she remembered seeing with Marion—standing tall, defiant, and threatening. Her eyes— bright blue eyes, *the same colour as Adie's*—were fixed upon Mr. Lilliecrip. She neither moved nor spoke for a space. Only her right arm slowly lifted, as if mechanically. Madame Rachel, a gipsy woman in a rage, a Hindoo whose husband has eaten her cakes, an Arab woman who is having an altercation with another lady of the same camp—alone could equal that gesture of unbounded and unstudied rage. Her lips were parted; her nostrils dilated; the flush of wrath upon her sunken cheeks filled them out, and made her look ten years younger.

Marion started from her chair, and placed herself between the woman and her sister.

"You dare to come here!" she cried—"*here*, of all places in the world?"

"Hush, Marion Revel!—hush!" the other said. "Don't be afraid. It is not to you I come. Tell me—tell me—why is *he* here? What is that man doing in this room? My God, what fresh misery is he preparing? Marion Revel, tell me before I kill him!"

At the voice of the woman, at the name she spoke, Mr. Lilliecrip seemed to shrink together and collapse. He did not change colour, because his ghastly pallor could not well grow whiter; but he grew suddenly six inches shorter of stature, and ten years older. His hair seemed to lose its silky flow, and fell over his face; his eyes grew crowsfooted, his cheeks wrinkled, his hands trembled. The youthful coat he wore looked like some horrid mockery.

"Tell me what he is doing here, Marion Revel—if not for your own sake, tell me for hers."

She pointed to Adrienne, who cowered with terror behind her sister.

"Revel!" murmured the man, with chattering teeth.

"Ay, Revel! You ought to know the name well—no one better. What have you to do here—and with *his* daughters? Yes, Captain Revel's daughters. And who am I? Do you remember me? Do I ever cross your thoughts? Am I changed? Am I wasted, worn, and miserable?"

"You are, Carry."

The answer came like a whisper from dry and trembling lips.

"Carry! Yes, Carry! Marion, do you know now who this man is? You do not. I see you do not. Perhaps you cannot even guess. But you know—oh! you know what I am; and he is the cause. He is the wicked cause, and I am the miserable, wretched victim."

She passed, in her swift way, from lamenting to threatening.

"I told you, Marion, that I should meet him some day. I prayed for this, and that makes the second prayer answered. I told you I should have my revenge."

The man who looked on, shivered, shook, and trembled, trying to stop the torrent of her words.

"Come upstairs, Carry. Not here. For God's sake, come away with me."

"Marion," the woman went on, "I came to tell you that the boy is dying. Better so—better so. I will have my revenge by the death-bed of his son."

He shrank back, as she stepped towards him, with a pitiable terror and horror.

"I did not know," he murmured—"I did not know who they were. Miss Revel, I give you my word of honour—"

"His word of honour! His word of honour! Come with me. Both the parents shall be at the bedside of their dying child. That is proper—that is right. The boy shall give you his blessing before he goes."

Marion, bewildered as she was, felt pity for the poor wretch, so utterly broken down, and at the mercy of this woman.

"Have pity on him," she said. "He is old—and—and—"

"Marion Revel, you are a fool. Shall I nurse my revenge for fifteen years, and lose it at last? Shall I suffer want and misery, shame and disgrace, and forgive him when I meet him after all this time? Come"—she seized him by the arm—"come!"

Then she turned, and saw Adrienne clinging to her sister, frightened. Suddenly her whole face changed. She let the man's arm drop, and, with a bitter cry, threw herself at the girl's feet.

"No, Marion—suffer me—only this once in all my life. Never again—oh! me—never again! Both your hands, my pretty—both your hands, my darling; both your hands for me to hold and kiss—and kiss. O Adrienne—little Adie—little, little Adie!—do you remember, Marion? And she never knew, did she?—never knew. What shall I say to her —what? She is as beautiful as the day; she shall be as happy as a princess; she shall have every blessing that the Lord has to give her; and she shall be—she shall be—good."

She went on like a mad woman, crying, talking, and kissing Adie's hands all the time. The girl yielded passively. The tears stood in her eyes; but they might have been tears of surprise, sympathy, or anything. She understood nothing, and suspected nothing. The miserable Hermit stood irresolute. There was a moment when he might have made his escape, when Mrs. Spenser was crying over Adie's hands. He lost that moment, looking at the woman with eyes of foreboding. All the uprightness was gone out of the man; he seemed shrunken into the semblance of a terrified and beaten cur. When it was too late, and her passion had somewhat spent itself, he bethought himself of the door, and stealthily moved in that direction.

Mrs. Spenser sprang from Adie, dashed away the tears from her eyes, and seized her prisoner once more with a clutch of steel.

"Marion," she whispered quickly, "I have not told her—never tell her. Make up something. Forgive me. Come, sir, come—we have something to see together."

She dragged him, resistless in her wrath, from the room.

"Marion," said Adie tremulously, "what is it? What does it all mean? Who is she, Marion?" the girl repeated. "Why did she kiss my hand? Why did she look so wild?"

But Marion made no reply. Her cheek was pale, and her lips dry. She *knew*. She knew without needing to be told, all that it meant. The man with the silky, white hair—the man whose face had inspired her with a distrust at first sight, was he who had brought ruin and wretchedness upon her father's happiness.

And the woman?

She soothed her sister as best she could. It was her great comfort, for herself, that Adie had no suspicion, not the slightest suspicion, of the truth. She was only frightened and curious.

"Is she mad, Marion?"

"Yes, dear, yes. She will not come back again. Adie, you are not afraid to be left alone, are you? I must go and look after that poor creature. Never ask me who she is, dear. Never speak of her, or think of her again. If you are nervous, go and sit in Mr. Owen's room. He is in the school, and you are quite safe there. Don't be frightened, dear. The poor woman has had a terrible life, and a fearful punishment for sin. The wretched man was, it appears, her tempter. Do not think harshly of her, Adie. I must go to her lodgings."

Marion found the unfortunate Hermit planted by the pallet of the boy, just where Mrs. Spenser placed him. His hands hung down his side; he looked sometimes at the woman, sometimes at the boy, and sometimes at the wretched room.

His face brightened when he saw Marion.

"Don't let them murder me," he moaned. "I will make expiation; I will pay something every week."

The mother was attending to the boy, still with her wild eyes and shaking limbs. She seemed to take no notice of the man, but if he moved she placed herself at once between him and the door.

Marion turned to the boy. He lay back upon the pillow, his cheek pale and thin, his frame wasted. Death was written, so plain that even his mother could see, in his bright and fixed eyes. His lips played with a thin, sweet smile, and his face wore the intensified, peculiar expression of absolute vacancy, which yet was not quite idiotic, but even pleasing. He did not belong to the world—he never had belonged to the world. There was no tie with humanity, except that with his mother, which it would pain the boy to break. There was no thought of the next world to excite in him the tears of terror, or those of a grateful trust. He was an infant still, although of fourteen years, on whom the ills of the world had passed over innocuously, because he did not know they *were* ills. He was that creature whom the Arab has ever regarded with respect, and the Christian, until the last few years, with loathing—a boy with half a brain. Nature had been very kind to him. He was to live for fourteen years only, and then to die. She gave him the gifts of gentleness, sympathy, and love.

"Look at him, Marion," said the poor mother. "Do you think he is looking easier?"

"Jem," said Marion, kneeling beside the child, "you know me, don't you? You have seen me here before."

He smiled. He would have nodded his head, but was too weak.

"I know," he murmured. "I told you the hymn—

> ' Adama Neave they turned him out,
>   'Cos he knocked the apples down.'

Mother, give me an orange. I say"—he turned feebly to Marion—"don't you wish you was ill? It's jolly to get oranges all day long, and all night too. I should like to see the boys again. There's one boy—tell him—"

He stopped and coughed.

"Yes," said Marion. "What shall we tell that boy? He is a friend of yours."

"Tell him," said Jem—the words were ferocious, but the meek manner of utterance redeemed their ferocity—"tell him that he owes me for two *Globes* and an *Echo*, and if he won't pay me, I'll cut his liver out. It's twopence altogether."

This seemed to Marion a poor way of starting for the next world; but the boy's childish face belied his sanguinary threats.

They watched—the three of them—while he had another fit of coughing, which seemed to tear him in pieces. Presently the fit ceased, and he sank back. His mother held his hand, and began, always with one eye on her prisoner, a sort of trembling monologue.

"When he was only a day old," she said, "I wished I was dead, and the child as well, till I felt those little fingers at my breast. Marion, I never felt so with the other two—not quite so. It was for this boy that I gave up my husband, and my home, and—and—you, little Marion, that I loved, only not my own. It was for him—for him. Ah! and he will never know what I gave up. He will never learn the madness of his mother and the wickedness of his father."

Mr. Lilliecrip moved uneasily, and in the direction of the door. A gesture from the woman stopped him, and he stood at the end of the bed, looking miserably, not at the boy, but at the woman who had found him out.   His dignity was gone; his figure was bent; his bearing was cowed.   It seemed impossible that so great a change should happen in so short a time.

"Look at him, Marion.   Look at this miserable creature. He has not even the common courage to brazen it out.   And it was with him—with him—that I ran away from the best husband in the world, and the dearest children—with this man.   Look at him well.   He was handsome, after his kind. He could do things.   He wore his uniform gallantly.   He was not so clever as my husband, and I was not afraid of him.   I was a fool—oh, heavens, what a fool I was!—and he persuaded me.

"My boy," she went on, after a while, "who was your mother?"

He was breathing slowly, and with difficulty.   The cold dews rested on his forehead, and his eyes were closed.

"She was a lady," he replied, slowly, and with pain.

"And who was your father?"

"He was a gentleman."

"What else, my boy?"

"Oh, hush!" said Marion.   "For pity's sake, spare him. The boy is—"

"What, Marion Revel—what?   The boy is going to have a quiet sleep; and then, perhaps, he will get better.   Say, my boy—what was your father?"

"A scoundrel!   When I meet him, I will kill him."

The man at the foot of the bed trembled in all his limbs.

"He was more than a scoundrel," said his mother.   "Plenty of greater men are scoundrels.   He was a coward—a convicted coward.   He was a disgrace to the cloth he bore, and to the army he belonged to.   He refused to go—the only officer in the service who ever did it—he actually refused—look at him well, Marion!—to go out on trench duty.   They tried to hide it in the regiment; but I knew it—oh! I learned it.   Only think, Marion, that for this miserable creature I lost my all!"

Marion was wiping the lips and forehead of the dying boy, and hardly listened to the poor frantic woman.

"Jem," she whispered—"Jem, dear boy. Say after me, my boy. Say, 'Our Father.'"

"That's my father—I'll kill him," the boy replied, in sullen words. "When I see him, I'll kill him. Mother says I am to."

"Say, then—'God help and forgive us every one.'"

"God help and forgive us every one," the boy repeated, dutifully. "What is your name?" he asked feebly.

"Marion."

"I'm Rickety Jem. Mother!"

His mother seemed stupefied. She sat stupidly gazing at her boy, trying by some superhuman effort to realise the full bearing of things. But she could not. It seemed like some dreadful nightmare. The years rolled away. She was with Marion, but Marion was a little girl. She was with this man, but he was a brave and gallant officer. She was—but no—the dream would go no farther.

"Mother," said Jem.

His senses swam about him. His eyes and lips lit up for a moment in a smile.

"One of the boys—" he began.

But he stopped short, laid his cheek on Marion's hand, and ceased to breathe.

Only Marion noticed that the boy was dead. But in a minute the mother's heart misgave her, and she stooped to kiss the boy. Then, with a bitter cry, she fell upon the body, kissing it a thousand times in her agony.

When Marion looked round again Mr. Lilliecrip was gone.

He had slipped away at the first relaxation of the woman's watchfulness. He crept noiselessly down the stairs, and he fled. The first thing that occurred to him was that he ought to get a hat; for Mrs. Spenser had dragged him through the streets hatless, an object of pity and derision to the world. He had his purse in his pocket. Provided with this necessary, he turned east, and, with furtive steps and much looking behind him to see if he was followed, he began a pilgrimage to some place—he knew not where—where he might be safe.

He marched, with downcast eyes and stooping figure—a strange figure—drawing the eyes of all after him, through the crowded streets. He was unused to walk abroad for so many years that he ran against people, got over crossings by a kind of miracle, drew upon himself the imprecations of cabmen and the warnings of policemen. But he kept on. He was so terrified that he could think of only one thing— the best way of escape, and only one way—escape to a foreign country. He would go down to the docks; he would take the first ship which was going to sail; he would go to America. Other purpose he had none—only to escape from those dreadful eyes of the woman he had wronged, from the memory of the scene he had just witnessed, from any future consequences that might arise. We do not, unhappily, repent of our sins; we only dread the consequences.

Then he found himself at the docks, and further flight seemed, for the moment, impossible.

He went to a hotel—there are some good hotels at the East End of London—and ordered a private room. It was getting on for evening. He ordered dinner as well. And then he sat down and began to think.

"It was an awkward position," he said—"most awkward. I do not know that I can remember a more remarkable situation in any novel. The old love—she—the old love, and actually her daughter, with the step-daughter—elements, if one had only gone a little farther, of an excellent French novel. Devilish unlucky thing her finding me out! And most disagreeable business that in her lodgings. However, it has forced me to leave my retreat. I will go back to the world. Not London—no, not there. In some place where I am not known —where there can be no chance of my being found out again, where the name of Lillingworth has never been heard."

He rose abruptly, and walked up and down the room.

"Curse the Crimean War! Curse my own folly in going! I might have sold out—lots of fellows sold out. I might have exchanged—lots of fellows exchanged. I might have come home on urgent private affairs—lots of fellows did. But I must needs go in for glory. And if I had done—if I had obeyed orders, I might have been snug, and been a general with a reputation by this time.

"Poor Carry! she's gone off terribly. Fancy my ever being in love with that little doll. I suppose I must have been once, else I shouldn't have run away with her. I was devilish afraid Revel would call me out. He didn't. Why didn't he? He wasn't afraid.

"And that's his daughter!—that splendid beauty; that glorious girl, with the deep brown eyes, that go through a man like a gimlet. Gad! and if it had not been for the cursed woman's interference, she might have been mine. We would have gone to Italy, she and I together, and practised Art. We would have lived at Spezzia—ah! I know it. I was there once with—with one of them, and looked over the blue waters of the bay, and drank the Chianti wine. Oh, what a chance to lose!"

He rang the bell.

"Waiter. If you have any curaçoa, give me a small glass. Dinner at six, if you can. And a bottle of Piper's Sec, if you have any. None of your sweet stuff. No, not a pint— a whole bottle.

"I am devilish low to-night. This curaçoa is not dry enough, but it is better than nothing. Poor Carry! she's like a devil to look at. Women are, when they go off in that shocking way, and neglect their dress.

"Hang her! Why should I trouble my head about her at all. What is she to me, or I to her, now? It is all past and gone. Let me forget the past. I am fifty-five years of age. I have ten years more of enjoyment before me, and then ten more of care and misery. I will go to America. If I don't like it, I will come back to Europe. Waiter, let me have dinner as soon as you can. I shall sleep here; and— waiter, get me a telegraph form."

He telegraphed to his lawyers; went out to the docks, hard by; found a steamer—the *Triton*—going to sail at twelve the next morning; returned to his house; had a good dinner; bought a novel, and read it with great enjoyment; went to bed, and dreamed of Marion Revel.

Not a thought of the woman he had ruined, or of the wrecked boy, his son. The woman was one instrument out of many which had subserved his selfish purposes. Why should he feel for her?

The next day he was steaming down the Pool, on board the *Triton*. In his pocket were letters of credit. In his hand was another novel.

He strolled forward. In the forecastle, a steerage passenger was sitting—a handsome young fellow, whose face struck him with terror, for that also was the face of Carry.

"Good God!" he cried. "Can I never escape her?"

And hurried back to the after-deck. His enjoyment was gone.

For the young man was Fred Revel, his fellow-passenger.

While Captain Lillingworth—we may as well give him his real name—was drinking brandy and water, and laughing over the novel, Mrs. Spenser was wandering up and down the streets. Not in search of him—he was not in her mind at all, save as some refrain to a song, or as a song which gets possession of the brain, and keeps singing itself over and over again, always in discord with the thoughts that pass backward and forwards.

Presently she wandered down to the Embankment—unconscious where she was, or how she got there.

She was past thinking—she could only remember. Her life passed before her in easy stages, beginning with the brief courtship, when the grave young widower asked her—her, the girl who thought of nothing but balls—to be his wife, and made her believe that she was clever.

"I wasn't," she said. "I was only silly—only silly."

Then she thought of her marriage. That took her a long time, because it was a happy thing to think of. Then she remembered the life in London, and at Portsmouth, where her husband got a ship. Then the quiet life in the country, while he was on the Mediterranean. Then the birth of the boy. Then the captain's return, and the coming of the little girl; and then—then—ah! then!

She was tired. There were no seats. The Embankment was deserted, because it was a rainy night. She went and sat down on the steps that overhang the water. The tide was rushing up through the arches of Waterloo Bridge before her with a loud swirl and sweep, tearing past the granite wall by which she sat, foaming against the steps, rushing inland, as if to escape some pursuer. There were lights beyond the river, which were reflected in the water; and as she looked across, there seemed to stand out upon the black water a face which the poor distracted creature knew too well.

It gave her a shock at first; but in a minute or two she grew accustomed to the sight of it.

And then she began to grow rational.

"My boy is dead," she began, speaking to the phantom. "I have been very miserable—almost starving, except for your daughter, who is the best woman in all the world. Forgive me. I have never been happy for a single day since I did it—never once. Oh! forgive me. I found him out for what he was the day after I left you. I knew then—but it was too late—what I had given up. I was so silly—so silly; and you thought I could understand when you talked about books. O God! I was so silly! And I got tired and cross because you would not see how stupid I was! And then he came, and then—oh, forgive me! Husband—say you forgive me!"

She stretched out her arms. The waves were flowing over her feet, but she felt nothing. Something seemed to lift her from the cold stones on which she sat, and to lay her softly in the water, which bore her swiftly—the face beckoning her always—past steps and granite walls, under the dark arches of the bridges, by barges and steamboats, rolling her over and over, beating her face and washing her limbs, carrying her, cold and insensible, to the land where her husband had long forgiven her.

CHAPTER XXXVI.

THE doctor came back to town thoughtful, but not, on the whole, depressed. It was true that the rightful heir was come back to his own. That was bad for himself and his succession. On the other hand, it was by the most blessed —by the most providential—arrangement of time and circumstance that the young prince should have arrived in the very nick of time, while Chauncey's demonstrative gratitude was in open evidence. There was very little fear, after this, that he would ever have to give an account of his stewardship at all; or, if any account, then such a one as would be best in his own interests. Two courses were open to him. He might simply declare that the Chacomb revenues had been spent on the Chacomb estate; or—it was an alternative of some moral importance—he might tell the actual truth. He might say, "I have received the rents. I have kept a careful and accurate statement of all incomings and outgoings. I have seen that my cousin was looked after, and the place properly kept up. I have borrowed four or five thousand for my own purposes, for which I am ready to give interest, and to pay it off in a reasonable time. And the rest is all lying in the bank, or invested in the funds, in my name, *as the trustee.*" No legal documents; no nasty binding conditions; nothing but the word of a gentleman and a cousin.

"And, by gad!" he said, after an hour's cogitation in the train, "there is nothing in the world like honesty. I will write to Gerald when I get back to town, and send him the real statement."

This he eventually did, with such heightening of favourable details as even the goddess herself, fresh from the well, could not avoid. The result was as satisfactory as he could wish for Gerald in person assured him that he valued his services to the owner of Chacomb at far more than the small sum (this remarkable young man called it "the small sum") which his father had lent him—the doctor was careful to set

the facts so as to make it appear that everything was done
by permission of the squire, after careful consideration—and
that no demand would ever be made upon him for the interest.
Travellers and colonials, when they come home to England,
are apt, as is well known, to be free of money, not rightly
knowing its value or the difficulty of getting it. No doubt
Gerald has learned better by this time.

The accounts which the doctor roughly drew up in his own
mind—he knew the value of a correct statement, from reading Balzac—formed, when set down, a remarkable record of
honest dealing. There was, first, the sum total of the rents
for four years—a trifle of fifteen thousand pounds. From
this sum was to be deducted the expenses of keeping up
Chacomb—amounting to no more, with the reduced establishment, than fifteen hundred a year. That left nine thousand
pounds. Now, of this sum he professed to have borrowed
four thousand, and invested the rest. He had not, it was
certain, embezzled, defrauded, made use of trust money, or
done any of the things by which men sometimes come to
grief. He had simply — being a self-appointed trustee,
answerable to no one, and acting in an inofficial manner
—taken the liberty of borrowing some of the money, and
investing the rest to what he considered the best advantage.
And he had prospered greatly—so greatly that, although
to repay the advances he had taken to start himself on his
successful career he would have to sacrifice nearly all his
earnings; yet he felt that he could do it, with a sure confidence that a few years more of work would put him in a
position to retire from active practice. He might, too, and
did, charge in his account for all those journeys undertaken
in his cousin's interest.

The moral of this novel, as, no doubt, everybody has found
out—it is absurd to append a moral in set terms—is that
prosperity, and not adversity at all, is needed to develop
the higher virtues of mankind. Some people have foolishly
taught that self-denial and maceration are the only virtues.
Rubbish! The most delicate flowers are fostered by the
warmest sunshine. Generosity, measured by a sense of

justice, prudence, thrift, common sense — all these fair
blossoms are produced by prosperity; and they are nipped
by the cursed east winds of ill-fortune. In the old days,
the doctor borrowed, spent, gave, lent, and scorned the
qualities which make collective man strong. In this his
wealthy time, he was actually proposing to charge his cousin
all his journeys to Barnstaple and back. Now the virtue of
thrift is very great. It makes England what it is. And it
is possessed far more largely by the rich than by the poor.

It is not to be disguised that he was strongly tempted to
evade the moral obligation of truth, and to enact the part of
the unjust steward. Gerald's return was, in itself, an act at
which he might fairly show some indignation. He had so
long been irresponsible, that it was almost intolerable to
resign his guardianship. And, besides, he had so accustomed
himself to regard the silence of Gerald as indicating his death,
that the rulings of Providence appeared a personal injury.
It must be marked, as a clear advance in the moral nature
of the doctor, that he shrank from the temptation as a dishonour; whereas, in his days of adversity, the unregenerate
times, such a temptation might—one is not quite sure—
might have been considered from the standpoint of risk. But
when the train rolled in at Waterloo terminus, the doctor's
brow was clear, and his resolution firm. His brow had
smoothed itself out, and he had resumed his ordinary aspect
of calm and thoughtful prosperity.

But there was another person to be considered. How
should he act to Marion?

He dismissed Gerald and the accounts from his thoughts,
and turned them in the direction of Marion. The doctor
had at least one gift—that of being able to shift his mind.
As with all clear-headed men, his subjects arranged themselves in pigeon-holes. Marion and Gerald were together
in one, separate in two others; Chauncey and his housekeeper
together in another; Gerald and the future auditing of
accounts in a third. And so on.

Marion. She had to be told of Gerald's return. Should
he tell her?

It seemed as if a crisis of his fate was approaching. For four years everything had prospered with him. If he borrowed money, it returned to him with interest wherever he invested it. If he started a speculation, it succeeded. If he wrote a book, it sold, and brought him credit. He was carried for four years along the tide of fortune, almost without effort of his own, save to guide his craft. All around him he saw the barks of other men—dismasted, rudderless, foundering, even keel uppermost—at best, making slow and uncertain headway, like a Thames barge when the flow is well-nigh spent. And now—the heir returned, the girl whom he had hoped to marry lost to him, and the borrowed money all to be repaid.

He resolved to see Marion that same evening.

He dined at a restaurant—things looking a little brighter after dinner—and drove home to Adelaide Street. Among the letters lying on his table, which he tossed over to be read the next day, was one which he seized and opened.

" I had forgotten that matter altogether," he said.

The letter was from a well-known artist.

" I am glad to tell you that your *protégé's* picture is accepted, and will be, if I can manage it, well hung. Come to the private view and see it, if you can find time. My opinion of it is vastly improved. There is force in the conception ; and, if some of the drawing is not too firm, it is correct. I do not think that the young lady will make a great artist, but she has gifts. The picture will sell. When you dine with me next, tell me all about her."

" By Jove ! " said the doctor. " If the news had only arrived before Gerald's return. Perhaps it is not yet too late. Gratitude is a strong passion with women ; as for men, they mostly wonder what it means. I will go at once."

He went, taking the letter with him, and found Marion alone, playing in the twilight such old music as she remembered—reminiscences which brought peace to her anxious heart.

She looked up as he entered, with those deep eyes of hers,

which always went straight to the doctor's heart. Adie's eyes were larger and brighter, but they never moved him— they were too bright and shallow.

"I have brought you news," he said.

"Is it good news, Dr. Chacomb?" she asked, with a little laugh. "It is such a long time since we heard anything good."

"Yes; it is very good news. I have a letter from ——, the Academician. May I read it to you? No; take the letter, and read it yourself. Shall I light your candles?"

"No, thank you. I like to sit in the twilight. And I can read it by the light of the street gas."

She took it to the window; and when she brought it back to the doctor, he noticed that her eyes were full of tears.

"Poor Fred!" she murmured. "If this had happened a week ago, perhaps he need not have gone abroad."

"Nothing ever happens when it ought," said the doctor, thinking over his own affairs. "People and things always arrive just too late, or just too early. If it's an even chance, as actuaries tell us, when a thing happens, I don't understand why it always happens wrong. We must not build too much upon the picture, Miss Revel. You have got into the Academy—that is a great thing. We will hope you will sell your picture, and a great many others. But all the pictures are not sold."

"No. I understand. Only"—she turned a face which looked, in the new light of happiness and hope, beautiful, even more than with the beauty of youth—"only, let me hope. Oh, Dr. Chacomb! do you think they will abuse the picture in the papers?"

"That's quite another thing. Art critics are perhaps the worst people of any that pretend to do work. I've known lots; and I never knew one—not one—on whom I could depend for a good judgment of a picture. They get up the slang—that's easy enough. You have got to find the proper adjectives. If you criticise a portrait, say it is 'wrought for strength and brilliancy.' Lug in the words arbitrary and self-assertive. Write that the artist has created difficulties

in order to conquer them. If you criticise a landscape, you
must have delicacy, neatness, fertility. Nothing is so easy
as to go in for Art. Do not worry your head about what
they say. And as to that, I can get hold of some of them."

"Oh, but I should like an independent judgment."

"That is just what you shall have. That is to say, no one's
mind shall be set against you. Remember that the Art critic
has first got to praise his own friends. When these are
cracked up, he has got to bully his enemies. After these are
well slashed, then come the general mob of painters, to whom
he is indifferent. All I shall try at, will be to guide one or
two of these gentlemen into the right groove for admiration."

It always grated on the girl's mind, this constant assump-
tion on the part of Dr. Chacomb that everything in the world
was done for some personal motive. He spoke out of the
depths of his own knowledge of evil; she out of her belief in
good.

"I will leave it all to you," she said. "How pleased Adie
will be! And, oh, Dr. Chacomb, how grateful I am to you
for all your kindness!"

She half held out her hand, but withdrew it again with a
blush, which the twilight of the room prevented the doctor
from seeing.

He was silent for a moment. For a great battle was
raging in his soul.

"Marion," he began presently, and in a strange, hoarse
voice—"I have worked for you, not without hope of a reward.
You know me now. I do not pretend to be what I am not.
My life has been that of most adventurers. Pirates and buc-
caneers in all ages live in much the same way. They fight,
drink, sing, gamble, and make love—those who live outside
the world, and do not work in the usual grooves. I was no
better than any of them—perhaps worse than most. But I
passed through it without harm to my name; and for four
years I have left the ranks, as you know. And I love you."

She made no answer.

This great, strong man, who had as much passion in his
soul as any young fellow of five and twenty, seemed to be

taking possession of her, whether she would or no. She trembled.

He stood over her, as she sat upon her music stool, his arms half open, as if for her to fall into them; his face, she could feel, looking down into hers; his eyes lit with that strange light of love which she had seen once, and only once, before, and remembered ever after.

"Marion!—I feel as if before to-night I only loved you a little. Now, when I feel that I may lose you altogether, I love you with all the strength of my heart. Have pity on me!

"When I asked you six months ago, you must have laughed to think what a half-hearted wooer I was. Because then I thought you safe, and now you may be snatched away from me. Remember, Marion, that it is I, and no one else, who has loved you all this time. To take away hope would be to take away the whole happiness of my life. Have pity!"

She did not answer.

"Marion, you *must* take me. I will not go away from you till you promise to be my wife.

"Oh! my dear"—his voice sank low—"my dear, who could watch you, as I have watched you, brave and strong, working for the others, always contentedly, and not love you? Who could talk with you, day after day, and read in those eyes of yours their truth and honesty, without loving you? Good Heavens! could I—*I*—who know all, go away for years, and come back, forgetting almost your very existence? Marion, love me, too, a little."

The doctor had his chance, but he threw it away. Marion was strangely moved by his sincerity—mesmerised a little, perhaps, by the impetuous current of his eloquence. She might perhaps have yielded, and engaged herself to Joseph Chacomb, but for the unfortunate allusion, covert though it was, to Gerald's return and Gerald's faithlessness.

She caught his words, and started to her feet, seizing him by the hand.

"Dr. Chacomb," she cried, "tell me what you mean! Why am I no longer safe? Why do you talk of losing me? Who

is it that has gone away and forgotten? Who—who—who
has come back?"

He did not answer.

She held him tighter; she cried and sobbed hysterically;
she implored him to tell her. As she wept and entreated,
the doctor's face, could one have seen it, exchanged its
passionate eagerness for a look of pity and sympathy, which
suddenly ennobled it. Was all this fidelity to be in vain?
Was this sweet remembrance of a brief love passage to be
smothered and marred? Was this loving and faithful heart
to be tossed aside like a worthless weed? It seemed too
cruel. His own passion vanished as he saw the quiet, self-
possessed girl shaken out of all reserve by the news that her
lover had returned; his own wrath at the dashing of the cup
from his lip was calmed when he saw her joy, and thought of
her coming misery. For of one thing he was very sure—as
sure as he was that Marion could never love himself—that
Gerald no longer thought of her.

He soothed her, stroking her soft hair with his hand, as
one would soothe a child.

"Hush, Marion!—hush, my child! Do not sob, and I will
tell you all. Gerald has returned."

"Oh!—Gerald!—Gerald!—Gerald!" she cried, falling on
her knees in a passion of weeping. "Oh, my love, my sweetheart! He has come back to me. Oh, God be thanked!"

"Forgive me," Joseph Chacomb went on—"I only saw
him last night. He returned unexpectedly. He is at
Chacomb with his father. I came here to-night to ask you
once more if you—"

"When will he come to see me?" She cared nothing for
his explanations. She even remembered nothing of his
passionate pleading. She could think of nothing but that
Gerald was returned. "Tell me what he said, and how he
looked, and everything. Sit down, dear Dr. Chacomb.
Let me put your hat on the table for you. You are always
so kind. Will you have candles? Tell me all about it—
exactly as it happened. Let me picture it all clearly in my
own mind."

" He is well, but has been ill with fever, and looks pale—older, perhaps, as you would expect; and certainly much graver. To be sure, there is not much to laugh at in Chacomb Hall just now. He asked particularly for your address, which I gave him. He will come to London shortly, and, of course, will visit you immediately."

" Perhaps he will write," said Marion. " There may be a letter coming for me now. But then it will be better to see him. Did he send no message, Dr. Chacomb? Surely, one little word."

" My dear young lady, how was he to know that I should arrive here to-night; and as for messages, he will bring them all himself."

" That is true," Marion replied thoughtfully. " He will come here, and we shall talk over the dear old days: of Comb Leigh and my father; the little cove where my father kept his boat—did I ever take you for a sail in our own boat, Dr. Chacomb? She was the neatest little craft, papa used to say, along all the coast of North Devon. Then there were the woods, where we used to wander when we were children. In the spring there were the birds; in the summer you could find wild strawberries; and always there was something to be seen and found. Gerald knew the woods as you would know a printed book. Oh, what we shall have to recall! Why, the past four years will seem just like a bad dream, when he sits here, and we talk about dear, dear Comb Leigh. The good old days!—they can now come back, can't they ? But we may make some new good days, and they may be better still." She stopped, and her eyes filled again with tears. " Dr. Chacomb, I am foolish; forgive me. The memory of—of those things always makes me cry. Adie was too young to remember it all so well as I. And how shall I thank you? What shall I say to you? What can I do to show my gratitude? I will tell Gerald. Yes, I will tell Gerald. It is all I can do. You were the only friend we had in our trouble. You came and helped us; you lent poor Adie money; you got my picture in the Royal Academy —oh! Gerald will thank you too."

She seemed to have forgotten that, five minutes before, the man was passionately praying her to forget the past, and to marry him.

"Forgive me, Marion," said the doctor, struck with contrition. "Tell Gerald any kind thing you please; but do not tell him that I tried to win you away from him."

"Oh no—oh no," she laughed and cried. She was *folle* —foolish in her joy. "All that is past shall be forgotten— all except kindness and sympathy; those we can never forget, Gerald and I, never. They will last with us all our lives. Dr. Chacomb, thank God with me that Gerald is returned."

"I would rather," thought the doctor afterwards, "have considered prayerfully a thanksgiving for the fact that he could not return any more."

"Will he come to-morrow? Will he come in the evening, do you think? Could Fred meet him at the station? No, Fred is gone—I forgot that. How shall I meet him? What shall I say to him? Shall Adie be here?"

"Miss Revel," said the doctor solemnly, "do not let Adie be present when you see Gerald first. You have never told her of your engagement, and how it was broken off—but just begun. Do not let her be with you. I will take her out in the afternoon, and bring her home to you in the evening, after you have seen him. Will you do this?"

"Will it be best so?" she asked eagerly. "Do what you think fittest and best for me, doctor—you are always right. Perhaps we should meet alone. We shall have much to say. I shall tell how we have suffered, and what you have done for us. He will tell me where he has been, and—and—oh! I do not know what I am saying, I think. It is all so strange—so strange."

"Where is Adie now?"

"She is with Winifred Owen, downstairs, trying to comfort her. Winifred has lost her lover too. It was Fred, poor girl! She has married him secretly."

"Do not tell her yet. Tell her nothing—not even of the Royal Academy. You shall go with me to the private view, and see your own picture. Tell Adie that, if she will trust herself with me, I will take her out to-morrow afternoon. You can let me give her a new dress, as a reward for the picture, can you not?"

She took his hand, and her tears burst out again.

"I pray only that you may be happy, Marion," said the doctor, with a softened heart—"there is nothing else for me to hope for. And, Marion, if not in one way, there is another. Tell me, if Gerald is not what you hope and expect, if—if—"

"Ah," said Marion, "there is no *if*. I know Gerald. It will be long to wait till to-morrow evening; but what is that compared to the four years we have been parted?"

"Be brave, my girl," he murmured.

They shook hands. Her cheek was bright; her eyes were dancing with happiness; her lips were trembling. Never, in all the promise of her happy youth, had Marion looked so beautiful.

CHAPTER XXXVII.

WHEN the great Atlantic liner, the *Bismarck*, homeward bound from New York to Hamburg, ran into the little steamer *Triton*, outward bound from London to Quebec, and that famous collision ensued which furnished material for such long and complicated litigation, it was Fred Revel's lot to be on board the smaller craft. Once resigned to that unlucky chance, he had reason to be thankful that when the disaster occurred he was on deck, and in the bows. The accident, as was fully demonstrated by the evidence, happened the Lord knows how. It was a clear, still night at the end of April. The water was smooth, save for a little choppy sea, which made no difference to a ship, and would have mattered little to a wherry. There was fine starlight, if no moon. The ships were on an even keel. It was long after the time of "all lights out," and some of the passengers on both vessels were still lingering on deck, loth to go below and exchange the air of the sea for that of the cabin, when the lights showed that two vessels were nearing each other. Then—but at this point the evidence was entirely contradictory. The passengers and crew of the *Bismarck* all swore that the *Triton* suddenly changed her course, and steered, as if purposely, athwart their bows. The few who survived from the *Triton* swore positively that the big ship put her helm hard a-starboard, and ran them down, with malice and deliberate intent to destroy.

Fred Revel's evidence to this effect was considered perfectly worthless. Also, he was unable to write a graphic account of the calamity, or even to give a verbal description. All he knew was that they were run down, without—as it seemed—time to steer out of the way; that there was a sudden grinding and crunching of beams, a rush of water, then a cry of drowning men, a shriek of the women from their cabins—and that was all. For the *Triton* went down like a stone, with all on board.

The disaster happened a few miles off the Cornish coast, and there was, of course, a rush of correspondents to the place nearest the scene, to write up the details of the "tragedy," and then collect the narratives of the survivors. Of course, too, there were pictures in the illustrated papers showing the sinking of the ship—with, in those sold for a penny—scenes in the ladies' saloon as the ship went down. Of course, there were letters from correspondents indignant, correspondents sarcastic, and correspondents calmly philosophical. Heraclitus and Democritus both have their innings at such articles; and, what with the sham tears and the sham derision, we manage to make the worst out of calamities which give us at first a comfortable thrill of horror. One man wrote out an elaborate system, which occupied a whole column of the *Times*, and appeared in leaded type. He said that sailors had only to provide themselves before going to sea each with a life-saving belt, which might be purchased of Messrs. Catch, Chance & Co., provided with a waterproof bag, in which were placed, in separate compartments, biscuits, preserved meat, cigars, lights, a spirit lamp and portable teapot, a pound of best Souchong, a flask of brandy, a pistol to fire at sharks, a rocket or two, and a chair to sit down in the water when it was desirable to change the position. This in case of wreck. As regards passengers, they would take not only the patent belt sold by Catch, Chance & Co., but also the patent guttapercha boat, manufactured by the same benevolent firm, combining at once the portmanteau, shaving apparatus, a bed, a mast and sail, Rob Roy cooking apparatus, and a small carronade for firing signals. Thus equipped, a whole family, the writer stated, might get ashore as easily as did the Swiss Family Robinson in their tubs, which, every one remembers, were lashed together by planks, Tommy being placed in the centre to prevent him getting into mischief. Further, with a view of preventing collisions, there was to be a grand division of the sea—ships going one way to take the North Atlantic, and the other way the South, and so on, and so on; with a hundred other patent inventions. It was beautiful, and only wanted sailors to be machines to be perfect. That is where all the systems break down. There is so much of humanity in things human. Philanthropists, religionists, social reformers, all the world of hobby-horse riders, break down through not considering this great fact. Have we not seen a great cause shattered, and the strongest Ministry of the day go to pieces, because its leaders forgot that the nation was made of men, and that the men are like the butcher's famous beefsteak, inasmuch as they may be humoured but cannot be drove?

A grinding up of iron ribs as if they were the bones of a partridge, a heeling over of the deck, a mighty wave of black water rushing in from all quarters—that was all Fred Rveel knew of the calamity. The whole of the tragic details, afterwards graphically described, were lost to him — perhaps because his berth was forward. He saw and heard nothing of the poor ladies rushing from their cabins, and falling at the captain's feet; he saw nothing of the captain himself, standing with folded arms on the broken bridge. Heroism, cowardice, resignation, faith, despair—all these things, which appeared in the daily papers, had no place in his memory, when he came to remember. He could think of nothing but a great horror, the swift destruction of the ship, and the sudden rush of black water. It was like a dream.

Everybody owned that the *Bismarck*, when the mischief was done, did her duty manfully. She steamed right over and through the vessel, whose stern she had cut in two, and kept way on for three hundred yards or so. Then she lowered the boats, and stopped the engines, being alive to the necessity of action. She picked up half a dozen sailors who were floating about, and then the boats, seeing no one else, returned to the vessel; and she went on her way, little the worse for the accident, the captain swearing in undisguised disgust at the stupidity of the other ship, and chiefly afraid that his licence might be suspended.

But the boats did not pick up all.

When Fred Revel returned to a consciousness of himself, and had done fighting his way upwards through the whirling waters, which rolled and eddied over the sinking *Triton;* when his head emerged above the surface, and he was able, like Neptune, "to look out over the main, and raise his head in majesty above the summit of the waters," it was a black prospect that he discovered. Floating near him were two oars from a deck boat. These he seized with such thankfulness as the dying man may hear the respite of his sentence, and partly resting on them, partly paddling, began to consider what next to do.

First he kicked off his boots; then, with a little manœuvring, he pulled off his coat, and let it go; then he picked up two more floating oars, which made four—almost a raft; and then, while he was binding them all together with a rope extemporised of his braces and his necktie—a feeble line, but sufficient for his purpose and a short voyage, unless bad weather should come—he tried to realise the position.

He never saw the boats at all. In his evidence at the inquiry, he declared that, so far as he knew, the *Bismarck* neither stopped nor sent out boats. That was not the case; but it was curious that in a starlight night, and with smooth water, the boats should not have seen him—perhaps some current hurried him away. He was not alone either; for presently there came floating past him, on an empty sheep-pen—a thing like a crockery crate whose bottom has fallen out—another human salvage. A crockery crate, as one may imagine, is not a comfortable craft for even the shortest voyage in the fairest weather. It travels without any regard to keel. It is useless to label it "this side up:" equilibrium is unstable. If it floats, it makes no pretence to support any one in an easy position; if it saves a passenger from drowning, it is careless about ducking him. On this coop was clinging a figure, with long arms, convulsively clutching the ribs of what had been a pen. Now and then it turned over, and the occupant would be seen, after a few moments of immersion, clinging on the other side.

Fred hailed him, and then paddled his raft of four oars towards this other shipwrecked mariner.

"Come," he said cheerfully, "let us lash your boat to mine, and make room for two."

The occupant of the coop was apparently too exhausted to reply. Fred got him alongside, and managed to pass one of the oars through the open bars. This gave an additional buoyant power to his raft.

"Now, then," he said, "you may take your fingers off the bars, and see if the oars will not keep us both up."

It was too dark to see the other man's face, but Fred made out that he was old; for he had very long hair, which shone in the glistening starlight like silver; with a heavy long white moustache. On his back there hung a bag.

The man, without saying a word, shifted his hands from the bars of the coop, and threw his body athwart the oars. The feeble raft was not calculated to keep up the whole weight of his body, and went under.

"Hold up!" Fred cried. "Don't hang on to it that way, man. Rest your arm over it—hang it! we can't sit upon the thing."

"I was first," said the newcomer, uttering the most bare-faced falsehood. "I was first, and the oars belong to me. You must go and find more oars for yourself. It won't bear both. Be off, I say."

Fred looked round upon the tranquil waters. There were no more oars, nor any trace of the ship floating about.

"That's pretty cool," he replied. "But I suppose you are frightened—don't know what you are saying. However, we are too heavy. What have you got round your neck? It's heavy. If it's nothing to eat, throw it off."

"I won't throw it off," said his companion. "It is the work of my life. My Memoirs."

"Damn your Memoirs!" cried Fred, in a great rage. He had got his knife in his right hand, the left holding on to the raft, and his body floating pretty easily. "Damn your Memoirs! Do you think I am going to be drowned to save your mouldy Memoirs?"

With a dexterous movement he cut the string of the bag, dragged it from the man's shoulders, and let it drop into the water.

As they drifted, the bag went with them for a little, gradually dropping astern, and finally disappearing.

The man cried aloud, and made a feeble dash at Fred, as if he would cast him off the raft.

"No, you don't," said the younger passenger coolly. "Try it on again, my friend, and off you go, if you were Jonah himself."

"Don't blaspheme," the other said, in a hollow voice. "There's only an oar between you and death."

"Four oars and a sheep-pen," said Fred. "Look—there is a light on land. How far can a light be seen? Three—four miles. We are only so far from the shore. Pluck up, old boy; you will live to write your Memoirs all over again yet."

"No," he said. "No—no. I shall not live. It is the curse of that woman. Carry cursed me solemnly, and the boy cursed me. I shall die. I shall be cut off in my prime. I am unprepared—oh dear! quite—quite unprepared; and too young—much too young to die."

"He's wandering," thought Fred.

"It's different for you," he went on, in a wandering way—choking now and then, when a wavelet dashed in his face.

" You are only a steerage passenger. You have no money. There is nothing to keep you to this world; and very likely you will be better off when you get to the other. I can't. I am happy as I am. Oh, dear! oh, dear!—if I was only safe back in Lowland Street. Why did I ever leave the room where I had lived happily for fourteen years?"

" Lord!" said Fred. " Are you the Hermit? I know you now."

" I was—I was. Everybody knows the Hermit of Lowland Street. I wish I was back there again. Ugh! I believe the wind is blowing up. Young man, there is not—there really is not room on these oars for two of us. I am the elder, and I was on the oars first. Take one or two bars from the pen, and go your own way. I rescued you from the sheep-pen, as you know. I daresay I shan't miss one or two sticks; but you must not take many. I saved your life, but not to be a means of destroying mine."

" That's a staggerer," said Fred. " Mr. Hermit, whatever you are, you are a coward. Don't cry and snivel, man. If we are to die, let us die like gentlemen."

" Oh, I never could think of dying. It's constitutional. I'm the bravest man in the world, except when it comes to dying. But this is worse than the Crimea—worse than the trenches. A man had a chance there—what chance has he here?"

A wave broke over his face; and in his terror he shrieked, and nearly fell off the slender support that kept them up.

" Come, old boy," said Fred cheerily. " It's cold and dark —it isn't pleasant for either of us. Can't you pretend, just for honour's sake, not to be a coward?"

" Three miles from land—only three miles—and to float about here, getting colder and colder, until we die! Young man, if you will swim ashore—you are strong, and swim well; I can spare you one of the oars; only three miles— and fetch out a boat for me, I will give you—whatever I can. I am Captain Lillingworth. I have served her Majesty. I am rich. Only help me to get ashore."

" If you are a soldier, you ought to face death without crying like a girl over it," said Fred. " I do not know

which way the current is carrying us; but we must hope.
It is about midnight now. When the day breaks, we shall
see if there is any hope."

For three hours Captain Lillingworth moaned and cried,
lamented and prayed. At intervals Fred remonstrated with
him. It was useless. The man had but one feeling—that
he might be drowned. He was a sensualist, and a coward.
He clung to life. He was religious, too, in the same sense
that the fallen angels are religious—because he trembled
when his thoughts wandered in the direction of his creed.

The night sped on. Fred clung silently to the oars, and
watched the east. His limbs were numb with cold, his
fingers stiff. He began to wonder how long he could continue to hold on. He ceased to take any further notice of
his companion, who went on moaning and crying unin-
terruptedly.

When they were lifted into the boat that saved them, the
sun was high. They were only a mile from the shore when
they were picked up. One of the boatmen had a little water,
which revived them. The elder of the two cried and sobbed,
lying in a heap at the bottom of the boat. The younger,
trying to warm his stiffened limbs, took an oar, and helped
to row the boat ashore.

They brought the first news of the disaster. A sort of
lerée was held in the evening, at the little inn of the fishing
town where they were landed. Captain Lillingworth had
the only private room; and received—after dining as well as
the resources of the place would admit—the special correspondents, the Coastguard officer, the parson, and the doctor.
He was quite recovered. Dressed in a rough boatman's
costume, lent him for the occasion, he sat in the only arm-
chair, and smoked affably, drinking brandy and water, while
the people plied him with questions.

In the kitchen, which was also the common smoking-room,
sat the other passenger—the steerage passenger. He wore
his own clothes, a good deal spoiled by the night's adventures. The sailors and fishermen sat round him while he

told the story, so far as he knew. He did not think it necessary to inform his auditors of the unbecoming way in which his companion passed the night. Captain Lillingworth, for his part, was improving the occasion. He told how, on the first intimation of the danger, he had rushed from his cabin, seized the helm, and dashed it hard a-port.

"She swung round, sir, with a will—the gallant craft! The steersman, as honest an old salt as ever chewed an inch of pigtail, seemed bewildered. But it was too late—too late!"

Here he paused, and wiped away a tear.

"Bah! I am a soldier. Let us face death manfully—eh, gentlemen? We can but die once. Happy he—you know, all of you—*dulce et decorum est pro patria mori.* That means, I take it, to die in the discharge of duty. Then came the crash. I cannot bear to think of it. There were three or four women on board. I seized a child in one hand and a woman in the other. I saw, just at the last, the captain standing near to the boat on the bridge. The engineers came running up the gangway. I endeavoured, in the few moments which remained, to effect a little organisation; but too late!—the boats were entangled. Well, there was the end of it. Nothing could have been finer than the behaviour of the officers. I hope some of them will prove to have been saved, and will bear me out. The ship struck, gentlemen. I held the child and the lady; but when I came to myself I was floating on the surface with my hands upon a spar, and I saw no one else. Stay, there was the young man below stairs—not a sailor, poor fellow—and his wits were well-nigh gone. I rescued him, at least—that is some comfort—and did my best to cheer him up all night."

There were many more details; in fact, the graphic account called "The Foundering of the *Triton*," done into the most picturesque English in the daily papers, which made so great a sensation at the time, was mainly due to details supplied by Captain Lillingworth. How he battled with the terrors of the night; how he nearly perished in the attempt to save a whole shipful of passengers and men; how he triumphantly brought ashore one out of all; how he made the deck of the sinking ship a field for the display of the most heroic courage and coolness—all this was fully set forth.

"This gallant officer," said the special, "does not talk of his exploits; they are forced from him by questions and cross-examination. Like all brave men, he is modest as regards his own achievements. We have yet to learn what other details will be supplied by those whom the *Bismarck* picked up. The young gentleman, Mr. Revel, whose life Captain Lillingworth was instrumental, under Providence, in saving, can remember very little of the disaster. We believe that Captain Lillingworth is already known as no carpet knight. He served in the Crimea."

The young man, indeed, was of no use to the reporters at all. When he read Captain Lillingworth's account he only laughed; and the half-dozen whom the *Bismarck* picked up were unable to confirm or contradict it. There were one or two who were struck by the name, and showed it to each other.

"Arthur Cleveland Lillingworth," said Colonel Firebrace to General Pyrgopolinices—"that's the fellow's name. Same man, of course."

"I remember him—bad business; hushed up, though. No one knew outside the regiment, except the chief. Let me read the story again. Lies, Firebrace, lies. You see his gallantry rests upon nobody's word but his own. He never did anything except lie. Here is a curious coincidence, Firebrace. The fellow saved with him was named Revel. Wonder if it is any relative to the man whose wife he ran away with. Gad! the fellow was always ready enough to run away. Old story now—husband in the navy, excellent good officer; wife pretty woman and a fool—Carry Revel, they called her. It was a year or so before the Crimean row. Some of the fellows wanted the colonel to take it up. Wish he'd gone to the bottom, Firebrace. Upon my soul, I wish he was at the bottom with the rest!"

The gold medal of the Royal Humane Society was presented the next year, by common consent of the council, to the brave and gallant officer who distinguished himself at the loss of the *Triton*, Captain Arthur Cleveland Lillingworth, formerly of the Royal 125th Regiment of Light Infantry, the Swashbucklers, or Isle of Wight Fusiliers. He was living in retirement in a small town on the Garonne in France. On the receipt of the intelligence, the Prefect gave an official banquet to do honour to their illustrious ally, his old brother-in-arms, and in memory of the *entente cordiale.*

Fred, of course, got no medal; and as he seldom read the papers, he heard nothing about it. Therefore he was saved from the emotions of envy, malice, or derision. He went straight back to Lowland Street, arriving there just as the news of the disaster, with the names of the survivors, reached the place. Marion and Adie had not begun to weep for him as a brand snatched from the burning. Winifred was still at the telegraph office; but the schoolmaster was sitting at the window reading the graphic account with mingled feelings.

"I sent him away," he said. "If he had been drowned, how could I ever have looked my girl in the face again?"

And then he saw him hastening along the street, and went out to be the first to welcome him.

"I know now," he said, his wrinkled old face lighting up with welcome. "I know now. Winifred told me all. And so you escaped, and swam ashore, like St. Paul at Malta, did you? Come in and see them all. I think they have not so much as heard that you were in danger."

"I am come back, like a bad half-crown," said Fred. "But I have not come back to loaf about again, Mr. Owen, you may be sure. Where is Winifred?"

And there was great rejoicing among the three loving hearts who welcomed back again this resolute pioneer of industry.

CHAPTER XXXVIII.

MARION sat in a sort of stupor when Joseph Chacomb left her at last, repeating the glad tidings to herself. Gerald home again! Her thoughts flew back to the day when they sat together on the cliff, and looked out upon the blue sea, flecked with the passing clouds. The wind fanned her cheeks again as they flushed once more at Gerald's burning words. His hand held hers close, close; again her heart leaped up with the unspeakable joy of a woman who loves her lover. All the present vanished. The twilight wrapped the mean lodgings of Lowland Street in obscurity, so that the room looked like the drawing-room of Comb Leigh. The cries of the children and footsteps of the passers-by fell on her ear unheeded, or resolved themselves into the dashing of the waves upon the mouth of the cove, and the long-drawn moan of the shingle as the waters rolled them up and down. Then the beating of her heart grew too violent, and she cast her thoughts back five years before, when she was yet a girl trembling on the brink of womanhood. Then she roamed with Gerald about the hillsides, clothed with lofty bracken; or the woods inland, where wild birds answered their call, and Gerald hunted strange creatures, unknown except to those versed in woodcraft. There together they wandered from morning to eve. And when they came home at sunset, there was the kindly face to meet them at the gate, with the voices and laughter of the children.

Far away, that vanished life, yet present still. And always her thoughts turned again to the evening when Gerald kissed his last good-night upon her lips, her cheek, her forehead, and her hands, when he drew her trembling to his arms, and kissed her all over again. Then came the next day—the day that broke deceitfully with radiant vest, ending in clouds and the blackness of a deep sorrow.

"Marion, are you asleep? Marion, dear, you are sitting all alone in the dark. Are you ill? Is there anything the matter?"

She roused herself, and came back to London. The room was shabby and mean; but the glamour of the trance was on her, and she was still in Devonshire.

"Is it you, Adie?" she answered. "Is it you? Come here, my darling, and let us talk. Do not light the candles."

Adie sat on the footstool at her sister's feet—the old attitude of love and trust—while Marion petted and caressed her face.

"Winifred is better to-night," said Adie. "She has been telling me all about it, and we have had a great cry. My dear, poor Fred has been living in an atmosphere of delusion. He thought he was going to get a good place somewhere through the interest of his old college friends. He promised Winifred to give her a great house and make her a fine lady. Poor Winifred! We will not desert her, Marion, will we?"

"No—poor Winifred! We will not desert Fred's wife, Adie. We have not been very happy for the last four years, have we?"

"Not your fault, Marion. Oh! not your fault, my best of Marions," she replied. "And you have forgiven me my impatience and bad tempers, have you not? Not your fault, my dear. You have worked for all, and we have been so helpless—oh! so helpless and exacting. Now Fred is gone, and there is only one left for you."

"Yes, dear, and I wish Fred was back again. Adie, I have had good news."

"Good, Marion?"

"Yes; so good—so good that I can hardly believe it true. My picture is accepted. Dr. Chacomb's friend writes everything that is kind of it. He says that it will sell, and that I shall do well yet. Are you pleased, dear?"

"Pleased? O Marion! And we can leave this place." She sprang to her feet, because she could no longer keep still. "We shall actually leave this dreadful place at last—where we have suffered so much sorrow? O Marion! can it really be that we shall live properly again?"

"I hope so, Adie—indeed, I think so. And—and there is another piece of news; but I will tell you that to-morrow evening."

"She is engaged to the doctor," thought Adie. "Is that good too, Marion?"

"Ah, yes!" she replied—"very good. Adie, do not ask me any more about it."

"Tell me more, dear, about the picture. Do let us talk about the future."

She sat down again. In the darkness you could not see the difference between the two faces. Marion's eyes were full of tears, and her lips trembled with the great and overwhelming joy of her soul. Adie, thinking of the new life that seemed to lie almost within her reach, talked with eyes aflame, and glowing cheeks. She looked like her brother on that night when he built his castles in the air in Lincoln's Inn Fields, and beguiled the heart of pretty Winifred.

"Marion, where shall we live? You do not want to be in London; we will go back to Devonshire. Not to Comb Leigh—not there, Marion; it would be too sad—but to some quiet place by the seashore, where we shall find a cottage just large enough for you, and me, and Winifred. We will have a garden with roses, like the roses of Comb Leigh. You shall paint the rocks and boats. We will have a village girl to wait on us. We will sit in the shade, and talk about these dingy old rooms, and all we have done and suffered. And think of being ladies again, among ladies—if there are any in our Devonshire village! Think of a country church, and the sweet air! O Marion, it seems too much that the old time should come back again to us."

"My dear, the old time is gone. The past never comes back again. But we may have happiness again. Sing me something, Adie—sing me a hymn."

She sang one of the newest. Most new hymns are irritating beyond expression with their pretence and their shallowness; but this was not. Adie sang it because the air pleased her; but the words fell upon her sister's ear like rain upon a thirsty soil.

As she sang, Marion sat with clasped hands, thinking. And to her crept, in the gloom, her new sister, Winifred. She stole up the stairs, listening to the hymn. She hesitated, because she was uncertain; it might be that Marion would not want her. But love, which casteth out fear, prevailed; and she timidly came into the open door, and laid her hand upon Marion's.

Her new charge! Surely the world was full of love to

her. Marion was so happy, that what Winifred meant as a mute appeal for protection and forgiveness, she took for sympathy with herself.

"My sister Winifred," she whispered.

All night she lay awake, till the red morning glowed through the windows; and then she fell asleep, praising God in her dreams.

The doctor came next day, in the afternoon, and took Adie out with him.

"You have not told your sister?" he whispered to her. "Gerald will call on you as soon as he comes to town, between five and six. Ah, Marion, be brave."

He repeated what he had said the day before, and the words fell upon her heart like frost upon the flowers of May. "Be brave." But why? What was there to be brave about? The doctor bade her be brave when her father opened his eyes to speak his last broken words of prayer and blessing.

"Be brave!"

She put the words by; they did not belong to her. They might have been spoken years ago, when all this trouble was coming on them; but not now—surely not now. The cause which parted her lover and herself was removed. It was but a ghastly dream, that hallucination of poor Mr. Chacomb's. The love that had never died would revive and flourish as if there had never been any interruption. She would see once more the light of passion, joy, and hope in the eyes of the man she loved; she would have again his arm about her. Pity poor Marion. She was only a woman, with all a woman's desire for the love of one man. She had never learned to unsex herself. She obeyed the instincts of her nature in thinking the wedded life the happiest and holiest lot. She did not hope for anything but the common lot of humanity. She lived in the dream which all good women feel, of universal love and sympathy. A most commonplace woman. Not a heroine at all; not even strong-minded; not even given to religious doubts. A woman born to be a wife and a mother.

Four o'clock. She made and took some tea, to quiet her nerves.

Half-past four. He would come in an hour.

She put her room in order, making it look as pretty as she could. She dressed herself—not that she had any choice of dresses—with an anxiety she had never felt before. She looked in the glass. The Spenser woman told her the truth when she said that her figure was gone, and her beauty faded. She saw a pale, thin cheek, with lines of care and suffering. She saw a wasted form. She saw eyes that seemed to have lost the capacity of happiness. What she did not see, and nobody saw but the doctor and poor Dicky Carew, was the steady light of steadfast love that burned there, and the seal of goodness on her forehead, set there by seven and twenty years of patient duty.

The afternoon seemed strangely silent. She missed the step of Mr. Lilliecrip overhead—the Hermit disappeared on the day when Mrs. Spenser had her revenge. Men came and removed his things, and the rooms were empty. She missed the anxious expectancy which was associated in her mind with her brother. The boys in school, downstairs, made a soft murmur over their lessons, through the closed doors; it sounded like the buzz of many bees. When the master's voice was raised in reproof, it was as if a thrush chirruped; and when he caned a criminal, it was like a peacock screaming. The very street for some reason of its own, seemed hushed and quiet. Her nerves were strung beyond the point of being touched by ordinary things, and she did not notice them. She tried to do some work, but her fingers would not hold a pencil. She tried to read, but it was just as when, four years before, the poet Pope took credit to himself because a nymph was reading the Essay on Man, inasmuch as the words floated before her brain, and she saw them not. And then she tried to play, and soothed her soul with some of the old things which never tire.

At five o'clock, the boys streamed out of the house, and began to play in the street—their only playing field—with a chorus of shouts. Leap-frog and fly-the-garter were "in," games which require, to bring out their full flavour, as much shouting as a Homeric battle. Marion did not hear them.

She wandered about the room restless. But the boys screamed so loud that Marion did not hear a cab drive up to the door. But she heard his step upon the stair. Was it likely that she should forget his step?

He came in—her Gerald!

As his eyes met hers, as his outstretched hand advanced to take her own, the words of Dr. Chacomb recurred to her with a force that drew the blood from her cheeks, and made her pulse stand still—

"Be brave, my girl!"

She was brave. She resolutely pushed away from her this pressure at her heart, which seemed to stop its beating. See took the offered hand, which had lost the remembered touch. She met the calm eyes, which looked as if they had never been stirred by the magic of love. She greeted him, as if no words of love had ever passed between them, with the warmth of an old friendship.

As for love, there was no more any thought of love. His face told her so much. It was set with a warmth which was different from the warmth of love.

"Marion," he said, taking her hand and holding it.

Did no thought of the past flash across his mind?

"Gerald," she replied.

Had they been lovers still, they could have said no more. As they were friends, they could say no less.

She saw that he was older, firmer of step and of face. She saw that his eyes had changed to her, and were now cold and hard. His lips had lost their smile. His very head, which used to bend as if with pleasure when he met her, was stiff and rigid. She had left a lover; she met a friend.

It came upon her with a suddenness which stunned her. She turned pale. Her face resumed its worn and wasted look. The ring of black colour returned to her eyes. Her happiness died swiftly out of her look.

Gerald saw a thin and prematurely aged woman—she was but seven and twenty; and—alas! for the quickness of poor Marion's perception, which showed her, at first sight, that love was dead, and so killed the beauty with which she was

prepared to meet him—he saw a wasted figure, a shaking
hand, eyes that were dimmed with tears which even that
brave heart could not wholly keep down, and—woe is me
that I must write it!—the first love-making seemed to him
like some impossible dream, which he had forgotten so long
that it was a pity to begin it again. And what he saw,
Marion read in his eyes.

This was their meeting. This was the end of her fidelity.
He cared no more to reopen the closed chapter. It was for
her to close it too with what speed and security she might.

She flushed a moment, thinking of Joseph Chacomb. Then
her pride came to her help, and she greeted him with a smile
—a thin, worn smile, like a gleam of sunshine in December.

"Tell me about yourself, Marion," he said kindly.

"First, tell me what you have been doing."

He talked, she listened; and the effort of listening and
trying to understand, and the tumult of bitter emotion,
hardened her nerves. He told her how he had been wandering on the uplands of Southern Africa; how his resolution at
first was never to come back at all; how he had lived among
the friendly savages, or among the simple Boers, uncorrupted
then by diamond fields; careless of civilisation, with England
like a far-off dream, and only the memory of that last dreadful interview with his father to trouble him; how, little by
little, the thirst for talk with his own kind drove him back
to Cape Town, and so home again. A simple story of a
simple journey, with no adventures to speak of, no sufferings
and privations, no hopes and no fears.

"I have discovered nothing," he finished, "or next to
nothing. I have returned as I went—empty-handed. Never
mind, now. Tell me about you and yours, Marion."

"My story is simple. I have been painting, to keep the
house together."

"And you have succeeded?"

Involuntarily he cast a glance at the shabby room, the
furniture of which—the old furniture from Comb Leigh—
fitted with the street and the house.

"I did not succeed—not very well, that is; but I think, I

hope, that I may succeed now. For I have a picture accepted at the Royal Academy."

Gerald did not seem much moved by the announcement. Colonial folk, as you may have observed, are provoking that way. They will not observe the nice gradations of success. If you tell an old Colonial friend that you have been discovered to rank with Tennyson or Browning, he is no more moved than if you told him that you have been compared with Tupper. To Gerald it seemed only proper that Marion's picture should be in the Academy.

"That's right," he said cheerily. "And where are Fred and Adie?"

"Fred is gone. He tried hard to get something to do, poor boy; and, as he could not, he has emigrated."

"A very good thing too. England is a bad place for men who have been brought up to nothing. I am very glad I went abroad. And little Adie?"

"She is not little Adie at all now. She is taller than I am. If you will stay and have some tea with me, you shall see her. She will be back again soon."

Gerald had not yet dined, but he stayed. Marion was glad that he did. She dreaded being left alone.

She made tea for him, Gerald helping in his old brotherly fashion; laughing, and telling her stories of his travels, in a pleasant, happy way which recalled the days even before he went to Brazil. Then he began to talk about Chacomb.

"My father is a good deal shaken," he said. "You will have heard about him from the doctor. The old hallucination, which gave us all such a shock once, is still strong upon him. And this miserable second marriage—but you know, probably."

"I know something," she said, wondering of what stuff men were made, that Gerald could talk so coolly of the great "shock," after all it had done to both. "I know something. Do not talk about it if it is painful to you."

"Not at all painful."

And then he began to take up the thread of his father's history from the funeral of Captain Revel, omitting all mention of the engagement.

Had the man no memory ? Was it possible that he had actually forgotten ?

Gerald had not forgotten. But the kiss which burned itself into the soul of the girl, and had become a part and parcel of herself, so that she felt it still upon her cheek like a brand, had long since gone out of his mind, or only lingered there as part of a pleasant day. There was an afternoon, and he kissed a pretty girl. Then came the evening, and he kissed her again. Then came a dreadful calamity, with the suspicion of worse disaster behind, and they parted.

Now they met again : he in the bloom and prime of early manhood, thirty years of age ; she faded and worn, the shadow of her former self—the fruit that had withered on its stalk, the flower that had never bloomed to its fullest beauty. The kisses had been forgotten—Marion was a memory only. In the savage and wandering life that he had led, bodily fatigue drove out sad thoughts. The long marches and thirsty stretches, the fierce African sun, the hunting days, the camp life—all these had killed and crushed the lingering shoots of tender love.

And what was there to revive his passion ? The *umbra* of what had been ; the shadow of sweet maid Marion ; the form without the light, and life, and laughter ; the face without— ah ! but he did not see her eyes—Marion's eyes—or else he would have loved again.

Eight o'clock struck, and they were still talking, when Adie came home with the doctor.

" Adie," said Marion, " I told you I had some good news. Here is Gerald come home again."

She had lit the candles by this time. Gerald rose to greet his old friend, who had been little schoolgirl Adie.

Heavens ! Was this glorious creature, this queen of beauty, on whose brow sat all the graces, as the poets used to say ; whose lips, and eyes, and dimpled cheeks were a multitudinous smile ; whose hair was a coronal of glory—was this little Adie ?

His eyes lit up as they had not done for her sister. Marion saw it, with a pang which struck her heart like a knife.

She beckoned the doctor to the window, and murmured, with dry lips—

"What was that you advised me yesterday? Did you know?"

"I guessed. I did not know."

"I have been brave. Keep my secret, doctor—dear Dr. Chacomb, I trust my secret with you. Keep it, and be my friend always."

"I will be whatever—good God! Marion, that it should be possible!—I will be whatever you let me be."

She touched his fingers with hers. It was a compact.

"We will always be as we are now, and always friends, dear Dr. Chacomb."

Then they joined the other two.

Presently the doctor, who had been very silent, went away, and they all began to talk of him—how good and great he was; how kind and unselfish. And because two were women, who believed what they wished to believe, and one was a stupid Colonial, who was inexperienced in the sin of great cities—the sin, namely, of selfishness, struggling to the front, trampling down those that are in your way, and appropriating to yourself the *kudos* that belongs to others— they all lauded, praised, and magnified the name of Joseph the Good, who had stood by his poor cousin Chauncey, sacrificed his own time and interests to the good of Chacomb, and been more than kind to themselves, till admiration of his virtue took away their breath, and they were fain to stop and admire him in silence.

When Gerald took his leave, it was in Adie's face that he looked last, with an admiration which Marion, taught by experience, construed into passion.

"Marion, he is splendid! It is delightful—it is happiness. O Marion!" cried the younger girl, clasping her sister round the neck, "this *was* good news."

It was, indeed, good news. Such good news as some people try to persuade us is the good tidings of the gospel—good news of sorrow, misery, and impossible salvation.

"Go to bed, Adie, dear," said Marion. "I will come pre-

sently." She was longing to be quiet. She yearned for some
place where she would be alone in her sorrow and bitterness.
"Go, Adie," she added, in a voice harsh with impatience.
"I will come—presently."

Adie left her at length ; and Marion sat down, and tried
to think.

Let us leave her to herself. There are some sorrows,
besides those of bereavement, which are of a life, and cannot
be told. Why paint the tortures of a man upon the rack ?
Why try to show how Marion battled with the agony that
rent her, all the night, until gleams of peace came when, in
the reddening east, God made a tender rose of dawn ?

CHAPTER XXXIX.

GERALD remained in town. He resumed the old brotherly
relations with Marion, talked about his projects and
his experiences, asked her advice, and, like all the world,
assumed her entire sympathy with him. He came daily, and
took them both for walks and drives. Joseph Chacomb it
was who secretly provided Adie with the means of procuring
a "proper" dress or dresses for these excursions. Perhaps
it was not only the pleasure of talking with Marion that
brought him to Lowland Street.

Fred, who, after his dash into virtue and energy, felt the
need of a little rest, resumed his loafing—except the billiards.
The very thought of that prophetic marker filled his soul
with horror. Gerald was good enough to lend him a little
money, with which he entertained himself in the daytime
and his wife in the evening.

Then the Academy opened. Whether Joseph Chacomb
was romancing when he offered to "square" the reviewers,
I do not know. I incline to think that he was. I love to
believe that there is as little envy, as little camaraderie, as
little malice, as much appreciation, brotherly love, and kindness in Art as there is in Literature. Let me never cease to
find cause for gratitude to critics, whether of pictures or of

books. No doubt, Joseph Chacomb exaggerated his powers of influencing Art criticism. However this may be, the fact is certain that, when of the leaders some had been slashed and some had been stroked, all the papers with one accord turned to Marion's picture, and said good things about it. It was only by reading all the reviews and combining her information that Marion found out all the faults in her work. Then, indeed, she learned that it was sketchy, laboured, heavy in colour, pedantic, frivolous, weak in drawing, unreal in light, too real in the light, with so many other contradictions, that she was fairly puzzled. And then the picture sold, and for a good price; and the great picture dealers, Messrs. Puffit, Pushem & Co., men to whom Burls was humble, and before whom such creatures as Hermann Gottfried tried to efface themselves, took her up, and gave her commissions.

Marion saw her way at last. It was not the fame of immortality that awaited her, nor the fortune of a Turner; but it was comfort, ease, and a life of ladyhood that came within her reach.

She went a good deal to the Academy—partly to look at her own picture. Gerald sometimes went with her. They walked among the thousand gaudy frames where the Don Quixotes, the boats on the river, the "bits" of Haslemere, betray the poverty of artists' reading and resource, and where the unmeaning portraits of commonplace people stare from the walls; and always to Marion's solace, a little crowd gathered round her own picture.

Every stroke in it was dear to her. She remembered the slow progress, the studies for the drawing, her hesitation about the colour, her desire to get things right, her anxiety about the costume. The people saw nothing of all this; they looked at the sweet face—Adie's face—with its *insouciant* look, its parted lips, and the light of youth in the careless eyes: they saw the result.

"It is splendid, Marion," Gerald whispered. "I like it better every time I see it. We are proud of you."

Marion smiled. She was no longer unhappy—only a little

sad and ashamed of herself; and she said to herself what the Emperor Alexander said to the Poles—

"Above all, no dreams."

"I should like to talk to you," said Gerald, quietly, "where there will be no one to interrupt us."

It was only ten in the morning, and the Academy was comparatively empty. He took her into the refreshment room, where there were two or three people taking breakfast.

"Marion," Gerald began with great solemnity, and then stopped.

"Have you ordered, sir?" asked a waiter.

Gerald glared. Then he remembered, and ordered an ice; and then he tried to start afresh.

Marion's pulse did not quicken, nor did her cheeks flush. Whatever Gerald was going to say, there would be nothing to move her from her tranquillity.

"When I came home, Marion," he said—it was only a fortnight since that event, but he spoke as if it had been a year at least—"when I came home I intended to stay long enough to shake off the fever, and then to get back to Africa for another spell. Now, you would hardly believe it, I have changed my mind. I no longer care for African travel. It seems to me that nothing can be better than life in England. I am thirty years of age; my father is feeble; I ought not to expect my cousin to go on giving up his time to the care of Chacomb Hall. I shall stay at home."

"I am very glad indeed," said Marion.

"Yes—yes. We have always been brother and sister to each other, have we not?"

"Always brother and sister."

"There was a time when it seemed"—(only "seemed," Gerald?)—"as if we might be something more to each other. But it is better as it is."

"Better as it is," Marion murmured.

"I am not worthy of you. No one is, for that matter. If you only knew, Marion, how we all respect and love you! However, what I want to say is this. My father has never let the Rosery. Come back there. Forget the trouble that drove you from the place. You will be able to work there better than in London. You will be back in the old place that you love. And besides—"

"What besides, Gerald? Let me hear everything."

"I have not spoken to her yet. I would not speak to her without your permission. But—O Marion!—will you let me be your brother indeed?"

Marion neither flushed nor turned pale. For a moment it seemed cruel to mock her; but she put the thought away.

"You mean Adie? Of course, you mean Adie. Gerald, she is dear to me. Examine your heart well. Four years ago—I am not reproaching you—you told another girl that you loved her. Now you love her no more. Remember, Gerald, I am not reproaching you. It is better so, as we said before. But—you have ceased to love her. How do I know that you may not cease to love my poor Adie?"

Quietly as the words were said, they went home to Gerald.

"I can say nothing," he replied. "Marion, if the past could return—"

"It cannot. Let me only think that you love Adie stead-fastly. Let us have no more mistakes. Life, Gerald, is not long enough for such blunders. They cannot be repaired."

"They cannot," he said. "You will believe me when I tell you that Adie's happiness is dearer to me than my own."

She laid her hand on his.

"I do believe you, brother Gerald."

And he never knew the effort by which she had enabled herself to say this honestly. He accepted the sacrifice, as everybody always accepted Marion's gifts, without asking what they cost.

"I wish you success, Gerald. And I will think over your proposal about the Rosery. I think we might afford to live there—Winifred, Fred, and I. It would be a great change for us, and almost too great happiness. Let me think it over."

It was no longer unhappiness to feel that Gerald had never loved her, as she once thought—that she could never love him again. Perhaps she would have been higher than human had she witnessed without a pang the transference of his affections to her sister. But she hardened her heart against the thought, and preserved, to Gerald's eyes, the frank smile with which she always met him. Lower than human would he have been had he not remembered something of the troth which should have been sacred by the memory of the dead man who sanctioned it. He did remember it, and with shame. But the past, as Marion said, can never return; and he was dazzled by the loveliness of her sister. Venus Victrix laughs at the pale charms of Vesta. One needs to be a monk to rank St. Cecilia above Phryne.

Gerald had forgotten. It humiliated and pained him to be reminded, even in terms as gentle as those in which Marion clothed her plaint. This served him right. It was just that he should have a glimpse, even a momentary and imperfect glimpse, of the ruin he had wrought. "Only a woman's hair," Swift wrote. Only a woman's heart, which Gerald Chacomb mocked and wounded. Had he known how deeply, there would have been small happiness for him in the after-years. But Marion smiled and passed on her way, no one but Joseph Chacomb knowing the truth.

She went back to the pictures, Gerald following with a sense of discontent and shame. Among the visitors was a fat man, with a large head, a flabby white face, and big white hands. He had a catalogue, on which he made notes with a big, square pencil. It was Mr. Hermann Gottfried. He took off his hat, and bowed politely.

"The pewtiful Miss Reffel," he said, loud enough for all the world to hear. "The sweet jung bainter. Ach! mein Gott!—what a bicture! what a bicture! You never painted zoch a bicture for me—neffer. But I forgif you. Ach! Herr Je—yes—I forgif you. Zo, Miss Reffel, I was wrong. You will not—no neffer—be one of my jung men. Eh? Ze jung men will make their gobies from you. Where is the most pewtiful of all young laties that effer was bainted? Where is the lofely zister?"

A week later, they were leaving the old lodgings. Once more the well-used furniture was to go back to Devonshire, and to the Rosery. Chauncey Chacomb, deprived of the society of his fond and loving wife, and awakened to the fact that his son was really restored to him, wrote a humble and contrite letter to Marion. He begged forgiveness for cruel words and for dreadful suspicions. He asked humbly to be allowed to see her again at Chacomb Hall. He expressed his joy at Gerald's engagement.

"Since," he wrote—"since I heard of it, a great thing has happened to me. I have ceased to see your poor father's face at night. So that I know now—what my cousin Joseph always told me—that it was hallucination. Perhaps I shall forget it, even the memory of it, in time; but I fear not. I have suffered greatly, Marion; and if you will all come back to your old cottage it will help me to greater peace of mind. I beg your acceptance of the greatest treasure in all my Collection. It is no less an heirloom than the identical dagger with which King Edward was stabbed. It was dug up at Corfe Castle by myself, and identified as of the period by the Council of the Swanage Archæological Institute. I give it to you as a pledge of my earnest desire to win back your friendship and forgiveness."

The treasure was very much like an old dinner knife rusted by lying in damp ground. By holding it so as to catch the light sideways, Marion once thought she saw the name of "Rogers, Sheffield," upon it. But we know that to be an old firm, and very likely it supplied the Court of the Wessex King with cutlery.

"Marion," said Adie, "let us jump for joy. Let us sing. Let us dance. We are going back to Comb Leigh. Oh, if only we could find everything there just exactly as we left it. Winifred, we will dance upon the lawn. Think. The wistaria will be all out in great purple bunches, like lovely grapes; and the yellow jessamine—it is too late for that. There will be the lilacs, and the laburnum, and roses all ready to burst into flower, directly they see me again."

"Then Mr. Owen crept into the room, looking as unhappy as if he were about to lose his scholars.

"I shall have no heart left for anything," he said. "What shall I do when you are all three gone?"

"You will have no one to tease you," said Adie. "You will read Plutarch and the Book of Proverbs, and smoke your pipe all by yourself every evening. There is always compensation, you know. You have often told us so."

"Compensation! what can compensate for losing my daughter?"

"But you shall come and see us. Shall he not, Marion?" This was Winifred.

"Nothing can compensate," he said, mournfully. "It is like the cow's tail. You know that the cow's tail, Miss Marion, was made to brush off the flies. *But it is not long enough.* That's the compensation of things. When are you going to be married, Miss Adie? Ah! There's more trouble. Why can't girls—no, Winifred, my dear, I won't say it."

"I shall miss Adie," said Marion. "But I have got Winifred instead. And we are all proud of Fred now, are we not, Mr. Owen?"

"Ay," he replied. "He's made a man of himself."

These simple folk believed that Fred had retrieved his character, and fulfilled entirely the promise of his youth, by simply embarking on board the *Triton*, and swimming ashore. Providence clearly intended him to remain in England. Its finger—as the clergymen say when they change a lean living for a fat one—was visible to the naked eye, pointing in the direction of superior material comfort.

"Poor Fred!" said his wife. "It makes me so happy to think that he has won back everybody's good opinion. I always said he was the noblest of men."

He was indeed—as Gerald was the truest.

There was a knock at the door.

It was Dicky Carew. He was attired in an entirely new suit of black cloth, with a large expanse of white shirt front. In his left hand he bore a bunch of roses. His face presented a mixture of pride and shame. Behind him came the portly person of Mrs. Medlar.

"Miss Revel," he said, "we have taken the liberty—allow me to present to you my wife, Mrs. Richard Carew, the late Mrs. Medlar—learning that you have at last taken the position your talents, as well as your birth and social qualities, entitle you to take—taken the liberty, I say, of calling to wish you, if we may, our most sincere congratulations and hearty hopes for the future, before saying farewell—"

He stopped, choked, laid the roses on the table, and added, in a broken voice—

" For ever."

" I've seen you, Miss Revel, every day a'most for three years and more," said Mrs. Carew, "and all Lowland Street knows you for the best of good women and the hardest worked. My husband is one of them that worship the ground you tread on—there's lots more—but we know our distance, and we keep it."

" Perhaps, Mr. Owen," said Mr. Carew, feebly—"perhaps you will bear me out in saying that I am not the only one in this respectable street who knows and values Miss Marion Revel."

" Indeed he can," cried Winifred, seizing Marion's hand.

" There's not one," said the schoolmaster—" I don't care where you look, high and low, in ancient and in modern history—there are no women in Plutarch—you won't find a woman—I beg your pardon, Miss Marion, a lady—that can hold a candle to Miss Marion Revel. 'She is a tree of life to them that lay hold upon her; she is like the merchants ships—she bringeth good things from afar; her price is above rubies; strength and honour are her clothing, and she shall rejoice in time to come. Let her own works praise her in the gates.' That's what the wise man said of the good woman; and he would have said it of Miss Marion Revel if he'd only known."

" And so he would," said Mrs. Medlar—we mean Mrs. Carew—"so he would. Miss Revel, we wish you the best of happiness, and—Richard, come away; don't you see you've made me cry? It's always the way with men—and their stupid compliments."

She nodded at Mr. Owen, as much as to say that his extracts from the Book of Proverbs were misplaced.

" No—no," said Marion. " But you are too good, all of you."

" The best woman in the world," said Richard. " I told them

down below in the street that you were all going, and there
is a little crowd assembled to wish you good-bye. Mr. Owen
here, who was going to cane Candy Secundus, has let him off."

"I hadn't the heart," said the schoolmaster. "It was
wrong; but I was obliged to forgive him. A wise son heareth
his father's instruction: Candy Secundus never hears any
instruction. A whip for the horse, a bridle for the ass, and
a rod for the fool's back."

"Miss Revel," Dicky continued, "there are all the women
you have helped crying because you go away and leave them;
there are the poor girls who looked to you when they were
starving and tempted. You cannot go without saying 'God
bless you' to them—can you?

"There's myself, too," he went on. "I came because I
couldn't help it, and Mrs. Carew because she wanted to
show that she wasn't jealous."

"Quite right, Richard," said his wife; "and to show Miss
Revel that it wasn't philandering with *her* that I was afraid
of." She transfixed poor Winifred with a look which spoke
volumes. "Go on, my Richard."

"Her Richard!" exclaimed Dicky. "Yes, Miss Revel.
The dream is o'er, the vision faded. I have been lazy, and I
am now rewarded. I have missed all my chances. I have
lost the reputation I might have won.

> 'Like a door on its hinges, so he with his head,
>   Turned round and winked at her, and went back to bed.'

You remember the hymn, Mr. Owen? I have deserted the
Muses, and am going in for business. The—ahem!—the
late lamented Mr. Medlar, a man of great weight and consideration—"

"He was only five feet two in his stocking feet, and he
weighed two hundred and twenty-five pounds," said his
widow.

"—was a distinguished purveyor. He left behind him a
connection—"

"In the pork and fancy pie line," said Mrs. Carew.

"Precisely." Dicky shuddered. "A connection which it

would be a sin to allow quite to drop. So we are going to reopen the—the emporium—"

"The pork shop," said his wife.

"And—in fact—my energies will be henceforth devoted to the retailing of murdered swine. I believe that I shall not personally stick those interesting and toothsome animals. No other ignominy, however, will be spared. I have also taken the pledge."

"For a second time," said Mrs. Medlar. "And he means to keep it, this time, or I'll know the reason why."

Dicky shook his head, and groaned—

"She will know the reason why!"

Then Fred arrived with cabs to take the luggage, and experienced persons came to pack up the furniture; and presently they all drove away, leaving Lowland Street, with its joys and sorrows, behind them.

CHAPTER XL.

MY story draws to an end, and is nearly told. All these things occurred in the spring of the year of grace 1870. In the summer of that year, as all the world knows, happened the overthrow of France, accompanied by such a cock-crowing on the part of the conquerors as may be expected when those who have been accustomed to defeat suddenly gain the victory. We have not forgotten, nor are any of us likely to forget, the honest rejoicing of the Fatherland. Socialism, junkerism, militarism, press-gagging, press-inspiring, absolutism, pedagogism, professorism, terrorism—all the other isms which make life in Prussia admirable, and Germany a land of sweetness and light—were forgotten in that great scream of rapture and astonishment which still echoes in our ears. The country of *Geist*, with a wonder that it has not yet overcome, saw itself in dreams the leading power in the world, and a living proof of the Great Frederick's creed that the God of battles sides with the bigger army.

The roaring of the cannon beat upon the ears of one

listener in a quiet little Devonshire village, rousing him from an indolence which seemed invincible to a wrath heroic. Day after day, as the tidings came to England of more disaster, Fred Revel bethought him more and more of the French blood in his veins. He could not sleep. He wandered up and down, with the news of each morning ringing in his brain. Day and night the force which drew him with invisible bonds grew stronger. He pored over the map; he reckoned the chances; he talked, dreamed, thought of nothing but the war. Marion watched him, suspicious; his wife watched him, suspecting nothing, but wondering at the passion which filled her husband's heart.

One night—it was after the crushing fight of Gravelotte, when the French might have won, had they been a few thousands stronger, or had—but they lost, and it was enough —he spoke.

The papers came in the evening, and Fred read the letters in the *Daily News*—the paper which first showed the world what a war correspondent ought to be—with flushing cheek and excited eyes.

"Marion," he said one evening, "have you read to-day's news?"

She knew what was in his mind, and waited.

"We are of French descent, Marion."

"Yes, Fred."

"We have been soldiers and fighting men from generation to generation—all but myself."

"Yes, Fred."

"Marion, tell me what you think. Say what I ought to do."

She trembled. It was a heavy responsibility that her brother threw upon her—the responsibility of his life.

"Can you bear to leave Winifred?"

"I can bear anything. Tell me I ought to go."

She obeyed the voice within her. She arose, went to her own room, and returned with her father's sword.

"Keep it for me, Marion," he replied. "If I come back, I will claim it as my right. If I never return, give it to Winifred, for—for the unborn child."

It was eleven o'clock. He stepped gently into his wife's room—where she lay asleep, poor girl—and kissed her on the forehead; but so lightly that it did not awaken her. Then he made up a small bundle of necessaries, and came back to bid farewell to Marion.

"Better so," he said. "Break the news to her to-morrow. Tell her—no—let her think that I am not so worthless as I seem. And God bless her—and you, too, Marion!"

Exactly four years before, under such a summer moon, he had taken the same road to catch the night train to town. Four years! He thought, as he strode along the quiet lanes, beneath the tall hedges, on whose leaves the moonlight lay in silver, of all that had happened since then. The misspent years might have followed his footsteps, accusing. But Fred's conscience was not so sensitive. He only thought that the time had been wasted. He only remembered that on one or two occasions—such as that bill of sale business—he had been imprudent. He did not repent of the past, because it never occurred to him that, with a few trifling exceptions, there was anything to repent about. But for the future he had no fear. He was going to be a soldier. He ought to have been a soldier from the first, like his fathers before him.

He joined Chanzy, and before many weeks gained his colours. It was the life for which he was best fitted. In the movement and continual change of the camp, spite of the disasters that crushed his cause, he was far happier than he had been, wasting his sister's substance in riotous living. His letters home were full of hope and enthusiasm; and the hearts at Comb Leigh were kept at ease through the infection of his good spirits.

Suddenly the letters ceased; and Gerald managed to find out that the Lieutenant Count de Reville—Fred, needless to say, enlisted under his French name—was among the missing after one of the battles, which were mostly skirmishes before Orleans.

Marion went herself in search of him. She sent Winifred to Chacomb Hall, in charge of Adie, comforted her with hope, and started alone to look for her brother.

Over the battle-fields and in the camps she sought. She

made her way among the Frenchmen, mad with defeat and
shame; among the jubilant Germans, anxious only now to
have an end of it, and fight no more for the madness of an
Empire tottering to her fall; where the ambulance corps
performed their duties under the protection of the much-
abused Geneva Cross. She searched for Fred as Evangeline
searched for Gabriel, but with a better result. For she found
him. To be sure, she had not to wander over the whole of
America; and the battle-fields of the Midi did not cover a
greater extent of ground than the county of Yorkshire.
She found him at last, lying in a farmhouse, stricken
grievously, but not unto death. Outside, the grapes hung
in ripe clusters, the corn was reaped, the autumn flowers
blossomed, and the convolvulus clambered about wall and
porch. Nature, in that unfeeling way of hers which I have
already noted, took no notice of the war, and went on with
her flowers, as if there were no weeping women and heart-
broken men. In the shade was a soldier, a German, smoking
a placid pipe, and thinking very likely of Gretchen. Why we
always associate a German soldier with Gretchen, I do not
know. When he clearly understood that the gracious lady
was not intent on slaughter, he informed her that they had
wounded men in the place—French and German. Might she
see them? The gracious lady might see the door open:
there was nothing to prevent her walking in.

Within the place lay, in half a dozen rooms, pallets filled
with the wounded. Some—but no, it is too near the end of
the tale. Among them, in one of the smaller rooms, lay her
brother Fred.

His right arm was gone—that was immediately apparent.
His forehead was tied up with a cloth, for it was laid bare to
the bone—perhaps a piece of shell, or a spent shot. He
had an open wound in the leg, and he was raving with fever.

Marion obtained permission to stay here. There were no
nurses in this farmhouse used for a hospital, only a young
army surgeon—a dreamy, expert German who talked a
brutal materialism and acted the highest Christianity. Him
Marion conquered. She was a very Venus Victrix for

reducing every man to a state of abject reverence and admiration; and in a day she was mistress of the hospital, and nurse-in-chief to all the poor fellows on the pallets, from Jacques Bontemps, the Auvergne peasant, to Max Herbst, from Posen. All knew that she was come after her brother; but every man felt that, next to him, he was himself the chief object of her solicitude.

In November, when the yellow leaves of Chacomb Park were heavy with autumnal dews, and the air faint with the odour of crushed and decaying leaves, Marion brought her brother home to his wife.

He was scarred. He had only one arm, and that the left. He was pale and wasted. But he was home again; and he was a hero.

Marion brought him once more his father's sword, and laid it in his left hand.

"Take it, my brother. It is yours."

"Yes, Marion," he said humbly. "I may claim it now, may I not?"

Winifred buckled it on for him, smiling through her glad and happy tears.

Fred was a hero. As long as he lives he will enjoy the honour and respect which men in all ages have agreed to pay to him who acquits himself manfully in the battles of his country. No other honour is equal to this. The poet's crown and statesman's statue are poor things compared with the praise and envy bestowed on a gallant fighting man. It is better to be Turenne than Colbert. Wellington seems a greater man than Pitt. Murat in his lifetime was a more gallant figure than Talleyrand.

Fred, for all the countryside, was a hero. The women remembered how he stood, brave and handsome, at his father's funeral, the prop and support of his house. No doubt he had propped it and supported it during the four years of exile from Devonshire. What but good was to be expected of one so handsome?

A hero. And yet it does not seem that his moral nature was altered. He had been as lazy as Lawrence, and he continued in his laziness—of course a man with only the left arm could not be expected to work. He is just exactly what he always has been—as indolent, as good-natured, taking as keen a delight in merely breathing the air of heaven, as affectionate, as avid of pleasure. Only his pleasures now cost nothing. He can fish with his left arm. He can sail with Gerald. He can go to Exeter with his brother-in-law for such dissipation as that city affords. He cannot, happily, play billiards. He can ride ; he can play with his children ; and he can be the joy and happiness of his wife and sister. Always a favourite with everybody. Great is amiability, and it shall prevail.

When Mr. Rhyl Owen comes down once a year to see his daughter, he allows himself to be overcome with shame at the folly of his former predictions.

"That man worthless, Winifred ? Why you ought never to forgive me. A fool talks folly. What says Solomon ? 'Whoso keepeth his mouth and tongue keepeth his soul from troubles.' And again: 'He that is void of wisdom despiseth his neighbour ; but a man of understanding holdeth his peace.'"

And yet, most certainly, had this young man remained in London, his end would have been like unto that of the prophetic billiard-marker.

And so the end of action has come—the problem of what each shall do with his life is solved. There will be no more anxiety for Marion and the rest till the little ones grow up, and a new generation begins its own troubles.

At Comb Leigh there is peace, and but little intercourse with the outer world. The most frequent visitor is Dr. Chacomb. Quite recently he has achieved his highest ambition. He has not only become the acknowledged leader in his profession for gout, but he has received the honour of a baronetcy. He is now Sir Joseph Chacomb, Bart., M.D. This distinction was acquired in pulling a certain exalted personage through an attack which threatened to fly to the stomach. Dr. Chacomb, who was called in at an early stage, manifested the very greatest devotion throughout. He sat up for four nights, without leaving the patient's bedside. He never left it at all, in fact, till the danger was over, and the great man safe. Then they knighted him. Of course, Dr. Porteous, of Savile Row, declared that there never had been the slightest danger; that the bulletins issued every two hours by his rival were quite unnecessary; and that all the racket was got up by himself, for his own ends. How hateful a passion is envy!

Sir Joseph has never renewed his suit to Marion. He knows, indeed, that it would be useless. But there is no one in the world in whose society he takes such pleasure, with whom he is less cynical, or more hopeful of his fellow-creatures. Like the wicked man, his eyes swell out with fatness; but Sir Joseph is a wicked man no longer. Observe that, like Fred, he has improved with prosperity. He owes not only his success, but also his present virtue, to the artful measures which I have had as historian to chronicle, and as moralist to deplore. All my people, indeed—except Marion, Adie, and Winifred—have been sinners; and nobody, somehow, except poor Mrs. Spenser, has been punished for his sins. My friends, it is only in copybooks that people get punished in the material manner. There are some sins which even carry their own reward, in the shape of prosperity, with them. There are some, on the other hand, which carry their own punishment. These latter, young candidate for worldly success, find out and avoid. Fred, you see, who never would work, any more than the Idle Apprentice, is comfortable and happy, provided with the best of wives, and kept in affluence by the painting of his sister. Gerald, who broke every pledge of love and constancy, never felt any repentance, never knows how great and glorious a woman he threw away, never institutes comparisons between the present and the possible past, and is perfectly happy with a wife of whom he is beyond measure fond and proud. The doctor, who found a way to greatness by paths tortuous and questionable, is on a pinnacle of fame. Dicky Carew is really eminent in his new walk. And even the second Mrs. Chacomb has been rewarded for her bold stroke by a comfortable annuity.

Compensation? Yes. But, like the cow's tail, it does not reach far enough. These sinners will never repent; they will never be punished. All that the moral philosopher can prophesy is that from time to time they may be reminded of the past, and feel a pang of remorse or shame, sharp in direct proportion to their present happiness.

Is Marion, the innocent scapegoat of all the sins and misfortunes of others, the only unhappy one?

No. Happiness—as people who have got everything they want are fond of telling us—does not depend always on obtaining what we vehemently desire. There is—only preachers very seldom know anything about it—a happiness independent of all human desires, which issues from the higher, unselfish life. In the years to come, Marion sees a long life of labour; but it is labour rewarded with some honour and sufficient pay. She will not be a great artist, like Rosa Bonheur; but she will command a sale for her works. She will not be remembered for ever, like Raffaelle; but she will please the better taste of the day, and advance, by her purity, truth, and sweetness, the highest interests of Art. Her house will not be lonely, for Winifred and the children will light it up; with Fred—the lazy, careless Fred, of whom his wife can never be too proud, or his sister too fond.

And all shall love her alike. As the children read of women to be worshipped, they shall think of Marion. When they grow up, and can understand something of the mystery and meaning of good works, they shall associate all good works with Marion. When they hear of those who give and spend for others, their thoughts will turn to Marion. She has—as Mr. Owen was fond of saying—she has the fruit of her own hands: her own works praise her in the gates. There is a CROWN for those who live for others, more glorious than any wreath of the Nemæan games. Hers is the golden HARP, with which to celebrate the victory over sorrow and disappointment—the solution of the problem, insoluble to the selfish world, the final triumph of Love over Pain.

PRINTED BY BALLANTYNE, HANSON AND CO.
EDINBURGH AND LONDON.

A LIST OF BOOKS

PUBLISHED BY

CHATTO & WINDUS,

214, PICCADILLY, LONDON, W.

Sold by all Booksellers, or sent post-free for the published price by the Publishers.

About.—The Fellah: An Egyptian Novel. By EDMOND ABOUT. Translated by Sir RANDAL ROBERTS. Post 8vo, illustrated boards, 2s. ; cloth limp, 2s. 6d.

Adams (W. Davenport), Works by:

A Dictionary of the Drama. Being a comprehensive Guide to the Plays, Playwrights, Players, and Playhouses of the United Kingdom and America, from the Earliest to the Present Times. Crown 8vo, halfbound, 12s. 6d. [*Preparing.*

Latter Day Lyrics. Edited by W. DAVENPORT ADAMS. Post 8vo, cloth limp, 2s 6d.

Quips and Quiddities. Selected by W. DAVENPORT ADAMS. Post 8vo, cloth limp, 2s. 6d.

Advertising, A History of, from the Earliest Times. Illustrated by Anecdotes, Curious Specimens, and Notices of Successful Advertisers. By HENRY SAMPSON. Crown 8vo, with Coloured Frontispiece and Illustrations, cloth gilt, 7s. 6d.

Agony Column (The) of "The Times," from 1800 to 1870. Edited, with an Introduction, by ALICE CLAY. Post 8vo, cloth limp, 2s. 6d.

Aïdé (Hamilton), Works by:
Post 8vo, illustrated boards, 2s. each.
Carr of Carrlyon.
Confidences.

Alexander (Mrs.), Novels by:
Post 8vo, illustrated boards, 2s. each.
Maid, Wife, or Widow ?
Valerie's Fate.

Allen (Grant), Works by:
Crown 8vo, cloth extra, 6s. each.
The Evolutionist at Large. Second Edition, revised.
Vignettes from Nature.
Colin Clout's Calendar.

Strange Stories. With Frontispiece by GEORGE DU MAURIER. Cr. 8vo, cl ex., 6s. ; post 8vo, illust. bds., 2s.

Philistia: A Novel. Crown 8vo, cloth extra. 3s. 6d ; post 8vo, illust. bds., 2s.

Babylon: A Novel. With 12 Illusts. by P. MACNAB. Crown 8vo, cloth extra, 3s. 6d.

For Maimie's Sake: A Tale of Love and Dynamite. Cr. 8vo, cl. ex , 6s.

In all Shades: A Novel. Three Vols., crown 8vo.

The Beckoning Hand, &c. With a Frontispiece by TOWNLEY GREEN. Crown 8vo, cloth extra, 6s.

Architectural Styles, A Handbook of. Translated from the German of A. ROSENGARTEN, by W. COLLETT-SANDARS. Crown 8vo, cloth extra, with 639 Illustrations, 7s. 6d.

Artemus Ward :

Artemus Ward's Works: The Works of CHARLES FARRER BROWNE, better known as ARTEMUS WARD. With Portrait and Facsimile. Crown 8vo, cloth extra, 7s. 6d.

Artemus Ward's Lecture on the Mormons. With 32 Illustrations, Edited, with Preface, by EDWARD P. HINGSTON. Crown 8vo, 6d.

The Genial Showman ; Life and Adventures of Artemus Ward. By EDWARD P. HINGSTON. With a Frontispiece. Cr. 8vo, cl. extra, 3s. 6d.

Art (The) of Amusing: A Collection of Graceful Arts, Games, Tricks, Puzzles, and Charades. By FRANK BELLEW. With 300 Illustrations. Cr. 8vo cloth extra, 4s. 6d.

Ashton (John), Works by:
Crown 8vo, cloth extra, 7s. 6d. each.

A History of the Chap-Books of the Eighteenth Century. With nearly 400 Illustrations, engraved in facsimile of the originals.

Social Life in the Reign of Queen Anne. From Original Sources. With nearly 100 Illustrations.

Humour, Wit, and Satire of the Seventeenth Century. With nearly 100 Illustrations.

English Caricature and Satire on Napoleon the First. With 120 Illustrations from Originals. Two Vols., demy 8vo, cloth extra, 28s.

Bacteria.—A Synopsis of the Bacteria and Yeast Fungi and Allied Species. By W. B. GROVE, B.A. With 87 Illusts. Crown 8vo, cl. extra, 3s. 6d.

Bankers, A Handbook of London; together with Lists of Bankers from 1677. By F. G. HILTON PRICE. Crown 8vo, cloth extra, 7s. 6d.

Bardsley (Rev. C.W.), Works by:
Crown 8vo, cloth extra, 7s. 6d. each.

English Surnames: Their Sources and Significations. Third Ed., revised.
Curiosities of Puritan Nomenclature.

Bartholomew Fair, Memoirs of. By HENRY MORLEY. With 100 Illusts. Crown 8vo, cloth extra, 7s. 6d.

Beaconsfield, Lord: A Biography. By T. P. O'CONNOR, M.P. Sixth Edition, with a New Preface. Crown 8vo, cloth extra, 7s. 6d.

Beauchamp. — Grantley Grange: A Novel. By SHELSLEY BEAUCHAMP. Post 8vo, illust. bds., 2s.

Beautiful Pictures by British Artists: A Gathering of Favourites from our Picture Galleries. All engraved on Steel in the highest style of Art. Edited, with Notices of the Artists, by SYDNEY ARMYTAGE, M.A. Imperial 4to, cloth extra, gilt and gilt edges, 21s.

Bechstein. — As Pretty as Seven, and other German Stories. Collected by LUDWIG BECHSTEIN. With Additional Tales by the Brothers GRIMM, and 100 Illusts. by RICHTER. Small 4to, green and gold, 6s. 6d.; gilt edges, 7s. 6d.

Beerbohm. — Wanderings in Patagonia; or, Life among the Ostrich Hunters. By JULIUS BEERBOHM. With Illusts. Crown 8vo, cloth extra, 3s. 6d.

Belgravia. One Shilling Monthly. The Number for JANUARY contains the First Chapters of a New Novel by SARAH TYTLER, Author of "Citoyenne Jacqueline," &c. entitled Disappeared, with Illustrations by P. MACNAB; and Stories by WILKIE COLLINS, Miss BRADDON, Mrs. ALFRED HUNT, the Author of "Phyllis," and other Popular Authors.

, *Just ready, the Volume for* NOVEMBER 1886 *to* FEBRUARY 1887, *cloth extra, gilt edges,* 7s. 6d.; *Cases for binding Vols.,* 2s. *each.*

Belgravia Holiday Number, 1887. Demy 8vo, with Illustrations, 1s.
[*Preparing.*

Bennett (W.C.,LL.D.),Works by:
Post 8vo, cloth limp, 2s. each.

A Ballad History of England.
Songs for Sailors.

Besant (Walter) and James Rice, Novels by. Crown 8vo, cloth extra, 3s. 6d. each; post 8vo, illust. boards, 2s. each; cloth limp, 2s. 6d. each.

Ready-Money Mortiboy.
With Harp and Crown.
This Son of Vulcan.
My Little Girl.
The Case of Mr. Lucraft.
The Golden Butterfly.
By Celia's Arbour.
The Monks of Thelema.
'Twas in Trafalgar's Bay.
The Seamy Side.
The Ten Years' Tenant.
The Chaplain of the Fleet.

Besant (Walter), Novels by:
Crown 8vo, cloth extra, 3s. 6d. each; post 8vo, illust. boards, 2s. each; cloth limp, 2s. 6d. each.

All Sorts and Conditions of Men: An Impossible Story. With Illustrations by FRED. BARNARD.
The Captains' Room, &c. With Frontispiece by E. J. WHEELER.
All in a Garden Fair. With 6 Illusts. By H. FURNISS.
Dorothy Forster. With Frontispiece By CHARLES GREEN.
Uncle Jack, and other Stories.

Children of Gibeon: A Novel. Three Vols., crown 8vo.
The World Went Very Well Then. Three Vols., crown 8vo. [*Preparing*
The Art of Fiction. Demy 8vo, 1s.

Betham-Edwards (M.), Novels
by. Crown 8vo, cloth extra, 3s. 6d.
each.; post 8vo, illust. bds., 2s. each.
Felicia. | Kitty.

Bewick (Thos.) and his Pupils.
By AUSTIN DOBSON. With 95 Illustrations. Square 8vo, cloth extra, 10s. 6d.

Birthday Books:—
The Starry Heavens: A Poetical
Birthday Book. Square 8vo, handsomely bound in cloth, 2s. 6d.
Birthday Flowers: Their Language
and Legends. By W. J. GORDON.
Beautifully Illustrated in Colours by
VIOLA BOUGHTON. In illuminated
cover, crown 4to, 6s.
The Lowell Birthday Book. With
Illusts. Small 8vo, cloth extra, 4s. 6d.

Blackburn's (Henry) Art Handbooks. Demy 8vo, Illustrated, uniform in size for binding.
Academy Notes, separate years, from
1875 to 1885, each 1s.
Academy Notes, 1886. With numerous Illustrations. 1s.
Academy Notes, 1875-79. Complete
in One Vol., with nearly 600 Illusts. in
Facsimile. Demy 8vo, cloth limp, 6s.
Academy Notes, 1880-84. Complete
in One Volume, with about 700 Facsimile Illustrations. Cloth limp, 6s.
Grosvenor Notes, 1877. 6d.
Grosvenor Notes, separate years, from
1878 to 1885, each 1s.
Grosvenor Notes, 1886. With numerous Illustrations. 1s.
Grosvenor Notes, 1877-82. With
upwards of 300 Illustrations. Demy
8vo, cloth limp, 6s.
Pictures at South Kensington. With
70 Illusts. 1s. [*New Edit. preparing.*]
The English Pictures at the National
Gallery. 114 Illustrations. 1s.
The Old Masters at the National
Gallery. 128 Illustrations. 1s. 6d.
A Complete Illustrated Catalogue
to the National Gallery. With
Notes by H. BLACKBURN, and 242
Illusts. Demy 8vo, cloth limp, 3s.

Illustrated Catalogue of the Luxembourg Gallery. Containing about
250 Reproductions after the Original
Drawings of the Artists. Edited by
F. G. DUMAS. Demy 8vo, 3s. 6d.
The Paris Salon, 1885. With about
300 Facsimile Sketches. Edited by
F. G. DUMAS. Demy 8vo, 3s.

ART HANDBOOKS, *continued*—
The Paris Salon, 1886. With about 300
Illusts. Edited by F. G. DUMAS.
Demy 8vo, 3s.
The Art Annual, 1883-4. Edited by
F. G. DUMAS. With 300 full-page
Illustrations. Demy 8vo, 5s.

Blake (William): Etchings from
his Works. By W. B. SCOTT. With
descriptive Text. Folio, half-bound
boards, India Proofs, 21s.

Boccaccio's Decameron; or,
Ten Days' Entertainment. Translated
into English, with an Introduction by
THOMAS WRIGHT, F.S.A. With Portrait
and STOTHARD's beautiful Copperplates. Cr. 8vo, cloth extra, gilt, 7s. 6d.

Bowers'(G.) Hunting Sketches:
Oblong 4to, half-bound boards, 21s. each.
Canters in Crampshire.
Leaves from a Hunting Journal.
Coloured in facsimile of the originals.

Boyle (Frederick), Works by:
Crown 8vo, cloth extra, 3s. 6d. each; post
8vo, illustrated boards, 2s. each.
Camp Notes: Stories of Sport and
Adventure in Asia, Africa, and
America.
Savage Life: Adventures of a Globe
Trotter.

Chronicles of No-Man's Land
Post 8vo, illust. boards, 2s.

Brand's Observations on Popular Antiquities, chiefly Illustrating
the Origin of our Vulgar Customs,
Ceremonies, and Superstitions. With
the Additions of Sir HENRY ELLIS.
Crown 8vo, cloth extra, gilt, with
numerous Illustrations, 7s. 6d.

Bret Harte, Works by:
Bret Harte's Collected Works. Arranged and Revised by the Author.
Complete in Five Vols., crown 8vo,
cloth extra, 6s. each.
Vol. I. COMPLETE POETICAL AND
DRAMATIC WORKS. With Steel Portrait, and Introduction by Author.
Vol. II. EARLIER PAPERS—LUCK OF
ROARING CAMP, and other Sketches
—BOHEMIAN PAPERS — SPANISH
AND AMERICAN LEGENDS.
Vol. III. TALES OF THE ARGONAUTS
—EASTERN SKETCHES.
Vol. IV. GABRIEL CONROY.
Vol. V. STORIES — CONDENSED
NOVELS, &c.
The Select Works of Bret Harte, in
Prose and Poetry. With Introductory Essay by J. M. BELLEW, Portrait
of the Author, and 50 Illustrations.
Crown 8vo, cloth extra, 7s. 6d.

BRET HARTE, *continued—*

Bret Harte's Complete Poetical Works. Author's Copyright Edition. Beautifully printed on hand-made paper and bound in buckram. Cr. 8vo, 4s. Cd.

Gabriel Conroy : A Novel. Post 8vo, illustrated boards, 2s.

An Heiress of Red Dog, and other Stories. Post 8vo, illustrated boards, 2s.

The Twins of Table Mountain. Fcap. 8vo, picture cover, 1s.

Luck of Roaring Camp, and other Sketches. Post 8vo, illust. bds., 2s.

Jeff Briggs's Love Story. Fcap. 8vo, picture cover, 1s.

Flip. Post 8vo, illustrated boards, 2s. ; cloth limp, 2s. 6d.

Californian Stories (including THE TWINS OF TABLE MOUNTAIN, JEFF BRIGGS'S LOVE STORY, &c.) Post 8vo, illustrated boards, 2s

Maruja: A Novel. Post 8vo, illust. boards, 2s. ; cloth limp, 2s 6d.

The Queen of the Pirate Isle. With 28 original Drawings by KATE GREENAWAY, Reproduced in Colours by EDMUND EVANS. Small 4to, boards, 5s.

Brewer (Rev. Dr.), Works by :

The Reader's Handbook of Allusions, References, Plots, and Stories. Fifth Edition, revised throughout, with a New Appendix, containing a COMPLETE ENGLISH BIBLIOGRAPHY. Cr. 8vo, 1,400 pp., cloth extra, 7s. 6d.

Authors and their Works, with the Dates: Being the Appendices to "The Reader's Handbook," separately printed. Cr. 8vo, cloth limp, 2s.

A Dictionary of Miracles : Imitative, Realistic, and Dogmatic. Crown 8vo, cloth extra, 7s. 6d ; half-bound. 9s.

Brewster (Sir David), Works by:

More Worlds than One: The Creed of the Philosopher and the Hope of the Christian. With Plates. Post 8vo, cloth extra 4s. Cd.

The Martyrs of Science: Lives of GALILEO, TYCHO BRAHE, and KEPLER. With Portraits. Post 8vo, cloth extra, 4s. 6d.

Letters on Natural Magic. A New Edition, with numerous Illustrations, and Chapters on the Being and Faculties of Man, and Additional Phenomena of Natural Magic, by A. SMITH. Post 8vo, cl. ex., 4s. 6d.

Briggs, Memoir of Gen. John.

By Major EVANS BELL. With a Portrait. Royal 8vo, cloth extra, 7s. 6d.

Brillat-Savarin.—Gastronomy

as a Fine Art. By BRILLAT-SAVARIN. Translated by R. E. ANDERSON, M.A. Post 8vo, cloth limp, 2s. 6d.

Buchanan's (Robert) Works :

Crown 8vo, cloth extra, 6s. each.

Ballads of Life, Love, and Humour Frontispiece by ARTHUR HUGHES.

Undertones.

London Poems.

The Book of Orm.

White Rose and Red: A Love Story.

Idylls and Legends of Inverburn.

Selected Poems of Robert Buchanan. With a Frontispiece by T. DALZIEL.

The Hebrid Isles: Wanderings in the Land of Lorne and the Outer Hebrides. With Frontispiece by WILLIAM SMALL.

A Poet's Sketch Book: Selections from the Prose Writings of ROBERT BUCHANAN.

The Earthquake ; or, Six Days and a Sabbath. Cr. 8vo, cloth extra, 6s.

Robert Buchanan's Complete Poetical Works. With Steel-plate Portrait. Crown 8vo, cloth extra, 7s. 6d.

Crown 8vo, cloth extra, 3s. 6d. each ; post 8vo, illust. boards, 2s. each.

The Shadow of the Sword.

A Child of Nature. With a Frontispiece.

God and the Man. With Illustrations by FRED. BARNARD.

The Martyrdom of Madeline. With Frontispiece by A. W. COOPER.

Love Me for Ever. With a Frontispiece by P. MACNAB.

Annan Water.

The New Abelard.

Foxglove Manor.

Matt : A Story of a Caravan.

The Master of the Mine. With a Frontispiece by W. H. OVEREND. Crown 8vo, cloth extra. 3s. 6d.

Bunyan's Pilgrim's Progress.

Edited by Rev. T. SCOTT. With 17 Steel Plates by STOTHARD engraved by GOODALL, and numerous Woodcuts. Crown 8vo, cloth extra, gilt, 7s. 6d.

Burnett (Mrs.), Novels by :

Surly Tim, and other Stories. Post 8vo, illustrated boards, 2s.

Fcap. 8vo, picture cover, 1s. each.

Kathleen Mavourneen.

Lindsay's Luck.

Pretty Polly Pemberton.

Burton (Captain), Works by:

To the Gold Coast for Gold: A Personal Narrative. By RICHARD F. BURTON and VERNEY LOVETT CAMERON. With Maps and Frontispiece. Two Vols., crown 8vo, cloth extra, 21s.

The Book of the Sword: Being a History of the Sword and its Use in all Countries, from the Earliest Times. By RICHARD F. BURTON. With over 400 Illustrations. Square 8vo, cloth extra, 32s.

Burton (Robert):

The Anatomy of Melancholy. A New Edition, complete, corrected and enriched by Translations of the Classical Extracts. Demy 8vo, cloth extra, 7s. 6d.

Melancholy Anatomised: Being an Abridgment, for popular use, of BURTON'S ANATOMY OF MELANCHOLY. Post 8vo, cloth limp, 2s. 6d.

Byron (Lord):

Byron's Childe Harold. An entirely New Edition of this famous Poem, with over One Hundred new Illusts. by leading Artists. (Uniform with the Illustrated Editions of "The Lady of the Lake" and "Marmion.") Elegantly and appropriately bound, small 4to, 16s.

Byron's Letters and Journals. With Notices of his Life. By THOMAS MOORE. A Reprint of the Original Edition, newly revised, with Twelve full-page Plates. Crown 8vo, cloth extra, gilt, 7s. 6d.

Byron's Don Juan. Complete in One Vol., post 8vo, cloth limp, 2s.

Caine (T. Hall), Novels by:

The Shadow of a Crime. Cr. 8vo, cloth extra, 3s. 6d.; post 8vo, illustrated boards, 2s.

A Son of Hagar. Three Vols., crown 8vo.

Cameron (Comdr.), Works by:

To the Gold Coast for Gold: A Personal Narrative. By RICHARD F. BURTON and VERNEY LOVETT CAMERON. With Frontispiece and Maps. Two Vols., crown 8vo, cloth extra, 21s.

The Cruise of the "Black Prince" Privateer, Commanded by ROBERT HAWKINS, Master Mariner. By Commander V. LOVETT CAMERON, R.N., C.B., D.C.L. With Frontispiece and Vignette by P. MACNAB. Crown 8vo, cl. ex., 5s.

Cameron (Mrs. H. Lovett), Novels by:

Crown 8vo, cloth extra, 3s. 6d. each; post 8vo, illustrated boards, 2s. each.

Juliet's Guardian. | Deceivers Ever.

Carlyle (Thomas):

On the Choice of Books. By THOMAS CARLYLE. With a Life of the Author by R. H. SHEPHERD. New and Revised Edition, post 8vo, cloth extra, Illustrated, 1s. 6d.

The Correspondence of Thomas Carlyle and Ralph Waldo Emerson, 1834 to 1872. Edited by CHARLES ELIOT NORTON. With Portraits. Two Vols., crown 8vo, cloth extra, 24s.

Chapman's (George) Works:

Vol. I. contains the Plays complete, including the doubtful ones. Vol. II., the Poems and Minor Translations, with an Introductory Essay by ALGERNON CHARLES SWINBURNE. Vol. III., the Translations of the Iliad and Odyssey. Three Vols., crown 8vo, cloth extra, 18s.; or separately, 6s. each.

Chatto & Jackson.—A Treatise

on Wood Engraving, Historical and Practical. By WM. ANDREW CHATTO and JOHN JACKSON. With an Additional Chapter by HENRY G. BOHN; and 450 fine Illustrations. A Reprint of the last Revised Edition. Large 4to, half-bound, 28s.

Chaucer:

Chaucer for Children: A Golden Key. By Mrs. H. R. HAWEIS. With Eight Coloured Pictures and numerous Woodcuts by the Author. New Ed., small 4to, cloth extra, 6s.

Chaucer for Schools. By Mrs. H. R. HAWEIS. Demy 8vo, cloth limp, 2s. 6d.

Chronicle (The) of the Coach:

Charing Cross to Ilfracombe. By J. D. CHAMPLIN. With 75 Illustrations by EDWARD L. CHICHESTER. Square 8vo, cloth extra, 7s. 6d.

City (The) of Dream: A Poem.

Fcap. 8vo, cloth extra, 6s. [In the press.

Clodd.— Myths and Dreams.

By EDWARD CLODD, F.R.A.S., Author of "The Childhood of Religions," &c. Crown 8vo, cloth extra, 5s.

Cobban.—The Cure of Souls:

A Story. By J. MACLAREN COBBAN. Post 8vo, illustrated boards, 2s.

Coleman.—Curly: An Actor's Story. By JOHN COLEMAN. Illustrated by J. C. DOLLMAN. Crown 8vo, 1s. cloth, 1s. 6d

Collins (Mortimer), Novels by:

Crown 8vo, cloth extra, 3s. 6d. each; post 8vo, illustrated boards, 2s each.

Sweet Anne Page. | Transmigration. From Midnight to Midnight.

A Fight with Fortune. Post 8vo, illustrated boards, 2s.

Collins (Mortimer & Frances),
Novels by:
Crown 8vo, cloth extra, 3s. 6d. each; post
8vo, illustrated boards, 2s. each.
Blacksmith and Scholar.
The Village Comedy.
You Play Me False.

Post 8vo, illustrated boards, 2s. each.
Sweet and Twenty.
Frances.

Collins (Wilkie), Novels by:
Crown 8vo, cloth extra, Illustrated,
3s.6d. each; post 8vo, illustrated bds.,
2s. each; cloth limp, 2s. 6d. each.
Antonina. Illust. by Sir JohnGilbert.
Basil. Illustrated by Sir John Gil-
bert and J. Mahoney.
Hide and Seek. Illustrated by Sir
John Gilbert and J. Mahoney.
The Dead Secret. Illustrated by Sir
John Gilbert.
Queen of Hearts. Illustrated by Sir
John Gilbert.
My Miscellanies. With a Steel-plate
Portrait of Wilkie Collins.
The Woman in White. With Illus-
trations by Sir John Gilbert and
F. A. Fraser.
The Moonstone. With Illustrations
by G. Du Maurier and F. A. Fraser.
Man and Wife. Illust. by W. Small.
Poor Miss Finch. Illustrated by
G. Du Maurier and Edward
Hughes.
Miss or Mrs.? With Illustrations by
S. L. Fildes and Henry Woods.
The New Magdalen. Illustrated by
G.Du Maurier and C.S. Reinhardt.
The Frozen Deep. Illustrated by
G. Du Maurier and J. Mahoney.
The Law and the Lady. Illustrated
by S. L. Fildes and Sydney Hall.
The Two Destinies.
The Haunted Hotel. Illustrated by
Arthur Hopkins.
The Fallen Leaves.
Jezebel's Daughter.
The Black Robe.
Heart and Science: A Story of the
Present Time.
"I Say No."

The Evil Genius: A Novel. Three
Vols., crown 8vo.

**Collins (C. Allston).—The Bar
Sinister: A Story.** By C. Allston
Collins. Post 8vo, illustrated bds.,2s.

Colman's Humorous Works:
"Broad Grins," "My Nightgown and
Slippers," and other Humorous Works,
Prose and Poetical, of George Colman. With Life by G. B. Buckstone,
and Frontispiece by Hogarth. Crown
8vo cloth extra, gilt, 7s. 6d.

Convalescent Cookery: A
Family Handbook. By Catherine
Ryan. Crown 8vo, 1s.; cloth, 1s.6d.

**Conway (Moncure D.), Works
by:**
Demonology and Devil-Lore. Two
Vols., royal 8vo, with 65 Illusts., 28s.
A Necklace of Stories. Illustrated
by W. J. Hennessy. Square 8vo,
cloth extra, 6s.

Cook (Dutton), Works by:
Crown 8vo, cloth extra, 6s. each.
Hours with the Players. With a
Steel Plate Frontispiece.
Nights at the Play: A View of the
English Stage.

Leo: A Novel. Post 8vo, illustrated
boards, 2s.
Paul Foster's Daughter. Crown 8vo,
cloth extra, 3s. 6d.; post 8vo, illustrated boards, 2s.

Copyright. — A Handbook of
English and Foreign Copyright in
Literary and Dramatic Works. By
Sidney Jerrold, of the Middle
Temple, Esq., Barrister-at-Law. Post
8vo, cloth limp, 2s. 6d.

Cornwall.—PopularRomances
of the West of England; or, The
Drolls, Traditions, and Superstitions
of Old Cornwall. Collected and Edited
by Robert Hunt, F.R.S. New and
Revised Edition, with Additions, and
Two Steel-plate Illustrations by
George Cruikshank. Crown 8vo,
cloth extra, 7s. 6d.

Craddock. — The Prophet of
the Great Smoky Mountains By
Charles Egbert Craddock. Post
8vo, illust. bds., 2s.; cloth limp, 2s. 6d.

Creasy.—Memoirs of Eminent
Etonians: with Notices of the Early
History of Eton College. By Sir
Edward Creasy, Author of "The
Fifteen Decisive Battles of the World."
Crown 8vo, cloth extra, gilt, with 13
Portraits, 7s. 6d.

Cruikshank (George):
The Comic Almanack. Complete in
Two Series: The First from 1835
to 1843; the Second from 1844 to
1853. A Gathering of the Best
Humour of Thackeray, Hood, May-
hew, Albert Smith, A'Beckett,
Robert Brough, &c. With 2,000
Woodcuts and Steel Engravings by
Cruikshank, Hine, Landells, &c.
Crown 8vo, cloth gilt, two very thick
volumes, 7s. 6d. each.

CRUIKSHANK (GEORGE), *continued.*

The Life of George Cruikshank. By BLANCHARD JERROLD, Author of "The Life of Napoleon III.," &c. With 84 Illustrations. New and Cheaper Edition, enlarged, with Additional Plates, and a very carefully compiled Bibliography. Crown 8vo, cloth extra, 7s. 6d.

Robinson Crusoe. A beautiful reproduction of Major's Edition, with 37 Woodcuts and Two Steel Plates by GEORGE CRUIKSHANK, choicely printed. Crown 8vo, cloth extra, 7s. 6d.

Cumming (C. F. Gordon), Works by:

Demy 8vo, cloth extra, 8s. 6d. each.

In the Hebrides. With Autotype Facsimile and numerous full-page Illustrations.

In the Himalayas and on the Indian Plains. With numerous Illustrations.

Via Cornwall to Egypt. With a Photogravure Frontispiece. Demy 8vo, cloth extra, 7s. 6d.

Cussans.—Handbook of Heraldry; with Instructions for Tracing Pedigrees and Deciphering Ancient MSS., &c. By JOHN E. CUSSANS. Entirely New and Revised Edition, illustrated with over 400 Woodcuts and Coloured Plates. Crown 8vo, cloth extra, 7s. 6d.

Cyples.—Hearts of Gold: A Novel. By WILLIAM CYPLES. Crown 8vo, cloth extra, 3s. 6d.; post 8vo, illustrated boards, 2s.

Daniel. — Merrie England in the Olden Time. By GEORGE DANIEL. With Illustrations by ROBT. CRUIKSHANK. Crown 8vo, cloth extra, 3s. 6d.

Daudet.—The Evangelist; or, Port Salvation. By ALPHONSE DAUDET. Translated by C. HARRY MELTZER. With Portrait of the Author. Crown 8vo, cloth extra, 3s. 6d.; post 8vo, illust. boards, 2s.

Davenant. — What shall my Son be? Hints for Parents on the Choice of a Profession or Trade for their Sons. By FRANCIS DAVENANT, M.A. Post 8vo, cloth limp, 2s. 6d.

Davies (Dr. N. E.), Works by:

Crown 8vo, 1s. each; cloth limp, 1s. 6d. each.

One Thousand Medical Maxims.
Nursery Hints: A Mother's Guide.

Aids to Long Life. Crown 8vo, 2s.; cloth limp, 2s. 6d.

Davies' (Sir John) Complete Poetical Works, including Psalms I. to L. in Verse, and other hitherto Unpublished MSS., for the first time Collected and Edited, with Memorial-Introduction and Notes, by the Rev. A. B. GROSART, D.D. Two Vols., crown 8vo, cloth boards, 12s.

De Maistre.—A Journey Round My Room. By XAVIER DE MAISTRE. Translated by HENRY ATTWELL. Post 8vo, cloth limp, 2s. 6d.

De Mille.—A Castle in Spain: A Novel. By JAMES DE MILLE. With a Frontispiece. Crown 8vo, cloth extra, 3s. 6d.; post 8vo, illust. bds., 2s.

Derwent (Leith), Novels by:

Crown 8vo, cloth extra, 3s. 6d. each; post 8vo, illustrated boards, 2s. each.

Our Lady of Tears.
Circe's Lovers.

Dickens (Charles), Novels by:

Post 8vo, illustrated boards, 2s. each.

Sketches by Boz. | Nicholas Nickleby
Pickwick Papers. | Oliver Twist.

The Speeches of Charles Dickens 1841-1870. With a New Bibliography, revised and enlarged. Edited and Prefaced by RICHARD HERNE SHEPHERD. Crown 8vo, cloth extra, 6s.— Also a SMALLER EDITION, in the *Mayfair Library*. Post 8vo, cloth limp, 2s. 6d.

About England with Dickens. By ALFRED RIMMER. With 57 Illustrations by C. A. VANDERHOOF, ALFRED RIMMER, and others. Sq. 8vo, cloth extra, 10s. 6d.

Dictionaries:

A Dictionary of Miracles: Imitative, Realistic, and Dogmatic. By the Rev. E. C. BREWER, LL.D. Crown 8vo, cloth extra, 7s. 6d.; hf.-bound, 9s.

The Reader's Handbook of Allusions, References, Plots, and Stories. By the Rev. E. C. BREWER, LL.D. Fifth Edition, revised throughout, with a New Appendix, containing a Complete English Bibliography. Crown 8vo, 1,400 pages, cloth extra, 7s. 6d.

Authors and their Works, with the Dates. Being the Appendices to "The Reader's Handbook," separately printed. By the Rev. Dr. BREWER. Crown 8vo, cloth limp, 2s.

DICTIONARIES, *continued*—

Familiar Allusions: A Handbook of Miscellaneous Information; including the Names of Celebrated Statues, Paintings, Palaces, Country Seats, Ruins, Churches, Ships, Streets, Clubs, Natural Curiosities, and the like. By WM. A. WHEELER and CHARLES G. WHEELER. Demy 8vo, cloth extra, 7s. 6d.

Short Sayings of Great Men. With Historical and Explanatory Notes. By SAMUEL A. BENT, M.A. Demy 8vo, cloth extra, 7s. 6d.

A Dictionary of the Drama: Being a comprehensive Guide to the Plays, Playwrights, Players, and Playhouses of the United Kingdom and America, from the Earliest to the Present Times. By W. DAVENPORT ADAMS. A thick volume, crown 8vo, half-bound, 12s. 6d.   [*In preparation.*

The Slang Dictionary: Etymological, Historical, and Anecdotal. Crown 8vo, cloth extra, 6s. 6d.

Women of the Day: A Biographical Dictionary. By FRANCES HAYS. Cr. 8vo, cloth extra, 5s.

Words, Facts, and Phrases: A Dictionary of Curious, Quaint, and Out-of-the-Way Matters By ELIEZER EDWARDS. New and Cheaper Issue. Cr. 8vo, cl. ex., 7s. 6d. ; hf.-bd., 9s.

Diderot.—The Paradox of Acting. Translated, with Annotations, from Diderot's " Le Paradoxe sur le Comédien," by WALTER HERRIES POLLOCK. With a Preface by HENRY IRVING. Cr. 8vo, in parchment, 4s 6d.

Dobson (W. T.), Works by :
Post 8vo, cloth limp, 2s. 6d. each.

Literary Frivolities, Fancies, Follies, and Frolics.

Poetical Ingenuities and Eccentricities.

Doran. — Memories of our Great Towns; with Anecdotic Gleanings concerning their Worthies and their Oddities. By Dr. JOHN DORAN, F.S.A. With 38 Illustrations. New and Cheaper Ed., cr. 8vo, cl. ex., 7s. 6d.

Drama, A Dictionary of the. Being a comprehensive Guide to the Plays, Playwrights, Players, and Playhouses of the United Kingdom and America, from the Earliest to the Present Times. By W. DAVENPORT ADAMS. (Uniform with BREWER'S " Reader's Handbook.") Crown 8vo, half bound, 12s. 6d.   [*In preparation.*

Dramatists, The Old. Cr. 8vo, cl. ex., Vignette Portraits, 6s. per Vol.

Ben Jonson's Works. With Notes Critical and Explanatory, and a Biographical Memoir by WM. GIFFORD. Edit. by Col. CUNNINGHAM 3 Vols.

Chapman's Works. Complete in Three Vols. Vol. I. contains the Plays complete, including doubtful ones; Vol. II., Poems and Minor Translations, with Introductory Essay by A. C. SWINBURNE; Vol. III., Translations of the Iliad and Odyssey.

Marlowe's Works. Including his Translations. Edited, with Notes and Introduction, by Col. CUNNINGHAM. One Vol.

Massinger's Plays. From the Text of WILLIAM GIFFORD. Edited by Col. CUNNINGHAM. One Vol.

Dyer. — The Folk - Lore of Plants. By Rev. T. F. THISELTON DYER, M.A. Crown 8vo, cloth extra, 7s. 6d.   [*In preparation.*

Early English Poets. Edited, with Introductions and Annotations, by Rev. A. B. GROSART, D.D. Crown 8vo, cloth boards, 6s. per Volume.

Fletcher's (Giles, B.D.) **Complete Poems.** One Vol.

Davies' (Sir John) **Complete Poetical Works.** Two Vols.

Herrick's (Robert) **Complete Collected Poems.** Three Vols.

Sidney's (Sir Philip) **Complete Poetical Works.** Three Vols.

Herbert (Lord) **of Cherbury's Poems.** Edited, with Introduction, by J. CHURTON COLLINS. Crown 8vo, parchment, 8s.

Edwardes (Mrs. A.), **Novels by :**

A Point of Honour. Post 8vo, illustrated boards, 2s.

Archie Lovell. Crown 8vo, cloth extra, 3s. 6d. ; post 8vo, illust. bds., 2s.

Eggleston.—Roxy: A Novel. By EDWARD EGGLESTON. Post 8vo, illust. boards, 2s.

Emanuel.—On Diamonds and Precious Stones: their History, Value, and Properties ; with Simple Tests for ascertaining their Reality. By HARRY EMANUEL, F.R.G.S. With numerous Illustrations, tinted and plain. Crown 8vo, cloth extra, gilt, 6s.

English Merchants: Memoirs in Illustration of the Progress of British Commerce. By H. R. Fox BOURNE. With Illusts. New and Cheaper Edit. revised. Crown 8vo, cloth extra, 7s. 6d.

Ewald (Alex. Charles, F.S.A.), Works by:

The Life and Times of Prince Charles Stuart, Count of Albany, commonly called the Young Pretender. From the State Papers and other Sources. New and Cheaper Edition, with a Portrait, crown 8vo, cloth extra, 7s. 6d.

Stories from the State Papers. With an Autotype Facsimile. Crown 8vo, cloth extra, 6s.

Studies Re-studied: Historical Sketches from Original Sources. Demy 8vo cloth extra, 12s.

Eyes, Our: How to Preserve Them from Infancy to Old Age. By JOHN BROWNING, F.R.A.S., &c. Fifth Edition. With 55 Illustrations. Crown 8vo, cloth, 1s.

Fairholt.—Tobacco: Its History and Associations; with an Account of the Plant and its Manufacture, and its Modes of Use in all Ages and Countries. By F. W. FAIRHOLT, F.S.A. With upwards of 100 Illustrations by the Author. Crown 8vo, cloth extra, 6s.

Familiar Allusions: A Handbook of Miscellaneous Information; including the Names of Celebrated Statues, Paintings, Palaces, Country Seats, Ruins, Churches, Ships, Streets, Clubs, Natural Curiosities, and the like. By WILLIAM A. WHEELER, Author of "Noted Names of Fiction;" and CHARLES G. WHEELER. Demy 8vo, cloth extra, 7s. 6d.

Faraday (Michael), Works by: Post 8vo, cloth extra, 4s. 6d. each.

The Chemical History of a Candle: Lectures delivered before a Juvenile Audience at the Royal Institution. Edited by WILLIAM CROOKES, F.C.S. With numerous Illustrations.

On the Various Forces of Nature, and their Relations to each other: Lectures delivered before a Juvenile Audience at the Royal Institution. Edited by WILLIAM CROOKES, F.C.S. With numerous Illustrations.

Farrer. — Military Manners and Customs By J. A. FARRER, Author of "Primitive Manners and Customs," &c. Cr. 8vo, cloth extra, 6s.

Fin-Bec.—The Cupboard Papers: Observations on the Art of Living and Dining. By FIN-BEC. Post 8vo, cloth limp, 2s. 6d.

Fitzgerald (Percy), Works by:

The Recreations of a Literary Man; or, Does Writing Pay? With Recollections of some Literary Men, and a View of a Literary Man's Working Life. Cr. 8vo, cloth extra, 6s.

The World Behind the Scenes. Crown 8vo, cloth extra, 3s. 6d.

Little Essays: Passages from the Letters of CHARLES LAMB. Post 8vo, cloth limp, 2s. 6d.

Fatal Zero: A Homburg Diary. Cr. 8vo, cloth extra, 3s. 6d.

Post 8vo, illustrated boards, 2s. each.
Bella Donna. | Never Forgotten.
The Second Mrs. Tillotson.
Polly.
Seventy-five Brooke Street.
The Lady of Brantome.

Fletcher's (Giles, B.D.) Com- plete Poems: Christ's Victorie in Heaven, Christ's Victorie on Earth, Christ's Triumph over Death, and Minor Poems. With Memorial-Introduction and Notes by the Rev. A. B. GROSART, D.D. Cr. 8vo, cloth bds., 6s.

Fonblanque.—Filthy Lucre: A Novel. By ALBANY DE FONBLANQUE. Post 8vo, illustrated boards, 2s.

Francillon (R. E.), Novels by:
Crown 8vo, cloth extra, 3s. 6d. each; post 8vo, illust. boards, 2s each.
One by One. | A Real Queen.
Queen Cophetua. |

Olympia. Post 8vo, illust. boards, 2s.
Esther's Glove. Fcap. 8vo, 1s.

French Literature, History of. By HENRY VAN LAUN. Complete in 3 Vols., demy 8vo, cl. bds., 7s. 6d. each.

Frere.—Pandurang Hari; or, Memoirs of a Hindoo. With a Preface by Sir H. BARTLE FRERE, G.C.S.I., &c. Crown 8vo, cloth extra, 3s. 6d.; post 8vo, illustrated boards, 2s.

Friswell. — One of Two: A Novel. By HAIN FRISWELL. Post 8vo, illustrated boards, 2s.

Frost (Thomas), Works by: Crown 8vo, cloth extra, 3s. 6d. each.
Circus Life and Circus Celebrities.
The Lives of the Conjurers.
The Old Showmen and the Old London Fairs.

Fry's (Herbert) Royal Guide to the London Charities, 1886-7. Showing their Name, Date of Foundation, Objects, Income, Officials, &c. Published Annually. Cr. 8vo, cloth, 1s. 6d.

Gardening Books:

Post 8vo, 1s. each; cl. limp, 1s. 6d. each.

A Year's Work in Garden and Greenhouse: Practical Advice to Amateur Gardeners as to the Management of the Flower, Fruit, and Frame Garden. By GEORGE GLENNY.

Our Kitchen Garden: The Plants we Grow, and How we Cook Them. By TOM JERROLD.

Household Horticulture: A Gossip about Flowers. By TOM and JANE JERROLD. Illustrated.

The Garden that Paid the Rent. By TOM JERROLD.

My Garden Wild, and What I Grew there. By F. G. HEATH. Crown 8vo, cloth extra, 5s.; gilt edges, 6s.

Garrett.—The Capel Girls: A

Novel. By EDWARD GARRETT. Cr. 8vo, cl. ex., 3s. 6d.; post 8vo, illust. bds., 2s.

Gentleman's Magazine (The)

for 1887. One Shilling Monthly. In addition to the Articles upon subjects in Literature, Science, and Art, for which this Magazine has so high a reputation, "Science Notes," by W. MATTIEU WILLIAMS, F.R.A.S., and "Table Talk," by SYLVANUS URBAN, appear monthly.

** *Now ready, the Volume for* JULY *to* DECEMBER, 1886, *cloth extra, price* 8s. 6d; *Cases for binding,* 2s. *each.*

German Popular Stories. Col-

lected by the Brothers GRIMM, and Translated by EDGAR TAYLOR. Edited, with an Introduction, by JOHN RUSKIN. With 22 Illustrations on Steel by GEORGE CRUIKSHANK. Square 8vo, cloth extra, 6s. 6d.; gilt edges, 7s. 6d.

Gibbon (Charles), Novels by:

Crown 8vo, cloth extra, 3s. 6d. each post 8vo, illustrated boards, 2s. each.

Robin Gray.	Braes of Yarrow.
For Lack of Gold.	The Flower of the
What will the	Forest. [lem.
World Say?	A Heart's Prob-
In Honour Bound.	The Golden Shaft.
Queen of the	Of High Degree.
Meadow.	Fancy Free.

Post 8vo, illustrated boards, 2s. each.
For the King. | In Pastures Green.
In Love and War.
By Mead and Stream.
Heart's Delight. [Preparing.

Crown 8vo, cloth extra, 3s. 6d. each.
Loving a Dream. | A Hard Knot.

Gilbert (William), Novels by:

Post 8vo, illustrated boards, 2s. each.

Dr. Austin's Guests.
The Wizard of the Mountain.
James Duke, Costermonger.

Gilbert (W. S.), Original Plays

by: In Two Series, each complete in itself, price 2s. 6d. each.

The FIRST SERIES contains—The Wicked World—Pygmalion and Galatea—Charity—The Princess—The Palace of Truth—Trial by Jury.

The SECOND SERIES contains—Broken Hearts—Engaged—Sweethearts—Gretchen—Dan'l Druce—Tom Cobb—H.M.S. Pinafore—The Sorcerer—The Pirates of Penzance.

Eight Original Comic Operas. Written by W. S. GILBERT. Containing: The Sorcerer—H.M.S. "Pinafore" —The Pirates of Penzance—Iolanthe — Patience — Princess Ida — The Mikado—Trial by Jury. Demy 8vo, cloth limp, 2s. 6d.

Glenny.—A Year's Work in

Garden and Greenhouse: Practical Advice to Amateur Gardeners as to the Management of the Flower, Fruit, and Frame Garden. By GEORGE GLENNY. Post 8vo, 1s.; cloth, 1s. 6d.

Godwin.—Lives of the Necro-

mancers. By WILLIAM GODWIN. Post 8vo, cloth limp, 2s.

Golden Library, The:

Square 16mo (Tauchnitz size), cloth limp, 2s. per volume.

Bayard Taylor's Diversions of the Echo Club.

Bennett's (Dr. W. C.) Ballad History of England.

Bennett's (Dr.) Songs for Sailors.

Byron's Don Juan.

Godwin's (William) Lives of the Necromancers.

Holmes's Autocrat of the Breakfast Table. Introduction by SALA.

Holmes's Professor at the Breakfast Table.

Hood's Whims and Oddities. Complete. All the original Illustrations.

Irving's (Washington) Tales of a Traveller.

Jesse's (Edward) Scenes and Occupations of a Country Life.

Lamb's Essays of Elia. Both Series Complete in One Vol.

Leigh Hunt's Essays: A Tale for a Chimney Corner, and other Pieces. With Portrait, and Introduction by EDMUND OLLIER.

GOLDEN LIBRARY, *continued.*

Mallory's (Sir Thomas) Mort d'Arthur: The Stories of King Arthur and of the Knights of the Round Table. Edited by B. MONTGOMERIE RANKING.

Pascal's Provincial Letters. A New Translation, with Historical Introduction and Notes, by T. M'CRIE, D.D.

Pope's Poetical Works. Complete.

Rochefoucauld's Maxims and Moral Reflections. With Notes, and Introductory Essay by SAINTE-BEUVE.

St. Pierre's Paul and Virginia, and The Indian Cottage. Edited, with Life, by the Rev. E. CLARKE.

Golden Treasury of Thought, The: An ENCYCLOPÆDIA OF QUOTATIONS from Writers of all Times and Countries. Selected and Edited by THEODORE TAYLOR. Crown 8vo, cloth gilt and gilt edges, 7s. 6d.

Graham. — The Professor's Wife: A Story. By LEONARD GRAHAM. Fcap. 8vo, picture cover, 1s.

Greeks and Romans, The Life of the, Described from Antique Monuments. By ERNST GUHL and W. KONER. Translated from the Third German Edition, and Edited by Dr. F. HUEFFER. 545 Illusts. New and Cheaper Edit., demy 8vo, cl. ex., 7s. 6d.

Greenaway (Kate) and Bret Harte.—The Queen of the Pirate Isle. By BRET HARTE. With 25 original Drawings by KATE GREENAWAY, Reproduced in Colours by E. EVANS. Sm. 4to, bds., 5s.

Greenwood (James), Works by: Crown 8vo, cloth extra, 3s. 6d. each.

The Wilds of London.

Low-Life Deeps: An Account of the Strange Fish to be Found There.

Dick Temple: A Novel. Post 8vo, illustrated boards, 2s.

Guyot.—The Earth and Man; or, Physical Geography in its relation to the History of Mankind. By ARNOLD GUYOT. With Additions by Professors AGASSIZ, PIERCE, and GRAY; 12 Maps and Engravings on Steel, some Coloured, and copious Index. Crown 8vo, cloth extra, gilt, 4s. 6d.

Habberton— Brueton's Bayou. By JOHN HABBERTON, Author of "Helen's Babies." Post 8vo, illustrated boards, 2s.; cloth, 2s. 6d.

Hair (The): Its Treatment in Health, Weakness, and Disease. Translated from the German of Dr. J. PINCUS. Crown 8vo, 1s.; cloth, 1s. 6d.

Hake (Dr. Thomas Gordon),
Poems by:
Crown 8vo, cloth extra, 6s. each.
New Symbols.
Legends of the Morrow.
The Serpent Play.

Maiden Ecstasy. Small 4to, cloth extra, 8s.

Hall.—Sketches of Irish Character. By Mrs. S. C. HALL. With numerous Illustrations on Steel and Wood by MACLISE, GILBERT, HARVEY, and G. CRUIKSHANK. Medium 8vo, cloth extra, gilt, 7s. 6d.

Halliday.—Every-day Papers. By ANDREW HALLIDAY. Post 8vo, illustrated boards, 2s.

Handwriting, The Philosophy of. With over 100 Facsimiles and Explanatory Text. By DON FELIX DE SALAMANCA. Post 8vo, cl. limp, 2s. 6d.

Hanky-Panky: A Collection of Very Easy Tricks, Very Difficult Tricks, White Magic, Sleight of Hand, &c. Edited by W. H. CREMER. With 200 Illusts. Crown 8vo, cloth extra, 4s. 6d.

Hardy (Lady Duffus). — Paul Wynter's Sacrifice: A Story. By Lady DUFFUS HARDY. Post 8vo, illust. boards, 2s.

Hardy (Thomas).—Under the Greenwood Tree. By THOMAS HARDY, Author of "Far from the Madding Crowd." With numerous Illustrations. Crown 8vo, cloth extra, 3s. 6d.; post 8vo, illustrated boards, 2s.

Harwood.—The Tenth Earl. By J. BERWICK HARWOOD. Post 8vo, illustrated boards, 2s.

Hawels (Mrs. H. R.), Works by:
The Art of Dress. With numerous Illustrations. Small 8vo, illustrated cover, 1s.; cloth limp, 1s. 6d.
The Art of Beauty. New and Cheaper Edition. Crown 8vo, cloth extra, Coloured Frontispiece and Illusts. 6s.
The Art of Decoration. Square 8vo, handsomely bound and profusely Illustrated. 10s. 6d.
Chaucer for Children: A Golden Key. With Eight Coloured Pictures and numerous Woodcuts. New Edition, small 4to, cloth extra, 6s.
Chaucer for Schools. Demy 8vo, cloth limp, 2s. 6d.

Haweis (Rev. H. R.).—American Humorists. Including WASHINGTON IRVING, OLIVER WENDELL HOLMES, JAMES RUSSELL LOWELL, ARTEMUS WARD, MARK TWAIN, and BRET HARTE. By the Rev. H. R. HAWEIS, M.A. Crown 8vo, cloth extra, 6s.

Hawthorne (Julian), Novels by. Crown 8vo, cloth extra, 3s. 6d. each; post 8vo, illustrated boards, 2s. each.

Garth.	Sebastian Strome.
Ellice Quentin.	Dust.
Prince Saroni's Wife.	
Fortune's Fool.	Beatrix Randolph.

Crown 8vo, cloth extra, 3s. 6d. each.

Miss Cadogna.

Love—or a Name.

Mrs. Gainsborough's Diamonds. Fcap. 8vo, illustrated cover, 1s.

Hays.—Women of the Day: A Biographical Dictionary of Notable Contemporaries. By FRANCES HAYS. Crown 8vo, cloth extra, 5s.

Heath (F. G.). — My Garden Wild, and What I Grew There. By FRANCIS GEORGE HEATH, Author of "The Fern World," &c. Crown 8vo, cloth extra, 5s.; cl. gilt, gilt edges, 6s.

Helps (Sir Arthur), Works by: Post 8vo, cloth limp, 2s. 6d. each.

Animals and their Masters.

Social Pressure.

Ivan de Biron: A Novel. Crown 8vo, cloth extra, 3s. 6d.; post 8vo, illustrated boards, 2s.

Heptalogia (The); or, The Seven against Sense. A Cap with Seven Bells. Cr. 8vo, cloth extra, 6s.

Herrick's (Robert) Hesperides, Noble Numbers, and Complete Collected Poems. With Memorial-Introduction and Notes by the Rev. A. B. GROSART, D.D., Steel Portrait, Index of First Lines, and Glossarial Index, &c. Three Vols., crown 8vo, cloth, 18s.

Hesse - Wartegg (Chevalier Ernst von), Works by:

Tunis: The Land and the People. With 22 Illustrations. Crown 8vo, cloth extra, 3s. 6d.

The New South West: Travelling Sketches from Kansas, New Mexico, Arizona, and Northern Mexico. With 100 fine Illustrations and Three Maps. Demy 8vo, cloth extra, 14s. [*In preparation.*]

Herbert.—The Poems of Lord Herbert of Cherbury. Edited, with Introduction, by J. CHURTON COLLINS. Crown 8vo, bound in parchment, 8s.

Hindley (Charles), Works by: Crown 8vo, cloth extra, 3s. 6d. each.

Tavern Anecdotes and Sayings: Including the Origin of Signs, and Reminiscences connected with Taverns, Coffee Houses, Clubs, &c. With Illustrations.

The Life and Adventures of a Cheap Jack. By One of the Fraternity. Edited by CHARLES HINDLEY.

Hoey.—The Lover's Creed. By Mrs. CASHEL HOEY. With Frontispiece by P. MACNAB. New and Cheaper Edit. Crown 8vo, cloth extra, 3s. 6d.; post 8vo, illustrated boards, 2s.

Holmes (O. Wendell), Works by:

The Autocrat of the Breakfast-Table. Illustrated by J. GORDON THOMSON. Post 8vo, cloth limp, 2s. 6d.—Another Edition in smaller type, with an Introduction by G. A. SALA. Post 8vo, cloth limp, 2s.

The Professor at the Breakfast-Table; with the Story of Iris. Post 8vo, cloth limp, 2s.

Holmes. — The Science of Voice Production and Voice Preservation: A Popular Manual for the Use of Speakers and Singers. By GORDON HOLMES, M.D. With Illustrations. Crown 8vo, 1s.; cloth, 1s. 6d.

Hood (Thomas):

Hood's Choice Works, in Prose and Verse. Including the Cream of the COMIC ANNUALS. With Life of the Author, Portrait, and 200 Illustrations. Crown 8vo, cloth extra, 7s. 6d.

Hood's Whims and Oddities. Complete. With all the original Illustrations. Post 8vo, cloth limp, 2s.

Hood (Tom), Works by:

From Nowhere to the North Pole: A Noah's Arkæological Narrative. With 25 Illustrations by W. BRUNTON and E. C. BARNES. Square crown 8vo, cloth extra, gilt edges, 6s.

A Golden Heart: A Novel. Post 8vo, illustrated boards, 2s.

Hook's (Theodore) Choice Humorous Works, including his Ludicrous Adventures, Bons Mots, Puns and Hoaxes. With a New Life of the Author, Portraits, Facsimiles, and Illusts. Cr. 8vo, cl. extra, gilt, 7s. 6d.

Hooper.—The House of Raby: A Novel. By Mrs. GEORGE HOOPER. Post 8vo, illustrated boards, 2s.

Hopkins—"'Twixt Love and Duty:" A Novel. By TIGHE HOPKINS. Crown 8vo, cloth extra, 6s.

Horne.—Orion: An Epic Poem, in Three Books. By RICHARD HENGIST HORNE. With Photographic Portrait from a Medallion by SUMMERS. Tenth Edition, crown 8vo, cloth extra, 7s.

Howell.—Conflicts of Capital and Labour, Historically and Economically considered: Being a History and Review of the Trade Unions of Great Britain. By GEO. HOWELL M.P. Crown 8vo, cloth extra, 7s. 6d.

Hunt.—Essays by Leigh Hunt. A Tale for a Chimney Corner, and other Pieces. With Portrait and Introduction by EDMUND OLLIER. Post 8vo, cloth limp, 2s.

Hunt (Mrs. Alfred), Novels by:
Crown 8vo, cloth extra, 3s. 6d. each post 8vo, illustrated boards, 2s. each.
Thornicroft's Model.
The Leaden Casket.
Self-Condemned

That other Person. Three Vols., crown 8vo.

Indoor Paupers. By ONE OF THEM. Crown 8vo, 1s.; cloth, 1s. 6d.

Ingelow.—Fated to be Free: A Novel. By JEAN INGELOW. Crown 8vo, cloth extra, 3s. 6d.; post 8vo, illustrated boards, 2s.

Irish Wit and Humour, Songs of. Collected and Edited by A. PERCEVAL GRAVES. Post 8vo, cloth limp, 2s. 6d.

Irving—Tales of a Traveller. By WASHINGTON IRVING. Post 8vo, cloth limp, 2s.

Jay (Harriett), Novels by:
The Dark Colleen. Post 8vo, illustrated boards, 2s.
The Queen of Connaught. Crown 8vo, cloth extra, 3s. 6d.; post 8vo, illustrated boards, 2s.

Janvier.—Practical Keramics for Students. By CATHERINE A. JANVIER. Crown 8vo, cloth extra, 6s.

Jefferies (Richard), Works by:
Crown 8vo, cloth extra, 6s. each.
Nature near London.
The Life of the Fields.
The Open Air.

Jennings (H. J.), Works by:
Curiosities of Criticism. Post 8vo cloth limp, 2s. 6d.
Lord Tennyson: A Biographical Sketch. With a Photograph-Portrait. Crown 8vo, cloth extra, 6s.

Jerrold (Tom), Works by:
Post 8vo, 1s. each; cloth, 1s. 6d. each.
The Garden that Paid the Rent.
Household Horticulture: A Gossip about Flowers. Illustrated.
Our Kitchen Garden: The Plants we Grow, and How we Cook Them.

Jesse.—Scenes and Occupa- tions of a Country Life. By EDWARD JESSE. Post 8vo, cloth limp, 2s.

Jeux d'Esprit. Collected and Edited by HENRY S. LEIGH. Post 8vo, cloth limp, 2s. 6d.

Jones (Wm., F.S.A.), Works by:
Crown 8vo, cloth extra, 7s. 6d. each.
Finger-Ring Lore: Historical, Legendary, and Anecdotal. With over Two Hundred Illustrations.
Credulities, Past and Present; including the Sea and Seamen, Miners, Talismans, Word and Letter Divination, Exorcising and Blessing of Animals, Birds, Eggs, Luck, &c. With an Etched Frontispiece.
Crowns and Coronations: A History of Regalia in all Times and Countries. With One Hundred Illustrations.

Jonson's (Ben) Works. With Notes Critical and Explanatory, and a Biographical Memoir by WILLIAM GIFFORD. Edited by Colonel CUNNINGHAM. Three Vols., crown 8vo, cloth extra, 18s.; or separately, 6s. each.

Josephus, The Complete Works of. Translated by WHISTON. Containing both "The Antiquities of the Jews" and "The Wars of the Jews." Two Vols., 8vo, with 52 Illustrations and Maps, cloth extra, gilt, 14s.

Kempt.—Pencil and Palette: Chapters on Art and Artists. By ROBERT KEMPT. Post 8vo, cloth limp, 2s. 6d.

Kershaw.—Colonial Facts and Fictions: Humorous Sketches. By MARK KERSHAW. Post 8vo, illustrated boards, 2s. ; cloth, 2s. 6d.

King (R. Ashe), Novels by:
Crown 8vo, cloth extra, 3s. 6d. each ; post 8vo, illustrated boards, 2s. each.
A Drawn Game.
"The Wearing of the Green."

Kingsley (Henry), Novels by :
Oakshott Castle. Post 8vo, illustrated boards, 2s.
Number Seventeen. Crown 8vo, cloth extra, 3s. 6d.

Knight.—The Patient's Vade Mecum : How to get most Benefit from Medical Advice. By WILLIAM KNIGHT, M.R.C.S., and EDWARD KNIGHT, L.R.C.P. Crown 8vo, 1s. ; cloth, 1s. 6d.

Lamb (Charles):
Lamb's Complete Works, in Prose and Verse, reprinted from the Original Editions, with many Pieces hitherto unpublished. Edited, with Notes and Introduction, by R. H. SHEPHERD. With Two Portraits and Facsimile of Page of the "Essay on Roast Pig." Crown 8vo, cloth extra, 7s. 6d.
The Essays of Elia. Complete Edition. Post 8vo, cloth extra, 2s.
Poetry for Children, and Prince Dorus. By CHARLES LAMB. Carefully reprinted from unique copies. Small 8vo, cloth extra, 5s.
Little Essays : Sketches and Characters. By CHARLES LAMB. Selected from his Letters by PERCY FITZGERALD. Post 8vo, cloth limp, 2s. 6d.

Lares and Penates; or, The Background of Life. By FLORENCE CADDY. Crown 8vo, cloth extra, 6s.

Larwood (Jacob), Works by:
The Story of the London Parks. With Illustrations. Crown 8vo, cloth extra, 3s. 6d.

Post 8vo, cloth limp, 2s. 6d. each.
Forensic Anecdotes.
Theatrical Anecdotes.

Lane's Arabian Nights, &c.:
The Thousand and One Nights: commonly called, in England, "THE ARABIAN NIGHTS' ENTERTAINMENTS." A New Translation from the Arabic, with copious Notes, by EDWARD WILLIAM LANE. Illustrated by many hundred Engravings on Wood, from Original Designs by WM. HARVEY. A New Edition, from a Copy annotated by the Translator, edited by his Nephew, EDWARD STANLEY POOLE. With a Preface by STANLEY LANE-POOLE. Three Vols., demy 8vo, cloth extra, 7s. 6d. each.
Arabian Society in the Middle Age: Studies from "The Thousand and One Nights." By EDWARD WILLIAM LANE, Author of "The Modern Egyptians," &c. Edited by STANLEY LANE-POOLE. Cr. 8vo, cloth extra, 6s.

Life in London ; or, The History of Jerry Hawthorn and Corinthian Tom. With the whole of CRUIKSHANK'S Illustrations, in Colours, after the Originals. Crown 8vo, cloth extra, 7s. 6d.

Linton (E. Lynn), Works by:
Post 8vo, cloth limp, 2s. 6d. each.
Witch Stories.
The True Story of Joshua Davidson.
Ourselves: Essays on Women.

Crown 8vo, cloth extra, 3s. 6d. each ; post 8vo, illustrated boards, 2s. each.
Patricia Kemball.
The Atonement of Leam Dundas.
The World Well Lost.
Under which Lord ?
With a Silken Thread.
The Rebel of the Family.
"My Love!" | Ione.

Longfellow:
Crown 8vo, cloth extra, 7s. 6d. each.
Longfellow's Complete Prose Works. Including "Outre Mer," "Hyperion," "Kavanagh," "The Poets and Poetry of Europe," and "Driftwood." With Portrait and Illustrations by VALENTINE BROMLEY.
Longfellow's Poetical Works. Carefully Reprinted from the Original Editions. With numerous fine Illustrations on Steel and Wood.

Long Life, Aids to: A Medical, Dietetic, and General Guide in Health and Disease. By N. E. DAVIES, L.R.C.P. Crown 8vo, 2s. ; cloth limp, 2s. 6d.

Lucy.—Gideon Fleyce: A Novel.
By HENRY W. LUCY. Crown 8vo,
cl. ex., 3s. 6d.; post 8vo, illust. bds., 2s.

Lusiad (The) of Camoens.
Translated into English Spenserian
Verse by ROBERT FFRENCH DUFF.
Demy 8vo, with Fourteen full-page
Plates, cloth boards, 18s.

Macalpine. — Teresa Itasca,
and other Stories. By AVERY MAC-
ALPINE. Crown 8vo, bound in canvas,
2s. 6d.

McCarthy (Justin, M.P.),Works
by :

A History of Our Own Times, from
the Accession of Queen Victoria to
the General Election of 1880. Four
Vols. demy 8vo, cloth extra, 12s.
each.—Also a POPULAR EDITION, in
Four Vols. cr. 8vo, cl. extra, 6s. each.
—A JUBILEE EDITION, with an Appendix of Events to the end of 1886,
complete in Two Vols., square 8vo,
cloth extra, 7s. 6d. each, is now in
the press, and will be ready shortly.

A Short History of Our Own Times.
One Vol., crown 8vo, cloth extra, 6s.

History of the Four Georges. Four
Vols. demy 8vo, cloth extra, 12s.
each. [Vol. I. *now ready.*

Crown 8vo, cloth extra, 3s. 6d. each;
post 8vo, illustrated boards, 2s. each.

Dear Lady Disdain.

The Waterdale Neighbours.

My Enemy's Daughter.

A Fair Saxon.

Miss Misanthrope.

Donna Quixote.

The Comet of a Season.

Maid of Athens.

Linley Rochford. Post 8vo, illustrated boards, 2s.

Camiola : A Girl with a Fortune.
New and Cheaper Edition. Crown
8vo, cloth extra, 3s. 6d.

"The Right Honourable:" A Romance of Society and Politics. By
JUSTIN MCCARTHY, M.P., and Mrs.
CAMPBELL · PRAED. Three Vols.,
crown 8vo.

McCarthy (Justin H., M.P.),
Works by:

An Outline of the History of Ireland,
from the Earliest Times to the Present Day. Cr. 8vo, 1s. ; cloth, 1s. 6d.

Ireland since the Union : Sketches
of Irish History from 1798 to 1886.
Crown 8vo, cloth extra, 6s. [*Shortly.*

MCCARTHY (JUSTIN H.), *continued*—

The Case for Home Rule. Crown
8vo, cloth extra, 5s. [*Shortly.*

England under Gladstone, 1880-85.
Second Edition, revised and brought
down to the Fall of the Gladstone
Administration. Crown 8vo, cloth
extra, 6s.

Doom ! An Atlantic Episode. Crown
8vo, 1s. ; cloth, 1s. 6d.

Our Sensation Novel. Edited by
JUSTIN H. MCCARTHY. Crown 8vo,
1s. ; cloth, 1s. 6d.

Hafiz in London. Choicely printed.
Small 8vo, gold cloth, 3s. 6d.

MacDonald (George, LL.D.),
Works by :

Works of Fancy and Imagination.
Pocket Edition, Ten Volumes, in
handsome cloth case, 21s. Vol. 1.
WITHIN AND WITHOUT. THE HID-
DEN LIFE.—Vol. 2. THE DISCIPLE.
THE GOSPEL WOMEN. A BOOK OF
SONNETS. ORGAN SONGS.—Vol. 3.
VIOLIN SONGS. SONGS OF THE DAYS
AND NIGHTS. A BOOK OF DREAMS.
ROADSIDE POEMS. POEMS FOR
CHILDREN. Vol. 4. PARABLES.
BALLADS. SCOTCH SONGS.—Vols.
5 and 6. PHANTASTES: A Faerie
Romance.—Vol. 7. THE PORTENT.—
Vol. 8. THE LIGHT PRINCESS. THE
GIANT'S HEART. SHADOWS. — Vol.
9. CROSS PURPOSES. THE GOLDEN
KEY. THE CARASOYN. LITTLE
DAYLIGHT.—Vol. 10. THE CRUEL
PAINTER. THE WOW o' RIVVEN.
THE CASTLE. THE BROKEN SWORDS.
THE GRAY WOLF. UNCLE CORNE-
LIUS.

*The Volumes are also sold separately
in Grolier-pattern cloth, 2s. 6d. each.*

Macdonell.—Quaker Cousins:
A Novel. By AGNES MACDONELL.
Crown 8vo, cloth extra, 3s. 6d.; post
8vo, illustrated boards, 2s.

Macgregor. — Pastimes and
Players. Notes on Popular Games.
By ROBERT MACGREGOR. Post 8vo,
cloth limp, 2s. 6d.

Maclise Portrait-Gallery (The)
of Illustrious Literary Characters;
with Memoirs—Biographical, Critical,
Bibliographical, and Anecdotal—illustrative of the Literature of the former
half of the Present Century. By
WILLIAM BATES, B.A. With 85 Portraits printed on an India Tint. Crown
8vo, cloth extra, 7s. 6d.

Mackay.—Interludes and Undertones: or, Music at Twilight. By CHARLES MACKAY, LL.D. Crown 8vo, cloth extra, 6s.

Macquoid (Mrs.), Works by:

Square 8vo, cloth extra, 10s. 6d. eac

In the Ardennes. With 50 fine Illustrations by THOMAS R. MACQUOID.

Pictures and Legends from Normandy and Brittany. With numerous Illustrations by THOMAS R. MACQUOID.

About Yorkshire. With 67 Illustrations by T. R. MACQUOID.

Crown 8vo, cloth extra, 7s. 6d. each.

Through Normandy. With 90 Illustrations by T. R. MACQUOID.

Through Brittany. With numerous Illustrations by T. R. MACQUOID.

Post 8vo, illustrated boards, 2s. each.

The Evil Eye, and other Stories.

Lost Rose.

Magician's Own Book (The): Performances with Cups and Balls, Eggs, Hats, Handkerchiefs, &c. All from actual Experience. Edited by W. H. CREMER. With 200 Illustrations. Crown 8vo, cloth extra, 4s. 6d.

Magic Lantern (The), and its Management: including full Practical Directions for producing the Limelight, making Oxygen Gas, and preparing Lantern Slides. By T. C. HEPWORTH. With 10 Illustrations. Crown 8vo, 1s. ; cloth, 1s. 6d.

Magna Charta. An exact Facsimile of the Original in the British Museum, printed on fine plate paper, 3 feet by 2 feet, with Arms and Seals emblazoned in Gold and Colours. 5s.

Mallock (W. H.), Works by:

The New Republic; or, Culture, Faith and Philosophy in an English Country House. Post 8vo, cloth limp, 2s. 6d. ; Cheap Edition, illustrated boards, 2s.

The New Paul and Virginia ; or, Positivism on an Island. Post 8vo, cloth limp, 2s. 6d.

Poems. Small 4to, in parchment, 8s.

Is Life worth Living? Crown 8vo, cloth extra, 6s.

Mallory's (Sir Thomas) Mort d'Arthur: The Stories of King Arthur and of the Knights of the Round Table. Edited by B. MONTGOMERIE RANKING. Post 8vo, cloth limp, 2s.

Marlowe's Works. Including his Translations. Edited, with Notes and Introductions, by Col. CUNNINGHAM. Crown 8vo, cloth extra, 6s.

Marryat (Florence), Novels by: Crown 8vo, cloth extra, 3s. 6d. each ; post 8vo, illustrated boards, 2s. each.

Open! Sesame!

Written in Fire

Post 8vo, illustrated boards, 2s. each.

A Harvest of Wild Oats.

A Little Stepson.

Fighting the Air.

Masterman.—Half a Dozen Daughters: A Novel. By J. MASTERMAN. Post 8vo, illustrated boards, 2s.

Mark Twain, Works by:

The Choice Works of Mark Twain. Revised and Corrected throughout by the Author. With Life, Portrait, and numerous Illustrations. Crown 8vo, cloth extra, 7s. 6d.

The Innocents Abroad ; or, The New Pilgrim's Progress : Being some Account of the Steamship "Quaker City's" Pleasure Excursion to Europe and the Holy Land. With 234 Illustrations. Crown 8vo, cloth extra, 7s. 6d.—Cheap Edition (under the title of "MARK TWAIN'S PLEASURE TRIP"), post 8vo, illust. boards, 2s.

Roughing It, and The Innocents at Home. With 200 Illustrations by F. A. FRASER. Crown 8vo, cloth extra, 7s. 6d.

The Gilded Age. By MARK TWAIN and CHARLES DUDLEY WARNER. With 212 Illustrations by T. COPPIN. Crown 8vo, cloth extra, 7s. 6d.

The Adventures of Tom Sawyer. With 111 Illustrations. Crown 8vo, cloth extra, 7s. 6d.—Cheap Edition, post 8vo, illustrated boards, 2s.

The Prince and the Pauper. With nearly 200 illustrations. Crown 8vo, cloth extra, 7s. 6d.

A Tramp Abroad. With 314 Illustrations. Crown 8vo, cloth extra, 7s. 6d. —Cheap Edition, post 8vo, illustrated boards, 2s.

The Stolen White Elephant, &c. Crown 8vo, cloth extra, 6s. ; post 8vo, illustrated boards, 2s.

MARK TWAIN'S WORKS, *continued—*

Life on the Mississippi. With about 300 Original Illustrations. Crown 8vo, cloth extra, 7s. 6d.

The Adventures of Huckleberry Finn. With 174 Illustrations by E. W. KEMBLE. Crown 8vo, cloth extra, 7s. 6d.—Cheap Edition, post 8vo, illustrated boards, 2s.

Massinger's Plays. From the Text of WILLIAM GIFFORD. Edited by Col. CUNNINGHAM. Crown 8vo, cloth extra, 6s.

Matthews.—A Secret of the Sea, &c. By BRANDER MATTHEWS. Post 8vo, illustrated boards, 2s; cloth, 2s. 6d.

Mayfair Library, The:
Post 8vo, cloth limp, 2s. 6d. per Volume

A Journey Round My Room. By XAVIER DE MAISTRE. Translated by HENRY ATTWELL.

Latter Day Lyrics. Edited by W. DAVENPORT ADAMS.

Quips and Quiddities. Selected by W. DAVENPORT ADAMS.

The Agony Column of "The Times," from 1800 to 1870. Edited, with an Introduction, by ALICE CLAY.

Melancholy Anatomised: A Popular Abridgment of "Burton's Anatomy of Melancholy."

Gastronomy as a Fine Art. By BRILLAT-SAVARIN.

The Speeches of Charles Dickens

Literary Frivolities, Fancies, Follies, and Frolics. By W. T. DOBSON.

Poetical Ingenuities and Eccentricities. Selected and Edited by W. T. DOBSON.

The Cupboard Papers. By FIN-BEC.

Original Plays by W. S. GILBERT. FIRST SERIES. Containing: The Wicked World — Pygmalion and Galatea — Charity — The Princess — The Palace of Truth—Trial by Jury.

Original Plays by W. S. GILBERT. SECOND SERIES. Containing: Broken Hearts — Engaged — Sweethearts — Gretchen—Dan'l Druce—Tom Cobb —H.M.S. Pinafore — The Sorcerer —The Pirates of Penzance.

Songs of Irish Wit and Humour. Collected and Edited by A. PERCEVAL GRAVES.

Animals and their Masters. By Sir ARTHUR HELPS.

Social Pressure. By Sir A. HELPS.

MAYFAIR LIBRARY, *continued—*

Curiosities of Criticism. By HENRY J. JENNINGS.

The Autocrat of the Breakfast-Table. By OLIVER WENDELL HOLMES. Illustrated by J. GORDON THOMSON.

Pencil and Palette. By ROBERT KEMPT.

Little Essays: Sketches and Characters. By CHAS. LAMB. Selected from his Letters by PERCY FITZGERALD.

Forensic Anecdotes; or, Humour and Curiosities of the Law and Men of Law. By JACOB LARWOOD.

Theatrical Anecdotes. By JACOB LARWOOD.

Jeux d'Esprit. Edited by HENRY S. LEIGH.

True History of Joshua Davidson. By E. LYNN LINTON.

Witch Stories. By E. LYNN LINTON.

Ourselves: Essays on Women. By E. LYNN LINTON.

Pastimes and Players. By ROBERT MACGREGOR.

The New Paul and Virginia. By W. H. MALLOCK.

New Republic. By W. H. MALLOCK.

Puck on Pegasus. By H. CHOLMONDELEY-PENNELL.

Pegasus Re-Saddled. By H. CHOLMONDELEY-PENNELL. Illustrated by GEORGE DU MAURIER.

Muses of Mayfair. Edited by H. CHOLMONDELEY-PENNELL.

Thoreau: His Life and Aims. By H. A. PAGE.

Puniana. By the Hon. HUGH ROWLEY.

More Puniana. By the Hon. HUGH ROWLEY.

The Philosophy of Handwriting. By DON FELIX DE SALAMANCA.

By Stream and Sea. By WILLIAM SENIOR.

Old Stories Re-told. By WALTER THORNBURY.

Leaves from a Naturalist's Note-Book. By Dr. ANDREW WILSON.

Mayhew.—London Characters and the Humorous Side of London Life. By HENRY MAYHEW. With numerous Illustrations. Crown 8vo, cloth extra, 3s. 6d.

Medicine, Family.—One Thousand Medical Maxims and Surgical Hints, for Infancy, Adult Life, Middle Age, and Old Age. By N. E. DAVIES, L.R.C.P. Lond. Cr. 8vo, 1s.; cl., 1s. 6d.

Merry Circle (The): A Book of
New Intellectual Games and Amusements. By CLARA BELLEW. With
numerous Illustrations. Crown 8vo,
cloth extra, 4s. 6d.

Mexican Mustang (On a),
through Texas, from the Gulf to the
Rio Grande. A New Book of American Humour. By ALEX. E. SWEET and
J. ARMOY KNOX, Editors of "Texas
Siftings." With 265 Illusts. Cr. 8vo,
cloth extra, 7s. 6d.

Middlemass (Jean), Novels by:
Post 8vo, illustrated boards, 2s. each.
    Touch and Go.
    Mr. Dorillion.

Miller. — Physiology for the
Young; or, The House of Life: Human Physiology, with its application
to the Preservation of Health. For
Classes and Popular Reading. With
numerous Illusts. By Mrs. F. FENWICK
MILLER. Small 8vo, cloth limp, 2s. 6d

Milton (J. L.), Works by:
Sm. 8vo, 1s. each; cloth ex., 1s. 6d. each.
    The Hygiene of the Skin. A Concise
    Set of Rules for the Management of
    the Skin; with Directions for Diet,
    Wines, Soaps, Baths, &c.
    The Bath in Diseases of the Skin.
    The Laws of Life, and their Relation
    to Diseases of the Skin.

Molesworth (Mrs.).—Hather-
court Rectory. By Mrs. MOLES-
WORTH, Author of "The Cuckoo
Clock," &c. Crown 8vo, cloth extra,
4s. 6d.

Murray (D. Christie), Novels
by. Crown 8vo, cloth extra, 3s. 6d. each;
post 8vo, illustrated boards, 2s. each.
    A Life's Atonement.
    A Model Father.
    Joseph's Coat.
    Coals of Fire.
    By the Gate of the Sea.
    Val Strange.
    Hearts.
    The Way of the World.
    A Bit of Human Nature.

Crown 8vo, cloth extra, 3s. 6d. each.
    First Person Singular: A Novel.
    With a Frontispiece by ARTHUR
    HOPKINS.
    Cynic Fortune: A Tale of a Man with
    a Conscience. With a Frontispiece
    by R. CATON WOODVILLE.

North Italian Folk. By Mrs.
COMYNS CARR. Illustrated by RAN-
DOLPH CALDECOTT. Square 8vo, cloth
extra, 7s. 6d.

Number Nip (Stories about),
the Spirit of the Giant Mountains.
Retold for Children by WALTER
GRAHAME. With Illustrations by J.
MOYR SMITH. Post 8vo, cl. extra, 5s.

Nursery Hints: A Mother's
Guide in Health and Disease. By N.
E. DAVIES, L.R.C.P. Crown 8vo, 1s
cloth, 1s. 6d.

O'Connor.—Lord Beaconsfield
A Biography. By T. P. O'CONNOR, M.P.
Sixth Edition, with a New Preface,
bringing the work down to the Death
of Lord Beaconsfield. Crown 8vo,
cloth extra, 7s. 6d.

O'Hanlon. — The Unforeseen:
A Novel. By ALICE O'HANLON. New
and Cheaper Edition. Post 8vo, illustrated boards, 2s.

Oliphant (Mrs.) Novels by:
    Whiteladies. With Illustrations by
    ARTHUR HOPKINS and H. WOODS.
    Crown 8vo, cloth extra, 3s. 6d.;
    post 8vo, illustrated boards, 2s.

Crown 8vo, cloth extra, 4s. 6d. each.
    The Primrose Path.
    The Greatest Heiress in England.

O'Reilly.—Phœbe's Fortunes:
A Novel. With Illustrations by HENRY
TUCK. Post 8vo, illustrated boards, 2s.

O'Shaughnessy (Arth.), Works
by:
    Songs of a Worker. Fcap. 8vo, cloth
    extra, 7s. 6d.
    Music and Moonlight. Fcap. 8vo,
    cloth extra, 7s. 6d.
    Lays of France. Crown 8vo, cloth
    extra, 10s. 6d.

Ouida, Novels by. Crown 8vo,
cloth extra, 5s. each; post 8vo, illustrated boards, 2s. each.

Held in Bondage.	Signa.
Strathmore.	In a Winter City.
Chandos.	Ariadne
Under Two Flags.	Friendship.
Cecil Castle-	Moths.
maine's Gage.	Pipistrello.
Idalia.	A Village Com-
Tricotrin.	mune.
Puck.	Bimbi.
Folle Farine.	In Maremma
TwoLittleWooden	Wanda.
Shoes.	Frescoes.
A Dog of Flanders.	Princess Naprax-
Pascarel.	Ine.

OUIDA, NOVELS BY, *continued*—

Othmar: A Novel. Cheaper Edition. Crown 8vo, cloth extra, 5s.

Wisdom, Wit, and Pathos, selected from the Works of OUIDA by F. SYDNEY MORRIS. Small crown 8vo, cloth extra, 5s.

Page (H. A.), Works by :

Thoreau: His Life and Aims: A Study. With a Portrait. Post 8vo, cloth limp, 2s. 6d.

Lights on the Way: Some Tales within a Tale. By the late J. H. ALEXANDER, B.A. Edited by H. A. PAGE. Crown 8vo, cloth extra, 6s.

Animal Anecdotes. Arranged on a New Principle. Crown 8vo, cloth extra, 5s.

Parliamentary Elections and

Electioneering in the Old Days (A History of). Showing the State of Political Parties and Party Warfare at the Hustings and in the House of Commons from the Stuarts to Queen Victoria. Illustrated from the original Political Squibs, Lampoons, Pictorial Satires, and Popular Caricatures of the Time. By JOSEPH GREGO, Author of "Rowlandson and his Works," "The Life of Gillray," &c. Demy 8vo, cloth extra, with a Frontispiece coloured by hand, and nearly 100 Illustrations, 16s.

Pascal's Provincial Letters. A

New Translation, with Historical Introduction and Notes, by T. M'CRIE, D.D. Post 8vo, cloth limp, 2s.

Patient's (The) Vade Mecum :

How to get most Benefit from Medical Advice. By WILLIAM KNIGHT, M.R.C.S., and EDWARD KNIGHT, L.R.C.P. Crown 8vo, 1s.; cloth, 1s. 6d.

Paul Ferroll :

Post 8vo, illustrated boards, 2s. each.
Paul Ferroll: A Novel.
Why Paul Ferroll Killed his Wife.

Paul.—Gentle and Simple. By

MARGARET AGNES PAUL. With a Frontispiece by HELEN PATERSON. Cr. 8vo, cloth extra, 3s. 6d.; post 8vo, illustrated boards, 2s.

Payn (James), Novels by.

Crown 8vo, cloth extra, 3s. 6d. each
post 8vo, illustrated boards, 2s. each.
Lost Sir Massingberd.
The Best of Husbands.
Walter's Word. | Halves.
What He Cost Her.
Less Black than we're Painted.
By Proxy. | High Spirits.
Under One Roof.

PAYN (JAMES), NOVELS BY, *continued*—

A Confidential Agent.
Some Private Views.
A Grape from a Thorn.
For Cash Only. | From Exile.
The Canon's Ward.

Post 8vo, illustrated boards, 2s. each.
Kit: A Memory. | Carlyon's Year.
A Perfect Treasure.
Bentinck's Tutor. Murphy's Master.
Fallen Fortunes.
A County Family. | At Her Mercy.
A Woman's Vengeance.
Cecil's Tryst.
The Clyffards of Clyffe.
The Family Scapegrace.
The Foster Brothers.
Found Dead.
Gwendoline's Harvest.
Humorous Stories.
Like Father, Like Son.
A Marine Residence.
Married Beneath Him.
Mirk Abbey.
Not Wooed, but Won.
Two Hundred Pounds Reward.

In Peril and Privation: Stories of Marine Adventure Re-told. A Book for Boys. With numerous Illustrations. Crown 8vo, cloth gilt, 6s.

The Talk of the Town: A Novel. With Twelve Illustrations by HARRY FURNISS. Cr. 8vo, cl. extra, 3s. 6d.

Holiday Tasks: Being Essays written during Vacation Time. Crown 8vo, cloth extra, 6s.

Pears.—The Present Depres-

sion in Trade: Its Causes and Remedies. Being the "Pears" Prize Essays (of One Hundred Guineas). By EDWIN GOADBY and WILLIAM WATT. With an Introductory Paper by Prof. LEONE LEVI, F.S.A., F.S.S. Demy 8vo, 1s.

Pennell (H. Cholmondeley),

Works by:
Post 8vo, cloth limp, 2s. 6d. each.
Puck on Pegasus. With Illustrations.
Pegasus Re-Saddled. With Ten full-page Illusts. by G. DU MAURIER.
The Muses of Mayfair. Vers de Société, Selected and Edited by H. C. PENNELL.

Phelps (E. Stuart), Works by:

Post 8vo, 1s. each; cloth limp, 1s. 6d. each.
Beyond the Gates. By the Author of "The Gates Ajar."
An Old Maid's Paradise.
Burglars in Paradise.

Pirkis (Mrs. C. L.), Novels by:

Trooping with Crows. Fcap. 8vo, picture cover, 1s.
Lady Lovelace. Post 8vo, illustrated boards, 2s. [*Preparing.*

Planché (J. R.), Works by:
The Pursuivant of Arms; or, Heraldry Founded upon Facts. With Coloured Frontispiece and 200 Illustrations. Cr. 8vo, cloth extra, 7s. 6d.
Songs and Poems, from 1819 to 1879. Edited, with an Introduction, by his Daughter, Mrs. MACKARNESS. Crown 8vo, cloth extra, 6s

Plutarch's Lives of Illustrious
Men. Translated from the Greek, with Notes Critical and Historical, and a Life of Plutarch, by JOHN and WILLIAM LANGHORNE. Two Vols., 8vo, cloth extra, with Portraits, 10s. 6d.

Poe (Edgar Allan):—
The Choice Works, in Prose and Poetry, of EDGAR ALLAN POE. With an Introductory Essay by CHARLES BAUDELAIRE, Portrait and Facsimiles. Crown 8vo, cl. extra, 7s 6d.
The Mystery of Marie Roget, and other Stories. Post 8vo, illust.bds. 2s.

Pope's Poetical Works. Complete in One Vol. Post 8vo, cl. limp. 2s

Praed (Mrs. Campbell-).—"The Right Honourable:" A Romance of Society and Politics. By Mrs. CAMPBELL-PRAED and JUSTIN McCARTHY, M.P. Three Vols., crown 8vo.

Price (E. C.), Novels by:
Crown 8vo, cloth extra, 3s. 6d. each; post 8vo, illustrated boards, 2s. each.
Valentina. | The Foreigners.
Mrs. Lancaster's Rival.
Gerald. Post 8vo, illust. boards, 2s.

Proctor (Richd. A.), Works by:
Flowers of the Sky. With 55 Illusts. Small crown 8vo, cloth extra, 4s. 6d.
Easy Star Lessons. With Star Maps for Every Night in the Year, Drawings of the Constellations, &c. Crown 8vo, cloth extra, 6s.
Familiar Science Studies. Crown 8vo, cloth extra, 7s. 6d.
Saturn and Its System. New and Revised Edition, with 13 Steel Plates. Demy 8vo, cloth extra, 10s. 6d.
The Great Pyramid: Observatory, Tomb, and Temple. With Illustrations. Crown 8vo, cloth extra, 6s.
Mysteries of Time and Space. With Illusts. Cr. 8vo, cloth extra, 7s. 6d.
The Universe of Suns, and other Science Gleanings. With numerous Illusts. Cr. 8vo, cloth extra, 7s. 6d.
Wages and Wants of Science Workers. Crown 8vo, 1s 6d.

Pyrotechnist's Treasury (The);
or, Complete Art of Making Fireworks. By THOMAS KENTISH. A New Edition, revised and enlarged, with 267 Illusts. Cr. 8vo, cl. extra, 5s. [*Shortly.*

Rabelais' Works. Faithfully Translated from the French, with variorum Notes, and numerous characteristic Illustrations by GUSTAVE DORÉ. Crown 8vo, cloth extra, 7s. 6d.

Rambosson.—Popular Astronomy. By J. RAMBOSSON, Laureate of the Institute of France. Translated by C. B. PITMAN. Crown 8vo, cloth gilt, numerous Illusts., and a beautifully executed Chart of Spectra, 7s. 6d.

Reade (Charles), Novels by:
Cr. 8vo, cloth extra, illustrated, 3s. 6d. each; post 8vo, illust. bds., 2s. each.
Peg Woffington. Illustrated by S. L. FILDES, A.R.A.
Christie Johnstone. Illustrated by WILLIAM SMALL.
It is Never Too Late to Mend. Illustrated by G. J. PINWELL.
The Course of True Love Never did run Smooth. Illustrated by HELEN PATERSON.
The Autobiography of a Thief; Jack of all Trades; and James Lambert. Illustrated by MATT STRETCH.
Love me Little, Love me Long. Illustrated by M. ELLEN EDWARDS.
The Double Marriage. Illust. by Sir JOHN GILBERT, R.A., and C. KEENE.
The Cloister and the Hearth. Illustrated by CHARLES KEENE.
Hard Cash. Illust. by F. W. LAWSON.
Griffith Gaunt. Illustrated by S. L. FILDES, A.R.A., and WM. SMALL.
Foul Play. Illust. by DU MAURIER.
Put Yourself in His Place. Illustrated by ROBERT BARNES.
A Terrible Temptation. Illustrated by EDW. HUGHES and A. W. COOPER.
The Wandering Heir. Illustrated by H. PATERSON, S. L. FILDES, A.R.A., C. GREEN, and H. WOODS, A.R.A.
A Simpleton. Illustrated by KATE CRAUFORD.
A Woman-Hater. Illustrated by THOS. COULDERY.
Singleheart and Doubleface: A Matter-of-fact Romance. Illustrated by P. MACNAB.
Good Stories of Men and other Animals. Illustrated by E. A. ABBEY, PERCY MACQUOID, and JOSEPH NASH.
The Jilt, and other Stories. Illustrated by JOSEPH NASH.
Readiana. With a Steel-plate Portrait of CHARLES READE.

Reader's Handbook (The) of Allusions, References, Plots, and Stories. By the Rev. Dr. BREWER. Fifth Edition, revised throughout, with a New Appendix, containing a COMPLETE ENGLISH BIBLIOGRAPHY. Cr. 8vo, 1,400 pages, cloth extra, 7s. 6d.

Richardson. — A Ministry of Health, and other Papers. By BENJAMIN WARD RICHARDSON, M.D., &c. Crown 8vo, cloth extra, 6s.

Riddell (Mrs. J. H.), Novels by: Crown 8vo, cloth extra, 3s. 6d. each; post 8vo, illustrated boards, 2s. each. Her Mother's Darling. The Prince of Wales's Garden Party Weird Stories.

Post 8vo, illustrated boards, 2s. each. The Uninhabited House. Fairy Water. The Mystery in Palace Gardens.

Rimmer (Alfred), Works by: Square 8vo, cloth gilt, 10s. 6d. each. Our Old Country Towns. With over 50 Illustrations. Rambles Round Eton and Harrow. With 50 Illustrations. About England with Dickens. With 58 Illustrations by ALFRED RIMMER and C. A. VANDERHOOF.

Robinson Crusoe: A beautiful reproduction of Major's Edition, with 37 Woodcuts and Two Steel Plates by GEORGE CRUIKSHANK, choicely printed. Crown 8vo, cloth extra, 7s. 6d.

Robinson (F. W.), Novels by: Crown 8vo, cloth extra, 3s. 6d each; post 8vo, illustrated boards, 2s. each. Women are Strange. The Hands of Justice.

Robinson (Phil), Works by: Crown 8vo, cloth extra, 7s. 6d. each. The Poets' Birds. The Poets' Beasts. Poets' Natural History. *[Preparing.*

Rochefoucauld s Maxims and Moral Reflections. With Notes, and an Introductory Essay by SAINTE-BEUVE. Post 8vo, cloth limp, 2s.

Roll of Battle Abbey, The; or, A List of the Principal Warriors who came over from Normandy with William the Conqueror, and Settled in this Country, A.D. 1066-7. With the principal Arms emblazoned in Gold and Colours. Handsomely printed, 5s.

Rowley (Hon. Hugh), Works by: Post 8vo, cloth limp, 2s. 6d. each. Puniana: Riddles and Jokes. With numerous Illustrations. More Puniana. Profusely Illustrated.

Runciman (James), Stories by: Post 8vo, illustrated boards, 2s. each cloth limp, 2s 6d. each. Skippers and Shellbacks. Grace Balmaign's Sweetheart. Schools and Scholars.

Russell (W. Clark), Works by: Crown 8vo, cloth extra, 6s. each: post 8vo, illustrated boards, 2s. each. Round the Galley-Fire. On the Fo'k'sle Head: A Collection of Yarns and Sea Descriptions.

Crown 8vo, cloth extra, 6s. each. In the Middle Watch. A Voyage to the Cape. A Book for the Hammock. *[Preparing.*

Sala. — Gaslight and Daylight. By GEORGE AUGUSTUS SALA. Post 8vo, illustrated boards. 2s.

Sanson. — Seven Generations of Executioners: Memoirs of the Sanson Family (1688 to 1847). Edited by HENRY SANSON. Cr. 8vo, cl. ex. 3s 6d.

Saunders (John), Novels by: Crown 8vo, cloth extra, 3s. 6d. each; post 8vo, illustrated boards, 2s. each. Bound to the Wheel. Guy Waterman. The Lion in the Path. The Two Dreamers.

One Against the World. Post 8vo, illustrated boards, 2s.

Saunders (Katharine), Novels by: Cr. 8vo, cloth extra, 3s 6d. each, post 8vo, illustrated boards, 2s. each. Joan Merryweather. Margaret and Elizabeth. The High Mills.

Crown 8vo, cloth extra, 3s. 6d. each. Heart Salvage. | Sebastian. Gideon's Rock.

Science Gossip: An Illustrated Medium of Interchange for Students and Lovers of Nature. Edited by J. E. TAYLOR, F.L.S., &c. Devoted to Geology, Botany, Physiology, Chemistry, Zoology, Microscopy, Telescopy, Physiography, &c. Price 4d. Monthly; or 5s. per year, post free. Vols. 1. to XIV. may be had at 7s. 6d. each; and Vols. XV. to XXII. (1886), at 5s. each. Cases for Binding, 1s. 6d. each.

Scott (Sir Walter), Poems by: Marmion. With over 100 new Illustrations by leading Artists. Small 4to, cloth extra, 16s. The Lay of the Last Minstrel. With over 100 new Illustrations by leading Artists. Sm. 4to, cl. ex., 16s.

"Secret Out" Series, The: Crown 8vo, cloth extra, profusely Illustrated, 4s. 6d. each. The Secret Out: One Thousand Tricks with Cards, and other Recreations; with Entertaining Experiments in Drawing-room or "White Magic." By W. H. CREMER. 500 Engravings.

"SECRET OUT" SERIES, *continued—*

The Art of Amusing: A Collection of Graceful Arts, Games, Tricks, Puzzles, and Charades. By FRANK BELLEW. With 300 Illustrations.

Hanky-Panky: Very Easy Tricks, Very Difficult Tricks, White Magic Sleight of Hand. Edited by W. H. CREMER. With 200 Illustrations.

The Merry Circle: A Book of New Intellectual Games and Amusements. By CLARA BELLEW. Many Illusts.

Magician's Own Book: Performances with Cups and Balls, Eggs, Hats, Handkerchiefs, &c. All from actual Experience. Edited by W. H. CREMER. 200 Illustrations.

Senior.—By Stream and Sea. By WILLIAM SENIOR. Post 8vo, cloth limp, 2s. 6d.

Seven Sagas (The) of Prehistoric Man. By JAMES H. STODDART, Author of "The Village Life." Crown 8vo, cloth extra, 6s.

Shakespeare:

The First Folio Shakespeare.—MR. WILLIAM SHAKESPEARE'S Comedies, Histories, and Tragedies. Published according to the true Originall Copies. London, Printed by ISAAC IAGGARD and ED. BLOUNT. 1623.—A Reproduction of the extremely rare original, in reduced facsimile, by a photographic process—ensuring the strictest accuracy in every detail. Small 8vo, half-Roxburghe, 7s. 6d.

The Lansdowne Shakespeare. Beautifully printed in red and black, in small but very clear type. With engraved facsimile of DROESHOUT'S Portrait. Post 8vo, cloth extra, 7s. 6d.

Shakespeare for Children: Tales from Shakespeare. By CHARLES and MARY LAMB. With numerous Illustrations, coloured and plain, by J. MOYR SMITH. Cr. 4to, cl. gilt, 6s.

The Handbook of Shakespeare Music. Being an Account of 350 Pieces of Music, set to Words taken from the Plays and Poems of Shakespeare, the compositions ranging from the Elizabethan Age to the Present Time. By ALFRED ROFFE. 4to, half-Roxburghe, 7s.

A Study of Shakespeare. By ALGERNON CHARLES SWINBURNE. Crown 8vo, cloth extra, 8s.

Short Sayings of Great Men. With Historical and Explanatory Notes by SAMUEL A. BENT, M.A. Demy 8vo, cloth extra, 7s. 6d.

Sheridan:—

Sheridan's Complete Works, with Life and Anecdotes. Including his Dramatic Writings, printed from the Original Editions, his Works in Prose and Poetry, Translations, Speeches, Jokes, Puns, &c. With a Collection of Sheridaniana. Crown 8vo, cloth extra, gilt, with 10 full-page Tinted Illustrations, 7s. 6d.

Sheridan's Comedies: The Rivals, and The School for Scandal. Edited, with an Introduction and Notes to each Play, and a Biographical Sketch of Sheridan, by BRANDER MATTHEWS. With Decorative Vignettes and 10 full-page Illusts. Demy 8vo, half-parchment, 12s. 6d.

Sidney's (Sir Philip) Complete Poetical Works, including all those in "Arcadia." With Portrait, Memorial-Introduction, Notes, &c., by the Rev. A. B. GROSART, D.D. Three Vols., crown 8vo, cloth boards, 18s.

Signboards: Their History With Anecdotes of Famous Taverns and Remarkable Characters. By JACOB LARWOOD and JOHN CAMDEN HOTTEN. Crown 8vo, cloth extra, with 100 Illustrations, 7s. 6d.

Sims (George R.), Works by:

How the Poor Live. With 60 Illusts. by FRED. BARNARD. Large 4to, 1s.

Rogues and Vagabonds. Post 8vo, illust. boards, 2s.; cloth limp, 2s. 6d.

The Ring o' Bells. Post 8vo, illust. bds., 2s.; cloth, 2s. 6d.

Mary Jane's Memoirs. Post 8vo, illustrated boards, 2s.; cloth, 2s. 6d. [*Preparing.*

Sister Dora: A Biography. By MARGARET LONSDALE. Popular Edition, Revised, with additional Chapter, a New Dedication and Preface, and Four Illustrations. Sq. 8vo, picture cover, 4d.; cloth, 6d.

Sketchley.—A Match in the Dark. By ARTHUR SKETCHLEY. Post 8vo, illustrated boards, 2s.

Slang Dictionary, The Etymological, Historical, and Anecdotal. Crown 8vo, cloth extra, gilt, 6s. 6d.

Smith (J. Moyr), Works by:

The Prince of Argolis: A Story of the Old Greek Fairy Time. Small 8vo, cloth extra, with 130 Illusts., 3s. 6d.

Tales of Old Thule. With numerous Illustrations. Cr. 8vo, cloth gilt, 6s.

The Wooing of the Water Witch: A Northern Oddity. With numerous Illustrations. Small 8vo, cl. ex., 6s.

Society in London. By A FOREIGN RESIDENT. New and Cheaper Edition, Revised, with an Additional Chapter on SOCIETY AMONG THE MIDDLE AND PROFESSIONAL CLASSES. Crown 8vo, 1s.; cloth, 1s. 6d.

Spalding.—Elizabethan Demonology: An Essay in Illustration of the Belief in the Existence of Devils, and the Powers possessed by Them. By T. A. SPALDING, LL.B, Cr. 8vo, cl. ex., 5s.

Spanish Legendary Tales. By Mrs. S. G. C. MIDDLEMORE, Author of "Round a Posada Fire." Crown 8vo, cloth extra, 6s.

Speight (T. W.), Novels by:
The Mysteries of Heron Dyke. With a Frontispiece by M. ELLEN EDWARDS. Crown 8vo, cloth extra, 3s. 6d.; post 8vo, illustrated bds., 2s.
A Barren Title. Cr. 8vo, 1s.; cl., 1s.6d.
Wife or No Wife? Cr. 8vo, picture cover, 1s.; cloth, 1s. 6d. [Shortly.

Spenser for Children. By M. H. TOWRY. With Illustrations by WALTER J. MORGAN. Crown 4to, with Coloured Illustrations, cloth gilt, 6s.

Staunton.—Laws and Practice of Chess; Together with an Analysis of the Openings, and a Treatise on End Games. By HOWARD STAUNTON. Edited by ROBERT B. WORMALD. New Edition, small cr. 8vo, cloth extra, 5s.

Stedman. — The Poets of America. With full Notes in Margin, and careful Analytical Index. By EDMUND CLARENCE STEDMAN, Author of "Victorian Poets." Cr. 8vo, cl. ex., 9s.

Sterndale.—The Afghan Knife: A Novel. By ROBERT ARMITAGE STERNDALE. Cr. 8vo, cloth extra, 3s. 6d.; post 8vo, illustrated boards, 2s.

Stevenson (R. Louis), Works by:
Travels with a Donkey in the Cevennes. Fifth Ed. Frontispiece by W. CRANE. Post 8vo, cl. limp, 2s. 6d.
An Inland Voyage. With Front. by W. CRANE. Post 8vo, cl. lp., 2s. 6d.
Familiar Studies of Men and Books. Second Edit. Crown 8vo, cl. ex., 6s.
New Arabian Nights. Crown 8vo, cl. extra, 6s.; post 8vo, illust. bds., 2s.
The Silverado Squatters. With Frontispiece. Cr. 8vo, cloth extra, 6s. Cheap Edition, post 8vo, picture cover, 1s.; cloth, 1s. 6d.
Prince Otto: A Romance. Fourth Edition. Crown 8vo, cloth extra, 6s.; post 8vo, illustrated boards, 2s.
The Merry Men, and other Tales and Fables. Cr. 8vo, cl. ex., 6s.

St. John.—A Levantine Family. By BAYLE ST. JOHN. Post 8vo, illustrated boards, 2s.

Stoddard.—Summer Cruising in the South Seas. By CHARLES WARREN STODDARD. Illust. by WALLIS MACKAY. Crown 8vo, cl. extra, 3s. 6d.

Stories from Foreign Novelists. With Notices of their Lives and Writings. By HELEN and ALICE ZIMMERN. Frontispiece. Crown 8vo, cloth extra, 3s. 6d.; post 8vo, illust. bds., 2s.

St. Pierre.—Paul and Virginia, and The Indian Cottage. By BERNARDIN ST. PIERRE. Edited, with Life, by Rev. E. CLARKE. Post 8vo, cl. lp., 2s.

Strutt's Sports and Pastimes of the People of England; including the Rural and Domestic Recreations, May Games, Mummeries, Shows, &c., from the Earliest Period to the Present Time. With 140 Illustrations. Edited by WILLIAM HONE. Crown 8vo, cloth extra, 7s. 6d.

Suburban Homes (The) of London: A Residential Guide to Favourite London Localities, their Society, Celebrities, and Associations. With Notes on their Rental, Rates, and House Accommodation. With Map of Suburban London. Cr. 8vo, cl. ex., 7s. 6d.

Swift's Choice Works, in Prose and Verse. With Memoir, Portrait, and Facsimiles of the Maps in the Original Edition of "Gulliver's Travels." Cr. 8vo, cloth extra, 7s. 6d.

Swinburne (Algernon C.), Works by:
Atalanta in Calydon. Crown 8vo, 6s.
Chastelard. A Tragedy. Cr. 8vo, 7s.
Poems and Ballads. FIRST SERIES. Fcap. 8vo, 9s. Cr. 8vo, same price.
Poems and Ballads. SECOND SERIES. Fcap. 8vo, 9s. Cr. 8vo, same price.
Notes on Poems and Reviews. 8vo, 1s.
Songs before Sunrise. Cr. 8vo, 10s 6d.
Bothwell: A Tragedy. Cr. 8vo, 12s.6d.
George Chapman: An Essay. Crown 8vo, 7s.
Songs of Two Nations. Cr. 8vo, 6s.
Essays and Studies. Crown 8vo, 12s.
Erechtheus: A Tragedy. Cr. 8vo, 6s.
Note of an English Republican on the Muscovite Crusade. 8vo, 1s.
Note on Charlotte Bronte. Cr. 8vo, 6s.
A Study of Shakespeare. Cr. 8vo, 8s.
Songs of the Springtides. Cr. 8vo, 6s.
Studies in Song. Crown 8vo, 7s.
Mary Stuart: A Tragedy. Cr. 8vo, 8s.
Tristram of Lyonesse, and other Poems. Crown 8vo, 9s.

SWINBURNE'S (A. C.) WORKS, *continued*—
A Century of Roundels. Small 4to, 8s.
A Midsummer Holiday, and other Poems. Crown 8vo, 7s.
Marino Faliero: A Tragedy. Cr. 8vo, 6s.
A Study of Victor Hugo. Cr. 8vo, 6s.
Miscellanies. Crown 8vo, 12s.

Symonds.—Wine, Women and Song: Mediæval Latin Students' Songs. Now first translated into English Verse, with Essay by J. ADDINGTON SYMONDS. Small 8vo, parchment, 6s.

Syntax's (Dr.) Three Tours: In Search of the Picturesque, in Search of Consolation, and in Search of a Wife. With the whole of ROWLANDSON's droll page Illustrations in Colours and a Life of the Author by J. C. HOTTEN. Med. 8vo, cloth extra, 7s. 6d.

Taine's History of English Literature. Translated by HENRY VAN LAUN. Four Vols., small 8vo, cloth boards, 30s.—POPULAR EDITION, Two Vols., crown 8vo, cloth extra, 15s.

Taylor's (Bayard) Diversions of the Echo Club: Burlesques of Modern Writers. Post 8vo, cl. limp, 2s.

Taylor (Dr. J. E., F.L.S.), Works by. Crown 8vo, cloth ex., 7s. 6d. each.
The Sagacity and Morality of Plants: A Sketch of the Life and Conduct of the Vegetable Kingdom. Coloured Frontispiece and 100 Illust.
Our Common British Fossils, and Where to Find Them: A Handbook for Students. With 331 Illustrations.

Taylor's (Tom) Historical Dramas: "Clancarty," "Jeanne Darc," "'Twixt Axe and Crown," "The Fool's Revenge," "Arkwright's Wife," "Anne Boleyn," "Plot and Passion." One Vol., cr. 8vo, cloth extra, 7s. 6d.
⁎ The Plays may also be had separately, at 1s. each.

Tennyson (Lord): A Biographical Sketch. By H. J. JENNINGS. With a Photograph-Portrait. Crown 8vo, cloth extra, 6s.

Thackerayana: Notes and Anecdotes. Illustrated by Hundreds of Sketches by WILLIAM MAKEPEACE THACKERAY, depicting Humorous Incidents in his School-life, and Favourite Characters in the books of his every-day reading. With Coloured Frontispiece. Cr. 8vo, cl. extra, 7s. 6d.

Thomas (Bertha), Novels by: Crown 8vo, cloth extra, 3s. 6d. each; post 8vo, illustrated boards, 2s. each.
Cressida. | Proud Maisie.
The Violin Player.

Thomas (M.).—A Fight for Life. A Novel. By W. MOY THOMAS. Post 8vo, illustrated boards, 2s.

Thomson's Seasons and Castle of Indolence. With a Biographical and Critical Introduction by ALLAN CUNNINGHAM, and over 50 fine Illustrations on Steel and Wood. Crown 8vo, cloth extra, gilt edges, 7s. 6d.

Thornbury (Walter), Works by
Haunted London. Edited by EDWARD WALFORD, M.A. With Illustrations by F. W. FAIRHOLT, F.S.A. Crown 8vo, cloth extra, 7s. 6d.
The Life and Correspondence of J. M. W. Turner. Founded upon Letters and Papers furnished by his Friends and fellow Academicians. With numerous Illusts. in Colours, facsimiled from Turner's Original Drawings. Cr. 8vo, cl. extra, 7s. 6d.
Old Stories Re-told. Post 8vo, cloth limp, 2s. 6d.
Tales for the Marines. Post 8vo, illustrated boards, 2s.

Timbs (John), Works by:
Crown 8vo, cloth extra, 7s. 6d. each.
The History of Clubs and Club Life in London. With Anecdotes of its Famous Coffee-houses, Hostelries, and Taverns. With many Illusts.
English Eccentrics and Eccentricities: Stories of Wealth and Fashion, Delusions, Impostures, and Fanatic Missions, Strange Sights and Sporting Scenes, Eccentric Artists, Theatrical Folk, Men of Letters, &c. With nearly 50 Illusts.

Trollope (Anthony), Novels by: Crown 8vo, cloth extra, 3s. 6d. each; post 8vo, illustrated boards, 2s. each.
The Way We Live Now.
Kept in the Dark.
Frau Frohmann. | Marion Fay.
Mr. Scarborough's Family.
The Land-Leaguers.

Post 8vo, illustrated boards, 2s. each.
The Golden Lion of Granpere.
John Caldigate. | American Senator

Trollope (Frances E.), Novels by Crown 8vo, cloth extra 3s. 6d. each; post 8vo, illustrated boards, 2s. each.
Like Ships upon the Sea.
Mabel's Progress. | Anne Furness.

Trollope (T. A.).—Diamond Cut Diamond, and other Stories. By T. ADOLPHUS TROLLOPE. Post 8vo, illustrated boards, 2s.

Trowbridge.—Farnell's Folly :
A Novel. By J. T. TROWBRIDGE. Post
8vo, illustrated boards, 2s.

Turgenieff. — Stories from
Foreign Novelists. By IVAN TURGE-
NIEFF, and others. Cr. 8vo, cloth extra,
3s. 6d ; post 8vo, illustrated boards, 2s.

Tytler (C. C. Fraser-). — Mistress Judith: A Novel. By C. C.
FRASER-TYTLER. Cr. 8vo, cloth extra,
3s. 6d. ; post 8vo, illust. boards, 2s.

Tytler (Sarah), Novels by :
Crown 8vo, cloth extra, 3s. 6d. each ;
post 8vo, illustrated boards, 2s. each.
What She Came Through.
The Bride's Pass.
Saint Mungo's City.
Beauty and the Beast.   With a
Frontispiece by P. MACNAB.

Crown 8vo, cloth extra, 3s. 6d. each.
Noblesse Oblige.   With Illustrations
by F. A. FRASER.
Citoyenne Jacqueline.   Illustrated
by A. B. HOUGHTON.
The Huguenot Family. With Illusts.
Lady Bell. Front. by R. MACBETH.
Buried Diamonds.

Van Laun.—History of French
Literature. By H. VAN LAUN. Three
Vols , demy 8vo, cl. bds., 7s. 6d. each.

Villari. — A Double Bond : A
Story. By LINDA VILLARI. Fcap.
8vo, picture cover, 1s.

Walford (Edw., M.A.), Works by :
The County Families of the United
Kingdom.   Containing Notices of
the Descent, Birth, Marriage, Educa-
tion, &c., of more than 12,000 dis-
tinguished Heads of Families, their
Heirs Apparent or Presumptive, their
Offices they hold or have held, their
Town and Country Addresses, Clubs,
&c.   Twenty-seventh Annual Edi-
tion, for 1887, cloth gilt, 50s.
The Shilling Peerage (1887).   Con-
taining an Alphabetical List of the
House of Lords, Dates of Creation,
Lists of Scotch and Irish Peers,
Addresses, &c.   32mo, cloth, 1s.
Published annually.
The Shilling Baronetage (1887).
Containing an Alphabetical List of
the Baronets of the United Kingdom,
short Biographical Notices, Dates
of Creation, Addresses, &c. 32mo,
cloth, 1s.
The Shilling Knightage (1887). Con-
taining an Alphabetical List of the
Knights of the United Kingdom,
short Biographical Notices, Dates of
Creation, Addresses, &c. 32mo, cl., 1s.

WALFORD'S (EDW.) WORKS, continued—
The Shilling House of Commons
(1887). Containing a List of all the
Members of Parliament, their Town
and Country Addresses, &c.   New
Edition, embodying the results of
the recent General Election. 32mo,
cloth, 1s. Published annually.
The Complete Peerage, Baronetage, Knightage, and House of
Commons (1887). In One Volume,
royal 32mo, cloth extra, gilt edges, 5s.
Haunted London.   By WALTER
THORNBURY.   Edited by EDWARD
WALFORD, M.A. With Illustrations
by F. W. FAIRHOLT, F.S.A. Crown
8vo, cloth extra, 7s. 6d.

Walton and Cotton's Complete
Angler; or, The Contemplative Man's
Recreation ; being a Discourse of
Rivers, Fishponds, Fish and Fishing,
written by IZAAK WALTON; and In-
structions how to Angle for a Trout or
Grayling in a clear Stream, by CHARLES
COTTON. With Original Memoirs and
Notes by Sir HARRIS NICOLAS, and
61 Copperplate Illustrations. Large
crown 8vo, cloth antique, 7s. 6d.

Walt Whitman, Poems by.
Selected and edited, with an Introduction, by WILLIAM M. ROSSETTI. A
New Edition, with a Steel Plate Portrait. Crown 8vo, printed on hand-
made paper and bound in buckram, 6s.

Wanderer's Library, The :
Crown 8vo, cloth extra, 3s. 6d. each.
Wanderings in Patagonia ; or, Life
among the Ostrich-Hunters. By
JULIUS BEERBOHM. Illustrated.
Camp Notes: Stories of Sport and
Adventure in Asia, Africa, and
America. By FREDERICK BOYLE.
Savage Life. By FREDERICK BOYLE.
Merrie England in the Olden Time
By GEORGE DANIEL. With Illustra-
tions by ROBT. CRUIKSHANK.
Circus Life and Circus Celebrities.
By THOMAS FROST.
The Lives of the Conjurers. By
THOMAS FROST.
The Old Showmen and the Old
London Fairs. By THOMAS FROST.
Low Life Deeps.   An Account of the
Strange Fish to be found there. By
JAMES GREENWOOD.
The Wilds of London. By JAMES
GREENWOOD.
Tunis: The Land and the People.
By the Chevalier de HESSE-WAR-
TEGG. With 22 Illustrations.
The Life and Adventures of a Cheap
Jack. By One of the Fraternity.
Edited by CHARLES HINDLEY.
The World Behind the Scenes. By
PERCY FITZGERALD

WANDERER'S LIBRARY, THE, continued—

Tavern Anecdotes and Sayings: Including the Origin of Signs, and Reminiscences connected with Taverns, Coffee Houses, Clubs, &c. By CHARLES HINDLEY. With Illusts.

The Genial Showman: Life and Adventures of Artemus Ward. By E. P. HINGSTON. With a Frontispiece.

The Story of the London Parks. By JACOB LARWOOD. With Illusts.

London Characters. By HENRY MAYHEW. Illustrated.

Seven Generations of Executioners: Memoirs of the Sanson Family (1688 to 1847). Edited by HENRY SANSON.

Summer Cruising In the South Seas. By C. WARREN STODDARD. Illustrated by WALLIS MACKAY.

Warner.—A Roundabout Journey. By CHARLES DUDLEY WARNER, Author of "My Summer in a Garden." Crown 8vo, cloth extra, 6s.

Warrants, &c.:—

Warrant to Execute Charles I. An exact Facsimile, with the Fifty-nine Signatures, and corresponding Seals. Carefully printed on paper to imitate the Original, 22 in. by 14 in. Price 2s.

Warrant to Execute Mary Queen of Scots. An exact Facsimile, including the Signature of Queen Elizabeth, and a Facsimile of the Great Seal. Beautifully printed on paper to imitate the Original MS. Price 2s.

Magna Charta. An exact Facsimile of the Original Document in the British Museum, printed on fine plate paper, nearly 3 feet long by 2 feet wide, with the Arms and Seals emblazoned in Gold and Colours. 5s.

The Roll of Battle Abbey; or, A List of the Principal Warriors who came over from Normandy with William the Conqueror, and Settled in this Country, A.D. 1066-7. With the principal Arms emblazoned in Gold and Colours. Price 5s.

Wayfarer, The: Journal of the Society of Cyclists. Published Quarterly. Price 1s. Number I., for OCTOBER 1886, and Number II., for JANUARY 1887, are now ready.

Weather, How to Foretell the, with the Pocket Spectroscope. By F. W. CORY, M.R.C.S. Eng., F.R.Met. Soc., &c. With 10 Illustrations. Crown 8vo, 1s.; cloth, 1s. 6d.

Westropp.—Handbook of Pottery and Porcelain; or, History of those Arts from the Earliest Period. By HODDER M. WESTROPP. With numerous Illustrations, and a List of Marks. Crown 8vo, cloth limp, 4s. 6d.

Whistler's (Mr.) "Ten o'Clock." Uniform with his "Whistler v. Ruskin: Art and Art Critics." Cr.8vo,1s. [Shortly.

Williams (W. Mattieu, F.R.A.S.), Works by:

Science Notes. See the GENTLEMAN'S MAGAZINE. 1s. Monthly.

Science In Short Chapters. Crown 8vo, cloth extra, 7s. 6d.

A Simple Treatise on Heat. Crown 8vo, cloth limp, with Illusts., 2s. 6d.

The Chemistry of Cookery. Crown 8vo, cloth extra. 6s.

Wilson (Dr. Andrew, F.R.S.E.), Works by:

Chapters on Evolution: A Popular History of the Darwinian and Allied Theories of Development. Third Edition. Crown 8vo, cloth extra, with 259 Illustrations, 7s. 6d.

Leaves from a Naturalist's Note book. Post 8vo, cloth limp, 2s. 6d.

Leisure-Time Studies, chiefly Biological. Third Edit., with New Preface. Cr.8vo, cl. ex., with Illusts., 6s.

Studies In Life and Sense. With numerous Illustrations. Crown 8vo, cloth extra, 6s.

Common Accidents, and How to Treat them. By Dr. ANDREW WILSON and others. With numerous Illustrations. Crown 8vo, 1s.; cloth limp, 1s. 6d.

Winter (J. S.), Stories by:

Cavalry Life. Post 8vo, illust. bds., 2s.

Regimental Legends. Crown 8vo, cloth extra, 3s. 6d.; post 8vo, illustrated boards, 2s.

Women of the Day A Biographical Dictionary of Notable Contemporaries. By FRANCES HAYS. Crown 8vo, cloth extra, 5s.

Wood.—Sabina: A Novel. By Lady Wood. Post 8vo, illust. bds., 2s.

Words, Facts, and Phrases: A Dictionary of Curious, Quaint, and Out-of-the-Way Matters. By ELIEZER EDWARDS. New and cheaper issue, cr. 8vo, cl. ex., 7s. 6d.; half-bound, 9s.

Wright (Thomas), Works by:

Crown 8vo, cloth extra, 7s. 6d. each.

Caricature History of the Georges. (The House of Hanover.) With 400 Pictures, Caricatures, Squibs, Broadsides, Window Pictures, &c.

History of Caricature and of the Grotesque In Art, Literature, Sculpture, and Painting. Profusely Illustrated by F.W. FAIRHOLT, F.S.A.

Yates (Edmund), Novels by:

Post 8vo, illustrated boards, 2s. each.

Castaway. | The Forlorn Hope. Land at Last.

NEW THREE-VOLUME NOVELS.

WILKIE COLLINS'S NEW NOVEL.

The Evil Genius: A Novel. By WILKIE COLLINS, Author of "The Woman in White." Three Vols., crown 8vo.

WALTER BESANT'S NEW NOVEL.

Children of Gibeon: A Novel. By WALTER BESANT, Author of "All Sorts and Conditions of Men," "Dorothy Forster," &c. Three Vols., crown 8vo.

ANOTHER NEW NOVEL BY WALTER BESANT.

The World Went Very Well Then. Three Vols., crown 8vo. [*May*, 1887.

MRS. HUNT'S NEW NOVEL.

That other Person: A Novel. By Mrs. ALFRED HUNT, Author of "Thornicroft's Model," "The Leaden Casket," &c. Three Vols., crown 8vo.

GRANT ALLEN'S NEW NOVEL.

In all Shades: A Novel. By GRANT ALLEN, Author of "Strange Stories," "Philistia," "Babylon," &c. Three Vols., crown 8vo.

HALL CAINE'S NEW NOVEL.

A Son of Hagar: A Novel. By T. HALL CAINE, Author of "The Shadow of a Crime," &c. Three Vols.

THE PICCADILLY NOVELS.

Popular Stories by the Best Authors. LIBRARY EDITIONS, many Illustrated, crown 8vo, cloth extra, 3s. 6d. each.

BY GRANT ALLEN.

Philistia.

BY W. BESANT & JAMES RICE.

Ready Money Mortiboy.
My Little Girl.
The Case of Mr. Lucraft.
This Son of Vulcan.
With Harp and Crown.
The Golden Butterfly.
By Celia's Arbour.
The Monks of Thelema.
'Twas In Trafalgar's Bay.
The Seamy Side.
The Ten Years' Tenant.
The Chaplain of the Fleet.

BY WALTER BESANT.

All Sorts and Conditions of Men.
The Captains' Room.
All in a Garden Fair.
Dorothy Forster.
Uncle Jack.

BY ROBERT BUCHANAN.

A Child of Nature.
God and the Man.
The Shadow of the Sword.
The Martyrdom of Madeline.
Love Me for Ever.

Annan Water.	The New Abelard.
Matt.	Foxglove Manor.

The Master of the Mine.

BY HALL CAINE.

The Shadow of a Crime.

BY MRS. H. LOVETT CAMERON.

Deceivers Ever. | Juliet's Guardian.

BY MORTIMER COLLINS.

Sweet Anne Page.
Transmigration.
From Midnight to Midnight

MORTIMER & FRANCES COLLINS.

Blacksmith and Scholar.
The Village Comedy.
You Play me False.

BY WILKIE COLLINS.

Antonina.	New Magdalen.
Basil.	The Frozen Deep.
Hide and Seek.	The Law and the
The Dead Secret.	Lady
Queen of Hearts.	TheTwo Destinies
My Miscellanies.	Haunted Hotel.
Woman in White.	The Fallen Leaves
The Moonstone.	Jezebel'sDaughter
Man and Wife.	The Black Robe.
Poor Miss Finch.	Heart and Science
Miss or Mrs.?	I Say No.

BY DUTTON COOK.

Paul Foster's Daughter.

BY WILLIAM CYPLES

Hearts of Gold.

BY ALPHONSE DAUDET.

The Evangelist; or, Port Salvation.

BY JAMES DE MILLE.

A Castle In Spain.

BY J. LEITH DERWENT.

Our Lady of Tears. | Circe's Lovers

BY M. BETHAM-EDWARDS.

Felicia. | Kitty.

BY MRS. ANNIE EDWARDES.

Archie Lovell.

BY PERCY FITZGERALD.

Fatal Zero.

BY R. E. FRANCILLON.

QueenCophetua.	A Real Queen.
One by One.	

Prefaced by Sir BARTLE FRERE.

Pandurang Harl.

BY EDWARD GARRETT.

The Capel Girls.

PICCADILLY NOVELS, *continued—*
BY CHARLES GIBBON.
Robin Gray. | For Lack of Gold.
What will the World Say?
In Honour Bound.
Queen of the Meadow.
The Flower of the Forest.
A Heart's Problem.
The Braes of Yarrow.
The Golden Shaft.| Of High Degree.
Fancy Free. |Loving a Dream.
A Hard Knot.

BY THOMAS HARDY.
Under the Greenwood Tree

BY JULIAN HAWTHORNE.
Garth. | Ellice Quentin.
Sebastian Strome.
Prince Saroni's Wife.
Dust. | Fortune's Fool.
Beatrix Randolph.
Miss Cadogna.
Love—or a Name.

BY SIR A. HELPS.
Ivan de Biron.

BY MRS. CASHEL HOEY.
The Lover's Creed.

BY MRS. ALFRED HUNT.
Thornicroft's Model.
The Leaden Casket.
Self-Condemned.

BY JEAN INGELOW.
Fated to be Free.

BY HARRIETT JAY.
The Queen of Connaught

BY R. ASHE KING.
A Drawn Game.
"The Wearing of the Green."

BY HENRY KINGSLEY.
Number Seventeen.

BY E. LYNN LINTON.
Patricia Kemball.
Atonement of Leam Dundas.
The World Well Lost.
Under which Lord?
With a Silken Thread.
The Rebel of the Family
"My Love!" | Ione.

BY HENRY W. LUCY.
Gideon Fleyce.

BY JUSTIN McCARTHY.
The Waterdale Neighbours.
My Enemy's Daughter.
A Fair Saxon.
Dear Lady Disdain.
Miss Misanthrope.| Donna Quixote
The Comet of a Season.
Maid of Athens.
Camiola.

BY MRS. MACDONELL.
Quaker Cousins.

PICCADILLY NOVELS, *continued—*
BY FLORENCE MARRYAT.
Open! Sesame! | Written in Fire
BY D. CHRISTIE MURRAY.
Life's Atonement. | Coals of Fire.
Joseph's Coat. | Val Strange.
A Model Father. | Hearts
By the Gate of the Sea
The Way of the World.
A Bit of Human Nature
First Person Singular
Cynic Fortune.

BY MRS. OLIPHANT.
Whiteladies.

BY MARGARET A. PAUL.
Gentle and Simple.

BY JAMES PAYN.
Lost Sir Massing-|A Confidential
berd. | Agent.
Best of Husbands|From Exile.
Halves. |A Grape from a
Walter's Word. | Thorn.
What He Cost Her|For Cash Only.
Less Black than|Some Private
We're Painted. | Views.
By Proxy. |The Canon's
High Spirits. | Ward.
Under One Roof. |Talk of the Town.

BY E. C. PRICE.
Valentina. | The Foreigners.
Mrs. Lancaster's Rival.

BY CHARLES READE.
It Is Never Too Late to Mend.
Hard Cash.
Peg Woffington.
Christie Johnstone.
Griffith Gaunt. | Foul Play.
The Double Marriage.
Love Me Little, Love Me Long.
The Cloister and the Hearth.
The Course of True Love.
The Autobiography of a Thief.
Put Yourself in His Place.
A Terrible Temptation.
The Wandering Heir. | A Simpleton.
A Woman-Hater. | Readiana.
Singleheart and Doubleface.
The Jilt.
Good Stories of Men and other
Animals.

BY MRS. J. H. RIDDELL.
Her Mother's Darling.
Prince of Wales's Garden Party.
Weird Stories.

BY F. W. ROBINSON.
Women are Strange.
The Hands of Justice.

BY JOHN SAUNDERS.
Bound to the Wheel.
Guy Waterman.
Two Dreamers.
The Lion in the Path.

BY KATHARINE SAUNDERS.

Joan Merryweather.
Margaret and Elizabeth.
Gideon's Rock. | Heart Salvage.
The High Mills. | Sebastian.

BY T. W. SPEIGHT.

The Mysteries of Heron Dyke.

BY R. A. STERNDALE.

The Afghan Knife.

BY BERTHA THOMAS.

Proud Maisie. | Cressida.
The Violin-Player.

BY ANTHONY TROLLOPE.

The Way we Live Now
Frau Frohmann. | Marion Fay
Kept in the Dark.
Mr. Scarborough's Family.
The Land Leaguers.

BY FRANCES E. TROLLOPE.

Like Ships upon the Sea.
Anne Furness.
Mabel's Progress.

BY IVAN TURGENIEFF, &c.

Stories from Foreign Novelists.

BY SARAH TYTLER.

What She Came Through
The Bride's Pass.
Saint Mungo's City.
Beauty and the Beast.
Noblesse Oblige.
Citoyenne Jacqueline.
The Huguenot Family.
Lady Bell.

BY C. C. FRASER-TYTLER.

Mistress Judith.

BY J. S. WINTER.

Regimental Legends.

CHEAP EDITIONS OF POPULAR NOVELS.

Post 8vo, illustrated boards, 2s. each.

BY EDMOND ABOUT.

The Fellah.

BY HAMILTON AÏDÉ.

Carr of Carrlyon. | Confidences.

BY MRS. ALEXANDER.

Maid, Wife, or Widow?
Valerie's Fate.

BY GRANT ALLEN.

Strange Stories.
Philistia.

BY SHELSLEY BEAUCHAMP.

Grantley Grange.

BY W. BESANT & JAMES RICE.

Ready-Money Mortiboy.
With Harp and Crown.
This Son of Vulcan. | My Little Girl.
The Case of Mr. Lucraft.
The Golden Butterfly.
By Celia's Arbour.
The Monks of Thelema.
'Twas in Trafalgar's Bay.
The Seamy Side.
The Ten Years' Tenant.
The Chaplain of the Fleet.

BY WALTER BESANT.

All Sorts and Conditions of Men.
The Captains' Room.
All in a Garden Fair.
Dorothy Forster.
Uncle Jack

BY FREDERICK BOYLE.

Camp Notes. | Savage Life.
Chronicles of No-man's Land.

BY BRET HARTE.

An Heiress of Red Dog.
The Luck of Roaring Camp.
Californian Stories.
Gabriel Conroy. | Flip.
Maruja.

BY ROBERT BUCHANAN.

The Shadow of | The Martyrdom
the Sword. | of Madeline.
A Child of Nature. | Annan Water.
God and the Man. | The New Abelard.
Love Me for Ever. | Matt
Foxglove Manor.

BY MRS. BURNETT.

Surly Tim.

BY HALL CAINE.

The Shadow of a Crime.

BY MRS. LOVETT CAMERON

Deceivers Ever. | Juliet's Guardian

BY MACLAREN COBBAN.

The Cure of Souls.

BY C. ALLSTON COLLINS.

The Bar Sinister.

BY WILKIE COLLINS.

Antonina. | Queen of Hearts.
Basil. | My Miscellanies.
Hide and Seek. | Woman in White
The Dead Secret. | The Moonstone.

CHEAP POPULAR NOVELS, *continued—*
WILKIE COLLINS, *continued.*

Man and Wife.	Haunted Hotel.
Poor Miss Finch.	The Fallen Leaves.
Miss or Mrs. ?	Jezebel's Daughter
New Magdalen.	The Black Robe.
The Frozen Deep.	Heart and Science
Law and the Lady.	"I Say No."
The Two Destinies	

BY MORTIMER COLLINS.

Sweet Anne Page.	From Midnight to
Transmigration.	Midnight.
A Fight with Fortune.	

MORTIMER & FRANCES COLLINS.

Sweet and Twenty. | Frances.
Blacksmith and Scholar.
The Village Comedy.
You Play me False.

BY DUTTON COOK.

Leo. | Paul Foster's Daughter.

BY C. EGBERT CRADDOCK.
The Prophet of the Great Smoky
Mountains.

BY WILLIAM CYPLES.
Hearts of Gold.

BY ALPHONSE DAUDET.
The Evangelist; or, Port Salvation.

BY JAMES DE MILLE.
A Castle in Spain.

BY J. LEITH DERWENT.
Our Lady of Tears. | Circe's Lovers.

BY CHARLES DICKENS.

| Sketches by Boz. | Oliver Twist. |
| Pickwick Papers. | Nicholas Nickleby |

BY MRS. ANNIE EDWARDES.
A Point of Honour. | Archie Lovell

BY M. BETHAM-EDWARDS.
Felicia. | Kitty.

BY EDWARD EGGLESTON.
Roxy.

BY PERCY FITZGERALD.
Bella Donna. | Never Forgotten.
The Second Mrs. Tillotson.
Polly.
Seventy five Brooke Street.
The Lady of Brantome.

BY ALBANY DE FONBLANQUE.
Filthy Lucre.

BY R. E. FRANCILLON.

| Olympia. | Queen Cophetua. |
| One by One. | A Real Queen. |

Prefaced by Sir H. BARTLE FRERE.
Pandurang Hari.

BY HAIN FRISWELL.
One of Two.

BY EDWARD GARRETT.
The Capel Girls.

CHEAP POPULAR NOVELS, *continued—*
BY CHARLES GIBBON.

Robin Gray.	The Flower of the
For Lack of Gold.	Forest.
What will the	A Heart's Problem
World Say ?	The Braes of Yar-
In Honour Bound.	row.
In Love and War.	The Golden Shaft
For the King.	Of High Degree.
In Pastures Green	Fancy Free.
Queen of the Mea-	By Mead and
dow.	Stream.

BY WILLIAM GILBERT.
Dr. Austin's Guests.
The Wizard of the Mountain.
James Duke.

BY JAMES GREENWOOD
Dick Temple.

BY JOHN HABBERTON.
Brueton's Bayou.

BY ANDREW HALLIDAY.
Every Day Papers.

BY LADY DUFFUS HARDY.
Paul Wynter's Sacrifice.

BY THOMAS HARDY.
Under the Greenwood Tree.

BY J. BERWICK HARWOOD.
The Tenth Earl.

BY JULIAN HAWTHORNE.

Garth.	Sebastian Strome
Ellice Quentin.	Dust.
Prince Saroni's Wife.	
Fortune's Fool.	Beatrix Randolph.

BY SIR ARTHUR HELPS.
Ivan de Biron.

BY MRS. CASHEL HOEY.
The Lover's Creed.

BY TOM HOOD.
A Golden Heart.

BY MRS. GEORGE HOOPER.
The House of Raby.

BY MRS. ALFRED HUNT.
Thornicroft's Model.
The Leaden Casket.
Self Condemned.

BY JEAN INGELOW.
Fated to be Free.

BY HARRIETT JAY.
The Dark Colleen.
The Queen of Connaught.

BY MARK KERSHAW.
Colonial Facts and Fictions.

BY R. ASHE KING.
A Drawn Game.
"The Wearing of the Green."

BY HENRY KINGSLEY.
Oakshott Castle.

BY E. LYNN LINTON.
Patricia Kemball.
The Atonement of Leam Dundas.
The World Well Lost.
Under which Lord ?

CHEAP POPULAR NOVELS, continued—
E. LYNN LINTON, continued—
With a Silken Thread.
The Rebel of the Family.
"My Love | Ione.

BY HENRY W. LUCY.
Gideon Fleyce.

BY JUSTIN McCARTHY.

Dear Lady Disdain.	Linley Rochford.
The Waterdale	MissMisanthrope
Neighbours.	Donna Quixote.
My Enemy's	The Comet of a
Daughter.	Season.
A Fair Saxon.	Maid of Athens.

BY MRS. MACDONELL.
Quaker Cousins.

BY KATHARINE S. MACQUOID.
The Evil Eye. | Lost Rose.

BY W. H. MALLOCK.
The New Republic.

BY FLORENCE MARRYAT.

Open! Sesame	A Little Stepson.
A Harvest of Wild	Fighting the Air
Oats.	Written in Fire.

BY J. MASTERMAN.
Half-a-dozen Daughters.

BY BRANDER MATTHEWS.
A Secret of the Sea.

BY JEAN MIDDLEMASS.
Touch and Go. | Mr. Dorillion.

BY D. CHRISTIE MURRAY.

A Life's Atonement	Val Strange.
A Model Father.	Hearts.
Joseph's Coat.	The Way of the
Coals of Fire.	World.
By the Gate of the	A Bit of Human
Sea.	Nature.

BY ALICE O'HANLON.
The Unforeseen.

BY MRS. OLIPHANT.
Whiteladies.

BY MRS. ROBERT O'REILLY.
Phœbe's Fortunes.

BY OUIDA.

Held in Bondage.	Two Little Wooden
Strathmore.	Shoes.
Chandos.	In a Winter City.
Under Two Flags.	Ariadne.
Idalia.	Friendship.
Cecil Castle-	Moths.
maine's Gage.	Pipistrello.
Tricotrin.	A Village Com-
Puck.	mune.
Folle Farine.	Bimbi.
A Dog of Flanders.	Wanda.
Pascarel.	Frescoes.
Signa.	In Maremma.
Princess Napraxine.	

CHEAP POPULAR NOVELS, continued—
BY MARGARET AGNES PAUL.
Gentle and Simple.

BY JAMES PAYN.

Lost Sir Massing-	Like Father, Like
berd.	Son.
A Perfect Trea-	A Marine Resi-
sure.	dence.
Bentinck's Tutor.	Married Beneath
Murphy's Master.	Him.
A County Family.	Mirk Abbey.
At Her Mercy.	Not Wooed, but
A Woman's Ven-	Won.
geance.	Less Black that
Cecil's Tryst.	We're Painted.
Clyffards of Clyffe	By Proxy.
The Family Scape-	Under One Roof.
grace.	High Spirits.
Foster Brothers.	Carlyon's Year.
Found Dead.	A Confidential
Best of Husbands.	Agent.
Walter's Word.	Some Private
Halves.	Views.
Fallen Fortunes.	From Exile.
What He Cost Her	A Grape from a
Humorous Stories	Thorn.
Gwendoline's Har-	For Cash Only.
vest.	Kit: A Memory.
£200 Reward.	The Canon's Ward

BY EDGAR A. POE.
The Mystery of Marie Roget

BY E. C. PRICE.

Valentina.	The Foreigner's
Mrs. Lancaster's Rival.	
Gerald.	

BY CHARLES READE.
It is Never Too Late to Mend
Hard Cash. | Peg Woffington.
Christie Johnstone.
Griffith Gaunt.
Put Yourself in His Place.
The Double Marriage.
Love Me Little, Love Me Long.
Foul Play.
The Cloister and the Hearth.
The Course of True Love.
Autobiography of a Thief.
A Terrible Temptation.
The Wandering Heir.
A Simpleton. | A Woman-Hater.
Readiana. | The Jilt.
Singleheart and Doubleface.
Good Stories of Men and other
Animals.

BY MRS. J. H. RIDDELL.
Her Mother's Darling.
Prince of Wales's Garden Party.
Weird Stories.
The Uninhabited House.
Fairy Water.
The Mystery in Palace Gardens.

BY F. W. ROBINSON.
Women are Strange.
The Hands of Justice.

CHEAP POPULAR NOVELS, *continued*—

BY JAMES RUNCIMAN.
Skippers and Shellbacks.
Grace Balmaign's Sweetheart.
Schools and Scholars.

BY W. CLARK RUSSELL.
Round the Galley Fire.
On the Fo'k'sle Head.

BY BAYLE ST. JOHN.
A Levantine Family.

BY GEORGE AUGUSTUS SALA.
Gaslight and Daylight.

BY JOHN SAUNDERS.
Bound to the Wheel.
One Against the World.
Guy Waterman.
The Lion in the Path.
Two Dreamers.

BY KATHARINE SAUNDERS.
Joan Merryweather.
Margaret and Elizabeth.
The High Mills.

BY GEORGE R. SIMS.
Rogues and Vagabonds.
The Ring o' Bells.

BY ARTHUR SKETCHLEY.
A Match in the Dark.

BY T. W. SPEIGHT.
The Mysteries of Heron Dyke.

BY R. A. STERNDALE.
The Afghan Knife.

BY R. LOUIS STEVENSON.
New Arabian Nights.
Prince Otto.

BY BERTHA THOMAS.
Cressida. | Proud Maisie.
The Violin-Player.

BY W. MOY THOMAS.
A Fight for Life.

BY WALTER THORNBURY.
Tales for the Marines.

BY T. ADOLPHUS TROLLOPE.
Diamond Cut Diamond.

BY ANTHONY TROLLOPE.
The Way We Live Now.
The American Senator.
Frau Frohmann.
Marion Fay.
Kept in the Dark
Mr. Scarborough's Family.
The Land-Leaguers.
The Golden Lion of Granpere.
John Caldigate.

By FRANCES ELEANOR TROLLOPE
Like Ships upon the Sea.
Anne Furness.
Mabel's Progress.

BY J. T. TROWBRIDGE.
Farnell's Folly.

CHEAP POPULAR NOVELS, *continued*—

BY IVAN TURGENIEFF, &c.
Stories from Foreign Novelists.

BY MARK TWAIN.
Tom Sawyer.
A Pleasure Trip on the Continent of Europe.
A Tramp Abroad
The Stolen White Elephant.
Huckleberry Finn.

BY C. C. FRASER-TYTLER
Mistress Judith.

BY SARAH TYTLER.
What She Came Through.
The Bride's Pass.
Saint Mungo's City.
Beauty and the Beast

BY J. S. WINTER.
Cavalry Life. | Regimental Legends

BY LADY WOOD.
Sabina.

BY EDMUND YATES.
Castaway. | The Forlorn Hope.
Land at Last.

ANONYMOUS.
Paul Ferroll.
Why Paul Ferroll Killed his Wife.

POPULAR SHILLING BOOKS.

Jeff Briggs's Love Story. By BRET HARTE.
The Twins of Table Mountain. By BRET HARTE.
Mrs. Gainsborough's Diamonds. By JULIAN HAWTHORNE.
Kathleen Mavourneen. By Author of "That Lass o' Lowrie's."
Lindsay's Luck. By the Author of "That Lass o' Lowrie's."
Pretty Polly Pemberton. By the Author of "That Lass o' Lowrie's."
Trooping with Crows. By Mrs. PIRKIS.
The Professor's Wife. By LEONARD GRAHAM.
A Double Bond. By LINDA VILLARI.
Esther's Glove. By R. E. FRANCILLON.
The Garden that Paid the Rent. By TOM JERROLD.
Curly. By JOHN COLEMAN. Illustrated by J. C. DOLLMAN.
Beyond the Gates. By E. S. PHELPS.
An Old Maid's Paradise. By E. S. PHELPS.
Burglars in Paradise. By E. S. PHELPS.
Doom: An Atlantic Episode. By JUSTIN H. MACCARTHY, M.P.
Our Sensation Novel. Edited by JUSTIN H. MACCARTHY, M.P.
A Barren Title. By T. W. SPEIGHT.
Wife or No Wife? By T. W. SPEIGHT.
The Silverado Squatters. By R. LOUIS STEVENSON.

J. OGDEN AND CO., PRINTERS, 29, 30 AND 31, GREAT SAFFRON HILL, E.C.